ForkBraid

The Price of Peace

By Michael Robert von Blucher-Altona

27-December-2009
and
01-November-2023

First published 2011
Revised edition 2023

Books by Michael Robert von Blucher-Altona

ForkBraid
Book 1: ForkBraid   - The Price of Peace
Book 2: ForkBraid II - The Cost of War
Book 3: ForkBraid III - Just Rewards

Table of Contents

Written for my Son Erick, whom I call Ulrick.

A fine Lad who likes to read weird stories written by his Dad.

It has long been said that the pathway to freedom
was paved with the blood of innocents.
So it was in the past and so it has been to this very day.
This was the price we humans have always paid.
In the future the price of freedom will be paid for with our
constant vigilance and so too shall be the price of peace.

Lord Folcrom Tafazah. Spring Equinox 2022.

1. Terror Attack on T.V

Catherine Swann walked briskly into the lounge room, her children Miranda and Chiron were watching the video screen wall. Her Husband, Peter was watching also, he had been getting ready for work. The news program was showing a devastating scene, only they hadn't been watching the news. The roof of a large auditorium had collapsed. To the right, rear of the auditorium, where the podium ought to have been, they could see a large crater.

"I thought you were watching the end of the induction ceremony at the Flinders Psychic Academy"

"We were, but there was some sort of explosion. The reporter is saying it's some sort of attack", replied Peter.

"An attack!" exclaimed Catherine, "What kind of attack?"

"They're saying it's a terrorist attack."

"There hasn't been a terrorist attack for well over fifty years?"

"Well, apparently that's changed. The news feed was saying some fundamentalist religious group had claimed responsibility."

"Really, I thought the remote viewing teams had put a stop to all that."

"So did everyone else, but there you have it", said Peter, pointing at the video screen which covered most of the wall.

"So what happened exactly?"

"Everything was normal. The officials had assessed the psychic potentials of each of the young children. Then they moved off to the right, to a teenage girl who had been brought in. They assessed her and then turned back to the podium, then Bang! Everything blew up!"

"Bang. Just like that?"

"It was a big explosion. Just as the explosion happened, there was this golden glow that suddenly appeared around the officials. Then the auditorium roof came crashing down."

A large section of the wall screen showed the scene of what had been an induction ceremony, at the Flinders Island Psychic Academy. A group of sixty-five, six-year-old children, were being inducted. The explosion had blown a large crater where the podium had been, the roof had collapsed and the children, their parents, and siblings lay buried underneath tonnes of rubble. Confusion and pandemonium were the order of the day, people were running and screaming everywhere.

Emergency services had started to move into the collapsed auditorium. Android attendants, already on the scene, were already helping the survivors. The two attending officials, a High Priest and High Priestess, were already helping as well.

"Who are the officials?", inquired Catherine as she walked over and took a seat.

"Lord Folcrom Forkbraid and Lady Folcrom Selene", replied Miranda.

"Aren't they the top psychics?", queried Catherine.

"Yes, they're supposed to be the two most powerful psychics on the planet", replied Peter, adding, "It makes you wonder, how they didn't see this coming. Or did they?", questioning himself, "There was that strange golden glow that appeared right before the explosion."

"It just goes to show, they can't be as powerful as people had thought. Maybe being psychic isn't all that special after all" as Catherine sat down to watch the unfolding scene.

"I don't know, I doubt that you or I could do that", said Peter gesturing towards the wall.

The Priest and Priestess were gesturing with their hands, moving them in a very precise manner. Large sections of rubble began to move. As they gestured, the rubble gently lifted and floated to the side, away from the buried victims. As rubble was removed, Android attendants moved in to check for survivors. They gently pulled bodies out of the wreckage, none showed any sign of life. No survivors had been found as yet. More and more rubble was shifted, more and more lifeless bodies were removed.

"We are the survivors?", inquired Catherine, "Chiron, leave the room, I don't want you watching this. You too Miranda, go on get moving. To your rooms now."

"No, Mum, I want to watch the Wizard", Miranda said of Forkbraid; Chiron didn't move either.

"Chiron, leave the room now!", Chiron sighed and left the room, Miranda refused to budge. Catherine sighed and resigned herself to the fact that Miranda, her pretty little golden haired and blue-eyed Daughter, was extremely stubborn and simply would not budge. She could be the most stubborn little girl when she wanted to be.

Finally, after several minutes of removing rubble, a survivor was found. The Android attendant gently handed the child to an emergency worker, who took her outside the auditorium, where the front lawn had been set up for triage. Lady Selene moved another section of rubble, another child was pulled alive from the wreckage. More psychics had moved into the auditorium and began to shift rubble aside.

"She's pretty", Miranda said of Lady Selene.

"I thought you were watching the Wizard?", Catherine's eyes came around to look at her Daughter.

"I am, but I'm also watching the Witches too. And the Androids. Doesn't Daddy make those?"

"Yeah, I do actually, they're Hyper Dynamics model three-o-three's. The newer ones anyway. Those older ones are model two-nine-five's. I think I even saw a couple of older two-seven-fives earlier as well."

"Look, they've found another survivor", Catherine pointed at the wall.

An Android had gently lifted a woman from under the rubble. She was screaming for her child.

"She's still alive, she's still alive, I can feel her, there, over there", pointing at a section of twisted steel and concrete with her bloodied right hand.

Lord Forkbraid wasted no time. He leapt forty or more feet across the wreckage and raised a hand towards where the woman had pointed. Slowly the rubble lifted, he gestured to an Android and pointed with his left hand. The Android crawled underneath the raised rubble and some long moments later, came back out, gently cradling a young girl. She was unconscious, but alive.

"There's another, there's more of them", he shouted with urgency. Lady Selene leapt quickly to his side and raised her hands. Together they moved the rubble aside. Androids were now stepping into the opening. Within minutes, three boys and two girls were gently pulled from the wreckage. This went on for more than thirty minutes, then finally they stopped.

The Witches and Wizards all gathered near the entrance to the collapsed auditorium. They were shaking their heads. Of the more than five hundred people who had been in the auditorium, it appeared as many as two hundred had died. Only eight children and twelve parents were in the triage area outside the damaged building. A group of school children on a tour had been at the very rear of the auditorium, fortunately all of this group had survived relatively unscathed, with only minor cuts and abrasions. More than two hundred had perished. It was the most shocking thing seen on TV in many, many years.

About now, Folcrom Forkbraid had noticed a TV camera crew was still recording the event. He quickly stormed over to the TV camera crew, a look of intense fury in his eyes. The TV camera crew focused their camera directly on him as he approached.

"Have you no decency. Turn off your camera. People, young children have died here. Turn it off!"

Forkbraid was a tall thin man, he wore a dark robe, almost black, its hood swept back. His hair was long, light brown and parted in the middle. What stood out most of all was his beard, a goatee, it was long, braided and split into two at the end. The camera crew did not turn off their camera.

Lord Folcrom Forkbraid froze for a long moment staring directly into the camera lens. It was as if he was suddenly camera shy. The TV crew also froze, not knowing what to think, they flicked quick glances at each other. Lady Folcrom Selene, watching the scene, quickly came to his side. Two minds met across the vastness of space. Forkbraid took a startled step back, turned to Selene and simply said one word "Miranda." He then turned back to the TV camera crew, clicked his fingers and the camera went dead.

The video screen wall went dark blue, showing a loss of signal. Catherine and Peter looked at each other, then looked at Miranda.

"That, that was really weird", still staring at his Daughter.

"Did I hear him say 'Miranda'?", asked Catherine.

"That's what I heard", still staring at his Daughter, "Did he say your name, Miranda?"

"Yes, Daddy, he looked straight at me, so I said *Hello Forkbraid*", Miranda replied.

"I didn't hear you say anything little lady", her Father replied with a curious look on his face.

"That's because I said it with my mind silly."

"Well I guess that explains everything then", stated Catherine, her husband turned to look at her, "Well he is a psychic, supposedly one of the most powerful on Earth, he reads minds."

"Darling, he's on Earth, we're in a cylinder at L-Five, three hundred and eighty-four thousand kilometres from Earth. Psychics can't operate in space! Every-body knows that."

"I didn't know that, Daddy". Both Catherine and Peter stared at Miranda, their little eight-year-old Daughter smiled back at them with a wide grin.

After a few moments Peter said, "Maybe they can s*ee* across space", he smiled, "Forkbraid is supposed to be the most powerful of them after all. Who knows how far he can see."

"What other explanation can there be", his Wife responded.

Peter nodded his head in agreement with his Wife.

Catherine switched channels on the video screen. A new video station appeared on the wall, it was showing an unplanned news break.

"*Breaking news from Earth. There appears to have been an explosion at a psychic induction ceremony on Earth. Sources are stating that it appears to have been a terrorist attack*", the young female newsreader stated.

Catherine quickly switched the channel again. Another video station appeared on the wall. Yet again there was *breaking* news, with another young newsreader telling the tale. Again and again Catherine switched channels. The news of the attack was breaking across all the video channels.

Catherine finally switched the video screen wall to random scenery. A lush jungle scene appeared across the entire wall, as if viewed from above on an escarpment. To one side of the scene a large waterfall appeared. The soft and relaxing sounds of flowing water, rustling leaves and chirping birds filled the room.

Catherine smiled as she looked into the scenery, "Much better", she said to herself.

"Peter, I don't think I'll send the children to school today. After watching that, that attack, I think I'll keep them home for the day. I'll shut all the video feeds off as well. This is going to be repeated on the news all day long, over and over and over. I don't want the kids watching that again."

"I expect it will be all the talk at work today as well. Which reminds me, I'd better get a wriggle on, or I'll be late. They have me working on the positronic sub-assemblies this week."

Peter got up and continued his preparations for work, the vision of the attack still fresh in his mind.

2. Terror Attack at the Academy

The bus trip from Whitemark was uneventful. It took only fifteen minutes to drive from the local airport to the Academy. From the buses the students could see the approaching buildings. The entire Academy was built in the style of a huge castle. Eight massive turrets marked the outer perimeter, each turret connected by very tall, strong, stone walls. Atop the walls were battlements, fashioned as one would expect with merlons and crenelles. Beyond the walls, the central keep could be seen. It had six stone turrets, each connected by stout walls, again topped with battlements.

The entire Academy was surrounded by a broad, deep moat. Someone had obviously had a passion for castle architecture. The central keep towered high above the other structures of the Academy. At the very top it was capped with a large central dome. Such an odd sight, this Academy on an island so far from the mainland. It was hard to imagine the entire structure had been built without machinery of any kind. Powerful minds had been at work here.

The road swung around so that the buses approached from the north-east. The entrance was a large archway in the north-east turret. The long drawbridge was down and portcullis raised. Each of the six buses drove through the arch and into the courtyard. The students noticed a second raised portcullis deeper within the arch. Once within the courtyard the students could see the other Academy buildings. These buildings had been barely visible from beyond the Academy walls. Here they could be seen clearly for the first time. There were eight buildings in all, they were quite large in their own rite, but not nearly as tall as the central keep, which itself was immense. They were each situated behind the tall stone walls within the courtyard, each equally spaced midway between the outer turrets.

The buses were circling the courtyard counter-clockwise, they made a full circuit, giving the students a complete viewing of the Academy grounds. The outer walls, it could be seen, were also buildings in their own rite. Each contained many rooms, dormitories, and corridors. Many trees were planted in the courtyard, these were mostly oaks. They were not overly tall and appeared to have been managed by a resident arborist. The students noticed that a moat also surrounded the inner keep.

Students at the Academy could be seen moving about the courtyard. They wore cloaks in various shades of grey, the trims of which were coloured. It seemed the older the student, the darker the shade of grey. The youngest students had the lightest shade of grey, being almost white. Emblems could be seen on the left breast of each cloak, perhaps reflecting some internal academic house structure, only the emblems themselves and the number of them appeared to be too complex.

They seemed like students anywhere else in the world, only here and there, you could see something clearly odd. One group of students was playing ball, only the ball never touched their hands or feet. Clearly they were controlling the ball with some kind of telekinesis. Further over, a student flew across the courtyard well in front of the buses, landing on her feet on the other side. Another teenager was holding an ornate staff, the top of which glowed an eerie red, Clearly this was no ordinary school.

The buses had performed a complete circuit of the courtyard and were now passing by the arched entrance they had come through. They drove up to a building within the north side of the courtyard and parked in the appropriate parking bays.

Their tour guide was standing on the lawn before them. She was of average height, thin but not overly so, with relatively short cropped reddish, auburn hair and incredibly green eyes. Her face was beaming with a smile that automatically put everyone at ease. The sign on the building behind here simply stated *"Auditorium"*. The teachers stepped out of the buses and approached their guide. They conversed for a few minutes and a few short moments later they were directing the students out of the buses and towards the auditorium. The guests had arrived, and the ceremony was due to begin shortly.

The tour guide led the group of teenage students into the foyer of the auditorium. There were just over one hundred and thirty of them in all. Six groups of students from different schools on the Australian mainland and Island of Tasmania. Each on an excursion to the Flinders Psychic Academy to view an induction ceremony. Class teachers led each group of twenty-five or so students into the foyer. A large door was open at the front of the foyer. The main auditorium could be seen through the door. To either side, there were two other doors, one to the left, the other to the right, both of which were closed. They stopped and waited for instructions from their tour guide.

"Okay, students, my name is Ms Charlene Fewkes. I'm a level five psychic and I will be your tour guide for today. Your teachers will be handing out your ear-phones. Here we call them ear-wigs. Please let your teacher know if your ear-wig doesn't work. The ear-wigs will enable me to communicate to you all directly and silently. Does anyone know why we need to use our ear-wigs?"

A sixteen-year-old Victorian school girl from Melbourne replied, "It's because the induction ceremony is completely silent".

"That is correct. Not a word is spoken during the entire ceremony. The entire ceremony is telepathic. Now students, when we enter the auditorium, you must all be on your best behaviour. Try not to speak, if you need to ask a question, either whisper it to your teacher to relay to me, or think your question to me directly, and I will reply through your ear-wigs."

"What if we all think at you at once?", asked a young lad from Tasmania.

"Ask your teacher first. If your teacher cannot answer your question, the question will be relayed to me. If you do need to ask me directly, please do so. Trust me, as a level five psychic, your thoughts will not flood me. I will answer them as I narrate the ceremony."

"What were those emblems those students were wearing out there in the courtyard?", asked a young school girl from Geelong.

"They are the insignia for our Academy's house structure, or at least our equivalent of one."

"Houses?", the young girl queried.

"It's a little more complicated than that. We essentially have four houses, although we call them elements. All students less than eleven years old are novices, they belong to no elements at all and wear the same coloured robes, all with the same insignia upon them. They are assigned quarters in the novitiate's dormitory, based upon their ages. The older students, who have turned eleven, are sorted into their appropriate elements and are known as elementals. Each of the elements has its own dormitory."

"Will we be seeing a Sorting Ceremony, Ms Fewkes?", another Girl asked.

"No, today you will be seeing an Induction Ceremony."

"What are the elements, Ms Fewkes?", asked another Tasmanian lad.

"The four elements are Air, Fire, Water, and Earth. The robes of each student have the insignia that represents their element, in the appropriate colour and with the appropriate symbol."

"What element was yours, Miss?", the same Boy asked.

Charlene pointed to her auburn hair, "What do you think?"

The Boy smiled, "Fire?"

"Very good. Fire was the element I was sorted into at eleven years of age. Remember, I said it gets complicated. At the age of fourteen, a student chooses between purely secular and religious training. If they choose religious training, they are elevated into a higher level of elements during their Initiation."

"What happens at the initiation, Miss?", asked a young Girl from Melbourne.

"I can't tell you that", waving her finger, "What I can tell you is the following. The religious elements are of course based upon the elements, but more correctly, their elemental guardians. So we have [1]Eurus, Notus, Zephyrus and Boreas, which correspond to the directions, East, North, West, and South in our hemisphere. The religious students have robes with insignia representing these guardians, complete with the appropriate colours and symbols. The students within these religious elements are then known as Sylphides, Salamanders, Undines, and Gnomes. The religious elements also have their own set of dormitories."

"Is there only one initiation?", asked another Girl.

"No. In this Academy, all secular students will undergo a Graduation Ceremony at eighteen. The religious students do so as well, but for them there are three more years of study. The final graduation for religious students occurs at twenty-one years of age. That's when they undergo their final Initiation. That's when they choose their Witch name and are presented with their coven names and titles."

"What if a student can't be sorted into an element?", asked another Boy.

"That is a good question. And I'm very glad you've asked that one. Remember I said it was complicated. There are exceptions to the rules."

Charlene was smiling now, "By the time a student reaches eleven years of age, we know fairly well what level they can achieve. Any child who shows the potential to reach above level nine, cannot be sorted into an element. They are destined to become a Folcrom."

Charlene did not explain the meaning of the term Folcrom, "Those who are destined to become a Folcrom, whether they stay secular or later become religious, are apprenticed to an appropriate Folcrom for individual training. They wear a special insignia that combines all the elements as one and represents spirit. There are two dormitories for our young apprentices, one for secular and one for religious students."

"What is the difference between secular and religious training?", asked one of

---

1   Pronounced: Euray-us, No-tay-us, Zephyr-rus and Boreay-us

the class teachers.

"Another good question. Firstly, let me state this, all students here undergo a school curriculum which is approved by our federal government. Above this, there is their psychic training. Secular students undergo a vigorous psychic training, to enhance and of course enable the full use of their psychic abilities. The religious students also undergo this same psychic training, but they also undergo religious education and training in the magical arts as well."

"So Witches get to use wands and staffs and other magical stuff. Cool.", stated another Boy.

"That's correct. Witches are trained in the use of all magical implements. Indeed, they are also trained to make and consecrate these magical implements."

"So what you're saying, Ms Fewkes, is that psychic students undergo a more rigorous training than ordinary students?", the same class teacher asked.

"Yes. That's precisely correct. Being a psychic student is no walk in the park. It is very demanding work", Charlene paused, "And if a psychic student chooses religious studies, their workload increases significantly."

"Isn't that hard on the students?", another class teacher asked.

"Yes it is", again pausing, "We do however, give the students all the support they could possibly need. The teachers here at the Academy, treat their students, as they would their own children. All the students in our care are precious to us, and we look after them accordingly."

Unheard to nearly all in the foyer a message was being relayed continuously. It wasn't a message in words, just an obscure feeling that only a psychic or someone with psychic potential could pick up. Usually only the tour guides and other psychic attendants could sense it. It would be very rare indeed for visitors to be aware of it. Only today was one very rare day indeed.

Roseanne Rhein, another sixteen-year-old student from Melbourne turned to her right. The closed door on the right of the foyer seemed to be somehow inviting her to walk through. The urge was strong, Roseanne resisted it, *"Come through the door, come through the door"*, the urge whispered. Roseanne took one tentative step towards the door, then another, then stopped.

An usher near the auditorium door noticed, he turned to Charlene, who caught the thought immediately. Carefully Charlene looked at a young girl who had stepped slightly out of her group, quickly Charlene skimmed the surface of her mind. Turning back to the usher, *"We have a candidate. She's very afraid though."*

Unheard to all, except for those who were psychic, the urging changed to silent whisper, *"Be not afraid, you will be perfectly safe, please step through the door"*. Roseanne looked at the door again, took another step and then hesitated.

Again the silent whisper, *"Be not afraid, you will be perfectly safe, please step through the door. It is your destiny."*

Roseanne bit her lower lip, walked quickly to the door, it opened and through it, she went. None of the students or teachers had noticed.

Charlene the tour guide smiled as she sent a thought to her superiors, *"We have a walk-in."*

After a few more minutes the visiting students entered the auditorium and were led to their seats. From here on Charlene communicated purely with her thoughts.

The students could see a small podium at the rear centre of the auditorium, on it stood a man and a woman wearing long black, hooded cloaks. Their cloaks had ornate symbols on them, but they weren't close enough for the students to see them clearly. The man was tall and thin, his hair long, brown and parted in the middle, he had the visage of a viper. He had a goatee that was long braided and split into a fork at the end. The woman was almost as tall, had long dark hair and the face of a goddess. An android attendant stood with them, carrying an array of brightly coloured sashes. In front of the podium was a group of children sitting on the floor, over sixty in all, split into two roughly equal groups of boys and girls. They all wore simple white robes. Behind them seated in chairs, were their parents and siblings. Behind the parents sat other people who had come to watch the ceremony. To the left of centre, on the other side of the entrance way, was a camera crew filming the proceedings. Induction ceremonies were usually televised.

"As you will all know from your studies, nearly all psychics are found during primary school testing, at the tender age of five or six. Those young children are then inducted into the Academy. Here, as boarding students, they will be taught to develop and use their abilities. It is during the induction ceremony, that the young students will be tested to grade their psychic potentials. Does anyone know how this grading is done?"

A Geelong boy raised his hand. Charlene flicked a thought at him, *"Yes, Mark"*.

"How did you know my name?", he whispered.

Charlene smiled and tapped her right temple, *"Psychic remember"*, she replied with a thought.

"Oh sorry", his face going red, before replying, "The head psychics are going to give the students the *Cold Hard Stare.*"

"Yes, precisely. The cold hard stare is used to ascertain the child's psychic potential. Once their potential is graded, they are given a sash, the colour of which denotes their grading. Today, arguably the two most powerful psychics on the planet are officiating. Both are not only psychics, but also Witches and hold the titles High Priest and High Priestess. Remember students, a Witch is a Witch, whether male or female. While it is common practice in the wider community to call a male Witch a Wizard, here among their peers, the term Wizard is frowned upon. Whether male or female, the term Witch is applied. On the podium you can see Lord Folcrom Forkbraid and Lady Folcrom Selene. Does anyone know what Folcrom means?"

No-one answered, not a hand was raised.

"Folcrom is just another title. It is based on the word fulcrum and only psychics who have attained the highest levels achievable are given this title. Those psychics who achieve greater than level nine are all titled Folcrom."

"Will you ever be a Folcrom, Ms Fewkes?", a boy named Axel asked.

"No, Axel, level five is as high as I can go. I will never achieve the title, Folcrom", there was a slight sadness in Charlene's thought.

"Are you a Witch, Ms Fewkes?", another boy asked.

"Yes, Timothy, I am a Witch. I am a religious psychic. The black and green trim on my robes tells you two things. Black is for religious and the green shows I'm level five. The levels are from one to nine, as follows, white, red, orange, yellow, green, blue, indigo, violet and black. If my trim was white and green, I'd be a level five secular psychic and not a Witch."

'*Getting back to the podium, you will notice an android attendant, holding a number of coloured sashes. As each child is graded, the appropriate sash will be placed over the child.*'

Just as Charlene finished the thought, a teenage girl was brought into the auditorium by an usher from their right. Someone said rather loudly, "That's Roseanne, what's she doing there?"

"Yes, Mrs Carrington. That is Roseanne Rhein. Remember I said before, that nearly all psychics are found during primary school testing. Well, not all psychics are found that way. Sometimes a child is not picked up during the tests. It is very, very rare, but it does happen. Sometimes young psychics fall through the gaps. Later, if they are lucky, they come to an establishment like this and here, we pick them up. Roseanne is what we call a walk-in. Today is a very special day, both for Roseanne and for us. We haven't had a walk-in for many years. Roseanne is now a part of the induction ceremony and will be graded for her psychic potential."

Astonished whispers sprung up among the students.

The usher led Roseanne towards the podium, but well off to the far right of it. The two Witches on the podium looked over to the teenager, they then looked at each other and smiled. They stepped off the podium and walked to the children in front of them. Lord Folcrom Forkbraid graded the girls and Lady Folcrom Selene graded the boys. One by one the children stood up as the two Witches moved among their respective groups. They would kneel in front of the child and stare coldly into their eyes. As coldly as they stared, the children did not seem to be afraid. After what seemed to be about a minute, they would hold up their hand and signal a number with their fingers. The attending Android would then pass the appropriately coloured sash, which would then be placed over the child's head and shoulder. The child would sit back down, and they would move onto the next nearest child. There did not seem to be any real order to how the children were processed.

At one point Selene stood up and Forkbraid came to her side. They both stared coldly at the child, a boy, then after several minutes looked at each other. Selene signalled to the Android, who passed her both an indigo and a black sash. Forkbraid stared at the boy again, then picked up the indigo sash and passed it back to the Android. Selene placed the black sash over the boy's head and shoulder. They moved onto the next child.

"That young boy was difficult to grade', explained Charlene adding, 'It took both of them to decide that he has the potential to be a level nine. It is quite rare to be graded so high at an induction ceremony. The boy must have enormous potential. This is a special day indeed."

One by one the children were processed, sashes handed out appropriately. Three more times, Selene and Forkbraid had both conferred over a child. Another boy was given a violet sash and two girls given indigo sashes. Eventually, all sixty-five children were graded. The Android returned to the podium, while Forkbraid and Selene walked over to Roseanne, the walk-in.

"Now students, they have finished grading the young children, and they are going to grade the walk-in, Roseanne. This is such a rare situation, that the Android attendant has returned to the podium and doesn't seem to realise that his job is not quite finished."

Off to the far right of the podium, Forkbraid and Selene began to give Roseanne the cold hard stare. At first Roseanne stepped back, she was scared, but her fear melted away as Forkbraid and Selene reassured her and then continued their assessment. It was many long minutes before they conferred among themselves and Forkbraid raised his hand signalling for a black sash. The Android was on the podium and completely oblivious to the signal. Forkbraid frowned, he looked at Selene and they both turned to look toward the podium and the Android standing upon it.

"Students, this is exceedingly rare. Not only is Roseanne a walk-in, but one with extremely high potential. This is not something that happens very often, we are indeed privileged today", informed Charlene.

As Forkbraid and Selene looked towards the podium and the Android standing upon it, something subtle shifted in the surrounding reality. A look of shock came over their faces as they realised what was about to happen. They quickly raised their arms, as they did so, the podium erupted. There was the loud crack of an explosion. Heat and flame exploded outward from the podium, debris flew into the air, the auditorium's structure began to buckle, and the roof came tumbling down.

Forkbraid and Selene had raised their defences just in time. A golden bubble of light encapsulated them. The blast wave was deflected around them, behind them stood Roseanne and the usher who had led her into the auditorium. Both were relatively safe, but not so the children, their parents, and the audience in the auditorium. Debris was everywhere, the roof had collapsed and people were screaming.

Charlene picked herself up off the floor, instinctively reaching for a painful cut on her temple, blood streamed down her hand and wrist. Already Androids and Ushers had started helping the students out of the auditorium.

An Android grabbed Charlene's arm, it was an older model two-nine-five, she was severely dazed, "This way. This way, you must leave the building. Danger, you must leave the building."

Charlene allowed herself to be led out of the building. As she passed through the doorway, she noticed the film crew had picked themselves up and begun filming once more. They refused to be led out of the auditorium, ignoring the requests of Android attendants. Students and their teachers had begun leaving the auditorium almost as soon as they had got to their feet. Bright light momentarily blinded her, it was a sunny day outside.

Still dazed and now sitting on the ground in front of the auditorium, Charlene could see that most if not all the older students had been led out of the auditorium. It appeared most were relatively uninjured, cuts and abrasions yes, but no serious injuries were seen. Frantic teachers were counting and checking their charges. Some had scratches, cuts, and abrasions from flying debris. Many were sitting on the ground in shock.

Charlene could not see any of the parents or other audience members who had been closer to the podium, then it dawned on her, *"Where are the little ones?"*

Tears were in her eyes.

An usher named Marcus brought Roseanne out of the auditorium, she appeared to be okay but somewhat shaken.

They came straight to Charlene, "We're lucky to be alive", he paused, "Lady Selene has asked you to take charge of Roseanne. She says that she is very special."

"Yes, of course", replied Charlene, still dazed, she reached out to grab Roseanne's hand. Roseanne collapsed into her arms in shock. Marcus the usher turned and ran back towards the auditorium. Charlene looked around, other psychics and Android workers had arrived on the scene. Emergency services were arriving from the local town of Whitemark. Charlene slipped backwards onto the grass and passed out.

3. Terror Attack for the Walk-in

Roseanne had entered the foyer of the auditorium. Today was a special day. Twenty-five students from her school had been flown in from Melbourne, to watch a psychic induction ceremony at the Flinders Psychic Academy. It was a privilege, there were usually only six induction ceremonies each year and only a limited number of students from a handful of schools could attend in the audience of each ceremony. They were on Flinders Island for the weekend. Here they would view the induction ceremony and then be guests of the Academy for the rest of the weekend.

Their tour guide, a level five psychic, Ms Charlene Fewkes had been explaining the intricacies of the Academy's house structure. Ushers, also psychics, were handing out earpieces, called ear-wigs. Roseanne Rhein stood patiently waiting to enter the auditorium and take her seat. The discussion about the Academy's house structure, if you could call it that, was most informative and Roseanne listened intently. Complex though it was, it seemed to make perfect sense to her. As Roseanne listened an unusual feeling came over her, something odd, something she did not understand, she could not put her finger on it, then it was gone. Yet it wasn't gone completely, it had drawn Roseanne out of herself, Roseanne was no longer listening intently. Roseanne's mind began to wander. Looking to her right, there was a closed door, it beckoned, it beckoned with an intensity that was hard not to notice.

"Come through the door, come through the door", came the silent whisper. The urging was strong, and a somewhat frightened Roseanne did all she could to ignore it. It was hard to ignore, it was hard to resist.

Yet still it beckoned, *"Come through the door, come through the door."*

Roseanne looked at the door once more, what was on the other side? No-one else seemed to notice the silent beckoning.

Still the silent beckoning came forth growing with urgency and intensity, *"Come through the door, come through the door"*, it called.

Slowly Roseanne took one tentative step towards the door, she paused then took another step, then stopped. Roseanne looked around her, no-one had noticed her move, at least that's what she thought. Others had noticed, others had seen.

The urging grew even stronger, *"Come through the door, come through the door."*

"No", Roseanne thought to herself.

Then the silent whisper changed completely, a small still voice with infinite understanding spoke within her mind, *"Be not afraid, you will be perfectly safe, please step through the door."*

Roseanne took one more tentative step, then stopped. *"No"*, Roseanne thought to herself again.

Again the silent whisper, *"Be not afraid, you will be perfectly safe, please step through the door. It is your destiny. You must come through the door."*

Roseanne bit her lower lip, looked about herself, then walked quickly to the door, it opened and through it, she went. The door closed silently behind her. Roseanne found herself in a small ante-room. An Usher walked straight up to her.

"Don't be afraid. You are perfectly safe here. My name is Marcus Greyhelm. I'll be your guide."

"Why am I here? Why didn't any-one else hear that, that whisper?"

"You're here because you were always meant to be here. You alone heard the whisper because you are a psychic and the other students with you are not", explained Marcus.

"I don't understand". Roseanne was confused.

Marcus explained, "Not all psychics are picked up by the usual screening process in primary school. A few, very few actually, slip though the gaps so to speak. If they're lucky, we pick them up later on in life as what we call a walk-in. Young lady, you are a walk-in and today is your luck day."

"I'm a walk-in?"

"Yes you are, you lucky girl. Now please come along with me."

"Why? Where are we going?"

"Why? To the induction ceremony of course. You are to be graded.", Marcus said with a smile.

Roseanne fell silent, a million scrambled thoughts clouded her mind, the predominant one, *"Graded?"*

Marcus took her left hand and looked into her eyes, "Don't be afraid, you are perfectly safe here. Your psychic potential is going to be graded, just like the others."

"My psychic potential?", Roseanne queried incredulously.

"Yes, your psychic potential", Marcus replied with a smile.

Roseanne allowed herself to be led out of the ante-room and into the auditorium proper.

Off to her left, Roseanne could see the other teenage students who were here to observe the induction ceremony. The astonished looks on the faces of her schoolmates was clearly visible. Her year level coordinator, who looked equally astonished, gave her a little wave.

Marcus led Roseanne towards the podium, stopping well off to the right of it. A small spotlight turned on and illuminated Roseanne and Marcus. Nervously Roseanne looked at her surroundings. A large group of children sat to her left, there were well over fifty of them. They weren't speaking, yet clearly she could hear some of them. Roseanne felt faint, her legs began to wobble.

Marcus sensed her unease and was quick to reassure her, '*It's okay. You'll be fine.*' He squeezed her hand and caught a stray thought.

"My hair must be a mess."

Marcus looked at Roseanne's long blond hair, *"No, your hair is fine. You'll be fine. Don't worry, it's okay to be a little nervous, it's only natural."*

On the podium stood two Witches, the High Priest and High Priestess. They glanced at her and smiled. Roseanne mentally noted that the High Priestess had the features of a Goddess.

"Yes, Lady Folcrom Selene does", Marcus thought, clearly sounding in her mind.

Roseanne looked at Marcus, who merely smiled, then looked back at the podium. The High Priest was tall and thin, his hair long and parted in the middle. His beard, a goatee, was strange. Long, braided and forked at the end. He had thin features, with the visage of a viper and yet an aura of kindness about him.

Roseanne recognised him, this was Lord Folcrom Forkbraid, largely believed to be the most powerful psychic on the planet. The head of the remote viewing teams that scour the Earth for any sign of potential malevolent behaviour. He and his [2]RV's had kept the Earth free of terrorism and other atrocities for decades. Yet to look at him, you'd think he would never hurt a fly.

Marcus smiled, he looked at Roseanne, *"He does give that impression doesn't he."*

---

2 Remote Viewers. Psychics whose abilities include remote viewing.

Lady Selene and Lord Forkbraid had begun to grade the children. Each being given a coloured sash, appropriate to their psychic potentials. Marcus explained that this was not their final grading, only their initial 'induction' grading and that their final grading would take many years. It would only be when their training is completed, many years from now, that their final grading would be bestowed. Then, at that distant time, it would be seen whether they reached their potentials, as graded during their inductions. It was not unusual for a child to achieve slightly higher or even slightly less, than their induction grading indicated. This induction grading was merely a guide, that would indicate what sort of training each child would receive and that each child was truly unique.

"What sort of training will I receive?", asked Roseanne in a whisper.

"That will depend on how they grade you", replied Marcus, adding, *"Remember also, you are a walk-in. You can't go through the normal training that these young ones will."*

"I don't understand. Why not?", her whisper growing louder.

"These children are being inducted at five and six years old. They will have ten or so years of training before they reach your age group. That's a lot of training, which you have not received. So your training cannot be the same as theirs."

"So I'm going to be in the *'dummies'* class?", she whispered with a sad look on her face.

"That's not what I mean. You'll undergo personal one on one training in an apprenticeship, rather than regular psychic schooling."

"An apprenticeship?", Roseanne thought.

"Yes. You'll be apprenticed to a fully trained psychic, who is one-or-more levels above your potential. They'll become your teacher and mentor."

"Do you get many walk-ins?", Roseanne was thinking rather than whispering now.

"Very, very few. In fact, you're the first walk-in we've seen here in many years."

"When was the last one?"

"If I remember correctly, the last walk-in we had was nearly ten years ago. A thirty-five-year-old delivery man, who delivered some goods to a Psychic centre in Melbourne."

"So walk-ins are quite rare?"

"Yes and no. There are probably many more out there in the community. At least that is the speculation, but unless they come into contact with one of our centres or a psychic who is trained to pick them up, they remain lost to us. It's a shame really."

Roseanne quietly watched the proceedings. It seemed to take forever. Each child took around a minute to be assessed. Roseanne counted the children, sixty-five?, yes sixty-five, that would be at least an hour, probably longer. Marcus tapped her shoulder and indicated that she should take a seat, "What?, Where?", she whispered rather loudly.

"While you were busy counting the children, I took the opportunity to grab a couple of chairs."

"Oh, was I that obvious?", slightly embarrassed.

"It's okay, no need to be embarrassed, we're all human after all."

The pair sat down and continued to watch the young children being graded. It was a slow process, but eventually the last of the little ones was processed.

At long last, Lady Selene and Lord Forkbraid began to walk towards them. Marcus motioned to Roseanne to stand and they both stepped slightly forward away from their seats.

Roseanne noticed that the Android attendant had returned to the podium. *"It doesn't know about walk-ins, so it doesn't know to follow them here"*, Marcus informed her.

Marcus took Roseanne's left hand once more and presented her to the High Priest and High Priestess. They nodded to him and began to process Roseanne with the cold hard stare. Roseanne stepped back, frightened. Both Selene and Forkbraid reassured Roseanne and her fear melted away. They continued with their assessment.

Flecks of light and swirls of colour appeared in Roseanne's mind, strange tones began to sound, none of it made any sense at first. Then the flecks began to form patterns, then the colours began to dance, forming intricate patterns and designs. The sounds took on new tones and formed into intricate notes. Before long Roseanne's mind was filled with a tapestry of light, colour, and sound.

She could no longer see Selene or Forkbraid standing before her, nor even the auditorium, for there was only the tapestry and the tapestry grew in vibrancy and complexity. This continued for several minutes, the light, the colours, the sounds, all growing in intensity, focusing and binding, until suddenly there was an enormous internal explosion of thought and knowledge. The tapestry dissolved, and the Earth appeared before her in all its majesty. Roseanne was above the world and she could feel its life. It was alive, a living conscious entity, it embraced her warmly and she embraced it in return. In her mind Roseanne stepped back from the Earth, slightly to her right she could feel many, many souls all separated from their mother earth, who seemed somewhat sad.

Roseanne could see the lights of the colonies at L-Five and felt herself drifting out further and further, beyond the Earth, beyond the Moon, towards a distant smiling redness that had turned blue-green with joy.

Roseanne could have sworn she had heard someone say, *"For, God's sake bring her back! Forkbraid, we'll lose her!"*

There was the sudden sound of a cracking whip and her knees began to buckle, everything began to go dark.

Selene had Roseanne's right arm and Forkbraid had her left, they steadied her gently. Roseanne was sweating profusely, Marcus was looking severely concerned, several minutes had passed.

"It's okay, Roseanne, everything is okay, we have you now, everything will be fine", Selene's soothing thoughts came flooding in.

"What happened? What was that?", Roseanne's voice was barely a whisper.

"That was you, Roseanne. You happened, you flew, and you soared", Forkbraid stated matter-of-factly, he did not elaborate.

"I flew?", Roseanne was feeling more than a little giddy and confused.

"Yes, Roseanne. You flew. You flew higher than any child I have ever assessed in all my years."

"We nearly lost you, you flew so high, so fast. We could never have known", Selene touched Roseanne's cheek and at once Roseanne felt flooded with a soothing bliss.

"Scared the pants off me, you did", added Marcus.

"Peaking, were you, Marcus?", a slight smile on Forkbraid's face.

"How could I not? When an untrained mind soars so high. Scary!"

Forkbraid and Selene turned to each other, Marcus held Roseanne's shoulders steadying her, grounding her, he could not hear their internal dialogue.

"That was close, Forkbraid. We could have lost her."

"Yes, yes very close. A walk-in too, who would have guessed?"

"She could be like one of us. No fear, no uncertainty, no doubts. Very rare and very precious."

"Yes, and we nearly lost her, Selene. I should have contained her."

"You were quick, Forkbraid, you roped her in, you brought her back."

"Yes, and her mind seems settled now, no damage that I can discern."

"Roseanne will need special training."

"Yes, yes, special training. A Folcrom must train her. Only a Folcrom can."

"Settled then, we'll need a black sash."

"Black indeed, there is none higher", Forkbraid raised his hand and signalled for a black sash.

Forkbraid frowned, the Android stood some distance away on the podium, completely oblivious to his signal. One of the new ones, it had only arrived the previous day and someone had been lax in its programming and conditioning. It knew not what to do when a walk-in was in the ceremony. He looked at Selene and gave a slight sigh. They both turned towards the podium and again Forkbraid signalled the Android.

As Forkbraid and Selene looked towards the podium and the Android standing upon it, something subtle shifted in the surrounding reality. A look of shock came over their faces, they hastily raised their arms, as they did so, the podium erupted. There was the loud crack of an explosion. Heat and flame exploded outward from the podium, debris flew into the air, the auditorium's structure began to buckle, and the roof came tumbling down.

The blast wave swept past them. Forkbraid and Selene had been quick, their defences were raised, an impervious golden bubble of light protecting them from the heat and flame erupting around them, debris flew past. Standing behind them, Marcus and Roseanne were knocked to the floor by the shock-wave but otherwise unharmed, it was several minutes before the pair were able to get back to their unsteady feet. When they did, all around them was absolute chaos. Forkbraid and Selene were directing Android attendants to look for survivors.

For a brief moment Selene came to their side, "Marcus!", there was no response, "Marcus!", still no response. Selene slapped his face hard, "Marcus!", she shouted.

"Yes, yes my Lady.", his head still spinning.

"Quickly, Marcus. Take Roseanne out of here. Take her to Charlene. Tell Charlene to look after her."

"Yes, my Lady, straight away", clearer now.

"And, Marcus, tell Charlene that Roseanne is special, very special."

With that Marcus helped Roseanne to her feet, and together they weaved their way through the debris of the auditorium. Before long they were pushing up against other people trying to extricate themselves from the collapsed building. Then the light of day was upon them and they were safe. Marcus scanned the lawn in front of the building, there was Charlene. Quickly he helped Roseanne to Charlene's side.

"We're lucky to be alive", he paused, noticing a deep, bloody laceration on Charlene's temple, "Lady Selene has asked you to take charge of Roseanne. She says that she is very special."

"Yes of course", replied Charlene, still dazed, she reached out to grab Roseanne's hand. Roseanne collapsed into her arms in shock.

"You'll be okay?", asked Marcus.

"Yes, I'll be fine. Help the others."

With that Marcus quickly turned and ran back towards the auditorium. Charlene looked around, other psychics and Android workers had arrived on the scene. Emergency services were arriving from the nearby town of Whitemark. Charlene slipped backwards onto the grass and passed out.

4. Aftermath

The council chamber was a large round room, capped by a large ornate dome. The circular base of the dome was carved with a dozen ornate astrological symbols. Beneath this was another circular layer carved with the twenty-four runes of the elder futhark. It was at the top of the central keep. In the centre of the chamber was a large circular desk around which were thirteen chairs. Here the Flinders Academy's Grey Council sat. Forkbraid entered the chamber. Already the other council members had gathered and taken their seats, he of course was the last to arrive, he always was, it was his way. In his hand he held a leather-bound folder. Forkbraid walked quickly across the chamber and placed the folder on the desk in front of the Academy's Dean, Folcrom Tobius, with an audible slap. Turning around quickly, Forkbraid walked over to his seat and sat down.

"You're not going to present me with a summary, I take it then, Forkbraid?"

"Scan the first page, Tobius, you'll get the basic gist of the situation.", Forkbraid replied.

Opening the folder, Tobius removed the first page and gave it a quick read, pausing only long enough to put his reading glasses on. It contained a quick summary of the situation, the number of deceased, the number of wounded, results of the preliminary investigation, damage report and conclusions / recommendations etc. Tobius placed the summary page back into the folder, quickly he leafed through to the section describing the source of the explosion. He looked up at Forkbraid.

"Is this true?", he did not believe what he was reading.

"Indeed it is. There can be no doubt about it.", Forkbraid's voice was colder than ice.

"The Robot?", Tobius shook his head, "How? They are all [3]three laws safe! Every-one knows the three laws. What you're saying is impossible! Absolutely impossible!", he wanted an explanation. Uneasy murmurs filled the chamber.

"No, it's not!", Forkbraid rose to his feet, "The explosion erupted from within the mid-section of a Hyper Dynamics three-o-three Humaniform Android. There is absolutely no doubt, both myself and Selene saw it. The auditorium's event recording system caught the moment of the explosion and recorded it as well. When the forensics investigation is complete, they will come to the same conclusion both myself and Selene have."

---

3   The three laws of Robotics as expressed by Isaac Asimov

"Selene, is that true? You saw the robot explode?"

"Yes, Tobius. The explosion erupted from within the Android, there is no doubt", Selene replied.

"But the three laws? How? Robots, Androids cannot harm, nor through their actions cause harm, to a human being", Dean Tobius was having a hard time swallowing Forkbraid's conclusion.

"They can", a slight pause, "if they have no knowledge of what they are about to do."

"I'm not sure that I understand you, Forkbraid? How can a Robot perform an action for which it has no knowledge?"

"It is my belief Tobius", again pausing, "That the Android in question was modified to contain a concealed explosive device within its body. The Android itself had no knowledge of the device and so the three laws have no effect. I suspect it was triggered to explode at the end of the induction ceremony."

More murmurs erupted throughout the chamber. Forkbraid raised his hand to silence them, with a strong voice stating, "I have already ordered all Androids within the Academy grounds be scanned for possible explosive devices. Starting with the new batch that was flown in from [4]Woomera yesterday. I've also notified the relevant authorities to check all recent Android imports."

"Do you expect to find any more?"

"I don't know what to expect Tobius, but we need to be sure, so we must treat all Androids as suspect."

"Do we know where the Android was tampered with?", asked Folcrom Andromeche.

"Andromeche", Forkbraid nodded to her, "Security at the spaceport is tight, really tight. They were transported directly here, still in their crates, straight to us. I don't see how they could have been tampered with during transport. The security seals on their crates showed no signs of tampering. There's only one possibility I can think of." Forkbraid reached for his goatee and thoughtfully tugged at it.

"Please, share your thoughts, Forkbraid", Andromeche could see where this was leading.

---

4 Woomera Spaceport in central South Australia.

"If they were tampered with on Earth, our [5]RV's would have scanned the perpetrators intentions while they were still making their plans. We would have caught them and stopped them in the planning stages. This attack would never have happened. It should never have happened."

"Android shipments are delivered straight from [6]L-Five, straight from the Hyper Dynamics Corporation", Folcrom Selene shouted out, looking particularly alarmed.

"Yes! This Android was modified off-world during the manufacturing process", Forkbraid stated boldly, then added, "The terrorists are up there at L-Five! The bastards are off-world."

The chamber fell silent.

Finally, some-one stated the bleeding obvious, "We cannot scan off-world!", it was Folcrom Janeth, a slightly built young woman with dark, deep penetrating eyes.

"Precisely, Janeth. *Fear, Uncertainty, and Doubt*. You all know the score, our fears, our phobias, our uncertainties, and doubts, bring us all undone."

"But off-world, Forkbraid, are you sure?"

"We can scan the entire globe, Janeth. If they were here, we would have found them."

"Some psychics can't use their gifts under certain circumstances, you know that, Forkbraid."

"Of course, I know it. Some fail on a plane, some on a ship, some underwater, underground, what-ever. It all depends on the individual's particular phobias, their particular disposition", it was all well known to them, "but we manage to cover the entire globe, we cover all bases. Where one RV fails, we have another RV to cover the gap and so on and so on."

"And all the gaps are covered?"

"On this world, yes, all the gaps are covered. There are no gaps down here. The one place we cannot scan is off-world!"

"This is unprecedented!", shouted Tobius, "We have never had an attack

---

5   Remote Viewer. A psychic whose main capability and/or occupation is remote viewing.

6   L-Five. A point in space approximately 384,000 km from Earth where the Earth & Moon's gravitational forces cancel each other out.

originating off-world. This is unprecedented!"

"And it's been such a long time since we've had an attack", added Janeth.

"It was bound to happen. I've said it countless times, four billion of our people don't live on the Earth. They live up there", Forkbraid pointed skywards, "scattered across the solar system in the inky black of the void. It was only a matter of time. The terrorists, the extremists, have simply moved to where we can't find them", he finished, shaking his head.

There was silence in the chamber again, then some moments later Selene spoke, "We are closing that gap too, Forkbraid."

"Yes, the Elysium colony. A thousand psychic families on Mars", Forkbraid smiled, then added, "But it still doesn't cover all the gaps."

"No, but it is another world. What we have accomplished here, we can duplicate there."

"I've said this before many times, Selene. Even if the colonists manage to settle in and use their gifts on Mars, even if they have complete use of their gifts, even if they do there, what we have accomplished here, it does not cover the gaps. It merely covers one more planet."

"Yes, but still, even that will be an accomplishment."

"Selene, it's the space between the planets we need to cover. The [7]Cis-Lunar reaches, the asteroid belt, the [8]outer satellites, the places that we fear to go."

"So few of us can use our gifts off-world, Forkbraid, you know this", Tobius stepped in.

"And there we have the problem, Tobius. We need to walk among the off-worlders. We need to be up there with them."

Again there was silence, before some-one else asked a curious question, "Do they know?"

Forkbraid turned to his left, "Tarquin?"

"Do they know, Forkbraid?", Folcrom Tarquin asked again, he was an old man, his long hair completely grey and straggly, he looked out from behind

---

7   Cis-lunar space. The region of space encompassing the Earth and Moon.
8   Outer Satellites. The moons of the outer planets, Jupiter, Saturn, Uranus, and Neptune.

sightless eyes, "Do they know?", he turned his head to face Selene.

"I don't think they could possibly know", Forkbraid was now looking at Selene as well, "We've kept that tightly under wraps."

"We can't cancel, everything is scheduled", Selene stated, "More than five years of hard work. We're so close to completing it, we're almost there. I simply won't allow it!"

The Mars project was Selene's, any hint of disruption would not be tolerated.

"If they know, you'll all be a target", Tobius gave Selene a concerned look while pointing his finger.

"They couldn't possibly know. It's just another Martian colony being set up."

"Not just another colony, Selene, a colony of psychics", stated Tobius adding, "And it's one hell of a long flight to Mars."

"Selene, we should really postpone the flight. At least until we know what we're up against."

"We can't postpone, Forkbraid. Nearly all the colonists are already aboard the Ptolemy, in high earth orbit. I'll be joining them myself with the last batch in two days."

"What do you think, Pandora?", Forkbraid had turned to his right and enquired of his old mentor.

Folcrom Pandora flicked her head, grey streaked hair flying in all directions, her eyes closed, her head lowered. Everyone in the chamber watched intently. Pandora was particularly gifted.

Pandora lifted her head and opened her eyes, "They don't know anything about Elysium. Our colonists should be safe."

"How can you be sure?"

"Simple logic Forkbraid. If you had the choice between taking out an interplanetary liner full of psychic colonists or a small psychic induction ceremony, the former being easy, the latter being hard..... which would you choose to destroy?"

"I would have chosen the liner, easy target, Pandora, more victims and far greater damage, more notoriety."

"Precisely, Forkbraid. Had they known, the induction ceremony would have gone without a hitch. They would have targeted the liner, and we would be having these deliberations in the future, several days from now, with much greater carnage to discuss. Things could have been worse!"

Forkbraid smiled, "I believe you're right, Pandora."

"Still, I recommend that security be tightened on the Ptolemy. Have the ship completely screened for anything suspicious, Selene. Bow to stern, have that ship completely checked, everywhere!"

"Yes, Tobius, I was going to do so as a precaution anyway."

"Good then, all we need to worry about is who we're going to send to hunt these mongrels down."

Silence in the chamber once more.

Forkbraid stroked his beard once again, "It can't be Selene, you'll be on your way to Mars", he glanced over to Selene.

"Well there are only two psychics qualified to hunt for terrorists off-world and if it can't be Selene, then that leaves you, Forkbraid."

"Then we'll need to settle a couple of other issues first."

"Other issues?", Tobius looked curiously at Forkbraid.

"Yes. Firstly I am very sorry to report that the attack killed fifty-seven children, among them a very promising level nine."

"Yes, we saw that not many of the children have survived. It is a terrible tragedy.", sadness clearly visible in his eyes.

"This morning's ceremony was special in so many ways. Two other level nines, both walk-ins survived the attack. They will both need very particular training."

"Two walk-ins, Forkbraid?"

"Yes, Tobius, two walk-ins. Both female, both level nines at least, one physically present, one not."

Selene looked up at Forkbraid and exclaimed, "The touch!".

He smiled gently at Selene, "The touch!"

"Firstly, we have the walk-in Roseanne Rhein", Forkbraid began, "Roseanne has the highest potential of any child I have ever assessed, well above level nine.", murmurs erupted in the chamber.

He raised a single hand in the air for silence and then continued "Ordinarily such a gifted teenager would be apprenticed to myself, but as I will be off hunting terrorists, someone else will need to be her Master and Mentor."

"I will teach her myself", offered Tobius.

"No, Tobius, it can't be you, there is only one other that can teach her", Forkbraid looked towards Selene, "You must teach her, Selene. You must teach Roseanne!"

"But, I'm leaving for Mars in two days."

"Yes, and Roseanne Rhein will be going with you."

"To Mars, what about her parents?"

"I've already checked. Roseanne Rhein is a ward of the state of Victoria. Her parents died in a car accident when she was only five years old. That's why she wasn't picked up during the psychic testing at primary school. At the time, Roseanne Rhein was in a coma in hospital."

"That explains a lot. That's probably why she was able to launch into such a powerful [9]OBE."

"Yes, all she needed was a trigger, and we provided it", Forkbraid smiled once more, then added, "And we must remember, Selene, during the cold hard stare, what did Roseanne's mind reach for?"

"Oh my God, the smiling redness that turned blue-green with joy. Mars!"

"Yes, Roseanne's destiny is on Mars", Forkbraid smiled again, "You'll need to take Charlene Fewkes and Marcus Greyhelm with you as well."

"Charlene and Marcus?"

"Yes. There's a nexus of sorts forming. I can't quite make it out yet. It's on Mars and all four of you are needed there."

Selene was deep in thought, "Yes, I'm beginning to see what you mean, I'll make arrangements."

"What about this touch?", Tobius interrupted.

"A child reached out to me through a television camera. A child of about eight, named Miranda."

"A television camera? Are you sure?"

---

9   Out of Body Experience. The experience of the mind, separated from the physical body.

"Oh yes, Tobius and it gets better. I was able to reach out and get a rough location for this child."

"Okay then, we'll just organise a pickup, and we'll bring her in. Two days tops!"

Forkbraid frowned, "That's not exactly going to work, Tobius. I'm definitely going to have to bring this child in myself."

"You? But you're going up to L-Five to hunt terrorists?"

"Yes, which is kind of ironic in a way because this child lives in a colony at L-Five. I don't know which one yet, but I will find her. I can kill two birds with one stone so to speak."

The chamber was filled with shocked faces, anyone would have thought they'd been slapped about the heads with wet fish. Every-one was literally gob smacked.

After several moments Janeth spoke, "This child is an off-worlder? .....and a psychic?"

"That does appear to be the case, Janeth. An off-world psychic, the first one we've ever encountered, and my initial assessment is that this child is at least a level nine."

The room was quiet now. Faces turned from one to another, off-world psychics didn't exist. To find one, even one would be a miracle, to find a level nine was a miracle beyond any other.

"You can't possibly bring her in, Forkbraid. You have terrorists to hunt down. It will be far too dangerous."

"And precisely who else would you send, Janeth?"

Janeth looked around at the other twelve Folcrom of the Grey Council about her. As powerful as they were, only two of their number could fully use their gifts off-world.

Janeth sighed, "There is no-one else."

"I don't know yet which colony this child lives in, but I will find her. This child is too special."

"You'd best deal with the terrorists first. Find this child after the terrorists have been dealt with."

"That's good advice Tobius, and it just so happens, that's precisely what I intend to do."

5. Travellers

Lady Selene entered the infirmary, Charlene was lying comfortably on her bed. The deep laceration on her temple had almost healed, barely visible now and partially covered by her auburn locks. On her left Roseanne was sitting up in her bed. Most of the beds were occupied, courtesy of the attack. Selene drew the curtains around both beds, then whispered a short incantation before sitting at the end of Roseanne's bed.

Looking at Charlene she said, "That wound is almost healed, they do great work here."

"I know, I was worried it would leave a scar."

"So, how have you two been?"

"Not too bad considering. Things could have been a lot worse", replied Charlene.

"I'm fine. They're just keeping me in here for observation", replied Roseanne.

"That, and I'm following your instructions to the letter Selene. Young Roseanne here has not left my side."

"We're both so lucky, considering how many didn't make it."

Selene patted Roseanne's leg, "In every tragedy, there are both victims and survivors. Fewer victims would have been better. Better still, having no attack would have been wonderful, but some things", Selene paused, "we simply can't control."

Selene looked at Roseanne for several moments, then asked "How would you like to go to Mars?"

"Mars?", Roseanne had a perplexed look on her face.

"Tomorrow I'll be going to Mars. We're setting up a colony, a psychic colony. It won't be much different from here. Charlene will be going as well, assuming you want to go Charlene?"

"Mars? Of course, I want to go. I was really miffed when I failed selection. Why am I going now?"

"Forkbraid says you need to go. So failing selection is irrelevant. Marcus will be going as well."

"What about my studies?", a confused Roseanne asked.

"You have been assigned as my apprentice. So I'll be teaching you personally. Of course, I'll be going to Mars, which means you'll need to come as well."

"I can't go to Mars. It's a whole other planet."

"Forkbraid says it's your destiny. He says that you also need to go to Mars."

"But Mars? I've never even been outside of Australia, this was my first trip outside of Melbourne."

"Roseanne, remember the induction ceremony?"

"How can I forget it? So much death."

"No darling. Not the attack, before that, when we assessed you. When you were *flying*."

Roseanne thought back to the ceremony, to her assessment, "I flew out of my body, up above the Earth and into space."

"Yes, yes, Roseanne", Selene encouraged her, "Where were you flying to?"

Roseanne remembered the smiling redness that had turned blue-green with joy, "Mars!", she shouted, "I need to go to Mars!"

"Well, then it's settled, we need to go to Mars, and I've already made the arrangements", Selene stood up and left the infirmary.

The next day, Lady Selene, Charlene, Roseanne, and Marcus travelled to Whitemark, where they boarded a [10]Hummer at the local airport. It was only a small eight-seat vehicle, but they all had plenty of room. They quickly took off for Woomera Spaceport. Within a few short minutes they were flying above Bass Strait and soon settled in for the two-hour flight.

Marcus turned the hummer north above the Spencer Gulf. They followed the Spencer Cut, a broad, deep man-made canal that connects Spencer Gulf to Lake Torrens and Lake Eyre. Both ethereal lakes, now permanently flooded, formed man-made inland seas in central South Australia. The Spencer Cut opened up the inland region of South Australia to shipping by sea. Before long they had landed on the tarmac at Woomera Spaceport, west of Lake Torrens in the South Australian desert, close to where the [11]HLT Achilles was being prepared for space flight.

---

10 Hummer. A small, light antigravity transport vehicle with a range of 6,000 kilometres.

11 Heavy Lift Transport equipped with antigravity lifters and photon thrusters with a range of 400,000 kilometres.

The Achilles wasn't much to look at, an ungainly looking vehicle built along similar lines to the old-fashioned ships known as space shuttles, but with more of a *lifting-body* shape and somewhat longer than she was wide. From bow to stern she was almost two hundred metres long. It was designed to lift cargo and passengers to and from high orbit. In high Earth orbit it would meet with the much larger vessel, the [12]IPL Ptolemy, which would take said cargo and passengers to Mars.

The four from Flinders Island were the last passengers to arrive and were quickly whisked through customs and onto the waiting Achilles. Marcus mentioned more than once that travelling with a VIP passenger always cuts through the red tape. He was right, only forty minutes after arriving at the spaceport they were aboard the Achilles and ready for launch. Less than twenty minutes after that the ship's captain instructed all passengers and crew to take their seats and fasten their seat belts. Interior scanners checked that all instructions had been followed and then the sixty-second countdown began. As the countdown reached zero, the loud humming of the Achilles [13]AGLs kicked in and the Achilles began to lift off.

Within minutes the Achilles was above the sparse cloud deck and approaching the vacuum of space. The captain instructed that all passengers remain in their seats, with their seat belt fastened, until they had docked with the Ptolemy. Crew personnel were allowed to go about their duties. A screen lowered at the front of the passenger cabin. The screen split into four sections showing different views from the ship. On one section there was a view of the retreating Earth. On another section a telescopic view of the colonies at L-Five, another section showed a telescopic view of the Moon. The final section showed a view of their destination, the IPL Ptolemy. The Ptolemy gradually grew larger as the Earth receded.

The Ptolemy was a large ship, nearly a kilometre long. It consisted of three sections, like most of the larger off-world vessels. At the front was a large spherical section, two hundred and fifty metres across. This was the command and passenger module. The Ptolemy could carry well over two thousand passengers and had a crew of two hundred. This trip she would be carrying one thousand psychic couples, colonists for the new Elysium colony on Mars, along

---

12 Interplanetary Liner. Large vehicle equipped with photon thrusters designed to travel from one planet to another.

13 Antigravity Lifters. Devices used to nullify gravity and allow vessels to fly.

with tons of other cargo and equipment. An array of sensors and communications booms extended from the equator of the spherical section.

At the rear of the ship was the drive module. Here there were three immense, powerful photon thrusters, two hundred metres long and over one hundred and fifty wide, that would propel the Ptolemy towards Mars. The ship would thrust towards Mars, accelerating for half its journey, before turning completely around and decelerating for the other half of its voyage. When close enough to Mars and at a slow enough speed, the ship would turn around again for orbital insertion. A one way trip would take a little over three weeks. During the flight, the entire ship would rotate about its central axis. This would generate a centrifugal force, providing an artificial gravity for the crew and passengers in the command module.

The central section of the ship was one long extended boom. It connected the command module with the drive module. Crew personnel could travel within the boom to go from bow to stern. It was strong enough to support the ship and was wide enough to allow for some storage of cargo. Arrayed around the boom at the rear of the command module were a series of HLTs. There were seven in all, the Achilles was to be the eighth. Each was docked to the boom and held in place by an elaborate framework of connectors which held each HLT firmly in place. Once at Mars the HLTs would ferry colonists and cargo down to the Elysium colony on the surface of Mars.

Selene was sitting with the others at the front of the passenger cabin, the VIP section as Marcus had put it. The seating at the front had a little more legroom and a closer view of the screen.

"That's a big ship", Roseanne was in awe of the scene before them.

"Yes, it's certainly that. Roseanne, look closely at the ship."

"Why? What am I meant to be seeing?"

"Look closely at it. And concentrate."

Roseanne did as she was told, she closed her eyes, "I can feel them."

"Feel who?", asked Charlene.

"The other colonists. They're all there on board that ship. Lots of them."

"I can't feel them", Charlene was concerned, "I can't feel any of them, not even the ones on board our ship."

"Neither can I", Marcus was also starting to worry.

"It's okay guys. I expect very few of us on this ship can use our gifts right now. Everyone else has already been briefed on this particular issue, so I guess it's up to me to brief you guys now. Off-world, your gifts", Selene paused, "will pretty much be useless."

"The fact that Roseanne can still use her gifts is very promising. It means that Forkbraid and I were right all along."

"Right about what?", asked Roseanne.

"That you're special, Roseanne. You need training, for sure, but you show so much promise."

"Roseanne. Look over at the colonies at L-Five", Selene was pointing to the telescopic view of L-Five, "Same deal, concentrate on one of the larger colonies."

Roseanne chose the largest colony, an enormous cylinder in the centre of L-Five and concentrated on it. Her eyes closed. A minute or two passed, then her eyes opened. Roseanne picked another, closed her eyes again and concentrated on it. After a couple of minutes, she opened them again. Twice more she did this, before stating, "Each colony, each one is like a tiny little Earth?" It was almost a question.

"Precisely. Very good. That is exactly what I wanted you to see", Selene smiled.

"I don't understand. What does she mean?", Marcus was confused.

He looked at Charlene, who was equally confused, simply shrugged, "Don't look at me, I don't know."

Selene explained, "Every off-world colony is like a tiny little Earth. You can't see it, but it's true. The fact Roseanne can see it is just wonderful. Let me explain."

Selene thought for a few moments and then began, "When you were back on Earth and you concentrated on the Earth itself, what did you feel?"

Charlene answered almost straight away, "Life!".

"Yes, like an immense tangled web", Marcus blurted out.

"And all of it connected, us to it, it to us", Charlene continued.

"Exactly. [14]Gaia. An off-world colony is just the same, but much, much, much smaller and very, very subtle. The immensity of the Earth, festooned as it is with life, is easily felt, even for a level one. The subtlety of an off-world colony is just so much", slight pause, "harder to feel, even for a level nine. It's a pocket of life, separated from mother Earth. Within itself, it's an interconnected web, but separated from its neighbours. The off-world colonies", again a slight pause, "are an incredibly small analogue of that tangled web of life we feel on the Earth."

Marcus and Charlene were trying to grasp the concept, Roseanne seemed to know instinctively.

"This is why the majority of psychics lose their abilities, the minute they step off-world. We are such an integral part of life on the Earth, that when we leave it, we become disconnected, disoriented. Our fears, our uncertainties, and our doubts take over and bring us undone."

"So that's why I feel so uneasy?", Charlene queried softly.

"Uneasy and somewhat lost!", replied Marcus.

"And now you see it. This is our failing. This is why Mars is so important to us."

"Won't Mars be just like the other colonies?", enquired Roseanne.

"Three centuries ago, before we started terraforming, yes. Now it's all different."

"How is it different?", Roseanne was curious.

"When we first went to Mars, there was a huge debate about whether we should even be there at all. Some groups wanted to lock the planet away and leave it as it was. Other groups wanted to exploit it, mine it for its minerals and put nothing back. There were some groups who wanted to terraform Mars, make it suitable for life, like we have back there on Earth.", slight pause, "Finally, someone did the most obvious thing."

"What was that?", enquired Roseanne.

"A Folcrom, the very first one actually, named Tafazah", another pause, "actually asked Mars what it wanted."

"What Mars wanted? How do you ask a planet what it wants?"

"Well, Roseanne, that's the question. Only one person could, only one person did, and after he shared his experience with the other psychics on Earth, every

---

14 Gaia – The Earth as a living conscious organism of which we are all a part.
Named after the goddess of the Earth.

psychic on the planet agreed with him. Simply put, Mars wanted to live. Mars smiled at the prospect of terraforming, Mars smiled at the prospect of being like Earth. That single event changed the course of human history, at least with respect to the planet Mars."

"Tafazah was a direct ancestor of Forkbraid wasn't he?"

"Yes, Marcus, that he was. His seventh or eighth great-grandfather I believe."

"So how is Mars now like Earth?", Roseanne curiously asked.

"Life, Roseanne, Life. First we imported huge quantities of volatiles and water to Mars, from the [15]centaur bodies orbiting between Saturn and Uranus. Huge quantities of carbon dioxide, nitrogen, oxygen, methane and other gases. This thickened the atmosphere and raised the temperatures, which in turn released much of Mar's own soil locked atmosphere. The water created oceans that now cover thirty-five percent of the surface. We seeded the oceans and land with a soup of nutrients and microbes. Genetically modified higher life forms to suit the new environments and transplanted them to Mars. As each milestone was reached, we stepped up to the next level of complexity. The life we transported became more and more complex. This all started three centuries ago, and it's continued beautifully until now."

"Until now?", Roseanne was still curious.

"Now Mars has tundras, grasslands, temperate forests, there are even a few rain forests around the equator. There are fish in all the oceans, seas, rivers, and lakes. Wild animals, large and small, roam the lands. Each specifically modified to be able to survive and prosper. So much so, they've had to introduce predators. At Elysium, one of the tasks our colonists will have is to introduce cetaceans. Can you imagine it, we will be introducing dolphins and porpoises to Mars! Later, they may even introduce whales."

"So this new Mars with all its life, is just like the Earth", stated Marcus.

"No", Selene looked somewhat disappointed, "It's a start though."

"A start? What more needs to be done?"

"People, Marcus! The terraforming is not complete until people take their place on Mars and complete the transformation."

"The tapestry", Roseanne nodded her head remembering the Earth's vibrant tapestry of life.

---

15 Centaur bodies – Small icy asteroids orbiting between Saturn and Uranus

"Don't get me wrong. There are people there now. We now have seven official colonies on Mars, including Elysium. Colonists are arriving all the time now. They bring with them seed stock and livestock. There are officially around fifteen thousand on Mars at the moment. All of these colonists live around the seven official colonies, spreading out across the Martian landscape as the colonies grow. Forkbraid says that the actual number is around twenty-five thousand or more."

"So where are all the others?", Marcus asked.

"Small unofficial colonies scattered around the Martian globe here and there. Some set up by squatters wanting to farm the land, others by unofficial mining operations and prospectors, others by smugglers. One of the tasks our colony will be performing is to put in place satellites, to scan the surface and report on the extent of human habitation."

"Why are we setting up satellites? Isn't Elysium going to be a colony of psychics?"

"Yes, Marcus, it is", Selene paused for a moment, "But it may take time for our people to adjust to Mars. It may take months or even years before our people are settled in enough and comfortable enough to use their abilities."

"What about the tapestry? How long will it take to complete?", asked Roseanne.

"Roseanne darling, the tapestry is never complete. Even back on Earth. It is always growing and evolving. The Martian tapestry is new. As our people spread across the Martian globe we all interconnect, even the [16]mundanes interconnect and bring the new tapestry to life. We'll all be inter-meshed with this tapestry of life on Mars, and it'll become so much closer to what we have back here on the Earth. That is the promise of Mars."

"So that's what we're trying to achieve?", Roseanne understood now and was smiling.

"And more. Forkbraid believes that one day, all the colonies will interconnect, right across the solar system. Only we humans have to first evolve to be able to perceive the tapestry of life in the absolute smallest of colonies, the smallest of places. Or as Forkbraid once put so succinctly, *When we perceive life in a single atom, we will truly perceive the truth, and truly we will understand life.*"

Roseanne looked up at the screen and pointed. The Ptolemy was much closer now. They could all see where the Achilles was going to dock very clearly now.

---

16 Mundane. Ordinary folk who lack psychic ability as opposed to "supramundane", or psychic.

On one side was the HLT Patroclus and on the other side the HLT Hector. Roseanne knew her history and smiling she said, "Patroclus and Hector. We're going to dock between friend and foe."

Charlene and Marcus both laughed.

Selene took out her [17]PDA and checked the reports. Security teams had swept every inch of the Ptolemy and its attached HLTs. Nothing was overlooked. Everything had been checked and everything was clear. Selene gave a slight sigh of relief.

"We'll be docked in about ten minutes."

Roseanne pointed to another screen. It showed the colonies at L-Five. In the bottom left corner a small object had appeared. It was quickly approaching the colonies.

"Lord Folcrom Forkbraid is on board that ship", she stated boldly.

"Really, Roseanne. How do you know that?", asked a curious Charlene.

"I can just feel him there", she paused, "It's hard to explain."

"Roseanne is right. Forkbraid is on board that ship. I can feel him too", stated Selene, there was a slight, but perceivable sadness in her voice.

"He said goodbye to you last night didn't he?", Roseanne gently asked.

"Yeah. He took his personal ship up to a colonial liner last night. That's the one, the Chimera I believe", a small tear slid slowly down Selene's cheek.

"You won't be seeing him again?", a concerned look was in Roseanne's eyes.

"No. Not unless he comes to Mars", replied Selene in an even sadder voice.

"You guys were really close", Roseanne held out a comforting hand.

"You never know", said Marcus, "Forkbraid is hunting off-world terrorists. There's no telling where his hunt might lead him".

"And even if his hunt doesn't take him out our way, Forkbraid does travel well. He might decide to come out and visit, just for the fun of it", added Charlene.

Selene smiled lightly, as the Captain announced the Achilles would be docked within minutes.

---

17 PDA – Personal Digital Assistant, although much more powerful than ours.

6. The Hunt Begins

Lady Selene walked out into the courtyard, in the evening before her emigration to Mars, it was ten thirty pm. The sky was overcast and the night was cold and dark. Forkbraid had taken his personal ship out of his workshop. It was an antique, a leftover from the long ago Outer Satellite Insurrection. A brutal rebellion that had been relatively short-lived, put down by the military might of Earth and L-Five. Forkbraid had painstakingly rebuilt the centuries old craft. The only real modifications he had made were modernisations to its drive and weapons. It was an interceptor, more commonly called a [18]Bat Wing.

"Are you really going to fly that thing?"

"Sure, I don't see why not. The council", Forkbraid cocked an eye-brow, "has a colonial liner waiting for me", he paused, "The Chimera. This little ship is the quickest way to reach it."

"You don't have to go on this hunt, you know? You could always come with me to Mars."

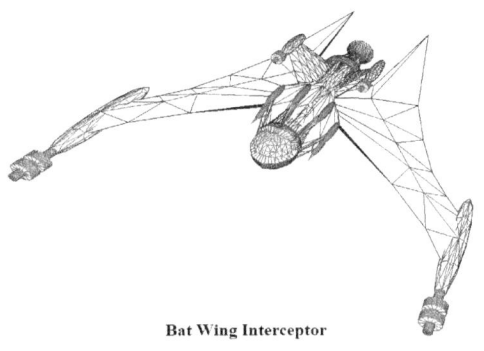

Bat Wing Interceptor

"We've had this discussion before Selene and besides, there is no-one else, they need me."

Selene reached forward and grabbed Forkbraid's arm, "You'll be up there in the inky black of space, on your own, with no backup. It's too dangerous.", almost angry with a deep look of concern.

"I have to go, if I don't, if we don't respond to this attack, they'll become bolder. Next time they'll rain hell down upon us and there'll be no-one, no-one to stop them. I'm doing this for you, for all of us. It's the only way to ensure that we're all safe."

"And if you survive? What then? Will you join me on Mars?"

"Selene", Forkbraid held her hands in his, "Mars is your baby. You chose to set up the Elysium colony. You made that choice."

"That was more than five years ago. I", she stuttered, "I hardly knew you back then", tears began to well up in her eyes.

---

18 Bat Wing Interceptor. Seven lasers, two wing mounted particle beams, two fin mounted pulsed plasma cannons.

"You knew this day would come. I've always said it would."

"I know", Selene was openly weeping now, "I just thought you'd change your mind, that you'd come with me."

Forkbraid placed his hands gently about Selene's head, he looked deeply into her eyes, "Don't cry", he whispered, "You know I'll always be with you, even when I'm not."

"You know I love you. I always have."

"I know. And you know I feel the same."

Forkbraid placed his forehead to Selene's and then they [19]shared. Long minutes passed then finally, "You see, I'll be with you always Selene."

"It's not the same", Selene embraced him and then they kissed deeply.

Long minutes passed once more, then Selene pushed Forkbraid gently away, "Go. Go now. Don't make this any harder for me. You're breaking my heart."

Forkbraid leant forward, he kissed Selene's forehead gently, turned and jumped into the Bat Wing. "Selene, when I find these mongrels, I'll deal with them. Once that's done, there's only the girl, Miranda to find. Then we'll see what the future holds", he pressed a button and the cockpit closed.

Seconds later the Bat Wings AGLs hummed into action and the Bat Wing lifted slowly into the sky. When it reached about one hundred feet, Forkbraid fired up the [20]Magneto plasma drive. The Bat Wing shot forward at high speed and Selene watched as it carried Forkbraid skyward. In less than a minute it was gone.

The Captain of the Chimera was frowning, he didn't like it when his ship was behind schedule. On this trip their departure was two hours late. His passengers were suitably angry and irritable. His crew were somewhat put out as well.

His only consolation was that it was not his fault. "John, are we still on launch hold?", he asked his co-pilot.

"Yeah. Still waiting for that [21]VIP", John replied adding, "Our cabin crew have been handing out refreshments, so that should keep the passengers happy for a while."

---

19 Sharing of consciousness, telepathic two-way transmission of memories, consciousness, and experiences.

20 Magneto Plasma Drive. Electromagnetic plasma drive.

21 Very Important Person, but every-one already knows that.

"Right. Just what we all need, a cabin full of drunken passengers", Captain Jenkins replied, "Wait a minute, what's that blip on the scanners?"

"It's", John the co-pilot paused for a moment, "It's a small ship", he paused again, "It's moving fast."

"Our VIP?", the Captain leant over to look at the scanner, "Christ! It's a Bat!"

"A Bat!", the co-pilot took a closer look, "Yeah, so it is."

"Our VIP's flying a Bat!", Captain Jenkins turned up the resolution on the scanners to maximum.

John the co-pilot exclaimed, "And she's carrying a full complement of weapons!"

"What the flaming hell is going on here?", Captain Jenkins flicked on the communicator to hail the approaching ship, the screen before him went blue *"Communications denied"* flashed up.

"Sir. Who ever it is, he's requesting [22]DCI"

The communications screen flicked an emblem into view, it was an ornate crest covered with various symbols, to one side of it was a dragon, to the other a gargoyle.

"Christ! Give him DCI. Ensure our VIP is directed to an internal dock", the Captain paused, giving thought, "In cargo bay three."

"Sir, what is that?", the co-pilot asked curiously.

"Something I hoped never to see. Something I never want to see again. Our VIP is a Wizard!"

"A Wizard? They never travel off-world."

"Sometimes they do. Very, very rarely, but sometimes they do. It's a harbinger of trouble."

"What do we do, Sir?", John, the co-pilot, appeared nervous.

"We. We do nothing. We let him on board, he takes his seat and we… we stay out of his way."

The Chimera's navigation computer took control of Forkbraid's ship, and within minutes it was safely docked within cargo bay three. The dock re-

---

22 Docking Computer Interlock. Interlocking of ships navigation computers for automated docking.

pressurised and Forkbraid jumped out. He headed quickly for the passenger cabin.

At the entrance a stewardess stopped him, "So you're the one we've been waiting for", her jaw dropped as she got a proper look at him.

Before her stood a tall man wearing a dark, hooded cloak. It had a strange insignia that she had never seen before. On his feet he wore simple leather sandals. The man threw back his hood and the stewardess regained her composure. For all his frightening attire and appearance, he seemed to have a friendly enough face.

"Sir, you can't take that into the cabin", she pointed to his staff.

Forkbraid was holding a six-foot-long staff. Its top was mounted with three equally spaced boars tusks, and a crystal was mounted into the centre of it. Forkbraid looked at her for a moment as if not understanding.

"Sir, it will be dangerous", she insisted.

"Ah. I see what you mean."

Forkbraid pointed the staff towards the aisle of the cabin, its base touched his robe. A pocket that had not been there before opened up and Forkbraid pushed the staff into it. When the top of the staff finally entered the pocket, it closed and vanished, as if it had never been. The stewardess's jaw dropped once more.

Forkbraid asked, "Is everything satisfactory now?"

"Yes, yes", she stuttered, "Please take your seat. It's the fifth seat on the left."

"Thank you, Angela", he bowed, before walking to his seat.

Angela the stewardess looked at her tunic, she had forgotten her name badge, *'How did he know my name?'*, she thought silently to herself as she fumbled about a draw to find her name badge.

Forkbraid walked down the aisle, passengers stared at him. Some were angry at the delay, others curious at his attire, a few were somewhat frightened, one was *"tired and emotional"*. Forkbraid took his seat and made himself comfortable.

Across the aisle from him a young boy named Thomas was growing increasingly excited, until finally, "Dad! Dad! Look, Dad, he's a Wizard."

His father turned around to look; Thomas father's eyes were bloodshot, courtesy of way too many double jacks on ice, "Na boy, he ain't no Wizard!", he slurred, "He's a clown in a fucking Halloween costume!"

"Don't be rude, Jethro!", his Wife scolded, "Sorry, Mister, my Husband's had far too much to drink I'm afraid. Please, just ignore him."

"Drunk! Drunk! Woman I ain't drunk! Jeez woman! Can't a man have a quiet drink!"

"Please, Jethro, don't make a scene", his Wife implored.

"Scene! I ain't making no scene! And he doesn't care either! The clowns all dressed up for trick or treat! Ain't yeah mate?"

Forkbraid looked intently at Jethro, he could see he meant no harm, it was the booze talking.

Calmly he said to the man, "You look tired, Jethro, it's a long flight, perhaps you could do with a nap?", his voice had a very unusual lilt to it.

Jethro became slightly agitated, "I ain't tired!", he yawned, "I don't", he paused and yawned again, "need", yawning again, "no nap", then gave off a gentle snore. He was fast asleep.

Jethro's Wife looked at Forkbraid, "That's a neat trick Mister. Mind teaching me that one."

Forkbraid smiled and shook his head.

Jethro's Son Thomas was still excited, he asked, "Are you a Wizard ,Mister?"

"Thomas, leave the man alone. He's had enough noise from your father."

"It's okay, I don't mind", he assured her, "Now Thomas I'm not a Wizard", to which Thomas looked disappointed. "I'm a Witch. Whether male or female, a Witch is a Witch."

Thomas eye's lit up "Core, that's cool!"

"Have you heard the tale of the Sorcerer's apprentice?" Forkbraid asked Thomas.

Thomas shook his head and said, "No."

"Okay then, well it goes like this" and Forkbraid launched into the tale.

Some while later Forkbraid had finished telling the story, as he looked up he noticed a crowd of children around him. Some adults had played musical chairs, changing their seats allowing the children to sit closer to the storyteller who was keeping them all so enthralled.

"Tell another one, Mister, please tell another one?", a girl with red hair and bright blue eyes asked.

Forkbraid smiled as he thought of a new tale, "How about ...."

This went on for most of the trip. Even some parents were listening intently. It was a twelve-hour flight to L-Five and the story telling was a perfect way to pass the time. It only stopped once for lunch and even then it was a quick lunch.

The stories varied from the mystical fairy tales from old Europe, to tales from the Indian epics, the Mahabharata and Ramayana, and tales of the Arabian nights. Sometimes between the tales, Forkbraid would perform magical tricks, at one time pulling a real gold doubloon from thin air. He quickly made it vanish and requested eight children to check behind their right ears. Each child reached up to their ears and pulled out a piece of eight. Dutifully they placed them into Forkbraid's outstretched hand. His sleeves were pulled up so they could see there was nothing up his sleeves.

He closed his hand and then re-opened it, the pieces of eight were gone. Astonished looks were on the faces of the children. Then he closed his hand again and then re-opened it, his hand was full of gold doubloons, The children screamed with glee. There was precisely one for each child in his audience, which had swelled by now to fifteen.

Thomas Mother bit her teeth into her Son's gold doubloon, "My God! It's real!", she shrieked.

Angela the stewardess had been watching intently, it was usually hard work to keep all the children entertained on these long flights. Forkbraid made their task much easier. She smiled at his doubloon trick, it was truly impressive. Forkbraid smiled back, he clicked his fingers and another gold doubloon dropped out of thin air just in time for Angela to reach out and catch it. "That one's for you", he said with a smile. Angela blushed and curtseyed, "Thank you kindly Sir", as she placed the doubloon into her blouse. The story telling went on for the whole flight and the time passed quite quickly indeed.

Soon they were approaching their destination, Colonial Central Command. It was an immense colony, its main cylinder was twenty kilometres long and four kilometres wide. At each end were hemispherical caps, two kilometres in radius. Three enormous mirrors extended out from the rear of the main cylinder at an angle, to catch the Sun's rays and reflect them towards immense window strips running the length of the main cylinder. Each end cap had a circular window running around it, where they joined the main cylinder. Mirrors reflected sunlight through these windows as well. The whole structure rotated to produce centrifugal force, creating an artificial gravity for its interior. Well over ten million people lived within this one cylinder. This was the Chimera's destination, an immense [23]O'Neil type colonial cylinder.

Scattered all around L-Five, other colonies could be seen and there were thousands of them. They were of varying sizes, all smaller than Colonial Central, some much, much smaller. Not all were cylinders either. Some were Bernal style spheres, others were huge Toroidal style colonies. Each a self-contained world in its own rite, complete with cities and towns, farms, forests, parks, rivers, mountains, and even weather. Some, the older, smaller colonies, had populations of around ten thousand, the larger ones had populations in the hundreds of thousands and even millions. One of these was Hyper Dynamics Corporation, a private corporate world where all the inhabitants were employees. This was to be Forkbraid's destination and where his investigation was to begin.

The Chimera had docked gently to the rear docking ring of Colonial Central Command. All the passengers were disembarking and would soon be going through customs. All ships from Earth and the other planets and satellites came to Colonial Central Command. This was L-Five's immigration centre, the clearing house for all travellers coming to and going from L-Five. From here passengers could, if they required, catch smaller transports to their ultimate destinations within L-Five. Forkbraid noticed Thomas Father Jethro had finally woken up, he appeared to be nursing one all mighty hangover. The customs gates approached.

Forkbraid approached the customs desk, the two officers looked at him curiously. He wore a black cloak over what appeared to be a simple black robe. His hood was drawn back, clearly they could see his face. His long hair was of a light brown, almost a sandy blond colour and parted in the middle. His goatee was long, braided, and forked at the end. His face was thin, and his features refined with a gentle look about it, yet underlying this was the visage of a viper. His eyes appeared as if they could pierce through the core of a neutron star.

On his cloak, upon the left breast was an emblem. It was intricate and they could not understand its meaning. There was a circle of runes, the runes of the elder futhark, then within this was another ring of runes, three phrases separated by colons. Those versed in runic lore would render the phrases as a single sentence thus, *Love and Light, Justice and Might, All things Good, Holy and Right*. This

---

23 O'Neil type colony cylinders as described by Gerard O'Neil in the early 1970s.

was the original motto of the first Folcrom, Lord Folcrom Tafazah, Forkbraid's ancestor.

Within this ring was a brightly coloured green dragon with wings outstretched. Its eyes looked towards the heart of the cloak's wearer. The torso of the green dragon was covered by a symbol. For those who were versed in runic lore, it was a bindrune, a very special one, known as the Sigil of Folcrom. The wearer of the cloak wore simple sandals of leather upon his feat. He carried no baggage of any kind. The two officers looked at each other, *hmm* they thought, *we have a right loony here, one of those days.*

"No baggage, Sir?", one of the customs officers, Larry enquired.

"Hmm, plenty of baggage actually", replied Forkbraid

"And where pray tell would that be?", pausing, "May we inspect it, Sir?"

Forkbraid smiled, "No, you may not."

Larry grinned, "Jeff, we have a live one here."

"Passport, Sir?", requested Jeff.

"Give me a moment", Forkbraid smiled, "I have it here somewhere."

He reached into his robe and a pocket appeared from out of nowhere, he reached into it and pulled out his staff. The six-foot staff was extracted, and he placed it beside him. It remained standing all by itself.

Forkbraid reached into his pocket once more and rummaged around, "It's in here somewhere, I'm sure of it", he smiled.

The two officers stared at the staff. It was six feet tall, crowned with three boar tusks and atop its centre was embedded a large crystal. Below this were three symbols, they were the *all seeing eye of Ra, the Pentacle and the Sigil of Folcrom*. Below this was a phrase written in runes, but also in Icelandic, for those who could read it, it read *Ek Vitki Rist Runa Odhinn!,* in a counterclockwise direction. Then below this were nine words and a phrase, again all in runes. For those who could read them, they read *Air, Fire, Water, Earth, Ice, Yeast, Iron, Salt and Venom*, the other phrase reading *Staff of lore and light.* Below this was the phrase *Ek Vitki Rist Runa Odhinn!,* yet again but in a clockwise direction. Below this were three names in runic, *Urdhr, Verdhandi and Skuld.* Finally wrapped around the base in a clockwise direction the phrase, *Yggdrasill's root.* The meaning of all this was completely unknown to the two customs officials. They stared with eyes wide and jaws agape, not comprehending what they perceived. It was quite the distraction.

"Ah, here it is", Forkbraid held up his passport, the pocket from whence it came, had vanished.

The two customs officials stopped staring at the staff and looked at the document. Larry opened it and turned to the identity page. There was a picture of Forkbraid, it matched perfectly with the man standing in front of him. Larry read his name, *Lord Folcrom Forkbraid. Count (Enchanted words that he could not read). Fehu and Othala. The Double Dragon who Flies Upon the Wings of Time. High Priest of the Golden Path, Master of Light and Darkness. The Magus who Stands Astride the Abyss, Dispenser of Justice. He who holds the Keys of Life.*

"Blimey, get a load of this!", Larry exclaimed.

Jeff had a look, "What the! What kind of name is that?"

"That would be mine", replied Forkbraid.

"What's this say then?", Larry pointed to the words he could not read.

"That's", Forkbraid paused, "a part of my name."

"I know that, but what does it say?", Larry asked.

"Can't you read?", Forkbraid was getting a little short with them.

"Sure, I can read", stated Larry a little embarrassed, "I want to hear you say it."

Forkbraid stated his name in full, including the section that Larry and Jeff could not read.

"I didn't get that bit in the middle there. Did you, Jeff?"

"No, I got the rest. Just not that bit in the middle."

"Could you say it again? In English this time", Jeff asked.

"That was in English", Forkbraid replied adding, "Would you care to turn to the visa section?", a strange lilt was now present in his voice.

Larry thumbed through the passport to the visa section. It was stamped with a single, coloured stamp. An ornate crest with three symbols emblazoned upon it in red, the same as on Forkbraid's staff. On one side of the crest was a dragon, on the other side a gargoyle. Larry's jaw dropped, he passed the passport to his colleague. Jeff took one look at the visa and froze. Many long moments later he slammed the passport shut and handed it back to Forkbraid, who quickly placed it back within his pocket.

Jeff gulped loudly, then said "Have a nice stay in the colonies Sir. You're free to go. Feel free to visit the duty-free shop while you're in the spaceport. Have a nice day."

Forkbraid walked off through the customs arrival gate and into the spaceport, his staff dutifully followed all by itself.

As he did so he caught part of Larry and Jeff's conversation. "He was for real. I thought his getup was a lark, you know another loony."

"Yeah. A right tosser I picked him for too. Never thought he'd really be a Wizard."

Forkbraid chuckled silently to himself, 'Wizard! Will they ever get it right', he sent a silent message to the pair, "*The correct term is Witch!*"

Larry and Jeff stood up straight, slowly turned and looked at each other.

On the other side of the arrivals gate, a lone man wearing a suit and trench coat held up a sign that simply read "Wizard."

"*Oh crap*", Forkbraid thought to himself, "*You too*", he said to the man with the sign.

"Beg your pardon, Sir?"

Forkbraid tapped the sign with his index finger, the man held the sign-up, now it said *"Witch."*

The man with the sign stared at it for a moment before regaining his composure.

"I'm Special Agent Murphy, James Murphy. I'm here to take you directly to the President's office. Where's your baggage, Sir?"

"It's being taken care of", it was easy to tell a small fib than go into a lengthy explanation.

"Excellent. I was never one for carrying bags", Special Agent Murphy smiled, "This way, Sir."

"My name's Forkbraid, I'd prefer not to be called Sir."

"As long as you call me Jim. Is it okay if I call you, FB?"

Forkbraid smiled, "Sure. Why not."

Agent Murphy, Jim, led Forkbraid to a waiting [24]Pod. The white egg-shaped vehicle had doors that opened like a gull's wing. They both stepped inside, Forkbraid taking his staff in hand. The doors closed automatically, and the transport started moving towards its pre-programmed destination.

Jim's PDA gave off a slight buzz. He flipped it open and quickly scanned the message. He smiled and shook his head, "You brought a Bat with you. Mate, that's going to piss off more than a few people. What possessed you to bring a Bat Wing?"

"Really", Forkbraid smiled back, "I hadn't really thought about it."

"Yeah, well anyway, it's been impounded. You'll get it back when you head home."

"Just so long as it's handy. I might need it for what's ahead."

Jim fell silent for a few moments, "Really", slowly asking, "Is it that bad?"

"Don't you watch the news Jim? What do you think I'm here for?

"I don't rightly know. I hadn't really thought about it."

"The attack, Jim. Remember it? That's why I'm here."

"The attack. Yeah, I remember it, but what's that got to do with L-Five?"

"The bomb originated at Hyper Dynamics Corporation. The mongrels are up here in L-Five. You have rats, Jim", Forkbraid wasn't smiling.

"Whoa", Jim fell silent once more. This was terrible news.

---

24 Pods, the main form of transport on the larger L-Five colonies capable of carrying six passengers.

7. Little Witchling

Miranda watched the scene before her. This Hyper Dynamics Corporation colony was not overly large, only seven hundred metres long and four hundred metres wide. It was in an early standard O'Neil configuration, complete with end caps. From her vantage point, Miranda could see through the cylinders strip windows to the second cylinder nearby. Hyper Dynamics Corporation consisted of a pair of connected cylinders. Both rotated in opposite directions, each producing enough centrifugal force to simulate one Earth gravity for their interiors.

The cylinders did not have proper names, they were simply called East cylinder and West cylinder. Miranda was looking down the length of the East cylinder towards the sunward end cap. The end caps themselves did not have proper names either, sunward was simply the Northern cap and the opposite end, the Northern cap. This was a common practice across the whole of the solar system for O'Neil-style colonies. The colonies themselves had names, but generally the components of the colonies did not. A similar situation existed with other styles of colonies as well. Those that had a toroidal configuration for instance had generic names such as Ring, Hub and Spokes.

Three window sections ran the length of each cylinder, and light streamed into the interior reflected by three large, well positioned window panels. The land sections on the interior of the cylinders were a patchwork of small farms and food production facilities. It was a beautiful site. A miniature world in its own rite, although rather a tame one.

Miranda had spent the day on an excursion to the Northern cap. Both Northern caps were in their scheduled winter now, complete with snow on the ground and ice on the artificial ponds and river. The children were learning about the juxtaposition of the weather systems in the colony and the children had taken delight in building snowmen and throwing snow balls. Both Northern caps had the opposite weather to the Southern caps, which currently enjoyed a balmy summer. The children had not thought that it was the least bit odd, that their colony could enjoy different seasons in different sections. Nor was it considered odd that the two main cylinders themselves were kept in perpetual spring, to enhance food production.

The windows, which were sheets of transparent aluminium, were tinted to absorb the most harmful sections of the spectrum, allowing in the most beneficial sun-rays for food production. They were thick, double-layered and between these layers were water filled sections. Between the thick, double-layered windows and the internal water layer, most, if not all the harmful sun-rays were absorbed. Beyond the windows, the children could see a handful of the many orbiting manufacturing modules associated with the Hyper Dynamics

Corporation colony.

It was in these that their colony's bread and butter product, humaniform androids were produced. Some of these modules were refineries, processing crushed ore, which was imported from the Moon. The ore was refined into the raw materials that would be used in the manufacture of Androids and other products. These raw materials were further processed into the parts from which the androids etc. were assembled. Other modules were required for android assembly, manufacturing of positronic brains, programming, testing, and storage. These manufacturing and storage modules all floated in controlled orbits about the colony cylinders. The void of space meant that no sound was transmitted from the factory floor to the residences in the cylinders. The only part of the manufacturing process that occurred within the cylinders, was the research and development, which was performed in offices and laboratories within the two Southern end caps. The two Northern end caps were for Corporate Administration.

The children stepped into the airlock, built into the bulkhead between the main cylinder and the Southern end cap. The atmosphere in the main cylinder was kept at seven hundred and seventy millibars with a slightly higher carbon dioxide content. The end caps on the other hand, had Earth standard atmospheres of one thousand millibars, with the atmospheric components at Earth optimal. The airlocks allowed for movement between the different colony sections, whilst enabling each component to have differing atmospheres. The children stepped out of the airlock and into the Southern end cap. Here was one of the four small towns, end caps, where the colonists actually lived. A large hemisphere, two hundred metres from centre to edge. It was set up as a small town built around the interior of a huge bowl. It had apartments, administration offices, research laboratories, schools, shops, restaurants, parks, and gardens etc. All the things you would expect in a small town of around three thousand or so people.

There were even artificial ponds and a river running around its centre. Shrubs and trees grew in the parks and gardens, and here and there amongst the buildings. No one thought it unusual to see trees growing sideways a quarter of the way around the town, nor upside down when viewed on the opposite side. Here the horizon did not curve around the outer edge of a sphere, but instead the inside edge of a bowl. This was where Miranda lived. Life in a colony was like living in paradise.

There was one final stop on the way back to the school. Their teacher, Mrs Harmon, had scheduled time at the colony's observatory. Here they would be able to view the realm outside their tiny, little, self-contained world. The students walked to where their bikes had been parked, it was only a short distance down from the airlock, over the bridge across the windows through which the Sun's rays shone. Nearly all the transport within these smaller colonies was peddle-powered. The only rapid transit systems, of which there were three, one on each land section, ran from one end of the main cylinder to the other.

Mrs Harmon requested that they mount their bikes and follow her to the Colony's observatory. Soon they were riding around the perimeter of the Southern end cap, under the constant glow of sunlight from the redirection mirror, set into the centre of the Southern end cap's bulkhead. It was the middle of a work shift, so bicycle traffic was reasonably light. Miranda's Mother worked in a research lab in the Southern end cap, her Father was currently assigned to work in the positronic matrix assembly plant, off cylinder in an orbiting manufacturing module. Nearly all the adults living in this colony were employees of Hyper Dynamics Corporation.

They turned up the laneway that led to the Colony's observatory. Minutes later they passed by their school and approached the observatory building itself. Another group of students was just leaving, so Miranda's group had only a short wait before entering. They parked their bikes in the observatory's bike racks.

The children took their seats in front of four large screens, two of which were active. The observatory's operator adjusted the screens. The Earth appeared on one of the active screens, the mega-colony Colonial Central Command was on the other. Mrs Harmon began talking about the differences between the larger colonies, the Earth and their small world. As she spoke, the screens would change, highlighting different aspects of the Earth and Colonial Central Command.

Complex cloud patterns could be seen on the Earth. Mrs Harmon explained that the Earth's weather was naturally driven by the Sun and was dependent upon its distance from the Sun, and its orbital and rotational parameters. That the Earth's weather could only be controlled in very limited ways, usually for the purposes of increasing or decreasing regional rainfall. As long as the Earth's atmospheric components remained within certain limits and the Sun's output remained unchanged, the system would remain stable and the planet habitable.

The explanation for the Earth's natural seasons was difficult to understand, the children had never considered that seasons could be anything other than scheduled. Having seasons reliant on the Earth's rotational axis and changing with the position of the Earth in its orbit around the Sun, was a totally alien concept to them. They found it a very difficult concept to swallow.

A close up view of clouds could be seen through the window sections of Colonial Central Command's main cylinder. Mrs Harmon explained that Colonial

Central Command was large enough to have naturally occurring weather within its main cylinder. This was also largely driven by the Sun, but it was controllable far better than on Earth, as its atmosphere was fully contained.

The children considered this something that their small world could never have. Here in their little Hyper Dynamics Corporate world, weather was completely artificially contrived. Here there were never any clouds, only clear skies. The rain always came when the valves were switched on, and it only snowed when the snow-makers were active, and all the seasons followed a strictly controlled temperature schedule. Here there were strictly speaking, no natural systems, yet there was still abundant life.

While Mrs Harmon was talking, the screen panned out for a deeper view of the central regions of L-Five. More and more colonies were coming into view. Mrs Harmon explained that this was their realm, this was where they lived. Here it was so much better than living on Earth or any other planet for that matter. Here we truly had control over our destinies. The children stared in awe at the number of colonies that could be seen, there were literally thousands of them. They varied in shapes and sizes. Most of them were O'Neil-style colonies, many others were Stanford Toroidal designs, quite a few were Bernal spheres. Very few appeared to deviate from these three basic styles.

Their own small world was further out than most, but nonetheless still a part of this grand collection of self-contained worlds. Ferries could be seen travelling here and there between the colonies, and off to the left heading towards Colonial Central Command was a large passenger liner. It was nearly quarter as large as their own colony. A large spherical passenger and command section attached to its drive unit, consisting of three photon thrusters, by an extended boom; it was a fairly standard passenger liner design. It was more than two hundred and fifty metres long, yet considerably smaller than its far larger interplanetary counterparts.

Miranda pointed to the liner, "Look, Miss. There's a Wizard on board that ship!", she exclaimed.

"Don't be silly, Miranda, Witches and Wizards never leave the Earth. They're afraid to."

"Yes they do, Miss", replied Miranda frowning, "Lord Folcrom Forkbraid is on that ship."

A shocked look came over Mrs Harmon's face, quickly she highlighted the ship on the screen, zoomed in and clicked a button. The observatory computer pinged the ship for identification and shortly there after the label [25]CL Chimera appeared on the screen, with other information about its schedule. "What makes you think that he's on that ship, Miranda?"

---

25 Colonial Liner. A mid-sized ship used for transport between orbital colonies and high planetary orbit.

"I don't know, Miss, I just know he is. He's there", came Miranda's reply as she stepped closer to the screen and pointed to the Chimera.

Mrs Harmon thought to herself, *"How can she know this? This child is too weird, she's an abomination before God!"*

Engrossed as she was with the view, little Miranda did not pick up on the thought. It was not the first time that Miranda had stunned her teacher with things that no child should know.

"Come along children, we have to leave now", Mrs Harmon instructed fearfully.

The children pulled themselves away from the view screens and followed Mrs Harmon out of the observatory. They quickly walked to the bike racks and mounted their bikes. Soon they were riding the short distance back to their school. The children arrived back at their school shortly before home time. The bell was due to ring shortly and already household androids had arrived to pick up their charges. It was not long before the bell rang, signalling the end of another school day. Miranda met her brother Chiron, and together they were taken home by Tonka, their family's android.

Mrs Harmon picked up her communicator and pushed the speed dial, within a few short moments a face appeared on the small screen.

The man was bearded, his dark hair short, he had what looked like a permanent scowl on his face, he almost snarled into his communicator, "What is it now, Mrs Harmon?"

"Leroy. We may have a problem!"

"A problem? What possible problem do we have now?", the bearded man was curious.

"Remember the strange child I mentioned some time ago? The one who *'knows'* things."

"Yes, yes, the abomination, I remember. What about this child?", he growled.

"She has seen", Mrs Harmon paused for a moment, "A Wizard on board a ship going to Colonial Central Command."

"A Wizard?", Leroy now had an incredulous look on his face.

"Yes. A Wizard. The little abomination has seen a Wizard coming from Earth", Mrs Harmon was most insistent about it.

"How did she see this?", again the curious look came over him.

"The child doesn't know how. She just knows that the Wizard is there, on the ship."

Leroy thought for a moment and considered the situation, then he asked, "Which ship?"

"The CL Chimera", she replied adding, "And the Wizard is Folcrom Forkbraid himself!"

Leroy looked stunned, "Say nothing to anyone about this. We'll take care of it."

A short while later Leroy met with the leader of his fundamentalist group. A highly charismatic individual whose knowledge of their religion was supposedly second to none. He was their Leader, their Mentor, a man they trusted with something more precious than their lives, their very souls. He was an older man, although his face looked far younger than his years. His bright blue eyes almost sparkled, reflecting both knowledge and intelligence. His hair was short-cropped and fair, his beard long and grey. Most members of their sect wore beards, following their leader's example. No one knew his proper name, they simply called him the Prophet. Leroy relayed Mrs Harmon's information to his master.

"A Wizard on the Chimera? Lord Folcrom Forkbraid himself?", the Prophet too was incredulous.

"Yes, that's what I thought as well", replied Leroy, "but the child, the abomination has seen him."

"We should not rely on the words of an abomination, Leroy", the Prophet was stroking his long grey beard now, thinking half to himself, "so this is how they answer our little gift. We need to verify this new information."

"Yes, yes, my Lord. We have people on Colonial Central", Leroy noted as he agreed.

"Good. Have them watch the passenger arrivals terminals. When the Chimera arrives, watch who gets off. If there is a Wizard amongst them", the Prophet paused considering their options, "Kill him. No mercy for this evil one. The Wizard must die! One cannot allow this evil to live and spread."

"Consider it done my Lord", Leroy left to make the arrangements.

He quickly returned to his apartment and made a b-line directly to his communicator. He sent an urgent message to their contact on Central, being careful to ensure that the message would be fully encrypted.

"Urgent! Wizard, Folcrom Forkbraid, suspected aboard the Colonial Liner Chimera. Watch the passenger arrivals. If the Wizard is amongst the passengers, terminate him."

It was only a few minutes before the reply was received.

"Terminate Wizard? Please confirm the message."

Leroy looked at the reply, they didn't believe it either, he clicked the resend icon. A minute later a new reply flashed up on the screen.

"Understood. It will be taken care of."

Leroy switched off the communicator and sat down to read his version of the bible.

8. Terror Attack on Colonial Central

Two men watched the spaceport's passenger arrivals. They noticed the man wearing a trench coat, waiting by the Chimera's arrivals gate, he held a sign that simply read, *"Wizard."*

The two men looked at each other. So there was a Wizard on board the Chimera and a Colonial Bureau of Investigations Special Agent was waiting for him; that was never a good sign.

The two men stepped much, much further back. A Wizard had to be handled carefully, they didn't want their intentions being read. Wizards had a reputation after all, and they did not want to be scanned. That would be a disaster for them. When they saw Forkbraid come through the gate, they knew their information was correct. They watched as the Wizard's staff followed dutifully after him, hovering and following him all by itself. They watched as the Wizard altered the wording on the Special Agents sign with a tap of his finger. This was all the conclusive proof they needed.

The two men quickly climbed into their Pod, they were gripped with fear. A stray thought now could give them away, would bring them all undone. Watching carefully from a distance, they noted down the number on the Special Agent's Pod. They dare not follow it. After the Special Agent's Pod was safely out of sight, they relayed their information onto another member of their sect.

This new operative took the information and used his computer skills to hack into the transport network. He quickly found the Pod's identification number and looked up its destination. He frowned, it was going straight to Colonial Central Command's government offices.

This would be no easy task. The operative thought to himself, *"Where would a CBI Special Agent take a Wizard?"*

The answer popped into his head almost straight away. Wizards and Witches so rarely left the Earth, so rarely came to L-Five.

If one was to arrive, they were invariably taken to the man in charge of the colonies, *"The President."*

This hit was getting more and more complicated.

Braddock sighed to himself, *"Why can't things ever be simple?"*

Braddock knew what he had to do, and it would probably cost him his life. Quickly he made his way to the bulkhead mountains between Colonial Central Command's southern end cap and its main cylinder. He had chosen his vantage point well. It was high on the Southern end caps terraced bulkhead wall. As far from his target as it could be, yet still well within range of his weapon.

The walls of Colonial Central Command's end caps were set up like artificial mountains, complete with terraces, and forests of conifers. He took his Pod as high as he could and then parked it before climbing out. He took out his satchel and threw it over his shoulder. Braddock would have to walk and then climb the rest of the way. Fortunately it was mid-autumn in Colonial Central Command's southern end cap, so it was neither too hot nor too cold for the climb. Better still, the higher he climbed, the lower the artificial gravity, and he was soon at his destination. He secreted himself in a covered position between some tall, pine trees and opened his satchel.

Braddock took out his weapon. It was a light rail gun. He took out the laser scope and mounted it, then aimed casually around him to check the sighting. All seemed in order. He focused his sights across the Southern end cap and scanned the government offices. He knew the President's office was on the sixth floor, and he quickly found it.

"Sweet!" he thought to himself.

He sat the gun down, took the heavy magazine belt of iron slugs out the satchel and unravelled it beside his weapon. Then carefully clipped the head of the magazine belt to the gun's magazine feed. He picked up his weapon once more and rested it on a branch. Carefully he scanned the President's office, his eyes glued watchfully to the cross-hairs. All he had to do now was wait.

Special Agent James Murphy's Pod arrived at the secure underground garage at Colonial Central Command's government offices. The trip had been uneventful. Both he and Forkbraid stepped out of the Pod and walked to the elevators. They travelled up to level one, where they checked in. Other agents and officers stared as they walked by, they had never seen a Wizard, nor a Wizard's staff, moving as it did, obediently behind its master. They walked to an elevator to take them to level six. Within a few minutes they had arrived at the President's office floor. The President's secretary was waiting for them as they stepped out of the elevator.

"Special Agent Murphy, Lord Forkbraid", she looked curiously at Forkbraid, her eyes focused, and her brow furrowed, "This way", she paused, "Gentlemen."

They followed the secretary a short distance to the President's office and entered.

"Thank you, Tanya. Gentlemen come in", President Banyan smiled, flicking a quick glance at the Wizard's staff floating as it did in its obedient way.

The President's office was quite large, it contained several desks. Tanya walked over to her desk and sat down.

The President beckoned them over to a pair of chairs in front of his desk, "Please gentlemen, take a seat."

They all took their seats. Forkbraid looked around, a large window ran almost the entire length of the office. The view of the Southern end cap was truly spectacular.

"If only we could have Psychic Academies up here", he thought to himself.

"I take it you had a good flight", he asked Forkbraid.

"It was okay", Forkbraid smiled, "Can't say much about the food though."

President Banyan laughed, "I believe that's standard right across the whole system."

Forkbraid smiled back.

"What about you, Murphy? Is everything okay?"

"Yes, Sir, everything is fine", Murphy replied.

"Good, Good. Let's get down to brass tacks shall we."

"So, what are you doing here, Wizard?", Banyan put on a more serious visage.

Forkbraid sighed, "Witch, Sir."

"Witch?", Banyan asked, "I'm not sure what you mean?"

"Wizard is not a term that we use. Male or Female, a Witch is a Witch, we are Witches."

"Oh, I probably should have known that", Banyan replied.

"It tends to slip most people's minds", Forkbraid replied adding, "In answer to your question, Sir, I'm here to track down terrorists."

Banyan sat back in his chair, "Terrorists you say? Up here in L-Five?"

"Yes, Sir, Terrorists, here in L-Five."

"You do know, of course, that… that is the most preposterous thing that I've ever heard."

"Perhaps it is, but it is also completely true. They are here, and I'm here to hunt them down."

"How can you be so sure?", Banyan asked, it was almost a demand.

"The attack at Flinders Psychic Academy. The bomb was planted in a Hyper Dynamics three-o-three humaniform android. A new one, freshly imported from Hyper Dynamics Corporation. The bomb was fitted during manufacture, so the android had no idea it was a weapon."

President Banyon was silent, this was difficult to digest. It was many long moments before he spoke.

Banyon changed tack, "You brought a fully armed Bat with you. Why?"

"I thought that I might need it", Forkbraid simply replied.

"A Bat! Do you know what kind of damage one of those things can do up here?"

"I have no intention of going *'gun'* crazy, if that's what you're worried about."

"No, no, that's not my worry. We just don't like weapons in private hands up here", replied Banyan adding, "And a Bat Wing is one very dangerous weapon."

"We've impounded the Bat Wing, Sir, so it's in safe hands", Special Agent Murphy offered.

"Good, Good", he replied to Murphy, then to Forkbraid he said firmly "You'll get it back when you leave for Earth."

"Now about these terrorists?", Banyan enquired of Forkbraid.

"I have to track them down", Forkbraid replied, "The android came from Hyper Dynamics, so that's my starting point. I'll begin my investigation there."

"Your investigation, Special Agent Murphy", President Banyan pointed to Jim Murphy, "You're in charge of this investigation now."

"Yes Sir., and I'll be starting at Hyper Dynamics, Sir."

"Good. Good", Banyan replied.

"You know, Forkbraid, L-Five isn't like Earth. Down there on Earth, you have the authority to come and go as you please. It's not like that up here."

"How so, Mr President?" Forkbraid asked.

"Every colony here is a separate world in their own right. We have agreements, of course. Colonial Central Command manages external affairs, immigration, emigration, even intercolonial police issues etc. Apart from that, each colony has its own sovereign laws and customs."

"That's not so different from Earth. We do have many separate nations down there you know."

"Yes, but by and large, your nations all co-operate. You have agreements dating back many centuries. Here things are different. Here each colony is fiercely independent. We don't always agree. The crime you're investigating occurred on Earth, not L-Five. Hyper Dynamics Corporation could very well decide not to co-operate with you at all and under our laws, they'd be well within their rights."

"That may be the case, Sir, but this crime was planned and instigated from here at L-Five. Whether they want to co-operate or not, I will track these mongrels down. They will be found and punished!", the coldness in Forkbraid's eyes told President Banyan that this would be so. There was no stopping this man. If Hyper Dynamics would not co-operate, this man would still find a way.

The President stood up and walked across the floor in front of the windows. As he did so he came into view of someone positioned two kilometres away, across the Southern end cap hidden amongst the pine trees.

"Where's the Wizard?", Braddock thought.

As if to answer, Forkbraid and Agent Murphy both stood up and walked over to President Banyan.

"There you are, Wizard! Die!", Braddock smiled.

It was as if time had frozen still, Forkbraid had caught that single stray thought, quickly his mind came into focus.

In his mind a perfect shimmering golden egg formed quickly about him.

His mind reached swiftly outwards and felt the Sun's super hot corona.

His mind drew upon it and imbued the golden egg with the corona's intense heat.

His mind pressed this golden egg outwards to encompass and protect the others in the office, being careful not to harm them as he did so.

Quickly his staff flew into his right hand.

His palm covered its pentagram.

His fingers wrapped about its Sigil of Folcrom.

The All Seeing Eye of Ra had a clear and open view.

The crystal atop Forkbraid's staff glowed an intense golden glow.

Forkbraid's eyes rolled back, showing only their whites,

Forkbraid's mind became a golden pillar of intense concentration.

Less than a split second had passed.

Braddock squeezed the trigger of his light rail gun. Iron shells flew in rapid succession.

The office windows directly in front of Forkbraid shattered. Iron shells flew into the office. They struck Forkbraid's extended shimmering golden egg and their momentum was arrested. They stopped dead as if they'd hit an impenetrable wall. Then they fizzled and melted, dropping harmlessly to the office floor in little pools of molten iron.

Still Braddock fired, strafing the President's office now, sweeping left and right. President Banyan was on the office floor, and Special Agent Murphy had thrown himself over him. Tanya the secretary was screaming wildly under her desk, fear ran through her tormented mind. More and more iron shells fizzled and melted. Long minutes passed as the onslaught continued. Officers and Special Agents quickly came to the President's office. They could not enter. They could not penetrate Forkbraid's protective shell. More and more iron shells fizzled and melted. Frustrated at not being able to strike down his target, Braddock stopped.

Braddock screamed, "Dam you Wizard! Damn you to Hell!", uselessly he strafed the President's office left and right once more, to no effect.

Then he looked down. He smiled a wry smile. Below him in front of the Southern end cap's bulkhead mountains, he saw the end cap's windows through which the Sun's light was reflected. He looked at his light rail gun and smiled again. Transparent aluminium was no match for this weapon. The President's office had no windows now, no protection, blow out a section or two of window panels and everyone, including the Wizard, would be breathing vacuum.

Forkbraid caught the thought as it formed in Braddock's heartless mind, *"No you fool!"*

Braddock heard the thought within his mind. He shook his head to clear it, then he aimed his gun at the transparent aluminium window panels below him. Iron shells ripped through both layers of transparent aluminium. Through panel after panel, left and right he strafed. The water between the layers bled out into space, and their precious atmosphere began to escape.

Braddock smiled at his handy work.

Forkbraid reached his mind deep into Braddock's. He reached into his very cells, reaching deep into his very DNA. He located Braddock's mitochondrial DNA. Then he located the centres of energy metabolism. He bound them all together in his mind.

Then Forkbraid let loose one single thought in Braddock's direction as the crystal in his staff turned a deep, rich bloody red, *"Burn!"*

Within Braddock's body, cell after cell burst into flames, a chain reaction of uncontrolled energy release. Braddock screamed in pain briefly as the wave of flames swept through his body, before his mind quickly went dead. His light rail gun dropped from his lifeless hands, and he crumpled to the ground, a burning mass of stinking flesh. A small intense fire could be seen upon the distant mountains of the Southern end cap. Braddock was dead!

Forkbraid's staff stomped once on the floor as his defences dropped. The office lights had dimmed to red, sirens through-out the Southern end cap were sounding.

"Take shelter. This is an atmospheric breach alert. This is not a drill. Repeat. Take shelter. This is an atmospheric breach alert. This is not a drill. Repeat."

The words repeated over and over and over. Outside people were running and screaming, trying to locate the nearest emergency shelters.

Forkbraid looked around him, the President's office was in total chaos. Tanya the secretary was screaming continuously under her desk. Her mind was a broken and tangled mess of terror.

An Administration Officer rushed to a computer, scanned the series of flashing lights on the screen, then he hurriedly screamed out, "Sir. Window section three-five-five, panels seven, eight, nine and ten, section three-five-six, all panels, section three-five-seven, panels one, two, three, and four have all been penetrated. Sir, we're bleeding our atmosphere out into space."

"Well don't just stand there. Get work crews onto it. Get caissons over those breaches!", the President shouted back at him.

"The damage is too great, Sir. We're losing atmosphere far too quickly. We've got mere minutes before those sections collapse and completely blow out into space."

Every-one in the room had horrified looks on their faces. They all turned and looked towards the distant end cap mountains. Vortices of precious air were circling and funnelling down through the bullet hole ridden panels. They didn't have long to live. Soon they would be sucked out into space and be breathing vacuum.

Forkbraid acted quickly, his eyes rolled back once more, the crystal in his staff glowed a coal fire red. The pools of melted iron shells that covered the office floor where his golden mind shield had been, began to coalesce. The President's people all stepped back as the mass of melted iron began to lift from off of the floor.

It wasn't enough, "I need more iron", Forkbraid yelled.

Special Agent Murphy caught on to what he was going to attempt. He stepped forward and pointed to a playground in a park six stories below in front of the administration offices.

"Yes, yes, perfect! Thanks, Jim", Forkbraid smiled.

The mass of molten iron flew down to the park. The park's play equipment melted and coalesced with it. Forkbraid directed the entire mass of liquid metal over to where the window panels had been breached. Sweat poured off Forkbraid's brow as he telekinetically manipulated the molten metal mass. The damage was two kilometres away and this was an enormous strain on him.

Everyone stared in sheer disbelief.

The liquid metal flowed onto the damaged panels one by one. It spread evenly, cooling slightly as it did so. The liquid metal filled every nook and cranny, hardening in place and sealing the bullet holes. One by one the panels were sealed. Lights on the computer screen slowly went from red to orange, and then green as each panel was sealed and stopped venting their precious air into space. It was a slow process, but soon all eighteen damaged sections were sealed off.

Outside the sirens could be heard still wailing their warning, *"Take shelter. This is an atmospheric breach alert. This is not a drill. Repeat. Take shelter. This is an atmospheric breach alert. This is not a drill. Repeat."*

An exhausted Forkbraid sank to his knees, "I've sealed the inner panels", he shouted, "Can you seal off the outside panels?", it was a desperate query; Forkbraid had little strength left in him.

Agent Murphy knelt down beside him, "No, we can't."

Forkbraid forced himself to his feet once more, "What do you need me to do?", he questioned.

"It's okay, FB. It's okay. It's the only inner panels that we need to worry about."

"What do you mean, Jim?", Forkbraid didn't understand the intricacies of a panel breach.

"Once the inner panels are sealed, we can cover the entire damaged sections with caissons. You've just bought us the time we need to get those caissons in place. Then we can begin repairs", Jim slapped a hand on Forkbraid's shoulder, "Thanks, FB, you've saved our lives."

Forkbraid gave off a slight sigh of relief. He turned to Tanya, the secretary who was still under her desk. She was silent now, the screaming had ended or had it. In her mind Tanya screamed every bit as loudly as she had before, only no-one but Forkbraid could hear it.

Forkbraid raised a hand and the desk lifted and moved out of the way. He walked over to Tanya and gently picked her up, carrying her over to a nearby couch positioned against the office wall. Tanya was near catatonic, her mind trapped in an endless silent scream. Forkbraid placed a hand on each side of her temple and looked deeply into her eyes. The President's secretary shook suddenly and then went limp. Forkbraid laid Tanya gently down upon the couch.

"Is Tanya okay?", asked President Banyan.

"Yes, Tanya will be fine", Forkbraid assured him, "She's asleep now. When she wakes up, she won't remember a thing."

"Is that a good thing?", Banyan asked.

"Yes", he paused for a moment, "If you could see what state her mind was in", Forkbraid paused again, "Yes, it's a very good thing."

Special Agent Murphy approached them, "They've found the assailant, Sir."

"They have. Good, good. When can you interrogate him, Jim?"

"That won't be possible, Sir", replied Special Agent Murphy.

"Why the hell not?", asked President Banyan.

"He's dead, Sir. The team that found him described him as a 'crispy-critter', Sir." President Banyan looked squarely at Forkbraid.

"I could see what he was trying to do. I was most harsh", Forkbraid stated without remorse.

Special Agent Murphy injected some more information, "Sir. It's just like we thought. The assailant had an [26]LRG", he noticed a querying look on Forkbraid's face, then added, "He had a Light Rail Gun."

"A very dangerous weapon to be carrying around in a colony in space", Forkbraid replied.

"Indeed. They are restricted weapons. Military use only", Special Agent Murphy replied adding, "And LRGs are another product manufactured under strict regulations by the Hyper Dynamics Corporation."

President Banyan reached for Forkbraid's hand, "Well that settles it then. All things considered, I'd say we're in your debt, Sir. You'll have our every co-operation. Hyper Dynamics Corporation will co-operate, I'll make sure of it. I am not giving them any choice."

"What kind of person could do this?", Special Agent Murphy asked, staring out the windows of the office, "What kind of person could recklessly endanger so many thousands of people?"

"One that cares not one wit for human life, Jim", Forkbraid replied.

---

26 Light Rail Gun. Light Electro-magnetic Rail Gun, hurls small iron projectiles at close to speed of light.

"There'll be more of them, Sir", Forkbraid told President Banyon.

"You mean that there's more than one of them?", President Banyan queried him.

"It's a certainty", Forkbraid answered, adding, "There'll be a whole nest of rats here."

"After this, they'll be wanting to jump ship", Special Agent Murphy stated.

"I'm here now. Once I've settled in, and that won't take me long, I can hunt them down."

President Banyan looked at Forkbraid, "Your reputation precedes you. They're going to run."

"Yes. That they will, but if we seal the bottle, where can they run too?", Forkbraid replied.

Special Agent Murphy flipped open his communicator, he pressed the speed dial. A familiar face appeared on the screen.

James Murphy was brief, "Seal the docks Delfino. All of them. Total and complete lock down. No-one gets in, and no-one gets out."

"Yes, Sir", came Delfino's short reply.

"Gentlemen, this bottle is sealed!"

Forkbraid smiled. The terrorists were going nowhere.

Just then Tanya, the President's secretary, awoke with a yawn and stretched, "I must have dozed off. Sorry everyone.", she looked quite embarrassed, before noticing the wreckage that was the President's office, "What the hell did I miss?", she enquired.

"Trust me, Tanya, you really don't want to know", President Banyan replied.

9. Sealed Bottle

News spread quickly, and it wasn't long before everyone in Colonial Central Command knew about the attack. Nearly everyone was outraged and many were fearful of another attack. For a small handful, there was also fear, but not from another attack. Rather their fear was of the Wizard.

Forkbraid had a reputation as a powerful remote viewer. It was said that Wizards couldn't use their powers off-world, yet Forkbraid had used his powers to great effect. Their comrade Braddock had paid the ultimate price. The docks had now been closed, and the Wizard would be hunting them. It would only be a matter of time before they were found. They had to flee.

News was spreading quickly off cylinder as well. All the L-Five colonies had heard about the attack. Integrated news feeds carried word of the attack far and wide. It was now being reported on Earth and the Moon. It would be less than an hour or two before the news reached Venus and Mars. Another two hours and the Belter colonies would know about it, soon after that, the outer satellites, within a day the whole system would have heard of the terrorist attack at Colonial Central Command.

Special Agent James Murphy sat in a room above the departure lounge, next to him sat Lord Folcrom Forkbraid. Together the pair watched the departure lounge through tinted class windows.

The docks had been closed for most of the day, while special security measures were being set up. All inbound flights had been cancelled until further notice and only those flights that were already in transit would be allowed to dock. Outbound flights had been put on launch hold until further notice. The rats would flee, but not before Special Agent Murphy had their security in place. Towards the end of the day, outbound flights were resuming. Outbound passengers were arriving at the spaceport for the now tightly controlled departure flights. One by one, each flight was given launch clearance, and Forkbraid watched over each and every flight and every passenger.

The flight of the [27]CF Lindstrom to Carson Torus had been cleared for launch. Forkbraid had scanned the minds of every single passenger and crew member who boarded her. The Lindstrom was cleared and allowed to leave. The process was slow and tedious, but it was working.

Colonial Agents had spent the day spreading rumours that Lord Folcrom Forkbraid and his remote viewing teams were searching the cylinder from bow to stern in plain clothes, scanning the minds of every citizen. There were no remote viewing teams, there was only Forkbraid, but the terrorists did not know this.

---

27 Colonial Ferry class ship designed for short inter-colony transport.

They would panic, they would try to flee. It was only a matter of time.

Several ships by now had been cleared and were allowed to launch.

Special Agent Murphy began to wonder if this gambit would pay off, "That's the fourth ship, Forkbraid. Are you sure this will work?", he enquired.

"Have a little faith, Jim. It's early days yet, and I reckon we'll have a result soon enough."

"How can you be so sure, FB?"

"Simple logic really. Put yourself in their shoes, Jim. Terrorists in a colony in lock down. There are remote viewing teams roaming around in plain clothes scanning everyone. There's no place to hide, no place to run. Where can they hide? What are they going to do?"

"Try to board a ship and leave. They're caught between a rock and a hard place."

"That's right, Jim. They either try to sneak off or worse, fight their way off. Either way, we are waiting for them."

Special Agent Murphy nodded in agreement, "As you said, FB. It's only a matter of time."

"If I was a betting man, Jim, I'd put my money on that ship", Forkbraid pointed to the flight schedule, tapping his finger on one particular ship.

The CF Nobel bound for Hyper Dynamics Corporation. It was due to launch the next morning.

Agent Murphy smiled at Forkbraid, "They couldn't be that stupid?", he paused, "Could they?"

"Jim, we'll find out tomorrow morning mate."

Three more ships were cleared for launch during the night, before the passengers began to arrive to board the CF Nobel. Most seemed to be fairly normal enough folk just going about their business, until one bloke turned up and joined the line. He seemed somewhat nervous and was constantly looking around.

"A likely looking lad if ever I saw one", Jim was on his feet and watching carefully.

Forkbraid was still seated, he carefully looked over the man on the screen, "No, Jim. He's just high on [28]Shaboo, but otherwise normal. Have him apprehended for treatment and rehabilitation."

"Thought we had one for a minute there", Special Agent Murphy replied, almost disappointed.

Forkbraid adjusted the view on the screen, panning out to take in more of the terminal. Another man was approaching, he appeared to be slightly nervous as

---

28 Shaboo, a powerful opiate based drug more powerful and addictive than heroin.

well.

"That one, Jim", Forkbraid pointed to the screen.

"Are you sure, FB? How do you know?", asked Agent Murphy.

"He's trying to hide his thoughts, Jim."

"How does someone hide their thoughts?", it was an obvious question.

"You can't, Jim. He's telling himself not to think, not to think of certain things. It's a dead bloody give away", Forkbraid rose to his feet and focused squarely on this newcomer.

Special Agent Murphy got straight to his communicator, "Miller!"

"Yes, Sir", Miller was quick to answer.

"Approaching from the left, wearing blue jeans and a beige top."

"We're on him, Sir", Special Agent Miller was moving his men into position.

Forkbraid carefully skimmed the surface of the man's mind, gradually reaching deeper and deeper into his mind.

"We've got one, Jim. His name is Thompson, Chuck Thompson. He's their communications man. He's the one who received word from the Hyper Dynamics Corporation colony. Someone named Leroy McGuvan gave him a message."

Forkbraid read the message directly from Thompson's mind, *"Urgent! Wizard, Folcrom Forkbraid, suspected aboard the Colonial Liner Chimera. Watch the passenger arrivals. If the Wizard is amongst the passengers, terminate him."*

"How did they know you were on the Chimera?", asked Special Agent Murphy.

"He doesn't seem to know. Somehow they found out, but he doesn't know how", Forkbraid moved closer to the screen and concentrated harder. "Jim. Watch this one. He's scared, but more scared of being captured than dying. He's a committed fundamentalist. Be careful, be very careful."

Special Agent Murphy was on the communicator again, "Miller. He's our man. Approach with caution. Forkbraid says he's dangerous."

Forkbraid was talking once more, drawing more information from Thompson's mind.

"The man with the rail gun was their *'fixer'*, Braddock was his name. There are two more men in their cell. Cotton and Martins. They were the surveillance at the passenger arrivals yesterday morning. They watched me come through and relayed that information to Braddock."

Special Agent Miller was back on the communicator, "We're in position and ready to move in."

Special Agent Murphy replied, "Do it. Do it now."

Eight agents sprung from their cover and quickly circled Thompson, their pulse pistols aimed squarely at him, "We are colonial agents! Raise your hands in the air and don't move!", Special Agent Miller commanded.

Thompson backed up slowly with his hands raised in the air. He looked left and then right, he had nowhere to run. A determined look came over his face. Miller's men were closing in, the circle was getting tighter. Thompson contorted his lower jaw slightly, and then bit down hard, real hard.

Special Agent Miller shouted, "Get back! Everybody get back!"

A pale yellow mist escaped from Thompson's mouth and dissipated in the air, his body convulsed violently, and then he collapsed to the ground dead.

Special Agent Murphy and Forkbraid watched the scene unfold on the screen.

"A poison pill secreted in his dental work!", Special Agent Murphy exclaimed.

"I did say he was committed, Jim. I expect the other two will be no different."

"Well, let's hope we can get at least one of them alive, FB".

"I wouldn't worry about that, Jim. Whatever they know, I'll take it straight out of their minds", the look on Forkbraid's face showed he was totally serious.

A few moments later a security alert was triggered on the other side of the docking ring. Special Agent Murphy was quickly onto the computer screen.

An entry alarm had been triggered in the private yacht moorings, "Some-ones trying to steal a private yacht."

"Can they do that?", asked Forkbraid.

"Not easily. Private ships are stowed in a mooring hold. They'd have to first get into a ship, and then get launch clearance to open the main airlock doors. Without that, they'll be stuck in the internal mooring hold."

"Do the main airlock doors have overrides, Jim?", Forkbraid cocked an eyebrow.

Special Agent Murphy thought for a moment, then was quickly on his communicator, "Miller. Some-ones in private mooring hold six. Get a team down there straight away."

"We're right on it, Sir", came Miller's quick reply.

Special Agent Murphy typed a few commands on his keyboard. Sensors showed two people in the private mooring hold. A few more commands later and the main airlock doors were sealed and locked. Special Agent Murphy brought the private mooring hold's internal sensors on screen. There were a number of private mooring holds built into the docking ring. Each one held literally dozens or more small personal private ships of varying sizes.

Special Agent Murphy started an automatic interrogation of the life support systems on the stowed vessels. One by one the ships reported their status. None were active as yet. Well over half of the ships in this hold had reported back before they received an active response.

"We have a hot one, FB", Special Agent Murphy directed the sensors to the ship in question.

It was a small ten person [29]colonial hummer. "The life support system on that Hummer is reporting two people on board. I think we may have just found Cotton and Martins."

"They've backed themselves into a corner, Jim. There's no way out of there."

"That's what worries me, FB", Special Agent Murphy replied.

"We should get down there, Jim. This could get ugly real fast."

Just then Special Agent Miller's voice was heard on the communicator, "Sir, I have my team by the private mooring hold's doors. We're awaiting your instructions."

"Miller. Our targets are in the hummer in bay seventy-two. I want them taken alive."

"Acknowledged. Proceeding into the mooring hold."

Special Agent Miller's men entered the mooring hold and cautiously approached bay seventy-two. Slowly, yet cautiously his men approached, taking cover at every opportunity as they did so. From his vantage point, Special Agent Miller could see the Hummer's rear hatchway was open.

This was as close as they would get, "We are colonial agents! Throw your weapons out of the hatch and come out with your arms raised high above your heads!", he barked out.

A face cautiously peaked out from the hatch, followed by a hand holding a submachine gun. The man opened fire. Special Agent Miller and his team ducked for cover, before returning fire with their pulse pistols. Bullets sprayed towards Special Agent Miller and his team, one was hit in the chest and dropped to the ground. Pulses of plasma burst against the metal skin of the hummer, the machine gunner backed away from the onslaught.

"You're not going anywhere, fuck wit. We have you all boxed in. Give yourselves up", Special Agent Miller shouted at the two men.

One of the men leapt from the hummer hatch and ran towards Special Agent Miller, his hand gun threatening. Miller fired his pulse pistol three times. Pulses of plasma struck the man hard in the upper torso. He dropped to the floor with three holes burned deeply into his chest.

"Come on man, give up. Your situation is hopeless. You can't get away", Miller yelled.

"Maybe not", the man screamed out, "but I can take a few of you infidels with me!"

The hummer's engine came online.

---

29 A small, light personal transport equipped with small plasma thrusters, having a range of 25,000 kilometres.

Special Agent Miller ordered his men back out of the docking hold, "Get out! Move it, get out! Run! Run!"

Special Agent Miller grabbed his fallen comrade and helped him to his feet. As fast as they could, they all ran towards the entrance. The hummer's engine throttled up, while the hummer itself remained moored to its docking bay. Cotton lifted the access panel that covered the hydrogen plasma feed lines. He aimed his weapon and squeezed the trigger. A burst of machine gun fire could be heard. Then there was a loud hissing sound, followed by a sudden cracking sound, which was quickly followed by a violent explosion, as the hummer was ripped apart.

Forkbraid and Special Agent Murphy were both thrown to the floor as the shock wave rippled through the docking ring. The noise was deafening. Several more deafening explosions were heard as several other ship's fuel tanks ruptured and exploded. There were more shock waves rippling through the docking ring. A klaxon sounded, giving a loud warning as the emergency systems overrode the airlock doors and exposed the private mooring hold to the vacuum of space. As the air vented into space the fires began to extinguish and an eerie calm descended over the mooring hold.

Forkbraid and Special Agent Murphy struggled to their feet. They were close to the private mooring hold now and could see that its main entrance doors remained firmly closed. Special Agent Murphy quickly made enquiries on his communicator.

"The private mooring hold is trashed. We're lucky we didn't have a hull breach. Fortunately, the bulkheads down here were designed to withstand this kind of", he paused, he was going to say accident, but quickly changed it to "explosion."

Agent Murphy looked at Forkbraid.

He understood, "No, Jim. I'm not picking up anyone alive on the other side of that bulkhead."

Special Agent Murphy nodded, "Yeah. It's a vacuum in there. The emergency system's designed to seal off the entire compartment and vent the air to extinguish any fires."

James Murphy paused a moment then added "Eight good men died in there today."

"I felt their passing, Jim", he paused, "It was mercifully swift", Forkbraid responded.

Emergency response teams began to arrive as the pair turned and walked back the way they'd come. Eight men died, and that's not counting the terrorists. It had been a terrible day.

A short while later they were back in the room above the departure lounge.

Colonial Central Command was again in lockdown. All departures were cancelled until further notice. Forkbraid and Special Agent Murphy had spent a long time on the [30]vid talking to President Banyan. President Banyan was extremely concerned about the latest events, to say the least, he was livid. Five ships had exploded in private mooring hold six. Eight Special Agents and the two assailants had died. The terrorists were endangering the lives of everyone in the mega-colony.

"Do you know just how many people could have died if those bulkheads had failed?", President Banyan screamed at them.

"Yes, Sir", Special Agent Murphy replied, "Perhaps several thousand, Sir."

"Several thousand, several thousand at the very least", the President screamed, "Forkbraid, I want you to personally hunt these evil bastards down and kill them", the President demanded.

"I can hunt them down, Sir, that's a given, but I'm no man's assassin. I'll only kill if it's absolutely necessary", Forkbraid replied.

"Well, damn you, it's looking awful bloody necessary to me", President Banyan replied coldly.

Forkbraid silently forgave the *"damn you"* remark and replied, "I'll hunt these mongrels down. Rest assured they will be found. Then your people can do what they will with them."

President Banyan smiled, "Good!", he exclaimed, and then he added, "Can't you predict what these mongrels are going to do?"

"I wish I could, Sir", Forkbraid did not elaborate, "I'll have to hunt them down the hard way."

"Do that", the President replied, then the video screen went blank.

"Forgive me for asking, FB, but why can't you predict these attacks? You are a psychic after all?"

"Psychic, yes, Jim, but I'm not a [31]precog", Forkbraid replied.

"So you can't see into the future?"

"Yes, and no, Jim", Forkbraid replied, "Sometimes I can see future events when they're imminent."

"When the events are imminent?", Jim enquired.

"Yeah. The closer they are to fruition, the more readily I see them", Forkbraid clarified.

"But not when they're some time off in the future?", Special Agent Murphy enquired.

"That's it, Jim", Forkbraid replied, "True precogs are very, very rare."

"True precogs?", Special Agent Murphy was curious.

---

30 Vid, video communications system.
31 Precog. A psychic whose specific skill is precognition of future events, i.e. prophecy.

"True precogs can predict the pattern of future events, Jim. It's an extremely rare gift, but even then, they're not perfect at it either."

"I don't understand. If they can see the future, surely it unfolds as they see it?"

"You'd think so, but the future is not fixed. It's fluid and it depends on current events. Change the current situation by just a smidgen and the future unfolds completely differently."

"That would make predicting the future very difficult, indeed", Special Agent Murphy realised.

"That it does, Jim, that it does", Forkbraid replied before changing the topic.

"Jim, we're going to need a ship", Forkbraid told Special Agent Murphy.

"That can be arranged. And no, you can't have your Bat Wing", Special Agent Murphy replied.

"My Bat Wing is no good for what we're going to do, Jim."

"And what is it that we're going to do?", Special Agent Murphy enquired.

"We are going to [32]skin-dance", Forkbraid replied, adding "Can you fly a [33]Gull Wing?"

"Yeah. No problem", Special Agent Murphy paused, "Interceptor or Skimmer?"

"A skimmer will do", Forkbraid informed him.

Forkbraid and Special Agent Murphy commandeered a Gull Wing Skimmer from mooring hold twelve on the opposite side of the docking ring.

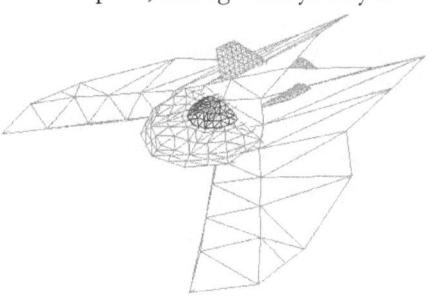

Gull Wing Skimmer

They were quickly given launch clearance and the small ship was soon being transported to the nearest mooring hold airlock. Once placed in the airlock and with the airlock door safely closed behind them, Special Agent Murphy brought the ship's plasma thrusters online. The air was quickly evacuated from the airlock and outer airlock doors opened. James Murphy pushed the throttle forward and the small ship shot swiftly into space.

"Jim, we need to take this ship as close to the colony's outer hull as you can manage", Forkbraid instructed.

"I'll do the best that I can, FB", Special Agent Murphy replied.

---

32 Skin-dance. Flying a small ship fast, just barely above the surface of a much larger vessel or colony.

33 Gull Wing Skimmer. A small, fast two person civilian runabout equipped with a single plasma thrust engine.

Forkbraid sat quietly in his seat, his staff was again in his right hand, his eyes rolled back. The crystal atop the staff glowed a cool shade of opalescent green. Forkbraid reached his mind outward into space, and then focused back towards the colony and penetrated deep into the colony's hull.

Special Agent Murphy concentrated on flying the small ship, skin dancing it across the colony's outer hull. It was slow and it was tedious. After two hours they had finished scanning the Southern end cap. Forkbraid was certain that the Southern end cap was clear of any more terrorists. They took a short break.

"What is it with your staff, FB?", Special Agent Murphy asked.

"I'm not sure if you'll understand the explanation, Jim", was Forkbraid's honest reply.

"Try me, I'm not a complete moron you know."

"Well, it's kind of like this", Forkbraid began his explanation, "You know, when you fly a ship, like this one. How do you feel about it?"

"I'm not sure if I understand what you mean?", Special Agent Murphy was puzzled.

"Well, when you fly a small ship like this, it becomes like an extension of you. You hold the controls and the ship in turn responds to your control", Forkbraid explained.

"Yeah, but a ship is just a ship."

"Ordinarily, yes, but not for the pilot. You're the pilot, and you toss around this ship like it's an extension of your arm."

It was a perplexing concept, "I think I get it, but what's that got to do with your staff?"

"Well, Jim. My staff is an extension of me. I can feel it, and it can feel me."

"How can your staff feel you?", Special Agent Murphy was having trouble following this one.

"We Witches generally make our own magical tools, staffs, wands, what-ever. In this case I inherited my staff, it's literally hundreds of years old. Anyway, we also consecrate our magical tools. The act of consecration, imparts a living essence into our creation."

"A living essence?", Special Agent Murphy gave Forkbraid an incredulous look.

"A living essence, Jim. It's difficult to explain. We can draw upon a number of different sources for these living essences. Elementals, Fairy folk, Deities, Phantasms, even ourselves and there are many, many other sources available to us."

"So what did you impart into your staff?", Special Agent Murphy enquired curiously.

"I imparted a very small piece of myself into it, Jim. What we call, a wight of my will, so to speak. My staff, though, is very special. It contains a wight of the will of every Witch that has ever owned it, starting with its original creator."

"A wight of your will?", Special Agent Murphy repeated questioningly.

Forkbraid could see that Jim was beginning to get the gist of it, "Yes, Jim, a wight of my will."

"And that's why your staff follows you around like a lost puppy?"

"Actually, no, Jim", Forkbraid explained further, "My staff is merely covering my six, you know, watching my back."

"It's protecting you? Can it do that?"

"Of course, it can. Otherwise, we all would have died back in Banyan's office."

"So you're telling me that your staff", Special Agent Murphy stopped mid-sentence before finishing, "Saved all of our lives?"

"Yes, and, no, Jim. A staff, a wand, any magical tool is also an amplifier."

"An amplifier?", Special Agent Murphy was beginning to look perplexed once again.

"Jim. It was nearly two kilometres from Banyan's office to those damaged window panels. Do you really think I'm powerful enough to move all that molten metal that far, without a little help?"

"I", Special Agent Murphy stuttered, "I, I never really thought about it."

"A magical tool like my staff, amplifies and enhances my abilities", Forkbraid paused, "It helps me focus, helps me reach deep inside myself to the primordial pools of power. It puts me in touch with that inner Well-Spring from which all reality, all phenomena emerge."

To which Special Agent Murphy replied, looking even more confused, "You were right, FB. I'm not sure that I will ever understand that. To me, your staff still looks just like a colourful, cleverly crafted piece of wood. Ornate and decorative, but honestly, I can't see anything beyond that."

"I understand, Jim. Colourful, cleverly crafted, even ornate and decorative. They all describe my staff, but there is so much more that you simply cannot see. And I can understand that, Jim."

After about fifteen minutes, Special Agent Murphy began to skin dance around the main cylinder of Colonial Central Command. It was again slow and tedious, taking much longer than before due to the shear size of the mega-colony's main cylinder. They stopped every two hours for a fifteen-minute break, continuing one again after each break where they had left off.

They had just started their forth scanning session on the main cylinder when Forkbraid started to note down some coordinates. It was on the gamma land strip. Forkbraid jotted down the longitude and latitude equivalents. He paused long enough to take a few notes, then instructed Special Agent Murphy to swing back and restart at that point.

They continued skin dancing over the outer hull of the mega-colony. Nearly seven and a half hours later they had finally finished. Only one set of coordinates had been noted down. Forkbraid was exhausted, he had spent nearly sixteen hours scanning for terrorists.

Special Agent Murphy was equally exhausted having concentrated on flying the skimmer for the whole time. After docking, they quickly made their way to Special Agent Murphy's office in Colonial Central Command's government administration offices. He sat down in his office chair to discuss the situation with Forkbraid, suggesting Forkbraid take a seat in front of his desk.

"I need to rest, Jim", Forkbraid insisted, instead taking a seat on the couch by the wall.

"What about these fundamentalists?", Special Agent Murphy enquired.

"They're not going anywhere, Jim", explained Forkbraid, "They think there are teams of remote viewer's, roaming around all over the place. These guys are lying low."

"You can be sure of that?", Special Agent Murphy queried.

"Yes. These people are shit scared of being found. They're avoiding all contact with anyone from outside their community."

"Still, we do have their coordinates", replied Special Agent Murphy, "I'll have a few surveillance teams set up to keep an eye on them just in case."

"Good. Do that, Jim. I'm going to get some rest", Forkbraid replied as he leant back into the couch, put up his feet and relaxed. "Wake me up in eight hours."

It was ever so long since he'd slept.

Special Agent Murphy rose to his feet and stepped out of his office. He walked down the corridor to a nearby room with a comfortable couch. He, too, was going to catch some shut-eye.

10. Rats Nest

Forkbraid was already awake when Special Agent Murphy came into the office to wake him.

He held two small packages of food, "Sandwiches I'm afraid. They're edible, but only just."

"They'll do", Forkbraid reached out a hand for one of the packages, asking as he took the package, "Do I have time to wash."

"Yeah, sure, We have showers on the floor lower down. You'd be surprised how many of my people sleep in their offices overnight."

"What? Workaholics?", inquired Forkbraid.

"No, not really. Just, well, a colony is really just one big building, isn't it. And our concept of day and night is, well, it's completely contrived. Up here we often work odd hours and strange shifts, so pretty much every office building has a place to grab a nap and a wash."

"That's certainly different from back home."

"Of course, it is", Special Agent Murphy had been leading Forkbraid down to the floor below, "but we're not complete barbarians up here, I've organised an apartment for you over in my building. Life up here can get pretty hectic, so there's no telling when you'll actually get to use it."

Special Agent Murphy slapped his hand on a door as he went past, "Showers are in there, FB. I'll meet you back down in the garage in say, twenty minutes or so/"

Special Agent Murphy waved with his hand as he walked down the corridor to the elevators.

Twenty minutes later Forkbraid was in the garage. Special Agent Murphy's pod pulled up alongside him and its passenger side gull-wing door opened up. Forkbraid jumped in. The pod left the garage and pulled out into one of the main radial roads leading towards the Southern end cap's bulkhead mountains. The mountains, although artificial, were every bit as beautiful as any mountains on Earth. They were covered with forests and the view was spectacular.

Forkbraid looked high up on the bulkhead mountains. Above the highest peaks was a grey metal bulkhead separating the mountain tops from the central solar redirection mirror. Squinting into the sunlight, Forkbraid could see the pattern of the mountain range repeated on the other side of the mirror, with mountains reaching high overhead back towards the opposite side of the Southern end cap. The mountains ninety degrees away from them were even more disturbing.

A slight feeling of vertigo swept over him, *"How do the colonists ever get used to this?"*

Forkbraid looked directly above them through the pod's sunroof. Jutting out from the very centre of the Southern end cap along Colonial Central Command's axis of rotation was a large cylindrical structure. Forkbraid new without thinking there'd be another just like it in the Northern end cap.

What was done in one end cap was always repeated in the other. Forkbraid knew from memory that the structure was the zero gravity recreational building. Constructed along the mega-colony's rotational axis meant the centrifugal force and therefore artificial gravity was minimal. It was a place where human powered flight was a reality, where low gravity diving and swimming were common recreational pursuits among the colonists. In the very centre would be a gravity free zone where colonists could play in zero g's. Nowhere like it existed on the Earth, nor any other planet for that matter.

Shortly before reaching the mountains, the radial road crossed over a river that seemed to run the entire circumference of the end cap. White sandy beaches lined its shores. Just beyond this river, the pod swung left into the main ring road and began travelling around the end cap. Forkbraid was surprised by the number of trees he had seen in the end cap. Parks and gardens, it seemed, were an integral part of the mega-colony's design. Hanging gardens of life were visible everywhere.

"They need all of this life", he thought to himself, *"Otherwise they'd all go insane."*

Eventually they came to another main radial road and the pod swung right, then the bulkhead mountains loomed before them once more. The radial road crossed over a broad bridge, across the circular end cap windows. A short time later they entered a large tunnel. Each of Colonial Central Command's end caps had three of these huge tunnels, which led into the main cylindrical centre of the colony. This particular tunnel led from the Southern end cap out into the main cylinder's gamma land section. Once out of the tunnel and into the main cylinder, Forkbraid looked behind them. The mountains of the end cap were perfectly repeated on both sides of the bulkhead.

Before them was a large valley, twenty kilometres long. At the far end was the Northern end cap bulkhead, complete with its ring of mountains. To the left and right of them were a pair of low mountain ranges. These were somewhat lower than those at the bulkheads, but equally forested.

These mountains partially obscured the main cylinder's long slit windows through which the sun's light was reflected and beyond the range of mountains was a high grey metal wall. A broad green valley filled the expanse between the mountains. Farms and small stands of trees filled the valley. Forkbraid looked above them, the same pattern was repeated on alpha and beta land strips, a hundred and twenty degrees to the left and right around the cylinder. Seeing land above their heads was such a strange thing for Forkbraid.

"I've been meaning to ask you, FB, how do you fit that staff of yours in that pocket? The damn thing must be nearly six feet long. And another thing, how is it that your pocket is there when you reach for it, but not there when you don't? You really must explain that to me?"

"Actually, no, I don't have to explain it, Jim", Forkbraid replied simply.

Special Agent Murphy gave him a perplexing look, "Why the hell not?"

"A Magus, Jim", Forkbraid stated, using a more ancient title, "has to keep some of his secrets."

In the central regions of each land section, was a large lake. Nestled between the mountains, it covered the broad expanse of the valley and was about two kilometres wide. A long bridge crossed the centre of each of these lakes. It wasn't long before Special Agent Murphy's pod approached the bridge. A sign before the bridge read simply *"Gamma Sea"*. Wide, white sandy beaches lined the southern shores. Sail boats could be seen sailing on the blue-green waters.

"We actually have Salmon and trout in our little rivers and seas", noted Special Agent Murphy.

"Really, I do have several fishing rods in one of my pockets", Forkbraid replied.

James Murphy glanced at Forkbraid and thought to himself, *"Several fishing rods?"*

Forkbraid heard the unspoken question and smiled, "Actually about fifteen fishing rods, with a complete set of reels and tackle as well.", he stated.

Special Agent Murphy gave him another glance, but said nothing in reply.

In the centre of the Gamma Sea was a town. It was simply called Gamma Central. A small town only a few hundred yards across in the centre of the sea. The road they were travelling on passed through its middle. This pattern, Forkbraid noticed, was repeated on the other land sections as well.

"Honestly, Jim, you guys have no imagination up here", Forkbraid mentioned.

"Why is that, FB?", Special Agent Murphy enquired, he honestly didn't understand.

"All these generic names, Southern end cap, Northern end cap, Gamma Sea, Gamma Central."

"Oh. Well, that has nothing to do with our imagination, FB. It's an efficiency thing."

"Efficiency?", it was Forkbraid's turn to be perplexed.

"Yeah. It doesn't matter which O'Neil-style colony you're in, the names are pretty much the same, so you can never really get lost."

"Really. That's it? The entire reason for the generic naming convention?"

"Yeah. It was something decided long ago. The original few colonies tried having separate names for everything, but as more and more colonies came online, it just got so damn confusing."

"So they just reverted to using generics?"

"Yep, they sure did", Special Agent Murphy replied, "Bloody good decision I reckon."

"Extraordinary", Forkbraid answered.

A short while later they had finished crossing the Gamma Sea and the pod swung right and headed towards the distant slit window mountains. Special Agent Murphy had called a map up on the pod's video screen. Their destination was a farm compound nestled at the foot of the mountains, just northeast of the Gamma Sea. Information on the side of the map indicated that the farm grew corn, barley, and wheat. They also produced goats, sheep, chickens, turkeys, and another animal called a slig, that Forkbraid was completely unfamiliar with.

"Jim, what's a slig?", Forkbraid enquired.

"A genetic experiment gone wrong if you ask me", Jim replied.

"What do you mean?", Forkbraid was curious.

"About a century ago, someone had the bright idea of splicing slug DNA into a pig", Jim explained.

"Really. Did that work? It sounds bloody awful."

"Not really. Oh, well, yes, and, no. And it was bloody awful. They ended up with a pig that couldn't support its own weight. They have small, tiny legs, and a weak bone structure, they're overly fat, and they drool the most vial snot. Furthermore, they spend nearly all their time in the water and mud, so they're highly aquatic animals as well."

"What were they trying to achieve?"

"To be honest, I don't really know", replied Jim, "and here in the colonies, I recommend that you don't eat pork. If you're ever on a liner, or anywhere else for that matter, and they serve up pork, don't eat it. We don't have pigs up here, we have sligs. Some folk say they taste just fine, personally, I stay well clear of slig meat. I reckon it tastes like crap. Awful damned stuff."

"I'll take that under advisement", Forkbraid replied, then having thought about it for just a moment, "Fundamentalists don't eat pork. And a slig isn't a pig, slig meat isn't pork."

"Now that's interesting. I never thought of it that way", Jim replied.

Special Agent Murphy's pod turned down a narrow laneway and pulled to stop behind a small stand of trees. Several other vehicles were also present and colonial agents could be seen in the tree line. They left their vehicle and quickly made their way to the waiting agents. Forkbraid pulled his staff from out of his robe, and it obediently followed behind him. As he did so, Special Agent Murphy watched, trying to figure out how Forkbraid's staff managed to fit in his *invisible* pocket.

"It's a community farm, Sir. About eight families live and work here", offered

Agent Spencer.

Special Agent Murphy put a pair of scanners to his eyes and viewed the farm compound, "It's going to be hard to approach without being seen."

Forkbraid was holding his staff before him, his eyes rolled back, "There are eight families living there, Jim. Hmm, polygamists. Eight men, fifteen women and a lot of teenagers and children. This is a recipe for disaster, Jim."

"Whatever we do, we'll have to be careful about it."

"They don't know we're here yet, but they do seem to be preparing for our imminent arrival."

"They know we're coming?", asked Agent Spencer.

"No, not at all. They're just assuming that we'll find them", replied Forkbraid.

"How will you be approaching their compound, Spencer?"

"Sir, we can approach without being seen through the corn fields on the north side. The barley fields in the east will give us no real cover, the same with the wheat fields in the west. However, there are irrigation channels south of both the barley and the wheat fields. I've sent some of our men into the woods to skirt around to the irrigation channels. South of the compound, well that's the slig ponds. It's probably best to stay clear of those."

"So we can approach unseen on three fronts?", Special Agent Murphy asked.

"Not quite, Sir", Agent Spencer replied, adding "There's a clearing around the compound. They have small goat and sheep lots around the compound, and free-range chicken and turkey pens as well. These are between the fields and the compound. So we'll have to break cover to approach the buildings. A distance of about two hundred feet."

"As I said before, Jim, a recipe for disaster", Forkbraid added.

"So we can get close, but not quite close enough to take them by surprise."

"That's pretty much it, Sir", Agent Spencer nodded.

"What do you think, FB?"

"They're preparing for us, even though they don't know we're here. These are committed fundamentalists. You go charging in, and it'll be a bloodbath."

Forkbraid scanned more deeply the minds of the fundamentalists, "They have guns, plenty of ammo, they aren't afraid to die, nor to sacrifice their children. They", Forkbraid paused, a concerned look came over his face, "have a small [34]flash vaporiser! Only one, fortunately."

"What! Are you sure?", Special Agent Murphy exclaimed.

"Yeah. They have one and all indications are that they will use it."

"Where'd they get one of those from? They've been banned for nearly two centuries!"

---

34 Flash vaporiser. A banned weapon capable of vaporising all biological matter within a hundred-metre radius.

Forkbraid concentrated a little harder, "It was made at Hyper Dynamics Corporation."

"Exploding androids, light rail guns, flash vaporising ordinance! What the hell kind of colony are they running over there?", Special Agent Murphy was completely livid.

This was not what he expected in *civilised* L-Five.

Agent Spencer threw in, "Hyper Dynamics Corporation does have Military contracts, Sir."

"Flash vaporisers were banned under the [35]O.S.I Armistice Treaty of twenty-one ninety-two! Just like nukes and land mines were banned in the United Nations Weapons Treaty of twenty thirty-five. Flash vaporisers are banned weapons, period!", Special Agent Murphy replied.

Special Agent Murphy looked coldly at Agent Spencer, "Every day up here, is beginning to look more and more like the old Earth, and that is not a good thing!"

Agent Spencer's communicator buzzed, he grabbed it and checked the messages, "My men are all in position, Sir. We should move a little closer to the action."

They moved silently through the small stand of trees and out into the corn field. When they were reasonably close to the edge of the clearing that surrounded the farm compound, Forkbraid grabbed Special Agent Murphy's arm, "Stop right here, Gentlemen."

"Why, Sir?", Agent Spencer quickly asked.

Special Agent Murphy looked at the ground before him, "This is it isn't it, FB?"

"Yeah. Any further, and we'll be within range of that flash vaporiser."

"We have to get closer, Sir. I have to be with my men", Agent Spencer stated.

"Spencer, have your men pull back. Set a perimeter, just outside the flash vaporiser's range", Special Agent Murphy instructed.

"Sir, are you serious? We can't take the compound, if we stay out here."

"We get any closer than this, and we'll all be within the range of their most effective weapon", Special Agent Murphy replied.

"We don't know that they'll use it, Sir. They may just be keeping it up their sleeve as a bluff."

"FB? What do you think?", Special Agent Murphy looked to Forkbraid for his opinion.

"These people are fundamentalists, they're psychopaths, Jim. They will use the weapon. I know this with absolute certainty."

---

35 The O.S.I Armistice Treaty officially ended the Outer Satellites Insurrection.
   A number of weapons were banned.

The three men looked at each other for a long moment. Agent Spencer picked up his communicator, telling his men to pull back to a safer distance, then Forkbraid lifted his head up with a startled look. "Trip wires!", he hastily said to the other two.

"Where?", Special Agent Murphy hastily enquired.

Several of Agent Spencer's men were already within range of the vaporiser, some were close to the inside edge of the corn field. They began to withdraw to a safe distance.

"Just inside the fields and just inside the...", there was a loud explosion, "clearing", Forkbraid swung his head in the direction of the sound.

Agent Spencer told his men to withdraw with caution. He then asked for a quick roll call. One by one his men signalled back, Agent Andrew Baxter failed to reply. "We've lost Baxter."

The crack of rifle shots was soon heard, bullets began randomly whizzing through the corn.

The three men threw themselves to the ground, "They know we're here", Agent Spencer stated.

"You really think so, Spencer?", Special Agent Murphy snapped back sarcastically, and then, "FB, can you disable that flash vaporiser?"

"Jim, that's easier said than done."

"Can you or can't you, FB?"

"Yes, but I have to work through them. Through their minds, see what they see, know what they know. They have to lead me to it. Then maybe, just maybe."

"Good, good, get straight on it."

"No guarantees, Jim. I can't guarantee a positive outcome."

Rifle and machine gun fire was now ripping wildly into the corn field. The colonial agents did not return fire. They were now too far back in the corn field to see their attackers. A few of the colonial agents in the irrigation channel were still in the danger zone.

Forkbraid's eyes had rolled back once more. He scanned the compound looking for information on where they kept the flash vaporiser. Soon he found the information he was seeking, it was in a conversation between two men. One was firing into the corn field, the other discussing with him whether they should martyr themselves. Forkbraid scanned more deeply looking for information on the location. A decision had been made.

The man at the window firing the gun turned and called to his Wife, "Lillian! Do it! Do it now!", he screamed out.

Forkbraid frantically pulled his mind away from the two men, in search of the woman, Lillian.

He found her in a hallway. Lillian was running into a back room Forkbraid followed her vision in her own visual cortex. He couldn't see the flash vaporiser,

"Where is it he thought to himself?"

Lillian ran into the room, she yelled at her Son, a boy of twelve "Mark! Do it! Do it now!"

Forkbraid searched the room for the child named Mark. There were five children in the room, all of them were boys. He found Mark too late, holding the flash vaporiser device. Mark's slender young hand slapped down hard upon the detonation button.

Forkbraid pulled his mind back, "It's too late!", he screamed out.

There was the sound of an enormous hissing crack, then a blinding flash of light. A pillar of light reached three hundred feet up into the sky. It hung there for several long seconds. Terrified colonial agents dove for cover, as a high-pitched squeal erupted in their ears.

Slowly at first, then more quickly, the pillar of light began to drop. The pillar expanded, growing wider and wider as it collapsed towards the ground. The high-pitched squeal began to lower in pitch and volume, until the pillar struck the ground hard. At ground level it had expanded to about fifty feet across.

There was another loud crack as the light pillar rebounded and spread quickly across the ground growing wider and wider once more. Ripples and waves of light were crackling like lightning, a visible expanding ring of death. Goats, sheep, chickens, and turkeys burst into flame and quickly vaporised as the ring of death passed through them. Sligs burned and vaporised in their ponds. Grass burned, weeds burned, wheat, barley, and corn burned. A few unfortunate agents in the irrigation ditch burned. Then there was silence once more. An eerie deathly silence.

When Agent Spencer and Special Agent Murphy opened their eyes once more, they were surrounded by a glowing golden egg of light. Forkbraid was already on his feet, standing, he allowed his defences to drop.

"Is that wise, FB?", asked Special Agent Murphy.

"It's okay, Jim", came Forkbraid's sombre reply, "Everyone in the compound is gone", he didn't use the word dead, this was worse than dead.

Agent Spencer stared wide-eyed at the devastation before them, "The buildings are all still standing?"

"Yeah, sure. The buildings are still standing, they're untouched, but inside that scorched circle, there's not a single living thing, not even a microbe", Special Agent Murphy was pointing to the burnt circle before them.

"That's why these weapons were banned", Forkbraid added, his voice still sombre, "You'd think, that after the last time, people would have learnt."

Special Agent Murphy nodded in agreement.

Agent Spencer's communicator buzzed into action, "Sir, we can't find

Hopkins or Tollis. And Bortman, Sir, he's dead, his entire top half is missing."

The circle of death had stopped where Agent Bortman had taken cover. Every living thing within the circle had been reduced to fine dust.

Leroy watched the news feeds from Colonial Central Command. He had watched the earlier feeds about the failed assassination attempt on the Wizard Folcrom Forkbraid. Now he was watching the details of the *"docking ring incident"*, as it was being called.

The Prophet spoke to him, "Leroy, you know that they're saying that Colonial Central Command's crawling with remote viewers."

"My Lord, we had no idea. We thought that only the infidel, Forkbraid, was on the Chimera."

"Whose idea was it to hit the demon while he was in the President's office?", but before Leroy could answer, the Prophet added, "And what moron authorised blowing out those window panels?"

"I don't know, my Lord. I left everything up to our people on Colonial Central Command. I assumed that they would handle things", he searched for the right words, "more or less, correctly".

Leroy was looking more than a little sheepish, and sweat began to form on his temples.

"More or less, correctly? Well, they certainly screwed up, didn't they", it was a statement, more than a question. "And now this debacle", the Prophet pointed to the screen, "Explosions in a private mooring hold?"

The Prophet looked squarely at Leroy, "Am I surrounded by complete idiots and morons?"

Leroy didn't answer, he remained quiet with his eyes focused on the floor in front of him.

Then the news feed altered, as a new news flash appeared on the screen.

A young female newsreader appeared on the screen, she looked frightened, "I'm Sandra Long with some breaking news in from Colonial Central Command. There has been some sort of explosion in the North Gamma Land Strip, just northeast of the Gamma Sea. The explosion was clearly visible from the Alpha and Beta Land Strips. Informed sources are saying that the explosion had all the characteristics of a Flash Vaporiser. A military weapon banned by legal conventions for nearly two centuries. We'll bring you full coverage in our evening news broadcast."

The newsreader, herself a native of Colonial Central Command with relatives still living there, had a partially terrified look on her face. The news flash hung on her frightened features for long seconds before the previous news feed re-appeared on the screen.

The Prophet looked up at Leroy, he closed his eyes and sighed, "And now this!", he then snapped angrily, "You know, they will come here now. That is a certainty."

"No, my Lord, how will they know?", Leroy quickly replied.

"Remote viewers, Leroy! The infidels most powerful Wizard, Leroy! Of course, they will come here", the Prophet's voice grew hard and cold, his eyes took on a steely look.

Again Leroy was quiet. Fear showed in his eyes, and he could not answer.

"They will come here, Leroy, and Colonial Central Command will help them. The events of the past three days are tantamount to war. We now have no choice. We will have to run", the Prophet stated with finality.

"My Lord, where will we go?", Leroy asked, finally finding his voice.

"We can't stay here, that's for certain. Now that the devils are up here in L-Five, we can't stay anywhere near here. They'll track us down and exterminate us like dogs", the Prophet thought for a moment, "Ah yes. We have people on Mars don't we?"

"Yes, my Lord, we do", Leroy replied.

"And our people on Mars, are they well-placed, Leroy?"

"Yes, my Lord. Our people on Mars are very well-placed."

"Good, good then. We will go to [36]New Tortuga. They won't find us there", the Prophet decided.

---

36 New Tortuga. A smugglers' colony on Mars named after the Caribbean pirate port town of Tortuga.

11. Fleeing Rats

President Banyan was livid, "Are you certain there are no more of these mongrels in my colony?" The detonation of the flash vaporiser was still fresh in his mind.

"Positive. That was the only rat nest", came Forkbraid's swift reply.

"You're absolutely sure?", President Banyan queried again.

"I've scanned this colony from stern to bow. There was only that one rat's nest."

"And you agree with his assessment, Special Agent Murphy?"

"I have to, Sir. Forkbraid is our only source of information", Special Agent Murphy replied.

"Hmm. Well, that leaves Hyper Dynamics Corporation doesn't it."

"Maybe not", Forkbraid replied, "There may be other colonies up here with rats."

"You think so? How do we find them?", concern showed on President Banyan's face.

"That won't be easy. I can scan a colony from close quarters, but I have to be close."

"Why is that, FB?", asked Special Agent Murphy

"Up here, is not like down there on Earth, Jim", Forkbraid replied.

"You might need to elaborate a little", Special Agent Murphy noted.

"I can't explain it. You wouldn't understand. It has to do with biomass concentrations."

"Biomass concentrations?", President Banyan looked at him with a confused stare.

"Yes, biomass concentrations and connectivity. On Earth life is everywhere, up here, life is in little discrete pockets, each separated from the next. On Earth scanning is easy, simply because of the sheer size of the biomass concentration and its interconnectedness."

"I don't know if I'm following you at all on this one, Forkbraid", President Banyan admitted.

"Mr President, I don't expect you to. Think of it this way. I can stand anywhere on the Earth and I can scan every nook and cranny, given enough time. It's the same up here, but as with Earth, I have to either be standing in each individual colony or closely skimming its outer hull."

"So you need to personally be present on each colony to scan it?", Special Agent Murphy queried.

"Exactly, Jim", came Forkbraid's simple reply, "There are exceptions to this rule though."

"What exceptions? Can we make use of one?", President Banyan quickly asked, his hopes high.

"The exceptions all require connections to other psychics on each colony to be scanned."

"But there are no other psychics in L-Five", President Banyan frowned.

"That's the problem, Gentlemen. I am the only one, and I need an army of psychics."

"Can we bring more of your people up here, Forkbraid?"

"Mr President, it would be a waste of time. Very few of us can use our gifts off-world."

"That was what we always thought about you psychics", Special Agent Murphy added.

"And it's largely true. Some of us can function off-world, with minimal problems, but very few of us. That's just the way it is. Although there are probably other psychics up here."

"How can there be other psychics up here?"

"Jim, psychics are born into every human population. It's just that, off-world you don't look for them. So they don't get trained. Their gifts atrophy. That and the fact that up here, they're behind the eight-ball to start with."

"Behind the eight-ball?", President Banyan didn't follow the metaphor.

"Most *native* psychics, most psychics born up here, can't use their gifts anyway. For the same reasons that most Earth born psychics can't use their gifts off-world."

"Why can't they use their gifts off-world, FB?"

"Jim. I can't explain that to you. You'd need to be a psychic to fully appreciate the explanation."

"Forkbraid, you did say most native psychics", President Banyan wanted clarification.

"There is one, Gentlemen. A young girl of about eight. The only one we've ever come across."

"And where is this young girl, Forkbraid?"

"Mr President, I don't know. Up here somewhere. It's my task, one of them anyway, to find her."

"What about the other colonies then?"

"Well Mr President. I suggest you have your colonial agents search the colonies thoroughly for any banned weapons. If any banned weapons are found, that demands an explanation doesn't it."

"Hmm. I guess that's all we can do for the moment. You're still going to have to go to Hyper Dynamics Corporation though. Murphy, have the [37]Cruiser Spartan prepared for the trip."

---

37 A colonial cruiser equipped for military action. The propulsion system includes three powerful fusion thrusters.

"I can't wait that long, Mr President", Forkbraid stated, "I have to get there very quickly."

"It will only take a day or so to prep the ship", Special Agent Murphy assured him.

"The longer I take, the more chance that they'll run. I have to leave as soon as possible."

"Forkbraid, take your Bat Wing", President Banyan decided, "You'll be on your own until the Spartan arrives, so you watch your back."

James Murphy smiled looking at Forkbraid's staff, "He's always got his back covered, Sir."

Leroy had some of his men stow aboard the [38]CEO's space yacht, the Delilah. It was a fast, sleek ship equipped with small but powerful photon thrusters and antigravity lifters, capable of making the run to Mars. It was also large enough to carry nearly all the Prophet's key people. The Prophet's fundamentalists quietly took control of the yacht and prepared her for its launch.

"Everything is ready, my Lord", Leroy reported to the Prophet.

"Good, excellent. We'll need some insurance, Leroy", the Prophet replied.

"Insurance? I'm not sure that I understand, my Lord."

"That abomination, Leroy. That abomination was able to see the demon coming."

"But, my Lord, the child is an abomination. She is one of them. If anything, we should kill her."

"She isn't quite one of them yet, Leroy. And, although she is an abomination, we can use her."

"My Lord, thou shalt not suffer a Witch to live", Leroy quoted from his Bible.

The Prophet could see the confusion on Leroy's face, "You are one hundred percent correct, Leroy", he replied, then after a short pause he added, "but desperate times require desperate measures. This abominable child will be our Witch, Leroy. We will use her to watch their movements, to track them, the way they track us. And when we are all safe, she will burn."

Forkbraid approached Hyper Dynamics Corporation colony, a twin pair of cylinders, surrounded by a flotilla of orbiting processing and manufacturing modules. He swung his Bat Wing in and around the colony, scanning the orbiting modules as he went. Several times the Hyper Dynamics Corporation tried to hail his little ship. His only response was to signal them with the official [39]Psi Corps crest.

Forkbraid had no time to discuss the issues with them, he wanted full

---

38 The Chief Executive Officer of Hyper Dynamics Corporation colony.

39 Psi Corps, the name of the organisation responsible for organising and controlling the remote viewing teams.

compliance now and without discussion. As expected, Colonial Central Command had already called ahead and Hyper Dynamics Corporation was expecting him.

After a few moments Hyper Dynamics Corporation replied with "We have been expecting you, Sir. You will have our full co-operation. Approach as you see fit."

Forkbraid continued his scans.

Forkbraid located suspect colonists on several of the orbiting modules. He noted down the module designations and suspects names. After completing his sweep, Forkbraid swung back to scan the suspects again, this time more closely. After scanning the suspects once more, but this time more deeply and confirming they were indeed extremists, he then moved his ship closer to the colony's main cylinders.

Forkbraid skin danced his Bat Wing along the full length of the West Cylinder, scanning as swiftly as he could.

He was surprised to find that only a few extremists were present, "*Where are the rest? There must be more of them?*", he thought to himself.

Forkbraid gave the West Cylinder a second pass to confirm his findings and make sure he hadn't missed any others. He noted down the names of those extremists he had located and their locations. Then, he swung his Bat Wing over to the East Cylinder and began to repeat the scanning process, noting down any suspected extremists as he went.

By now, the news of a Bat Wing Interceptor buzzing around the colony had spread quickly across the small community. People were afraid. The extremists especially so. They, of course, were being hunted.

The internal colony news feeds were following the movements of Forkbraid's ship as best as they could and televising them to the colonists. Video walls across the colony were watching Forkbraid's progress. News announcers were doing their best to calm the inhabitants, telling them that the Bat Wing was not a threat, that they were being routinely scanned to ensure that no banned weaponry was present in the colony.

A small girl of eight named Miranda Swann was watching the television wall screen with her family in their lounge room. The small ship flew in closer to the cylinder. Closer to the outer hull than any other ship had ever flown, except perhaps by the colony's maintenance bots. It was both exciting to watch and at the same time frightening. Only one person could truly see who was on board this ship and that it was a psychic from Earth hunting extremists. Miranda smiled a wide smile, as she realised who was aboard the Bat Wing Interceptor.

"Lord Folcrom Forkbraid is aboard that ship", the little girl stated with conviction.

"How could you possibly know that Miranda?", her Father Peter asked.

"I just do, Daddy. The Wizard is on board that ship, and he's hunting."

"Don't be silly, Miranda. You couldn't possibly know that", her Mother Catherine chided.

"But he is, Mummy, he is on that ship", Miranda insisted, "I can feel him, Mummy!"

It was at that very moment that two men burst into their lounge room. They were armed with stun guns and once inside the room, they fired quickly at Miranda's startled parents.

The surprised words "Leroy McGuvan", were the only words Peter spoke before he and his Wife Catherine collapsed unconscious on their couch. Miranda's younger brother Chiron began to scream. He was quickly stunned and collapsed onto the floor. The two men aimed their stun guns at a terrified Miranda.

Behind the two men, Miranda's teacher, Mrs Harmon, stepped into the room, "Come with us Miranda! Come now!"

Mrs Harmon grabbed Miranda by the arm and began to drag her out of the room. Miranda's eyes brimmed with tears, and she screamed out as loudly as she could, "Help me, Forkbraid! Help me!"

A startled Forkbraid was still skin dancing down the East Cylinder's hull when the image of a frightened young girl with tear filled eyes popped into his mind.

The words "Help me Forkbraid! Help me!", resounded loudly in his mind. "*Miranda? She's here!*", he quickly thought to himself.

"*Help me Forkbraid! Help me!*", Miranda was now screaming out with her mind. Forkbraid reached out quickly once more, "*Miranda, I'm on my way.*"

Forkbraid swung his Bat Wing quickly towards the Southern end cap's docking ring and requested [40]DCI. Hyper Dynamics Corporation space dock quickly granted Forkbraid's request and his ship was soon approaching the docking ring. As his ship closed in on the docking ring, Forkbraid reached his mind deep inside the East Cylinder, scanning far and wide.

"*There they are*", he thought to himself, "*Like rats preparing to abandon ship.*"

He noted the name of the vessel, the Delilah. He had found them, but was he too late?

Within minutes Forkbraid's Bat Wing was docked, and he was preparing to disembark from his ship and enter the spaceport.

Miranda had been dragged roughly to a waiting pod by her captives, kicking and screaming all the way. Several innocent bystanders who were witnessing the event, were shot with the stun guns and dropped to the ground. They quickly jumped into the waiting pod. It was only a matter of minutes before the pod

---

40 Docking Computer Interlock. Interlocking of ships navigation computers for automated docking.

whisked the four away towards the Southern end cap's docking ring. A short while later, they were approaching the private mooring bay of the space yacht , the Delilah, the personal ship of the CEO of Hyper Dynamic's Corporation.

Forkbraid had stepped into the spaceport facilities. While Hyper Dynamics Corporation security guards watched, Forkbraid whisked out his staff and tossed it behind him. It then followed him obediently. He then reached into his invisible pockets once more and pulled out a wand in each hand. The one in his left-hand hand was made of rosewood and deeply coloured, the one in his right-hand was made of oak. Forkbraid's cloak billowed about him, he was a terrifying sight to behold. The security guards were all confused, and they aimed their pulse pistols at him.

Forkbraid spoke harshly in a voice with the oddest lilt, "Idiots", he sent an image of the official [41]Psi Corps crest deep into their minds, "You will obey me!"

All gentleness disappeared from Forkbraid's face, as the visage of the viper hardened into his features. Forkbraid continued his march down the corridor.

The frightened guards turned to their commander, Dean Beck, who simply told them, "Do as he says. Holster your pulse pistols."

The frightened security guards holstered their pulse pistols.

By now the pod had arrived at the Delilah's mooring bay. Miranda was dragged out of the pod, kicking and screaming into the waiting ship, the Delilah.

Leroy stopped at the open hatch, "Has the Prophet arrived, yet?"

"He came on board fifteen minutes ago, Sir", replied one of the men standing guard at the hatch.

"Good", Leroy then ordered five of his men to defend the bay, "Kill anyone that approaches."

Forkbraid issued his orders to the corporate security guards, "There's a yacht just around the ring, a fair size one, it's called the Delilah. It must not leave this colony!"

Commander Beck gulped, "The CEO's yacht. I'll take care of it."

Commander Beck called through to the spaceport's control centre, "Lock down the Delilah! Repeat, lock down the Delilah!"

Several gun shots could be heard through the communicator.

"Shit!", Forkbraid exclaimed, "You", he pointed at Commander Beck, "Take half your men and secure the control centre. Lock down that ship! It must not leave this colony!", he ordered. "The rest of you come with me!"

Commander Beck ran quickly towards the spaceport's control centre, six men followed behind him. Forkbraid continued on to the Delilah, with six security guards close behind.

---

41 Psi Corps, the name of the organisation responsible for organising and controlling the remote viewing teams.

A golden glow filled the air around Forkbraid as he approached the CEO's yacht, the Delilah.

The crystal in his trailing staff glowed a deep orange. The security guards gave his staff a wide berth. A hail of bullets and plasma shot towards him. Bullets fizzled in the air and plasma exploded in little balls of scintillating light. Forkbraid's shield held. The security guards threw themselves behind the nearest cover.

Forkbraid's wands swung around in his hands once and pointed at his assailants. Streams of bright blue light shot out of the wands and two of the assailants dove for cover as blue light streaked past them, audibly rippling through metal walls as it went.

"He means business", one of his assailants shouted to the other, who simply nodded in return.

In the distance behind them gun fire could be heard. Commander Beck had reached the spaceport's control centre and a gun fight now ensued.

Forkbraid continued walking towards the Delilah's mooring bay doors. The inner mooring bay doors had been closed, and five men stood guard at the entrance. They continued their hail of bullets and plasma. Again streams of blue light shot out of Forkbraid's wands. Two men turned momentarily transparent as the blue light struck them hard, they then crumpled lifeless to the floor.

Then there were three.

The distinct hum of the Delilah's antigravity lifters could be heard above the hail of gun fire. '*I don't have much time*', Forkbraid thought to himself.

He again aimed his wands and streams of blue light shot forward once more. They lashed two more assailants, who flashed into writhing transparency before collapsing to the floor.

Then there was one.

Gun fire could still be heard in the distance behind them. The spaceport's control centre was still not secured. Forkbraid could hear the outer mooring bay doors opening beyond the bulkhead. Forkbraid frowned as he dispatched the last assailant with another streak of blue light.

Then there were none.

Forkbraid quickly approached the inner mooring bay doors. It was too late. The outer mooring bay doors were now fully open. There was a sudden eerie vibration as the Delilah launched itself swiftly into space.

"Miranda, child, I am too late. Be brave, child. I will find you", Forkbraid transmitted to the frightened child.

In the distance gun fire could still be heard. Forkbraid swung about and began making his way back towards the spaceport's control centre. The final shots rang out as he approached. Commander Beck lay dead on the floor, as were three of his men. There were four dead extremists lying on the floor close to the control centre's entrance.

Forkbraid swung his wands back into his impossible pockets. He flicked his hand at the control centre door, and it burst wide open. Stepping inside he found the three controllers dead at their seats. Forkbraid walked up to the control screens and quickly located the Delilah on one of them.

Forkbraid took some readings, then after waiting a few minutes he took some more. It seemed that the Delilah was heading away from L-Five.

"They aren't running to another colony. They can't run to Earth, my people will be waiting for them. Where are they going?", Forkbraid thought to himself.

The remaining security guards behind him stood still awaiting orders. By now the corporation's CEO had arrived on the scene.

"What the hell is going on down here?", Clinton Usarian shouted at Forkbraid.

Forkbraid stood up and looked coldly into his eyes, "Cleaning up your fucking mess, Usarian!"

"What? How do you know my name?", the CEO quietly queried.

"Are you stupid? Who do you think I am? Fucking Santa-Claus?"

"You're a Wizard", Clinton Usarian stated simply, adding "You were supposed to be scanning my colony for extremists. You weren't supposed to start a fucking war!", he was now openly screaming at Forkbraid with his hands waving in all directions.

Forkbraid held up his hand and squeezed his fingers shut in front of Usarian's face.

Clinton Usarian's mouth shut tightly as Forkbraid replied, "Firstly, I'm a Witch. Male or female, a Witch is a Witch! Get it right! Secondly, I'm here to do whatever it takes! This is Psi Corps business. These were terrorists, not Santa's fucking Elves!", he burned an image of the Psi Corps crest deep into Usarian's mind, "My will be done! And you will comply!"

Again that strange lilt in his voice. Forkbraid dropped his hand and Clinton Usarian's mouth opened once more. A frightened look appeared in his eyes.

"Have your men take care of the dead, Usarian", Forkbraid requested.

"Yes, Sir, I'll have it taken care of straight away, Sir", a far more compliant Clinton Usarian responded.

"Get some men down here", Forkbraid continued. "That ship of yours, the Delilah", Forkbraid pointed to the fleeing ship on the screen, "I want to know precisely where she's going."

Usarian stared at the screen, "I'll have it taken care of straight away, Sir."

"Another task for you, Usarian", Forkbraid looked coldly into his eyes, "Your corporation has been making banned and illegal weapons. And androids with concealed explosive devices."

Clinton Usarian looked up at Forkbraid with a truly shocked look on his face, he didn't know anything about this. The remark about androids with concealed explosive devices was particularly disturbing to him. All robots and androids must under universal system law be three laws safe. A rumour of this nature could destroy his entire company, send it into bankruptcy.

"I want this colony searched from top to bottom, every which way you can. I want every illegal weapon found and destroyed. I want every single robot and android checked. Got that!"

Clinton Usarian gulped deeply, "That's a given. I'll personally oversee that myself, Sir."

"One final thing, Usarian", Forkbraid reached into his pocket and pulled out a notepad.

He pulled the front page off and memorised the names inscribed upon it, before passing the page to Clinton Usarian.

"These people, they're all extremists. Pick them up, lock them up. Do it quickly, don't let any of them escape. Be careful about it, they may be armed and dangerous. I'll have my people extradite them back to Earth as soon as possible. They will all undergo psychic demolition."

Those two words, psychic demolition, hung in Usarian's mind for long moments.

"There must be more than fifty people on this list!", Clinton Usarian finally exclaimed.

"Yes, Usarian", Forkbraid replied, "and you have to catch them all. Every single one of them."

Usarian nodded compliantly to Forkbraid, then gave a command to his head of security, "Barrows! Have these people arrested and locked up. Do it quietly, do it quickly and get them all. No-one, no-one escapes!"

"Yes, Sir. I'll get straight on it, Sir", Barrows turned and walked out of the control centre.

Forkbraid quickly scanned Barrow's mind to make sure that Barrows was the right man for the job, *"Good"*, Forkbraid thought to himself, *"He'll get the job done."*

A short time later three people had been brought to a large office that Forkbraid had commandeered near the spaceport's control centre. A small four-year-old boy and his parents.

Forkbraid quickly scanned their minds, *"Chiron, Catherine, and Peter Swann"*, he silently thought to himself.

Chiron was scared and sobbing, his eyes were streaming with tears. His Mother, Catherine, comforted him, her eyes were also red and teary. His Father,

Peter, stood behind them, his hands on their shoulders. Forkbraid indicated the chairs in front of the desk for them to sit on.

"You're the Wizard?", Peter questioned, "You're the one Miranda felt on that ship?"

Forkbraid sighed slightly, "Please use the term Witch, not Wizard. And, Yes, I am Folcrom Forkbraid, the one your Daughter felt on the ship."

"They have my child, Miranda", Catherine sobbed.

"I know they do", Forkbraid's face displayed its gentleness once more, "I tried to stop them, but I wasn't quick enough."

"Can you help us get her back?", Peter asked, his voice breaking slightly.

"I will do my best to get her back", Forkbraid replied, adding, "They will pay for their crimes."

"Why did they take my Child?", Catherine asked, choking back her tears.

"Miranda is special. Your Daughter is a highly gifted individual. They somehow see an advantage in keeping her close."

Then Forkbraid asked, "Peter Swann, what do you know about these extremists?"

Peter looked stunned, he looked to his Wife and his Son, then back to Forkbraid.

"It's alright, Peter, I know you're not one of them. But you do know them."

"I, I know that they are a very religious group", Peter stuttered. "We've met them a few times", he indicated he and his Wife, "They're a growing group and always looking for new members, new converts. They are not our cup of tea, though."

Catherine quickly added, "They were far too religious for our liking. We never really clicked, if you know what I mean. There was", Catherine paused momentarily, "something odd about them."

"Yes, Catherine. I know exactly what you mean. They all seem so nice enough, but just that little-bit too strict, religiously strict. And perhaps you could see an underlying intolerance, for certain other groups and individuals."

"Yes, that's exactly it", Catherine replied, nodding her head.

"What can you tell me about their leader?"

"We've never met him", there was no lie in Peter's voice, "They call him the Prophet."

Forkbraid looked surreptitiously into their minds, they were telling him the truth. He carefully assessed them for psychic potential. Catherine would have been around level four. Peter would have been about level three. Chiron could be a level seven? He needed a proper assessment.

It was far too late for the parents. Their gifts had already atrophied long ago. Alas, any adult walk-in whose original potential was less than a level five, could not be trained. Chiron was another matter though. He was a child and his potential could be realised.

Forkbraid smiled, being careful not to smile too much considering the current situation, he spoke gently, "Your Son, Chiron, is also special. He has the same gifts as Miranda, although perhaps not nearly as strong."

"Really?", Peter looked at his young Son.

"Yes. Given the proper training, he has the potential to become quite the powerful young psychic", Forkbraid informed them both.

"But, you said Chiron's not as strong as Miranda", Catherine asked with a concerned look.

"Miranda is very special. Highly gifted. Her mind reached out across the vacuum of space, all the way to Earth and touched mine. That's very, very special. Not many psychics can do that. Miranda will need highly individualised training. She is very special."

Miranda's Mother and Father looked slightly shocked, their jaws dropping slightly. They stole a quick glance at each other.

"It's okay. Miranda is a perfectly normal child, just somewhat more gifted in one very special department. With the proper training, your Daughter will be outstanding."

Peter's voice took on a serious tone, "We have to get her back first."

"And that we will, Peter", Forkbraid replied equally seriously, "The Cruiser Spartan will be here in a few short hours", Forkbraid indicated to all of them, "We will give chase. We will get her back."

Just then the colony's CEO Clinton Usarian walked into the office, "Sir, we've calculated their course. We know precisely where they're going."

"Spit it out man. Where are they going?", Forkbraid demanded.

"They're going to Mars, they're going to Mars, Sir."

"Mars!", Forkbraid exclaimed, "Well, then, that's where we're going, all of us", Forkbraid indicated himself and the family before him.

"Not you, Usarian. You have a right unholy mess to clean up here. Colonial Central Command tells me that they're sending another Cruiser, the Corinthian, as well. They're going to help you sort out this unholy mess of yours."

Clinton Usarian gulped, he could see himself losing his job at the next shareholders' meeting.

Forkbraid picked up the thought and quickly suggested, "Usarian, perhaps at your next shareholders' meeting, you should fall on your sword", again with that strange lilt in his voice.

'*So we're going to Mars!*', Forkbraid thought to himself.

12. Three Ships

The Cruiser Spartan was now in close proximity to the Hyper Dynamics Corporation. She was a large ship, resembling a long stretched triangular wedge in shape. The widest part of the ship was the aft section where her three powerful fusion thrusters resided. The ship's superstructure sat atop the wedge, projecting up and out from the stern, then forward along and above the two angled top decks. Interceptor and Hummer launch tubes and landing bays lined her top and lower decks.

The Spartan's equally angular bottom decks contained within them two large shuttles designed for transporting squads of colonial troopers. These shuttles could be used for boarding other ships, boarding colonies and could even be used as drop-ships to land troops on planetary surfaces. They were equipped with both antigravity lifters and photon thrusters.

Her identical sister ship, the Cruiser Corinthian was close behind her. Both ships were too large to dock at the smaller colonies like Hyper Dynamics Corporation. The Captain of the Spartan had dispatched a Hummer to pick up the Swann family. Forkbraid had decided that they would need to accompany him on the trip to Mars.

Peter and Catherine Swann had agreed to go to Mars for the sake of their kidnapped Daughter, Miranda. Although Forkbraid also had other ideas. The new Elysium colony on Mars did need colonists after all and the Swann's children were psychics, fitting the bill beautifully.

Forkbraid himself, flew his Bat Wing interceptor across to the Spartan. The Delilah already had a good head start, and it would be very difficult to catch up with her. Fortunately, although the solar system is a big place, trajectories can be calculated with accuracy and the destination of any fleeing ship can be plotted.

The Corinthian had dispatched both of her shuttles, one to each of the cylinders in the Hyper Dynamics Corporate colony. Eight squads of the colonial troopers were to go aboard each colony cylinder and oversee its security for the next few weeks. The Hyper Dynamics Corporate colony was now officially under martial law.

All the extremists on Forkbraid's list had already been rounded up and arrested by Hyper Dynamic's security teams and placed in holding cells. Very little resistance had been encountered thus far and only a few minor skirmishes had occurred, resulting in the deaths of two more extremists. Nonetheless, there was considerable unease among the remaining colonists at the Hyper Dynamics Corporation. It was the task of the colonial troops to maintain both the peace and continue the search for illegal weaponry. Prisoner interrogation would also begin with the arrival of the colonial troops. Upon the end of its current mission, the Cruiser Corinthian was then to deliver the prisoners to Earth, where they would undergo criminal prosecution and appropriate treatment.

So far a total of one hundred and seventy-five Androids had been discovered with explosive devices concealed in their torsos. These had been scheduled to be exported to Earth during the next two weeks. Each Android appeared to have a specific target on Earth. The first attack on the Flinders Psychic Academy appeared to have been a trial run. If it was deemed successful, as it was, other attacks in greater numbers were to follow. These Androids were already being disarmed when the first of the two cruisers, the Spartan, arrived.

Forkbraid stepped out of his Bat Wing. A Colonial Officer and two Colonial Troopers were waiting for him. The Officer did not offer his name, simply asking Forkbraid to follow him to the conference room. It didn't take very long to get to the conference room, as it was the landing bay where Forkbraid docked his Bat. Forkbraid was ushered inside where he found two men waiting for him, one of whom he was already acquainted with.

"Jim, good to see you again", Forkbraid offered.

"Good to see you too, FB. This is Captain Bartholomew Carmichael", Jim replied.

"Captain", Forkbraid nodded, "Might I ask where the Swann family is?"

"They are currently being debriefed. After that, they will be given a short orientation tour of their quarters", Captain Carmichael replied. "They are to be billeted in a compartment close to the officers quarters. Your own room and that of Special Agent Murphy is in the same compartment."

"Good. If you could take good care of them, I'd appreciate that", Forkbraid requested.

"Lord Forkbraid, I don't like civilians on my ship. Whilst on my ship, both Special Agent Murphy, the Swann family and yourself will be confined to the guest compartment so to speak. This is a military vessel, and we can't have civilians wandering around. When outside your compartment, you'll be escorted by a Colonial Officer at all times."

Forkbraid gave a slight, barely noticeable sigh, "Captain, this is your ship. We will be following your rules. The most important thing is that we catch up with the Delilah and all those on board."

"I've been talking to the Captain about that, FB. Catching the Delilah is not going to be so easy."

"How so, Jim?", Forkbraid enquired.

"Their yacht is fast, and they have a two-day head start", Jim replied.

"My ship is faster, but she's also so much bigger. So it takes a while to get her going", Captain Carmichael added.

"What does that mean exactly? Can we catch them or can't we?", Forkbraid enquired.

"Based on our current projections, it will take the Delilah around three weeks to reach Mars. Once the Spartan is up to speed, we'll be much faster, but she's also much bigger. So getting to top speed takes a bit longer. We'll arrive at Mars within a day or two of the Delilah."

"We can't get there any quicker, Captain?", Forkbraid asked with a frown on his face.

"No. That's as quick as we can get there", Captain Carmichael confirmed.

"Hmm. So we'll have to track them to a colony, either in orbit or on the surface."

"FB, Mars is a blue planet now remember", Special Agent Murphy was referring to the terraformed Mars, "They can land pretty much anywhere they like on the surface. They don't have any need to land at a colony. Any patch of level ground will do."

"That's not good, Jim. Mars has a surface area as great as the Earth's entire land area."

"Gentlemen", Captain Carmichael butted in, "Let us assume that they will not land in any of the Martian Oceans or Seas. So I believe we can rule out a water landing."

"That's still a big area to search, Captain", Special Agent Murphy noted.

"Can't you use your talents? Scan the entire planet and find them that way", the Captain asked.

"I'm only one psychic, Captain. The area to search is simply way too big. It would take too long."

"What if they try to make it to one of the Belter colonies?", asked Special Agent Murphy.

"Unlikely, Agent Murphy. I've had my people study the Delilah's schematics. Even with a full load of fuel, the Belter colonies are simply too far. They'd have to refuel at Mars and even then, they'd be taking a huge risk", came Captain Carmichael's reply.

"How so?", asked Forkbraid.

"If they refuel at Mars, we can request the Martian authorities pick them up, which incidentally, we're going to do anyway. Even if the Martian authorities don't co-operate, as is the case on many occasions, if they try to run again, we'll be more than close enough to track them."

"Then we'll be back at square one. Just chasing them further out into the solar system", Special Agent Murphy noted in reply.

"Ah, but the Belter colonies are scattered all over the Asteroid Belt. Once we calculate their trajectory, we'll know precisely which colony they're going to. They'll have nowhere to run. We'll be able to simply adjust our course and get to their destination well ahead of them."

"I can't see them doing that. They'd have to be completely stupid", Forkbraid replied.

"They wouldn't. Their safest bet is a Mars landing. Somewhere well away from any of the colonies. A smuggler base probably", Special Agent Murphy replied, "That's what they'll do."

"Precisely, Gentlemen. Mars is their destination", the Captain replied with certainty.

"What's the status of Hyper Dynamics Corporation?", Jim asked Forkbraid.

"They've found a huge number of rigged Androids, Jim. The first attack was just a test. They were going to hit us real hard, Jim. Another week and there would have been bombs exploding all over Earth at every Psychic Academy. We've managed to avoid a huge catastrophe."

"Seems you've stopped them just in time, Gentlemen", Captain Carmichael noted.

"Yes, Captain, this time. A dozen of those Androids were even fitted with flash vaporisers", Forkbraid paused for a moment, "Let's hope there's no other rat nests up here."

The Captain and Special Agent Murphy looked shocked.

"Gentlemen, the colonial armed forces are on full alert. We've organised a priority search of the colonies. Colonial troops will be searching each and every one, in order, starting with those colonies that export products to Earth first. Every single container heading to Earth is going to be scanned and searched."

"Let's hope that's enough, Captain", Forkbraid replied.

"I believe it will be", the Captain replied.

Catherine Swann stared into the video screen at the receding Cis-Lunar system. The blue Earth, the grey Moon and the multitude of sparkling lights of the colonies of L-Five and L-Four were receding slowly behind the ever accelerating Spartan.

"I've never been out of L-Five before", she said with sadness.

Peter looked into the video screen, "Catherine, think of Miranda. When you hold her in your arms again, you'll be happy once more."

Catherine smiled slightly and tucked herself into her husband's arms, "I just hope our little girl is going to be okay, she has been kidnapped by terrorists after all."

"Forkbraid seems to think so. He says that the extremists need our Daughter for some reason."

"I hope he's right", Catherine Swann stared into the video screen once more.

Special Agent Murphy and Forkbraid were standing well back away from the screen, "Do you really think she'll be okay, FB?", Jim Murphy asked.

"I'm hoping she will be, Jim", Forkbraid quietly replied, "The extremists do seem to need her and that gives me hope. When I reach out to her, I can just feel her at the edge of my mind's eye."

"So we know for sure that the girl is alive?", Jim whispered in reply.

"Yes, Jim, young Miranda is alive and well", Forkbraid replied.

Special Agent Murphy looked back towards the video screen, "I've never been this far from L-Five either. I've been to many of the colonies, I've been to the L-Four [42] mining catch-alls and ore processing stations. I've even been to the Lunar mining colonies. Hell, I've even been to the Earth. But to be this far from home. The whole system looks so awfully small."

"Well, Jim. Remember this is my first trip into space. My first trip off-world", Forkbraid noted.

James Murphy looked at Forkbraid, "Yeah. I nearly forgot. How's that going by the way?"

"I'm really surprised. I thought it would be harder. I mean, we psychics have this big thing about being away from our Mother Earth. Many psychics would never consider going off-world at all, not ever. Nearly all those that would consider it, would find their talents, their gifts, useless. I feel a little, I don't know, disconnected? But I can still use my gifts, I can still function as a psychic, as a Witch. It's not as bad as I thought it would be."

"Well, that's something then isn't it", James Murphy replied, then pointing to the video screen he said, "You know, FB, we're lucky to get that view. This ship has fusion thrusters, so if the rear scanners weren't mounted up high on the superstructure, all we'd see is the glare from the Spartan's fusion exhaust, it's three fusion torches."

"Then we should be thankful, Jim. Being able to see that view of our home system, so small, and so fragile as it is. It kind of puts things into perspective, doesn't it?"

"Hmm. That it does. That it does", James Murphy replied.

The space yacht Delilah sped swiftly along its course ahead of the Cruiser Spartan.

"Are we being followed, Leroy?", the Prophet asked.

"I can't say, my Lord", Leroy replied, adding, "This ship has no rear scanners."

"No rear scanners?", the Prophet enquired.

"It's the ship's photon thrusters, my Lord", Leroy explained, "We'd only see the glare of our own exhaust. That being the case, and this being a civilian vessel,

---

42 Specially designed transports, designed to catch compressed lunar ore
launched from the surface of the moon.

it has no rear scanners."

"So we have no way of knowing if we're being followed", the Prophet asked.

"That's pretty much it, my Lord", Leroy replied, "Until we cross the halfway mark."

"Halfway mark?", queried The Prophet, "You'll need to explain that one, Leroy."

"Well my Lord. When we've crossed the halfway point in our course, our pilot Matthew, will turn the ship around to reverse thrust. That way, we'll be decelerating and slowing down as we approach Mars. We need to do this for Martian orbital insertion. At that point, we can scan back towards L-Five and then, we'll know if we're being followed."

"I have a better idea, Leroy", the Prophet stated, "Bring me that abominable child."

"My Lord?", Leroy was caught by surprise.

"Bring me that abominable child, Leroy", the Prophet stated again.

A few minutes later Leroy returned with Miranda. The little girl was still somewhat frightened, but had to some degree gotten used to her surroundings.

"Child", the Prophet looked at Miranda, "Are we being followed?", he demanded.

Miranda did not answer.

"Child! Are we being followed?", the Prophet demanded again.

"Yes", Miranda's voice was little more than a whisper.

"Speak up, child!", the Prophet shouted.

"Yes. We are being followed", tears were welling in Miranda's eyes.

"And who is following us, exactly?", the Prophet demanded anew.

"My Mum and Dad, and my little brother Chiron", Miranda sobbed in reply.

This caught the Prophet by surprise. Her family was giving chase.

"Anyone else?", the Prophet demanded once more, "Speak child!", he shouted.

"Lord Folcrom Forkbraid", Miranda replied, the sobbing making her difficult to understand.

The Prophet knelt down in front of Miranda, "How are they following us?", he demanded.

"They're in a big ship, with a lot of soldiers. They call it the Spartan", Miranda took a step back.

Leroy gasped, "The Spartan!"

They were being chased by a colonial cruiser, a heavy colonial cruiser at that.

The Prophet stood up once more. "There, you see, Leroy. We are being followed. Now take this abominable child back to her quarters."

Leroy obediently took Miranda back to her quarters and locked her in.

Leroy thought to himself, *The Prophet was right, the child was useful after all.*

The next day a Colonial Liner was picked up on the Delilah's scanners. The ship's pilot Matthew had summoned Leroy to the bridge. Leroy in turn had summoned the Prophet.

"My Lord there's a Colonial Liner seven thousand kilometres off the starboard bow. I've already pinged the liner, it's the [43]IPL Ptolemy. We'll be overtaking her soon", Matthew informed the Prophet when he arrived at the Delilah's bridge.

"Probably just on her regular Mars run", the Prophet replied, asking, "Why was I summoned?"

"My Lord, that was my idea", replied Leroy, "I thought it might be a good idea to have the abominable child", Leroy paused for a moment before continuing, "have the child scan that Liner."

"I don't see how the Liner could possibly be a threat, Leroy", the Prophet replied.

"I wasn't thinking of that, my Lord. I was thinking more of", Leroy paused again, "more of testing her abilities. It would be useful to know how accurate the child really is. We can have Matthew here access their passenger manifest, and we can check her accuracy that way."

Matthew nodded, "Piece of cake my Lord."

The Prophet thought about this for several moments, "Leroy. That's actually a good idea. Bring the abominable child, let's see what she can tell us."

"I've already taken the liberty, my Lord", Leroy replied as Mrs Harmon quickly appeared and dragged Miranda onto the bridge.

"Child!", the Prophet snapped, "I want you to concentrate on that ship!", he demanded, pointing to the Interplanetary Liner on the screen.

Miranda focused on the screen. At first, she seemed a little confused, then a small smile came over her face. Miranda quickly hid the smile.

"Well, child, what's the name of that ship?", the Prophet asked.

Miranda focused again, "The Interplanetary Liner, Ptolemy."

"Who is the Captain of that ship?", the Prophet asked.

Miranda focused again and replied, "Captain Samuel Lewis Brixton."

"Who is the Pilot on duty on that ship?", came the Prophet's next question.

Miranda focused again and replied, "Ensign Brett James Laraby."

The Prophet cocked an eyebrow and barked, "How many passengers are onboard that ship? Passengers not crew", he qualified his original demand.

Miranda focused again and after a few moments replied, "Two thousand and four."

The Prophet stared long and hard at Miranda, then asked softly, "What's their destination?"

---

43 Interplanetary Liner

"Mars", Miranda replied quickly.

"I know that, child!", the Prophet shouted, "Which colonies are they going to?"

Miranda focused once again then answered, "All to the one colony. Elysium."

The Prophet looked at Matthew, who answered the unasked question, "Five for five my Lord."

So far so good, the child appeared to be very accurate.

The Prophet queried Matthew, "Elysium?"

"It's that new colony, my Lord", Matthew answered, "On the Elysium subcontinent in the Martian Northern Hemisphere", a wealth of information was Matthew.

The Prophet stared at Miranda once more. The child was accurate, capable of providing detailed information, but just how detailed.

He had a use for this child, *"Five for five"*, he thought to himself.

The Prophet looked at Miranda once more, *"Just how much info can she provide?"*, he thought.

"Child! Starting with the first class cabins, who are the first five passengers on that ship?", the Prophet demanded.

Miranda focused again, but this time did not answer.

Matthew spoke, "My Lord. I just tried to access the passenger manifest. It's been classified!"

"Classified? Why would their passenger manifest be classified?", the Prophet queried.

"I don't know, Sir", the Pilot Matthew looked perplexed, "Passenger manifests are never classified", he paused, "except on military vessels."

"Can you hack the passenger manifest?", the Prophet asked.

"Yes, my Lord", Matthew replied, "Of course, I can, Sir. Just give me a minute or two."

Several minutes passed before Matthew responded, "Okay. I now have access, Sir."

"Child!, those names I asked for. Give them too me. Now!", the Prophet barked.

Miranda skipped over the first name and started the list "Charlene Fewkes, Marcus Greyhelm, Roseanne Rhein, Miriam Devree and Jason Phelps."

"My Lord, the child skipped over the first passenger on the manifest", Matthew stated.

"Why would you do that child?", the Prophet asked, then before she could answer, "Matthew, who is the first passenger?"

Matthew gulped, he looked up at the Prophet, "My Lord, it's the Lady Folcrom Selene!"

"Lady Folcrom Selene? Are you sure?", the Prophet queried.

"Yes, my Lord, the Lady Folcrom Selene", Matthew confirmed.

The Prophet stared coldly at Miranda, "Is this true child? Is Lady Folcrom Selene on that ship?", he screamed at her.

Miranda was crying once more, through her sobbing she answered, "Yes, yes she is."

"Why would a Witch be on board an Interplanetary Liner bound for Mars?", the Prophet asked.

"I don't know, my Lord", Leroy responded, "Why would their passenger list be classified?", he asked in return.

"How many Witches and Wizards are on board that ship?", the Prophet barked at Miranda.

Miranda sat down on the floor, her tears flowing freely, "About half", she whimpered.

"Half the passengers are Witches and Wizards?", Leroy asked incredulously.

Miranda simply sobbed a single word, "Yes."

Matthew the Pilot then asked, "What about the other half?", the sound of panic in his voice.

The Prophet grabbed Miranda's arm and lifted her to her feet, "What about the other half Child?"

"They're all psychics", Miranda cried.

The Prophet looked at Leroy, "Have her taken back to her quarters. Now!"

Leroy waved his hand and Mrs Harmon dragged Miranda away.

The Prophet demanded, "We must destroy that liner! Now!"

"My Lord, this is a space yacht. We don't have any weapons on board capable of taking out an Interplanetary Liner."

"What about our light rail guns?", the Prophet asked.

Matthew the Pilot shook his head, "No, my Lord. They're seven thousand kilometres away. Even if we could use the rail guns in an airlock, at that distance, we'd never hit the Ptolemy."

"There must be a way", the Prophet demanded, "We can see her on the screen. Surely there must be some way to strike at her?"

Leroy answered, "My Lord. We're looking at a magnified scan. Unmagnified, she'd be just a speck. Barely visible at all."

"Leroy. They're so close. When will we ever have such an opportunity again?"

"My Lord. We don't have anything on board that can accurately reach her", Leroy responded.

"There has to be a way?", the Prophet asked again.

Leroy then answered in the affirmative, "There is, my Lord", Leroy was smiling now.

The Prophet smiled back, "Leroy. How pray tell, are we to destroy her?"

"My Lord, we will arrive at Mars ahead of the Ptolemy", Leroy answered.

"Hmm. Now, that does give one food for thought, doesn't it, Leroy?"

"My Lord. It certainly does", Leroy replied as he noticed the Ptolemy was now off their stern.

Mrs Harmon dragged Miranda back to her cabin. It was a small room with a single bunk, a closet, a wash basin and a toilet. Roughly Miranda was shoved through the cabin door.

"You'd do well to obey the Prophet child", Mrs Harmon spat, "He says jump, you jump!"

"Why is everybody so mean?", Miranda sobbed.

"People are trying to kill us, Miranda. Why do you think we behave this way?"

Miranda's voice firmed as she asked, "Wasn't it your people that did all those horrible things?"

Mrs Harmon stared at Miranda through frightened eyes, "How could you possibly know that?"

"It was, wasn't it?", Miranda was no longer sobbing, "Your people started the killing first!"

"Shut up child!", a frightened Mrs Harmon screamed, "You couldn't possibly know!"

"Oh, but I do know. I know everything", Miranda's eyes had rolled back showing only their whites.

Mrs Harmon panicked and slammed the door shut, before running to her own cabin.

Lady Selene watched the video screen above the bar in the Ptolemy's main dining lounge. The ships captain had placed a scan of a space yacht on the screen. It was a rare passing of another ship in space, the Delilah, as the label on the sidebar of the screen showed. The smaller, much faster ship approached from behind and was now overtaking them, en route to Mars. Many of the passengers, currently eating their lunch, watched in fascination at this rare event.

Marcus was eating the chef's special, roast pork, "Hmm, I won't recommend this to anyone. It's supposed to be roast pork, but it's somewhat odd tasting."

Lady Selene was uneasy, "I have an ill feeling about that ship", she stated to no-one in particular while looking up at the video screen.

Charlene, who was sitting on her right, asked, "What is it, Selene?".

"I'm not sure. I had the feeling we were being watched. It was just a fleeting feeling, but it was there nonetheless, and then it was gone."

"I felt it too", stated Roseanne, "Like the feeling you get when a small child is sneaking a peek at you, when they're hidden behind something."

"Yes, that's it", Selene replied, "That's exactly it."

Selene concentrated on the screen and the ship it displayed, then thought, *"Miranda?"*

Roseanne heard the unspoken name, "Miranda?"

Marcus and Charlene had also heard Selene, "Who's Miranda?", Marcus asked.

"Miranda is a young child. A psychic child. We had two walk-ins at the induction ceremony. You were one, Roseanne, physically present, but the other was only their in spirit so to speak. One of Forkbraid's tasks is to locate her, locate Miranda at L-Five."

"At L-Five? A psychic child at L-Five?", Charlene questioned.

"Yes, the first we've ever encountered. Anyway, I'm surprised either of you picked that up", Selene indicated Charlene and Marcus.

"Well, I think it was more you were transmitting than us reading", Marcus answered.

Charlene nodded in agreement.

Selene pointed to the ship on the screen, "Miranda is there, I'm certain of that", then she sighed, "I'm too far from the Earth, unfortunately. I can't pick up much more from that ship, except a very odd ill feeling."

"Perhaps her family is immigrating to Mars", Charlene offered.

"No, no Charlene. I get a very strong ill feeling from that ship. Something is definitely amiss and Miranda is very frightened", Selene replied.

The small, fast ship was now ahead of them and leaving the Ptolemy in its wake.

"Forkbraid will have to come to Mars now", Roseanne stated.

"To Mars?", Selene looked at her young apprentice.

"Yes, of course", Roseanne replied, "He can't complete his mission until he finds Miranda."

"And Miranda is on her way to Mars!", Charlene quickly added, reaching out her hand.

Selene took Charlene's hand and smiled a broad smile, "Forkbraid will be coming to Mars", her smile turning into a wide grin.

This was the happiest they'd all seen her in days.

Roseanne had another thought, and she tried to keep it to herself, *"What if Forkbraid is still hunting?"*

Selene heard this thought and her smile dropped slightly, "It's okay, Roseanne. That thought had crossed my mind as well. And that ill feeling from that ship does not bode well", Selene smiled once more, "Still, Forkbraid will be coming to Mars and that is a good thing."

The Prophet and Leroy were back on the bridge of the Delilah. They were still some distance from Mars and needed to make their plans.

"My Lord, I recommend that we bypass Phobos completely", Leroy advised.

"We need to refuel, Leroy. Matthew has already told us that much."

"That is correct, my Lord, we do need to refuel", Matthew the Pilot confirmed.

"Yes, my Lord. Granted, we do need to refuel, but Phobos will be too dangerous. If word has arrived from Earth, we'll be walking into a trap", Leroy countered.

"You said you had men on Phobos, men in the communications centre", the Prophet noted.

"Yes, my Lord. We have three men in the communications centre, each working different shifts, but what if they didn't intercept the messages from Earth? What if a message or two got through?"

"You trust your men, don't you, Leroy?", the Prophet queried.

"Yes, my Lord, but after the fiasco at Colonial Central Command. I'd prefer not to push our luck at this time", Leroy explained.

The Prophet paced back and forth across the bridge for several minutes before replying, "We need another course of action, Gentlemen."

Matthew knew Mars better than anyone else on the ship and made a suggestion, "My Lord", he paused for a moment, "We could always do a smugglers' run."

Leroy questioned Matthew, "A smugglers' run?"

"Yes, Sir. There's an old naval base on Deimos. It was abandoned long ago, but it still holds a huge stockpile of fuel. Smugglers use it to bypass Phobos Command all the time. If we alter course at the last minute, Phobos will just assume that we are smugglers."

"How is that any better, Matthew?", asked the Prophet.

"My Lord, since Mars turned blue, with its breathable atmosphere and all, the colonists are abandoning Mars orbit in their droves. They all want their own slice of Mars.", Matthew replied.

"Yes, but how does that help us?", the Prophet was curious.

"Well, my Lord, Phobos Command is severely short on manpower. It's become a transit station for colonists and cargo going down to the surface colonies. They don't have the personnel to check every ship that bypasses them. Many of them are just unofficial colonists, some of them are smugglers. They don't have the manpower to check us out. We can refuel and just slip on by."

Leroy listened intently to this, "Just like that? Refuel, and slip on by?"

"Just like that, Sir", Matthew reiterated.

"So we can refuel at Deimos, no questions asked and just take the Delilah down to New Tortuga?", the Prophet double-checked that he'd heard correctly.

"That is correct, my Lord", Matthew replied.

"How far ahead of the Ptolemy will we be Matthew", the Prophet enquired.

"My Lord, according to my calculations, taking into account time to refuel at Deimos and time to land at New Tortuga. We'll be five days ahead of the Ptolemy."

"So, that will give us five days to organise an attack on the Ptolemy?", the Prophet questioned.

Leroy gave the Prophet two scenarios, "My Lord, we can attack as the Ptolemy as she approaches Phobos or", he paused for a long moment, "we can attack the Ptolemy's [44]HLTs as they ferry passengers and cargo to the surface of Mars. We have two avenues open to us."

Matthew interrupted, "My Lord, we can't attack the Ptolemy as she approaches Phobos!"

"Why not, Matthew?", the Prophet asked.

"Mr Lord. The day after we arrive at New Tortuga, the Cruiser Spartan will be approaching Phobos. The Spartan will arrive four days ahead of the Ptolemy."

"So the Spartan will protect the Ptolemy from any attack that we mount", Leroy added, slamming his fist into the console before him.

"Yes, Sir. Of course, it will be much harder to protect the HLTs. Once they hit the Martian atmosphere, they'll be vulnerable", Matthew paused, "And very difficult to protect."

"That sounds like a plan, my Lord", Leroy added.

"So we'll hit the demons as they're landing. Excellent!", the Prophet decided.

Roseanne was watching the video screen in her cabin when an announcement interrupted the program. Yet another ship was going to be overtaking them en route to Mars. Usually this was a rare event, but this was the second such occurrence during this flight, something almost unheard of. The space lanes between Earth and Mars were frequently very quiet. The announcer pointed out that the ship passing by was a majestic Colonial Cruiser, the Spartan. Roseanne switched to the appropriate channel; she wanted to watch the Spartan fly past.

"Selene. You might want to come look at this", Roseanne called Selene's cabin just across the hall from hers.

Selene hung up the communicator and was quickly in Roseanne's cabin, "What is it, Roseanne?"

"Another ship overtaking us. A Colonial Cruiser, the Spartan", Roseanne replied.

"Now that is odd", Selene said as she walked over to a chair and sat down, "First that small space yacht speeding by several days ago and now this Colonial Cruiser?"

"It does seem to be too much of a coincidence, doesn't it", replied Roseanne.

---

44 Heavy Lift Transport equipped with antigravity lifters and photon thrusters with a range of 500,000 kilometres.

"Yes. That's what I'm thinking. There's a connection between those two ships, I'm sure of it."

"Like one chasing the other?", Roseanne replied adding, "Is that what you mean, Selene?"

Lady Selene did not answer.

Selene's eyes were rolled back, only their whites were visible. Roseanne was at first shocked when she saw this, but then felt a wave of calm sweep through her as she heard Selene's thoughts "*I'm fine*", inside her mind.

Selene's mind reached out towards the approaching Colonial Cruiser, only to find another mind reaching back towards her. "*Forkbraid!*", Selene exclaimed in her mind.

"*Yes, my love. I'm here on the Spartan*", came Forkbraid's reply.

"*I thought you were hunting extremists in L-Five? I saw the news feeds. Was it really that bad?*"

"*I was and yes, it was really that bad. The Colonial Troopers are now clearing out the remaining rats from L-Five as we speak.*"

"*You're going after the child, aren't you? Miranda passed by us on the Delilah several days ago.*"

"*Yes, but it's not so simple. A few of the extremist rats fled L-Five aboard the Delilah. Miranda was kidnapped by them as some sort of insurance.*"

"*That explains the ill feeling that came from that ship. Miranda was okay, frightened but okay.*"

"*Yes. They need her for something. I suspect that they are using her to keep track of me.*"

"*They may know about us! I felt Miranda scan us as they flew past.*"

"*It is possible. Take precautions as the Ptolemy approaches Mars. We'll arrive ahead of you and hopefully clear a safe passage.*"

Then the Spartan was passed the Ptolemy and Forkbraid's mind let go, "*Take care, my love.*"

"*You too, my love*", Selene sent in reply.

Then finally, one last thought came across from Forkbraid, "*PS. Don't eat the pork!*"

Lady Selene then called the others to Roseanne's cabin and told them about the encounter with Forkbraid aboard the Spartan, finishing with, "Forkbraid also said we shouldn't eat the pork".

"Did he say why?", asked Marcus.

"No, he didn't. He just said PS. Don't eat the pork", replied Lady Selene.

Marcus frowned, "Well it tastes like crap anyway, so I certainly wouldn't recommend it to anyone. It tastes nothing at all like the pork back home."

"I wish you wouldn't do that, FB", James Murphy stated.

"What's that, Jim", Forkbraid enquired.

"When your eyes roll back like that", Jim shivered, "It gives me the willies. What were you doing anyway, FB?"

"Well, Jim. I've just given Lady Selene a quick heads up on the situation", Forkbraid replied.

"Lady Selene?", Jim was taken by surprise, "Is Lady Selene on the Ptolemy?"

Forkbraid smiled, "Yes, Jim, along with a thousand psychic couples, all colonists."

"One thousand psychic couples!", Jim exclaimed.

"Yes, Jim, one thousand psychic couples for the new Elysium Colony", Forkbraid smiled, "It was Selene's little pet project. She's worked for five long years to set it all up. When Lady Selene arrives, it will be given the name, New Flinders Psychic Academy."

"Couples? What, just men and women? Are there any children?"

"Couples, Jim", Forkbraid explained, "Couples without children. The children will, of course, follow later, but they will be born on Mars."

"One thousand psychic couples", Jim restated, "And they're going to produce little psychic Martians?", he queried, a wry smile on his face.

"That's the idea, Jim. Psychic families on Mars producing little psychic children. That's what we're hoping for, at least. As on the Earth, so too on Mars."

"I thought most of you guys had problems using your gifts in space?", Jim queried.

"Generally, Jim, that is the case", Forkbraid confirmed, "but Mars is a planet, not a colony. And a planet that has undergone centuries of extensive terraforming. It's much more like Earth now."

"Ah. I see, so you think that your psychic couples will work just as well on Mars as on Earth?"

"Well, not at first, Jim. Some of them, the more confident and powerful, perhaps. The others, we believe, will adapt over time."

"How long will it take for them to adapt?", Jim enquired.

"How long's a piece of string, Jim?", Forkbraid replied, "We don't really know. Lady Selene has put together an exercise program to facilitate the adaptation, but how long will it take? That's a good question. I could take days for some, weeks, perhaps months or even years for others. Only time will tell, Jim."

"What about the children?", Jim asked.

"Ah. Now the children will be born on Mars, so they won't know any different. So the Flinders Psychic Academy's Grey Council is hoping, and so Lady Selene believes, that they will have no trouble at all. However, that is yet to be seen."

"What do you believe, Forkbraid?", Jim asked.

"Jim, I believe that Lady Selene is entirely correct", Forkbraid answered.

"Then why don't we have psychics in the off-world colonies?", Jim queried.

"I've told you that before, Jim. It has to do with biomass concentrations and connectivity. Mars has developed what we believe is the critical level of biomass concentration. With human habitation on the surface growing, the level of connectivity is increasing rapidly."

"But", Jim paused, "There are no psychics on Mars, FB."

"Even the mundanes connect, Jim. Lady Selene's psychic couples will increase their connectivity."

"Mundanes?", Jim Murphy was confused and felt somewhat insulted.

"I'm sorry, Jim", Forkbraid assured him, "Mundane is just a word we use for ordinary non-psychic folk. As opposed to supramundane or psychic folk. Please, no insult was intended."

Jim put up his hand, "It's okay, FB. I fully understand. I'm getting the picture. And besides, it's certainly better than being called a muggle."

"Hang on", Jim Murphy paused once again looking a little perplexed, "I still don't understand why we don't have psychics in the colonies."

"You do, Jim", Forkbraid explained, "but only the most powerful are active psychics. So far we've found two, Miranda and her little brother. The less powerful ones atrophy once they reach adulthood. The colonies are simply far too small for the right concentrations of biomass and connectivity to develop. An off-world colony would have to be at least ten times the size of Colonial Central Command, before it was suitable for the average Earth based psychic."

"But surely the colonists adapt?", Jim argued, "Just like your guys on Mars will?"

"Ah, Jim", Forkbraid smiled a broad smile, "That's exactly the point. Humans will adapt, it will just take a little longer, generations in fact. And it is happening as we speak. Remember, Jim, we've already found two. Now, Jim, my people will be actively looking for others."

13. Histrionics

Mars appeared much closer on the display screen now. The fleeing space yacht, Delilah was only a few days ahead of them and with the right magnification could just be made out on the display. The Swann family were constantly keeping tabs on the fleeing space yacht's position.

"Forkbraid, why don't you like being called a Wizard?", Catherine Swann enquired.

"It's not so much that I don't like it. It's just that", Forkbraid thought for a moment, "more correctly, the term should be, Witch."

"But don't they really amount to the same thing?"

"Yes, and no", Forkbraid explained, "The word Wizard originally meant wise-one and back in those days Wizards were both male and female. Then you have the word Witch, which originally meant shaper, and, of course, they could be both male and female as well."

"So, if Wizards could be both male and female, and Witches could be both male and female, how did we end up with the current situation?", Catherine enquired further.

"Well, in practice Catherine, most Wizards were in fact men and most Witches were indeed women. So over time the two terms became delineated along gender lines of, Wizards being male and Witches being female."

"So, when we ordinary folk use the terms Witch or Wizard and link them with specific genders, we're just using their modern definitions."

"Catherine, both terms can be equally applied to both men and women. Perhaps I'm just being pedantic, but I do get annoyed when either term is exclusively used for only one gender."

"And as everyone calls you a Wizard, you just like to correct them?", Catherine enquired with a smile on her face.

"You've noticed that I see", Forkbraid replied smiling back, "Am I a wise-one? I'd like to think so, so yes the term Wizard can be applied. Am I a shaper? Definitely, so the term Witch is given. I do prefer to be called a Witch rather than a Wizard though. That's just my preference", he paused for a moment, "And it just so happens to be the preference of all those religious students, who pass through the halls of Flinders Psychic Academy back on Flinders Island on Earth."

"Are all the Psychic Academies like that?", Catherine's husband Peter enquired.

"No, not at all. Some Psychic Academies prefer the term Wizard for their religious students. Most of the psychic Academies in the US are like that. There are even a few that use the terms Witch and Wizard in their gender-specific roles as well."

"Which Academies would they be?", Catherine enquired further.

"Mostly the British and a few of the European Psychic Academies", replied Forkbraid adding "Over in Iceland, they use the terms Vitka and Vitki."

Peter cocked an eyebrow. "So", Peter paused to gather his thoughts, "If the Psychic Academies themselves use different terms and can't agree, how can you expect anyone else to?"

Forkbraid frowned, "I see your point, Peter, and you are right. I'd never thought about it that way before. I've probably been hunting extremists far too long to have noticed. You know, before the attack on Flinders Psychic Academy, it was more than five decades since the last successful attack anywhere on Earth. Even so, we've been busy. You never hear about all the failed attempts. There's usually about seven or eight a year around the planet. I guess it's made me, I don't know, a little cynical and judgemental. Maybe I've been a bit too sensitive about this. From now on instead of correcting people, I'll be more diplomatic and tell them I prefer the title Witch instead of Wizard", he finished with a smile.

"That's probably a good thing", Peter suggested, quickly adding "Anyway, I always thought a male Witch was a Warlock."

"Ah, Peter, that is indeed a word that all the Psychic Academies can agree on."

"How so?", Peter enquired.

"We don't use the word Warlock at all. It's an old Anglo-Saxon insult, a derogatory term that quite literally means traitor. Call any male Witch or Wizard a Warlock and they will be most displeased."

"Well then, we will try to avoid that one, won't we?", Peter smiled.

"Why do they hate psychics so much, Forkbraid?", Catherine queried.

"It's a long story, Catherine. It has to do with history, bigotry, misconceptions, and religion", Forkbraid replied.

"Well, we have plenty of time", Catherine replied, "You can tell it."

Forkbraid sighed, "It's not a story that tells well. It's complex and ugly."

"Why is it ugly?", Chiron, who was sitting on his Mother's lap, asked.

Forkbraid smiled, "Man's inhumanity to his fellow man, Chiron. That's always been ugly."

Forkbraid continued, "Religion has painted a false and terrible picture of psychics over the millennia. Not knowing or understanding what psychic abilities are, they condemned many to death simply for being different. It was cruel and unjust, it was the way that the world was."

"The way that the world was?", the little boy, Chiron, asked.

"Yes, Chiron, the way that the world was. Times changed and people got smarter, the age of reason came, and all the myths came tumbling down."

"This is a boring story", Chiron stated, then jumped off his Mother's lap and went off to play.

Forkbraid smiled, "Not the right kind of story for a four-year-old I suspect."

"That's okay, I'm still listening", Catherine replied.

"Many religious texts falsely condemn Witches to death and all psychics get tarred with that same brush. This is especially true for the three peoples of the book, Judaism, Christianity, and Islam. The animosity between the three groups has existed for many, many centuries."

"But why, Forkbraid? Surely there must be a reason?", Peter who had now joined in asked.

"None that truly makes sense I'm afraid", replied Forkbraid, "You need to look into a very tangled web of history, full of bloodshed, pogroms, and warfare. The hatred, animosity, and an irrational need for revenge goes back many centuries. The crusades were a large part of it."

"But they were such a long time ago?", Peter questioned.

"Yes, Peter, they were", Forkbraid replied, "and yet, to this day extremists on both sides still see a need for revenge! But there was much more to history than just the crusades. The Muslim and Christian civilisations were at each other's throats for much of their history. A good thousand years of it at least. Even the middle eastern conflicts from the mid-twentieth, through to the early twenty-first centuries, arguably, could be seen as a more recent extension of a much earlier conflict."

Peter nodded his head in agreement, "Yes, you could say that I suppose, but how does that tie in with modern day psychics?"

"The remote viewing teams, Peter", Forkbraid replied, "At first they were set up by governments to help track down the terrorists. They worked well. Plots were uncovered, terrorist cells located and teams of commandos were sent in to clear out the terrorist networks and cells."

"Then of course psychics came together in social groups. Different groups, some were religious, you know: Asatru, Wiccan, Pagan, whatever, others were secular, simply exploring their abilities. In the early days this was largely at universities, where their abilities could be studied and programmes set up to practice and enhance their abilities. Other groups set up covens and magical schools of Wizardry and the Art Magic. A myriad of diverse groups spread across the globe. Eventually they all came together under one umbrella, so to speak."

"The Psychic Academies", Peter stated the obvious.

"The original Psychic Academies weren't anything like the ones around today", Forkbraid lamented, "They were open institutions of study and learning scattered all over the place in cities, and anyone could just walk in off the street."

"So what happened?", Catherine asked.

"Fundamentalists happened. The remote viewing teams were doing too well.

The Islamic extremists were in decline. Governments around the world were cooperating to eliminate the problem of terrorism. The remote viewing teams located the extremists, then the relevant government would take over and eliminate them. The Arab nations were extremely harsh in their treatment of terrorists. Find a cell of terrorists in a village and the troops would move in and wipe out the entire village. The Islamic extremists blamed the remote viewing teams for all their troubles, so the psychics got the blame every time."

"Homegrown Islamic terrorists in the western nations turned their attention to their own countries and launched attacks. They started by attacking the Psychic Academies where the remote viewing teams had been set up. Then Christian fundamentalists blamed the psychics for bringing terrorism into their home countries, and they began to turn extremist as well. There were tit-for-tat bombings of churches, mosques and synagogues, even bombs going off in public places. Extremist on extremist violence was springing up everywhere and innocent people were being caught in the cross fire. Terrorism, which had been in decline everywhere, suddenly sprung up with a vengeance in the western nations. With the remote viewing teams out of action, the violence continued unabated for several years."

"So how did it all stop?", asked Peter.

"It didn't stop, Peter, it's always there waiting to rear its ugly head. It's simply being controlled and minimised. The price of freedom is eternal vigilance", Forkbraid replied.

"Eventually we psychics regrouped. The Psychic Academies were rebuilt, and the remote viewing teams were set up once more. The difference, this time, is that the Psychic Academies are fortresses, built in awkward, out of the way places. They are not so easy to get to, and they're very well defended. We currently have thirteen Psychic Academies around the Earth. In places like the Island of Molokai, Iceland, Baffin Island, the Falkland Islands, the Outer Hebrides, the Orkney Islands, the Kerguelen Islands, Flinders Island in Australia, Stewart Island in New Zealand. Places that aren't so easy to get to. The Psychic Academy I'm based at on Flinders Island in Australia, is only a short distance from a major capital city like Melbourne, but you have to get there by air or sea. It's not so easy, and we'll see them coming."

"Most importantly, the remote viewing teams now scan the whole planet. Not like back in the old days, when they scanned only those countries that had a known problem or where terrorists were known to be hiding. We check every country now. We check everywhere that we can."

"Isn't that a bit extreme, I mean checking every country?"

"Well you might think so, Catherine, but", Forkbraid raised his finger as if to stress the point, "if we don't check every nook and cranny, an extremist could slip through the gap and then people die."

"Besides, there are other benefits as well", Forkbraid continued, "We also find serial killers, people planning murders, robberies, and other criminal offences. We actually help to catch criminals and prevent crimes from taking place. We also find missing persons and pinpoint people that need rescuing. There are a lot of things that remote viewing teams do, not just catching terrorists."

"So the extremists actually hate psychics for doing good works!", Catherine exclaimed.

"It does seem that way doesn't it", Forkbraid replied, "They hate us for saving lives."

"It actually does seem a little absurd, Forkbraid", Peter noted.

"That it is, Peter", Forkbraid replied, "but you have to remember, these are fundamentalists and extremists. Their rule is simple *'Thou shalt not suffer a Witch to Live'*. More importantly, when we stop them, what are we actually doing?"

Neither Peter nor Catherine answered.

"We are preventing them from carrying out their mission", Forkbraid continued.

"And what is their mission?", Catherine enquired.

"Their mission is to spread their particular brand of fundamentalism, to convert everyone to their particular belief system. It does not matter whether the extremist is Muslim or Christian or whatever. They all believe that they are right, God is on their side and that the whole Earth is destined to fall under their religion and their beliefs. The ones we're chasing now just happen to be Christian fundamentalists."

"But that is just so absurd", Peter pointed out, "Freedom of belief and freedom of thought are fundamental human rights."

"That's the problem, Peter. Under fundamentalist and extremist beliefs, we only have the right to believe what they tell us. Their very strict interpretations of their particular religious texts. They would control our very thoughts if they could."

"But that's just another form of fascism!", Catherine stated loudly.

"And fundamentalist religious extremism is indeed religious fascism", Forkbraid summed up.

Then Catherine asked a peculiar question, "Why is it, I've never seen any Muslims at L-Five?"

Forkbraid was taken aback by this question. It was fundamentally true, Muslims did not live off-world. There was a simple reason for it, again religious, but very few people actually understood it. Catherine continued when Forkbraid failed to answer, "I mean, we have lots of religious groups up here. Christian groups are quite prolific, but we also have Jewish groups, Hindus, Zoroastrians, and many other religious groups. So why no Muslims?"

After a long moment, Forkbraid finally answered, "It has to do with definitions, Catherine."

"Definitions?", Catherine enquired.

"Yes. The definition of Heaven and Earth to be precise", Forkbraid replied.

"I don't follow you, Forkbraid. How can the definition of Heaven and Earth dictate whether, or not there are Muslims in space?"

"Well, Catherine, it's not so much the definition itself, but which version of it is accepted."

"How so Forkbraid?", asked Peter.

"The old definition of Heaven and Earth was simple. The Earth was the Earth and Heaven was everything above the Earth. Muslims accept and follow only that definition."

"So why don't they live off-world?", asked Catherine.

"That's because under their beliefs, the Earth belongs to Man and the Heavens belong to God."

"So they won't go off-world?", Peter asked incredulously.

"Oh, they go off-world, but never for long. They won't live off-world. That's the constraint."

"I don't get it. Don't Christians have the same religious belief?", asked Catherine.

"Yes, they do, but their definition of Heaven and Earth is slightly different", Forkbraid replied adding "The new Heaven and the new Earth, for the old Heaven and old Earth have passed away."

"I don't follow you, Forkbraid", Peter stated.

"My ancestor Folcrom Tafazah wrote the new definition back in the early twenty-first century. He wrote, '*The Earth spelled with a capital E, is the Earth our home planet. The earth spelled with a small e, represents all of manifest reality. The Earth is just one small world in the vastness of the physical cosmos, or earth. Above the Earth, again spelled with a capital E, our home world, is just more earth, small e, that and vacuum. The Heavens are not above the Earth as such. The Heavens are beyond the earth, in that they are beyond physical manifestation. The Heavens are a metaphysical realm beyond the manifest earth realm. The Heavens encompass all manifest physical reality.*' That was the new Heaven and the new Earth that my ancestor penned onto paper."

"Whoa, that's deep", Peter exclaimed.

"Yes, and it's basically just a semantic change in a simple definition", Forkbraid replied.

"But why was that so important?", Catherine asked.

"It fulfilled the Biblical prophecy of the new Heaven and the new Earth. The passing away of the old Heaven and the old Earth, was just the passing away of our primitive notions and the developing of new understandings. Yet at the same time it kept to the old saying, that the Earth belongs to man and the Heavens belong to God. It's just, under the new definition, the Heavens are no longer equated with space, instead they're a spiritual realm beyond the physical realm."

"And the Muslims don't accept this new definition?", Peter enquired.

"And that is why they only live on Earth", Forkbraid answered.

"Obviously everyone else accepts the new definition", Catherine tossed out.

"Exactly. Whether they realise it or not. That's why we have so many colonies up here now."

"So on Earth, you only have to worry about Muslim extremists?", Peter enquired.

"I wish that was true, Peter. It might make the task a little-bit easier. Unfortunately, back on Earth, we have a whole swag of different extremist religious groups. There's really no telling which one will try to pull off something next. We have to watch them all very, very closely."

"Well, it's one less extremist group up here anyway", Peter exclaimed.

"True enough, Peter, but the ones you've got up here are making up for it", Forkbraid finished.

"How does Mars fit into this? I mean now it's been terraformed and all", Peter asked.

"In what way Peter?", Forkbraid queried.

"Well, now that Mars is habitable, won't the Muslims want to colonise it?", Peter clarified.

"Ah, well, Peter, time will tell. Last time my people checked, there was some disagreement."

"Disagreement?", Catherine queried.

"Yes, disagreement on whether to accept the new definition of heaven and earth."

"I thought you said they don't accept the new definition?", Catherine quickly questioned.

"They don't. That's the current situation, but there are some more moderate Islamic leaders who want to accept the new definition so that they can send colonists to Mars. They don't want to be left behind", Forkbraid explained.

"So the situation could change?", Catherine noted.

"Yes, it could, Catherine, but not for a long while yet."

"Why do you say that, Forkbraid?", Peter asked.

"Peter, there aren't anywhere near enough moderates who want to change. Change requires momentum, and that momentum takes time to develop", Forkbraid replied.

Lady Selene stepped quietly into Roseanne's cabin. Charlene was seated watching over Roseanne as she practised. Roseanne was sitting cross-legged, levitating about two feet above the floor of the cabin. In front of her on a bench was a metal disk. Slowly the disk lifted off the bench. It climbed about two feet, then slowly descended once more. As soon as Roseanne felt Selene's presence in the cabin, the disk dropped like a lead balloon. It fell the last few inches landing with an audible thud. Roseanne simultaneously dropped to the floor.

"You need to learn to concentrate on what you're doing, Roseanne, irrespective of the surrounding distractions", Lady Selene lectured.

"Roseanne hasn't done too badly, Selene, considering her lack of formal training."

"Yes, you're right, Charlene. When we get to Mars, we'll organise proper training sessions. For now, we'll just have to make do."

Roseanne stood up, rubbing her bruised right buttock, "I think I'll be organising thicker cushions. That's my first priority."

Lady Selene and Charlene both chuckled.

"Roseanne, pick up that disk", Selene instructed.

Roseanne walked over to the bench. The circular metal disk was about six inches across and a centimetre thick. It weighed about a hundred grams. Roseanne picked it up.

"Roseanne, what symbol is that on that disk?", Selene asked.

Roseanne looked at the symbol inscribed on the top of the disk, "It's a pentagram."

"It has a circle around it. More correctly, it's called a pentacle", Selene corrected.

Roseanne nodded and repeated the word, "Pentacle."

"It doesn't really matter, Roseanne. We are actually interested in the pentagram within the circle", Selene explained.

Roseanne nodded once more.

"Do you know what a pentagram is, Roseanne?", Selene asked.

"It's just a five pointed star", Roseanne answered.

Selene smiled, "It's far more than that, Roseanne. For those who know how to read it, a pentagram is a complete book of knowledge."

Selene sat down in a chair next to Charlene. Roseanne stared at the pentagram, she couldn't read it. It seemed to be impossible. How could it possibly be a complete book of knowledge?

"Look closely at the pentagram, Roseanne. You notice within the five points there's a pentagon?"

"Yes, I see it", Roseanne replied.

"There's a special ratio", Selene stated, continuing, "When you measure the length of one side of that pentagon in the middle, and then compare that length to the length of the side of one of the points, you get a very special number. That number is called the golden ratio. It's the ratio of one to one point six one eight."

"I'm not sure that I understand.", Roseanne admitted. Charlene smiled.

"The golden ratio is reflected right throughout the natural world. Even in the human face. The ratio of the width of the base of the nose, to the width of the mouth for instance. Or the width of the mouth to the width of the chin. Or the spacing of the eyes to the width of the head."

Roseanne was listening intently, but still did not follow.

"The more closely the ratio of our facial features matches the golden ratio, the more pleasant or beautiful our facial features are considered to be. The greater the difference, the less pleasant and less beautiful. If you look very carefully at the most beautiful of people, you can see a pentagram inscribed in their facial features. It's such a strange thing, but the human concept of beauty has been tied to the golden ratio by evolution."

"Why is that?", Roseanne asked.

"I don't really know, Roseanne", Selene replied, "but there you have it nonetheless. That's just one of the many secrets hidden within the pentagram."

"In the old days, before the age of reason. When the early Christians were persecuting the pagans of old Europe. Women whose facial features closely matched the golden ratio, found themselves with both a blessing and a curse. They were more desirable in the eyes of the men-folk, which was wonderful if they caught the eye of a rich young noble and wanted to marry well. However, if they caught the eye of a Christian priest, who could see the image of a pentagram within their facial features, well that was another matter entirely."

"Why? What would happen to them?", enquired Roseanne.

"They would be declared a Witch, tortured and then burned at the stake", Selene replied.

Roseanne had a shocked look on her face.

"It didn't matter that the young woman was just an ordinary girl. It didn't matter whether, or not she had any psychic potential at all. Once declared a Witch, she would be tortured and burned alive. That was just the way of things before the age of reason."

"That's terrible! Why would they do such a thing?", Rosanne asked.

"Superstitious and I should say, entirely fallacious religious beliefs. In those days, there was no real science to speak of. They didn't understand the nature of psychic potentials. They feared what they didn't understand. People were accused of the most ridiculous crimes. Superstition, ignorance, fear and I should also say abject stupidity, caused the deaths of untold thousands, quite literally millions of people. Those were the burning times."

"And these are the kind of people Forkbraid is hunting?", Roseanne enquired.

"Precisely Roseanne", Selene replied, "People who have thrown away reason, for insanity."

"Anyway, back to the pentagram. Each point on the pentagram represents an element. Starting at the right-hand point and working your way clockwise around the pentagram, you have Water, Fire, Earth, Air and finally the top point, Spirit, which is the amalgam of all the elements combined."

Roseanne nodded in understanding.

"When you hold a pentagram inverted, with the top point facing down", Selene turned the disk around in Roseanne's hands, "It's sometimes called Horns Raised. Superstitious folk would call this an evil sign, a devil's sign. It has nothing to do with either good or evil, nor any devil for that matter. It is just a statement of humanity's normal state of affairs, Spirit buried beneath and within the elements. The normal, mundane Human condition."

Selene turned the disk around once more, "With the point raised, this is simply a statement of how we Humans should aspire to be. Spirit having risen above the elements and in control of the elements. We Humans, whether mundane or supramundane, should always aspire to live in Spirit."

Again Roseanne nodded in understanding.

"The lines of the pentagram running from one element to the next, represent alchemical and transformational processes. You can also relate the points on the pentagram to the quarters on the Celtic cross. You have to take into account which hemisphere you're standing on, of course, but they basically go element for element, with spirit in the centre. Each of these points also represents elemental guardians, classes of elemental creatures, colours, sounds, metals and so much more. Now turn over the disk. What do you see now, Roseanne?"

"It's a six pointed star", Roseanne replied.

"It's the six rayed star. It's comprised of two equilateral triangles, one overlaying the other and rotated with respect to the other", Selene explained, "And yes, it is yet another complete book of knowledge, which also has its own ancient and arcane meaning."

"Just how many of these books are there?", Roseanne enquired.

"Roseanne, my dear, there are many, many of them, and you must learn to read them all."

Roseanne was starting to look a little worried now, she had no idea how to read these books.

"Don't worry about it, Roseanne", Selene reassured her, "Charlene is going to teach you how to read them. It just takes time."

Roseanne turned to Charlene who was smiling at her, "It's okay. It's not as hard as it sounds. Once you have the knack of it, you'll be able to read the knowledge in every new symbol you see."

Selene smiled at Roseanne, "And once you've mastered the reading of symbols, I can begin your studies on Ancient Runes. Those are so much more fun."

Roseanne smiled a weak smile and mouthed one simple word, "Runes?"

"Yes, child, the Ancient Runes of the Elder Futhark to be precise", Selene replied.

It seemed to Roseanne that school had just begun.

Miranda Swann sat in her cabin aboard the space yacht Delilah. There wasn't much to her cabin. It was a smallish room, only twelve feet by five feet. The cabin door opened into the ship's main passageway, except, of course, the door was always securely locked.

Secured against the wall was a bunk. It was comfortable enough, but nowhere near as comfortable as her bed back home in the Hyper Dynamics Corporate colony. On Miranda's bunk, was the luxury of a mattress and a special sleeping bag with a built-in pillow. Special webbing on the bunk allowed the mattress and sleeping bag to be held in place against zero gravity. When sleeping, this webbing also held the occupant firmly in place.

Secured against the wall nearest the cabin door was a wardrobe, just big enough to put in a few changes of clothes, had her captives bothered to bring any with them. Instead, it contained a few simple articles of clothing, adult clothing that had been altered to fit Miranda by Mrs Harmon. None of it fit very well; Mrs Harmon was a terrible seamstress.

Secured against the wall at the end of the bunk, was a small single seat desk. It wasn't much, but it provided Miranda somewhere else to sit apart from on her bed. Secured within its draws were four books. One on spaceship navigation and celestial mechanics. Another on the physics and mechanics of photon thrust drives. The novel War and Peace by Leo Tolstoy. Finally, there was a copy of the Bible, the version used by the Prophet's sect. The last had been placed in the room by Mrs Harmon. None of these books were of interest to Miranda, who found herself totally bored.

At the rear of Miranda's cabin was a small bathroom. It wasn't much of a bathroom. All it contained was a zero vacuum toilet, a small wash basin with a spray unit, a mirror, and a small bathroom cabinet. There was a drain inbuilt into the bathroom's deck plating floor. There was barely enough room for an adult to move around, fortunately Miranda was much smaller than an adult.

This was Miranda's existence. Miranda could sit on her bunk and be bored, she could sit at the desk and be bored or if she felt like it, Miranda could sit on the toilet and be bored there as well.

On occasions Miranda would pick up one of the books in the desk drawer and read some of it. None of the books was written with a child in mind, so reading them was most difficult. Still Miranda persisted, reading as much as her young mind could understand.

Twice a day Mrs Harmon would bring Miranda food. Breakfast would arrive about nine o'clock. There would be no lunch, which the members of the Prophet's sect used as a time to fast, and then at around six pm, Miranda's dinner would arrive. Even Miranda's meals were boring. Generally taken straight out of the ships rations, most of Miranda's meals were either from a tube or a tin, or [45]MRE packs. Fortunately, the manufacturers had at least given the rations decent flavours.

Miranda spent most of her time sitting on her bunk letting her mind wonder. At first Miranda allowed her mind to wonder about the ship. The people aboard the Delilah were terrible people, cruel and ill minded, not to her liking at all. It didn't take long for Miranda to decide not to mentally wander around the Delilah.

Occasionally Miranda would search with her mind back along the ship's path for Forkbraid and her parents. Miranda was just able to make out her parents' minds, following far behind in the Spartan. First Miranda would sense the Spartan's personnel, then carefully search for her parents. They of course were unable to recognise her at all. Forkbraid on the other hand was always able to sense Miranda's fleeting presence. He would quietly reassure Miranda that they would find her and rescue her, and that she must remain brave and calm.

On occasion, Miranda allowed her mind to drift back towards the Earth and Cis-Lunar L-Five. It was becoming harder and harder to do, the farther the Delilah got from Earth. On one particular occasion, it had taken Miranda more than an hour to locate the Earth. Then from the Earth, her young mind reached out to find Cis-Lunar L-Five. There Miranda found familiar territory, the thousands of floating colonies of Cis-Lunar L-Five.

On this particular occasion, something was not quite right. Miranda had a sense of trouble and her mind sought it out. Her mind approached a smallish colony of the Bernal Sphere design. One of the older colonies in the outer reaches of Cis-Lunar L-Five, in a broad halo orbit.

Miranda's mind sensed a dread that she had never felt before. As if thousands of people were suddenly horrified by a singular shared event. In unison, thousands of minds screamed out in sheer terror and panic.

Miranda's mind reeled back as she sensed a sudden flash of light, of harsh energy and then shortly thereafter pure silence. It was as if thousands of minds had suddenly vanished from existence. Miranda's eyes opened wide with shock and terror, her small body was covered in sweat.

It would be many, many days before Miranda would let her mind wander again and never again did Miranda allow her mind to drift back towards the Earth and Cis-Lunar L-Five.

---

45 Meals Ready to Eat

14. Phobos and Deimos

Captain Carmichael and Special Agent Murphy entered the guest's compartment aboard the Spartan, "We have some good news and some bad news, FB", Jim stated without a smile, "Which would you like to hear first?"

"Always best to start with the bad and finish with the good news, Jim."

"We've had word from L-Five. Illegal weapons have turned up on several of the other colonies. The owners of those weapons have all been apprehended. Interrogations have led to the discovery of twenty-seven other extremist cells", Jim informed Forkbraid.

"I'd call that good news, Jim", Forkbraid stated, before asking, "So what's the bad news?"

"One of the terrorist cells had another of those flash vaporisers. It was set off in one of the smaller colonies, a Bernal Sphere called Skye, in a crowded public space."

"Oh, my God!", Forkbraid was shocked, "those smaller colonies are tightly packed aren't they?"

"Yes, Forkbraid", Jim replied, "They do tend to be more densely populated. Over three-thousand people are still missing, all presumed dead."

"Gods, Jim that is bad news", Forkbraid replied.

"Yeah. Centrals trying to keep a lid on it, so it hasn't hit the news feeds just yet. When it does, there's going to be sheer panic", James Murphy was seriously worried.

"I can image", Forkbraid reached for his goatee with his right hand and gave it a thoughtful tug, "So what's the good news then?"

"Well", James Murphy began, "When the news leaks out, every colony in the system will be taking this seriously. Colonial Troops will be on alert everywhere."

"That's a good thing at least, but I've heard that a lot of the colonies up here are a law unto themselves", Forkbraid noted.

"Too many of them I'm afraid. They're all like little nations and fiefdoms, each with their own sovereign bloody rights", Jim frowned, the lack of co-operation from a few of the colonies was truly frustrating, even for him, and he was used to it.

"Then, of course, our interrogations have shed light on their plans as well", Jim continued.

"Good, so what do we know, Jim?", Forkbraid enquired.

"They were planning to ship those modified Androids to Earth. Many of them were destined for Psychic Academies. Apparently, they thought that you wouldn't be able to trace the source of the bombs, at least not so quickly. They thought they had much more time."

"Well, then, they didn't know us very well, did they?", Forkbraid replied, then he quickly added, "When you have a bomb blow up in your face, you get to see it all happen up close and personal."

"You're lucky to be alive, FB", Captain Carmichael stated.

"Yeah. Fortunately, we sensed the explosion a split second before it happened and brought up our defences just in time. We actually saw the source of the explosion, it was like in slow motion."

"They would never have considered that", Captain Carmichael noted.

"No, they didn't, Captain, no they didn't. They had no idea.", Forkbraid confirmed.

"They didn't consider something else as well, FB", Jim commented.

"What was that, Jim?", Forkbraid asked.

"They didn't think that you'd come after them. You caught them completely by surprise, FB."

"That's why I moved so quickly, to catch them off guard", Forkbraid noted.

"They apparently had plans for L-Five as well. They were going to slip flash vaporisers into several key colonies and hold Colonial Central Command to ransom. Not for money, mind you, but for control and leverage. Your turning up spoiled all of that", Jim informed him.

"What were they hoping to achieve?", Captain Carmichael asked.

"Control, Captain, as I just noted. If they controlled Colonial Central Command, they could prevent anyone from coming up to stop them. If they'd thought to put their flash vaporisers in place first, they could have achieved just that. We were lucky this time, things could have turned out much, much worse", Jim Murphy explained.

"It wasn't luck, Jim, it was their mindset", noted Forkbraid.

"Their mindset?", Captain Carmichael queried.

"They were so focused on attacking us, they neglected to think tactically", Forkbraid replied.

"I hope you've got some more good news than that, Jim", Forkbraid enquired, "What you've mentioned thus far hardly balances the ledger."

"Well, the rest of the good news, does little better. Trust me, FB", Jim admitted.

"Let us have it, Jim, it can't be any worse than the bad news", Forkbraid suggested.

"We've also sent word to Phobos Command, to intercept the Delilah", Jim informed him.

"Good", Forkbraid replied, "Maybe we can catch them before they land."

"No such luck I'm afraid", Captain Carmichael stated, "According to our latest projections, they changed course."

"Changed course! They haven't got the fuel to go anywhere else", Forkbraid replied, "You said so yourself, Captain."

"They're still going to Mars, Forkbraid, they're just using a slightly different path, is all."

"A different path?", Forkbraid enquired with a confused look on his face, "How can they use a different path, Captain?"

"All shipping in Martian orbit generally goes through Phobos Command. Just like at L-Five, all shipping goes through Colonial Central Command, or for Earth, everything goes through the gateways in high Earth orbit", Captain Carmichael explained, before noting, "The Delilah is simply bypassing Phobos completely."

"They can do that?", Forkbraid enquired, "Won't Phobos send a ship after them?"

"That's why we sent them the message, FB", Jim added.

"Ordinarily, we'd ask Phobos to apprehend them when they dock", Captain Carmichael continued, "but as they're bypassing Phobos completely, we've requested an intercept."

"FB, their pilot knows what he's doing", Jim slipped in.

"Yes", Captain Carmichael agreed, "They're making a run for Deimos."

"You know what that means?", Jim asked Forkbraid, not expecting an answer.

Captain Carmichael continued, "There's an old naval supply base and depot on Deimos. It hasn't been used officially for decades. Smugglers and criminals have been using it as a refuelling station. It helps them bypass Phobos and a lot of customs and legal red tape."

"I don't get it. Why do they need to refuel? They're just going to Mars aren't they?"

"That they are, Forkbraid. They're still going to Mars, but they need to refuel, so that they can land. With a full load of fuel, they can pretty much land anywhere on the planet."

"Well, let's see how well Phobos Command does its job", Forkbraid stated.

James Murphy and Captain Carmichael looked at each other, "You can tell him, Jim."

"Tell me what, Jim?", Forkbraid enquired.

"Phobos Command, FB. We've sent them word. We've stressed to them how important intercepting the Delilah is, but", Jim began explaining.

"But what, Jim?", Forkbraid demanded, he did not like where this was going.

"It is possible that they might just ignore us", Jim quickly explained.

"Ignore us, Jim? Why the hell would they ignore us?", Forkbraid questioned.

"Mars, FB! They have a whole blue planet beneath them now", Jim noted.

"I don't get it. Sure we terraformed Mars. It's blue! So what?", Forkbraid asked.

"Phobos Command is the only official transit point to the Mars colonies", Jim explained, "Everyone is wanting to go down to the surface, to colonise and settle the planet. Everyone, FB. Even their own staff are abandoning their contracts and colonising the planet."

"So they don't have enough staff?", Forkbraid was beginning to get the picture.

"They don't have enough staff, FB. They've been running on a skeleton crew ever since the planet was opened up for colonisation, they're severely undermanned", Jim confirmed.

"So there's every chance that Phobos Command is just going to ignore us?", Forkbraid asked.

"Welcome to the colonies, Forkbraid", Captain Carmichael said as he slapped him on the back, "This is the sort of crap we in the military have to put up with all the time up here."

Lieutenant Roberts watched the incoming scanners, "What are those extra blips on my scanners Private Smith?"

"We have three ships coming in, Sir", Private Smith replied.

"Three ships? We're only scheduled to receive one. The IPL Ptolemy."

"Yes Sir. Correct, Sir. The IPL Ptolemy is the only ship on the schedule, Sir."

"Then what are those other two?", Lieutenant Roberts gestured to the smaller blips on the screen.

"The Heavy Cruiser is the Spartan, Sir. The other ship is a space yacht of some kind, I'm still trying to access its designation, Sir."

"You've pinged that ship, haven't you?", Lieutenant Roberts asked.

"Yes, Sir, but I'm getting no response. They appear to have disabled their pulse identification beacon, Sir."

"What's their trajectory?", Lieutenant Roberts enquired.

"They're outside the pipe, Sir", Private Smith replied.

"Outside the pipe? Could you be a little more specific, Smith?"

"Mars inbound, with a Deimos intercept trajectory, Sir. They're doing a smugglers' run, Sir."

"A smugglers' run, are they? Well, that explains their disabled pulse identification beacon. What else is new? What about that Cruiser? Have they made contact?", Lieutenant Roberts enquired.

"No, Sir", Private Smith lied, he was a sect member, "I can hail them, Sir, if you wish?"

"Do that, Smith. Find out what those Mother-fuckers are doing in my space lanes."

Lieutenant Roberts walked off to check on another console, displaying local flight schedules.

Lists of flights in chronological order were displayed. A load of ferries were scheduled for departures to the colonies in Martian Ultra High Orbit, with an even larger number scheduled for arrival. Over a dozen HLTs were scheduled for departures and arrivals, transferring cargo to the new Elysium colony on the surface. A dozen other cargo flights to and from the other surface colonies were scheduled as well. The local flight schedules were a tightly controlled, hot mess.

"I'm sure glad that space yacht's doing a smugglers' run, Smith", Lieutenant Roberts shouted, "I won't need to shuffle them into this scheduling nightmare. It's a right shit-hole at the moment."

"Sir, the Ptolemy does have its own HLTs", Private Smith shouted back.

"Still, they'll want fuel for their landings and the Ptolemy itself will want fuel for her return trip. So we have to schedule dock time for them all. The last thing we need is an unscheduled bloody Heavy Cruiser."

Private Smith contacted the space yacht, Delilah, while his Lieutenant was occupied with his scheduling problems, "Previous message received. STOP. You're officially classed as smugglers. STOP. Spartan communique intercepted. STOP. Need to spin a line about the Spartan's arrival. STOP", Private Smith typed into the console.

Another message was soon on its way back, "Tell them that the Spartan is arriving for extra security for the Ptolemy. VIPs onboard the Ptolemy. Tell them, VIPs are expecting royal treatment. STOP. Continue interception of all messages from the Spartan. STOP."

Private Smith smiled as he thought to himself, "*VIPs expecting royal treatment. Lieutenant Roberts is going to have a flaming fit.*"

Lieutenant Roberts was back at Private Smith's console, "Well, Smith! What do they have to say for themselves?", he bellowed.

"Extra security for the Ptolemy, Sir", Private Smith lied.

"Extra security? What do they need extra security for?", Lieutenant Roberts demanded.

"VIPs, Sir. Apparently the Ptolemy's packed full of them, Sir", Private Smith lied once again.

"VIPs? We weren't told about any bloody VIPs!", Lieutenant Roberts shouted.

"Sir, we've been asked to provide them all with Royal Treatment", Private Smith lied again.

"Royal Treatment, Royal bloody Treatment! I'll give them bloody Royal Treatment*"*, Lieutenant Roberts stormed off, his face bright red and fuming, with foam sputtering at the sides of his mouth "This is a bloody space dock, not the fucking [46]Venusian Cloud Resorts!"

Private Smith smiled to himself as he watched Lieutenant Roberts storm out of the control centre, he noticed the other controllers, their heads hanging lower

---

46 Venusian Cloud Resorts. Cities floating in the upper atmosphere of Venus where conditions are more Earth-like.

than usual. Morale was about to slump even further amongst Phobos's stressed and overworked crew. All the pay in the world couldn't make up for all the crap these workers had to put up with.

Phobos's entire docking system was going to be in absolute turmoil for days. Handling a scheduled Interplanetary Liner along with Phobos's usual stressed domestic port duties was bad enough. Having a Heavy Cruiser full of Colonial Troops dropping in unannounced was even worse. Add the imminent arrival of a load of smart ass VIPs expecting royal treatment and no-body would be giving a rat's backside about smugglers. That was for sure.

The Delilah approached the Martian moon Deimos right on time. Matthew, the pilot, brought the space yacht in real close and circled the moon once before approaching the old supply depot. The depot wasn't much to look at on the surface, numerous circular landing pads of varying sizes spread across a levelled section of the moon's surface. Most of the infrastructure was buried deep inside the moon itself.

Originally built during the Outer Satellite Insurrection for refuelling warships on their way outbound to the six Jovian Realms. It was also used as a repair dock for those returning vessels in need of maintenance, repairs, rearming and refuelling. Its space-docks were capable of handling quite large ships. Abandoned for over eighty years now, it had been closed down purely for economic reasons. It was simply far cheaper for the fleet to be maintained and outfitted at L-Five.

Matthew kept a close eye on the little Moon's surface. He flew extremely low to avoid being scanned by Pirate vessels that also frequented the region around Deimos. Once he was sure that they were safe, Matthew settled the Delilah down on a small pad well away from the main space-docks. It took several minutes of adjusting the docking computer before it could talk to the antiquated facilities on the little moon. Eventually, the docking computer interlocked with the landing pad's control systems and Matthew commanded the landing pad to refuel their ship.

Three sensor arrays lifted out of the ground at the edge of the landing pad, each equally distant apart. The Delilah was scanned, but the landing pad was understandably unfamiliar with the ship's modern configuration. Matthew gave it the relevant information that it required. The location of the ship's refuelling connectors, the type of fuel hose those connectors required, the pumping pressure and how much fuel they were to take on board.

Two pumping stations lifted from either side of the landing pad. They oriented their position to line up with the ship, then two flexible refuelling tubes extended, one from each pumping station. These slowly approached the Delilah from either side of the ship. A few minutes later they accurately locked onto the ships refuelling connectors. Matthew smiled as the ship registered the flow of fuel into its tanks.

"How long will we be refuelling?", Leroy, who had been quietly and patiently waiting, asked.

"Give me a second, Sir", Matthew checked the actual flow rates against the specified flow rate and sighed when he realised they were much lower than he had anticipated. He did a quick calculation, then reported back to Leroy, "It will take four hours, Sir."

"Four fucking hours! Can't it go any faster?", Leroy enquired loudly.

"No, Sir", Matthew answered, explaining, "This is an old depot, Sir. Old equipment. It's as much as I could hope for, that it worked the first time without manually intervening."

Leroy looked at him, "I just don't want to be caught here when the Spartan arrives is all."

"Sir", Matthew explained, "We'll be long gone before the Spartan arrives. I'm more worried about pirates myself."

"Pirates?", Leroy questioned.

"Yes, Sir", Matthew answered, "This is one of their haunts. Don't worry though, I've been scanning this little moon hard since we arrived. I think we'll be fine this time round."

"What if you're wrong, Matthew?", Leroy demanded.

"I've got one eye on the scanners as we speak, Sir", Matthew reassured him, "If pirates do show up, I can disconnect the fuel lines real quick. This is a sweet ship, Sir. The Delilah is really fast. We'll be off and on our way before they can catch us."

"Sir, aren't we going to New Tortuga?", Matthew enquired.

"Yeah, what of it?", Leroy snapped back.

"New Tortuga was named after an ancient Caribbean pirate town, Sir."

"That's a misnomer, Matthew. Tortuga simply means turtle", Leroy replied, "but this New Tortuga is more of a smugglers' base. So, sure, there may be the odd pirate down there, but we have our own people down there as well. Quite a few of them, actually. The Prophet has sent word to them, and they'll be putting things in place for us."

"So, in theory, we'll only have to worry about the pirates up here?", Matthew asked.

"Yeah", Leroy replied, "Assuming that there are any up here to worry about. I didn't know that this was one of their haunts until you mentioned it."

"Yes, Sir, it's one of their haunts alright", Matthew replied, "We just have to make sure we're faster than them if any of them turn up."

"Make sure we are, Matthew", Leroy replied, "I wouldn't mention pirates to the Prophet if I were you. He doesn't like surprises, and he absolutely hates stuff ups."

Matthew gulped, "Perhaps I should have broached the subject when we were making our plans?"

"Might have been an idea", Leroy tossed back, "too late now though. Just watch those scanners."

Four hours later the Delilah was fully fuelled. The Pilot Matthew flipped a switch and the refuelling tubes automatically disconnected and retracted. Once the tubes were fully retracted, the pumping stations and sensor arrays withdrew back beneath the surface of the little moon, Deimos. Matthew smiled as he prepared the Delilah for take off.

All was well and soon the distinct hum of the antigravity lifters was heard throughout the ship. The Delilah lifted off from the landing pad. Then when only fifty feet from the surface, the Delilah's four photon thrusters came online and the ship launched into space once more.

Matthew took the ship in a sweep past Deimos, giving one final sensor sweep. A small flicker of a reading was picked up from a space dock on the other side of the sprawling complex from where they had landed and refuelled.

Matthew sighed with relief, *"So there were pirates down there. Damn lucky they didn't spot us"*, he thought to himself as he altered course for Mars.

"The Delilah has left Deimos, Jim", Forkbraid pointed out the image on the screen.

"No sign of any intercepting ships?", Jim inquired.

"Nothing is showing up on the display. Either they're leaving things real late or they're ignoring us, just like you said they would, Jim", Forkbraid noted.

"I thought that would be the case", Jim lamented, "Co-operation up here is sometimes hard to come by. You know, shaky at the best of times."

"The Captain will be tracking them, I'm sure of that, Jim", Forkbraid assured him.

"He can only track them until they hit the cloud deck. Once they get below the clouds, we can't follow them. We're simply not close enough for that", Jim informed him.

"That won't be long, Jim", Forkbraid pointed again at the screen, "at the rate they're travelling, they hit atmo in a couple of hours."

"They managed to pick the right time for it", James Murphy sneered.

"What do you mean, Jim?", Forkbraid asked.

"Deimos is known for more than just smugglers. Pirates have been known to prey around Deimos", James Murphy stated.

"Pirates?", replied Forkbraid in a querying tone, "We have pirates up here as well, Jim?"

"Yeah. Sure do", James Murphy replied, "They've been known to attack ships bypassing Phobos. Their usual prey is the odd ship load of unofficial settlers heading for Mars and wanting to avoid officialdom. Sometimes they'll take a smuggler's ship as well."

"I always thought pirates were a thing of the past", Forkbraid remarked.

"We still have them up here. There are a few places in the system where pirates can be found. There aren't that many attacks, but they still do happen. The Delilah cruised through during a quiet time, so to speak. Not much pirate activity around Deimos of late."

"Where else do you find pirates up here?", Forkbraid enquired.

"Well, there are a few places, FB", Special Agent Murphy thought for a moment, "Jupiter's fore and aft Trojan asteroid fields. They may be a part of the Jovian Realms, but they are a wild and lawless place, nonetheless. Rough mining colonies, not much in terms of law and order. Then there's Saturn's outer moons. They're another lawless place as well. Much farther out there are the Neptunian Trojans. Where you have the smaller more isolated colonies, you tend to find more issues of lawlessness and pirates do tend to appear."

"I hadn't thought of that, Jim", Forkbraid admitted, "Pirates! Of all things!"

"Yep, pirates", James Murphy reiterated.

The Delilah had dropped into the atmosphere and was now cruising high above the Isidis Gulf. By the time they reached the cloud deck they were flying above the shallow Elysium Channel.

Matthew took the Delilah across the Amazonis Sea, taking great care to stay hidden beneath the clouds. The Delilah skirted north of Olympus Mons taking full advantage of the thick cloud cover surrounding the enormous volcano, the peak of which stood well above the clouds.

Crossing low over the Tharsis Bulge at Olympica Fossae and passing north of Uranius Tholus and Uranius Petera, Matthew then turned the ship south along the swamp lands Kasei Valles. Matthew kept the Delilah as close to the ground as he could, keeping the bulk of the highland region of Lunae Planum between them and Chryce Colony. They would not be detected.

The Delilah flew into the narrowing Echus Chasma just barely above its shallow, flooded, marshy surface and at its southern extremity, turned east once more. Matthew then flew the ship across the hummocks separating Echus Chasma from Hebes Chasma, a deep chasm flooded with water, with Hebes Island sitting in its middle.

Matthew took the Delilah to her destination, New Tortuga, built inside a huge cavern complex in the cliffs on the island's south side. The cavern was almost impossible to see, its entrance was camouflaged to look like the surrounding cliffs. Matthew, however, knew its location, as did several members of his family and he had no problems in finding the cavern entrance.

Matthew slowed the Delilah right down and took her into the port of New Tortuga under the gentle thrust of her antigravity lifters. Within minutes the Delilah touched down at New Tortuga.

Lieutenant Roberts stomped into the control centre, "Where the hell is Private Smith?", he bellowed.

"I don't know, Sir", Private Kelso replied, "He didn't turn up for his shift this morning."

"Did he call in sick?", Lieutenant Roberts enquired.

"No, Sir. We haven't heard from him since yesterday", Private Kelso replied.

"Great. Just what we need, another bloody deserter", Lieutenant Roberts snarled, "We need every man at his station and this dick head pisses off."

"He might not have deserted, Sir", another man, Private Borthwick stated.

"Really, Borthwick", Lieutenant Roberts replied angrily, "In that case you won't mind working his station as well as your own, until he returns."

Private Borthwick looked over at Kelso, they both knew that Private Smith would not be back. More and more personnel had abandoned their stations and jumped ship for the surface colonies.

"Borthwick, hail the Spartan", Lieutenant Roberts yelled, "I want to know just how many VIPs we can expect"; he shook his head, "Bloody royal treatment. I'll give them bloody royal treatment."

"Yes, Sir. Right away, Sir", Private Borthwick replied and then quickly messaged the Spartan.

Captain Carmichael was on the bridge of the Spartan when the message came through.

"Captain, Sir", the Communications Officer called out.

"Yes, man, what is it?", the Captain replied.

"It's Phobos Command, Sir", the Communications Officer hesitated, he was confused, "They want to know how many VIPs to expect, Sir."

"VIPs?", Captain Carmichael questioned, "What are they on about?"

"I'll find out, Sir", the Communications Officer replied, before sending a message back to Phobos Command.

"Lieutenant!", Private Borthwick called out, "It's the Spartan, Sir. They don't know what we're talking about, Sir."

"What!", Lieutenant Roberts screamed, "Ask them again. The extra security for the Ptolemy, the VIPs and their bloody royal treatment. Confirm it."

Private Borthwick sent the message.

On the Bridge of the Spartan, the Communications Officer informed his Captain

"Sir. Phobos Command is under the impression", he paused, "That we're the extra security for the Ptolemy and its", he paused again, "VIPs, Sir. There was also something about royal treatment?"

"What in the blazes are they on about?", Captain Carmichael exclaimed, "Tell those idiotic knuckleheads why we're here."

"Oh, shit!", Private Borthwick let slip, "Sir. It's the Spartan. They're saying they're here chasing a stolen space yacht full of terrorists."

"Terrorists?", Lieutenant Roberts queried.

"Yes, Sir", Private Borthwick replied, "That other ship yesterday."

"The smugglers?", Lieutenant Roberts queried again.

"Yes, Sir", Private Borthwick then explained, "That ship, the Delilah, was stolen from an L-Five colony, Hyper Dynamics Corporation. There are at least three dozen terrorists on board and a hostage, a small child."

"They", Private Borthwick stopped for a moment, "They requested that we perform an urgent intercept yesterday, during Private Smith's last shift, Sir."

"They did, did they?", Lieutenant Roberts' face was glowing red with fury, "What was that bullshit that Smith spouted out yesterday then? That lying sack of shit!"

"I don't know, Sir", Private Borthwick gulped, "I assume it was exactly that, Sir. Bullshit."

"Captain, Sir. Phobos Command is saying that they didn't get the message that we sent them yesterday", the Communications Officer stated, "They're saying that one of their men intercepted the message and fed them a load of bullshit before going AWOL and jumping ship for the Martian surface, Sir."

"Well, isn't that just great then?", Captain Carmichael replied, "The terrorists have people at Phobos Command as well. Tell them to keep an eye out for other personnel trying to jump ship", he paused, "Tell Phobos Command to expect visitors ahead of our arrival as well", he said as he stormed off the Bridge.

The boarding shuttle sped ahead of the Spartan. Folcrom Forkbraid and Special Agent Murphy were aboard the ship along with eight squads of Colonial Troops. It was only a two-hour flight to Phobos and the shuttle was soon docked at Phobos Command's main space-docks.

Special Agent Murphy stepped through the airlock wearing the typical dark trench coat that all Special Agents wore. Lieutenant Roberts was there to meet him. He automatically knew that he was in trouble, the preceding two days had been decidedly pear-shaped.

Special Agent Murphy looked over at the man standing before him, "Are you, Roberts?"

"Yes, Sir. Lieutenant Roberts, Sir", the Lieutenant replied.

"Well, Lieutenant, here are your fucking VIPs", Special Agent Murphy replied as the Colonial Troopers marched through the airlock and into the space-docks.

"Men. You have your orders. Secure this facility", Special Agent Murphy commanded, "If anyone resists, shoot first ask questions later."

The men split up into five-man teams and spread out into the complex.

Lieutenant Roberts was about to protest the takeover of his facility, until he saw Forkbraid step through the airlock. "Sweet Mother of God", the Lieutenant's jaw just dropped.

"Roberts", Special Agent Murphy snapped, "This is Lord Folcrom Forkbraid. You will give him complete cooperation. Do you understand?"

Lieutenant Roberts was in shock, he hesitated.

Special Agent Murphy pressed him further, "It would be a huge mistake to disobey this man Roberts. Do you understand me?"

Lieutenant Roberts came to attention, "Yes, Sir. Complete cooperation, Sir."

"How many personnel have jumped ship in the last three days Roberts?", Special Agent Murphy demanded.

"We've lost twelve people, Sir. They all jumped ship sometime before the current shift."

"You've searched for them?", Forkbraid enquired.

"Yes, Sir. We found no trace of them in the facility."

"Anywhere they can hide?", Special Agent Murphy asked.

"Plenty of places, Sir", the Lieutenant replied, "We've searched most of them, Sir."

"But not all of them?", Forkbraid added.

"No, Sir. I expect they probably stowed aboard the last HLT to leave for the surface yesterday."

"Lieutenant Roberts, my friend Forkbraid here, he will be the judge of that."

"We'll need to know the name of that last HLT", Forkbraid advised.

"It was the Hypolita, Sir", Lieutenant Roberts replied.

"Do you sense anything, FB?", Special Agent Murphy asked.

"No, Jim. I'm reaching out, deep into this facility. I can't find any extremists within a hundred yards. I need to look much deeper though", Forkbraid replied.

"Whatever you need, FB, I'll have Roberts here, provide it", Special Agent Murphy stated.

"We just need to lock down this facility", Forkbraid replied, "Lock it down and stop all traffic. Once that's achieved, I can wander through every section and scan everyone."

"How long will that take?", Lieutenant Roberts enquired, thinking of his schedules.

"As long as it takes", Special Agent Murphy replied.

"Sir, we have flight schedules, and deadlines to meet", Lieutenant Roberts insisted.

"They're all on hold until further notice", Special Agent Murphy snapped back.

Forkbraid smiled, "I'll need about eight hours, Lieutenant. I'll let you know if

I need any longer."

"Thank you, Sir", Lieutenant Roberts replied.

A little over eight hours later, Forkbraid had finished scanning the facility. All spaceport personnel had fully cooperated. He had not located any extremists on Phobos. That was expected. The HLT Hypolita was long overdue for her arrival at the Chryse colony on Mars. A sprawling complex built above the shoreline of the Chryse Sea, just northwest of the ancient Viking One landing site in the Sharanov Delta. The ship, its crew and cargo of earth moving and construction equipment were all missing. Special Agent Murphy was first to suggest that it had been hijacked by the twelve missing personnel. It was now becoming quite clear that they were indeed extremists.

"Where will they go?", questioned Forkbraid.

"They could go anywhere", Special Agent Murphy replied, "Mars, as you pointed out before, is a bloody big place."

"I don't know, Jim", Forkbraid was tugging his goatee again, "The Delilah, the Hypolita, what's the bet they're both going to the same destination."

"I'm not a betting man, FB", Special Agent Murphy replied, "but I do agree with you."

"Are we certain there are no extremists here on Phobos?", Special Agent Murphy queried.

"As certain as I can be, Jim", Forkbraid replied, "I've scanned the whole of the facility. There are some outlying stations, but they're not directly connected. I can scan those from space before we head back to the Spartan."

"Good, good", Special Agent Murphy then hesitated a moment, "It's just, I'm not so certain that I want the Ptolemy docking here at all. Your people are on board, and they are a prime target."

"The Ptolemy could refuel at Deimos?", Forkbraid offered.

"It's a real possibility. That old depot does l have plenty of fuel."

"There's just that slight issue of pirates, Jim?" Forkbraid reminded him.

"I'm pretty sure that any pirates will flee when they see the Spartan coming their way", Special Agent Murphy smiled.

Forkbraid smiled back, "It will certainly make Lieutenant Roberts happy. He won't have to slot us into his all important docking and flight schedules."

"Deimos it is then", Special Agent Murphy replied, "I'll make the recommendation to Captain Carmichael."

Captain Carmichael accepted Special Agent Murphy's recommendations. Lieutenant Roberts was pleased with their decision, now he didn't have to worry about making room for two rather big ships in his already overcrowded and busy spaceport. The [47]IPL Ptolemy and Heavy Cruiser Spartan both altered their

---

47 Interplanetary Liner. Large vehicle equipped with photon thrusters designed

respective courses to rendezvous at Deimos. Special Agent Murphy, Folcrom Forkbraid and eight squads of Colonial Troops were already en route aboard the boarding shuttle to secure the complex ahead of the Ptolemy's and Spartan's arrival.

It was difficult to say whether it was the approach of the Spartan's boarding shuttle or the approach of the Heavy Cruiser, the Spartan, itself that spooked the pirates more. One thing was for certain, Special Agent Murphy was right, half a dozen small ships fled the old supply depot at Deimos ahead of their arrival. They flew out of one of the space-docks and each took a separate trajectory towards Mars.

"You see, FB", Special Agent Murphy pointed at the scanner screen, "I told you they'd flee."

"It's a pity really, Jim", Forkbraid replied, "They were here when the Delilah refuelled. Interesting that. They didn't attack her. To me that speaks volumes. They might have had useful information. Information that I could have lifted straight out of their minds."

"Hmm. Now that's a thought", Special Agent Murphy replied, "There running for Mars, but just where on the surface they'll hide is anybody's guess."

"It would be nice to know wouldn't it, Jim?"

"That it would, FB, that it would."

"Request the Captain scan the trajectories of each of those ships. I'd like to know where each of those ships breaches atmo, Jim."

"Good idea, I'll make that request straight away, FB"

The boarding shuttle landed at the main space-docks on Deimos and Special Agent Murphy quickly sent in the colonial troops to secure the complex. Less than two hours later the Spartan's other boarding shuttle landed and quickly offloaded her complement of colonial troops.

It wasn't long before the abandoned naval base was entirely under their control. The Heavy Cruiser, Spartan, took up a synchronous orbit above the old naval base, awaiting the arrival of the IPL Ptolemy. It was decided this would be their base of operations for both the unloading of passengers and cargo to the Elysium colony, as well as their off-world base for hunting down the terrorists. Deimos was now completely at their disposal.

---

to travel from one planet to another.

15. New Tortuga

Leroy McGuvan stood before the Delilah, looking south towards the Martian horizon and the majestic, now flooded Valles Marineris. Blue Martian skies as far as the eye could see. The ancient Hebes Chasma lay before the mouth of New Tortuga's cavern, it too was flooded deep with water. Over his right shoulder thick white, snow laden clouds were rolling off the high plateau of the Tharsis Monts. Over his left shoulder, the Aurorae Chaos Sea at the mouth of the Valles Marineris was partially shrouded by massive thunderstorms.

"Awesome sight", Leroy thought to himself.

"What a sight, absolutely breathtaking!", Matthew said as he approached from the Delilah.

"You said it boy", Leroy replied.

"My sixth great-grandfather was here on Mars back when the skies were all salmon pink", Matthew stated.

"Your sixth great-grandfather?", Leroy gave Matthew a look of disbelief.

"Yeah, he was a surveyor at the beginning of the terraforming project", Matthew gestured with his hand, "He surveyed this very place."

"Really, what for?", Leroy was actually curious.

"Back then, Hebes Chasma was being considered for a colony", Matthew informed him, "It was rejected though. The region was considered far too isolated and too rugged."

"Well, someone definitely thought it had merit", Leroy considered as he scanned his eye around the port of New Tortuga.

"Yeah, the Russians built a base here nearly three hundred years ago before the early terraforming phase", Matthew informed him.

"So why aren't they here now?", Leroy questioned.

"There was an economic downturn shortly after they completed it. They ran out of money, so the whole place was abandoned. Then later, the terraforming ramped up and with all those huge chunks of ice dropping out of the sky like falling comets, no-one came back here. No-one official anyway."

"How do you know all this stuff, Matthew?", Leroy asked.

"I read a lot, Sir", Matthew replied simply.

What was once an enormous cavern in the south side of Hebes Island had been excavated and expanded. It now extended deep inside the island, well beyond its mouth in three distinct directions. The walls were re-enforced and lined with reinforced concrete, then coloured to match the surrounding terrain. Behind Leroy's right shoulder, sitting well within the cavern was the Delilah. Sitting further down on the right was by far the largest vessel in the cavern, the HLT Hypolita, which had been hijacked en route to Chryce colony. An assortment of smaller vessels, some as large as the Delilah, most somewhat smaller, were positioned on landing bays to the left and right. There were quite a few ships in good-old New Tortuga. With a quick glance, one could not count them all.

As Leroy stood observing the awesome scene before him, his keen eye picked out what he'd been waiting for. He pointed to the approaching ship, it was a [48]Talon, it was a deep blue-coloured ship, smallish, sleek and fast.

"There's one of them now, Matthew", he stated.

"One of what, Sir?", Matthew queried.

Talon Class Interceptor

Leroy let loose a slight chuckle, "Our pirates, Matthew, our pirates."

"Our pirates?", Matthew queried anew.

"Yes, Matthew. Those pirates you were so worried about on Deimos. Turns out, they're our comrades in arms", Leroy informed him.

"Why didn't you say so before, Sir?", Matthew asked, a slight hint of annoyance in his voice.

Leroy smiled once more, "I didn't know myself until after we landed."

"Just how many pirates do we have, Sir?"

"Well, Matthew, we have this one and another five to follow. Then we have another dozen or more parked over that way", Leroy pointed further into the left branch of the cavern.

"That's impressive, Sir. It's kind of like having an air force", a surprised Matthew commented.

"What about the HLT, Sir?", a curious Matthew asked of the Hypolita.

"Well, that was just a bonus", Leroy replied adding, "Our people on Phobos needed an escape route, so they planned ahead to commandeer the Hypolita, complete with her cargo, I might add."

"Smart thinking, Sir. We now have our own HLT", Matthew replied.

"Complete with cargo, remember, Matthew. Apparently our people on Phobos were quite astute. They planned the hijacking of the Hypolita to pay for the services of our pirates."

"So we get the ship, and they get the booty?", Matthew smiled.

"Yes, indeed and the Prophet is most pleased", Leroy replied as the first of the six new pirate ships entered the cavern and slowly taxied past. As they watched another two pirate ships, both Talons, appeared on the horizon.

---

48 Talon Class Interceptors. Two plasma thrust nacelles mounted under the wings, four particle beams, twin pulse cannons.

Matthew strolled into the enormous central branch of the cavern. This was where the inhabitants of the port of New Tortuga lived. The other two branches, simply designated east and west, were mainly taken up with docks and landing bays for the storing, refuelling and servicing of ships. Here in the cavern's main central branch, buildings had been carved out of the rock on both sides. The cavern was quite high, with terraces reaching up six stories high. The cavern roof was far higher.

Rectangular cut openings in the rock walls indicated entrances and windows to shops and businesses on the ground level. Some of these man made caves were of impressive size. Between the rock walls was a large town square, behind which in the very centre of the cavern were several large buildings built of stone and plasteel. Again these appeared to be business establishments. Some of these business establishments were quite large inside. The largest being the taverns, of which there were four. Matthew strolled past these buildings and deeper into the cavern itself.

Matthew scanned his eyes along the terraces above the ground level, nearly all appeared to be used for housing and apartments, most of which were also carved out of the rock itself. The only real indication of their existence, again the rectangular cuts for their doors and windows. Just how far these apartments extended into the rock was any one's guess. On the broader terraces, a few smaller structures made of stone and plasteel had been built, here and there extending out from the rock walls.

More than a few had clothes lines extending from the rock face, upon which hanging clothes were drying. A considerable number of gardens were also visible and Matthew could recognise most of the vegetables being grown. Many gardens had climbing vegetables growing up the rock faces and even dangling over the terraces themselves. The sheer amount of greenery was surprising to see. New Tortuga literally had hanging gardens.

Strolling much deeper into this branch of the cavern behind the buildings, the gardens became far more extensive and the apartment entrances became fewer. The deeper regions of the cavern appeared to be set up for intensive farming, as hydroponics equipment was set up everywhere in layer upon layer of plasteel scaffold, reaching for the cavern's roof.

Sheer walls of verdant greenery stood before him. He could not see how deep these *"farms"* extended into the cavern, nor how far the cavern itself extended, but looking more closely, he believed it could be a mile or perhaps much more.

Matthew understood instinctively that in the early days before Mars had a breathable atmosphere, the only place to grow food would have been inside caverns, with airlocks separating the colony from the deadly Martian environment outside. Back then these gardens not only produced the food for this unofficial colony, but they also helped to scrub the air of carbon dioxide. Redundant now, the airlocks had long been dismantled.

New Tortuga was an underground town of verdant green, hanging gardens, bathed in the glow of bright lights suspended from the cavern roof some ten or more stories up. This was not what Matthew had expected at all. Looking back the way he'd come, he could see now that New Tortuga was a vibrant growing town with a population of more than a thousand souls.

"How many other unofficial colonies like this are scattered across Mars", he thought to himself, *"There could be many dozens of them."*

Slowly Matthew strolled back towards the town square. Passing through the centre of town once more, Matthew located what he was looking for. New Tortuga's largest and most notorious tavern, it was called the Kraken.

Leroy McGuvan was standing by its entrance, "Took you long enough lad", he said as Matthew approached, then the two men walked inside.

Mrs Harmon had little Miranda in tow, and together they walked towards the far end of New Tortuga. They had seen Matthew and Leroy enter the Kraken, but neither man had noticed them. In front of them walked a man named Cormac Farmer. He was tall and thin, with wispy blond hair hanging loosely from his balding head. His eyes were blue with an ever slight shading of green. He was not a young man and was somewhat rough looking in appearance, with a definite need to shave. He was their guide so to speak and every once in a while he would stop to allow them to catch up.

Mrs Harmon seemed oblivious to the beauty of New Tortuga's hanging gardens; Miranda, however, was not. Miranda did her best to study the cavern with its verdant greenery and dawdled as best she could.

Mrs Harmon frequently dragged her forward, shouting "Come on girl, get a move on."

Cormac, however, seemed to dislike this and frowned regularly when he heard Mrs Harmon's loud, demanding voice. Mrs Harmon was all kinds of unpleasant.

Miranda could not see Cormac's face, she caught the thought, *"Poor child"*, several times.

On one occasion, when Cormac had turned around, Miranda caught the thought *"Damned cow"*, directed at Mrs Harmon.

This caused Miranda to laugh, which in turn caused Cormac to smile; his teeth were stained a light brown, more than a few looked rotten. His smile was gap-toothed. It was not a pretty sight.

Mrs Harmon said one word, "Yuck."

Cormac frowned once more, *"Damned cow"*, he thought to himself.

Miranda laughed again and Cormac smiled once more, as he turned and continued leading them deeper into the cavern.

Eventually they arrived at the hydroponics farms at the very rear of the main cavern and all three of them stopped at the sheer wall of verdant greenery and plasteel scaffolding. Only now did Mrs Harmon stop and stare in awe.

"This way. Come on woman", Cormac said as he led them down a path and deep into the farm.

Sheer walls of green stood on either side of them, rising up more than a hundred feet. Looking up Miranda could see many lights dispersed within the scaffold providing ample lighting for this artificial forest of sorts. Vegetables and fruits hung from the vines, bees buzzed from flower to flower. Even humming birds were seen flying here and there. Miranda's spirits lifted as she smiled at each new sight before her.

Miranda found herself staring at a peculiar looking fruit. It hung in bunches from slender stems, was about the size of a larger than normal apple and was a deep rose colour. Miranda reached up and grabbed one of the fruits.

"Child! Leave that alone", Mrs Harmon scolded.

Cormac turned around, *"Damned cow"*, he directed a thought at Mrs Harmon, but said to Miranda, "It's okay, little one, you may have one if you wish."

Miranda smiled back at Cormac, who smiled in return.

"What is it, Cormac?", Miranda enquired.

"It's a cherry, of course", Cormac replied.

"But it's huge", Miranda stated as she looked at the cherry.

"Well, yes, of course, it is. Martian cherries are like that. Something to do with the gravity and the qualities of the nutrients we extract from the Martian soil", Cormac informed her, continuing, "Well, what are you waiting for, try it."

Miranda took a bite of the cherry. It tasted as a cherry should, except it was much sweeter and by far the best cherry Miranda had ever tasted.

"Well, how does it taste then, little one?", Cormac asked.

"Delicious", Miranda replied.

"You think the cherries are good, you should try the grapes next", Cormac replied.

"Why do you grow so much produce?", Mrs Harmon questioned, "I doubt New Tortuga has enough people to consume all of this."

"It's mainly for the colonies in high Martian orbit", Cormac replied, "We get a pretty penny exporting our produce off-world. It really is quite lucrative. You should try our wine range."

"We never saw cherries like this in L-Five", Mrs Harmon remarked.

"And you won't. They wouldn't survive the trip to L-Five, it's way too far.", replied Cormac.

Miranda continued eating her cherry while Mrs Harmon stared at the hanging gardens all about them. She had never seen anything like it.

"Come along then, there'll be plenty of other fruits for you to try later", said

Cormac as he turned and continued leading them through the hydroponics.

The forest of hydroponics seemed endless; it followed the cavern, which continued deeper and deeper into the rock. After nearly thirty minutes of walking through it, they came to the end. A sheer wall of rock stood before them, into which a doorway had been carved. Miranda looked up at the rock wall. Every ten feet or so, there appeared to be a small window.

Cormac led them into the doorway, and they found themselves walking up a spiral staircase carved into the stone. As they walked up, small windows let them look out over the hydroponics farm. Eventually, they reached the top of the stairs, which opened up onto a large rock ledge seventy feet above the floor of the cavern. The ledge was about thirty feet across, and the rock wall on the far side was full of openings for doors and windows.

Cormac led them into the main doorway in the middle, and they found themselves inside a house carved into the rock. Cormac led them down a deep corridor with doorways leading into other rooms carved here and there into the rock, then up another spiral stairway. They walked up two levels and came out into another corridor.

Cormac led them down the corridor and into the last room on the right. Miranda walked over to the window and looked out, the smell of the hydroponics was amazing at this height and the view was incredible. The cavern roof was not too far above them and Miranda could see across the tops of the hydroponics towards the port of New Tortuga. It was small and difficult to see in the distance.

"This will be your room, little lady", Cormac informed her.

Miranda curtseyed and replied, "Thank you kind, Sir."

Cormac smiled at Miranda, then turned to Mrs Harmon, he frowned, "Your room madam, is through the opposite door. If you need me, my quarters are on the lower floor", he informed her.

"Thank you, Cormac. I'll tell my Lord how helpful you've been", Mrs Harmon replied.

"Damned cow", Cormac thought to himself.

Miranda laughed once more, and Cormac smiled once more.

There were footsteps behind them as Cormac's Wife walked into the room. A small chubby woman with a pretty, although slightly fat face and rosy red cheeks.

"Hello there. I'm Candace, but everybody calls me Candy", she said with a slight laugh, "You must be Mrs Harmon and little Miranda. I thought you might like some fruit."

Candy walked over to a table by the wall and placed a large bowl of fruit she'd be carrying on it.

"I see you've already tried the cherries", Candy said as she looked at Miranda's face, still stained with cherry juice.

Candy gave Miranda's cheek a firm but not overly firm squeeze, "Sweet child."

"You have a Wife?", Mrs Harmon stated a little surprised.

"How could he not with those good looks", Candy answered for Cormac.

Cormac smiled his gap-toothed smile with its rotten teeth once more.

Mrs Harmon said a silent *"Yuck"*, in her mind, as a slightly audible "Ugh" was let loose.

This time it was Candy's thought, *"Oh, you damned cow"*, that Miranda picked up as Candy said to Mrs Harmon, "Looks aren't everything, Mrs Harmon, and my Cormac, does have the sweetest of hearts."

Cormac gave his Wife a gentle tap on the behind, "Come on, Candy. We have things to do, and our guests do need their rest."

"Yes, of course, Cormac", Candy replied to her Husband. "If you need anything, just give me or Cormac a yell", Candy said to Mrs Harmon and Miranda as she left the room.

Cormac waved goodbye as he turned about, and as he left the room he let one thought trail behind him, *"I'll do my best to protect you, little one, and so will my Wife, Candy."*

Miranda's jaw dropped slightly, her eyes opened wide, *"Cormac is a psychic! A Martian psychic!"*, she thought to herself.

The Prophet sat surrounded by his salivating sycophants. The room they were in was large, they had commandeered the Kraken for their meeting. The Prophet's people held a tight grip over New Tortuga, it was now their town, and they could do with it as they pleased or at least they thought.

Leroy strode over to his Master, "My Lord, we should burn the abomination now."

"We still need her, Leroy", the Prophet replied, "With her, we can keep tabs on Him."

Leroy knew who his Master was referring to, he referred to Folcrom Forkbraid.

Leroy merely nodded in understanding, before remarking "We should keep her locked away my Lord. We can't have a little Witch wandering around in our midst."

The Prophet smiled, "That's already been taken care of, Leroy. Our little Witch is being locked away at the very rear of the caverns, behind the farms, where she can do no harm."

Another man approached, he was a squat fellow, not more than five foot four. He was thick set and rough looking, his face covered with a dark shaggy beard, flecked with grey and a thick scar across his left cheek.

Leroy introduced the man to the Prophet, "My Lord this is Mort Kendal, here abouts they call him Captain Scar."

"Scar?", the Prophet queried, "Well, that's original. Where'd you get it from?"

Mort replied, his voice as deep as he was squat, "My third misses, my Lord. She took a severe dislike to my affection for the tavern wenches."

The Prophet showed a distinct distaste for the man, "Perhaps, we can reform you of that particular behaviour, Captain Scar?"

Mort Kendal lifted his head at this remark, "No need, my Lord. We'll all behave right gentlemanly during your administration, Sir", he smiled.

"So why are you here, Mort Kendal?", the Prophet asked bluntly.

"My men and I just got in from Deimos, my Lord. The old naval base has changed hands it seems. We thought it prudent to leave in a hurry."

"Changed hands?", the Prophet was interested in this new development.

"That Heavy Cruiser, the Spartan, has taken over the base, my Lord. And that Interplanetary Liner, the Ptolemy, was on a trajectory for Deimos as well when we last tracked it."

"The Ptolemy is headed for Deimos?", the Prophet questioned.

"Yes, my Lord, it sure is", Mort confirmed.

"Interesting", the Prophet replied, "It puts them a little further beyond our reach, but it changes nothing. The colonists still need to land here on this planet."

"It does change a few things, my Lord", Leroy informed him.

"What would that be, Leroy?", the Prophet enquired.

"Our men on Phobos had made plans for the Ptolemy's arrival, my Lord."

"What plans were those, Leroy?"

"They booby trapped the refuelling stations, specifically the ones the Ptolemy would have been using for her HLTs", Leroy replied, "With the Ptolemy using the old naval base, those booby traps will be next to useless."

"More than useless, Leroy", the Prophet scowled, "Those booby traps will be awfully dangerous. The folks on Phobos may lose more than a few people, none of whom we intended to kill."

Leroy nodded, "Yes, they may have some collateral damage, my Lord."

"Never mind, Leroy. A disaster or two on Phobos might keep the Spartan occupied for a while."

Leroy smiled, "That thought had crossed my mind as well, my Lord."

Leroy pushed Matthew forward slightly as he spoke, "My Lord we have a bold plan for destroying the devils", he stated.

"Yes, my Lord", Matthew added.

"Well, then, Matthew, what is this plan of yours?"

"Well, my Lord, we have at least eighteen pirate vessels at our disposal, perhaps even a few of the smugglers' ships as well", Matthew smiled at Captain Scar who nodded in agreement, "We also have the HLT Hypolita."

"I am aware of this, Matthew, so what's the plan?"

"The Ptolemy's HLTs will have to bring the colonists down to the Elysium colony at some point. When they do, they will be vulnerable. We will have two avenues of attack at our disposal."

"Two avenues of attack?", the Prophet queried.

"Yes, Sir. Our pirate friends here", Matthew again indicated the pirates gathered in the tavern for the meeting, "can attack the HLTs as they breach atmo and bring them down. While this is happening, we can use the Hypolita itself, as a weapon."

"Use the Hypolita as a weapon?"

"Yes, Sir, if we load the Hypolita up with explosives, we have three options available. We can use her to attack either the Spartan, the Ptolemy, or the Elysium colony itself."

"Which option have you chosen, Matthew?"

"I haven't, my Lord. I thought you might like to make that decision yourself."

The Prophet smiled at Matthew as he considered the targets, he was in silent contemplation for several long minutes thinking about the proposed plan.

"They will recognise the Hypolita and surely suspect something", he finally stated.

"I have thought of that, my Lord. I've modified the Hyplolita's pulse identification beacon. She'll now identify herself as one of the Ptolemy's HLTs."

"Which one?"

"My Lord, I've put in place the identifiers for the Odysseus, the Ajax, and the Agamemnon. We can choose which one we want the Hypolita to be, when the time comes."

"That's impressive, Matthew", the Prophet smiled, "Now all we need to consider is the target."

"Yes, my Lord. The target?", Matthew was curious as to which target the Prophet preferred.

Again The Prophet was in deep thought, before replying "If we attack the Spartan, they'll send the whole fleet after us. If we attack the Ptolemy, the result will likely be the same."

"My Lord, if we attack the Elysium colony, we will still have the Spartan, a Heavy Cruiser, to deal with", Leroy stated.

"Yes, Leroy, but they don't know where we are and Mars is a big place after all. We just have to make sure that they don't find us."

"If it becomes necessary, Sir, it is far easier to slip past one ship than a whole fleet of ships", Mort Kendal added with his deep voice.

"Exactly", the Prophet replied, "We don't want a whole fleet to contend with."

"My Lord, we can drop the Hypolita straight down on top of Elysium. Blow it to smithereens."

"Yes, Matthew, that's my thought exactly. Wipe out the colonists as they try to land and wipe out their expensive new colony at the same time. Mars will be ours, not theirs."

Leroy was concerned, "The Spartan will send her interceptors after us, my Lord."

"The Spartan's interceptors won't be a problem, my Lord", Mort Kendal butted in, "She's a Heavy Cruiser, her interceptors are, by law, only space rated. They can't fly in atmo, Sir."

Matthew added, "Mort's right, my Lord. Once the HLTs hit atmo, the Spartan's interceptors will have to fall back. They'll have no choice, Sir, their [49]Wisps don't have any heat shielding."

"Their drop-ships do!", Leroy stated with concern.

"Yes, Sir, they do, but they're only good for landing their colonial troops and for that, they'd need our location."

Leroy nodded at Matthew's reply, "Well lad, we'll make sure they don't get that then, won't we?"

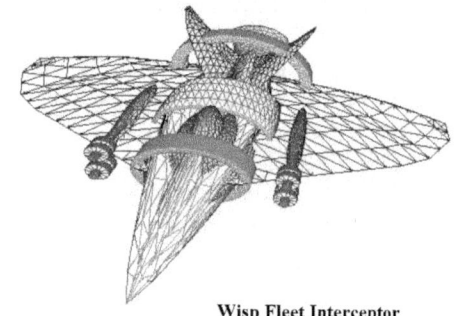

Wisp Fleet Interceptor

The Prophet smiled, "It's settled then. Leroy, prepare the Hypolita for the attack on Elysium."

"Yes, my Lord. Right away, Sir", Leroy replied.

"Matthew, keep a close eye on the Ptolemy. I want to know when their HLTs make a move. When they bring their colonists down, I want us to be ready for them."

"Yes, my Lord. I'll set up some auto-scopes to keep watch on her", Matthew replied.

"And, Captain Scar, make sure you and your comrades are ready."

"Where always ready for action, Sir", Mort Kendal replied.

"Just to make sure you are, henceforth this port is dry", the Prophet stated.

"Dry, Sir?", Mort queried, "Even pirates need a bit of Dutch-courage if you know what I mean."

"I need you all sober for the task", the Prophet replied, his intense eyes staring coldly at him.

Mort Kendal looked around at some of his comrades before replying, "Some of my men aren't going to be very happy with that, Sir."

---

49 Wisp. Fleet interceptor. Short range plasma drive and longer range EM drive, armed with two particle beams.

The Prophet looked around the room at the gathered privateers, rough men all of them, "Very well then. After the task is done, the bar will be reopened", he stated diplomatically.

"We drink after we work then, Lads", Mort Kendal looked around at his comrades once more, receiving a nod here and there in reply.

Mort looked back to the Prophet, "So be it, Sir. Sober it will be. The port will be dry for now."

The Prophet smiled back at Mort, "I'm glad we have your agreement."

Mort Kendal walked through the east branch's landing bays. As he went, he pointed out the ships to be used in the attack.

"There are only eight HLTs, so we don't need to use all the ships at our disposal. These dozen Talons should be plenty for the task."

"You sure they'll be enough, Mort?", Leroy questioned.

"Sure they are. A dozen Talons is overkill", Mort replied.

Matthew agreed, "Sir, HLTs don't have any weapons or defences, a dozen Talons should be plenty. As Mort said, it is overkill."

Leroy nodded, "That leaves us with six in reserve then."

"Nine", Mort tossed back, "There are three more ships over that way."

Mort pointed to three rough looking Talons a bit further over, all obviously in need of work.

Both Leroy and Matthew looked at Mort with incredulous looks on their faces.

"You've got to be joking, Mort", Matthew stated.

"Sure, they ain't pretty. They're space worthy though", Mort replied.

Matthew cocked an eyebrow; he didn't think that could possibly be true.

"Okay, okay, they need a bit of work. We'll have them ready in time. Don't worry, Lad."

Matthew caught sight of something else and quickly bolted off down the landing bays.

"What is it, Matthew?", Leroy hollered out.

"Over here, Sir", Matthew shouted back as he ran further down the bays.

Leroy and Mort quickly ran to where Matthew had stopped.

"What is it, Matthew?", Leroy asked once again.

"They're [50]Gull Wings, Sir. Gull Wing

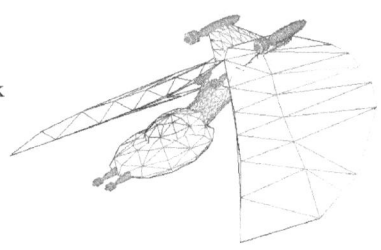

Gull Wing Interceptor

---

50 Gull Wing Interceptor. Small two person military ships equipped with six particle beams and a single plasma thruster.

Interceptors."

"They're in working order, Lad, if you think that we'll have a need for them. We only have the two though", Mort Kendal informed him.

"I'm more concerned about where they came from", Matthew replied.

"Deimos", Mort Kendal replied quickly and without any further explanation.

"Deimos!", Matthew shouted back.

Leroy stepped up to Matthew, "What is it, boy?"

"How many of these are still up there?", Matthew quickly asked Mort.

"I don't know, Lad. Maybe ten or twelve", Mort replied.

"Ten or twelve?", Matthew's face was growing redder by the minute.

Leroy was not used to being ignored, "Matthew! What is it?", he shouted.

"Sir! There are ten or twelve more of these ships up there on Deimos", came Matthew's loudly shouted reply.

Leroy looked at Matthew, he had not caught the drift of his words.

"They are atmo rated, Sir. And they are up there at Deimos."

It finally dawned on Leroy what Matthew was on about.

Mort Kendal reassured the two men, "It's okay. It's okay. The ones we left behind were empty shells. These were the only two that actually worked."

"You can be sure of that?", Leroy asked.

"Absolutely! We scavenged parts from the others to get these two working", was Mort's reply.

Matthew was unconvinced, "Describe the condition of the other Gull Wings", he demanded.

"The others were completely gutted", Mort replied.

"Completely gutted?", Matthew asked, "go on tell me more."

"We pulled them apart to rebuild these two."

"So the ones you left behind can't be rebuilt?", Matthew questioned.

"Maybe with the right parts, but all the useful parts, everything of value, was salvaged long ago", Mort assured him, "We didn't leave much of anything behind."

Leroy looked at Matthew, then back to Mort, "How much of that base have you actually ransacked?"

"Me personally or everyone else as well?"

"You personally, you and your men anyway", Leroy clarified.

"Me and my men have ransacked most of it", Mort told him.

"Most of it?", Matthew queried.

"I'd say most of it", Mort replied.

"But not all of it?", Leroy queried.

"It is a bloody huge base, enormous", Mort answered, adding "It would take more than a decade and then some to go through it all."

"So there could be more Gull Wings up there?", Matthew asked.

"Maybe. Potentially", Mort replied, "Maybe other ships as well, but I doubt it though."

"You doubt it? Why is that?", Leroy questioned.

"People have been ransacking and salvaging stuff from that base ever since it closed", he replied, "I'd be very surprised if there are any ships left up there in serviceable condition."

"Sir, Wisps are no threat to us once the HLTs hit atmo, but Gull Wings are another matter", Matthew told Leroy, adding "Sir, the Prophet will need to be told of this."

"Yes, Lad, and I don't particularly relish the task", Leroy replied.

Leroy and Matthew hurried back into the town. They quickly made their way to New Tortuga's second-largest tavern, its sign was disconnected on one side and hanging down. It read, *"The Black Pullet"*. The Prophet was standing in front of the tavern. Debris and fixtures from inside the tavern were strewn around him in the street. The Prophet was orchestrating the tavern's renovations.

Matthew asked him, "My Lord, I thought that we were commandeering the Kraken?"

The Prophet smiled at Matthew, "We were, Matthew, however, the meeting we had earlier showed me that we need to tread gently here. If we turn their biggest tavern into a church, we could well have a rebellion on our hands."

Matthew nodded showing that he understood.

The Prophet continued, "I think we can get away with converting this one with little resistance. Besides, I didn't like the name of it anyway."

"My Lord, we may have a problem with our plans", Leroy informed the Prophet.

"What problem would that be, Leroy?", the Prophet enquired.

"Matthew found a couple of Gull Wing Interceptors in the docks", Leroy told him.

"Why would they be a problem, Leroy?"

"Gull Wings are atmo rated, my Lord. These two came from Deimos. Mort Kendal says there are more up there. They are dismantled, empty shells, or so Mort Kendal says", Leroy explained.

"I don't see how dismantled, empty shells can be a problem, Leroy."

"There is a small chance that there might be more ships up at Deimos, my Lord."

"What does Mort Kendal have to say about that?"

"He says that it's unlikely. That any ships left lying around the base will have been scavenged long ago."

"So we're looking at an unknown?", the Prophet summed up.

"Precisely, my Lord", Leroy replied, "There may or may not be other intact ships at that base."

"If there are any intact ships at that base, they're probably not easily found. If they were, then Mort Kendal would be correct, wouldn't he? They would have been stolen long ago."

"Yes, my Lord. I'd expect that to be the case", Leroy replied.

"What's your take on this, Matthew?"

"My Lord, if there are any ships lying around up there at Deimos, then the Ptolemy's HLTs could well be flying in with an armed escort. Something that we were not planning for."

"Yes, but it does seem highly unlikely, doesn't it?"

"Highly unlikely, my Lord, yes, but still a possibility", Matthew replied.

"It's irrelevant anyway", the Prophet finally decided, "The attack will go ahead as planned."

"And if there are more ships up at Deimos, my Lord", Leroy asked.

"Then perhaps we'll lose a few pirates, Leroy. Nothing to worry about really, is it?", the Prophet replied with a wry smile.

Matthew had climbed to the highest point above New Tortuga. It had been a gentle climb, as a narrow track had long ago been carved into the cliff face to facilitate access to the cliff tops high above New Tortuga. It wasn't a perfect track, but it did make the task much easier.

From here Matthew could look down upon the large sea that now flooded Hebes Chasma. The colony of New Tortuga was not visible from this vantage point. Turning towards the centre of Hebes Island, he found that it was largely a plateau, with many small hills and a couple of east-west mountain ranges scattered here and there. Nothing that could pose a strenuous climb in Mars thirty-eight percent gravity.

Matthew found scanners already mounted at this relatively high point, New Tortuga's early warning system. All he really needed to do was patch his own equipment into this antiquated system. Before he did so, he first made some modifications to the older systems so that they'd be able to handle the extra load.

Quickly Matthew set up his equipment, a small yet powerful automated telescope capable of keeping a close eye on Deimos. He fixed the scope to the ground, then aligned the scope correctly and double-checked its data feeds, before connecting them into the existing communications cables.

Matthew's only concern was that Deimos would not always be in view. There were occasions when Deimos's orbit would take it around the other side of Mars, well below the horizon. During those occasions, they would not be able to watch Deimos at all. That was unavoidable.

It had only taken him a couple of hours to climb the cliffs, install and configure the scope. Now making his way back down the track, he realised how narrow the track truly was. On his way up, he had not noticed. It is hard not to look down when climbing down. That's when he noticed how truly dangerous the track was. By the time he entered New Tortuga once more, his usually well tanned face was almost ashen white.

Matthew felt much better when he'd made his way to New Tortuga's Port Control Centre. It really was just a room with a vantage point near the cavern entrance. He entered the room and nodded to the Port Controller who sat watching the scanners screens. A boring job, nothing much ever happened in here. The only ships that approached New Tortuga were generally all members of their own small community, outsiders were usually shunned.

Only recently had there been any real excitement and that was the arrival of the Hypolita, the largest ship they'd had in their port in many a year. That was then followed by the arrival of the Delilah, a sleek, modern space yacht. On both occasions the Port Controller had been drunk and fast asleep. Suitably punished for his lack of diligence, he was now glued to the monitor and alert.

Matthew set up his screen and patched it into the communications lines. Within a few minutes his screen was showing a perfect image of Deimos. The auto-scope tracked the little moon perfectly as it travelled along its orbit. Clearly the Ptolemy and the Spartan could be seen on the screen.

Matthew pulled up his chair and sat down to keep a close eye on the Ptolemy. When Deimos sank below the horizon, Matthew could sleep, returning to his vigil once more when it rose fifteen hours later.

It could be several Martian days before the Ptolemy sends her HLT's down to Elysium to offload the colonists and their cargo. The Martian day was thirty-nine minutes longer than the system standard twenty-four-hour day and Matthew had not yet adjusted to the difference.

Spaceship lag was a drag.

16. Deimos

Christopher Rolson waited to board the Vanguard. It was one of the smaller ferries, not much room for passengers, far more room for cargo. Christopher's Mother and Father were impatient, the port facilities at Phobos were as busy as always and not the cleanest port facilities around either. In all twelve passengers would be boarding the Vanguard. As per usual procedures, the cargo pods were installed first, forcing the passengers to stand around waiting in the stifling air of the busy spaceport. The cargo pods contained raw iron hauled up from Mars, to be processed at Consolidated Martian Steel, a corporate colony in high Martian orbit.

The Rolson's were going to visit their Son Garth, a young corporate hot shot, relatively high up in the corporation's managerial chain of command. After a long wait, that seemed almost endless to the Rolsons, the airlock was finally opened and the first mate of the Vanguard, a jovial fellow named Carl, beckoned them all in. The twelve passengers entered the mooring bay and quickly boarded the Vanguard, making their way to the passengers' concourse where they made themselves comfortable.

The Captain of the Vanguard, an equally jovial fellow named Sam, clicked into the docking computers command interface. Quickly he highlighted the refuelling subsystem and activated it. Two flexible refuelling tubes extended from the mooring bay's refuelling stations. They made a beeline for the Vanguard's refuelling receptacles. The spaceport's computers already knew the specifications of the Vanguard, her class of ship was common in these parts. Once connected, Sam checked the refuelling details and seeing that they were all correct, gave the go ahead for refuelling. Quickly liquid hydrogen fuel began flowing into the Vanguard's fuel tanks.

A very bored Christopher Rolson looked out of the porthole. Not much was happening out there in the mooring bay. The refuelling tubes were doing their thing as expected. It would be at least thirty minutes, probably longer, before the Vanguard would be ready for launch. Then the young lad noticed something, he wasn't sure what it was, but he was quite certain that it didn't look right.

Something attached to the starboard side refuelling station. Right at the point where the refuelling tube connected. It was hard to see, he'd almost missed it.

"What's that", he thought to himself, as the Vanguard was engulfed in a sudden flash of light.

Forkbraid was sitting comfortably watching the view screen. A landing pad was displayed, upon which an HLT had landed. A team of security personnel had swept this landing pad and its equipment prior to the refuelling, to ensure that everything was safe. One by one the Ptolemy's eight HLTs had landed at this landing pad and been refuelled. The last one, the Ajax, was almost ready to lift off and join its siblings back at the Ptolemy. Everything was going smoothly. Special Agent Murphy entered the landing pad's control room.

"We've just had word from Phobos", Special Agent Murphy informed Forkbraid.

"What's the word, Jim?", Forkbraid enquired.

"They've had a problem with one of their refuelling stations", Special Agent Murphy replied.

"A problem?", Forkbraid cocked an eyebrow.

"Yeah, FB. One of their refuelling stations. The one that would have been used by the Ptolemy's HLTs, has exploded."

"Exploded, Jim?", Forkbraid enquired, but before Special Agent Murphy could answer the question, he continued, "I assume it was booby trapped, yeah?"

"It appears so. One of the local ferries, the Vanguard, was destroyed."

"Loss of life? Casualties?", Forkbraid enquired.

"All hands were lost, FB. Crew of fifteen, along with twelve passengers."

"More crew than passengers?", Forkbraid queried.

"Yeah, apparently the ship was mainly a cargo carrier. It was taking a load of raw iron and a few passengers to a manufacturing colony in high Martian orbit."

"Didn't Roberts do a security sweep of the facilities?", Forkbraid asked.

"Apparently not. The good Lieutenant didn't think he had enough manpower for it."

"Manpower or not, he should still have checked", an astonished Forkbraid replied.

"Yeah, well he didn't. Carmichael has sent some of the Spartan's security personnel over to Phobos to sweep their remaining facilities."

"That's good at least. I hope Robert's has closed the port until the all clear is given."

"He has, but only after Carmichael threatened to have him court marshalled for negligence."

"Don't tell me, Jim. He was worried about his precious bloody schedules."

"You guessed it", Special Agent Murphy replied.

Several hours later Forkbraid and Special Agent Murphy had flown back to the Spartan aboard a hummer. The Ptolemy's HLTs had all been fuelled up for the landing at the Elysium colony, yet Captain Carmichael wanted to delay. They didn't know why. Upon arriving at the Spartan and docking, both men were then led to the Captain's briefing room. They waited there for numerous long minutes before the Captain arrived.

Captain Carmichael strode into the room, Forkbraid and Special Agent Murphy stood up to greet him. After shaking hands and exchanging formalities, they sat down and got down to brass tacks.

"We have a small problem, Gentlemen", Captain Carmichael informed them.

"What would that be, Captain?", Special Agent Murphy enquired.

"When the Ptolemy sends its HLTs down to Elysium, we'll only be able to escort them as far as the Martian stratosphere."

"The Martian stratosphere? That will leave them nearly a hundred kilometres above the surface and still thousands of kilometres from the Elysium colony", Forkbraid noted with concern.

"FB, you're thinking of the Earth's stratosphere. Mars has only thirty-eight percent gravity. Its atmospheric pressure at ground level is over fifteen hundred millibars."

"What are you telling me, Jim?"

"Well, the Martian atmosphere is more, I don't know, buoyant, fluffy and puffed up", Special Agent Murphy struggled for the right words that described the Martian atmosphere.

"Buoyant, fluffy and puffed up?", Forkbraid struggled for understanding.

"Yeah, the Martian stratosphere starts a lot higher up, closer to a hundred and fifty kilometres."

"For crying out loud, Jim, that's, that's much worse", Forkbraid finally understood.

"Yeah, that was the point I was trying to make", Special Agent Murphy agreed.

"Unfortunately gentlemen, our only interceptors are [51]Wisps", the Captain explained.

Forkbraid knew exactly what this meant, "Wisps don't have any heat shielding and their particle beams would be useless in Mars's thick atmosphere."

"Exactly, Forkbraid and their particular EM drives are useless in atmo as well", the Captain confirmed.

"But why do you only have Wisps anyway?", Forkbraid questioned.

Wisp Fleet Interceptor

"It's the same for all Colonial Cruisers", Captain Carmichael replied.

---

51 Wisp. Fleet interceptor. Short range plasma drive and longer range EM drive, armed with two twin particle beams.

"Under the [52]O.S.I Armistice Treaty of twenty-one ninety-two, Colonial Cruisers are not allowed to carry interceptors, nor bombers for that matter, that are capable of atmospheric operations", Special Agent Murphy added in sombre tone.

"Precisely", Captain Carmichael confirmed, adding "It protects the Earth from some forms of attack. All the atmo rated fighters at Cis-Lunar L-Five are short range, they couldn't reach the Earth, unless they were transported there. Wisps are longer range, but only space rated."

"But this is Mars, Captain", Forkbraid pointed out.

"Yes, but the old rules still apply. Our legislators have yet to catch up."

"So your fighters will escort the colonists until they reach the Martian stratosphere and then leave them hanging in the wind?"

"FB, they'll have no choice. Once the friction starts heating up their skin, they have to fall back. Either that or they'll burn up", Special Agent Murphy stressed.

"Can we outfit hummers with weapons?", Forkbraid enquired.

"In short, Forkbraid, no. Trying to put weapons systems on a hummer, would be disastrous", Captain Carmichael countered.

Forkbraid had to agree, the idea was a stupid one. Weapons on a hummer, he almost laughed.

"I still have my [53]Bat Wing Interceptor", he stated, "She has a polyceramalloy hull."

"Yes, you do. Which I might mention is a violation of the O.S.I Armistice Treaty. By rights, your little Bat Wing should not be on my Cruiser", the Captain informed him.

"Ah, but it is, Captain. It is", Forkbraid stressed.

Bat Wing Interceptor

"One Bat Wing is not going to be able to protect eight HLTs FB", Special Agent Murphy pointed out.

Forkbraid closed his eyes and sat in silent contemplation for several minutes. Special Agent Murphy had seen Forkbraid do this before, it was simply how Forkbraid concentrated.

---

52 The O.S.I Armistice Treaty officially ended the Outer Satellites Insurrection. Numerous weapons were banned.

53 Bat Wing Interceptor. Seven lasers, two wing mounted particle beams, two fin mounted pulsed plasma cannons.

54 Polyceramalloy (Poly-Ceramic-Alloy) Stronger than any steel, far more heat-resistant than titanium or ceramics, far more flexible than any plastics.

Captain Carmichael, however, had not, "Is he alright?", he enquired.

"Yeah, sure he's fine, he's just thinking", Special Agent Murphy replied.

Finally after several minutes Forkbraid stood up, reached over to a console and flicked on the view screen. A view of Deimos flashed up immediately. The sprawling naval base was clearly visible.

Forkbraid walked up to the screen and pointed to the base, "Lots of fuel down there", he stated.

"Yeah", the Captain agreed; he was perplexed, *"What are you thinking?"*, he thought.

Then as if Special Agent Murphy had heard his thought, "What are you thinking, FB?"

Forkbraid smiled, he had heard both questions, "What else was left down there?"

Now it was Captain Carmichael's turn for silent contemplation.

It didn't last long, the Captain slapped open a communications channel to the ship's bridge, "Bridge! The Captain here. Get me Lieutenant Hans Blixen."

He flicked the channel closed, "Gentlemen, we'll find out precisely what the Colonial Fleet has left behind on Deimos."

A few minutes later a Lieutenant stepped into the briefing room. Hans Blixen was a gangly looking fellow, quite thin, with long ropy arms. On his left forearm was strapped what was commonly known as an [55]A.I. Grip. "

"Captain", Hans greeted Captain Carmichael.

"Lieutenant. I need you to access the Colonial Fleet data on the Deimos base. I want to know if any ships were left behind when the base was abandoned."

Hans held his left forearm before him, he turned his palm up and flipped open the grip. A small keyboard of sorts lit up and a holographic screen appeared. Hans deftly moved his fingers across the keyboard. Various lists and images appeared in the holographic screen.

"I'll have the information for you in just a moment, Sir", Hans Blixen replied.

After a few more minutes Lieutenant Blixen had the information the Captain required, "I have that data now, Sir. I'll put it on your screen for you."

A pop-up window overlaid the Captain's view screen, lists of data appeared. Hans moved his hands across the keyboard once more and the lists rearranged themselves into groups, categorised by class of vessel.

The lieutenant began to read off the data, "As you can see, Sir,. Quite a few ships were abandoned along with the base. Now this is old data, so I can't vouch for its accuracy, nor can I tell you what condition these craft will be in given the length of time that they were unattended."

---

55 A.I. Grip. A small personal computer, communicator, and analyser that
   "grips" itself around the operator's forearm.

"Yes, we understand that, Lieutenant, but you can give us an indication of what was left?"

"Yes, of course, Captain", the Lieutenant pressed a key and a particular list was highlighted, "At least two dozen Talon Class Interceptors were left down there, Sir. They would be my first concern with regards to the threat."

"Threat?", the Captain hadn't thought of that, these abandoned ships could also be a threat.

"Yes, Sir. If these ships have been, shall we say salvaged, they could constitute a definite threat."

"Those pirate ships we saw fleeing Deimos, Captain. They were Talons", Special Agent Murphy informed him.

"Yes, they were", Captain Carmichael replied, "And now we know where those pirates got a hold of them."

"At least two dozen did you say, Lieutenant?", Forkbraid queried.

"At least two dozen, Sir", the Lieutenant replied, "How many are still functional, I couldn't say."

"Twin pulsed plasma cannons, four particle beams and polyceramalloy coated, solid titanium hull", Forkbraid, ever the connoisseur of all things interceptor, mentioned.

"Yes, and with twin, under wing magneto plasma drives", Special Agent Murphy added.

Captain Carmichael looked at the two men, even he would have a hard time remembering the details of these old-style vintage fighter craft, "Well, Gentlemen. I figure we now know what to expect from our opposition."

Special Agent Murphy and Forkbraid both nodded in reply.

Lieutenant Blixen touched a few more keys and another list was highlighted, "There were fifteen Gull Wing Interceptors down there."

"Single plasma thruster, six particle beams and a solid titanium hull", Forkbraid stated.

Special Agent Murphy nodded, "Add these to our worry list, Captain."

Captain Carmichael nodded then replied, "The Gull Wings are only a problem, gentleman, if someone has replaced their particle beams with high intensity lasers."

"Yes, Captain, but that's not so hard to do if they've got the parts", Special Agent Murphy noted.

"The same goes with the Talons as well. Replace the particle beams with high intensity lasers, and they'd be so much more of a threat. Stock standard, only their pulse cannons would be a problem in atmo", the Captain added to Special Agent Murphy's statement.

Forkbraid looked at the Captain, he was right, if the enemy had replaced the particle beams with high intensity lasers, they'd be so much more of a threat. Particle beams aren't so useful within an atmosphere, as the surrounding air absorbs the beam. High intensity laser weapons, however, were an entirely different matter.

"Any other ships left down there, Lieutenant?", the Captain enquired.

"Yes, Sir", Lieutenant Blixen replied, "Two dozen [56]Switch Blades."

"Well that's definitely not a good thing", Forkbraid replied with signs of deep concern showing on his face.

"No, it's not. Nose and wing mounted twin pulsed plasma cannons set inside a fuselage of polyceramalloy", Special Agent Murphy stated as he lowered his head, rubbing his eyes.

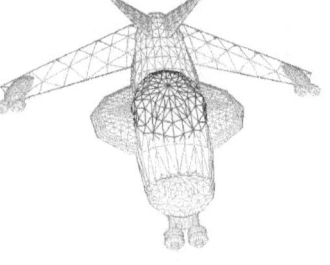

"What idiot left this stuff lying around an abandoned naval base", the Captain asked of no-one in particular.

Switch Blade Interceptor

"Economics, Captain. Cheaper to leave them behind than pack them all up and take them back to L-Five. When the base was abandoned, Deimos was in the middle of nowhere", Forkbraid replied.

"I still find that so hard to believe", the Captain replied.

"Hard to believe or not, Sir, that is what was left behind", Lieutenant Blixen assured him.

"Do you have any other bad news for us, Lieutenant", Captain Carmichael asked.

"No, Sir. All the other ships were transports and freighters. Most of those appear to have been salvaged and are now servicing the colonies in Martian high orbit", Lieutenant Blixen replied.

"Good. Now I want you to search that naval base. I want to know the status of those ships."

"Captain, Sir. The base was abandoned eight decades ago. I doubt that any of those ships are still there. They would have been salvaged long ago", Lieutenant Blixen replied.

"That is precisely what I want you to ascertain, Lieutenant", Captain Carmichael ordered.

"Yes, Sir", Lieutenant Hans Blixen then left the room.

"I got the distinct impression that you weren't simply thinking of threat vectors, Captain?", Special Agent Murphy questioned.

"No, Agent Murphy I wasn't. I was thinking more along the lines of your

---

56 Switch Blade Interceptor. Nose and wing mounted twin pulsed plasma cannons, and a single plasma thruster.

friend here", the Captain indicated Forkbraid.

"Remember, Jim, you said it yourself, one Bat Wing Interceptor isn't enough to protect eight HLTs", Forkbraid reminded him, "Those abandoned ships could come in very handy if they're still to be found, and if they are still functional."

"I can see that, FB, but what are the odds of finding any of them intact?", Jim enquired.

"Long odds, Jim, long odds, but still better than zero ", Forkbraid replied.

"Don't worry, Gentlemen, Lieutenant Blixen is a good man, one of my best. If there are any ships left down there intact, he will find them. And, Gentlemen, when he does, the colonists will have their escort", Captain Carmichael told them both.

Forkbraid nodded, "My Bat Wing Interceptor and whatever else we find at the old base."

Jim laughed, "It'll be a raggedy bunch of old ships, but certainly better than nothing."

Forkbraid and Special Agent Murphy had been waiting for news from the base. Searching the old naval base was taking longer than either of them had liked, even with all the men at their disposal. Lieutenant Blixen knew from the records precisely where to look, but what they had found didn't necessarily match the records.

Eight decades of vandalism had taken its toll on many sections of the base. In several places there had even been bulkhead breaches. The base had been ransacked so many times over the decades and much of what had been abandoned had been stolen, what hadn't been stolen had shifted around. Much of the base was in complete shambles.

Special Agent Murphy checked his communicator. Lieutenant Blixen had found the Gull Wing Interceptors. There were twelve in all, but they were of no use and of little value. All that had been found were their empty hulls, their parts having been scavenged long ago for other purposes. Three of them were also unaccounted for. It was another three hours before Jim received the next message.

The Talons were not where they had been left. Lieutenant Blixen had checked and found no trace of them at all, at their assigned storage hangar. Instead, he found them in another section of the base, on the opposite side. Lieutenant Blixen had correctly guessed that he'd find them close to the section from which the pirates had fled.

Of the two dozen Talons left behind, only three were found. These had been scavenged for parts. They were more than empty shells, but they would never fly again without weeks of work and a good supply of spare parts. Most alarmingly, in a corner of the hangar where they had been found, was a pile of old parts. Particle beam assemblies to be precise. It appeared that the surviving Talons had been modified. Their tail fin particle beams were now something else, probably high intensity lasers. Special Agent Murphy let out an audible sigh when he read this.

One of the missing Gull Wings had been found in the same hangar. It was inoperable, partially rebuilt, but it would take a lot more work to complete. Forkbraid claimed dibs on it; vintage interceptors were his hobby. Forkbraid had requested that the Gull Wing be taken to the Ptolemy for transport back to Earth, or perhaps Mars, wherever he ended up next.

It wasn't until the next day that Lieutenant Blixen found the Switch Blades. This surprised him immensely. They were precisely where they had been left, but it was easy to see why they had not been stolen. This section of the base had been heavily damaged. A series of explosions of some sort had occurred in the main access tunnels leading to the hangar.

The entire section was de-pressurised. Twisted metal and collapsed beams from the explosions made accessing this section of the base both difficult and dangerous. Apart from the main explosions in the tunnels, smaller explosions had occurred along the fuel tubing and power conduits. Whole sections had collapsed. There was no easy, nor safe way to access the hangar.

Finally, Lieutenant Blixen decided that to access the hangar they would have to excavate down to its roof and break through. This took the rest of the day and when they finally reached the hangar, they found it was also in total disarray. Its roof had collapsed in many places.

Many of the Switch Blades were severely damaged and beyond repair. Those Switch Blades that were not damaged beyond repair, still required repairs, however, the spare parts that were simply not available.

By the following morning, Lieutenant Blixen had retrieved only eight functional interceptors, all Switch Blades. One for each of the Ptolemy's HLTs. The rest were of little value. Captain Carmichael nether the less had them transferred to the Ptolemy for transport back to Earth, along with all the remaining interceptor hulks.

"Well, Gentlemen", the Captain began, "We know they have six Talons, possibly as many as twenty-one. They may have a couple of Gulls as well. We also know the Talons have been retrofitted with lasers. That much we can glean from the old base, but there are still a lot of unknowns."

"Knowing where they are would be useful", Special Agent Murphy mentioned.

"Well, Agent Murphy, we do have the trajectories of those pirate ships", the Captain replied as he called up a display of the trajectories onto the screen.

The video screen now displayed a map of Mars over which the trajectories of the six pirate ships were shown. These trajectories stopped at the point where the ships dropped below the cloud layers.

"Captain, the course those pirates took, once they breached the cloud layer could be completely different from their original trajectories", Special Agent Murphy stated.

"Exactly, Agent Murphy, but look at those trajectories", Captain Carmichael insisted.

Forkbraid had caught on, "They were trying to emulate random approach patterns, weren't they?", he asked rhetorically, before exclaiming, "What idiots!"

"Precisely, Forkbraid. And you know what happens when people try to emulate randomness?"

"They fail abysmally. They actually create patterns", Special Agent Murphy had just caught on.

"Exactly, Gentlemen", the Captain confirmed.

"Looking at these trajectories, we can not only see that our pirate friends were acting in concert, but all aiming for the same general region. They all dropped under the cloud layer around the perimeter of a vast region of Mars", Captain Carmichael explained.

The Captain was right, all trajectories formed a boundary around a vast Martian land region.

"The Tharsis Bulge and Valles Marineris regions", Forkbraid replied.

"That would be my bet, Gentlemen. Our target is hidden somewhere in that vast region. A rugged region of towering volcanoes, sinkholes and lava tubes, mountains, high plateaus and broken escarpments. Then further to the east you have deep, flooded valleys and untold thousands of islands right up to the Argyre River. All of it isolated and virtually unexplored", the Captain explained.

"Argyre River?", Special Agent Murphy queried.

"Yeah. It's a major river that drains the Argyre Sea basin. It flows north from the Argyre Sea to the inland sea at Aurorae Chaos", Captain Carmichael replied.

Forkbraid looked carefully at the map, "You do know, Captain, that you're talking about a region of nine or ten million square miles. It's a region as big if not bigger than North America."

"It may be a big area, Forkbraid, but it does reduce our original search zone somewhat", the Captain countered, "To about one quarter of what it was before, if my calculations are correct."

"That is an improvement, FB", Special Agent Murphy added.

Forkbraid considered the map before them, "It's an improvement, Jim, that's for sure, but I think we can improve on it a bit further."

"Forkbraid is right, Agent Murphy, we can improve on it further", the Captain tossed in, "Looking at their approach vectors, I'd say that those idiots aimed for the centre."

"The Valles Marineris region", Forkbraid agreed.

"Still we can't discount the rest of the region. They may have played a bit of misdirection", the Captain replied.

"Assuming they're smart enough, Captain", Forkbraid replied adding, "I have a good feeling about this. It's a good starting point."

"The downside, Gentlemen, is this region has to be one of the most isolated and rugged regions on Mars", Captain Carmichael informed them, not wanting them to get overconfident.

"We can see that, Captain", Special Agent Murphy replied, adding, "there must be ten thousand places to hide in that area."

"Easily, double that and then some", the Captain replied.

Forkbraid looked at the Captain more closely, "Tell us the other problem, Captain."

Captain Carmichael looked back at Forkbraid, *"He always seems to know"*, he thought to himself.

"How many colonists do you think live on Mars, Gentlemen?", Captain Carmichael asked.

"Officially there are about fifteen thousand in seven colonies", Special Agent Murphy replied

Forkbraid added, "There are probably another ten thousand more unofficially down there."

"That's the problem, Gentlemen", the Captain replied, noting, "You think that there are only twenty-five thousand people down there. Trust me, the true figure is easily three times that and probably even higher still."

"That's a little hard to believe, Captain. Mars has only been opened up for colonisation for less than twenty years now", Special Agent Murphy replied.

"Gentlemen, back when the first phase of the terraforming began, people kept well clear of the place. Operation ice drop, with all those thousands of chunks of ice dropping out of the sky, was really dangerous. But after that operation finished and the oceans and atmosphere stabilised, things changed. Colonists have been landing on the planet and setting up little unofficial colonies down there for a hundred years, and probably even longer", Captain Carmichael explained.

Forkbraid considered this, "And don't tell me, Captain. Those colonies are scattered throughout the more isolated equatorial regions of Mars. Coastal regions with lots of valleys and islands."

"Exactly my point", the Captain confirmed, "Just because we find a colony down there that's not on any map, doesn't mean we've found the one they're hiding at."

Finally, Special Agent Murphy spoke, "There could be dozens, scores of unofficial colonies down there."

Captain Carmichael nodded in agreement, "Proverbial needle in a haystack."

"Captain. You said people have been colonising Mars for a hundred years or more."

"That's right, Forkbraid. I'd say for at least that long, perhaps longer", the Captain replied.

"So, that's what, three, four generations?", Forkbraid inquired.

"I'd say so, three or four generations, maybe more", the Captain agreed.

Special Agent Murphy could tell by the look on Forkbraid's face that another unforeseen problem had arisen, "What is it, FB?", he asked.

"Lady Selene has come to Mars to set up a colony of psychics, Jim", Forkbraid began, "But people have been down there far longer than we'd thought. Perhaps four or more generations."

"I don't get it, FB? How can that be a problem?", Special Agent Murphy asked.

"That's more than enough time to adapt, Jim. There may be psychics down there already."

"Isn't that a good thing?", Captain Carmichael asked.

"It's a double-edged sword, people. It will be far harder to scan for Miranda if there are other psychics down there", Forkbraid explained.

"But why, FB? Surely they can help", Special Agent Murphy suggested.

"It doesn't work that way, Jim. They'll all be untrained. At best, they'll cause psychic interference that we'll need to filter out."

"You said at best, Forkbraid", a concerned Captain enquired.

"Yes. At best. Remember three or four generations, maybe even longer. These will be native Martian psychics. They may not agree with what Selene and the Flinders Psychic Academy Grey Council are trying to achieve."

"So they could actually work against us?", Special Agent Murphy questioned, "They could deliberately interfere?"

"Exactly, Jim", Forkbraid replied, "And we won't know what to expect until we meet them."

"If they exist, Gentlemen. If they exist", Captain Carmichael stressed.

"If", Forkbraid paused, "If they exist."

Catherine Swann was anxious, neither she nor her Husband, Peter, had been to Mars before, nor to any other planet for that matter, not even Earth. They were true spacers. Now they waited for a hummer to be fuelled and prepared, specifically to take them down to the planet Mars. Ordinarily a hummer, even a long range one, would not have the necessary range to reach Mars from Deimos. Special Agent Murphy was supervising the installation of an expendable external fuel tank to make the trip possible.

"What will it be like down there?", Catherine asked Forkbraid.

"Well, I can't really say that myself. I've never been there either", Forkbraid replied.

"Yes, but you've been on Earth, Forkbraid. Mars is just another planet after all."

"Mars won't be much like Earth I'm afraid. You're used to one standard gravity and so am I. Martian gravity is much weaker, only thirty-eight percent of standard. You'll need to be mindful of your walking and any movement in general, at least until you get used to it", Forkbraid informed her.

Catherine nodded and Peter, who had also been listening said to his Son Chiron, "You hear that Chiron. You'll need to be careful. No running around until you're used to the gravity down there."

"Then there's the air. On Earth the air is one thousand millibars. That's the standard for all colony habitats as well, I believe. Down there on Mars, the air is much thicker, currently more than fifteen hundred millibars", Forkbraid continued.

"So the air will be thicker?", Peter enquired.

"Definitely thicker", Forkbraid replied, "And I have no idea what it will smell like."

"What do you mean smell like?", asked Catherine.

"On Earth, the air smells different depending on where you are. Cities smell different to the country for instance and even different to each other. I've been told that the colonies have their air so heavily processed and regulated, that they all tend to smell the same."

"Not always", Peter replied, "The smaller colonies like Hyper Dynamics Corporation, sure, they all use the same processing techniques, but the really big colonies have their own smells. I noticed that the last time I went to Colonial Central Command on business."

"I noticed that as well", Forkbraid agreed, "When it comes to smell, Colonial Central Command is probably the closest analogue you have to a planet. Still, I can't guarantee how Mars will smell. It could be unique. I really don't know."

"So we can expect lower gravity, thicker air and funny smells", Catherine summed up.

"Well, yes, but then there is also the weather", Forkbraid told them.

"The weather?", Catherine enquired with a more confused look on her face.

"The weather in the colonies is pre-programmed and controlled. You only have the more natural weather on the largest colonies like Colonial Central Command, and even then only in its main cylindrical habitat", Forkbraid replied.

"That's right, honey, Colonial Central Command's our best analogue for weather as well", Peter Swann told his Wife.

"On Mars, as with Earth, you'll experience natural seasons", Forkbraid explained, "Wind, rain, snow, they'll all follow the natural cycles, driven by the Sun and Mars's axial tilt."

"Natural cycles?", Catherine enquired.

"Summer and winter at opposite times of the year, with spring and august in between. You have to remember, as well, that the Martian year is six hundred and eighty-seven days long."

"Yeah, I know that, Forkbraid, but it still snows in winter, and we'll still have hot balmy days in summer won't we?", Catherine asked.

"In the higher latitudes, yes, of course, but towards the equator, snow might be a rarity."

"So the weather changes depending on how close you are to the equator, as well?", an even more confused Catherine Swann asked.

"Pretty much. Rain will vary somewhat as well. In some areas, there will be too little rain and in other areas, far too much. Elysium has what's commonly called a Mediterranean climate, at least that's what I have been told."

"Is that a good thing?", Peter enquired.

"I believe so. On Earth, people enjoy living in regions that have a Mediterranean type of climate", Forkbraid informed them.

"This is all going to be so overwhelming!", Catherine exclaimed.

"No, no honey, you'll be just fine", Peter assured her.

"Yes. I'm sure that you'll find the weather's spontaneity and lack of predictability refreshing", Forkbraid stated reassuringly, "It'll be new, different, interesting, and exciting. Think of it that way."

"Is there anything else that we need to know?", Catherine finally asked.

"Well, there is day and night", Forkbraid mentioned.

"Don't tell me, natural cycles?", Catherine responded questioningly but knowing the answer.

"Day and night on Mars will follow twenty-four-hour thirty-nine-minute cycles", he replied.

"See, that's not so bad, honey. It's almost the same as the standard day, just a little bit longer. You always say that there aren't enough hours in the day.", Peter again reassured her.

"Oh. I nearly forgot to mention. On Mars, life will be different as well", Forkbraid stated.

"Well, thank you, Forkbraid, but I think we're getting that already", Catherine assured him.

"That's not what I meant. On Earth, we have farms and gardens like you're used to, but we also have fields, forests, jungles, swamps, and deserts. Living environments where life is free and unregulated by humans. Places where life does its own thing; goes wild so to speak. The closest analogue you have to it in

L-Five would be the forests on Colonial Central Command, but they are really tame in comparison. Then again, Mars will be more similar to Earth but not the same. Because Mars is all newly terraformed, it's difficult to tell you what to expect, but I will say this, it should be both interesting and exciting", Forkbraid informed them.

"Interesting and exciting! You've said that a couple of times already, Forkbraid. This, interesting and exciting, is going to take a lot of getting used to", Catherine told them both.

"That it will, my darling, and I'm going to be with you every step along the way", Peter reassured his Wife, Catherine.

Just then Special Agent Murphy stepped into the room, "The hummer is all ready, we'll be leaving shortly."

"Good work, Jim", Forkbraid replied, "The Swanns are a little anxious, so I'd like you to stay close by them for a few days. At least until they get acquainted with some of our people in Elysium."

"FB", Special Agent Murphy said to him softly, "Did I forget to mention to you, that I was more than a little anxious myself. I have never been planetside either."

Forkbraid smiled at him, slapped him on the shoulder, "Stop being a woos, Jim, you'll be fine."

With that, Special Agent Murphy led the Swann family into the hummer. Once they were all strapped in, the Special Agent launched his hummer and plotted its course for the Elysium colony. It was only a little over four hours away.

17. Landings

Captain Carmichael and Forkbraid were together in the Captain's briefing room hatching their plans for landing the colonists at Elysium.

"I have some concerns, Captain. When the Ptolemy's HLTs reach the Martian atmosphere, they won't have a lot of protection. My Bat Wing and eight Switch Blades aren't going to be nearly enough", Forkbraid told him.

"There isn't a lot we can do about that, Forkbraid", the Captain replied.

"You could have a dozen of your Wisps shadow us from space", Forkbraid suggested.

"You know as well as I do, my Wisps are useless in atmo", Captain Carmichael replied.

"They'll be above the atmosphere, Captain, shadowing us from space. It might make the enemy think twice", Forkbraid explained.

"A show of force is all it will be", the Captain replied, "Even their particle beams won't be much good to you, Forkbraid."

"Yes, but, Captain, we have all those damaged Switch Blades. Can we salvage their pulsed plasma cannons and retrofit the Wisps with those?"

"Forkbraid, that's a bloody good idea. Sure, my men can do that", the Captain replied adding,

"My Wisps may only be able to shadow you from space, but they'll be able to rain hell down on your attackers from above."

"That was exactly my thought, Captain", Forkbraid replied, "We'd have to maintain a high altitude path to stay close enough for it to be effective though."

"Not necessarily. My men can dip their Wisps in and out of atmo. As long as they don't go too deep they shouldn't burn up", the Captain replied, "it will be dangerous, but it is possible."

"I'm also concerned about the Hypolita, Captain", Forkbraid stated.

"Yeah, that one is a wild card", the Captain replied.

"My worry is that they might try to pass the Hypolita off as one of our HLTs."

"I've already thought of that, Forkbraid. Under no circumstances are any of the HLTs to approach the Spartan. If any of them do, I'll be shooting first and asking questions later. No apologies."

"Understandable, Captain", Forkbraid replied.

"The same goes for the Ptolemy. None of the HLTs are to return to the Ptolemy once they've departed, until I personally give them the all clear."

"That leaves the Elysium colony, Captain", Forkbraid replied.

"I'll be shadowing your path from space in the Spartan as well Forkbraid. If I can pick out the Hypolita. If I decide she's a threat, I'll have her taken out."

"That sounds too dangerous, Captain. You might accidentally shoot down one of our own HLTs."

"I have thought of that possibility, Forkbraid. It is a calculated risk."

"It's not an acceptable risk, Captain. Lady Selene will be on the Achilles. The thought of you accidentally shooting down her ship is not pleasant."

"Do you have any alternatives?", the Captain enquired.

"As a matter of fact, Captain, I do", Forkbraid replied.

"We all believe the enemy is hiding out in the Tharsis or Valles Marineris regions. If we launch the Ptolemy's HLTs from orbit on the other side of Mars, they won't see them coming until the very last moment", Forkbraid explained.

"That will force them to scramble into action", Captain Carmichael agreed, adding "It won't give them a whole lot of time."

"Precisely. It will catch them off guard and hopefully give us an advantage."

"I don't see how this will help with our Hypolita problem, Forkbraid."

"I'm getting to that bit now, Captain", Forkbraid assured him.

Forkbraid explained the rest of his plan to Captain Carmichael. It was a simple plan, it involved subterfuge and dwarves. He explained that he had already informed Special Agent Murphy of the plan before he had flown the Swann family to the Elysium colony. He had also transmitted the plan to Lady Selene telepathically on the Ptolemy.

Lady Selene would inform the Captains of the eight HLTs of their plan during their flight to Elysium. It would all be done at the last minute, so no-one would know about it, least of all the Prophet, his henchmen and his pirates. Captain Carmichael considered Forkbraid's plan. It was novel, it was different, it would catch their enemy off guard. He agreed to the plan and gave it the thumbs up.

Special Agent Murphy had flown his modified hummer on the most direct route to the Elysium colony, breaching the atmosphere high above Arabia Terra. He flipped the switch that dropped the expendable external fuel tanks as they approached the Isidis Gulf. The external fuel tanks tumbled out of the Martian sky into the waters of the Gulf.

Soon they passed over the Isidis Gulf and approached the shallow Elysium channel. The many thousands of islands of the Elysium channel were an incredible sight. Once over the channel Special Agent Murphy adjusted course slightly and flew his hummer towards the Elysium subcontinent.

A large circular basin was before them. Previously it had been an impact crater simply named Eddie, now it was a flooded basin along the coast of the Elysium subcontinent. A large artificial canal cut into the south wall of the crater connected Lake Eddie to the Elysium channel, turning the lake into a rather large bay, destined to become a major seaport. The Elysium colony lay slightly to the north of Eddie Bay, further inland.

Clearly visible now, the Elysium colony complex was below them. Most of the complex was underground, with many of its buildings poking up through the Martian regolith. It was a large sprawling complex, much like the other colonies on Mars. Fields close to the colony were being prepared for crops. These were being tended by android workers, older Hyper Dynamics model two-seven fives. Much of the drudge work in the official Martian colonies was performed by androids. Instead of landing at the Elysium colony, Special Agent Murphy adjusted course and headed further to the north.

Surrounding the Elysium colony to the north was a vast expanse of undulating hills covered in well grassed meadows. Large, young forests of conifers were clearly visible to the north and east on the higher ground towards the Elysium Mons and Albor Tholus. A few of the trees in these forests grew tall, to well over three hundred feet, and they were expected to grow even taller, due to the much lower Martian gravity.

The higher altitudes of the peaks were covered with deep snow and relatively young glaciers. The Swann family stared in awe at the terrain surrounding them. Herds of grazing herbivores, mainly sheep, goats, and smaller deer species, were clearly seen in the pastures north of the colony. There were even small herds of cattle, but they were much closer to the Elysium colony itself.

Sitting atop of a large rise towards the edge of the Elysium Plateau, a mere three hundred kilometres to the north of the Elysium colony was their destination. The large stone construction grew larger and larger as they approached it. It appeared to be fashioned in a very similar style to the Flinders Psychic Academy back on Earth.

A large castle-like structure with eight massive outer turrets and stout stone walls. A deep, wide moat surrounded the outer walls. The inner keep with its eight tall turrets and stout stone walls was capped with a beautifully built dome. This onion dome was far more elaborate and ornate than the dome atop the keep at Flinders Psychic Academy on Earth and none of the hummers passengers could have known this.

The lower Martian gravity allowed its unique and unusual construction. The inner keep was surrounded by a somewhat smaller moat. The hummer approached a large tarmacked landing zone set up two kilometres southeast of the castle.

"Welcome to the New Flinders Psychic Academy", Special Agent Murphy stated simply as he hovered the hummer above the tarmac before landing.

As their hummer landed, Catherine Swann asked Special Agent Murphy, "What kind of animals were they? The ones grazing in those fields?"

"I'm not sure myself. If I had to guess, I'd say they were goats, sheep, and cattle", he replied.

"Goats and sheep make sense, but cattle?", Catherine questioned.

Special Agent Murphy replied, "I think so. We don't have them in L-Five, they're far too big and unproductive, but I have seen videos of cattle on Earth, and they did look similar."

After they had all unstrapped from their seats, Special Agent Murphy asked the Swann family to follow him outside. Once on the tarmac, they all took a deep breath of the Martian air. It was different, definitely thicker, laden with moisture and somewhat cooler than they'd expected. As they breathed out small clouds of water vapour condensed from their breath.

"It must be the depths of winter", Catherine remarked.

"No. I believe it's nearly the beginning of spring", Special Agent Murphy replied pointing to the grass in the meadows and the distinct greenness that was visibly present.

"It smells similar to the air on Colonial Central Command, just thicker", Peter remarked.

"Similar but not the same", Special Agent Murphy replied, "It smells less processed, more like the air on Earth I guess but then again, probably not the same. Very clean and very crisp."

"Well, whatever the smell, it's not unpleasant, but it is definitely crisp", Catherine added.

"Here comes our ride now", Special Agent Murphy stated as a six wheeled vehicle approached from the castle to the northwest.

Catherine Swann took a few steps towards the approaching vehicle and stumbled in the lower Martian gravity. Quickly her Husband, Peter, stepped forward to catch her.

"Careful, darling, lower gravity remember", Peter reminded his Wife.

"Yes, yes, I know. I'm just not used to it yet", Catherine replied.

Little Chiron chuckled to himself as he skipped forward to meet the approaching vehicle.

"Careful, Chiron", his Father shouted after him.

A man stepped out of the vehicle, flanked by three androids. He was tall, very tall, just a shade under seven feet. His heavily muscled frame and ebony skin clearly visible under his thin layer of clothing. Prominent cheeks stood out below his dark piercing eyes.

"Hello, I am Varakhan Utana", the tall man stated, then continuing with a questioning look, "I was expecting a far larger vessel than this one, eight in fact."

"Well hello, Varakhan, I'm Special Agent James Murphy from L-Five, Colonial Central Command", Jim introduced everyone, "These are the Swanns, Catherine, Peter, and Chiron."

Chiron quickly asked, "Aren't you cold, Mr Utana?"

"Yes, little man, but it is cosy and warm inside my [57]chariot."

"My names, Chiron and I'm big, not little", Chiron replied.

Varakhan smiled, "I am so sorry, Chiron. Please call me Varak. Now where are my colonists?"

"There has been a change of plans, Varak", Special Agent Murphy explained, "They'll be landing soon enough, but via a slightly different route."

"Ah, and the reason for this, is all this turmoil we are hearing about at Cis-Lunar L-Five?", Varak replied

"Yes, precisely, Varak. I'll give you the details when we're safely inside the Academy."

"Good then. Now we best be getting into my chariot. Spring has only just begun here in the Elysium subcontinent and as you can see, it is still quite cold", Varak informed them.

They all quickly climbed into Varak's chariot. Once the gull wing doors were closed, the chariot's heating system quickly began warming them up. One of the three androids had loaded their baggage into the back of the chariot. Varak instructed another of the three androids to drive them back to the Psychic Academy. The remaining android had walked over to their hummer and climbed inside. Their hummer was now being taxied over to a hangar in the distance.

"How will he get back to the Psychic Academy?", asked Chiron.

"He'll run back after he's parked your hummer", Varak replied.

"I don't get it, Mr Utana. I thought we were going to the Elysium colony?", Catherine queried.

"Call me, Varak, Mrs Swann", Varak replied adding, "Technically the New Flinders Psychic Academy is a part of the Elysium colony."

"Then why is it so far away from the colony complex?", Peter enquired.

"Psychic Academies are never built close to major cities and the Elysium complex will become a major city one day", Varak replied, "That's why the Academy was built above the escarpment on this plateau."

"But wasn't the Elysium colony built for psychics?", asked Catherine.

"This part of it was", replied Varak, "The rest of the complex on the coast is for the [58]mundanes."

"Mundanes?", queried Peter.

"You know, the ordinary folk, like us", Varak replied.

"We can expect a lot more colonists to arrive in the next few years", Jim commented.

"The main complex down on the coast is still some years from completion, so

---

57 Chariot. Standard Mars personal transport. Six wheeled all terrain vehicle with the capacity to seat ten.

58 Mundane. Ordinary folk who lack psychic ability as opposed to "supramundane" or psychic.

our colonists here in the Academy will have plenty of time to settle in before the mundanes arrive", Varak explained.

"If the colony is still years from completion, what were all those crop fields being prepared for?", asked Catherine.

"They are all being prepared well in advance", Varak replied, "All the irrigation systems and pumping stations for the farms. They are sowing crops well before the colonists arrive to ensure our grain silos are all full. By the time the mundanes arrive, there will be seasons of good harvests in storage. It is the same with the cattle herds, the sheep, and the goat flocks. The managers are building them all up in readiness. When the mundanes arrive, our primary industries will be in full production. Our food supplies will be plentiful."

"I assume the colonists on the Ptolemy will be taking advantage of those very same stores as well", asked Special Agent Murphy.

"Yes, of course, they will", Varak replied, "When they land here they will have brought with them enough supplies for two [59]Sols. After those supplies have been used up, we will be drawing upon the stores from the main colony on the coast, and they are being planted in the next weeks."

Chiron looked to his right, there was a clear view to the snow covered peaks of the Elysium Mons. He turned around to look out the back of the chariot. Past his left shoulder was a clear view to Albor Tholus, equally covered in snow.

Chiron turned back around, "How high are those mountains?"

"Very high, Chiron, very high. They almost reach into space", Varak replied.

"Almost into space?", he enquired further

"Yes, almost into space, Chiron", Varak replied, "The Elysium Mons are perhaps forty thousand feet or more high."

"That's really high", Chiron exclaimed.

"No, young Chiron. These volcanoes are only small ones. The ones on the Tharsis Bulge are much, much higher and Olympus Mons reaches above seventy thousand feet. Its caldera is in air so thin, it may as well be in space", Varak informed Chiron.

"Are any of these volcanoes actually active, Varak?", asked Catherine.

"Our scientists think that the three large ones on the Tharsis Bulge and Olympus Mons are still active, but the ones here on Elysium plateau are definitely extinct. Although, I monitor them for seismic activity nonetheless", Varak replied.

"Well, that is good to know", Catherine replied with a slight sigh of relief.

The Psychic Academy's southeast turret was now very close. They watched as the draw bridge lowered and the portcullis raised. Within a few short minutes the

---

59 Sol. One Martian year, approximately 687 days long.

chariot had passed through the entrance archway and into the New Flinders Psychic Academy.

Special Agent Murphy sent a single message to the Spartan, "The Swanns are in our nest."

Forkbraid sat snugly in his Bat Wing Interceptor. Behind his odd looking craft were eight Switch Blades and twice as many modified Wisps. They all flew in a formation orbit around the Ptolemy. One by one the Ptolemy's eight [60]HLTs detached and took up appropriate parking orbits. Forkbraid dispatched one Switch Blade and two Wisps to each HLT, as they prepared for their flight to the Elysium colony.

Forkbraid had chosen to plot the fastest, most direct route. He made one final check of his vessel. A last minute change had been made, his vessels wing mounted particle beams had been replaced by pulsed plasma cannons. The weapons console lit up with green lights on all systems. Forkbraid ordered the Wisp pilots to check their weapons systems as well. They had undergone similar modifications. Each Wisp pilot replied that all weapons systems were good to go.

Then when all the HLTs were ready, at the appointed moment, with Forkbraid's Bat Wing leading the way, the landing convoy began its flight. Forkbraid glanced above them, the Spartan was already on the move. The Spartan didn't shadow the convoy as Captain Carmichael had suggested. Instead, the Spartan sped ahead of the convoy to take station above Elysium ahead of them. Forkbraid gave his braided goatee a tug for good luck.

Deimos was behind Mars when the convoy had launched. By the time it had become visible to Matthew's scanners, the convoy was close to breaching atmo.

"Shit!", Matthew exclaimed as he switched on the warning klaxon, "I knew they'd do that."

The siren wailed and the Prophet's private navy of pirates scrambled for their craft. Swift, sleek Talons, capable of doing enormous damage. Their captured HLT, the Hypolita was already starting to lift off and hover above its launching pad. Soon all required ships would be in flight.

"Matthew", the Prophet's voice was heard on the communicator.

"Yes, my Lord", Matthew replied hurriedly.

"How much time do we have", the Prophet enquired.

"Not much, my Lord. A little over thirty minutes to set up an intercept", Matthew replied.

"Weren't we expecting more time than that?", the Prophet demanded.

"We were, my Lord. They launched while Deimos was below the horizon. They've just been picked up by our scanners now."

---

60 Heavy Lift Transport equipped with antigravity lifters and photon thrusters with a range of 400,000 kilometres.

"Can we catch them in time?", the Prophet asked.

"Yes, my Lord", Matthew replied, "I'm just plotting their course now. If they stay on their current trajectory, they'll pass by us to the north. We can intercept them just after they breach atmo above Arabia Terra."

"Good Matthew. Make sure we catch them", the Prophet finished.

"Mort Kendal", Matthew called into his communicator, "I've plotted their course, and I'm transmitting it to you now. You'll be intercepting them above Arabia Terra."

"Thanks, Lad, got that", Mort Kendal replied.

"And, Mort, they have an escort. Three fighters per HLT", Matthew informed him.

"What kind?", Mort enquired.

"They're too small to say. My equipment doesn't have the resolution", Matthew replied.

"Small eh. Wisps", Mort Kendal replied, "They're no never mind to us, they're not atmo rated. No threat to us at all."

"Keep a watch-out for them anyway", Matthew finished.

The convoy breached atmo above Arabia Terra as planned. The Wisps having stayed aloft in space and shadowing the convoy from above. Only Forkbraid in his Bat Wing Interceptor and the eight Switch Blades followed the eight HLTs into the thick Martian atmosphere.

They stayed on their original course for several minutes, then Forkbraid gave the order, "Alter course on my mark", he paused "Mark."

As one, the convoy changed course to the northeast and began making their way to the Arabia Terra coast.

"Mayday! Mayday!", a call came across the coded communicator channel.

Forkbraid checked his scanners. The HLT Agamemnon had failed to change course.

Forkbraid quickly responded, "Agamemnon, this is Convoy Leader, I acknowledge your mayday. What is the problem?"

"Convoy Leader, our port rear and central [61]AGLs have shut down. We are unable to change course! Repeat. We are unable to change course!"

"Can the AGLs be rebooted?", Forkbraid enquired.

"No, Sir. The AGLs' power conduits on the port side appear to have burned out", the Captain of the Agamemnon replied.

"Agamemnon, reroute power from your other systems", Forkbraid suggested.

"No can do, Sir. The AGLs are all on isolated circuits. We'll need repairs on the ground to correct the issue", the Captain explained.

"Agamemnon it is imperative that you alter course. Can you alter course?", Forkbraid enquired.

---

61 Antigravity Lifters. Devices used to nullify gravity and allow vessels to fly.

"Convoy Leader, we are doing all we can just to stay aloft", the Captain replied.

"*Shit! Shit!*", Forkbraid thought to himself, "Agamemnon, can you make it to Elysium?"

"We're flying on a wing and a prayer, Sir, but I think we can make it", the Captain replied.

"Agamemnon, continue on your current course to Elysium. I'll leave the Switch Blades to cover you", Forkbraid replied.

"Thank you, Convoy Leader. We'll touch down as close to the colony as we can, Sir.", the Captain of the Agamemnon replied.

Forkbraid then flicked to another coded channel and gave the order, "All Switch Blades to protect the Agamemnon, repeat, all Switch Blades to protect the Agamemnon."

Quickly the eight Switch Blades left their charges and altered course to escort and protect the Agamemnon.

Forkbraid switched back to the HLT's communications channel.

"HLTs, HLTs, this is Convoy Leader. The Agamemnon has suffered a major malfunction and can not change course with us. We will, however, continue as planned. Increase altitude to seventy thousand feet and stay within range of our Wisp's cover fire", Forkbraid ordered.

As the gap between the convoy and the Agamemnon grew wider Forkbraid sent the Captain of the Agamemnon one final message, "Good luck, Agamemnon! May the Gods be with you!"

Mort Kendal, alias Captain Scar, led his twelve Talons on an intercept course for the convoy of HLTs from the [62]IPL Ptolemy. They rapidly approached their target location.

"Any sign of them?", Captain Scar asked of his fellow pirates.

"Nothing on our scanners yet, Captain", the other eleven pilots replied.

Then just a few minutes later Mort looked down at his own scanners, and a blip had appeared.

He increased the resolution and focused in, "Men we have an HLT dead ahead of us."

A few minutes later they had closed the gap significantly. Mort checked his scanners again and noticed the escorting fighters, "*Now that was unexpected*", he thought to himself.

"Caution, Lads", Mort Kendal transmitted to his comrades, "The HLTs are being escorted by Switch Blades."

Mort pinged the HLT ahead of them, his scanner lit up the words

---

62 Interplanetary Liner. Large vehicle equipped with photon thrusters designed to travel from one planet to another.

Agamemnon.

"*Where are the rest of them?*", Mort Kendal thought to himself.

The twelve Talons swooped in upon the stricken Agamemnon. Quickly the escorting Switch Blades took up positions to block their approach. The Talons opened up, their high intensity lasers and pulsed plasma cannons flared into action. Switch Blade pulsed plasma cannons responded with rapid fire pulses of super heated plasma.

The whole battle scene quickly developed into an uncoordinated dog fight with fighters on both sides flitting in and out of the zone around the Agamemnon. Laser and pulsed plasma fire lit up the sky with blue streaks of coherent light and fast tracking radiant, blue balls of plasma. There were midair explosions of fighter craft resembling eerie fireworks.

Eventually the Agamemnon was struck, a high intensity laser beam cutting deeply into its port hull. The Agamemnon continued on, smoke streaming from its fuselage. Again and again the Agamemnon was struck, this time on the starboard side and also across the bow.

The Agamemnon began to flounder as one by one her systems began to fail. Again and again she was struck, high intensity lasers cutting deeply into her hull, pulsed plasma cannons pummelling her at will. Then in one almighty burst of light the Agamemnon was no more. Debris rained down upon the mountainous region of Arabia Terra. There could be no survivors, it was total devastation.

Upon the demise of the Agamemnon, the remaining four Switch Blades pointed their noses up and headed for space. Once they were certain they weren't being followed, they plotted a course to rendezvous with the convoy of HLTs north of the Elysium colony. Outnumbered and outgunned, they had little hope of saving the Agamemnon, her fate being sealed the moment her port rear and central AGLs had failed. Mort Kendal had lost only two of his comrades; they'd been victorious!

"Men, break off the attack", Captain Scar ordered.

"Cowards. Watch them run", one of his comrades shouted into the mike.

The cheers of his fellow pirates soon followed.

"Into formation men. We still have work to do", Captain Scar ordered before switching to another secure channel.

"Scar here", Captain Scar shouted, "We located and destroyed the HLT, Agamemnon. No sign of the others. Repeat. No sign of the others. Awaiting orders."

"No sign of the others?", Matthew questioned.

"Correct. No sign of the others", Captain Scar replied.

It was a couple of minutes before Matthew responded, "They must have changed course. Perhaps running along the coast and approaching Elysium from the northwest."

Captain Scar replied, "That will make it hard to intercept them, won't it?"

"Yeah. Interception is no longer possible", Matthew replied.

"Orders, Lad, what are your orders?", Captain Scar bellowed into the mike.

It was a few more minutes before Matthew responded, "Rendezvous with the Hypolita, she's now going to play the Agamemnon. Make for the Elysium colony. Take out the colony and the other seven HLTs when they arrive."

"I like the way you think, Lad. A bit slow on the uptake, maybe, but you get there", Captain Scar replied before signing off.

Captain Scar flicked channels once more, "Men. We rendezvous with the Hypolita and make for the Elysium colony. It's time to rain death and destruction on Elysium."

Forkbraid led the convoy along the northern coast of Arabia Terra, high above the fractured coastline of Deuteronimus Mensai. Flying further to the east, they crossed high above the thousands of small islands of Protonilus Mensai. It wasn't very long before they found themselves flying high above the Utopia Sea. Halfway across the Utopia Sea they adjusted course once more and headed southeast. As they approached the Elysium subcontinent, they began reducing their altitude. The seven remaining HLTs cruised low around the northern and western flanks of Elysium Mons.

Finally, they were approaching the New Flinders Psychic Academy on the southern edge of the Elysium plateau, each of the HLTs signalled the Spartan stationed high above them. The Spartan cross-checked their pulse identification beacons and their call signs.

"Achilles requesting an approach vector to New Flinders. Call sign, Snow White."

"Achilles cleared for approach", the Spartan replied.

"Patroclus requesting an approach vector to New Flinders. Call sign, Happy."

"Patroclus cleared for approach."

"Odysseus requesting an approach vector to New Flinders. Call sign, Dopey."

"Odysseus cleared for approach."

"Ajax requesting an approach vector to New Flinders. Call sign, Dock."

"Ajax cleared for approach."

"Menelaus requesting an approach vector to New Flinders. Call sign, Bashful."

"Menelaus cleared for approach."

"Hector requesting an approach vector to New Flinders. Call sign, Sleepy."

"Hector cleared for approach."

"Paris requesting an approach vector to New Flinders. Call sign, Sad."

"Paris cleared for approach."

One by one the seven remaining HLTs touched down on the landing zone not far from the New Flinders Psychic Academy.

Forkbraid circled high above the Elysium plateau, keeping a watchful eye out over his charges.

Four blips appeared on his scanners. He watched carefully as they approached, *"Switch Blades"*, he thought to himself.

Quickly he flew out to meet them high above the Elysium Chasma.

Mort Kendal, alias Captain Scar, held his men back as the Hypolita approached the Elysium colony. Kendal wanted it to appear that they were chasing the HLT. The Captain of the Hypolita switched the Hyplolita's pulse identification beacon to transmit the identity code of the Agamemnon before opening a communications channel to the Elysium Colony.

"Elysium colony, this is the Agamemnon, requesting permission to land. Elysium colony, this is the Agamemnon, we are requesting permission to land."

"Captain, Sir. We have another HLT approaching the Elysium colony from the west. They're saying that they are the Agamemnon and are requesting to land", the Communications Officer reported.

"Are they giving us the correct pulse identity code?", the Captain asked.

"Yes, Sir. Their pulse identity beacon matches the Agamemnon, Sir", the Officer replied.

Captain Carmichael walked over to his Communications Officer, "Have they given us their designated call sign?"

"Lord Forkbraid reported that the Agamemnon suffered a malfunction of two of their AGLs. They flew along a more direct easterly route. That could explain their approach vector, and why they are landing south of their target field", the Communications Officer replied.

Captain Carmichael repeated his question, "Have they given us their designated call sign?"

"No, Sir, they have not", the Communications Officer replied.

"Ask them for their designated call sign", Captain Carmichael ordered.

"Agamemnon. What is your designated call sign?", the Communications Officer requested.

"Elysium colony, this is the Agamemnon. We are urgently requesting permission to land", the approaching HLT replied, "We have hostiles on our six. Repeat. We have hostiles on our six."

"Agamemnon. What is your designated call sign?", the Communications Officer requested again.

"Elysium colony, this is the Agamemnon. We are urgently requesting permission to land", the approaching HLT replied, "We have hostiles on our six. Repeat. We have hostiles on our six."

"So, they don't know their designated call sign. That is very telling, isn't it now?", Captain Carmichael questioned rhetorically before clipping a mike to his ear.

"To the approaching HLT. This is the Captain of the Colonial Heavy Cruiser Spartan. If you were, in fact, the Agamemnon, you would know that your assigned call sign was Grumpy! You are, in fact, the Hypolita!", the Captain transmitted to the approaching HLT.

"Weapons con. Lock onto the Hypolita. Single burst [63]GPL. Maximum power output. Strike them hard on my mark", Captain Carmichael paused, then, "Mark!", he commanded.

A single, powerful and intense flash of light shot out from the underside of the Spartan. The beam of light shot through the Martian atmosphere, down through the thick cloud layers. Striking the HLT Hypolita squarely amidship and cutting her in half. There was an enormous flash of light as the Hypolita burst into a brilliant ball of fire and debris. Burning debris from the Hypolita rained down upon the rolling hills of the Elysium subcontinent, slightly west of the colony itself.

Captain Scar watched the Hypolita erupt into fire before them, "*Sweet Mother of God, they certainly saw us coming*", he thought to himself.

"Men! Attack the colony. Attack the colony now!", he bellowed into his mike.

The remaining ten Talons swooped down upon the Elysium colony and began firing at will, striking anything that looked like volatile targets. High intensity laser beams sliced through buildings and pulsed plasma balls pummelled targets with deadly explosive force. Repeatedly they attacked. Repeatedly they struck. Over and over, destroying target after target.

"*They dare not hit us with the Spartan. We're too small and too close to their precious colony*", Captain Scar thought to himself.

Picking their targets at will, they continued firing again and again at the Elysium colony.

From high above them, Forkbraid in his Bat Wing led the remaining four Switch Blades into the fray. Pulsed plasma cannons firing rapidly at their targets. The first five Talons were caught completely unaware, bursting into fireballs, as each was struck hard by pulsed plasma cannon fire.

Captain Scar looked about, "What the fuck!", he exclaimed.

Forkbraid's Bat Wing swept down from above, his seven fuselage mounted high intensity lasers blazing into action. Intense beams of coherent light shot

---

63 GPL – Giant Pulsed Laser. A colonial cruiser's most devastating weapons system.

across the nose of Captain Scar's Talon. He rolled his ship, took her close to the ground, then pulled the nose up and took her skyward.

Forkbraid swung about locked onto another target and fired his lasers one more. This target was not so lucky. It did not survive, exploding in a ball of fire. The battle quickly descended into a wild and crazy dog fight. Forkbraid sliced another target in two. Both sections of it burst into flames.

Captain Scar swept in once more, looking for the Bat Wing that almost took him out.

His Talon was faster, but Forkbraid's Bat Wing was far more manoeuvrable. Dodging volley after volley of pulsed plasma cannon fire, Forkbraid dodged left and then right, before pulling his Bat Wing's nose up into a full loop, coming down behind Captain Scar's Talon, right on his six.

Forkbraid's pulsed plasma cannons flared into action.

Pulses of superheated plasma passed by Captain Scars Talon on every side.

"Sweet Jesus!", Scar thought to himself as he barely evaded death a second time.

Then again, those seven beams of coherent light cut across his ship's nose, nearly ending his life.

Beads of sweat poured off his brow. Captain Scar rolled his ship up and over, then pulled its nose up and headed skyward once more.

Captain Scar checked his scanners. He blinked and checked them again. None of his Talons were visible. Only two Switch Blades and that accursed Bat Wing still following hot on his heels.

"My men, they're all gone!", he thought, as he levelled off his ship and booked a ticket for home.

Captain Scar turned his Talon's nose west and punched the throttle real hard. The g forces pushed Captain Scar back hard against his seat, he was on his way out of there at high speed.

Forkbraid dropped back, and then swung about. He grabbed a quick glance at the fires raging throughout the Elysium colony far below him, before heading north towards the New Flinders Psychic Academy.

Forkbraid landed his Bat Wing Interceptor on the tarmac near the surviving seven HLTs, making sure that he was closest to the Achilles. A few crew members had stepped out of each of the ships, along with a couple of team leaders from each group of colonists. A dozen chariots were swiftly approaching from the New Flinders Psychic Academy to begin ferrying passengers to their new home. It had been a harrowing flight, and they were one HLT down, the Agamemnon was lost.

Lady Selene had stepped out of the HLT Achilles and watched eagerly as Forkbraid landed his Bat Wing Interceptor. Even before Forkbraid had stepped out of his ship, Lady Selene had begun running towards him. The lower Martian gravity caught her off guard, and she stumbled slightly, before quickly regaining her footing.

Lady Selene then covered the final distance quickly and threw herself into Forkbraid's eagerly awaiting arms. Their embrace lasted for several long minutes while Marcus, Charlene, and Roseanne watched them from the Achilles. All three smiled at the scene before them.

"I had a feeling that something like this would happen when they finally caught up with each other", Charlene said to the others.

Roseanne replied, "Lady Selene has missed him far more than she was letting on."

"Indeed", stated Marcus, "We'd better get over there, before they need a room."

Charlene smiled as she began walking and led the others over to Forkbraid.

As they approached, Lady Selene and Lord Forkbraid disengaged and turned to meet them. Lady Selene's face was flushed red with embarrassment.

"How was the flight?", Forkbraid asked them.

"It was interesting", Charlene replied, adding, "But apparently not as interesting as yours."

"Yes, well, that's a long story", Forkbraid replied, "I'll tell you all about it later."

Marcus had been looking around the tarmac, "I count only seven HLTs", he stated.

"Yes, Marcus. The Agamemnon was lost", Forkbraid replied.

"How?", Selene, who had now regained her composure, demanded.

"They suffered a malfunction during their flight from Deimos", Forkbraid answered, "Two of their five AGLs shut down shortly after we breached atmo."

"With three out of five AGLs running, they should have been able to limp here", Marcus stated.

"Yes, Marcus", Forkbraid answered, "But they lost all manoeuvrability. They could not change course and follow us in. I re-assigned our fighter escort to cover them, but…", Forkbraid's stopped mid-sentence, he lowered his eyes and shook his head.

Marcus finished the sentence for him, "They would have been fucking sitting ducks!"

"Yeah, Marcus, sitting ducks. They didn't stand a chance", Forkbraid agreed.

"How many?", Charlene asked as tears began streaming down her cheeks.

"Two hundred and eighty-six passengers plus the thirty crew", Forkbraid replied.

"So we lost three hundred and nineteen people?", Lady Selene noted with anger in her voice.

Forkbraid took her hand and added, "plus six fighter pilots", as he pointed to the two remaining Switch Blades that had landed nearby on the tarmac.

Forkbraid then pointed south towards the Elysium colony complex, "We have yet to tally the dead and wounded at the colony, it took a lot of damage."

Lady Selene's eyes followed to where Forkbraid pointed. The fires in the Elysium colony were barely visible at this distance. Slim pillars of smoke were rising high into the sky three hundred kilometres to the south of them.

Lady Selene threw Forkbraid's hand down and raised her fists in anger. Her face was red, contorted in anger, with tears steaming freely down her cheeks. Choking with grief and anger, Lady Selene brought her arms down violently.

"They will pay!", she shouted, as bolts of blue fire shot from her fingertips into the ground before her, "They will pay!", she shouted again, as blue fire shot from her fingertips once more.

Again and again Lady Selene shouted "They will pay!"

Again and again blue fire struck the ground before her, scorching the tarmac into molten tar.

Forkbraid took Lady Selene by the shoulders and turned her around. He buried her face into his robe and hugged her tight.

"Shush my, darling", Forkbraid whispered, "They will pay. I will make damned sure of it.", he assured Selene as he stroked her hair.

Forkbraid lifted his head. His eyes were white, and his face had fully taken on the visage of the viper. All softness had disappeared from his features. Few had seen him like this. Charlene and Roseanne shuddered at the sight, he was truly frightening to behold. Even Marcus took a step back.

"Marcus! Ensure the colonists get to the Academy, quick smart. Get everyone moving."

Forkbraid looked to the west and the sun sitting low on the horizon, "I want everyone safely inside by nightfall", he ordered.

Mort Kendal, alias Captain Scar, landed his Talon at an appropriate landing pad in the caverns of New Tortuga. Leroy and Matthew quickly ran through the port to meet him.

"Kendal! What happened?", Leroy screamed at him.

Mort stepped back slightly as they approached, "We had a few problems is all", he replied.

"A few problems! Did we get the HLTs or not?", Leroy demanded.

"In a few words. Yes, and No!", Mort replied.

"What happened Kendal?", Leroy demanded.

"Like I said. We had a few problems", Mort began, "First we intercepted the Agamemnon and dispatched her, blew her to smithereens we did, but the other HLTs were nowhere to be seen."

Matthew interrupted, "That is correct, Sir. The Agamemnon was on her own."

"A decoy?", Leroy asked.

"No, Sir", Mort replied straight away, "She wasn't manoeuvring properly. Something was wrong with her, I'd say. When we took her down, she was like a sitting duck. No evasive manoeuvres at all."

"What about the other seven?", Leroy demanded.

"Sir", Matthew interrupted again, "We believe they altered course before the interception."

"Yeah", Mort quickly added, "We didn't have any chance of intercepting them, so the young lad here, ordered us to take them out as they landed at the Elysium colony."

"No other choice, Sir", Matthew added, "We didn't know their precise course; however, we did know their destination."

"And?", Leroy questioned.

"We had a few more problems, Sir", Mort replied.

"What happened this time, Kendal?", Leroy demanded.

"We got to Elysium, no problem. We had the Hypolita playing the Agamemnon and all, just as we'd planned. Only they didn't fall for it, did they. The Spartan took out the Hypolita from low orbit. One shot was all it took", Mort Kendal replied.

"What about the other HLTs, Kendal?", Leroy demanded.

"Well, they just weren't there, were they. Nowhere to be seen", Mort replied, adding, "So we did the only thing we could do. We attacked the colony instead and blew the shit out of everything."

"So, the other seven HLTs survived?", Leroy asked.

"Yes, Sir. I assume they did", Mort replied adding "they were nowhere near the colony."

"You said you attacked the colony. How did that go with that?", Leroy queried.

"It went quite well, actually. We took out a lot of buildings and caused a hell of a lot of damage. Aimed at all and everything that was vulnerable, we did. The whole place was a smouldering ruin when I left it. Lots of damage, I'd say."

"Where are your other men, Kendal?", Matthew questioned.

"Well, that's the thing, isn't it", Mort rubbed his face, "We got jumped by fighters."

"Fighters?", queried Leroy.

"Yes, Sir", Mort replied, "A number of Switch Blades and a Bat Wing."

Leroy and Matthew looked at each other, then back to Mort.

"That's right, Switch Blades and a Bat Wing", Mort confirmed, adding "We met the Switch Blades first when we took out the Agamemnon. We thought we had them on the run, we did. They scuppered right-smart when the Agamemnon died. Then they turned up out of the blue, along with that Bat Wing, when we were attacking the Elysium colony."

"And your other men?", Matthew asked once again.

"Didn't make it back, Sir", Mort replied, "I'm lucky to get back myself. That damned Bat Wing nearly killed me thrice, it did."

"You weren't followed were you, Kendal?", Leroy asked.

"No, Sir, of course, not", Mort replied, "I came back flying low through the deep valleys."

Matthew looked about the landing bay, "Kendal, we're going to need those Gull Wings of yours and any other ships you can muster. Commandeer whatever you can."

Matthew then turned back to Leroy.

"Partial success, Sir", Matthew suggested to Leroy adding "It's better than nothing."

"Yes, yes. Partial success, Lad", Leroy replied, commenting, "Let's just hope the Prophet sees it that way."

18. Aftermath Two

Special Agent Murphy stood upon a small hill overlooking the Elysium colony. Fires still raged out of control and damage was visible everywhere. The main power plant had been hit, the main fuel depot and waste treatment facilities as well. Many of the major buildings in the colony had been destroyed or damaged to some degree, the colony's new hospital being completely destroyed by fire. Androids were busy fighting the fires, as rescue workers searched for any wounded colonists, the ones who'd been working really hard to build the new colony.

The bodies of the dead were being bagged and stored temporarily in portable freezers over by the spaceport's landing field. A large triage tent housed those wounded thus far found, and a mobile hospital tent had been erected for those wounded requiring urgent attention. Special Agent Murphy shook his head in shame; he blamed himself. This should never have happened.

Forkbraid put his right hand upon his shoulder, "I know, Jim, it's a mess. Remember though, it could have been far worse, and none of this was your fault."

His words failed to reassure him.

"How many?", Special Agent Murphy asked.

"Three hundred and nineteen dead, seventy-six wounded, so far", Forkbraid replied.

"How's, Lady Selene?", Special Agent Murphy asked.

He remembered seeing Lady Selene being brought into the Psychic Academy, distraught and inconsolable, her face a grey, ashen colour.

"Selene is resting", Forkbraid replied, adding "under sedation."

"Under sedation?", Special Agent Murphy asked.

"Yes, Jim. It was necessary", Forkbraid replied, "With our kind of power, it's prudent to take precautions, especially when one of us is so distraught."

"I heard about the blue fire", Special Agent Murphy stated curiously.

"The blue fire. Oh, yes", Forkbraid answered softly, "Selene was distraught, Jim, a momentary loss of control on her part."

"I thought it would take time for your people to adapt to Mars", Special Agent Murphy queried.

"Selene is a Folcrom, Jim", Forkbraid answered, "She's like me, she can use her abilities off-world as well."

"So you can do that too?", Special Agent Murphy queried.

"Yes, Jim", Forkbraid replied, "A few of us have that capability. It's not used very often, except for defence. Though sometimes it manifests through anger or intense emotion."

"Intense emotion you say", Special Agent Murphy repeated as he viewed the devastation before him, "I can understand that."

"You have to remember, Jim, Lady Selene handpicked every couple aboard the Ptolemy. Selene personally knew every colonist who died on the Agamemnon. They were her friends, her charges, her responsibility."

Special Agent Murphy didn't reply, he simply nodded in understanding.

Forkbraid turned around as he sensed Captain Carmichael approach, "Captain Carmichael."

"Forkbraid, Agent Murphy", Captain Carmichael greeted them.

"Captain", Special Agent Murphy replied.

"They certainly did the job, didn't they", Captain Carmichael stated as he scanned the devastated Elysium colony.

"That they did, Captain, that they did", Special Agent Murphy lamented.

"I've stationed the Spartan directly above us, Gentleman", Captain Carmichael began, "If they come sniffing around here again, we'll see them coming. Every approaching ship is being watched."

"That's good to know, Captain, but I'm not sure how it will help. I believe we have only three fighters left to defend the colony, early warning or not", Special Agent Murphy replied.

"True enough ,Agent Murphy", the Captain replied, "But the Spartan can take out some of those targets as they approach."

"Talons make very small targets, Captain, and they are very fast", Special Agent Murphy replied.

"That they are, that they are", the Captain agreed.

"We do still have those Wisps, Captain. The ones that were retrofitted with the pulsed plasma cannons", Forkbraid mentioned.

"Yes, but they're not atmo rated, Forkbraid", the Captain replied.

"On the Ptolemy there are seventeen damaged Switch Blades, Captain", Forkbraid continued.

"Yes, but we have no way to repair them. And honestly, some of them are complete write-offs", the Captain answered him.

"They do all have polyceramalloy hulls, Captain", Forkbraid stressed.

"What are you thinking, Forkbraid?", Special Agent Murphy enquired.

"Ah, Jim, just an idea I have, that's all", Forkbraid replied.

"Well, Forkbraid, spit it out", Captain Carmichael requested.

"Well, Captain. If you atomise some of those Switch Blade hulls, you can use the [64]polyceramalloy to coat the Wisps. Coating their hulls will make them atmo rated. I'd be inclined to coat the ones that have been retrofitted with pulsed plasma cannons", Forkbraid explained.

---

64 Polyceramalloy (Poly-Ceramic-Alloy) Stronger than any steel, far more heat-resistant than titanium or ceramics, far more flexible than any plastics.

"That would be illegal", Captain Carmichael replied, "You do remember the [65]O.S.I armistice treaty, don't you?"

"Yes, I do remember that, Captain", Forkbraid replied "But I have a way around that too."

"Really?", the Captain enquired.

"Yeah. Once the modifications are done, transfer the Wisps and their pilots to the Elysium colony. Then it's no longer your problem", Forkbraid advised.

The Captain cocked an eyebrow, "So, I'd be seconding a dozen Wisps and pilots to Elysium?"

"Yep, that's it", Forkbraid replied, adding "They'll become part of the Elysium Defence Force."

"And for how long would my pilots be on secondment?", the Captain asked.

"For as long as it takes to sort things out down here, Captain", Forkbraid replied.

The Captain thought long and hard about Forkbraid's idea, "We'd have to adjust their EM drives as well. Assuming you want them truly atmo rated."

"So, it can be done?", Forkbraid asked.

"Forkbraid, it's not as easy as removing particle beams and retrofitting pulsed plasma cannons."

Forkbraid smiled, "How long will it take?"

Captain Carmichael talked them through the process, "Well, we'd have to retrieve the Switch Blades from the Ptolemy, strip them right down and atomise their hulls. Coating the Wisp's hulls with polyceramalloy will require stripping them down completely as well. We'd have to do that anyway to pull out the EM drives and rework them. So it's a pretty big job."

Forkbraid smiled again, "Yes, it will take time captain, but just how much time?"

"Honestly, Forkbraid, I'd say about two weeks to ready a dozen Wisps, but don't hold me to that. It is not my field of expertise", Captain Carmichael replied.

"Then we'd better get started", Forkbraid suggested.

"Yeah, we'd better get started", Captain Carmichael agreed.

Special Agent Murphy smiled, "Woo-hoo! We have an air force!"

"Soon enough, Jim, soon enough", Forkbraid reminded him.

Captain Carmichael's hummer had just taken off when another hummer landed nearby. Varakhan Utana climbed out and rushed over to Forkbraid and Special Agent Murphy.

"Varak", Forkbraid nodded to him.

"Forkbraid, Agent Murphy", Varak returned the greeting.

---

65 The O.S.I Armistice Treaty officially ended the Outer Satellites Insurrection. A number of weapons were banned.

"What's the estimate?", Forkbraid asked.

"It is too early to say. Eighteen months at least, perhaps two years, maybe longer", Varak replied.

"That's not going to sit well with Selene", Forkbraid frowned.

"Indeed. This will be quite a setback. Lady Selene will be most upset", Varak agreed.

Special Agent Murphy pointed towards Lake Eddie, "I heard a report that the subsurface facilities near the port were flooded."

"There has been extensive flooding, yes, but they have it under control now", Varak replied, adding, "Although, it will take some time to pump all of that water back out."

.Forkbraid shook his head, "It's amazing what damage a few antique interceptors can do."

"Talons FB, Talons", Special Agent Murphy replied, "Very effective little buggers."

Forkbraid nodded in agreement.

"Lord Forkbraid, Governor Anderson is flying in from Chryce Colony", Varak informed them.

"Governor Anderson?", Forkbraid queried.

"Yes. He is the Governor of Chryce Colony", Varak replied, adding "although he fancies himself the governor of the whole planet."

"How's that Varak?", Special Agent Murphy asked.

"Chryce was the first official colony on Mars and it is the biggest. Anderson thinks that gives him primacy over the whole planet" Varak replied.

"Yes, but why is he coming here?", Forkbraid enquired.

"He has offered us the use of the Chryce medical facilities", Varak replied, before noting, "We are expecting several ambulances to follow him in to ferry the more critically wounded back to the hospital at Chryce."

"Well that's a good thing at least", Special Agent Murphy replied.

"But why is he coming here?", Forkbraid asked.

"It is his way. He likes to take control of things", Varak replied.

"Well, that's not going to happen here", Forkbraid was adamant.

A few minutes later another hummer landed at the landing field, followed by ten ambulances. Ambulance crews climbed out of their ambulances and made their way to the triage tents. A short, rotund, balding man climbed out of the hummer. Forkbraid led Special Agent Murphy and Varak across the landing field to meet him.

"Gentleman, I'm Governor Anderson, Governor John Anderson", his voice was stern.

Varak, having met Anderson previously, quickly returned his greeting and introduced Special Agent Murphy and Forkbraid.

Governor Anderson looked past the landing field to the Elysium colony. Fires still ravaged the colony, devastation was visibly apparent. A short distance away ambulance crews were transferring injured colonists to their vehicles on stretchers. Black plastic body bags were lined up next to freezers by the landing field. Androids were carefully stacking them for cold storage.

He frowned and turned to Forkbraid, "You brought this carnage to our peaceful little world."

Forkbraid frowned, *"Yet another bureaucrat looking for a scape goat"*, he thought to himself.

Special Agent Murphy replied angrily, "If not for Lord Folcrom Forkbraid, the carnage would have been much worse!"

"How could it be much worse!", Governor Anderson also replied angrily, "I want this man off my planet by nightfall! We don't need his kind meddling here."

Forkbraid responded diplomatically as he surreptitiously scanned Anderson's mind, "I have several points I'd like to make, Governor. Firstly, I did not bring this carnage here. Those who committed this carnage were already present here and have been here for a long time. I merely tracked their leader here from L-Five. Secondly, you are not the ruler of this planet, you have no authority beyond the borders of Chryce. The Elysium subcontinent is under the governance and authority of Lady Folcrom Selene. Thirdly, I have all the authority necessary to deal with the terrorists in whatever manner I see fit, and I have no intention of leaving this planet until my job is done. Get that through your thick skull!"

Special Agent Murphy quickly added, "Governor Anderson, as a duly appointed Cis-Lunar Bureau of Investigations Special Agent, I am licensed to kill. As I am in the field and the terrorists have attacked this colony and killed so many innocent people, I am at liberty to act in accordance with my mandate."

Governor Anderson's face went bright red, his authority was being challenged, "Who do you think you people are? What right do you have to talk to me like that?"

"I am Lord Folcrom Forkbraid, head of the Earth's Remote Viewing Teams. I am sanctioned under the United Nations of Earth and the United Colonies of Sol to hunt down and eliminate terrorist threats wherever they may be", Forkbraid paused and placed an odd lilt into his voice, "That sanction demands your immediate cooperation!"

Questions asked and answered, Governor Anderson took a step back. His face was still bright red, but he was lost for words. It had been a long time since anyone had challenged his authority, and never in this particular manner. Mars had been his little fiefdom for such a long time.

Governor Anderson turned and pointed to the air ambulances on the landing field, stuttering as he replied, "You, you, you have my cooperation already. What else do you need?"

Forkbraid replied, his eyes focused, his face viperous, "I will need whatever I will need, and I will take whatever I need. And you will comply!", again that strange lilt in his voice.

Forkbraid sent an image of the Psi Corps crest deep into his mind.

Governor Anderson's face was no longer red, all colour had been drained from his face, "I will comply", he gulped softly.

"I'm glad to hear that, Governor", Forkbraid replied, "Your colony's medical assistance is greatly appreciated, thank you."

"Yes, yes, thank you. It's the least that we could do", Anderson replied, "I'll send over some construction crews to help with the rebuilding as soon as possible. Anything else you need, just ask and I'll make the arrangements for it."

"Good. Thank you, Governor", Forkbraid replied.

Governor Anderson walked back to his awaiting hummer, he looked over his shoulder several times before getting inside. As the Governor's hummer lifted off, Varak smiled, his white teeth gleaming, and he said, "I've never seen the man so rattled!"

Special Agent Murphy replied, "Forkbraid can have that effect on people, Varak."

"Don't make light of it, Jim. It's not something that I enjoy doing, and I prefer not to do it", Forkbraid replied.

Special Agent Murphy slapped him on the shoulder, "That may be so, FB, but it saves a lot of time and gets things done. In these dangerous times, FB. It is very effective."

The Prophet sat quietly thinking about Leroy's report. He was sitting in the old pub, the Black Pullet. Only it had now been fully converted into a church. Partial success. One HLT, the Agamemnon destroyed, and the Elysium colony in ruins.

"An eighth of the demons will have been on the Agamemnon", the Prophet stated.

"Yes, my Lord. That would be a good estimate", Leroy replied.

"So we sent about three hundred of them straight back to hell", the Prophet smiled.

"There's no telling how many we eliminated at the colony, my Lord", Leroy replied.

Matthew added, "If we include the colony, their casualties would have to be at least double that, my Lord. Easily double that and then some."

The Prophet looked to Mort Kendal, "Captain Scar", he addressed him, "The sacrifice of your men has been greatly appreciated. They are martyrs. All of them."

"Thank you, my Lord", Mort Kendal replied, thinking to himself how he no longer had to split their payment twelve ways.

"It's been a good start, Gentlemen", the Prophet continued, "It is unfortunate that we lost so many ships and men, but nonetheless, a good start."

"My Lord, I'm certain we can commandeer more ships and press more pilots into service", Leroy replied.

"Yes, my Lord", Matthew added, "We've already started rebuilding our forces."

"Already. Good lad", the Prophet replied, "So how is that going?"

"Well, my Lord, we still have the seven Talons we held in reserve. We have two Gull Wings and Mort here, has managed to wrangle several small freighters into service."

"How many small freighters?", the Prophet enquired.

"Eight so far, my Lord", Matthew replied.

"And what can we do with these freighters?", the Prophet asked.

"I was thinking of fitting them out as Raiders, my Lord", Matthew told him.

"Raiders?", the Prophet queried.

"Yes, my Lord", Matthew began, "Those other colonists had to land somewhere. And the Elysium colony will need repairs." Matthew stopped.

"Go on, Matthew", the Prophet urged.

"Well, my Lord, at some point the other colonies will offer assistance to Elysium. When they do, we can slip our Raiders in amongst these assistance flights. That will give us access to the colony again. So we should be able to strike at them again and take out more of the demons", Matthew explained.

"That is an idea", the Prophet replied adding, "How will we slip into these assistance flights?"

"That will be easier than it sounds, my Lord", Leroy began, "We have people in the Chryce colony and as Chryce is the largest colony on Mars, it will offer the most assistance."

"Can we be sure of that?", the Prophet asked.

"Yes, my Lord", Matthew replied, "Nothing happens on Mars that Chryce isn't involved in."

The Prophet smiled, "Make sure these Raiders of yours are capable of performing a kamikaze run, Matthew."

"Yes, my Lord", Matthew replied, "That was my intention."

Mort Kendal smiled a wry smile, "It may be difficult to get crews for these Raiders, if they know that they're flying on suicide missions, my Lord."

"That's easily fixed, Captain Scar", the Prophet replied, "We'll offer them riches in payment and simply not tell them of our full intentions."

"We'll lie to them?", Mort Kendal queried.

"We'll do what is necessary to perform God's will", the Prophet corrected.

Mort nodded, "It's all good with me, my Lord", again thinking of reaping even higher profits.

"My Lord, I can definitely rig those freighters", Matthew informed the Prophet.

"What do you mean Matthew?", the Prophet enquired.

"Well, my Lord, the Raiders fly into battle and attack with their pilots in control. All's well, then when the battle heats up, we send in a signal that locks the pilots out of the control systems. Then the ship's autopilot takes over, only it's been modified to lock onto the nearest large surface target and makes a beeline straight for it. All pretty simple really", Matthew explained.

Mort Kendal stood back a step and looked at Matthew, "Blood thirsty little bugger ain't yeah, Lad. You'd make a bloody good pirate!"

"Captain Scar, I'd say that Matthew here, is highly resourceful", the Prophet corrected.

Leroy and Mort Kendal nodded in agreement.

"There is only one thing that puzzles me gentlemen", the Prophet stated, "Where did the other seven HLTs land?"

Mort Kendal shrugged his shoulders, "Beats me, my Lord. They weren't at the Elysium colony."

Leroy looked at Matthew, "Any ideas, Lad?"

"Actually, yes. I have an idea", Matthew replied.

All eyes looked upon Matthew with expectation.

"Back on Earth, the Psychic Academies are never close to major population centres", he stated.

"Yes, Matthew, but this colony was being built for psychics", Leroy replied.

"Yeah, sure, but what if it was built with more than one component", Matthew conjectured.

"More than one component?", the Prophet queried.

"Yes, my Lord. One for the ordinary population and another for the psychics", Matthew replied.

"Using the same mould as on Earth?", the Prophet asked.

"That's what I'm thinking, my Lord", Matthew replied, "The Elysium colony complex is just the main population centre. The psychics will have their own refuge somewhere separate from the main colony. It will be further afield."

"It could be anywhere on the subcontinent", Leroy noted.

"Or even across the Elysium channel, the islands of Nepenthis Mensai or Aeolis Mensai perhaps", Mort Kendal suggested, before raising his index finger and adding, "Or even east of Elysium on one of the Tartaris or Phlegra Islands."

"It could be any one of a thousand places", Matthew added.

"If such a refuge exists, we'll need to know where it is", the Prophet told them.

"I'll get right on, my Lord", Leroy replied.

Candy dropped three backpacks down on the floor in front of Cormac.
"What is this then, Candy?", he asked.

"We can not stay here any longer, Cormac", Candy replied, "Get that lot packed, we're leaving."

"We can't just get up and leave, Candy", Cormac told her.

"Of course, we can. It's not safe here any more, Cormac", Candy insisted.

"I know this new lot is a little iffy, but we've always managed to survive, no matter who's in charge of this place", Cormac reminded her.

"This new lot, are down right evil, Cormac", Candy replied, adding, "These are not just opportunistic bastards, these people are evil, plain, and simple. You know they are. You've seen what's in their minds."

Cormac stared at the backpacks. His Wife was right. He had seen what was in their minds. They were evil. They planned to tie young Miranda to a stake and burn her alive.

Cormac looked back at his Wife, "*I know what they plan to do, Candy*", he thought back to her.

"*It gets worse, Cormac. I was in town today. There was talk of an HLT full of colonists being shot down. Talk of an attack on that new colony at Elysium*", Candy thought back to him.

This was disastrous. New Tortuga had always been a rough, even violent place, run by smugglers, with pirates and privateers frequently dropping in, but as rough as it was, it was home. Cormac's and Candy's families had lived in New Tortuga for generations. The coming of this new element, these religious militants, was going to bring hell down upon them. It was only a matter of time. The location of New Tortuga was a closely guarded secret, but with the new goings-on, how long would that secret last. Reprisals would be coming and coming big time.

"We can't leave that little girl. We can't leave Miranda", Cormac told his Wife.

"Cormac! What do you think of me! Of course, we're taking Miranda with us", Candy replied.

"I'll get this lot packed, Candy", Cormac told his Wife, "You take care of Mrs Harmon."

"Good then. Meet me on the top floor when you're ready", Candy replied.
With that Candy left the room and headed up the stairs.

Candy entered Miranda's room, Mrs Harmon was there as usual keeping a close eye on the little girl. Miranda was staring out the window at the hydroponics, but quickly turned around when Candy came in. Her frown quickly turned into a beaming smile.

"I thought you might like some hot cocoa, Mrs Harmon", Candy told them as she placed the tray with two cups of hot cocoa on a table.

"Thank you, Candy", Mrs Harmon replied as she reached for a cup.

Miranda walked over to the table and reached for a cup as well.

"*Miranda, pick up the cup, but don't drink it*", Candy sent her a thought.

Miranda nursed her cup and watched as Mrs Harmon drank hers, "It tastes delightful", she said.

After only her third mouth full Mrs Harmon slumped forward onto the table unconscious.

"Is Mrs Harmon alright, Candy", Miranda asked.

"She's fine, little darling, sleeping sort of, although when she wakes up tomorrow, she will have the most awful headache."

Miranda looked up at Candy, a look that asked a thousand questions.

"We have to get you away from these terrible people, Miranda", Candy told her.

Cormac stepped through the door. He had a large backpack on his back and was carrying a couple of others. He passed one to Candy, who quickly slung it onto her back.

"We're going on a little trip, Miranda", Candy told her.

Cormac passed Miranda a somewhat smaller backpack, "Put this on, little one. We need to leave straight away."

Cormac led them back into the corridor and deeper into the house. He opened the door to a room next to the stairs, and they all stepped in. Cormac locked the door behind them. It was a small room and appeared to have no other way out. It appeared to be used for the storage of various items, mostly junk had been stored there.

There was a large closet against the rear wall. Cormac opened the closet door and stepped inside. Candy asked Miranda to follow Cormac. Inside the closet, the rear panel had opened, and a tunnel led deep into the rock. Miranda followed Cormac into the tunnel, with Candy following close behind. Once all three of them had entered the tunnel, Candy flicked a switch and the panel sealed itself once more. Another stone door then slid across the tunnel opening, completely hiding the tunnel entrance. Cormac turned on his glow light and lit the path before them.

"This house has been in my family for generations, Miranda. We are the only ones who know about this tunnel. From back there, it just looks like more rock", Cormac smiled his broad gap-toothed smile.

They followed the tunnel for about thirty feet, and it opened up into a long, narrow, natural cave. They then followed the marked course of the cave for what seemed an eternity, deeper into the rock of Hebes Island. At some point the cave had turned eastward. Eventually the tunnel began to angle upwards and after another half hour they came to its end.

Cormac flicked a switch in the cave wall and the rock in front of them slid out of the way. They now found themselves inside a fair sized cavern. Light could be seen gleaming through the entrance, and they walked towards the light.

"We'll rest here for fifteen minutes", Cormac told them as he took off his backpack.

Candy took off her backpack and quickly rummaged through it to get some food for them to eat.

"How far are we from town?", Miranda asked.

"We're about eight miles from New Tortuga", Cormac replied.

Cormac explained how his great-grandfather had bored out the rock to make the house that they lived in. Later, Cormac's grandfather had bored another tunnel through the rock to expand the house. Only this new tunnel only reached thirty feet into the rock when it struck the cave system.

Cormac's grandfather then acquired original surveyors maps of the region and these showed the cave formations that he had bored into. Using these maps he was able to follow the cave system deeper into the hill country, north and then east of New Tortuga, all the way to the cave's entrance.

Cormac's grandfather had decided that having a rear exit to New Tortuga might come in very handy one day, so he marked the direct passage from the house to the caves entrance. He then concealed both entrances to the cave system with large sliding stones.

To hide the cave system from view, Cormac's grandfather planted a thicket of pine trees and brush around its entrance. The terraforming project, with its seeding program, ensured that the slopes of the hill country on Hebes Island would one day be well forested, so no one would notice the slight thickening of the pine forest around the cave's entrance.

Cormac and Candy quickly finished their meals and slung their backpacks onto their backs once more. Little Miranda followed their lead and did the same. Then all three stepped out of the cave and into the narrow rock crevasses around its entrance. They pressed themselves against the rock-wall and pushed through the thicket with its tightly packed trees, and then finally into the pine forest. Cormac quickly pulled out his [66]GPS compass and quickly gained his bearings, then he led them down a narrow trail that led southeast towards the coast. The trail was narrow and not at all well-marked, resembling more of a rough goat track than a trail. Cormac, however, seemed to know it, only stopping once or twice to check his compass.

"We have to get to the hamlet before nightfall", Cormac advised them.

"The hamlet?", Miranda queried.

66 GPS – Global Positioning System via satellites in Martian Geo-stationery orbit

"Krell. It's a small fishing village", Candy informed her, "Cormac has a cousin there."

"My cousin Joseph has a boat. We can get off Hebes Island with it", Cormac added.

Candy giggled quietly and Cormac sighed, but neither explained why.

The trail continued downwards through the hills. The coast could be seen through the gaps in the trees now, the blue waters that filled Hebes Chasma gleaming in the sunlight. The high, steep cliffs in which New Tortuga was hidden lay in the distance to their right. To their left, the southeast, the cliffs gradually reduced in height, until they finally merged with the coast. Their path led them towards the coast, to where the cliffs finally ended. It was still several miles off in the distance.

Miranda began to tire and Cormac bent down, sweeping her up, placing her on his shoulders.

"We'll be there soon, little one", Cormac reassured her.

"Cormac, we mustn't be seen", Candy advised him, "best we approach through the orchards."

"Good idea, Candy, good idea", Cormac replied.

The trail had opened up, and the trees were less numerous now. They were in a small, narrow valley that led all the way to the coast. In front of them on their left were small ploughed fields, ready for planting. On their right, small orchards of apples, apricots, peaches, and nectarines. Beyond the fields and the orchards was the little hamlet of Krell. It consisted of perhaps a dozen small houses, scattered about the mouth of the valley, along the narrow strip of coastal land.

They quickly moved into the orchards and quietly moved amongst the trees. Slipping behind most of the hamlet and coming out close to a house that was slightly further away from the others.

It was one of two houses in the hamlet that were right next to the beach. Both of these houses had small jetties projecting out into the water of the Hebes Sea and a small boat lay birthed at the end of each jetty. Cormac led them to the nearest of the two houses.

They stopped behind a small shed near the back door. Cormac focused on the house in front of them. Little Miranda began to pick up a series of discrete, carefully focused thoughts.

"Joseph! Are you in? It's your cousin Cormac. We need your help, urgently."

"Yeah, Cousin, I'm in. Give me a minute."

The back door opened, and they ran quickly from the shed to the house. Within seconds, they were through the door and into the house itself. Cormac took Miranda down from his shoulders and placed her on the floor, before giving his cousin a huge hug.

Miranda looked up at the two men, they looked so very similar, "Cormac. You and your Cousin look more like Brothers than Cousins", Miranda told them.

Cormac smiled his gap-toothed smile and Candy began to laugh.

"Joseph's Mother was my Mother's sister, so we are Cousins", Cormac explained, "But we both had the same Father."

Joseph smiled as he added, "Cormac's my cousin and also my younger half-Brother, little one."

"Miranda darling, relationships get a little funny out here in the wild country", Candy explained.

"Joseph, you had the right idea", Cormac told Joseph.

"How so, Cormac?", Joseph enquired.

"Five years ago when the first of those fundamentalist types turned up. You said then that no good would come of it, and you left", Cormac told him, "You were right. More and more of them turned up. Now they damn well run the place. They've even turned the Black Pullet into a Church."

"You don't say, Cormac!", Joseph replied, "We had plenty a good times in that old pub."

"Well, we won't be having good times in that old pub any time soon", Cormac told his Cousin.

"And they're down right evil", Candy told Joseph, "They wanted to burn little Miranda here alive. Evil bastards I tell you."

Joseph shook his head, "*Did I hear that right?*", he thought to himself, then he looked over at little Miranda, "What? Just why?"

"Because she has the gift, Joseph! Thou shall not suffer a witch to live and all that crap. You know how these fundamentalists are", Candy explained.

"That's just monstrous!", Joseph exclaimed.

"It gets even worse", Cormac said to Joseph, and then they had a long discussion about what had been happening of late in New Tortuga.

After several tens of minutes and when Joseph was fully informed of the situation, he said "Well then, you can stay here as long as you need. No problem."

"We can't stay here, Joseph", Candy replied, adding, "When they find Miranda is missing, they'll come looking for her."

"They won't come looking for her here", Joseph replied.

"You don't know these people. They will come looking for her. Even here", Cormac insisted.

"We have to get off Hebes Island, Joseph", Candy stated, "And we have to do it tonight."

"Tonight! Is it that urgent?", Joseph asked.

"Yes, Joseph. It is that urgent", Candy insisted.

"We need to be as far away from here as possible, before they realise we're not in New Tortuga", Cormac added, "We need to get Miranda to Elysium."

"Why Elysium? It's on the other side of Mars, and across open sea waters", Joseph asked.

"Miranda's people are there at the new colony", Candy replied, "They're gifted ones from Earth."

"My Mum and Dad are there too, and my little Brother, Chiron", Miranda told Joseph.

"He's there as well", Cormac told him.

"He? Who is he?", Joseph enquired.

"Lord Folcrom Forkbraid!", Cormac replied.

Even on Mars people knew of Forkbraid. Joseph looked at his Cousin / half Brother.

"Why would Earth's most gifted be here on Mars, Cormac?", he enquired.

"He's here hunting those evil bastards who have taken over New Tortuga", Cormac told him.

"So history has come full circle", Joseph stated.

Cormac and Candy both nodded in agreement.

Miranda didn't understand and gave the three adults a curious look.

Candy explained, "Lord Folcrom Forkbraid is a distant kin of ours, little one."

"It's a long story Miranda", Cormac took over, "To tell it quickly, an ancestor of Forkbraid's came to Mars long ago, before the terraforming. During his time here on Mars there was a great deal of political instability. The Troubles as we call it. Anyway, he never expected to return to Earth or to his Wife and six Children again."

"So he took another Wife here on Mars", Candy continued, "and he had another six Children with her."

Cormac took over once more, "Only a decade later, his people came for him and took him back to Earth leaving his Martian family behind. He never saw his Martian family again after that."

"So he founded two lineages, one on Earth and one here on Mars", Candy continued, adding, "And that makes Forkbraid and us distant Cousins so to speak."

"So Forkbraid's ancestor was your ancestor as well?", Miranda asked to ensure she heard it right.

"Yes, little one. We share a common ancestor", Cormac replied.

"Why did he come to Mars in the first place, if there were all those troubles?", Miranda asked.

"He came to Mars to ask a question, little one", Candy replied.

"Yes. He was the one who asked *The Great Question* that actually led to the terraforming in the first place", Joseph added, "Amongst us gifted, he is called *He who Asked The Great Question.*"

"What was *The Great Question?*", Miranda asked.

"It's difficult to say exactly what the question was as such or how it was asked for that matter", Joseph replied, stroking the side of his face as he thought about it.

Candy answered for him, "He asked the planet whether it wanted to remain as it was, a cold lifeless world, or to be terraformed and made life bearing like the Earth."

"He asked the planet?", Miranda looked up with a surprised look on her face.

"Yes, little one", Candy replied, "He gave Mars the option. He asked *The Great Question.*"

"How did he ask *The Great Question?* How did he talk to the planet?", Miranda asked.

"No-one rightly knows, little one", Cormac replied, adding, "We know he went into the deepest depths of the old Hellas Planitia to ask it though."

"Hellas Planitia?", Miranda was looking puzzled now.

"Hellas Planitia is one of the old names, little one", Cormac replied, adding "It's now a deep, cold sea called Hells Ocean."

"Cold and deep, those are the right words. Eight miles deep, in fact", Joseph added, before noting, "And Forkbraid, a descendant of *He who asked The Great Question,* is now back on Mars."

"Forkbraid is here on Mars looking for me", Miranda told them.

"And we will help him find you, Miranda", Candy replied reassuringly.

Joseph pulled out his maps, "The quickest way to Elysium would be to go north to the big colony at Chryce and then catch transport from there. Up through Echus Chasma and the Kasei Swamps. It's not an easy trail though, and you'll need a long canoe."

"They'll expect that anyway", Cormac replied, "It's also the way smugglers fly in and out."

"It's also dangerous marsh and swamp country", Candy informed them.

"Well, trekking over the bulge is out of the question", Joseph pointed to the map, "So that leaves Valles Marineris." Cormac and Candy nodded.

Joseph explained the details. "At the far eastern end of the Hebes Sea there's a village called Shira. I can take you there in my boat. Over here in the northern reaches of Valles Marineris there's another larger village called Jericho. It's more of a trading port really. You should be able to get transport to Jericho from Shira. Once you're in Jericho you can catch a ship to the Aurorae colony, over here on the big island just east of Aurorae Planum."

"And from there we can catch a hummer to Elysium", Cormac concluded.

"We'd better get cracking then", Candy advised them, "It'll be dark soon, and we'll need the cover of darkness to slip out of here."

Forkbraid was back at the New Flinders Psychic Academy visiting Selene. The pair sat on a low bench atop the battlements of the inner keep, looking south over the Elysium plateau. The air was crisp and refreshing, although somewhat cold and they had both dressed accordingly.

"I can't see any smoke", Selene stated as she searched the horizon in the direction of the colony.

"The fires have all been put out, Selene", Forkbraid informed her, "It took most of the day and half of the night."

"So many deaths", Selene lamented.

Forkbraid looked carefully at Selene, "How are you feeling, Selene?"

"Better than yesterday", Selene replied softly, "Before they knocked me out, apparently I blew a hole in the infirmary wall with a scream."

"I know. I was there", Forkbraid told her, carefully adding, "You were quite the handful."

"I feel so embarrassed", Selene quietly confided.

"Don't be. I don't know what I would have done if I'd lost so many friends like that", Forkbraid assured her.

"I lost control, Forkbraid!", Selene shouted back at him.

"Yes, Selene. You lost control. It happens", Forkbraid replied softly.

"But why? I never lost control back on Earth, when the induction ceremony was bombed!"

"That was different. You were there in the thick of it. People needed your help, everyone was depending on you. You had lives to save and there was no time at all to feel grief or anger then", Forkbraid replied.

"The people on the Agamemnon, they depended on me too!", Selene shouted back.

"Yes, but you weren't there. It happened and neither of us was there. There was nothing we could do about it. You couldn't take charge of the situation and that made you angry. It made you feel helpless, helpless and angry", Forkbraid replied.

"It made you angry too! I can feel it!", Selene spat, with a slight bitterness in her voice.

"Yes, it makes me angry, Selene. Of course, it does", Forkbraid replied.

"Yet you didn't lose control?", Selene replied questioningly.

"No I didn't. I've learnt to become a cold, hard bastard, Selene", Forkbraid answered back.

He looked deeply into Selene's eyes and said with tenderness, "That you became so distraught that you lost control, tells me you still have a heart. And that's a good thing, Selene, a good thing."

"You're not the cold, hard bastard you make yourself out to be ,Forkbraid", Selene replied, reaching for his hand, "I know your heart, Forkbraid and I know what's in your heart."

They sat there for several minutes in silence before Selene asked, "Was there truly nothing that we could do?"

Forkbraid shook his head, "Nothing, Selene. I've thought it over many, many times."

"There must have been something we could have done", Selene asked again.

"Selene. Don't torture yourself about it. There was nothing we could do", Forkbraid assured her.

"Could the convoy have stayed with the Agamemnon?", Selene asked.

"Selene. Let it go", Forkbraid requested.

"Could the convoy have stayed with the Agamemnon?", Selene asked again.

"No", Forkbraid replied flatly, "If we had stayed with the Agamemnon, we would have lost more HLTs and many more lives. That just wasn't an option."

"Could they have landed somewhere else?", Selene enquired

"No. Apart from the Elysium subcontinent and Arabia Terra, they would have been over open ocean", Forkbraid replied.

"Why couldn't they land in Arabia Terra?", Selene enquired.

"The Agamemnon was malfunctioning and barely staying aloft, they had zero manoeuvrability. Arabia Terra is very rough and rugged terrain. They needed a good clear landing field to put down on and all the emergency facilities of a spaceport. Even if they could have found a place to land, their crippled ship would never have made it down safely", Forkbraid explained adding, "It's doubtful they could have landed safely at all, even at the Elysium spaceport."

"There must have been something we could have done?", Selene asked again.

"There was, Selene", Forkbraid replied, "I sent them our fighter escort and hoped for the best. That's the only thing I could do."

"It wasn't enough", Selene lamented.

"No, it wasn't enough", Forkbraid agreed.

"So many deaths", Selene lamented again.

Selene leant her head into Forkbraid's left shoulder and looked out over the Elysium plateau. Forkbraid placed his arm about her and kissed her gently on the forehead. Above them the clouds began to stir. Claps of thunder began to sound and lightning flashed through the sky. Forkbraid reached out with his right hand and directed a bolt of lightning to the ground several hundred yards beyond the Psychic Academy's outer walls. Thrice more he did this, each time exercising greater and greater control.

"You're angry, Forkbraid", Selene whispered.

"Oh, I am definitely angry, Selene", Forkbraid replied softly in a tightly controlled voice.

Forkbraid drew his index finger across the sky in front of them and lightning flashed along the line drawn by his outstretched finger. Several more times he made the lightning dance to his will. Back and forth it danced like a puppet on a string.

Selene lifted her head off of Forkbraid's shoulder and looked into his eyes.

"The more angry you get, the more controlled you become?", Selene questioned.

"Yes. To a point", Forkbraid replied calmly, but without emotion.

"To a point?", Selene queried.

"Yes. To a point, Selene", Forkbraid replied once more, adding, "At the right time. At the right place. I will unleash a rage so wrathful, that those who perpetrated these atrocities will most certainly wish they had not. They will rue the day that they committed those crimes."

Selene turned to look out upon the Elysium plateau once more, then leant her head back into Forkbraid's shoulder. For the first time ever since she'd met Forkbraid, she felt frightened of him.

19. On the Run

The little fishing boat had crossed the Hebes Sea in the night. Quietly the fishing boat had pulled out of the little hamlet of Krell. Not a soul had seen her leave, nor the passengers she carried. A strong westerly breeze was blowing and Joseph had remarked that they were blessed. The Gods be with us tonight, Joseph had said.

First they had skirted the coast of Hebes Island eastward, then they had crossed the sea towards the southern shore. The sea was quiet that night and the crossing had been uneventful. Joseph sailed his little boat eastward along the southern shoreline. It was nearly morning when Joseph gently nudged his boat onto the beach. The Sun had not yet risen, but its glow was beginning to show.

"Shira is just around that point", Joseph told his Cousin Cormac pointing along the coast to a small headland, "It's a small village, heaps bigger than Krell, but small nonetheless."

"Will we have trouble getting transport?", Cormac enquired.

"I shouldn't think so, Shira trades with Jericho all the time.", Joseph replied, "Just to be on the safe side, trek inland a mile or two and approach the village from the landward side."

"Is that necessary?", asked Candy.

"It's prudent", Joseph replied, "If anyone comes here looking for you, which would you prefer people to remember. That you arrived by land or that you arrived by sea?"

Candy thought about that for a very brief moment, "If we came by sea, they'll know it was us for sure. By land, they could never be sure, could they?"

"Precisely, Candy, precisely", Joseph replied.

"Cormac. Try not to be seen by too many people. The fewer who see you, the better", Joseph advised his Cousin.

"Good advice as always, Cousin", Cormac replied.

"Use your gifts if you have to", Joseph added, "It wouldn't hurt to obscure a few memories here and there. The fewer people that remember you, the better."

Cormac nodded, "We'll be doing just that, Joseph."

Cormac helped his Wife to the shore, carrying her across the few feet of water from the boat to the beach itself, a perfect gentleman. He had no sooner put Candy down on the beach, when Joseph passed them their backpacks.

"Wait here while I get the little one", Joseph told them.

Joseph walked back to his boat and gently lifted the still sleeping Miranda from her seat. He gently held Miranda against his shoulder and carried her small backpack and another parcel in his other hand. Once back on the beach again he passed Miranda to Candy, and the backpack and parcel to Cormac.

"What's in the parcel, Joseph?", Cormac asked.

"Some smoked fish, some dried fruit and a good-sized slice of cheese. Not much really, just stuff for the road", Joseph replied.

"Thanks, Joseph", Cormac replied as he held out his hand.

"No need to thank me, Cousin", Joseph replied as he took Cormac's hand and gave it a strong shake, "Just make sure you take care of those two."

"No problem there", Cormac replied.

"I can take care of myself you know", Candy replied, "What are you going to do now, Joseph?"

"Me. I'm a fisherman, Candy. I'm going to sail my boat back to Krell, catch me some fish and pretend that this little adventure never happened", Joseph replied smiling.

"Thanks again, Joseph", Candy told him.

"You just take care of yourselves", Joseph replied as he strode back to his boat and gave it a shove.

Joseph shoved his boat hard three more times, then jumped into it and began sailing back to his little hamlet, Krell.

The Prophet was furious, his captive Witch was missing. All morning his people had been searching through New Tortuga, thus far no sign of the child had been found. He had questioned Mrs Harmon several times, each being pointless. The woman had been drugged and remembered nothing from the day before. Cormac the hydroponics manager and his Wife, Candace, were both missing as well. It didn't take long to figure out what had happened, but where the three had gone was a mystery. There was only one way into New Tortuga and it was the only way out.

"Are you certain they haven't left?", the Prophet asked Leroy.

"My Lord. I don't see how they could have. We have sentries at the port. It's the only way in and the only way out. No one has left since we launched the attack", Leroy replied.

"Can you be sure, Leroy? Do we know for certain our sentries were awake?", the Prophet asked.

"We have six sentries, my Lord. Matthew himself set up scanners to watch the entrance as well. He has viewed the data files himself. My Lord, no one has left this colony. They must still be in here somewhere", Leroy replied.

"Then turn this colony upside down and inside out. I want them found", the Prophet demanded.

"Yes, my Lord. Your will be done", Leroy replied before leaving to supervise the search.

On his way out of the Church, he met with Matthew, "Any news?"

"Nothing, Sir", Matthew replied, "Our men are searching building by building, house by house. No sign of them has been found so far."

"They haven't left. They have to be in here somewhere", Leroy stated.

"Assuming the port is the only way out", Matthew replied.

A look of horror came over Leroy, "Have our men search for hidden rooms, hidden tunnels, passageways. Anything that they could have used to hide in or escape."

"Yes, Sir. I'll get right on it", Matthew replied.

By the end of the day, New Tortuga had been searched from top to bottom, left to right, and front to back, with still no sign of the three fugitives being found. Several boltholes had been discovered, all empty. Various hidden tunnels and passageways had been uncovered, none of these led to the outside of New Tortuga. Cormac's hidden passage remained undiscovered. Leroy was worried, Matthew was calm and logical.

"They have to be here somewhere, Matthew. No one has left the colony", Leroy stated boldly.

"Assuming there is no other way out, Sir", Matthew replied.

"And if there is?", Leroy queried.

"Then we have a problem, Sir", Matthew replied with a thoughtful look on his face.

Leroy thought for long moments before replying, "The location of New Tortuga is a carefully guarded secret. That's what makes this place so perfect for a base of operations. Now, we have three people on the loose, two of whom know our precise location."

"Sir, even if they got out of the colony, they still have to get off Hebes Island", Matthew replied.

Leroy smiled, "That's right, Lad. Even if they get out of here, they still have to get off the island."

"And we are in one of the most isolated and rugged regions of Mars, Sir", Matthew added.

"The odds of them reaching civilisation are quite slim aren't they?", Leroy speculated.

"It would be very difficult, Sir", Matthew replied adding, "However, Cormac is a local."

"Yes, he is, Matthew", Leroy considered, "We can't take any chances, Lad. We must find them."

Leroy's men had searched all night. No sign of the fugitives had been found. Leroy had reported the situation to the Prophet, who was not at all pleased with the situation.

"So, they're not in New Tortuga", the Prophet stated, being uncertain how this could happen.

"No, my Lord. They are not in New Tortuga", Leroy answered.

"How can this be so, Leroy?", the Prophet asked, "You yourself said they could not have left."

"They didn't pass through the port, my Lord", Leroy replied, adding "There has to be another way out of here, that we don't know about yet, and our men have not been able to find it, either."

"We must find them, Leroy", the Prophet ordered, "Before our enemy does!"

"We're doing everything we can, my Lord", Leroy replied.

"And what would that be, Leroy?", the Prophet demanded.

"It is possible they're hiding in the hills, my Lord. I've ordered our remaining Talons to scan the island for any sign of them. I've also sent our men out into the local villages to make enquiries. If they are still on this island, we will find them."

"Leroy", the Prophet began, then paused as he looked at the surrounding men, "If they had a hidden way out of here, I suspect they had a way off the island as well."

"That is also possible, my Lord", Leroy replied.

"Matthew", the Prophet called out, then when Matthew stepped forward, "If you were Cormac, what would you do?"

"If I were, Cormac?", Matthew asked.

"Yes, Lad. If you were Cormac, what would you do?", the Prophet asked again.

"Well, if I was Cormac and I had a way out of here, I would also have a way off this island as well. It goes without saying, my Lord", Matthew replied, adding "He's a local. He knows the terrain and the people. He also has a good day and a half head start."

Leroy nodded, he had to agree with Matthew's assessment thus far.

"I doubt very much that we'll find them hiding in the hills", Matthew added.

"You think searching the island is a waste of time?", the Prophet asked.

"Not at all, my Lord", Matthew replied, "We have to cover all of our bases, and it is possible that they're hiding in the hills. It's just that, I think it's very unlikely."

"So, what would you recommend, Matthew?", the Prophet enquired.

Matthew looked at Leroy and then back to the Prophet, "We should continue our search of the island, my Lord, at least for now."

"At least for now?", the Prophet queried.

"Well, my Lord. If we find a means of getting off this island that would have been accessible to Cormac, then we have to assume that he used it or at least a similar method. At that point we'd have to assume they're on the mainland and our search would have to widen considerably."

"What you're saying is that, if they get off this island, they could be anywhere?", the Prophet surmised and questioned.

"Yes, my Lord", Matthew replied, "Once they're off this island, they have any number of different routes they can take."

"If you were them, which one would you take?", the Prophet enquired.

"I couldn't say, my Lord", Matthew replied, "There's no telling which route they will have taken. Personally, I would head north to Chryce. It's the largest colony and the seat of power on Mars. It's also a major transport hub. Furthermore, it would be the quickest way for them to get to the Elysium colony. Honestly though, there's no guarantee they went that way."

"Elysium is on the other side of Mars, Matthew", Leroy remarked.

"Yes, Sir, but the child, Miranda, is a psychic", Matthew replied, "And the Elysium colony was built for psychics. I'd be willing to bet that that little Witch is heading for Elysium."

"They can't be allowed to reach Elysium. That would be a disaster", the Prophet reminded them.

Both Leroy and Matthew nodded in agreement.

Matthew then stated, "One good thing, my Lord."

"What's that, Matthew?", the Prophet queried.

"They won't have access to anything that flies in these parts", Matthew informed the Prophet confidently, "As far as we know, New Tortuga has control of every aircraft in this region."

"And we can be sure of this?", the Prophet queried.

"Yes, my Lord. Our agents checked for any aircraft in the area weeks ago. They found none", Matthew replied.

The Prophet considered Matthew's remarks, "I'm going to assume they've already left the island. We don't have the manpower to check every possibility. Leroy, have our Talons check the northern trails to Chryce. Also have our people check the coastal villages. See if anyone remembers seeing three strangers fitting their descriptions in the last couple of days. That should tell us which direction they went in."

"Straight away, my Lord", Leroy replied.

"Matthew, we have people at Chryce, yes?", the Prophet queried.

"Yes, my Lord", Matthew replied, "We have people at all the official colonies."

"Good, we need to have them watch out for our three fugitives. Get pictures of the girl out to our people. If they find her, they are to kill her and everyone she's with."

"Yes, my Lord. I'll send out word straight away", Matthew replied.

Cormac slowly eyed the village of Shira. He had chosen a vantage point high on a hill overlooking the village, with a good coverage of trees. It was a fair size village, larger than Krell, with more than two dozen houses and other buildings. A smallish inn was located near the edge of the village on the landward side.

Close to the inn was a large shed-like structure which Cormac assumed was a storage facility. From there the main road ran southeast.

A large vehicle was parked at the edge of the road in front of the inn. It was a Mog, a large six wheeled, all terrain vehicle. The rear section was a covered flat bed, loaded with goods and a covered Trailer was attached to its rear tow-bar. It was still early morning and a cold mist hung over the village, not a soul stirred.

Cormac concentrated on the inn, for several minutes as he scanned the minds of the people within. Finally, he looked back at Candy.

"There's a Mog and Trailer down there Candy. The drivers are heading to Jericho after they finish their breakfast. There doesn't appear to be any other transports to Jericho for at least another week, so this looks like the one. The only one."

"What's the plan then, Cormac?", Candy whispered as Miranda stirred slightly in her arms.

"I'm thinking we just climb aboard the trailer and hide amongst the goods", Cormac told her.

"A good plan", Candy agreed, "If we're quick, no one will see us."

"And no one will know that we were here", Cormac replied with his gap-toothed smile.

Cormac and Candy quickly snuck down from the hill. Hiding amongst the trees to ensure they would not be seen. They approached the inn. Cormac looked up and down the street, it was still quiet and no one was about. Swiftly and silently they crept up to the back of the trailer, pulled back the tarpaulin cover flap and climbed in. Cormac took one last look up and down the street. It was still quiet, no one and nothing stirred.

Smiling Cormac led Candy toward the front of the trailer. In front of them was a wall of sacks, all containing surplus corn from the previous autumn's harvest. He carefully moved the front sacks out of the way, making a good-sized cavity amongst the remaining stack. It took Cormac several minutes to make sure that their hiding place would be both safe and comfortable.

Once finished, he gave their hiding place the once over, then turned to Candy, "After you, misses", he said with a whisper.

"Why thank you kindly, Cormac", Candy whispered back in reply.

Candy entered their hiding place and carefully placed Miranda down upon some sacks.

Miranda awoke and yawned "Where are we?"

Candy put her finger to her lips, to signal Miranda to be quiet, "We're hiding in a Mog Trailer, little one. It will be leaving for Jericho shortly."

"Did I sleep through all the fun?", Miranda asked quietly

"Yes, little one. That long trek we took yesterday seems to have completely worn you out", Candy whispered back.

"Where's Joseph? Isn't he with us?", Miranda enquired.

"No, little one. Joseph has gone fishing, then he'll return to Krell", Candy replied.

Cormac had finished covering the entrance to their hiding place with sacks of corn, leaving only a narrow, barely noticeable passage, he looked at Miranda.

"Glad to see you're awake, little one", he greeted, and Miranda smiled back at him.

Cormac looked up at the canvas roof and then took out his belt knife, carefully he cut a few small slotted holes in the canvas, "We'll need light, and air, won't we?"

"That we will Cormac, that we will", Candy replied before leaning back into the corn sacks and nodding off to sleep.

Cormac smiled at his Wife, then put his feet up to rest, "We need to be quiet for this trip, Miranda. The drivers will be leaving shortly."

It was nearly fifteen minutes later when they heard the slamming of the Mog's passenger side door, followed shortly after that by the slamming of the driver's side door. Candy woke immediately upon hearing the door slam and reached for Miranda, then settled back down when she realised Miranda was alright. Then the engine started, and the Mog began to move forward. Slowly the Mog crawled up the road and out of the village, dragging its Trailer behind it.

Candy looked carefully in the dim light and noticed Miranda was eating dried fruit and cheese.

"A nice breakfast", Candy said softly.

Cormac passed some dried fruit and cheese to his Wife, "Thank you kindly, Cormac."

"How long will it take to get to Jericho?", Miranda asked.

Cormac concentrated on the Mog's two drivers, "A little over three days according to our driver", Cormac replied, "And we should be arriving in the middle of the night."

"Well that should suit us just fine", Candy replied with a smile.

"Can't we get there any sooner?", Miranda, not wanting to be stuck in the back of a truck trailer for three days, queried.

"Well, little one. I could put that notion into the driver's mind, but it wouldn't be a very good idea", Cormac replied.

"Why not?", Miranda, not understanding, enquired.

"Well, if I make them drive faster, they might get reckless and that wouldn't be good, would it now?", Cormac replied.

"We all want to get to Jericho in one piece, Miranda", Candy added.

"Oh, I see", Miranda replied, but with a slight frown.

The road out of Shira was all uphill and the Mog continued at a slow and steady pace. About two hours out of Shira, Cormac squeezed through the passage out of their hideaway and carefully looked out of the back of the trailer.

"Miranda", Cormac called, his voice barely above a whisper, "You might want to see this."

Miranda slipped through the passage, followed by Candy. Cormac had pulled back the tarp, and they all looked out of the back of the trailer.

"Wow!", was Miranda's only word as she stared at the vista from the rear of the trailer.

The road they were on had crawled up into the hill country. Before them was a view stretching all the way back to the Hebes Sea. Hebes Island was all but hidden in the sea's morning mists. The forest of pines and other conifers had become thinner and thinner, until finally the trees had become scarce. The forest, now being some distance behind them, concealing the village of Shira from sight. Only occasional stands of trees were seen in the immediate area.

The Mog's tire tracks dug deeply into the snow which covered the road. The road they were travelling on was marked on both sides with special marker posts every twenty meters or so. On both sides of the road, in places where the snow became patchy, the red Martian soil could clearly be seen. Otherwise, the snow covered pretty much everything else. The air was cold and sharp.

"Lucky we wore our warm clothes", Candy remarked with a slight shiver.

Cormac smiled his gap-toothed smile and pointed to a large patch of red soil, "That was the colour of nearly everything in the old days, when the sky was all salmon pink."

"When the sky was all salmon pink?", Miranda enquired.

"Back before the terraforming, little one", Candy sighed.

"The air was so thin back then, almost a vacuum and unbreathable", Cormac informed Miranda.

"How did people live?", Miranda asked.

"There weren't any hamlets and villages back then, little one", Cormac replied, "New Tortuga was one of only a handful of colonies back then, and they were all underground in caverns."

"And they were all sealed in, in those days. Every colony", Candy continued, "You needed to wear a special suit and go through an airlock just to go outside."

"Special suit?", Miranda who was familiar with modern space suits asked, "You mean a Mechanical Counter Pressure Environment Suit, an [67]MCPES?"

"Yes, little one", Candy replied, "It was a harsh environment back then."

"How long ago was that?", enquired Miranda.

"Oh, long ago, little one, centuries", Cormac replied, "It was before the sky fell, the coming of the long rains, back when Mars released its ancient breath."

---

67 MCPES – Mechanical Counter Pressure Environment Suit.

"Falling sky? Long rains? Ancient breath", Miranda asked, looking puzzled.

"Yes, little one", Candy replied, "The terraformers dropped pieces of icy asteroids on Mars back then. They fell right out of the sky, they did."

"Those chunks of ice contained a lot of water", Cormac continued, "And the sky couldn't hold onto it all. It rained for a long time, almost continuously for many, many years. That's where Mars got all of its oceans and seas from Miranda."

"And its air. The ancient Martian atmosphere was released as well", Candy added.

"It must have been very frightening", Miranda stated.

"I figure it was for those who lived here back then. Terribly frightening", Cormac replied.

"Wasn't it dangerous for the colonists?", Miranda asked.

"Yes, it was, little one", Candy answered, "Very dangerous."

"If it was so dangerous, why did they allow it?", Miranda enquired.

"There weren't supposed to be any colonists on Mars during that stage of the terraforming project", Cormac replied, "They were supposed to have been evacuated into high Martian orbit."

"Except, many of the colonists refused to leave", Candy added, "And they hid themselves in the older colonies, the ones not registered on anyone's books."

"Like New Tortuga", Miranda smiled.

"Like New Tortuga", Candy smiled back in confirmation.

Miranda looked out at the desolate landscape, "Why are there no trees up here?"

Cormac looked about at the vista before them, "The forests have yet to spread this far, little one."

Candy could see Cormac's short answer would not suffice, "Around the official colonies, a lot of time and effort was put into the seeding process. So the forests and pastures are far more developed there and quite extensive. For the rest of Mars the seeding was more sporadic. Most of the official seeding was done along the coastal regions, places where the rainfall would ensure their growth."

Candy continued, "Then many of the smaller towns and villages continued the process unofficially, spreading the forests and pastures even further. The forests are essentially self seeding now. Unfortunately, the process is quite slow and in the more isolated and rugged regions like this, the forestation process has yet to spread and take hold."

"But it is happening", Miranda pointed out, her small hand pointing to the odd small saplings starting to grow here and there in the Martian soil.

"Yes, little one. It is happening. Very slowly, but it is happening", Candy replied with a smile.

"One day this will all be forest", Miranda stated with certainty.

Cormac and Candy looked about the desolate landscape before them.

Then Candy replied, "Dare I say it, Miranda darling, by the time you have little ones of your own, this forest will stretch all the way to Jericho."

Leroy was back in the Church building formerly known as the Black Pullet, meeting with the Prophet. Leroy's people had spent two days checking the local villages and scanning the northern trails to Chryce. Night had descended once more and no sign of the fugitives had been found.

"My Lord", he addressed the Prophet, "Captain Scar and his men have scanned nearly all the trails leading north to Chryce. They have yet to find any trace of our fugitives."

"No trace?", the Prophet questioned.

"No trace, my Lord", Leroy reiterated, "It's the tail end of winter and still very cold out there. No one is abroad on the northern trails at the moment. They've even tried thermal imaging scans."

"Then they aren't heading north?", the Prophet questioned.

"Perhaps, my Lord. They could be using a trail that we don't know about, or perhaps they're just lying low. Until we get a positive sighting there's no way to know for sure", Leroy replied.

While the Prophet mulled over this news Leroy gave him further information, "Our men have checked the local villages along the island's coast, my Lord."

The Prophet looked up, "What have they found, Leroy?"

"Many of the villages have small fishing boats", Leroy replied, "More than capable of reaching the mainland. So I think we can safely assume that they've made it off the island. So far though, not a single villager remembers seeing them."

"Would they tell us if they had?", the Prophet asked.

"With the reward we're offering, my Lord, a man would sell out his own Mother", Leroy replied.

"And yet no one has seen them?", the Prophet questioned.

"Correct, my Lord", Leroy replied.

"We've also had our men checking the villages on the outer coast", Leroy told the Prophet.

The Prophet did not reply, instead he waited for Leroy to give him more information.

"No sign of them there either", Leroy continued.

"I was hoping you might have some good news for a change, Leroy", the Prophet scolded.

"I do, my Lord", Leroy quickly replied, "The only vehicles available in all of these villages are land and sea-craft. Nothing that flies, my Lord, just as Matthew told us."

"So they haven't jumped into a hummer and flown to Elysium then?", the Prophet asked.

"Extremely unlikely, my Lord", Leroy smiled, "We have the only aircraft in this region."

"That is at least good news, Leroy", the Prophet smiled back.

Finally, Leroy remembered a snippet of information, "The only thing our men have come across was news of a truck transporting surplus corn from the village of Shira to Jericho."

"A truck?", the Prophet enquired.

"Yes, my Lord", Leroy replied, "A six wheeled all terrain Mog and Trailer."

"Any passengers?", the Prophet asked.

"No, my Lord", Leroy replied, "Just the two drivers and twelve tonnes of corn. No one in Shira remembers seeing any strangers about and no boats have birthed at their jetties since winter began."

"It would be well worth following up on that truck, Leroy", the Prophet ordered, "It is our most promising lead."

"Yes my, Lord, I'll get my men on it at first light", Leroy replied.

Matthew stepped forward to report on the infiltration of the Chryce colony by their converted freighters. He also had information with regards the Elysium colony and the whereabouts of its Psychic Academy.

"My Lord", Matthew addressed the Prophet, "Six of our freighters are now in the process of entering the service of Chryce colony."

"That is good news, Matthew, tell me more", the Prophet replied.

"Well, my Lord. I had our pilots volunteer to help with the cartage of supplies to Elysium. Ostensibly for the repairs to the Elysium colony. They're now in the process of going through the red tape, as we speak."

"Excellent. How long will it be before we can attack?", the Prophet enquired.

"Not that long, my Lord. In three or four days we'll have our first opportunity", Matthew informed him.

"Won't they find our modifications?", Leroy asked.

"No, Sir", Matthew replied, "The Raider modifications have been carefully hidden within our freighters outer hulls."

Leroy looked at Matthew, a look that requested more detail.

"Specifically, sliding hull plating and pop up weapons blisters, complete with high intensity lasers and pulsed plasma cannons", Matthew informed Leroy.

"Well done, Lad", Leroy replied, "That ought to pack a wallop."

"Yes, Sir. That was my intention", Matthew replied.

"Indeed, Matthew, well done", the Prophet added.

"Thank you, my Lord", Matthew replied.

"I do have more news, my Lord", Matthew then told the Prophet.

"Yes, Matthew, I am listening", the Prophet replied.

"Our people in Chryce have been looking for information on the Elysium colony, specifically for the whereabouts of their Psychic Academy", Matthew began.

"Have they found anything?", Leroy asked.

"Not yet, Sir", Matthew replied.

"If they haven't found anything, what are you reporting?", the Prophet asked.

"My Lord, forgive me", Matthew began again, "They haven't found the Psychic Academy itself, but we now know for certain that it exists."

"Really? Please explain", the Prophet asked.

"My Lord", Matthew started, "Numerous androids were used on a special project during the building of the Elysium colony. These androids weren't used in building the main colony itself. They were taken elsewhere. When they were returned to the Elysium colony, all knowledge of what they had been working on had been removed."

"Removed", Leroy questioned, "They wiped their memories?"

"No, Sir", Matthew replied, "Wiping their memories wouldn't be thorough enough. The pathways would still be traceable. Their entire positronic brains were removed."

"Removing their brains! That would certainly hide the secret", Leroy answered.

"My Lord", Matthew addressed the Prophet once again, "Here's the thing. They were transported to this special project by land. The Psychic Academy has to be on the Elysium subcontinent."

"So we know it exists, we know it's on the subcontinent, we just don't have its precise location?", the Prophet stated, requesting confirmation.

"That is precisely the situation, my Lord", Matthew replied.

"But we will have it soon enough, my Lord", Leroy assured his master.

Cormac had been preparing their little hide away for their departure since dusk on the third day. They'd cleaned up the trailer and removed any obvious signs of their having been there. Then Cormac placed all the corn sacks back in their original positions, removing their hidden nook. Quietly they waited at the rear of the trailer by its tarpaulin cover flap.

They had no idea precisely when they'd reach Jericho and so Candy and Cormac took turns skimming the surface of the drivers' minds. First Cormac scanned the drivers' minds for an hour, then Candy would take her turn. Fours hours had slowly passed in this fashion, with Cormac and Candy switching turns and with little Miranda quietly watching them.

It was long after dark on the third day of travelling when the Mog approached the outer limits of Jericho. Candy had taken her turn at skimming the drivers' minds some thirty minutes earlier and had carefully scanned their minds almost continuously.

Then one of the drivers had said to the other, "Just over that next hill, and we'll be able to see Jericho's lights."

Candy smiled, it was almost time to leave, "Cormac!", she whispered.

Cormac looked up at his Wife.

"We get off at the top of this hill", Candy told him.

Cormac smiled, then nodded and carefully pulled back the trailer's tarpaulin cover flap.

Cormac looked out the back of the trailer and then carefully up both sides of the road.

He then turned to Candy "It's all clear, Candy. Can you sense anything?"

"No, not a thing, Cormac", Candy replied, "It's all clear to me as well."

"Good", Cormac replied as he carefully dropped their backpacks out of the back of the trailer.

Cormac was quick to follow the backpacks out of the trailer, then he quickly turned and ran up to the back of the trailer as Candy passed little Miranda out the back.

Cormac stopped on the road with Miranda in his arms as he watched Candy drop over the rear of the trailer. Candy landed awkwardly, but was otherwise okay. Quickly they gathered their backpacks and moved off to the side of the road. They quickly concealed themselves behind some trees and foliage, as they watched the Mog and Trailer go over the hill and disappear out of sight.

"So far so good", Cormac said to the others.

"Yes, Cormac, so far", Candy replied, "But let's not get cocky."

Cormac nodded to his Wife then he turned to Miranda, "How are you doing, little one?"

"I'm okay", Miranda replied, "But it is a bit cold."

"Yeah, lucky there's no snow here. It would be much colder", Candy replied, "Cormac we'd better get into town."

"Then we'd better start walking", Cormac told them, "Jericho shouldn't be too far off."

The trio walked through the trees on the side of the road, again being careful to conceal their presence. They reached the peak of the hill and looked down into the valley before them. Jericho sat at the mouth of a river on its western shore. It was a good-sized village, more of a town really, far larger than either Krell or Shira and probably as large as New Tortuga.

Cormac carefully eyed the town in the distance, "Lucky it's on this side of the river."

Candy nodded in agreement, crossing a bridge would mean being seen, even at night.

"The docks are way down the river. We'll have to go through town to reach them", Cormac informed them, pointing to the docks in the distance on the other side of town.

"Then we'll need to be careful, Cormac", Candy replied as she turned back to Miranda, "We may have to alter your appearance somewhat, Miranda."

"My appearance?", Miranda questioned.

"Yeah. We'll do that when we get closer to town, little one", Candy told her.

It took them nearly an hour to walk to the township of Jericho, stopping just outside of town behind a stand of trees. Candy called Miranda over to her, and she quickly began adjusting Miranda's clothes.

"Good", Candy said as she looked at her handy work, "Now let's dirty up that nice pretty blond hair of yours."

Miranda stepped back as Candy reached for some mud.

"It's okay, Miranda, we just need to hide your pretty blond hair a little-bit", Candy reassured her.

Candy ran her muddy fingers through Miranda's hair, dirtying it. Then having finished dirtying Miranda's hair, Candy carefully tied Miranda's back and clipped it up into a bun, finally hiding what had once been pretty blond locks under a boy's cap.

"There. All done", Candy stated as she passed Miranda a small mirror.

"I look like a boy!", Miranda exclaimed in disgust.

"That's exactly the look I was looking for, little one", Candy replied smiling, before asking her Husband, "What do you think Cormac?"

Cormac took a good look at Miranda, "Yeah, that should do it alright, Candy."

Cormac led Candy and Miranda into Jericho. They walked quickly and quietly through the silent, narrow backstreets of the town. They passed by a tavern, aptly named The Travellers Rest, with a Mog and Trailer parked out back. The very same Mog and Trailer they'd used to transport themselves from the village of Shira. They very carefully passed by as quietly as they could.

It didn't take them long to reach the docks and Cormac was certain that they weren't seen.

Carefully he scanned the docks, seeking minds that might have any information that he could use with regards transport to their next destination, the colony of Aurorae. For the most part the docks were quiet, nearly everyone was asleep, except Cormac came across a couple of startling thoughts.

"Over there", Cormac pointed to a schooner at the far dock, "The Shilo, she's leaving just a little after dawn."

"Is she going to Aurorae?", Candy enquired.

"Yep, she sure is", Cormac answered.

"Good, Cormac", replied Candy, "Are they taking on passengers?"

"Yeah", Cormac replied, adding, "They haven't fully booked yet, and they have more than enough room for us. We have a little problem though."

"Problem?", Candy queried, "What problem, Cormac?"

"Over there", Cormac pointed to a building and the laneway next to it.

Candy looked over at the lane way and concentrated, "Oh, I see, Cormac."

The Shilo was being watched. It was the only ship scheduled to leave Jericho that morning, and it was being watched by agents of the Prophet. Two men eyed the ship, all and everyone going aboard her would be seen.

"That's our little problem, Candy", Cormac told his Wife.

"More than a little problem, Cormac", Candy replied, then sending him a silent thought, *"They're looking for Miranda."*

Cormac replied silently, *"They're assassins Candy! Fucking assassins!"*

Candy looked at Cormac, *"Language, Cormac"*, then she looked at Miranda, *"They mustn't get her, Cormac. They mustn't!"*

"They won't, Candy", Cormac replied, assuring her, *"I'll deal with them myself."*

"What's wrong", Miranda asked with an agitated look on her face.

"Nothing you need to worry about, little one", Cormac replied.

Candy held Miranda closely to her, "It's okay, Miranda. Cormac is going to take care of everything", she said as Cormac disappeared into the misty night.

Candy also had a worried look on her face, she didn't like what Cormac was about to do.

Cormac crept silently through the docks and soon found himself behind the building where the Prophets men were watching the Shilo. He looked around and soon found himself a comfortable place to sit and wait.

About forty minutes into Cormac's vigil, one of the men said to the other, "I'm going for a leak."

A few minutes later the man walked past Cormac, further down the laneway where he began to pee against an old warehouse.

Cormac crept through the shadows and came up behind the man. Quietly he took out his belt knife, then with one deft move he placed his left hand over the man's mouth, while his right hand came up and plunged the knife deep into the man's neck. Cormac pushed the knife forward and out through the man's throat. There was a quiet gurgling sound as the man drowned in his own blood. Cormac carefully laid the now deceased man down on the ground.

Having dispatched the first man, Cormac now silently moved though the shadows once more towards the other. It took him just a few seconds to come up behind the second man, who was carefully watching the Shilo with all his attention. Cormac came up behind the man, placed his left hand over the man's mouth and pushed his knife deep into the man's back, piercing his heart. Carefully, Cormac lowered the man's corpse to the ground.

Cormac hid the second man's body with the first, then he quickly found some rope and made his way to the waters edge just down from the docks and away from the ships. Quickly locating a likely spot, Cormac tied some knots in the rope and a rock to its end.

He shone a small flashlight into the water, it was turbid, *"Good"*, he thought to himself.

Slowly he lowered the rope into the water. Counting each knot as he lowered the rope.

He soon found that the water to be thirty-five feet deep, *"Even better"*, he thought to himself.

Then, when he brought the rope back up again, he noted the thick mud covering the rock at the end of the rope, *"Excellent"*, he thought to himself.

Cormac quickly made his way back to the two dead men, looking for materials he could work with along the way. He gathered some more rope and some heavy steel beams. Quietly he assembled everything he needed by the waters edge.

He tied the corpses to the beams with the rope and when he was certain that they were securely tied on, he rolled the bodies into the deep, turbid waters of the river. They quickly sunk down to the muddy bottom. Cormac sighed with relief when he had finished the task and quickly returned to the laneway to clean up any remaining mess, before quietly returning to Candy and Miranda.

"Everything okay, Cormac", Candy thought out as Cormac approached.

"Everything is fine, Candy. Sweet as candy, in fact", Cormac replied as he sat beside his Wife.

Miranda lay sleeping in Candy's arms.

"What did you do with them?", Candy asked with a thought.

"I dropped them into a vile bog where they belong", Cormac replied, a serious look on his face.

"It was necessary, Cormac", Candy told him, *"What would they have done to this precious little one if they'd caught her?"*, Candy added as she looked down at Miranda, sleeping in her arms.

"I know it was necessary, Candy", Cormac replied with a frown, *"I just wish it wasn't."*

As the Sun rose on the eastern horizon Candy woke Miranda. Cormac was already gone, he had already disappeared again in the night to find the Shilo's ticketing office. He had used his gifts to surreptitiously awaken the sleeping ticket master.

Candy and Miranda stayed out of sight and waited for Cormac's return. Just after dawn Cormac arrived back from the ticketing office. He returned with three tickets in his hand, one for each of them. At the ticketing office they were recorded on the books as a Man, a Woman and a young Boy.

No-one was watching the Shilo when the three boarded the ship shortly after dawn. Once their tickets were checked they made their way straight to their cabin, where they decided to stay until the ship was well out to sea.

The Shilo was due to set sail later that morning at ten-forty-five am. Candy and Cormac took turns scanning the ship's passengers and crew for any more of the Prophet's men. The ship was clear each time they did a complete scan. None of the Prophet's men had boarded the Shilo.

Then at ten-forty-five a loud whistle blew, signifying the gang plank being retracted and Candy gave a sigh of relief. That was it. They were safely on board with nothing to worry about. Soon they would be at sea and on their way to the Aurorae colony.

John Smith had once upon a time been a private in the services of the Mars Colonial Command's Phobos space-docks. He was, of course, also a member of a militant fundamentalist Christian sect.

Now he was a fugitive from justice and a known terrorist. None of this mattered in the wild, lawless and rugged back country of Mars. Here, he was an agent of the Prophet tracking down three fugitives, whose capture and/or death was deemed a necessity. John Smith was now an assassin.

He had tracked a Mog and Trailer from the village of Shira to the township of Jericho. Upon his arrival, he had found the Mog and Trailer parked at the rear of a tavern, The Travellers Rest. He found the two drivers of the Mog at the rear of the tavern. They had just finished their breakfast and were looking to unload their cargo later that day.

"Have you two just come in from Shira?", Smith asked as he approached the two drivers.

"Yeah, mate", the older of the two replied, adding, "We arrived last night around eleven pm."

"Either of you seen this child?", Smith asked as he handed them a photograph of Miranda.

Both men eyed the photograph carefully, "No, mate. Haven't seen her", the older man replied.

"Are you sure?", Smith questioned again, "She was travelling with a man and a woman."

"Na, mate", the younger man replied, "We haven't seen them."

"This child was kidnapped", Smith lied, "There is a reward for her safe return", again a lie.

The older man considered this, "The reward would be nice, but mate, we haven't seen her."

He was sincere, Smith could see it in his face, "Could they have stowed away on your Mog?"

Both men looked at each other, before the younger one replied, "It's possible, but still, we haven't seen them."

Then the older driver added, "If they did stow away on our Mog, we never saw them."

Smith walked over towards the Mog as he asked, "Mind if I have a look at your vehicle?"

"Be my guest", the older driver replied.

Smith carefully looked over the Mog, checking out the covers and then jumped up on the back, folding back the tarpaulin cover flap and looking into the back of the flat bed. Everything seemed in order. He moved down to the Trailer and checked it carefully. Again jumping up at the back and folding back the tarpaulin cover flap. He eyed the back of the trailer carefully. Nothing seemed out of place. Sacks of corn stacked from floor to roof. Everything appeared to be in order. Smith jumped back down. He'd been certain that he'd find something.

"I told you, mate", the older driver told him, "We haven't seen them."

"So you say", Smith replied, "The question is whether, or not you had stow-a-ways."

Smith shook his head, if they were stowed aboard there had to be some sign of them. He carefully checked the Trailer once more. This time looking more closely for anything that might give the fugitives away, then he noticed something in the Trailer's tarpaulin.

Smith looked more closely. High up on the side of the Trailer there was a small, cut hole. He climbed up onto the Trailer and looked more closely, yes, it was definitely cut. Then he looked further along, there was another small, cut hole. In fact, he found three. Quickly he jumped down and ran to the other side of the Trailer. The pattern was repeated, three small, cut holes, high up on the tarpaulin.

"Air holes", he thought to himself, and then he jumped back down.

"Were these holes in your tarpaulin before you left Shira?", he asked the two drivers.

Both men had watched as Smith found the small, cut holes, three on each side of the Trailer.

"No", the younger driver replied, "Our tarpaulins had no holes in them when we left Shira."

"The Lads right", the older driver added, "Those holes are new."

"Now, that is very interesting, isn't it", Smith replied adding, "Do you mind if I have a quick inspection of your Trailer?"

The older driver replied straight away, "I'd prefer it if you didn't disturb our goods, Mr."

Smith turned his head slightly sideways as he looked at the man.

He rested his right hand gently on his pulsed plasma pistol as he said, "Oh, I insist, Gentlemen.''

The older driver gulped slightly then replied, "Well, since you insist, yeah sure."

Smith said to the younger man, "You! Climb in and move some of those sacks out of the way. Look for anything that's out of the ordinary, anything odd."

The younger driver climbed into the Trailer and began shifting sacks of corn out of the way. As he did so he checked for anything odd. He managed to move nearly fifteen sacks out of the way before he noticed something. On the floor was a piece of dried fruit, an apricot to be precise. He held it up and looked at it, before passing it to the older driver, who in turn passed it to Smith.

Smith eyed the dried apricot and smiled, "Gentlemen, it appears you had stow-a-ways on board."

"So it would seem", the older driver now agreed.

"What time did you say you arrived?", Smith asked.

"Around eleven pm last night, just like we said before", the younger driver replied.

"Thank you for your co-operation, Gentlemen", Smith said as he marched off to the docks.

Smith reached the docks quickly and checked which ships were due to leave that day. There were only two ships. The Shilo was due to leave at ten-forty-five am that morning, with another ship, the Carpenter, due to leave at six pm that night. It was already gone ten am and as Smith checked the docks he noticed something just a little odd.

They were supposed to have men watching the docks. They were supposed to have men checking the ships. Look as he might, he found no sign of the Prophet's men. He quickly checked the docks again, this time looking more closely, perhaps their men weren't terribly diligent. Perhaps they were sleeping on the job so to speak. There was still no sign of their men.

Something was wrong. Something was terribly wrong. It was now ten-thirty am.

Quickly Smith ran to the ticket office.

He asked to check the ship's passenger manifest.

The Clerk had said no, and told him to fuck off.

Smith insisted in the same manner as he had with the two Mog drivers.

The Clerk gulped silently and passed him the ship's manifest.

He ran his finger over the passenger list. He did not recognise any of the names.

"They'd use aliases. Of course, they would", Smith thought to himself.

He checked for families, two adults and a girl. He found none.

"They have to be here. They have to!", Smith thought.

Smith stepped back from the counter rubbing his chin. He scratched his head and then looked at the manifest once more.

"They have to be here", he said quietly under his breath.

Still nothing. He stepped back from the counter once more and then looked at the clerk.

"Give me a fucking ticket!", he demanded.

"That will be ninety credits", the Clerk lied, doubling the price out of spite.

Smith pulled out a hundred credit note and handed it to the clerk, "Keep the change", he said as he grabbed the ticket.

He then quickly turned around and bolted out the door for the Shilo.

It was ten-forty-eight am when John Smith reached the Shilo. The gang plank was already in the process of being retracted from the Ship.

"Shit", Smith swore under his breath as he bolted at full speed past the workers and up the retracting gang plank.

He leapt over the five-foot gap to the ship and landed with a thud onto its deck.

The ship's Bosun grabbed Smith to steady him as he stood up.

Smith reached into his pocket, pulled out his ticket and waved it in the Bosun's face.

"Running a bit late are you, Sir?", the Bosun queried.

"Better late than never, hey", Smith replied.

"No baggage, Sir?", the Bosun queried.

"I always travel light", Smith replied.

"I'll have a crewman show you to your cabin, Sir", the Bosun told him.

"No need", Smith replied as he walked off, "I'll find it myself."

20. A Call in the Night

Forkbraid stood on the landing field's tarmac, southeast of the New Flinders Psychic Academy. As he watched the northern skies, four modified Wisps and a Hummer approached the landing field.

Special Agent Murphy was standing beside him, also watching, he remarked, "They didn't burn up on entry. That's always a good sign."

"No, they didn't", Forkbraid replied smiling, "Looks like we have some atmo rated Wisps."

One by one the ships landed on the tarmac, close to the two already parked Switch Blades and Forkbraid's own Bat Wing.

Captain Carmichael was quickly out of his Hummer, the pilots of the Wisps followed quickly behind him.

"Captain", Forkbraid greeted him with a nod, then "I thought we were getting a dozen Wisps?"

"Four now, four more in a few days, then another four a few days after that", the Captain replied adding, "I thought you might want them sooner rather than later, so I brought down the ones we have ready right now, rather than wait until they're all finished."

"A wise move, Captain, a very wise move", Forkbraid replied, "There's no way to know when the enemy will attack."

"My thoughts exactly, Forkbraid", the Captain replied, "That's why I brought these down early."

Special Agent Murphy had wandered over to the closest of the Wisps and was inspecting it.

"Pulsed plasma cannons, polyceramalloy coated hull and an atmo rated EM drive", he stated loudly as he looked over the Wisp.

"Fully tested as well, Agent Murphy", the Captain shouted out to him, "They'll do the job."

"That they will, Captain", Special Agent Murphy replied.

Forkbraid called to Varak, who had been overseeing the unloading of supplies from the HLTs. Varak quickly came over to the three men.

"Varak, have your men deliver the interceptors to the Academy", Forkbraid instructed him.

"Yes, Sir", Varak replied, then for clarification, "All of them or just the Wisps?"

"All of them, Varak", Forkbraid replied, "House them in one of the larger vehicle hangars. Billet the pilots close by the ships. We'll want them close if an attack occurs."

"Yes, Sir, I'll organise it straight away", Varak replied before taking charge of the Wisp pilots and leading them off, "You four, come with me."

Captain Carmichael watched his pilots head off with Varak as he asked Forkbraid, "How are your people settling in?"

"So far so good", Forkbraid replied, "Martian gravity is taking a bit of getting used to, but otherwise everything is going smoothly."

"Point three eight gs is different for sure, but that's not what I meant", the Captain stated.

"Oh. You mean their gifts?", Forkbraid replied.

"Yeah, their gifts", the Captain confirmed.

"It's a bit hit, and miss at this stage", Forkbraid replied, "Some of our people seem relatively unaffected. Some of our other people can't use their gifts at all. The latter are in the majority."

"Unaffected?", the Captain queried.

"Yeah Captain", Forkbraid replied, adding, "Some of our people are as functional here as they were one Earth."

"But not all?", the Captain asked.

"No, not all", Forkbraid replied, "As I just said, the majority are affected to some degree. It's going to take time for many of them to adapt to Mars."

"Shame that", the Captain replied, "I was hoping your people would be able to scan the planet."

"So was I, Captain", Special Agent Murphy agreed.

"We did know this was going to be the case, guys", Forkbraid reminded them.

"Still, it would have been nice, FB", Special Agent Murphy lamented.

"That it would have", Forkbraid replied, adding, "Remote viewers require specialist training as well, which adds to the timeline."

"How long then?", the Captain asked.

"That's like asking, how long's a piece of string?", Forkbraid stated.

"Hard to say then?", the Captain queried.

"Yep, hard to say", Forkbraid confirmed before stating with confidence, "We might have our first rudimentary Remote Viewing team ready in a month or so, if we're lucky, touch wood."

"That long?", the Captain queried with a sigh.

"Yeah", Forkbraid replied.

"How capable will they be?", the Captain asked.

"Again, difficult to say", Forkbraid replied, "I mean, it all depends on who adapts the quickest."

Captain Carmichael gave Forkbraid a confused look which beggared an answer.

"If the first to adapt are also more highly graded, then the first team will be very capable", Forkbraid explained, "but if they're of a lower grade it will be far less capable. There's no way to know at this stage. We will just have to wait and see what the trend is."

"That doesn't sound very promising", Captain Carmichael stated.
"Unfortunately it's just the way it is", Forkbraid replied.

"Just out of curiosity", Special Agent Murphy began, "Just how many Remote Viewing teams do you need to cover a planet this large?"
"Well, on Earth, there are seventy-two active Remote Viewing teams scattered around the globe at any given time", Forkbraid replied, "Each team is called a Wyvern coven and contains thirteen members. They give a more or less, complete overlapping coverage of the whole Earth."
Captain Carmichael was astonished, "That's nine-hundred and thirty-six psychics!"
"Yes, Captain", Forkbraid replied, "And they're all very, very capable. The best in fact."
"So, we never really had any hope of scanning all of Mars?", Special Agent Murphy asked.
"No", Forkbraid replied, "That was never Selene's initial intention, anyway."
"Selene's initial intention?", Captain Carmichael queried.
"The Flinders Grey Council hoped to eventually have enough Remote Viewing teams set up to cover the whole of Mars, but that was expected to take maybe a decade or even longer. It is a very slow process, Gentlemen. Initially Selene had envisioned that given a year or two, we'd have enough Wyverns set up to cover the Elysium subcontinent", Forkbraid replied, "That would be sufficient to defend the Psychic Academy."

"Just how many Wyverns would that take, Forkbraid?", the Captain asked.
"My estimate?", Forkbraid replied.
"Your estimate?", Captain Carmichael requested.
"Assuming the same level of capability as on Earth, around eight to ten Wyvern covens", Forkbraid replied.
"What if they're less capable?", Special Agent Murphy asked.
"That is really difficult to say", Forkbraid began, "Perhaps as many as fifteen depending on their levels of capability."
"A definite lack of foresight here, Gentlemen", Captain Carmichael suggested.
"Not at all, Captain", Forkbraid corrected, "You have to remember, Gentlemen. When the plans were laid down, there hadn't been a successful terrorist attack in several decades and off-world terrorists were simply unheard of."
"There's a lot to be said about the best laid plans of mice and men, Gentlemen", Special Agent Murphy pondered.
"That there is Agent Murphy. That there is", Captain Carmichael agreed.

Leroy walked across the Church hall, formally the pub known as the Black Pullet, and approached his master the Prophet.

"My Lord", Leroy began, "We've had news from the township of Jericho."

"Jericho?", the Prophet queried.

"My Lord, it's a small town on the northern coast of the Valles Marineris Sea", Matthew answered.

Leroy continued, "My Lord, one of our operatives, John Smith, has gone missing in Jericho."

"John Smith?", the Prophet asked.

"Yes, my Lord. Private John Smith, the man who hijacked the Hypolita", Matthew replied.

"Yes, of course, I remember him", the Prophet replied.

"My Lord, our men found his Hummer on the outskirts of Jericho township. Smith appears to have abandoned it", Leroy continued.

"Why would he abandon his Hummer?", the Prophet queried.

"We aren't sure, my Lord", Leroy replied, "He was checking up on that truck shipment from the village of Shira to Jericho."

"Ah, yes", the Prophet replied, "I did ask you to check up on that didn't I."

"Yes, my Lord", Leroy continued, "He appears to have checked on the truck. From what our people have been told, he questioned the two drivers and inspected the truck's Trailer. He found signs that someone had stowed away in the Trailer during its trip from Shira."

"Our three fugitives?", the Prophet quickly asked.

"More than likely, my Lord, but we don't know for certain", Leroy replied.

"So what happened to Smith?", the Prophet demanded.

"We think he may have possibly boarded a ship bound for the Aurorae colony, my Lord", Leroy informed him.

"How did you come to that conclusion, Leroy?", the Prophet asked.

"We had men watching Jericho's port, my Lord", Leroy answered, adding "The night before Smith reached Jericho, two of our men on watch went missing. They haven't been seen or heard from since."

"Really. So we've lost two more men?", the Prophet replied, questioningly.

"Yes, my Lord", Leroy replied, "We think our fugitives are on a ship, the Shilo. It left Jericho just before eleven that morning."

"And Smith is on board the Shilo?", the Prophet asked.

"We believe so, my Lord", Leroy answered, "He was last seen jumping on board the Shilo, shortly before she set sail for the Aurorae colony."

"This is good news, Leroy", the Prophet smiled.

"Yes, my Lord", Leroy agreed, "We can blow the Shilo straight out of the water."

"No, no, Leroy", the Prophet began, "We have already created a huge stir on Mars since our arrival here. The Elysium colony is one thing, the other colonies are another altogether. We don't want the authorities thinking that this is a Martian problem. Let them continue to think it's isolated to Elysium. I don't want the whole planet hunting for us."

"What are your instructions, my Lord?", Leroy asked.

"Leroy, this is what I want you to do. Have our people in the Aurorae colony watch the ports for the Shilo's arrival. If Smith doesn't kill them at sea, our people will kill them when they reach port. I want this done quickly and quietly. Make it look like a simple case of robbery gone wrong. Most importantly, we don't want this to look like another attack."

"Yes, my Lord", Leroy replied, "I'll make arrangements."

"Matthew", the Prophet called out, "How close are we to getting our Raiders to Elysium?"

"Two days, my Lord, then we'll be in quite a good position", Matthew replied.

The Prophet looked around at his men before asking Leroy and Matthew, "Do we know where their Psychic Academy is yet?"

"No, my Lord, not yet", both Matthew and Leroy answered in unison.

"Matthew, I don't want your Raiders to attack Elysium just yet", the Prophet instructed him.

"My Lord", Matthew enquired, "I'm not sure that I understand."

"If we attack the Elysium colony", the Prophet began, "We'll be killing construction workers and little else. That would be very bad optics."

Matthew nodded in agreement.

"We want to hit the Psychic Academy itself and hit it hard", the Prophet continued, "We want to wipe out the demons. They're our primary target."

Matthew nodded again in agreement.

"Here's what I want you to do", the Prophet continued again, "Use the Raiders for just what they're being contracted to do. They're freighters, delivering building supplies to the Elysium colony. That's a perfect cover arrangement."

Matthew nodded again in agreement.

He was beginning to understand what the Prophet had in mind.

"On each flight into the Elysium colony and on each flight back to the Chryce colony, I want your Raiders to carefully scan the region around the Elysium colony. I want our pilots to scan for anything out of the ordinary, for anything that stands out."

Matthew now fully understood, "Yes, my Lord. I understand. If we scan the Elysium subcontinent methodically, we may learn the location of their Psychic Academy."

"Precisely Matthew", the Prophet replied.

"That could take quite a while, my Lord", Leroy noted.

"We could end up making more than a few runs delivering their supplies, but I think ultimately, we will find the location of their Psychic Academy", the Prophet replied.

"Maybe not as many runs as you'd think, Sir", Matthew informed Leroy.

"How so, Matthew?", Leroy asked.

"We have six Raiders lined up at Chryce colony, Sir", Matthew replied to Leroy, then he said to the Prophet, "My Lord, if our ships methodically scan separate strips of the subcontinent, both on the way in and on the way out, we will cover the territory much more quickly."

"Can you set up a schedule to perform the scanning in the most efficient manner, Matthew?", the Prophet enquired.

"Yes, my Lord", Matthew replied, "It... It depends on where their Psychic Academy actually is mind you, but we may be able to discover the whereabouts of their Psychic Academy in as little as four runs. Maybe."

"That would be most excellent, Matthew", the Prophet replied with a smile, "Make it so."

"Yes, my Lord, consider it done", Matthew replied confidently.

The Shilo sailed southward from Jericho through the network of flooded interconnecting chasms north of Valles Marineris. The ship was making good headway with a strong northwesterly pushing her along at a good pace. There was only a slight swell and the ship's journey thus far was surprisingly smooth. Cormac kept Candy and Miranda in their cabin for the whole first day, just to be on the safe side, worrying that the Prophet's men might fly past and spot them on their scanners.

Candy made herself busy cleaning the mud and dirt out of Miranda's hair. Having cleaned the young girl up somewhat, Candy decided Miranda should still pretend to be a boy, so she instructed Miranda to continue wearing boy's clothing and to keep her golden blonde locks tied up neatly under her cap.

On the second day, only Cormac and Candy would cautiously leave the cabin, making short sojourns to the passengers' lounge and other passenger areas of the ship below deck. Cormac and Candy kept to themselves as much as possible, only speaking to other passengers when spoken to or when absolutely necessary. It wasn't until well past noon of the third day, before they decided it should be safe to go up on deck.

Candy and Miranda walked through the hallway from the port cabins towards the deck. Cautiously Candy opened the door and stepped out into the sunlight. Miranda quickly followed Candy through the doorway. They found themselves on the deck towards the stern of the ship. It was a bright and sunny day, with the strong northwesterly from the previous few days still pushing them along at a good clip. Miranda wondered about the deck, exploring the ship for the first time. Candy kept a close watch over Miranda as she followed her about the deck.

There were a few other passengers on the desk enjoying the midday sun, but it appeared that many had either stayed in their cabins or were in the passengers' lounge enjoying the ship's entertainment. The Shilo was somewhat bigger than she had appeared when tied up at Jericho's docks, but even so there was surprisingly little to see, unless one was interested in sails, rigging, and other ships fittings.

Crew members went about their work, both on the deck and up amongst the rigging, rugged up against the last of the fading winter's chill.

Miranda had soon made her way over to the starboard side of the ship, with Candy following close behind. Having caught up with Miranda, the pair stood by the starboard railing looking out to sea. The sea appeared relatively calm, with the Shilo lifting gently up and down with a rhythmic motion upon the swell.

In the distance Miranda could just make out the outline of a few distant islands in the west. Turning around once more and looking across the deck and past the port railing, a distant headland could be seen. The Shilo was navigating the passageway between the headland and the islands. Every now, and then the wind gusted and passengers quickly grabbed for their hats.

After about thirty minutes on deck, Candy, who had been staring out to sea, looked towards Miranda and said, "Not much to see up here, little one."

Looking back at Candy, Miranda agreed, "Not a whole lot."

"We'll be in Valles Marineris proper soon", Candy told Miranda.

Miranda gave Candy an inquisitive look.

"It's the biggest valley in the solar system Miranda", Candy informed her, "Carves across Mars, eastward from the Tharsis Bulge for thousands of kilometres. The sea will get a bit rougher then."

"Why will the sea get rougher, Candy?", Miranda asked.

"The prevailing westerly wind that blows off the Tharsis Bulge", Candy replied, "It makes the valley an interesting place to sail."

"If there's a prevailing westerly blowing, how do the ships sail back to Jericho?", Miranda curiously enquired.

"Not easily, little one. On the way back, the Shilo will have to tack back and forth across the valley. It will take four times as long to sail back to Jericho, as it does to sail to the Aurorae colony", Candy answered.

"How long will it take to get to Aurorae?", Miranda asked.

"Twelve or thirteen more days", Candy replied.

"Why don't they just use Hummers?", Miranda enquired.

"The ordinary folk on Mars don't have Hummers, little one", Candy replied, "We don't have any aircraft of any kind."

"What about in the colonies?", Miranda asked.

"Yeah, they have them in the big colonies", Candy replied, "But they've used for transport from one big colony to another. They don't go anywhere near the wild country where we ordinary folk live."

"What about New Tortuga?", Miranda queried.

"The pirates and smugglers own all the aircraft in New Tortuga, little one", Candy replied, "And they charge like wounded bulls to haul cargo. It costs me and Cormac a small fortune to ship our produce to the off-world colonies. Fortunately our produce gets top dollar off-world."

The northwesterly suddenly became turbulent as it met with a strong westerly wind. Within a few short minutes, the wind had completely altered direction and the ship began to alter course towards the east. The swell was rougher now and the Shilo began to pick up speed. The westerly gusted strongly in short bursts and at one point Miranda's cap blew off, her blonde locks spilling out into the wind.

Across the deck towards the bow on the port side of the ship, a watchful pair of eyes noticed a young boy's hat blow off in the wind. Much to his surprise, the boy had a head full of golden blonde locks.

Carefully, John Smith eyed the child, "*That's her! That's Miranda!*", he thought to himself.

Candy picked up on the thought straight away. Even Cormac who was in the passageway on his way up from below deck, picked up on the thought.

John Smith pulled out his pulsed plasma pistol, he aimed, he fired. Zing.

A pulse of plasma shot across the deck.

Candy was far quicker than she looked, automatically leaping in front of Miranda, she caught the plasma pulse squarely on her left shoulder. Candy collapsed to the deck with an audible thud.

Miranda screamed a primal scream as she fell to the deck right beside Candy. Miranda's eyes rolled back, her hair flying backwards against the wind, her mind screamed out for Forkbraid as her right hand stretched out before her, with her palm held up as if willing the plasma pulses to stop.

Zing, Zing, Zing, Smith squeezed the trigger again and again, Zing, Zing, Zing.

Pulse after pulse flew towards Miranda only to stop eight feet from her outstretched right palm, exploding into brilliant blue fireworks.

Zing, Zing, Zing, Smith continued to squeeze off pulse after pulse. Zing, Zing, Zing.

More pulses exploded into brilliant blue fireworks, this time a mere six feet from Miranda's outstretched palm.

Zing, Zing, Zing, Smith again squeezing off pulse after pulse. Zing, Zing, Zing.

More and more plasma pulses exploded into fireworks. Miranda's mind still screamed.

Cormac burst through the passageway door, shattering it. Swiftly Cormac leapt onto the deck.

Quickly he assessed the situation, his Wife Candy was down, little Miranda was somehow holding off a pulsed plasma pistol attack.

"Miranda can't keep that up for much longer", Cormac thought to himself as he quickly reached for his belt knife.

Quickly Cormac raised his right hand, as he took careful aim.

"Hoi! You!", Cormac yelled as loudly as he could across the deck.

John Smith was startled by a shout to his right, and he turned in the direction of the shout. As he did so Cormac threw his knife. It tumbled through the air, point over hilt. Smith was now facing Cormac square on and taking careful aim with his pulsed plasma pistol.

"Ugh!", Smith gasped in surprise as the knife struck him in the right chest, burying itself deeply into his flesh just below the collar bone.

John Smith crumpled to his knees, dropping his pulsed plasma pistol as he did so.

"I'll take care of that for you, Mr Smith", said the Bosun to Smith as he picked up the pulsed plasma pistol and aimed it squarely back at Smith.

Two men came quickly to the Bosun's side, then grabbed Smith roughly by the arms.

"Careful, Lads. He does have a knife stuck in his chest", the Bosun instructed them.

A crewman approached Cormac with a bailing pin, "I'd stay right where you are, if I were you, Mister. Don't you make a move."

"I think not", Cormac replied as he brought up his elbow and king hit the crewman, knocking him to the ground.

Without looking back Cormac ran to his unconscious Wife's side.

Cormac checked Candy's neck pulse, "Thank the Gods, she's still alive."

"Is Candy going to be alright?", Miranda asked.

"I don't know, little one", Cormac replied, then shouting "Someone get the ship's doctor."

The Ship's Captain was now by their side.

"You'll need to come with me, Mr Farmer", he said as he pointed a hand gun at him.

"Not before your doctor takes care of my Wife", Cormac replied.

"The doctors with Mr Smith", the Captain replied, adding "You know, the guy you just knifed."

"Screw that bastard. Let him die. He doesn't deserve to live. Have your doctor see to my Wife."

"A knife wound is more life-threatening than a plasma burn", the Captain replied.

"He wouldn't have that knife wound if he hadn't been trying to kill my Wife and our little one."

The Captain conferred with the Bosun for a moment, "Is this true?"

"Yes, Captain", the Bosun replied, "I believe it is."

"Get the doctor up here and have him attend to Mrs Farmer first. He can sort out Smith later, if he's still alive", the Captain ordered.

"The Bosun is going for the doctor now, Mr Farmer. My men will escort you to the brig."

Cormac rose to his feet, "Very well then. Make sure you look after my misses and our little one."

"They will be well taken care of, Mr Farmer. Our doctor knows his trade", the Captain replied as Cormac was led off to the brig.

Cormac turned once and told the Captain coldly, "You'd better look after them, Captain. There'll be hell to pay if you don't."

"So much for a quiet, uneventful trip", the Captain thought to himself as he watched Cormac being led below deck.

Forkbraid lay fast asleep in Selene's apartment at the New Flinders Psychic Academy, when a sudden scream entered his mind, *"Forkbraid!"*

It was little Miranda Swann.

Forkbraid's mind began to awaken, then just as his mind strove for full consciousness, split seconds from fully awakening, it halted. In this partially awake, quiescent state, Forkbraid realised he was still asleep and quickly pulled himself out through his crown chakra, his astral body stretching up and out of his physical body. He looked down at his still sleeping body momentarily, before allowing himself to be drawn out further in the direction from whence the scream had come.

It took him only a moment to cover the distance from Elysium to Valles Marineris and Forkbraid found himself floating high above a schooner at sea, being pushed along swiftly by a brisk westerly wind. He noted the name of the ship written upon its prow, the Shilo. There were people on the deck of the ship, passengers and crew. A scene of pandemonium was unfolding beneath him.

Forkbraid quickly made out the form of Miranda Swann on the starboard, midsection of the ship.

Her small frame was fending off an attack.

Pulses of plasma exploded in brilliant blue scintillations, like fireworks before her.

"Miranda", Forkbraid thought to her.

The young girl was fully focused on her attacker and could not easily respond.

Forkbraid looked at the fallen woman in front of Miranda, a chubby woman with rosy cheeks, lying unconscious upon the ship's wooden decking.

A soft thought popped into Forkbraid's mind, pushed in as if it was a great effort, *"Candy is hurt. Plasma burns."*

Forkbraid scanned the unconscious woman, *"Candy lives"*, he transmitted back to Miranda.

Forkbraid looked over at Miranda's attacker, on the diagonally opposite side of the ship, remembering the man from photographs of the deserters from Phobos,

"Private John Smith!", he exclaimed within his mind.

More commotion broke out below as another person appeared on the ship's deck. He was tall and thin, with wispy blonde hair upon his balding head.

This new man yelled out at Smith. "Hoi! You!", Forkbraid clearly heard him yell.

Forkbraid cautiously probed this new man's mind. His name was Cormac Farmer, he was Candy's Husband and Miranda's protector.

A knife flew out of Cormac's hand, point over hilt, it spun swiftly through the air. Private Smith had turned to square off against the newcomer, only to have the knife strike deeply into his chest. Forkbraid watched as Smith crumpled to the deck, dropping his pulsed plasma pistol as he fell.

Forkbraid scanned Smith with his mind. Smith was wounded, but not dead. Forkbraid scanned Smith's wounded form, it seemed to Forkbraid that Smith would live. He could still be a threat.

The ship's crew was quickly taking charge of the situation now. Forkbraid watched as Smith was led away by crewmen and taken below deck. Cormac too was also led off and taken below deck. Miranda stayed by Candy's side as a doctor appeared on deck to tend to her wounds.

"Miranda!", Forkbraid shouted with his mind, *"I will come for you."*

Miranda looked up into the sky with hope in her eyes, as Forkbraid withdrew from the scene.

It was like the snapping of an elastic band. Forkbraid's astral body snapped quickly back into his physical body as it lay in bed in the Psychic Academy. So quickly did Forkbraid return, that he awoke fully and sat bolt upright in his bed.

Selene, who had been sleeping peacefully in bed beside him, awoke and sat up, "Are you alright Forkbraid? What's wrong?"

"We've had a call in the night", Forkbraid replied.

"A call in the night?", Selene questioned.

"Miranda Swann!", Forkbraid exclaimed as he turned to face Selene.

"What about Miranda?", Selene questioned.

"Miranda just summoned me", Forkbraid answered.

"Summoned you?", Selene replied confused, "Miranda is an eight-year-old child."

"Yes, and, she summoned me", Forkbraid confirmed, explaining, "I followed the summons back to its source. It was Miranda, she is aboard a ship called the Shilo and I know exactly where she is."

"You know where she is?", Selene queried.

"Yes, Selene", Forkbraid replied, "I know exactly where Miranda is and she needs our help. Private John Smith is on board the Shilo as well."

Forkbraid quickly leapt out of bed and began to get dressed.

Selene climbed out of bed and told him, "I'm coming with you", as she slipped a night gown over her naked body.

"No, not this time, Selene", Forkbraid replied, "You are needed here."

"You'll need me with you", Selene insisted, "Who's going to watch your back?"

Forkbraid laughed loudly, "Since when has my back ever needed watching."

Selene gave off a low growl, "You know what I mean."

"I'll take Special Agent Murphy and Marcus with me Selene", Forkbraid told her, "They can watch my back."

Forkbraid gave off a small chuckle as he finished dressing and grabbed his communicator.

Selene growled again and followed him out of the bedroom and into the lounge, "I'm coming with you and that's that!"

Forkbraid placed his forehead against Selene's and then they [68]shared.

Long minutes passed then finally, "You're needed here at the Academy Selene."

"There's nothing so pressing that I can't come with you", Selene insisted.

Forkbraid pulled his head back, "Selene, you still have to train Roseanne."

"Roseanne is progressing nicely", Selene replied, "She could do with a break from training."

Forkbraid countered with, "What happens if the shit hits the fan?"

Selene's face became serious, "You mean an attack?"

"Yes, Selene, an attack", Forkbraid replied, "If there's an attack, here at the Academy, your skills will be needed."

"No! No, Forkbraid! That doesn't bear thinking about", Selene replied, shaking her head.

"You have to think about it, Selene", Forkbraid insisted, "If they find out our location, they will attack and how many of our people are prepared to repulse it."

Selene allowed herself to fall gently back into a lounge chair, "There's me and

---

68 Sharing of consciousness, telepathic two-way transmission of memories, consciousness, and experiences.

maybe a couple of others. Not that many, actually."

"Exactly, Selene", Forkbraid answered, "You are needed here."

There was a sudden knock on the door of Selene's apartment. Forkbraid gave the knocker permission to enter telepathically. The door opened and Marcus Greyhelm stepped in. Selene quickly pulled her night gown about her, covering her body from view.

"Lord Forkbraid", Marcus began, "One of our Watchers detected a psychic intrusion."

Forkbraid turned to Selene, "You see, Selene. A Watcher detects an intrusion and only now is someone actually doing something about it."

"You're right, Forkbraid", Selene agreed, "We would never have been this sloppy on Earth."

Forkbraid turned back to Marcus, "We know all about the intrusion, Marcus."

"What? How?", Marcus queried.

Forkbraid gave Marcus a *"Like dah"*, look.

Marcus noted the look, "Oh, of course. Silly of me."

"It was Miranda Swann", Forkbraid informed Marcus, "She needs our help."

"I'm ready when you are, my Lord", Marcus stated quickly.

"Good, Lad", Forkbraid replied, "Head down to the hangar. Grab Special Agent Murphy on your way down. I'll meet you there shortly."

"Right away", Marcus replied and started for the door.

"And, Marcus", Forkbraid called out to him, "Commandeer a long rang Hummer."

"Consider it done, my Lord", Marcus replied as he left the apartment.

Forkbraid stepped in front of Selene and dropped on his haunches. He put his hands on her knees and said, "I'll be fine, Selene. We'll be back before you know it."

Selene gave him a disbelieving look, "You take too many risks, Forkbraid."

Forkbraid smiled and gave Selene a passionate kiss, then when they'd finished, "I do what needs to be done, my love."

"I know. I just wish there was someone else to do it instead of you", Selene replied.

"I'll be careful, Selene", Forkbraid whispered gently into Selene's ear, "I promise."

"Just make sure you are", Selene replied, "Now, get out of here and save that little girl."

Forkbraid kissed Selene tenderly on the lips, then he stood up and strode out of her apartment.

As the door closed behind him, Selene's eyes brimmed with silent tears.

Six of the Prophet's modified freighters had made their first run to the Elysium colony, delivering building materials for the colony's repairs. They had then returned to Chryce and upon their return, dutifully transmitted their scans of the Elysium subcontinent to New Tortuga. Matthew received the data streams with glee and was quick to begin deciphering them.

He had written an algorithm to read through the voluminous data searching for anything man made in the regions beyond the Elysium colony. Just over an hour later, when the algorithms had finished, Matthew checked the results. Nothing! Matthew was disappointed, but realised the first run was unlikely to yield any results anyway.

Matthew called up the source code of his algorithm onto the screen. He took a copy and then began tweaking the code to create a second version that would do more strenuous tests, looking for any signs of construction or human habitations. When he'd finished, he ran this new algorithm over the same dataset. It took a little longer to run than the first time, but when it had finished the result was the same. Nothing! Matthew sat back into his chair and threw his hands behind his head in silent contemplation.

A few minutes later Leroy walked into Matthew's little workshop, "Find anything, Lad?"

"Not so far, Sir", Matthew replied.

"Well, I guess it was too much to ask for", Leroy replied, "First run and all."

"Yeah", Matthew replied, "I wasn't expecting much on the first run."

"How long do you think it will take before we find them?", Leroy asked.

Matthew thought for a moment then replied, "I don't expect anything on the next run either. That would be too much to ask for. If we're really lucky, maybe the third, but I wouldn't hold my breath."

"You did tell the Prophet four runs", Leroy reminded Matthew.

"Sir, that I did", Matthew replied, "But I also added, maybe. The odds are good, but it still could take five or even six runs."

"You'd better pray we get the location in four, Matthew", Leroy replied, "The Prophets looking forward to bombing their precious little Psychic Academy."

"Yeah, Sir", Matthew replied with a smile, "I'm kind of looking forward to that myself."

Leroy smiled back, "Then, Lad, find their damned demon den. When we have that, we've got them", he replied before walking out the door.

Matthew called up his original algorithm once more on the screen. He took another copy of it, then began to tweak the code yet again. This time, to search the data for any signs of agricultural activity beyond the Elysium colony. When he was satisfied with the code, he ran the algorithm over the huge dataset once more. Just over an hour later it had finished and Matthew checked the results once more. Nothing! Again Matthew sat back into his chair and threw his hands behind his head in silent contemplation once more.

After several minutes Matthew thought to himself, *"There's nothing for it, I'll just have to view the data for myself."*

Matthew quickly began putting together an algorithm to display the data scans on his view screen in high definition colour. It took him well over an hour to write the new algorithm. When he'd finished, he got up from his desk and walked over to his microwave oven to heat up some popcorn. Two minutes and thirty seconds later, Matthew sat back down in a comfortable chair and activated his new algorithm. The data scans revealed brilliant vistas of the Elysium subcontinent and Matthew began watching for the slightest hint of the Psychic Academy.

He sighed to himself as he thought, *"This could take quite a while."*

Special Agent Murphy flew their hummer high above the Valles Marineris Sea. Marcus watched the screen carefully as he scanned the sea below them. It didn't take very long, soon they had found what they were looking for. Five thousand feet below them was a schooner, sailing swiftly along with a strong westerly. Marcus pinged the ship below them. There was no response.

Marcus was surprised by this, *"It must be an unregistered local vessel"*, he thought.

Forkbraid concentrated on the schooner, "That's the one. Take us down closer, Marcus."

"We can't land on her, FB", Special Agent Murphy informed Forkbraid, "We're far too big to land on her deck without capsizing her."

"It's okay, Jim", Forkbraid replied, "We're not going to land."

Special Agent Murphy dropped their altitude down to five hundred feet and followed along slightly behind the schooner. Magnified images of the schooner showed the passengers and crew had spotted them, they were staring curiously upward at them in surprise. Forkbraid moved to the rear of the hummer and opened the rear hatch.

"Jim, bring us ahead of the Shilo", Forkbraid began, "Then take the Hummer to the Aurorae colony. Find out where the Shilo is going to berth, then set up house nearby."

"What are you thinking, FB?", Special Agent Murphy asked

"I'm going down to the ship", Forkbraid replied, "You and Marcus wait for us at the Aurorae colony. The Shilo's moving at a good clip, we'll be there soon enough."

"What are you doing?", Marcus shouted at him, "Are you crazy?"

"I'll be fine, Marcus", Forkbraid replied, "This is Mars. Point three-eight gs remember."

Marcus gave him a look of disbelief.

"Truly. I'll be fine, Marcus", Forkbraid told him, then as he leapt from the

Hummer's rear hatch, he turned around and said to them, "Don't do this on Earth boys and girls."

Marcus turned to Special Agent Murphy and said, "Who's the girl?"

Special Agent Murphy smiled back at Marcus, "Don't look at me, I'm the boy."

Forkbraid fell towards the schooner Shilo, his black cloak billowing out behind him. Passengers and crew aboard the Shilo watched in disbelief as Forkbraid approached their ship. With a mere fifty feet to the deck, Forkbraid began to slow his descent telekinetically, then swung his feet beneath him and landed upon the decking with an audible thud. The Captain of the Shilo quickly approached Forkbraid.

"I'm Captain Swanson", the Captain informed Forkbraid, "The Shilo be my ship."

Forkbraid routinely scanned the man's mind, "That it is, Captain", he replied.

"That was an interesting trick, Mr", the Captain stated, then he asked, "Do you mind explaining how you did it?"

Forkbraid ignored the question and quickly scanned the passengers and crew around him.

Forkbraid quickly concluded that he was relatively safe.

"Sir!", the Captain began, "Who would you be and what would you be doing, here on my ship?"

Forkbraid reached for his robe, a pocket appeared from out of nowhere. Forkbraid's hand disappeared into the pocket and then pulled out his passport. He then passed it to the Captain.

Captain Swanson opened the passport and read the contents, his eyes opened wide when he read Forkbraid's name.

"You're the heir!", the Captain exclaimed.

"Whose heir?", Forkbraid questioned.

"The heir to, he who asked The Great Question", the Captain replied.

Forkbraid caught the reference to his ancestor and then asked, "Then, I have your cooperation?"

"Absolutely, Sir", the Captain replied, "You'll have our every cooperation", as he passed back the passport to Forkbraid.

Forkbraid reached into his pocket again and pulled out a package.

"Give this to your ship's doctor. It contains the latest medicinal treatments for plasma burns. Have your doctor treat Mrs Farmer with it", Forkbraid instructed.

"Straight away, Sir", the Captain replied, before passing the package to one of his crewmen and issuing instructions to him concerning the package.

"Would that be all, Sir?", the Captain asked Forkbraid.

"Not by a long shot, Captain", Forkbraid replied, "Have your men bring

Cormac Farmer and Private John Smith to me."

The Captain nodded and turned to the Bosun, "You heard the man. Make it so."

"Yes, Captain", The Bosun replied before heading off below decks.

It was several minutes before the two men were brought back up on deck. During his journey up from the brig, Private Smith, who had heard the news about the Hummer above them, had assumed it was the Prophet's men. Smith was taunting the crewmen and Cormac all the way back up to the deck, telling them he would be freed, and they were all going to die.

Then, when the door was opened, and they all stepped out onto the deck and into the Sunlight, Smith exclaimed, "Holy Mother of God!"

Forkbraid said one word to Private John Smith, "Silence!", applying an unusual lilt.

Smith found himself unable to speak. He was quite literally speechless.

Forkbraid stepped forward and scanned Cormac.

"Cormac Farmer", Forkbraid began, "You have killed before, haven't you? Many times."

Shocked faces looked to each other as Cormac nodded in reply.

"Yet I can see inside your mind, that every time you killed someone, you did so either in self-defence or the defence of others", Forkbraid continued.

"I did what needed to be done at the time to survive", Cormac replied softly.

"To kill out of necessity in self-defence or the defence of others is not a crime nor is it a sin", Forkbraid told Cormac, then to the Captain, he said, "Release this man at once."

"Make it so", the Captain told the Bosun who then took off Cormac's shackles.

Forkbraid turned to Smith, "Private John Smith. I am sanctioned by the authority of the United Nations of Earth and United Colonies of Sol, to judge you for your crimes and if you are found guilty of said crimes, I am sanctioned to execute you."

Loud murmurs rose up amongst the passengers and crew, Forkbraid raised his right hand and said to the crowd, "You will all bear witness to his deeds", and everyone fell silent.

Forkbraid stood before Smith, "Private John Smith. You have been charged in absentia with the crime of conspiracy, with regards the plot to bomb the Flinders Psychic Academy on Earth. An action which resulted in the deaths of nearly two hundred innocent men, women, and children."

The faces of the crowd looked truly shocked when they heard the charge.

Forkbraid scanned Smith's mind, "I find that you have no memory of the planning of this event. On this charge, I do find that you are innocent."

Forkbraid brought forth the next charge, "Private John Smith. You have been charged in absentia with the crime of conspiracy, with regards to the plot to black mail the authorities of L-Five, using flash vaporising ordinance. A plot which resulted in the deaths of well over three thousand innocent men, women, and children."

Jaws dropped once more when the crowd heard this charge, incredibly shocked looks were all around them. That was understandable, news was slow to travel to the backwaters of Mars.

Forkbraid scanned Smith's mind yet again, "I find that you have no memory of the planning of this event as well. On this charge, I also find that you are innocent."

Forkbraid continued with the next charge, "Private John Smith. You have been charged in absentia with the crime of conspiracy after the event with regards to the kidnapping of the eight-year-old girl, Miranda Swann. Furthermore, you have also been charged with aiding and abetting the perpetrators of this kidnapping, by interfering with the investigation and hindering the capture of said perpetrators, by use of your position in the communications centre at Port Phobos."

Forkbraid scanned Smith's mind yet again, he found the relevant memories and transmitted them to every adult passenger and crewmen upon the deck. The adults in the crowd were able to see with their own minds, Private John Smith's guilt, having watched Smith's own memories of the events.

Anger was now clearly visible in the faces in the crowd.

Forkbraid pronounced, "On these charges, I find you guilty as charged."

Forkbraid continued on with the next charge, "Private John Smith. You have been charged in absentia with the crimes of committing the hijacking of the HLT Hypolita and the crimes of planning and bombing of the transport ship Vanguard, in which twelve passengers and fifteen crewmen perished."

Again Forkbraid scanned Smith's mind, he found the relevant memories and again transmitted them to every adult passenger and crewmen upon the deck. The horror of Smith's crimes were evident for all to see.

Again Forkbraid pronounced, "On these charges, I find you guilty as charged."

Forkbraid then began with the next charge, "Private John Smith. You have been charged in absentia with the crime of conspiracy with regards the attack upon the HLT Agamemnon resulting in the deaths of three hundred and twenty-one innocent men and women. Furthermore, you are also charged with the crime of conspiracy with regards the attack upon the Elysium colony resulting in the deaths of three hundred and nineteen innocent men and women, and the wounding of seventy-six others."

Forkbraid scanned Smith's mind yet again, he found the relevant memories and again transmitted them to every adult passenger and crewmen upon the deck. Now the crowd could clearly see how evil this man before them was. There was simply no denying it.

Yet again Forkbraid pronounced, "On these charges, I find you guilty as charged."

Forkbraid indicated to the Captain that he had pronounced the last of the charges.

Captain Swanson then stated, "Sir, as the Captain of this ship, I have charges of my own to lay."

"As you will, Captain Swanson", Forkbraid replied.

"Captain John Smith. I hereby charge you with the attempted murder of the young child Miranda Swann, the attempted murder and grievous wounding of Mrs Candace Farmer and the attempted murder of Cormac Farmer."

Forkbraid reached into Smith's mind once again and transmitted to the adults in the crowd, Smith's own memories of the instructions given to him by the Prophet. The planning and plotting of the murders and the attempts from the previous day.

Having viewed Smith's own memories of these events, Captain Swanson pronounced, "Smith! I find you guilty as charged."

The Captain turned to Forkbraid, "Sir, I believe you have proven this man to be guilty of truly horrendous crimes. This is one very evil man."

"Indeed he is, Captain, and now I must sentence him", Forkbraid replied.

"Private John Smith", Forkbraid began, "You have been found guilty of actions leading to the deaths of many innocent men, women, and children. You are hereby sentenced to death. Do you have any last words?"

Smith was unrepentant, "They weren't innocent men, women, and children. They were demon spawn. Children of the devil. They all deserved what they got."

Forkbraid pointed out to him, "The passengers and crew on the Vanguard weren't psychics Smith. They were ordinary folk just like you. As were the crew of the Agamemnon and the workers in the Elysium colony."

Smith was still unrepentant, "In war, sometimes sacrifices have to be made. The innocent will become martyrs in heaven. God will recognise his own."

Forkbraid shook his head, he had seen this kind of reckless disregard for humanity many times before, "I pity you, Smith."

"Pity me!", Smith spat at Forkbraid, "Don't pity me. I may die, but we're going to win this war and all of your kind will be dead. Slaughtered to the last child."

Forkbraid replied, "My kind! My kind! Smith, do you even know where my kind comes from?"

Smith spat out, "Your kind are the spawn of demons!"

"Oh, you deluded bastard!", Forkbraid began, "Psychics are born from the loins of ordinary folk, ordinary humans, just like you. Your kind and my kind are the same, you deluded git!"

Private John Smith had a chest injury, courtesy of Cormac's belt knife. As a result he wasn't shackled in the same fashion as Cormac Farmer had been. Instead, Smith's right arm had been strapped to his chest and a ball and chain had been shackled to his left ankle. On his way to the deck, he carried this heavy metal ball in his left arm. It now lay on the decking before him.

Forkbraid pointed to the shiny metal ball with his right index finger, and it began to rise off the deck. He levitated it into Private John Smith's left hand and then used his gifts to force Smith to hold onto it once more.

"Captain", Forkbraid began, "You'd best have the children go below deck."

The Captain gave the order and the deck was cleared of all children.

"Captain. How deep is the Valles Marineris Sea?", Forkbraid enquired.

"Oh! It varies quite a bit. Around these parts it's up to four miles deep", he replied.

"Splendid", Forkbraid replied, "That will do nicely."

Forkbraid reached his right hand out towards Smith and closed his fist as if to grab him. Slowly Forkbraid raised his hand and moved it towards the port side railing. Smith levitated off the deck and followed the movements of Forkbraid's hand precisely.

Smith was uncommonly quiet during this entire procedure, which wasn't surprising as Forkbraid was silencing him telepathically. Then, when Smith was about twenty metres past the port side railing, Forkbraid released his telepathic control of Smith's voice.

Straight away Smith screamed, "You can't do this. I demand a fair trial. I demand due process."

When he finally realised that Forkbraid truly meant to drop him, he shouted out, "I'll be avenged you bastard demon spawn!", were his final words.

Forkbraid opened his right hand. The shiny metal ball fell from Smith's left hand, then seconds later Smith fell as well. Smith screamed his final scream. There was a small splash as Private John Smith hit the water and disappeared beneath the waves.

Forkbraid looked over to Captain Swanson, "Duly executed for his crimes", he said.

"Duly executed", Captain Swanson nodded in agreement.

After Private John Smith's execution, it didn't take long for Cormac to head below deck, to be by his Wife, Candy's, side. He found the doctor had just finished redressing Candy's wounded left shoulder and nearly bowled him over as he bolted into the cabin. Cormac sat on the bed beside his Wife and gave her a huge, yet gentle hug.

Forkbraid had followed Cormac down the passageway and into their cabin. Upon entering the cabin he found Cormac and his Wife Candy hugging on their bed, then Forkbraid looked around. Sitting on a chair on the other side of the bed was a pretty little girl with golden blonde hair.

The little girl looked up at Forkbraid and smiled, "I know who you are."

"You must be Miranda Swann", Forkbraid replied to her, "I think it's about time we met."

21. A Glint of Light

Selene stood on the landing field's tarmac, southeast of the New Flinders Psychic Academy. A Hummer was approaching from the north, behind it were four modified, atmo rated Wisps. A second instalment of the twelve ships promised to Forkbraid by Captain Carmichael. Charlene Fewkes and Varak stood beside Selene as the five ships landed nearby. No sooner than the last Wisp landed, the group of three briskly walked over to the new arrivals.

"Greetings, my Lady", Captain Carmichael greeted as he stepped out of his Hummer.

"Greetings, Captain", Selene replied, "It's good to see you again."

"It's good to see you as well", the Captain replied, "These are the latest four Wisps as promised. Where would Lord Forkbraid be? I was expecting to see him."

"Thank you for the Wisps, Captain", Selene replied, "They will come in very handy I'm sure. As for Forkbraid, he's somewhere on the other side of Mars."

"On the other side of Mars. Is he okay?", the Captain enquired.

"I'm sure he is. Forkbraid is following up on a lead with regards Miranda Swann's whereabouts."

Captain Carmichael nodded in reply.

"Varak, instruct the pilots to take their Wisps over to the Academy. Have them stow them with the others and billet them nearby", Selene instructed.

Varak quickly moved off to instruct the pilots on where to take their craft.

"Captain, Charlene here tells me the HLTs have been fully unloaded and can return to the Ptolemy any time they wish", Selene informed Captain Carmichael.

"Is that so?", the Captain enquired.

"Yes, Captain", Charlene replied, "The last cargo pods were unloaded this morning."

"Very well then. I'll give them flight clearance for this afternoon", the Captain replied.

"You said you were expecting to see Forkbraid, Captain?", Selene enquired.

"Yes, my Lady", the Captain replied, "I wanted to let him know that I have concerns about these cargo flights from Chryce."

"Concerns?", Selene queried.

"Yes", Captain Carmichael began, "As you know, Chryce colony has organised supplies and cargo to be air freighted in from their colony."

"And a lot of valuable help our neighbours are providing as well", Selene added.

"My concern is, Chryce have contracted quite a few private operators to help them haul the supplies on these cargo flights", Captain Carmichael informed Selene.

"Chryce does have security procedures in place, does it not?", Selene asked.

"Yes, they do", the Captain replied, "but I'm not certain that their security measures are up to scratch. I'm not certain they've vetted all the private operators sufficiently."

"Have you found any security breaches?", Selene enquired.

"Not as yet", the Captain replied, "So far everything checks out and everything seems to be running smoothly."

"Then, I'm not sure what your concerns are, Captain", Lady Selene stated.

"It's hard to put my finger on", the Captain replied, "Just a gut feeling that we're being given a false sense of security."

Selene raised an eyebrow, "Do you trust your gut feeling?"

"Yes, I do, my Lady", the Captain replied.

"Good, then act on it", Lady Selene replied, "Your gut feeling is a low level psychic awareness."

This time Captain Carmichael raised an eyebrow, "I already have, my Lady."

"In what way?", Selene asked.

"I have my people watching every convoy into Elysium. These freighters are small, but we can still keep tabs on them. If one deviates from its designated course, my people will know about it."

"And shortly thereafter, so will we", Selene finished for him.

"Yes. Precisely", the Captain replied, using a metaphor, "If there are any wolves in sheep's clothing, we'll know about them pretty damn quick."

"It's good to know you're watching over us, Captain", Lady Selene replied.

Shortly after noon that day, Lady Selene and Charlene watched from the southeast tower. One by one the seven HLTs lifted off and began their flight back to the Ptolemy. The Interplanetary Liner was already days late for its return flight to Earth and the return of the remaining HLTs would be a welcome sight to the Ptolemy's Captain. One by one, each HLT circled in front of the New Flinders Psychic Academy before turning northwest and thrusting skywards towards space.

Lady Selene said to Charlene, "There's no turning back now."

"No", Charlene agreed, "With the HLTs gone, there's no turning back."

The psychic colonists were on Mars to stay.

The Prophet's six modified freighters had made their second run to the Elysium colony. Another load of building materials and supplies had been delivered. On their way into the colony and again on their way back out, the freighters scanned their assigned sections of the Elysium subcontinent. Strip by strip they were searching for the Psychic Academy, it was only a matter of time before they found it. Upon their return trip to Chryce, the freighter's Captains dutifully transmitted all of their scans of Elysium to Matthew at New Tortuga.

Just as with the first run, Matthew received the data streams with glee and was quick to begin deciphering them. One by one he ran his three algorithms over this new data set. The first to check for any man-made objects, such as buildings or landing strips. The second to check more rigorously, looking for anything that could possibly be of human construction. The third algorithm was checking for any possible signs of agriculture.

After each run Matthew viewed the results. The first algorithm had turned up nothing. Matthew had expected this, he didn't really expect a positive result until after the third or fourth run. He was pleasantly surprised to find a positive result from his second algorithm, only to be disappointed when he checked the data on the view screen. His algorithm had picked up a large natural, pyramidal shaped hill.

"Lucky I didn't call Leroy", Matthew thought to himself.

The results from his third algorithm had found nothing useful.

It had taken close to four hours to process the voluminous data. Leroy had not come to check if anything had turned up, after all Matthew had told him not to expect anything on this run. As with the first data set, Matthew made himself some pop corn and then sat down to view the scans for himself. It had taken him nearly twelve hours to view the last dataset, he expected this new set of data to take just as long and made himself comfortable for the viewing.

It was now in the wee small hours of the morning, about eight hours into the viewing, a now very tired Matthew caught sight of a small flash of light on the view screen. It was quick and fleeting, Matthew rubbed his eyes and reached for his keypad. Matthew fumbled several times with the keypad before he finally got control of it. Quickly he ran the data in reverse until he was sure he was positioned well before the mysterious flash of light. He then ran the data forward once more and scrutinised the data on the view screen.

There it was, *"A glint of light"*, Matthew thought to himself.

"A glint of light!", he let himself exclaim.

A huge, beaming smile appeared on Matthew's face. The glint was real, it was there, no mistaking it. Matthew zoomed in on the mysterious glint. Suddenly its source became apparent, Matthew's eyes lit up brightly, as he reached for his communicator.

Leroy was not used to being woken up in the middle of the night. He was cranky and irritable, more so than usual. When he arrived at Matthew's workshop, he was still wearing his pyjamas and a night shirt. Leroy was in a terrible mood.

"This had better be bloody good, Matthew", Leroy snarled.

"It is, Sir", Matthew replied, "It most certainly is."

Leroy took note, his irritability began to subside, "Did your programs turn up something?", Leroy inquired curiously of Matthew.

"No. Not at all, Sir", Matthew replied.

"Then what in the bloody blue blazes am I doing here?", Leroy demanded.

"Watch, Sir. Just watch!", Matthew instructed Leroy as he reran the data on the view screen.

There was a small flash of light. Leroy almost missed it.

Leroy rubbed his eyes, "Let me see that again, Matthew."

Matthew reran the same section of data again. The flash of light reappeared and Matthew was quick to stop the viewer precisely on it.

"What is it?", Leroy enquired.

"It's a glint of light, Sir", Matthew stated without explanation.

"A glint of light?", Leroy asked Matthew, his face searching for understanding.

"Yes, Sir", Matthew replied, "A glint of light reflecting off an HLT in the afternoon Sun."

"An HLT!", Leroy exclaimed, "I thought you said your programs hadn't found anything?"

"They didn't, Sir", Matthew replied, "They were searching the terrain for surface features."

Leroy looked again at the screen, "This HLT is flying", he stated as he noted, the glint was clearly well above the ground.

"Precisely, Sir. This HLT is clearly flying", Matthew agreed, "If I hadn't been viewing the data myself, we would have missed it."

Leroy smiled a wry smile, "Can we use this, Matthew?"

"Oh, yes. That we can, Sir", Matthew replied as he zoomed in on the HLT.

Slowly the glint began to resolve. An image of an HLT became clear on the screen.

Matthew zoomed in even closer, the name labelled on the side clearly read, HLT Achilles.

Leroy laughed out loudly, "We know where that came from now don't we, Lad."

"That we do, Sir", Matthew replied, "Their Psychic Academy."

Still laughing loudly, Leroy sat down on Matthew's couch, "We'll find their precious Psychic Academy on the next run."

"Actually, Sir", Matthew began, "I've already found it!"

Leroy stopped laughing, "Found it! How?"

Matthew panned the screen back out and adjusted the settings. A total of seven images appeared on the screen.

Leroy turned to Matthew and gave him an enquiring look.

"It's not the same HLT seven times, Sir", Matthew assured him, "It's all seven of the Ptolemy's HLTs heading back into space. One after the other, all on the same course."

"All of them?", Leroy queried.

"Yes, Sir, all of them", Matthew smiled back.

Leroy was still lost in thought when Matthew finally stated, "And I've calculated their trajectory! Having all seven HLTs lined up on the same course made that possible."

Leroy's jaw dropped before he quickly composed himself, "Their trajectory! You've found them! You know where they are!"

Matthew's smile beamed back at Leroy, "Yes, Sir, I have, and I do. I've locked them down to an area of less than four hundred square kilometres."

Leroy smiled a huge smile, "God in heaven, you've found the demon's nest! Wait till the Prophet hears about this!"

Roseanne Rhein was in deep concentration. Some of the other women amongst the colonists, those who were quickly regaining their abilities since arriving from Earth, had decided to teach Roseanne how to play battleball, psychic style. A brutal form of dodgeball where one player is pitted against six others.

At first Lady Selene had thought that this was a terrible idea, but Roseanne had insisted that she was up to the challenge, and so Selene decided to let the game go ahead.

'I might be able to assess how Roseanne functions under pressure', was Selene's thought.

It also struck Selene, that she might be able to assess how well Roseanne's opponents were adapting to conditions on Mars at the same time. Now the game was about to begin.

Roseanne stood alone on one side of the rectangular court. On the other side stood six women, all armed with balls. The rules were very simple. If Roseanne caught one of the balls thrown at her, the player that threw the ball changes to Roseanne's side of the court. If Roseanne picks up a ball and throws it back, hitting an opposing player with it, that player changes to Roseanne's side of the court as well.

No matter how many players Roseanne is able to gather on her side of the court, only Roseanne is allowed to throw balls back at her opponents. The gathered players are only allowed to dodge. If any of the players gathered on Roseanne's side of the court is hit by a ball, that player returns to the opposing side to pelt balls back at Roseanne once more.

Roseanne can be hit as many times as it takes to make her give in and call the game off. The game only ends when all the opposing players have been hit by Roseanne and gathered to her side of the court or Roseanne gives up. Whichever comes first.

All of a sudden the women threw their balls at Roseanne. Quickly Roseanne moved, dodging as many as she could. Two balls struck her, one in the leg and another in the chest.

The older women laughed and chuckled, *"This won't last long"*, was a common thought.

"Roseanne! Use your gifts!", Charlene Fewkes shouted to Roseanne from the side line.

Roseanne looked up, just in time to catch another ball square in the face. Awkwardly Roseanne fell to the floor, landing on her side with a loud thud.

Lady Selene stood up and was about to rush out onto the court to stop the game, but Roseanne sent her a quick thought, *"No! I can do this!"*

Roseanne quickly regained her footing and stood before her opponents. Balls came flying at her from every angle. Roseanne ducked and weaved, then with a wave of her hand deflected the last three balls. Some of the women on the other side of the court smiled, the young Witchling was learning fast. Quickly they used their telekinetic abilities to retrieve their balls before Roseanne could grab any of them.

"Not so fast", Roseanne thought as she ripped a ball straight out of the hands of an opponent, using nothing more than sheer will power.

Roseanne's opponent looked shocked, that move wasn't expected. Once again the balls began flying at Roseanne. The first was blocked using the ball she was holding. Some of the other balls were dodged. The remainder of them were deflected with a sharp look. Roseanne pelted back the ball she was holding, it struck an opposing player hard and that player changed sides.

The balls came flying at Roseanne again. Roseanne ducked and weaved, dodging several balls, whilst picking out two, controlling them with hand gestures. Quickly Roseanne pelted the two balls back. Another opposing player was hit and changed sides.

More balls came flying at Roseanne, who again ducked and weaved, catching one of the balls at the last moment. The ball had curved in mid-flight as Roseanne had drawn it straight to her hands, using the power of her mind alone. Another opponent changed sides.

The balls flew back and forth across the court. Players changed sides, from one side to the other and then back again. So fast now was the flow of the game, that barely a hand touched a ball, yet the balls flew quickly from one side of the court to the other all the same. Roseanne had been struck many times by balls, yet as the game progressed, the number of times she was being hit grew fewer and fewer.

Eventually Roseanne was moving in fluid motion, her mind tightly focused on controlling the six flying balls in mid-flight. Ducking and weaving those balls that she could not control, tossing back those that she could. Then after twenty-five minutes of ducking, weaving and coercing the movement of balls in mid-flight, Roseanne had the upper hand.

Five of Roseanne's opponents were now dodging balls on her side of the court, only one remained on the opposing side. Roseanne's opponent Joanne, a twenty-eight-year-old, level nine psychic, with auburn hair and vivid green eyes. Three balls floated in front of Joanne at the ready. Roseanne had control of the other three balls in front of her.

Without warning Joanne sent her three balls hurling straight at Roseanne. With less than a split seconds reaction, Roseanne's mind pushed two of her balls out to block two of the balls flying at her. Joanne's third ball came straight at Roseanne, who stopped it, stock still in mid-flight and simply plucked it out of the air, while Roseanne's third ball struck Joanne square in the face.

"I think that's game don't you?", a now cheeky Roseanne asked.

"It certainly looks that way", a smiling Joanne agreed.

The other players patted Roseanne on the back and congratulated her on her win, before heading off to the showers.

Selene walked onto the court, "You started off a little slow, but finished well."

"I forgot to use my gifts at first", a somewhat bruised and battered Roseanne replied.

"That's what it looked like, Roseanne. You have to remember, your gifts are with you always", Selene explained, "You need to be able to call upon your gifts without even thinking about them."

Roseanne gave Lady Selene an enquiring look.

"Remember back on Earth, the explosion at the Academy?", Selene asked Roseanne.

"How can I forget? It was a black day. So many deaths", Roseanne replied, a sad look appeared on her face at the memory.

Selene painfully pushed all thoughts of the dead and wounded out of her mind and asked Roseanne, "Remember how Forkbraid and I brought up our defences?"

"Yeah. I remember. That was awesome", Roseanne replied.

"It was a reflex defensive manoeuvre. In less than a micro second, we both had our defences up. If we had stopped to think about it, we'd both be dead right now. That's what I'm trying to explain to you, Roseanne. Sometimes, you don't have time to think about it, you just have to do it."

"I don't know if I'll ever be able to do that", Roseanne replied with uncertainty in her voice.

"It takes practice, Roseanne. Practice and certainty in your own abilities. You, yourself have been taught the very defensive techniques that Forkbraid and I both used that dark morning. Know yourself, know your abilities, be certain that you can do it and you will. It's as simple as that."

"So I have to have faith?", Roseanne asked.

"No. Not faith. You have to know you can. You have to be certain", Selene replied, "No fear, no uncertainty, no doubts. Throw your fears, uncertainties, and doubts aside, and you can achieve miracles. Being in control of everything that holds you back, that is the key."

"I think I understand", Roseanne replied.

"Good then. Now, off to the showers, you smell a little overripe", Selene instructed Roseanne.

"They were really going for it", Charlene stated.

"That they were, Charlene", Selene replied adding, "I'm fairly certain, that these very same women were having difficulty adjusting just a week ago. So it makes me wonder, what's changed?"

"Joanne Seato", Charlene quickly replied.

"Joanne Seato?", Lady Selene enquired, "Yes, she was just playing battleball. What about her?"

"A little over a week ago, Joanne mentioned to me that maybe we were all just trying too hard."

"Trying too hard?", Selene asked, "You mean the training schedule?"

"Yes. I believe so", Charlene began, "Anyway Joanne had this theory, that maybe we just needed to forget that we're all on Mars, and then maybe our abilities would just shine through."

"Forget we're on Mars", Selene replied, "I'm not sure what you mean, Charlene?"

"It's simple really", Charlene explained, "Joanne thought that by playing a rough game like battleball, they'd become so engrossed in the game, that they'd forget they're on Mars."

"And they're abilities would just resurface naturally", Selene finished off Charlene's sentence.

"Yes. Joanne and a few of the other women have been playing battleball daily for the last week or more. From what I saw here, I'd say that Joanne was definitely on to something."

"I'm inclined to agree with you, Charlene", Selene replied smiling.

"Just how many women have been playing regularly?", Lady Selene enquired.

"There's a core group of around twenty or so", Charlene replied.

"Good. Talk to Joanne. I want the pair of you to incorporate sports like battleball into the training schedule. Let's see if this theory can be scaled up to include more colonists, both male and female."

"I'll see what we can come up with", Charlene replied.

Leroy and Matthew were back in the church, formerly the pub called The

Black Pullet, in New Tortuga. The Prophet was with them, as well as Mort Kendal, alias Captain Scar.

"So you've found them?", the Prophet enquired.

"My Lord, we've pinned them down to an area of four hundred square kilometres. So we've locked down their region", Leroy replied.

"That's still a big area", Mort Kendal stated abruptly.

"Have you confirmed their location, Matthew?", the Prophet asked.

"Unfortunately, no, my Lord", Matthew replied, "The area wasn't included in our last scans. I was able to track the HLT's trajectories back to that area though."

"So, we know they came from that region, but we haven't yet confirmed their precise location", the Prophet reiterated for confirmation.

"Yes, my Lord", Matthew immediately replied.

"Okay", the Prophet began, "Captain Scar. How many ships do we have up our sleeve?"

Mort Kendal rubbed his beard thinking aloud, "Well my Lord, we have the two Gull Wings, then there's the nine Talons we held in reserve plus my one, that's ten Talons all up. Then, of course, Matthew has those six Raiders he sent to infiltrate Chryce, and we have another two in reserve."

Matthew quickly cut in, "My Lord, two Gull Wings, ten Talons and eight Raiders."

"Yep. My Lord, that seems about right", Mort Kendal agreed.

The Prophet rolled his eyes and shook his head, "Okay, we need confirmation of the Academy's precise location. Matthew, can we get our Raiders to concentrate their scans on that area during their next run into Elysium?"

"Yes, my Lord", Matthew replied, "That shouldn't pose any problems."

"Good. Good", the Prophet began, "Can they transmit the data to you before they land?"

Matthew tilted his head in thought, "We'd have to encrypt it and bounce it off a satellite or two, but yeah, we can do that, my Lord", he replied.

"Good Matthew, make it so", the Prophet replied.

The Prophet pulled out a map of Mars, "Captain Scar. I'll need yourself and five of your men to fly over to Nepenthis Mensae. Find a safe place to land and stay hidden."

Mort Kendal looked at the map, "It's rough territory around that area, my Lord. Aeolis Mensai would be far safer, it's also much closer to Elysium."

"Very good then. Aeolis Mensai it is", the Prophet accepted Captain Scar's advice.

"As I said, stay hidden. Our Raiders will fly into the Elysium colony and make their scans as they approach. Once they've sent the data to Matthew here, he will quickly analyse it for the exact location of their Psychic Academy. Once we have the exact location, we can begin our attack."

"I'm thinking that I understand your plan, my Lord", Matthew stated.

"Good then, Matthew", the Prophet replied, "I'll let you flesh it out."

"Once we have confirmation of the Academy's exact location, I'll transmit this data back to our Raiders", Matthew began, "We can then signal Captain Scar here to attack the Elysium colony."

"The Elysium colony?", Mort Kendal enquired.

The Prophet nodded silently as Matthew replied, "Yes, the Elysium colony."

"Captain Scar will attack the Elysium colony, causing as much damage and confusion as he can", Matthew continued, "This will draw out any defenders that they might have protecting their precious Psychic Academy."

"So, we're the decoys", Mort Kendal stated in understanding.

"Yes, Mort", Matthew agreed, "You have to be careful not to attack any of the cargo freighters. Remember our Raiders will be in amongst them. Everything else in the Elysium colony is fair game though."

Mort Kendal nodded in understanding.

"Once their Psychic Academy's defenders turn up, break off the attack and fly south. Try to get them to follow you. Keep them busy as long as you can and try not to get yourselves killed", Matthew explained to Captain Scar.

Mort Kendal nodded once more, understanding the plan, "That goes without saying, Lad."

"Now once the attack finishes, it makes sense that the Freighters will try to leave the colony before anything else happens, this, of course, will include our Raiders. So, it will all look perfectly natural when our six Raiders take off and attempt to flee a confused battle scene", Matthew explained.

The Prophet took over, "And our Raiders will flee north, flying fast and low straight to their Psychic Academy to unleash the real attack!"

Leroy nodded as he let loose a single short sentence, "Brilliant, my Lord, brilliant!"

22. The Shilo

Lord Folcrom Forkbraid sat watching young Miranda playing on the deck of the schooner Shilo.

Standing ever watchful behind Forkbraid's back was his rune covered staff. Cormac sat in a chair on Forkbraid's right. Cormac's Wife, Candy, was sitting on Cormac's right.

Candy leant across Cormac and asked, "That was his staff wasn't it?"

"His staff?", Forkbraid queried.

"Yes. *He who asked The Great Question*", Candy clarified.

Forkbraid smiled, "Yes, it was his. How did you know?"

"We were all shown pictures of his staff when we were younger", Candy replied.

Forkbraid gave Candy an odd, curious look, "You were all shown pictures of his staff?"

"Yes", Candy replied without further explanation.

Cormac looked up and clarified, "All of his descendants, at least. His known descendants, Cousin."

"Cousin?", Forkbraid enquired.

"It's true", Cormac replied, "We three are all descendants of him. That makes us all distant Cousins."

There was no lie in Cormac's voice.

"You speak truthfully. I detect no lie in your voice, Cormac", Forkbraid replied casually, adding "There was a myth among my family, that Tafazah had a Martian Wife, as well as his Earth Wife. He, of course, was cautious in the extreme. He carefully chose which memories he shared with his children. Nothing was passed on about his Martian family and as no facts were available, it was always relegated to myth."

"It's not a myth, Cousin", Candy stated boldly, "It's all fact."

"Did Tafazah share his memories with his Martian children?", Forkbraid enquired.

"That he did, Cousin, that he did", Cormac replied.

"Few are able to follow the trail of sharing though and even fewer can unravel the memories", Candy added.

"You can follow them though can't you, Candy, you and Cormac?", Forkbraid asked.

"Yeah we can, both of us, but unravelling the memories is much harder", Candy replied.

"We can read maybe a fifth of what memories he passed on. The rest of his sharing is well warded, well guarded, very cryptic", Cormac added.

"I wonder?", Forkbraid asked of no one in particular.

Both Cormac and Candy gave Forkbraid a curious look.

"If our mutual ancestor was so precise in his sharing, specific memories for specific children. What would be discovered if all of those memories were put back together?", Forkbraid asked.

"Like a jigsaw puzzle?", Candy queried.

"Yes. Just like a jigsaw puzzle", Forkbraid replied.

"There's only one way to find out", Candy stated, adding, "Most of his memories are of little use to me, Cousin. Perhaps you can make better use of them", Candy leaned over to Forkbraid.

Forkbraid leaned his forehead against Candy's, as he did so Candy stated, "I share with you, whatever memories you would take."

Forkbraid's mind reached deep into Candy's mind, following the trail of sharing. There were Cousins and parents, aunts, uncles and also Candy's Husband, Cormac. Forkbraid perused the memories of the living and the deceased from Candy's mind, downloading all and any memories related to Folcrom Tafazah.

Further and further back in time he travelled, jumping from one individual's bundle of memories to another, searching for the memories of his long deceased ancestor, downloading each in turn as he found them. The journey culminated with the memories deposited long ago by Folcrom Tafazah himself, Forkbraid's eighth great-grandfather.

There were a multitude of strands, each following different, yet intertwined lineages. Each strand was indeed highly specific. Discreet memories well filed and shared with specific children and grandchildren. Forkbraid downloaded all that he found. It was nearly fifteen minutes before Forkbraid finally lifted his now weary head.

"It will take quite a while to collate all of this lot", Forkbraid stated as he wiped the sweat from his brow.

"Will you need to download my memories as well?", Cormac questioned.

Forkbraid reached back into the recently acquired memories, "No need, Cormac, scion of Cedric, seventh child and fourth Son of Tafazah. You shared your memories with your Wife, remember", Forkbraid explained. "So, I acquired your store of Tafazah's shared memories from Candy, scion of Freyja, twelfth child of Tafazah and sixth Daughter."

"So, now you see for yourself. Not a myth at all. All facts. We are all distant Cousins", Cormac replied.

"Yes, indeed, and Mars has had colonists on her far longer than officially believed as well", Forkbraid smiled, "It gets even better."

"How?", enquired Candy.

"Lady Selene is also a descendant of Tafazah, yet another distant cousin of ours", Forkbraid replied.

"And you have her store of His memories as well?", Cormac enquired.

"Yes, indeed, Cormac", Forkbraid replied adding "Maybe now I should attempt stitching these memories together and try deciphering them."

"That sounds like a plan, Cousin", Candy agreed, "Seek out the knowledge that neither Cormac nor I could unravel. Seek the answers, seek the truth."

Forkbraid rolled his head around on his neck, he had downloaded a hell of a lot of memories, "Maybe, first I should seek some aspirin?"

Marcus Greyhelm stared out of the window of his dark and dingy room above the tavern, at the docks, in the old quarter of the Aurorae colony. The door opened and Special Agent Murphy stepped into the room.

"I suppose you've already claimed the top bunk", Special Agent Murphy remarked.

"No, not at all", Marcus replied, "I've always preferred the bottom bunk myself."

"Good then, the top bunks mine", Special Agent Murphy replied with a smile.

"I don't think I've ever stayed in place as crappy as this one", Marcus told Agent Murphy.

"Yeah, it's pretty rough. Even calling it quaint isn't going to help", Special Agent Murphy replied laughing, "It has history though."

"History?", Marcus queried.

"Yeah. This is the old quarter of Aurorae", Special Agent Murphy replied, "This section of the colony was already here before Mars was officially opened up for colonisation after the terraforming was completed."

"Really. So this place pre-dates the official colony?", a now curious Marcus questioned.

"Sort of", Special Agent Murphy replied, "When the Aurorae colony was being planned, it was going to be built on the mainland to the west. Only someone pointed out there was already a town, with a good-sized, deep harbour and primitive port facilities on an island just to the east of their preferred location. So they decided to build the Aurorae colony here instead."

"So it does pre-date the colony", Marcus pointed out.

"It may pre-date the official Aurorae colony", Special Agent Murphy replied adding, "But the old quarter itself, was the original Aurorae colony, long before officialdom stuck its beak into it."

Marcus looked back out the window once more, "Well, they haven't improved it much, have they? This place really is quite a shit-hole."

The long pier at the docks was obviously quite new. As was the roadway leading up to it and the facilities at its base. To the south was the old pier. Made of timber, stone and concrete, it was a third as long as the new pier and no longer used for docking ships. Instead, the disused old pier was being used as a recreational fishing platform by the locals. Several youngsters could be seen prising mussels from its rotted, old pylons. It showed signs of its age and was in serious need of repairs. The Shilo was scheduled to dock at the new pier, on its south side in a few days time.

All around the tavern was a confusing mess of narrow streets, lined with old, dilapidated, wooden and stone buildings, terrace cottages and small houses. Many of them appeared to be quite old. Marcus was quite sure some were well over a century or more old. This contrasted greatly with the new modern colony that bordered the old quarter, with its broad tree lined avenues and relatively new, colourful modern buildings and apartments, made of reinforced concrete, [69]plasteel and other exotic alloys and materials. The change from old to new was so sudden and abrupt.

The new colony's planners dearly wanted to bulldoze the entire old quarter and rebuild it from scratch, but the locals who'd lived here for generations fiercely resisted any change. The locals were also backed by a newly created Martian historical society, who lobbied hard against any changes to the historic precinct as they called it. It had taken a Herculean effort of persuasion simply to get the new pier approved and built. The old pier had to stay, it was a historic landmark.

"Our Hummer was alright then I take it?", Marcus enquired.

"It's still in the hangar at the spaceport on the other side of the colony. No changes there", Special Agent Murphy confirmed.

"Good. I'd hate to have to walk all the way back to Elysium", Marcus explained.

Special Agent Murphy laughed, "Don't worry, Marcus. If anyone steals it, I'm sure I can find us a few pack mules and some floaties."

Marcus looked over to the new pier once more. He noticed several armed men standing by the ticketing office. He had seen them there many times before. None of them were uniformed or wore any insignia. It was hard for Marcus to pick up their thoughts, he was still a little out of sorts, courtesy of their trip from Earth. One thought that did come through was *"Shilo"*. These men were keeping tabs on the schooner Shilo.

"Those three men are back again", Marcus informed Special Agent Murphy.

Special Agent Murphy came to the window and looked over at the ticketing office, indeed these three blokes had been hanging around the docks and ticketing office for several days now.

"Are you picking up anything useful?", Special Agent Murphy enquired.

"Just the odd thought here and there", Marcus replied, "Nothing useful. My

---

69 Plasteel. A polymerised form of steel refined and processed in high Martian orbit.

head's still not right when it comes to my abilities."

"Has your head ever been right, Marcus?", Special Agent Murphy stirred, "Well, they are a bunch of likely looking Lads. We'd better keep tabs on them."

"I agree", Marcus replied, "They are definitely up to no good."

As they watched another armed man joined the three by the ticketing office.

"You see that scrawny blonde bloke", Marcus pointed out, "He comes and goes."

"Some sort of relay", Special Agent Murphy considered, "You know, running information and orders, back and forth."

"Maybe", Marcus replied, "He seems to be worried about a man named Smith."

"John Smith?", Special Agent Murphy enquired.

Marcus concentrated on the scrawny bloke, his brow furrowed, "Yes. John Smith."

"If that man knows Private John Smith, then these are seriously bad people", Special Agent Murphy stated.

Marcus nodded, "We definitely need to keep an eye on them."

Forkbraid slept comfortably in his cabin. It wasn't much of a cabin, quite smallish, containing only a wash basin, cracked mirror and a hammock. Still it was all Forkbraid required. Hunting down terrorists and other evil people had been his main task for many a year now. As a consequence, Forkbraid had learnt to sleep whenever time permitted and wherever he could.

Forkbraid was never fussed about his surroundings. Neither the room nor the rolling of the Shilo upon the swell disturbed Forkbraid's sleep, especially not in a hammock.

Within his sleeping mind, Forkbraid entered into the familiar realm of dreamscape. Here in this quiescent state of mind Forkbraid could work on the task of stitching and gluing together the myriad of memories from his long dead ancestor, the first Folcrom.

Memories that had been carefully separated, carefully divided and shared down specific lineages in specific batches. Forkbraid at first began to analyse the images contained within the memories. He was searching for commonalities that might aid him in his task.

Forkbraid's ancestor, Tafazah, had had twelve children by two separate Wives. His first Wife on Earth, his second on Mars. Each Wife had born Tafazah six children. In total Forkbraid's ancestor had Fathered six Daughters and six Sons.

"Will I need to accumulate the shared memories given to all twelve children?", was Forkbraid's main concern.

If his ancestor's memories had been split into twelve streams of sharing, that would pose a major hurdle in Forkbraid's efforts to stitch them together. For then, he might have to gather eight more streams of sharing before such an attempt could even be considered.

One by one, commonalities amongst the memories began to appear. There was a definite cross-over of sharing between the Martian descendants. Cormac and Candy had also shared their memories with their Cousins and some of Cormac's and Candy's Cousins contained separate streams of sharing. Yet, when Forkbraid traced these memories back to their ultimate source, Tafazah, he found just below that source, was a different child each time.

Conclusion, *"Some of these streams of sharing are identical"*, Forkbraid smiled in his sleep.

Forkbraid analysed the streams of Martian sharing. Indeed, they were identical. As Forkbraid traced the various streams back to their source, he quickly realised there was a Martian key.

"One stream of sharing is female, the other stream is male", Forkbraid concluded.

Each of Tafazah's three Martian Daughters had received one complete stream of sharing and each of Tafazah's three Martian Sons had received another.

"Does this pattern repeat for the Earth descendants?", Forkbraid considered in his still sleeping mind.

Forkbraid quickly focused his mind upon the streams of sharing from his own lineage and that of Lady Selene's. On Earth, the sharing of memories between Cousins was not as common as on Mars, nonetheless it did happen, although to a far lesser degree.

One by one Forkbraid located the separate streams of sharing and one by one he traced them back to their ultimate source, again Tafazah. Some of those streams started with the same children. Forkbraid continued to trace the others and one by one, he found that all of Tafazah's Earth children were accounted for. Again, he analysed the streams for commonalities and he found them.

"He used the same key! The Earth and Martian keys are the same!", Forkbraid again smiled in his slumber.

Again, one stream of sharing was female, and the other stream was male.

As with Mars, each of Tafazah's three Earth Daughters had received one complete stream of sharing and each of Tafazah's three Earth Sons had received another.

Forkbraid compared the Earth and Martian streams of sharing.

"They're different! Two streams of sharing for Mars and two for Earth", Forkbraid's realisation that he had the complete set of shared memories caused him to wake up.

"Two for Mars and two for Earth!", Forkbraid shouted out loud.

Twenty seconds later Cormac burst into the cabin, "Are you all right?", he quickly asked.

"Fine, Cormac", Forkbraid replied, "Half left in fact."

Cormac missed the joke, "Maybe you should join us up on deck. You can't spend the whole trip in your hammock."

Forkbraid climbed out of the hammock, "I suppose you're right, I've slept way too long."

On the way up to the deck, Forkbraid asked Cormac, "You don't want me to know where New Tortuga is, do you Cormac?"

"You know the name, I suppose you already know its location", Cormac replied.

"Yes, Cormac", Forkbraid replied, "From the sharing, remember."

Cormac nodded, "From the sharing."

As they stepped out onto the deck Cormac told Tafazah, "It's not an evil place you know."

Forkbraid turned to Cormac and gave him a questioning look.

"New Tortuga!", Cormac replied, "It's not an evil place."

"Tell me about it then, Cormac?", Forkbraid questioned.

"New Tortuga's a rough place, is all. I admit, it does attract a rough crowd, but it ain't evil."

"It does have some rather evil people there, doesn't it, though?", Forkbraid questioned further.

"Sure it does", Cormac replied, "But by and large, most of the folk are just ordinary folk, just like you and me. These other evil sligs came later."

Forkbraid caught the remark about evil sligs, thinking, *"It's a good metaphor"*, he replied aloud, "Slippery bastards."

"Yeah, evil slippery bastards", Cormac agreed.

"What would you have me do, Cormac?", Forkbraid asked, "I can't let the terrorists go free. They have to pay for their crimes."

"Yeah, they do. I agree one hundred percent", Cormac replied, before commenting, "There just has to be another way, Cousin."

"Another way, Cormac?", Forkbraid enquired.

"Yeah, another way", Cormac stated again, "I don't want you and the colonial troops going into New Tortuga and blowing everyone to hell!"

"Another way", Forkbraid stated with a smile, "Cormac, I promise you, I will find another way."

"You can do that, Cousin?", Cormac asked.

"Sure, I can do that", Forkbraid replied, "I know where New Tortuga is. Now, I just have to come up with a plan that will limit the damage, to just those bastards who deserve it."

"That's what I'm talking about, Cousin", Cormac smiled his gap-toothed smile, "Dealing with the Prophet and his arseholes without harming the ordinary folk. You find a way to do that and me and Candy will feel much happier about it."

Forkbraid recalled one of Cormac's own memories into focus, "The cave system, Cormac", he stated quietly.

"The cave system?", Cormac enquired.

"Yes. The cave system at the back of New Tortuga", Forkbraid replied, "I think we can use that."

"Ah, yes. The cave system", Cormac agreed with a huge smile on his face.

Special Agent Murphy had been gone for most of the day and Marcus was beginning to worry. All day long Marcus had been watching the docks. Not much had changed. The three armed blokes who had been hanging around the docks had been replaced by three new armed blokes. All of them seemed to be following the directions from the scrawny blonde bloke. It was nearly dark when Special Agent Murphy came through the door of their room.

"Where have you been, Jim?", Marcus enquired.

"I've been a little busy, Marcus", Jim replied as he placed a large parcel of take away food on the table in front of Marcus.

"At least you brought lunch", Marcus replied, not bothering to hide his sarcasm.

He got up from the window and checked out the food on the table, "Fish and chips, not bad."

"Better late than never, hey, Marcus", Jim replied.

"Seriously, Jim, where the hell have you been?", Marcus asked again.

"I've been following Blondie down there", Jim replied.

"And what do we know about him?", Marcus enquired.

"We know he has a place just down the road from here", Jim informed Marcus, "It's about a couple of hundred metres over that way", Jim pointed in a northeasterly direction.

Marcus nodded, "What else do we know?"

"There's a hell of a lot more of them, Marcus", Jim began, "Dozens at least, perhaps more."

"That is not good, Jim", Marcus replied, with a concerned look on his face.

"Well, it's certainly going to be problematic", Jim understated.

"I also hired a chariot", Jim informed Marcus.

"A chariot?", Marcus queried.

"Yeah, an eight seater. I thought we might need to head straight to the spaceport when Forkbraid arrives", Jim replied adding, "I've parked it in the Tavern's yard behind the gates."

"Good, that'll be handy", Marcus replied, "I'm thinking we'll need a speed boat as well."

"A speed boat?", Jim enquired with a curious look on his face.

"Yeah, a speed boat", Marcus replied, explaining, "I'm fairly certain Forkbraid can handle that lot down there, not a problem. What concerns me are the civilians he'll have with him. He won't want to be walking into a meat grinder while he's baby sitting a bunch of mundanes."

Special Agent Murphy didn't take offence at the mundanes remark, instead he simply asked, "What's your plan, Marcus?", he was now back in Special Agent tactical mode.

"I'm thinking that we get a speed boat or better yet, a motor launch and dock it over at the old pier. Now, we know roughly when the Shilo's due to dock, so I'll begin transmitting a signal to Forkbraid long before then."

"Transmitting a signal?", Jim queried.

"Yeah. A telepathic signal that Forkbraid will pick up on", Marcus continued, "He'll respond and when he does, I'll follow his response straight to the Shilo in the speed boat."

Special Agent Murphy had caught on, it was a sound plan after all, "So you'll speed out to the Shilo, pick up the mundanes he's protecting and bring them back here."

"Not quite", Marcus replied, "I'll be bringing them back to the old pier, and we'll wait there for the Shilo to dock."

"I don't get it. Why wait at the old pier?", a confused Special Agent Murphy questioned.

"Well, that's because when Forkbraid steps off the Shilo, all Hell's going to break loose", Marcus began, continuing, "And in the confusion, I'll bring our mundanes straight to the Tavern."

"A distraction! That lot out there won't have a clue", Special Agent Murphy realised.

"That was the general idea", Marcus replied.

Special Agent Murphy suddenly began to feel like a third wheel, "When all of this goes down, exactly what will I be doing?"

"Ah. Good question, Jim", Marcus replied, "I was kind of thinking, you might like to take out Blondie's humble abode. Maybe a small implosion or something equally deadly."

"I think I can arrange something like that", Special Agent Murphy replied.

"Excellent", Marcus replied with a grin, "Then on the way back here, you might consider eliminating as many of those goons as happens to cross your path as well."

"Another good plan, Marcus", Special Agent Murphy replied.

"There are a couple of points to remember", Marcus stated.

"And what would those be?", Special Agent Murphy queried.

"We'll need your help here as well to clear a path to the spaceport", Marcus replied.

"Yeah, it does look like I'm going to be busy. I'll be wearing multiple hats it seems", Special Agent Murphy replied, "What was the other point?"

"Oh, don't get yourself killed. You're our pilot remember", Marcus stated with a slight chuckle.

"Great", Jim laughed as he went through the list, "Procure a speed boat. Take out a rat's nest. Whack some rather nasty goons. Clear our path. Don't die. Anything else I can do for you?"

"No. That should just about do it, Jim", Marcus replied.

"Good, then. I'd better start with that speed boat", Special Agent Murphy smiled.

Forkbraid was in his hammock once more. Again in dreamscape, he carefully reviewed and analysed the streams of shared memories, all of which originated with his distant ancestor Folcrom Tafazah. One by one and piece by piece, Forkbraid slowly stitched the memories together. The complex jigsaw was slowly coming together.

The Martian male and female memory streams formed a double helix and Forkbraid quickly worked out the correct method for combining them. It was like zipping up a pair of DNA strands. Likewise, the Earth memory streams, male and female, also constituted a double helix. They zipped together in precisely the same fashion. It was a complex process, but any Folcrom, any psychic above level nine, ought to have been able to do it. Soon both planetary pairs were combined.

Forkbraid now had two planetary memory streams to deal with.

Combining the Earth and Mars memory streams was going to be much, much harder. The sequences were all out of kilter. The memories from before Tafazah travelled to Mars could appear in both planetary streams, as could the memories from when Tafazah was on Mars. The memories that followed Tafazah's return to Earth, however, could only appear in the Earth stream. Forkbraid could see no easy method of combining those two streams. There had to be another key, and it appeared to be missing; it was not in any of the shared memories. Tafazah had hidden it.

Cautiously, Forkbraid probed the memory streams. His careful analysis of the planetary streams revealed that with the right key, both streams would simply begin turning into each other. It was as if a single key could be placed into the midst of the two planetary memory streams, and they would simply turn as if they were tumblers in a lock.

It had to be the right key though, the exact precise key, for Forkbraid could see a wee little pitfall. If Forkbraid used the wrong key, a damaged key or tried to force the memory streams to join together, the result would likely be highly detrimental to his mind. Instinctively, Forkbraid knew that insanity would quickly follow. He had to get this right, else his mind would be lost.

"My ancestor was a right piece of fucking work", Forkbraid thought to himself.

Forkbraid spent the next several hours attempting to deduce what the correct key would be. No matter how many times he analysed the two planetary memory streams, the key refused to reveal itself. Over and over again Forkbraid analysed the two memory streams and over and over again the key remained hidden. Every which way Forkbraid turned those two memory streams in his mind, he found no solution. Forkbraid tried ever increasingly complex solutions and scenarios, all to no avail.

Then Forkbraid had the simplest of thoughts, *"Occam's razor. All things being equal, the simplest solution should be the correct solution."*

Forkbraid awoke, "I need a simple fucking solution!", he spat out.

There was none, he had no solution.

For long minutes Forkbraid stared at the wall of his cabin, being careful not to breach the ship's wooden hull with the sheer disdain he felt for his long deceased ancestor.

Forkbraid lost track of all time, he sat quietly, slowly letting the problem slip from his mind.

Then all of a sudden, there was a familiar voice, *"Lord Folcrom Forkbraid"*, it rang out in his mind like a calling bell.

"Marcus Greyhelm", Forkbraid transmitted back with far more power than was necessary.

23. Terror Attack at the Academy Two

Matthew waited patiently as the final satellite data stream downloaded to his computer. No sooner had the data finished downloading when Matthew began running his three algorithms. Each algorithm was run side by side, processing their own copies of the data. Matthew had instigated this change to process the data more efficiently.

After ten minutes of processing, Matthew was beginning to worry that he had calculated the wrong trajectory and subsequently calculated the wrong region. He was about to review his previous calculations when after a further two minutes of processing, just into the beginning of the fourth data stream, the first algorithm stopped. It gave off a sharp audible beep.

Matthew quickly eyed the screen, only to be distracted by a second sharp audible beep from algorithm number two, which was quickly followed by another beep from algorithm number three. All three algorithms had found something. All three screens beckoned for Matthew's attention.

At first Matthew looked from one screen to the next as if in a state of confusion, then he shook his head and checked the screen running the first algorithm. There on the screen was a structure that was not naturally found in the Martian terrain. Matthew zoomed the screen in on the object. There at the top of a large rise, overlooking the edge of the Elysium Plateau was a large building. It looked like a large castle!

A huge smile came over Matthew's face, "Holy mother!", he exclaimed.

Quickly Matthew checked the other two screens. On all three screens was the same vista, a large castle-like structure with a nearby air field complete with hangars, set amongst rolling pastures, with forests in the background. They'd found it, the location of the Psychic Academy was theirs.

It took several minutes for the discovery to fully sink in before Matthew reached for his communicator and called Leroy McGuvan.

Leroy answered in his usual gruff and surly tone, "What is it, Matthew?"

"Sir", Matthew replied, "We've found it! We have the location of their Psychic Academy!"

"We have?", Leroy replied as if questioning.

"Yes, Sir, we have their precise location, Sir", Matthew confirmed.

There was a long silence over the communicator before Leroy ordered, "Well, Lad, what are you waiting for? Relay that location to Captain Scar and our Raiders! We have an Academy to destroy."

"Yes, Sir", Matthew replied, "I'll get on it straight away."

"Good then, I'll let the Prophet know that the operation has begun", Leroy informed Matthew adding, "And Matthew, good work, Lad, excellent job."

Matthew smiled as he placed his communicator back on the desk.

Matthew jumped onto his keyboard once more and put together an encrypted message. It was a simple enough message, containing little more than a precise set of coordinates and the phrase, Time to go to work. Matthew bounced the message to Captain Scar at Aeolis Mensai via satellite, who received it within seconds.

Matthew then put together a second encrypted message, almost the same as the first, only this one contained just the Psychic Academy's Martian coordinates. He didn't need to provide more details, his Raider Captains had already been briefed on the attack plan. All they needed were the coordinates. Matthew bounced his message to his six Raiders and within seconds the Raider Captains were informed of the Psychic Academy's location. Matthew sat back in his chair, placed his hands behind his head, relaxed and smiled a broad smile.

Mort Kendal, alias Captain Scar, had chosen to position his little squadron of six Talons on an island in the centre of the flooded crater, Knobel, in the Aeolis Mensai region on the south coast of the shallow Elysium Channel. The terraforming process had played out well in the Aeolis Mensai region and Captain Scar had secreted his squadron in a clearing surrounded by thick coniferous forests. Tall trees surrounded them on all sides.

Captain Scar received the message from Matthew with glee.

Quickly he gave the order to his five comrades.

"Boys", Captain Scar began, "Time to go to work."

One by one the small squadron of Talons lifted off from the crater, Knobel. They quickly set their course for the Elysium Colony and headed north.

"Remember, Lads, keep well clear of the spaceport", Captain Scar reminded them, "Everything else in the colony is fair game."

It was a short twenty-minute flight to the Elysium Colony and Captain Scar had kept his little squadron flying very low over the beautiful, turquoise waters of the Elysium channel. It wasn't long before the flooded crater, Eddie, was in sight and just beyond that the colony itself. Swiftly the six Talons fell upon the Elysium colony with all of their high intensity lasers blazing and their pulsed plasma cannons firing at will.

Pulses of plasma exploded in long strafing runs, destroying everything they struck. Lasers cut deep into buildings, installations, and facilities. Once more massive explosions and firestorms erupted in the new colony. In and out Captain Scar's squadron of Talons flew, hammering the Elysium colony hard.

There was an urgent knock at the door of Lady Selene's apartment at the New Flinders Psychic Academy. Over and over the knocker knocked. An annoyed Lady Selene dropped the colony repair reports she was reading down on the table, then hurried over to the door, yanking it open.

"Lady Selene", the frightened young woman at the door began, "There's an attack happening at the Elysium colony, my Lady."

The annoyed look on Selene's face disappeared and was replaced by shock, "An attack?"

"Yes, my Lady, an attack!", the young woman quickly confirmed.

Lady Selene stepped out of her apartment, slamming the door behind her and headed off down the corridor. The now very nervous young woman followed closely behind.

"What's Charlene doing about it?", Selene asked the nervous young woman.

"Charlene's issued an order to launch the Wisps, my Lady", the young woman replied.

"And then she sent you to get me?", Lady Selene asked.

"Yes, my Lady", the young woman replied.

Lady Selene turned and gave the young woman a quick glance, *"Not one of my colonists"*, Selene thought to herself.

"You're not a psychic, are you?", Lady Selene asked.

"No, my Lady", the young woman replied, "I'm just one of the custodians, Ma'am."

Selene thought to herself, *"One of Varak's people looking after the Academy"*, then she asked, "What's your name?"

"Carol, my Lady", the young woman replied.

"Well, Carol", Lady Selene began, "I have a job for you."

"Yes, my Lady", Carol replied.

"Spread the word around", Lady Selene began, "We need everyone ready."

"Everyone ready?", Carol enquired.

"Yes, everyone's ready to go down to the bunkers at a moment's notice", Lady Selene explained.

"The bunkers", Carol thought so loudly that Selene picked it up.

"Yes, my Lady, I'll do it straight away", Carol stated, then ran off down another corridor.

Lady Selene reached the grand gallery in the centre of the keep and leapt over its balustrade.

Selene's cloak billowed out behind her as she dropped towards the floor ten stories below.

Stunned faces looked up at her and watched as Selene glided to a gentle landing.

"All of you, be prepared to go to the bunkers. Spread the word. Now move it", Selene shouted out before heading for the keeps entrance at a blazingly quick pace.

It wasn't long before Selene was at the building where the Wisps had been housed. All eight Wisps had already been launched and Charlene was now discussing the attack with Varak and Roseanne Rhein.

Lady Selene walked over to the trio, noticing that Forkbraid's Bat Wing was still present and questioned, "Don't we need every available fighter in the air?"

"We can not do anything with this one, my Lady", Varak replied adding, "It's DNA locked."

Lady Selene understood, but queried, "Only, Forkbraid can fly it?"

"That's right, Selene", Charlene replied.

Selene closed her eyes for a second, frowned, then upon opening them said one word, "Typical."

"What's happened so far?", Selene asked.

Varak replied, "Half a dozen or so Talons have attacked the colony. They are being hit pretty hard."

"So we've launched the Wisps to deal with the Talons?", Selene questioned.

"Yes", Charlene replied, "They'll be there in a few minutes."

"Let's hope they're enough", Selene replied.

"Why don't we have any communications in this place?", asked Roseanne.

"Psychic Academy remember", Charlene replied.

"We're not supposed to need them, Roseanne", Selene replied adding, "We do have communications, but they're all geared for contacting and dealing with the outside world. Within the Academy itself we're supposed to be using our gifts."

"Yes, I know, but this is Mars, not Earth. Things are different here", Roseanne replied.

"No-one was expecting terrorist attacks on Mars, Roseanne", Selene replied, "Had we known, things would have been different."

"We do have a warning system in place though", Varak replied.

"We do?", Selene asked.

"Oh, yes", Varak replied, "It was set up in the last few days along with other defensive measures. Courtesy of Captain Carmichael, of course."

"Good", Selene replied, "I've had one of your girls spread the word around to be prepared to head to the bunkers at a moment's notice."

"Excellent", Varak replied, "When the sirens go off, everyone will know exactly what to do."

"I don't get it", Roseanne stated, asking, "We have no communications, but we have bunkers?"

"Every Psychic Academy has bunkers, Roseanne", Charlene informed her.

Roseanne gave Charlene a questioning look and Selene explained, "We learned those lessons long ago on Earth Roseanne. Deep under every Psychic Academy, we have bunkers and escape passages. We know how to protect ourselves in our own home."

"What other defensive measures have you and Captain Carmichael set up,

Varak?", Selene enquired.

"Out well beyond the outer walls. We have set up eight anti-aircraft batteries", Varak replied.

"Really, I don't remember anyone mentioning that to me", Selene stated with surprise.

"Forkbraid requested them that very first day after you arrived", Varak informed Selene.

"When I was indisposed?", Selene queried.

"Yes", Varak replied, adding softly, "When you were indisposed."

Lady Selene sighed, "Typical. Forkbraid has the good sense to request anti-aircraft defences, but neglects to inform me about them."

"And he left his Bat Wing on a DNA lock", Charlene added.

"Yeah, typical", Selene replied.

"Perhaps, he just expected to be here to fly it himself?", Varak speculated.

"Exactly, Varak", Selene replied, "He expected to be in the air and in the thick of it. He always expects to be in the thick of it. It's his way. He always has to deal with everything personally. He spreads himself too thinly. Now he's on the other side of Mars dealing with something else."

"Are we expecting him back any time soon?", Roseanne asked.

"No, not really", Selene replied smiling slightly, "If things go pear shaped, we'll just have to manage as best we can. Just us girls dealing with whatever those evil bastards throw at us."

"In case you three hadn't noticed, I am not a girl", Varak informed them.

Captain Scar and his comrades continued to blast the Elysium colony.

Thus far they had found no air defences to worry about.

"Easy pickings", was the thought that crossed the Captain's mind.

Hell, *"Easy pickings"*, was the thought on the minds of Captain Scar's comrades as well.

Then Captain Scar noticed a small squadron of craft approaching from the north on his scanners.

"Careful, Boys, we have company", Captain Scar advised his comrades.

"What are they?", one of his comrades questioned, "They don't look like Switch Blades."

"I'm not sure, Lads", Captain Scar replied as he glanced again at the scanners.

"They're Wisps!", another of the Captain's comrades exclaimed.

"Atmo rated Wisps?", Captain Scar questioned, "There ain't no such fucking thing!"

"I suggest you look again, Captain", the same comrade recommended.

Captain Scar looked again, "Shit, Boys! They're atmo rated Wisps alright!"

"They're coming up fast, Captain. Real fast", another comrade advised.

"Damn, they're fast!", Captain Scar exclaimed.

"Break off the attack, Boys, we're heading south", Captain Scar ordered.

"Roger. Roger that. Roger. Roger. Roger that", came a series of replies from the Captain's men.

Then as one, the squadron of Talons turned tail and ran, leaving a trail of destruction in their wake. The approaching Wisps followed them.

"Keep ahead of them, Lads", Captain Scar ordered, "We want them to follow us."

"Keep ahead of them", one of the Captain's comrades replied, "Man they're fast, we'll be damn lucky if they don't overtake us."

"If they catch up", Captain Scar thought for a second, "We'll fight a running rear guard action", he then ordered.

"Running rear guard action?", one of the Captain's comrades questioned, "In a Talon?"

"Just keep them busy for as long as we can, Lads", Captain Scar replied.

The skies above the Elysium colony were soon clear of aircraft after the Wisps flew past. Taking full advantage of the lull in fighting, one by one the transports at the spaceport lifted off. They flew to the west, leaving Elysium airspace as fast as they could. All except a handful of ships, six freighters, held back, deliberately lagging behind. Once the main group was far enough ahead of them, those six freighters dropped altitude and turned north.

Charlene, Roseanne, and Lady Selene were atop the battlements of their Psychic Academy's central keep when Joanne Seato came running up to them. Far in the distant south, smoke from the fires at the Elysium colony billowed high into the sky. The amount of damage must have been enormous. Just as Joanne arrived, the sirens began to sound.

"We just got word from The Spartan", Joanne spat out, "Six freighters have gone missing."

"What do you mean missing?", Lady Selene enquired.

"The attack", Joanne replied as she caught her breath, "The attack. Our fighters chased off the attackers and the freighters at the spaceport decided to make a run for Chryce. Six of them went missing. Captain Carmichael says they dropped right off the scanners."

"Shot down?", Charlene asked.

"No. No. The Captain doesn't think so", Joanne replied, "All the action was in the south, well away from the freighters. The Captain says they dropped altitude, turned north and then vanished from his scanners. He thinks they're flying at low altitude, below his scanners' thresholds."

"Then they're coming here", Lady Selene responded.

"Charlene, take Roseanne down to the bunkers", Selene ordered.

"I'm on it. Come with me, Roseanne", Charlene replied.

"No!", Roseanne shouted, "I want to fight!"

"No. No, you don't, Roseanne", Selene replied, "We'll deal with this. Go to the bunkers."

"Joanne, get all the level nines, the ones who can use their gifts", Selene ordered, "We're going to put up one hell of a fight. Tell Varak to recall our damned Wisps, we're going to need them."

"Consider it done my, Lady", Joanne replied and ran back the way she'd come.

"Why are you still here, Roseanne?", Selene questioned, "I told you. Go to the bunkers!"

Then without warning Lady Selene leapt from the battlement and glided downwards towards the outer southern tower.

Charlene pulled hard at Roseanne's arm, "Come on, Roseanne. We have to go now."

To no avail, "No!", Roseanne shouted as she broke free and leapt from the battlement.

"Roseanne!", Charlene shouted after her.

Roseanne found herself falling quickly towards the ground, she raised her head and concentrated on the outer southern tower. Fully focused upon her chosen target, Roseanne glided swiftly to the tower's battlements. A surprised Selene turned around just in time to watch Roseanne Rhein land.

"Where'd you learn to do that?", Selene queried.

Roseanne shrugged her shoulders, "Just learnt it then."

"You're not going to go to the bunkers are you?", Selene asked.

"No, no matter how many times you order me", Roseanne replied.

"Stubborn, little Witch", Selene told her with a wry smile.

Roseanne smiled back.

Lady Selene reached into her robe and a pocket mysteriously appeared. Quickly Selene pulled out her staff. It was only about five feet tall and topped with a crystal sphere. The crystal sphere being held firmly in place by webs of golden metal thread. Three words glowered in red around the centre of the staff. On the right in the runes of the Elder Futhark was the name Artemis, in the front was the name Selene and on the left, the name Hecate. Just below the top of the staff was the symbol of the full moon, with half moon crescents connected on either side. Below this was the symbol of another crescent moon. Selene let loose her staff, and it drifted obediently to take up position behind her back.

Lady Selene reached into her robe once more and from the pocket that magically appeared pulled out her wand. Like her staff, Selene's wand was also mounted by a crystal sphere. It was smaller and mounted on the pommel, held in place again by a web of golden metal thread. Images of the elements were carved into the hilt, they glowered red to her touch. Selene held her wand before her and gently kissed the crystal sphere. It immediately glowed a golden yellow glow, then

Selene's staff responded in kind.

"Awaken, Gnomulus", Selene spoke to her wand, "Blessed be thee, defender of the righteous."

"Roseanne, stay behind me at all times", Selene instructed her stubborn apprentice Witchling.

Roseanne nodded to her Master then asked, "Your wand has a name?"

"Of course, it does, Silly girl", Selene replied, "Now hold out your hand, you'll be needing this."

"Needing what?", Roseanne queried.

"Gnomulus, my wand", Selene replied.

"What are you going to use?", Roseanne asked.

"Oh I won't need a wand, dear Child", Selene replied, a terrifying visage coming over her face, "I'm going to let loose and give them all hell."

"Gnomulus!", Selene addressed her wand, "This be Roseanne Rhein. Wight of my will, know Roseanne, harm Roseanne not. Gnomulus know my will. Cursed be those who would harm Roseanne. Protect her from all foes and the evils they perpetrate."

Selene then passed her wand to Roseanne who slowly, as if frightened of it, reached out with her right hand and took hold of it.

As Roseanne took hold of Gnomulus, Selene reached out with her left hand and pricked Roseanne's arm, drawing a small trickle of blood. Just as quickly, Selene wiped the blood onto Gnomulus's hilt.

"Ouch!", Roseanne exclaimed.

"Good", Selene stated, "Just point and shoot."

"Point and shoot?", a confused Roseanne questioned.

"Yes. Point and shoot", Selene replied, "Gnomulus will know your will."

It was just then that Joanne Seato appeared on the battlement. Behind her was Varak, who was holding a large thing. It was a really, really large thing.

"What is that, Varak?", Selene asked Varak.

"It's a light pulsed plasma cannon", Varak replied.

Selene looked at the weapon, it was anything but light, quite large in fact, "Light pulsed plasma cannon, you say?"

"Well, it is normally mounted on an interceptor, you know, like a Wisp", Varak replied, "I had to lighten it just a little."

The light pulsed plasma cannon appeared heavy, yet Varak's strongly muscled arms seemed to hold it quite well.

"It suits you, Varak. Just be careful where you point that thing", Selene advised Varak.

Lady Selene looked around the Psychic Academy's battlements. There were at least two dozen psychics standing ready to fight.

"Not as many as I'd hoped for", Selene remarked.

"It's all the level nines who can control their gifts to any great degree", Joanne replied.

"Then they will have to do", Selene stated.

"Those eight anti-aircraft batteries are sure going to come in handy", Varak replied.

"Yeah. I'll have to thank Captain Carmichael for those", Selene replied adding, "I'll thank Forkbraid when he gets back as well, after I've thumped him a few times."

Captain Scar and his squadron of six Talons were still running south, hotly pursued by the eight defending Wisps. The Wisps were closing in fast, and it wasn't long before the Captain's squadron came within firing range. Pulsed plasma cannons opened fire.

Captain Scar's Talon was rocked by explosions, he checked his scanners and noted two of his comrades were already gone.

"Evasive action, Lads", Captain Scar ordered, "No more running."

The remaining four Talons turned on their attackers and a crazy dog fight quickly ensued. Pulsed plasma cannons were being fired on both sides. The Talons having the added advantage of blazing away with their high intensity lasers. The two destroyed Talons were quickly avenged.

Again and again the two squadrons swept into the buzzing hornets nest that was their battle zone. Another Talon had been destroyed, exploding in a ball of brilliant flames. Then all of a sudden, as quickly as it had begun, the battle stopped and the Wisps all broke away from the battle and turned north once more.

"Well, Lads, what's the bet they've been ordered back to defend their precious Psychic Academy?", Captain Scar bellowed into the mike.

"No bet, Captain", one of the Captain's remaining comrades replied, "It's a sure thing."

"Yeah, a sure thing, Captain", his other remaining comrade replied, "It's too damn bad they won't get back in time."

Captain Scar chuckled into the mike, "Sure is a shame, ain't it, Lads. Let's go home, Boys, our job is done."

With that the three remaining Talons set course for New Tortuga.

Towards the distant horizon, six freighters appeared, and they were approaching fast.

As the freighters approached the New Flinders Psychic Academy, hull plating slid back and weapons blisters popped out. The six freighters were now in their Raider configurations. Joanne, who had been watching through binoculars, caught a glimpse of this metamorphosis.

"Holy crap!", Joanne exclaimed, "They're bristling with pulsed plasma cannons."

"We'd better bloody well get ready then", Selene replied.

Joanne pulled her own wand from out of her robe, Roseanne held Selene's wand, Gnomulus, in her outstretched hand and Varak stood firmly in place with his light pulsed plasma cannon. Lady Selene herself stood in front of Roseanne protectively, her hands outstretched, fingers aiming in the direction of the approaching Raiders. Blue fire arced from fingertip to fingertip, a viperous visage upon her face, her eyes fully focused upon the Raiders.

Joanne Seato caught a glimpse of Lady Selene's face, no longer the face of a beautiful Goddess, now the face of Hecate incarnate. Death lay imminent in Selene's intense gaze. A frightening visage to behold, even for a well-trained and seasoned level nine like Joanne, an involuntary gulp was loose in her throat.

The antiaircraft batteries had already begun firing. The six Raiders quickly returned fire. One by one the Raiders passed by the defender's outer ring of death. Two of the Raiders were badly damaged in the crossing, one exploding in midair in an enormous blue flash and red fireball. The second survived longer, veering to starboard and crashing violently into the rolling meadows of the Elysium plateau, with multiple explosions ensuing. Debris rained down upon the Academy's air field, setting fire to the aircraft hangars and the facilities.

Then there were four.

Pulses of super-heated blue plasma arced towards the Psychic Academy. The level nine psychics quickly raised their defences. Explosions rocked the Academy as the first pulses were blocked in blue and red scintillating fireworks.

"We won't hold against too many of those", Selene thought to herself.

"The best defence is a brilliant offence", Lady Folcrom Selene yelled from the battlements with an amplified voice.

Another barrage of super-heated plasma arced towards the Psychic Academy. Varak was returning fire with his light pulsed plasma cannon. Again the Psychic Academy shook violently as plasma exploded in scintillating fireworks.

Lady Selene dropped her shield momentarily to let loose arcs of blue flame at the approaching Raiders. Small explosions rippled along the outer hull of the nearest Raider. One by one, the other psychics returned fire with their wands, blue streams of light zipping across the gap between their Academy and Raiders. Ripples of flame and fire spread across the Raiders' hulls.

Roseanne stepped out from behind Selene and pointed, Gnomulus, twin arcs of red and blue fire rippled out of the tip of the wand. They struck the lead Raider square on, taking out its bridge. It dropped quickly and heavily to the ground, exploding across the meadows in massive balls of fire.

"Good work", Joanne yelled out to Roseanne in encouragement, as she herself launched blue fire from her own wand.

Then there were three.

Another barrage of super-heated plasma arced towards the Psychic Academy. Again the psychics put up their defences. Several of the pulses were aimed high, racing high above the defender's shields. One pulse struck the ornate onion dome atop the central keep.

Masonry exploded outward as the pulse of super-heated plasma struck home. The onion dome quickly buckled and collapsed inwards into the central keep's grand gallery.

"I liked that dome you, fucking bastards", Lady Selene yelled out in defiance.

Burning debris rained down across the Psychic Academy. Pieces of shrapnel and super-heated plasma shot like bullets across the inner bailey. A sudden thud to Roseanne's right drew her attention. Slowly Roseanne turned around to see Joanne Seato had been hit from behind by flying shrapnel. It was as if Roseanne was watching in slow motion.

Standing there in shock, Joanne put her hands to her stomach. A useless gesture, for a large piece of shrapnel had ripped into her back and out through her abdomen, taking with it most of her internal organs with it. Joanne's intestines hung down from the ragged open wound to the ground before her. Blood was splattered everywhere.

Joanne slowly turned her head looking toward Roseanne, a stream of blood trickling from her mouth. Roseanne could see the intense fear in Joanne's horrified face, horrified by the absolute knowledge that she had mere seconds left to live. Slowly Joanne's wand slipped from her right hand's grasp, it clattered lightly to the floor. A gentle tear rolled down her cheek. Joanne's eyes implored Roseanne to help her, yet she knew herself that there was no hope.

Another trickle of blood escaped from the corner of Joanne's mouth, she coughed, and her knees slowly buckled beneath her, her head slowly titled forward and ever so slowly Joanne Seato collapsed to the floor dead. Joanne's mutilated body was surrounded by a growing pool of crimson blood, it spoke entire volumes about the impermanence of life.

All that lives, must surely die.

Still the slow motion that was Roseanne Rhein's reality continued. Stepping out again from behind Lady Selene's shield, Roseanne pointed Gnomulus once more. Again twin arcs of red and blue fire rippled out of the tip of the wand. Another Raider, now side-on and preparing to broadside the Psychic Academy, was struck midships. The rippling red and blue arcs carving through its hull like hot knives through butter, and slicing the Raider cleanly in two.

"Die you murdering fucking arseholes", Roseanne's mind shouted out so loudly that everyone involved in the battle heard her, friend and foe alike.

Each section of the Raider slipped out of the sky and collapsed to the ground in massive explosions that shook the Psychic Academy to its very foundations.

Then there were two.

Lady Selene was truly taken aback by the ferocity of Roseanne's attack. Looking to her right, Selene could clearly see Joanne's crumpled and mutilated body. Roseanne was now slowly collapsing to the floor herself, unhurt, but in shock, with tears streaming freely down her cheeks. Roseanne's knees buckled as she fainted and collapsed to the floor. Varak continued to fire his light pulsed plasma cannon at their attackers, strafing them left and right; he was completely oblivious to the surrounding destruction.

"By the Gods, this ends now!", Lady Selene shouted, her voice reverberating through the very stone work of the Psychic Academy.

Bracing herself, Lady Selene aimed her fingertips at one of the two remaining Raiders. Blue fire shot from her fingertips once more, leaping out at her chosen Raider. Striking the Raider hard, the blue fire rippled along the Raider's hull. The blue fire wrapped around the Raider, as it burned deep into its hull. Lady Selene grimaced as she pulled her hands across the field of battle, dragging with them the crippled Raider.

Slowly the Raider moved sideways across the sky against the thrust of its own engines, striking the other remaining Raider in a collision that ultimately destroyed both ships. Crippled beyond any ability to stay aloft, both Raiders fell from the sky, exploding upon the verdant green meadows of the Elysium Plateau. The Psychic Academy shook violently once more in the wake of the explosions. Lady Selene herself collapsed to the ground from pure exhaustion. A long streak of hair at the front of her head had turned pure white.

Then there were none.

Varak looked around him. The skies were clear of attackers. Slowly he released his finger from the trigger of his light pulsed plasma cannon and stopped strafing the skies. He allowed his light pulsed plasma cannon to fall from his exhausted hands to the battlement floor. It landed with a heavy thud. Looking to his left, he noticed Joanne's crumpled remains surrounded by a pool of blood, obviously dead.

Then seeing Roseanne collapsed on the ground and Lady Selene prone from pure exhaustion, Varak yelled out as loudly as he could, "Medic! Medic!"

As Roseanne was being carried away unconscious on a stretcher, Varak helped a recovering Selene to her feet. Another stretcher arrived to carry away the mutilated body of Joanne Seato.

"No! No! Don't move her!", an angry and emotional Lady Selene ordered.

"My Lady, we can not leave her here", Varak insisted.

"No, Varak!", Selene replied, "We don't move any of the dead, until we've videoed them."

"Video the dead?", Varak questioned.

"That's right, Varak, you heard me", Selene confirmed, "I want the dead videoed. I want everything videoed", she gestured around her, "This is all evidence of the barbarity of their crimes!"

Lady Selene explained, "I want all of this destruction videoed. Here at our Psychic Academy, down there at our colony", Lady Selene pointed to the south.

"I want the dead videoed and recorded", Lady Selene continued, "Then I want this evidence, all of it, replayed over and over again, on all the news feeds, until every single person on this planet understands how evil these militant, fundamentalist bastards are! Do you understand me?"

"I understand, my Lady", Varak replied with a shaky voice, he did not approve, but he did understand, "The world will see their evil deeds. The whole system will see their evil deeds."

Lady Selene reconsidered her order for a moment, it had been hasty.

"Varak, just a thought. When we release the images of the deceased, only let them see the women. Not the men."

"I don't understand", Varak replied.

"If the general public sees only the murdered women, they'll get the impression our antagonists are murderers of women. Misogynists. It might play into our favour", Lady Selene explained.

"We should honour the dead, my Lady", Varak replied with obvious disgust in his voice, "Not use them in some disgusting, propagandising freak show."

"Varak", Selene replied softly, "I do understand your disgust, Varak, but this is War and we have to win. It will be done, Varak."

Varakhan Utana nodded in compliance, "It will be done, my Lady, but I do not approve."

Lady Selene looked around her Psychic Academy and the surrounding destruction.

'I can not let those evil bastards think they've won', Lady Selene thought to herself, before adjusting her previous order once more, "Varak, don't release any images showing damage to our Psychic Academy, just images of the destruction at our Elysium colony."

Varak gave Lady Selene a questioning look.

"I don't want our enemies to think that they've succeeded. I want them to think that they've failed", Lady Selene explained.

Varak gestured with his hand across the southern horizon, "I would hardly call that a failure."

Lady Selene nodded, "Yes, Varak, but that's an ordinary colony with ordinary folk. They hit our Elysium colony, as a diversion, so that they could hit us here. Let them think that they're diversion failed."

Varak nodded, "They will think that they have killed ordinary folk for nothing."

"Exactly, Varak", Lady Selene agreed, "That's exactly what I want them to think."

24. Aurorae

Marcus Greyhelm reeled back in his chair with the force of Forkbraid's response.

Special Agent Murphy looked up from his vigil by the window, "Are you right there or what?"

Marcus picked himself up off the floor and replied, "I've made contact."

"Contact?", Special Agent Murphy replied, "You've contacted, Forkbraid?"

"Yes, I have", Marcus replied, adding "Now give me a few minutes while I give Forkbraid a heads-up on our situation here."

Marcus allowed himself to relax and slowly put himself into a meditative, trance like state. Once he had reached the required level of relaxation, he reached out for Forkbraid once more. This time Forkbraid, having been contacted just minutes before, was ready waiting for him.

Marcus focused his mind as best he could, *"Problem at the docks, expect terrorists... Stop. I'm coming out to pick up Miranda by motor-launch... Stop. Jim Murphy will run interference at the docks when the Shilo arrives... Stop. We have a chariot organised... Stop. Will follow your mind out to the Shilo ASAP... End message."*

Over and over Marcus transmitted the message with his mind, only stopping when he received acknowledgement from Forkbraid.

"Message received and understood", Forkbraid replied five times.

Marcus Greyhelm smiled to himself, his message had been received. Slowly but surely he was rediscovering his psychic talents once more.

"Well then, Jim, I'm off to see the Wizard", Marcus informed Special Agent Murphy.

Special Agent Murphy looked around at Marcus, "I thought you guys preferred the term Witch."

"I was using a metaphor", Marcus replied, adding, "It'll be dark when I get back to the old pier. Keep an eye out for my signal."

"Three flashes of your torch, flashed three times over?", Special Agent Murphy questioned.

"That's it", Marcus confirmed, "When you see that signal, you'll know I'm back."

Special Agent Murphy nodded.

As Marcus walked to the door he stated, "The Shilo is due at the main pier at eight am. As soon as you see her masts on the horizon, you know what to do."

"Oh, yeah", Special Agent Murphy replied smiling, "I know exactly what to do. It's all prepared, and these bastards won't know what hit them."

With that Marcus walked out the door.

A short while later Marcus was at the old pier. It was a dark night, as all Martian nights were. The small Martian moons provided little moon light even when they were both up together. The motor-launch Special Agent Murphy had commandeered was a sleek machine with powerful twin inboard engines.

Marcus boarded the boat and gave it a quick once over. Everything appeared to be in order. Marcus started the engines and then untied the bow and stern lines. Slowly and quietly Marcus manoeuvred the motor-launch away from the old pier and into the bay. Once well away from the pier, Marcus opened up the throttle and sped out into the night and the Eos Sea, an eastern branch of the larger Aurorae Chaos Sea.

Marcus had wondered how he would find his way to the Shilo in the dark of night. It was his every intention to use Forkbraid's mind as a guide and simply lock onto it, following Forkbraid's mind like a beacon out to the Shilo. The big quandary was whether Marcus could concentrate on the beacon that was Forkbraid's mind, whilst at the same time driving the motor launch. It turned out far easier than Marcus had dreamed. Forkbraid's mind was more like a bright beam of consciousness than a beacon and Marcus barely had to concentrate to find his way.

The trip to the Shilo was uneventful and took a little over two hours. As Marcus approached the Shilo, he noticed that the Shilo was running her night lights as all ships did on the dark Martian seas at night. The Shilo's sails had also been fully furled, and she was barely moving in spite of the prevailing westerly. The Captain of the ship was running a sea anchor to slow her progress until his special passengers had been picked up.

Marcus manoeuvred his motor-launch alongside the Shilo, securing her to the starboard side. He looked up at the deck railing to see a face he did not recognise staring down at him.

Thoughts penetrated his mind, "*Don't panic, Lad, I'm on your side.*"

Marcus didn't have time to react, his jaw had dropped, and before he could even compose himself, Cormac had already climbed down into the motor-launch.

"You're a psychic!", Marcus managed to spit out.

"All my life, Lad", Cormac replied, "Now stop your gawking, we have things to do."

A large bundle of something dropped over the side. Cormac carefully caught the bundle in his outstretched arms. The bundle started giggling and Cormac placed it upon the deck. It was a young girl with golden, blonde hair.

"*Miranda Swann?*", was the thought that crossed Marcus's mind.

"*Yep, that's me*", a thought rapidly came back to him from the little girl.

One after another, three more bundles dropped over the side of the ship. Cormac caught each in turn and placed them on the motor-launch's decking. They were backpacks. Then while Marcus was still watching Cormac's commotion another passenger climbed down from the Shilo and boarded the motor-launch. It was a small chubby woman with rosy cheeks.

Cormac slapped Marcus on the shoulder, he pointed to Candy, "This is my Wife, Candy, the little one is Miranda, and I'm Cormac."

"Right, then, you three are my passengers", Marcus replied.

"Yep, and we're all psychics", Cormac informed Marcus.

Marcus gave Cormac a confused look.

Candy caught Marcus's look and remarked, "We do have psychics on our pretty little planet you know, Lad."

Marcus caught another thought from above and looked up, it was Forkbraid.

"*Look after this lot for me, Marcus. They are all depending on you*", Forkbraid transmitted.

"You could always come with us", Marcus replied verbally.

"No, Marcus", Forkbraid replied, "We have people waiting for us at Aurorae and I have no intention of keeping them waiting. It would be impolite of me."

Forkbraid was right. The terrorists would ransack the Shilo looking for them. No telling how many innocent passengers would get hurt or worse, killed.

"You be careful then", Marcus replied, "They are not nice people."

"I know that, Marcus", Forkbraid replied, "I'm going to give them merry hell."

Cormac and Candy waved to Forkbraid, *"Don't worry, Cousin, We'll look after the little one"*, they both transmitted to Forkbraid in unison, *"The Lad too, if needs be."*

"Hoi! I can look after myself you know, Cormac", Marcus told them, adding "And you lot as well I'll have you know."

Cormac and Candy looked at each other and both smiled, "Of course, you can Lad, of course, you can", Cormac replied.

"Good. Just so you know", Marcus replied, "Now let's get going."

With that Marcus untethered the bow and stern lines and manoeuvred the motor-launch away from the Shilo. A short distance from the sloop, Marcus opened up the throttle and turned the motor-launch east. The Aurorae colony was just over two hours away. Finding his way back would not be hard. Marcus simply locked the motor-launch navigation system onto Aurorae's navigation beacon and homed in on it.

It was still dark when Marcus approached the Aurorae colony. The lights of the new pier were standing out brightly against the dark of the Martian night. A lesser light to the south indicated the position of the old pier. Marcus steered his motor-launch even further south of the old pier, his intention being to approach the old pier from along the coast. Less than fifteen minutes later, Marcus had slowly and quietly nudged his motor-launch alongside the old pier. Without being asked Cormac jumped up and secured the bow and stern lines.

Marcus looked at Miranda, her blonde locks would be a dead give away.

"Candy, it might be an idea to hide Miranda's pretty blonde hair", Marcus suggested.

"Oh, yes", Candy replied, "I have a cap that will cover the little one's hair perfectly."

Marcus climbed up onto the old pier and searched along the coast for their tavern. Once he'd located the tavern, Marcus took out his torch and placed a cylinder over its lens. Flash, flash, flash, Marcus paused, flash, flash, flash, Marcus paused once more, flash, flash, flash, Marcus stopped signalling and waited.

"*Three flashes, thrice flashed*", Special Agent Murphy silently thought, "*That's Marcus alright.*"

Special Agent Murphy took out his own torch and placed some red cellophane over its lens, then covered the lens with a cylinder, he gave Marcus one long flash in reply.

"What was that red light?", Cormac who had climbed up onto the rickety old pier asked.

"That's a friend of mine letting me know that he got my signal", Marcus replied.

"Okay", Cormac replied, "What now?"

"Now, Cormac… We sit back and wait", Marcus replied, and then they climbed back into the motor-launch.

"What do we wait for?", Candy enquired.

"For morning", Marcus smiled, adding "My friend is going to clear out some rats for us."

Cormac nodded, "Always good to clear out the rats", he smiled.

A little after Sun up, Special Agent Murphy caught sight of the Shilo's masts upon the horizon.

"Time to get the work", Special Agent Murphy said to himself.

Special Agent Murphy quickly made his way to the rat's nest. He took with him a radio-control detonator and a [70]needle-gun.

The rat's nest was a wooden, clap board terrace house, amidst a long line of similar terrace houses in that particular street. Special Agent Murphy had crept into the rat's nest earlier, before Marcus had left in the motor-launch. He'd carefully placed implosion charges at the base of strategically selected support pillars in the basement of the terrace house. Now he was preparing to detonate them.

Special Agent Murphy quietly entered into a narrow laneway and climbed up onto the roof of a terrace house across the street from the rat's nest. From this vantage point, Special Agent Murphy had a clear view of all the streets down to

---

70 Needle-gun. A small rifle that fires needle thin poison darts, capable of deep penetration.

the new pier and a perfect view of the nearby rat's nest.

As the Shilo approached the coast from the west, it became clearly visible to the nasty folk watching the new pier. The scrawny blonde bloke he'd been keeping tabs on, came running up the street from the pier. Special Agent Murphy took out his remote-control detonator from his trench coat's pocket. He then watched as Blondie entered the terrace house that was the rat's nest. Special Agent Murphy counted to thirty, and then flipped the switch on his detonator.

There was barely a sound. Just a few small, almost inaudible, muffled implosions. Then there were eerie, cracking sounds, followed by several much louder cracks and bangs. Then all of a sudden, within a matter of seconds, the entire five-story terrace house collapsed inwards and downwards, into a crumpled, mangled heap. Special Agent Murphy noted that the terrace houses on either side had been left undamaged. He nodded to himself, mentally noting a job well done.

Special Agent Murphy watched the rat's nest carefully. He didn't expect many of the rats to be able to crawl out of the collapsed mess that was once their safe house. Just in case though, he'd brought with him his needle-gun. He slipped his remote-control detonator back into his trench coat's pocket, and then he slipped his needle-gun out from under his trench coat. Carefully, Special Agent Murphy aimed the needle-gun at the collapsed rat's nest.

There was some noise coming from the collapsed terrace house. Watching through his needle-gun's scope, Special Agent Murphy watched as the scrawny, blonde bloke scrambled from out of the wreckage.

Zing, Zing, Zing! Special Agent Murphy shot three thin needle-like darts into the man's neck.

The scrawny blonde bloke dropped to the ground dead; the needle-gun darts were poison tipped.

Another man managed to push his way out through what had been the attic's dormer window.

Zing, Zing, Zing! Special Agent Murphy quickly eliminated this new militant.

Nothing else stirred in the collapsed rat's nest; Special Agent Murphy's implosions had brought the safe house down and done the trick.

By now householders had come pouring out onto the street. They stared in disbelief at the collapsed terrace house. Some of those folk began to poke around the rubble looking for survivors. Others checked on the two dead men who were lying in the street. Special Agent Murphy noticed that some people in the growing crowd were carrying hand guns holstered at their hips.

Most weren't a problem. Carrying guns was apparently quite normal in the older Martian outposts. Some of them, however, made a beeline towards the new pier. They were an issue.

Special Agent Murphy turned in his vantage point to scan his eyes over the streets leading down to the port. Several gunmen were running towards the pier.

Zing, Zing, Zing! Three shots. Three kills.

Another gunman appeared. Special Agent Murphy recognised him as one of the scrawny, blonde bloke's men. He stopped by his fallen comrades and checked the pulse on one. Cautiously he looked up and scanned the rooftops.

Zing, Zing, Zing! Three shots to the neck and the gunman dropped dead.

"Time to leave", Special Agent Murphy thought to himself as more and more people appeared in the street where the collapsed rat's nest lay in ruins.

Special Agent Murphy slipped the needle-gun back under his trench coat, and then climbed down from his vantage point.

"You there", a voice sounded out behind him.

Special Agent Murphy turned around. In one fluid motion, his needle-gun slipped out from under his trench coat. Zing! Then just as quickly, his needle-gun disappeared again.

The man caught the single needle-gun dart in the mouth, then collapsed to the ground dead. It was another face Special Agent Murphy recognised from his surveillance activities. Quietly and without further incident, James Murphy slipped out of the narrow laneway and made his way back to the tavern.

By now it was approaching eight am and the Shilo was approaching the new pier.

"Captain Swanson. You would do well to anchor a good fifty metres from the pier", Forkbraid recommended.

"Are we expecting that much trouble?", Captain Swanson enquired.

"Perhaps. It's difficult to say", Forkbraid replied, "Still, it would be prudent."

"The safety of my passengers is paramount", Captain Swanson replied, "Your recommendation is accepted."

Captain Swanson had the Shilo anchor in the bay fifty metres off the north side of the new pier, just as Forkbraid had recommended. Forkbraid scanned the pier carefully. It appeared to be safe.

Forkbraid scanned further down the pier, around the docks. It was anything but safe, a hornets nest in fact. Forkbraid frowned as he reached into his robe, pulling his six foot, rune carved staff out from one of his impossible pockets. Captain Swanson cocked an eyebrow as the staff appeared.

Forkbraid let the staff float free, and it quickly positioned itself behind him. The crystal atop the staff began to glow an intense golden glow, as Lord Folcrom Forkbraid himself was engulfed in golden light, with an intensity that rivalled a hot midday Summer's Sun. Forkbraid held the edges of his cloak, took three long strides and leapt across the fifty metres from the Shilo to the pier, his obedient staff following quickly behind him. Crossing the gap in seconds, Forkbraid landed lightly upon the pier. He slowly rose to his feet.

Forkbraid scanned the water front around the base of the pier once more. There appeared to be trouble further back in the narrow streets of the Aurorae colony's old quarter.

Special Agent Murphy's handy work, *"That helps just a little"*, Forkbraid thought to himself.

Reaching both hands into his shimmering black robe, the colour of raven's feathers, Forkbraid retrieved two wands from his impossible pockets.

The wand in his left hand was made of rosewood and deeply coloured, the wand in his right hand was made of oak. Forkbraid's cloak billowed about him, blue sparks crackled in the air a few feet above his head. Once more Forkbraid was a terrifying sight to behold. Slowly, ever so slowly, Forkbraid walked down the length of the pier toward his enemies.

Many eyes had watched the tall, dark figure leap from the Shilo to the pier. They all watched now with alarm as the tall, dark figure walked slowly down the pier towards them.

"That's no little girl!", one of the militants exclaimed.

"There's not supposed to be a wizard on the Shilo", another remarked.

"This ain't right, we've all been deceived", said another as he started to back away.

"You ain't going nowhere", stated another man, pushing the man in the back and forcing him back to his post, "Stand your fucking ground, or I'll beat the tar out you and tattoo a yellow stripe down your fucking back."

The man who had started to back away, stared back down the pier with fear in his eyes.

Forkbraid had heard all of this, he'd been scanning the minds of the people at the base of the pier. Innocent bystanders were also about. To those he scanned he sent images of fear, hoping they'd leave the area before the shooting started. And start, it would, as soon as one of the militants lost their nerve and opened fire.

It didn't take long, *"Yellow stripe"* lost his nerve and fired his automatic pistol. The bullet struck Forkbraid's defence field, fizzled, melted and dropped onto the pier with a light splattering sound.

Forkbraid stopped, looked down at the molten lead and smiled, "You'll need to do better than that", he shouted down the pier, amplifying his voice so that they could hear him.

"Shit!", Yellow stripe exclaimed as he opened up, firing shot, after shot, after shot.

When he'd emptied his clip, his comrades turned and stared at him. The one who'd threatened to tattoo him asked, "Are you quite finished?"

Yellow stripe, laughed a nervous laugh, "My clip's empty."

"Then bloody well reload it, you stupid Yellow bastard", the larger man replied before reaching into his coat and pulling out a laser pistol, "Open fire", he ordered.

The intense beam of red, coherent light struck Forkbraid's defences. The air in front of Forkbraid crackled and fizzled with the intense heat that the collision of laser beams against shields generated. Then the red beam of light stopped. Forkbraid began moving forward once more. The sound of gun fire echoed across the water front.

Bullets fizzled and melted upon striking Forkbraid's defences, falling harmlessly onto the pier in little molten pools of lead. Again and again the bullets struck, again and again the laser beam lanced out. All to no avail, Forkbraid's defences were impenetrable.

Forkbraid was close to his enemies now, and he didn't hesitate. Forkbraid swung his wands about in his hands and blue light erupted from their tips and streaked down the pier. Two assailants caught the brunt of the blast, flashed into transparency and then crumpled to ground in writhing agony, dying only moments later.

Yellow stripe screamed, turned about and started running for his life.

Yellow stripe's larger comrade turned on him, called out, "Coward", and shot him in the back with his laser pistol.

Yellow stripe collapsed to the ground dead. Yellow stripe's killer looked beyond his fallen victim and noted that more of his comrades were arriving on the scene. Reinforcements had arrived and they had heavier weapons.

He turned back to the pier and shouted to Forkbraid, "We have you now! You can't kill us all!"

Forkbraid replied in his amplified voice, "Oh, I beg to differ!", and then he let loose with his wands once more.

Beams of blue light streaked down the pier once again, striking two more assailants. Again they flashed into transparency, their knees buckled, and they dropped lifelessly to the ground.

Special Agent Murphy was watching from the tavern. It had begun, all hell was breaking loose by the new pier. He looked over to the old pier where Marcus had docked his motor-launch. There was no sign of Marcus and the others.

Jim focused his mind as best he could and thought, "What's keeping you", hoping that Marcus would pick up on his thoughts.

Marcus picked up on the thought, so did his charges, "It's time to move", he said.

"Here grab this", Cormac replied as he tossed Marcus his backpack.

Cormac then turned to Miranda, "Piggy back time, little miss."

Miranda quickly climbed onto his back.

Candy quickly put on her backpack and reached down for Miranda's backpack, "Where ready, what's keeping you?", she questioned Marcus with a grin.

Marcus didn't reply, he simply climbed up onto the pier and waited for the others to join him before leading them to the tavern.

Special Agent Murphy watched as three people came running cautiously down the old pier.

It took him several moments to notice the child clinging to the older man's back, *"That'll be them"*, he thought to himself.

Special Agent Murphy turned back to the chaos erupting over by the new pier. Everyone was focused on the battle on the waterfront, no one was paying any attention to the old pier at all.

"Perfect", Special Agent Murphy thought.

As quickly as they could, Marcus and his three charges navigated the water front and approached the tavern. No one bothered with them. All eyes were on the battle further up the waterfront. Marcus led the others down the narrow lane at the south side of the tavern. He slid out two fence planks and led the way into the tavern's rear yard. Once they were all inside the yard, he carefully slipped the fence planks back into place.

On the far side of the rear yard by its gate was a chariot. It was an eight seat, all terrain people mover with its bulletproof windows all darkly shaded. Marcus led the others over to it and ordered them inside. One by one they all climbed in.

"What do we do now?", Cormac questioned.

"We wait", Marcus replied.

"What for?", asked Candy.

"We have two more passengers", Marcus explained, "They'll be along shortly."

Special Agent Murphy watched as Marcus led his three charges into the laneway beside the tavern. He then turned his attention back to the battle on the water front. Sitting well back from the window, he focused his needle-gun's scope on the battle scene. Picking out militants near the rear of the battle scene, Special Agent Murphy carefully took aim.

Zing! Zing! Zing! Zing! Zing! Zing! Six dead militants.

Carefully Special Agent Murphy scanned the battle scene once more.

No one had noticed where the shots had come from.

"One more bunch should do it", he thought to himself as he carefully took aim once more.

Zing! Zing! Zing! Zing! Zing! Zing! Another six dead militants.

Again Special Agent Murphy scanned the battle scene. There was too much chaos.

No one had noticed his handy work.

"Time to go", Special Agent Murphy whispered to himself as he hid his needle-gun under his trench coat and headed downstairs to the chariot.

The waterfront had descended into total chaos, militants were appearing from every direction. Lasers flared, and light rail guns blazed away, bullets were flying at Forkbraid from every direction. Forkbraid's defence shield held firm, and he returned fire with his wands. Here and there militants flashed into transparency and crumpled dead to the ground.

Forkbraid had lost count somewhere above twenty. So ferocious was the attack that it became difficult for Forkbraid to make out his targets. Too many bullets and too many iron shells fizzled and melted against Forkbraid's shield. The intensity of the light from more than a few lasers added their own eerie glare and intense heat.

Forkbraid concentrated on his defence shield and then replaced his wands back into the impossible pockets in his robe. From out of one of his impossible pockets, Forkbraid pulled out a bag full of amulets. He carefully chose an amulet and hung it around his neck, placing the bag back inside his impossible pocket. Magically attached to the amulet was a ring. In place of his wands, Forkbraid pulled out two samurai swords from within his impossible pockets.

Carefully Forkbraid reached out with his mind. His enemies were closing in on him, they were only a mere few metres away. There were a great many of them as well. Their air about his defence shields was growing intensely hot, white-hot. With one almighty thrust of his mind, Forkbraid sent the outer layers of his defence shield flying outwards. It caught the militants completely by surprise and knocked them off their feet. Dazed, stunned and slightly burned, they lay prone on the ground. The air was clear once more and the visibility was good.

With swift and fluid motion, Forkbraid went to work with his swords. His balance was good, his hands were swift, his aim was deft. In close quarter combat, one by one, Forkbraid sliced and diced his assailants to death.

Barely had the militants managed to stagger to their feet, when they were confronted by the swift, slashing of tempered steel. Forkbraid's swords sung in his hands as his foes fell before his slicing blades. Again and again his enemies swarmed upon him, again and again, Forkbraid fought them off with his swift, slicing blades.

When the last swarm of militants faltered and Forkbraid finally stopped with his swords crossed before him, the entire battle scene around him was a gory mess of blood, severed body parts and grisly death. Forkbraid wiped his blades on the clothes of the nearest headless torso and replaced them once again into his impossible pockets.

Then the bullets began to fire once more, the light rail guns began to spit their iron shells. The lasers were silent amongst his foes, their owners having fallen in battle, their severed bodies buried amongst the gore and severed limbs. Forkbraid's shield held once more, he was unassailable.

Forkbraid looked around at the carnage as he carefully fingered the amulet around his neck.

With one yank, Forkbraid pulled off the ring that was attached to the amulet.

"Enough!", Forkbraid shouted in his amplified voice, "No more! No More! Death has visited this place enough this day!", a strange lilt in his powerful booming voice.

Taken aback and confused by this proclamation, the militants stopped firing their weapons.

Slowly the air cleared once more. Forkbraid stood before them completely unharmed.

Slowly Forkbraid slipped the ring upon his finger.

Forkbraid vanished.

The militants looked to where Forkbraid had stood, he was gone. Impossible, yet he was gone.

Forkbraid looked at the ring on his finger. He had made it and the talisman around his neck long ago during his student days, along with many other talismans. His old mentor, Lady Folcrom Pandora and his own Father, Lord Folcrom Mandrakus had taught him how. Each talisman and ring being precisely crafted and precisely inscribed. This particular pair, were the ring, and talisman of invisibility, all from that ancient magical tome, The Black Pullet.

Forkbraid looked around him at the stunned militants. They were all confused, confounded and looking at one another. None of them knew what had happened, none of them knew what to do.

Forkbraid stood before them in plain sight, yet they saw him not. Slowly and quietly Forkbraid walked away, unseen from the battle scene.

Straight past the militants, Forkbraid walked away, making a beeline for the tavern. Soon he was in the rear yard of the tavern and preparing to climb into the chariot. Before climbing into the chariot Forkbraid replaced his staff into his impossible pocket once more. Forkbraid then climbed into the chariot and pulled the ring of invisibility off his finger.

"What happened?", Special Agent Murphy asked as Forkbraid magically appeared from out of nowhere inside their chariot.

"Oh, Jim. I got sick of all the carnage and decided to put a stop to it", Forkbraid replied.

"We're all here now. We'd better go", Marcus advised them.

"I agree", Forkbraid replied, "Jim, we'd better get moving."

Forkbraid then took the talisman from around his neck, reconnected the ring to it and popped it back into its bag and then back into his impossible pocket, once more.

Candy had watched closely as Forkbraid removed and pocketed the talisman and ring, "Are they what I think they are?"

"Why, yes, indeed, Candy", Forkbraid smiled, "You're a clever Witch."

Cormac smiled, "Candy always has been."

Candy smiled back and winked, "Yes, indeed."

Forkbraid noticed that Miranda was sleeping soundly, "It's a wonder that little Miranda could sleep through all of that commotion down at the pier."

"I do try to ensure that the little one doesn't see or hear things, that she ought not see or hear", Candy replied adding, "I think it's better that way."

Forkbraid nodded, "I agree with you on that one hundred percent."

Special Agent Murphy pushed a button on the remote control he was holding. The gate to the tavern's rear yard slid open. Special Agent Murphy drove their chariot out into the street and headed towards the Aurorae colony proper. They had only driven a few kilometres when numerous police vehicles passed them by at high speed, heading towards the port.

"Gee, I wonder where they're going?", Marcus asked sarcastically.

"Yeah, they are a little slow to respond around here", Special Agent Murphy commented.

"I counted at least a dozen of them as they went past", Cormac informed them.

"Right about now, those lousy sligs will be crawling back under their rocks", Candy replied.

"With a bit of luck, maybe the police will catch a few of them", Special Agent Murphy replied.

"One can only hope, Jim, one can only hope", Forkbraid replied, noting, "I honestly don't want to have to come back here and clean up this place."

Within thirty minutes they'd reached Aurorae's spaceport. Special Agent Murphy pulled their chariot up at the hangar where he'd stowed their long range hummer. It was all fuelled and ready to go. They all quickly climbed aboard the hummer and prepared for their flight.

It didn't take long for Special Agent Murphy to taxi their hummer out to a nearby launch pad. A few minutes after that, they had launch clearance, and they took off on their flight to the Elysium subcontinent and the New Flinders Psychic Academy.

Sanctuary was only a few hours flight away.

Special Agent Murphy had his headset on and was listening to the local weather conditions.

Several news flashes came over the channel and an alarmed look came over his face.

Special Agent Murphy looked around at Forkbraid.

"What is it now, Jim?", Forkbraid enquired.

"There's been an attack, FB", Special Agent Murphy replied.

"An attack?", Forkbraid asked for clarification.

Special Agent Murphy placed the hummer on autopilot and switched on the video screen.

Quickly he selected a news channel.

The news feed came up on the screen.

The big headline for the day was the attack on the Elysium colony.

All eyes in the Hummer were glued to the video screen.

Their sanctuary was in trouble.

25. Aftermath Three

Special Agent Murphy flew their Hummer on a course passing by the Elysium colony itself. Smoke billowing from hundreds of fires was clearly visible as they approached. As the seconds passed by, the devastation from the attack became clearer and clearer. Collapsed buildings, destroyed facilities. Fires raged uncontrolled over vast areas of the sprawling colony complex that was meant to be the seed of a fast-growing metropolis. There would be years of rebuilding ahead for the Elysium colony. Even their cattle herds had been wiped out, burnt into smouldering carcasses.

"The news feeds really don't give you a full enough picture", Special Agent Murphy remarked.

"No, they don't", Marcus Greyhelm replied, "From up here, the destruction is so... evident."

"They did this", Cormac commented, "Those evil fucking sligs did this."

"And you didn't want to leave New Tortuga", Candy replied, giving Cormac an I told you so glare.

"You were right, Candy", Cormac replied meekly, "Then again, you usually are."

Lord Folcrom Forkbraid said nothing, Elysium had been hit hard and the casualties were high, over four hundred dead and missing. No psychics were among these casualties, merely ordinary folk going about the daily business of rebuilding a colony after the previous attack. The entire complex had been evacuated, the only signs of movement below were Androids fighting the fires.

Little Miranda reached out for Forkbraid's hand, "Why?", Miranda asked as she looked out their hummer's window.

Finally, Forkbraid spoke, "Sometimes I wonder about that myself, Miranda", tears brimmed in his eyes, he straightened himself and held them back.

The New Flinders Psychic Academy was on Forkbraid's mind.

Looking at the devastation below them, he could only wonder how bad things were at the Psychic Academy itself. It wasn't long before they found out.

In the distance to the north, the billowing smoke from yet more fires became visible. The shock of the devastation at the Elysium colony was suddenly compounded by the fear and apprehension of what was awaiting them at the Psychic Academy.

The closer they flew, the more their apprehension grew.

It was Special Agent Murphy who first commented on the approaching fires, "There seems to be a lot of fires around the Academy. It's hard to make out at this distance, but it looks like ship wreckage as well."

"Ship wreckage?", Forkbraid queried.

"Yeah, FB", Special Agent Murphy replied, "It looks like we took out their strike force."

Forkbraid moved closer to the cockpit and looked out of the cockpit windows.

"All the hangars at the air field have gone up", Special Agent Murphy remarked upon seeing their charred and smouldering remains for the first time, "There's a trail of wreckage and debris leading right up to the air field."

"A downed ship no doubt", Forkbraid correctly guessed.

"I'd say so, FB", Special Agent Murphy replied.

"It's hard to say, but it looks like maybe five or maybe as many as eight ships were taken down", Special Agent Murphy speculated.

"The dome is gone!", Marcus Greyhelm quickly pointed out.

"Yes, I've noticed that, Marcus", Forkbraid replied adding, "It looks like it took a direct hit."

"And collapsed into the grand gallery", Special Agent Murphy suggested.

"There must be significant internal damage to the keep", Forkbraid considered.

"I'd be inclined to agree with you there", Special Agent Murphy replied.

"There's significant damage to the outer walls as well", Cormac pointed out.

"It's like you can tell where our defenders were standing simply by looking at the damage pattern", Marcus noted.

"Yes, indeed, they were mainly on the tower battlements", Forkbraid replied, "We put up one hell of a fight. Our psychic's had their defence shields up. They blocked far more than got through I'd be inclined to say."

"I'll circle around the entire Academy", Special Agent Murphy informed them, "We'll be able to assess things better that way."

Special Agent Murphy flew their hummer in a full circle around the Academy. It was easy to see that the attack had come straight in from the south. Most of the northern side of the Academy was unscathed, or so it appeared.

"Interesting", Forkbraid commented, "I would have thought they'd attack from multiple directions at the same time."

"That's what I would have done", Special Agent Murphy commented, "It would have stretched our defences thin. Our response would have been so much weaker."

"Yes, but by the same token our anti-aircraft batteries would have coped much better", Forkbraid noted, pointing out, "Their attack was only really confronted by three batteries head on."

Special Agent Murphy nodded in agreement.

"In the news feeds, the only victims I saw were women?", Candy questioned. It was so unlikely that only women would have been killed in the attack.

"Lady Selene will have been very selective in what she showed the world", Forkbraid replied, explaining, "The news feeds only showed the devastation at the Elysium colony, not the Academy."

"But why only show the female victims?", Candy asked again.

"It makes the militants look like murderers of women. Women haters and misogynists", Forkbraid explained, adding "I'm quite certain that's not the kind of image that the militants wanted to give to the world."

"It does paint them in an extremely bad light, Candy", Cormac pointed out to his Wife.

"I would have thought that their actions alone were enough to do that, Cormac", Candy correctly pointed out.

Special Agent Murphy put the Hummer down in the Academy's inner bailey, in the less damaged northern section, taking great care to avoid the debris still lying on the ground. Lady Selene and Charlene stood a short distance away near the entrance to the outer northern tower. Just behind them were Peter and Catherine Swann, with their little Son, Chiron.

As soon as the door of the Hummer opened, little Miranda Swann jumped through it and bolted straight to her Mother.

"Mummy, Mummy", Miranda cried out as she leapt into her Mother's arms.

Catherine Swann sobbed as she held her little girl, "Miranda", she cried.

Tears welled up in Peter Swann's eyes as he picked up his Son, Chiron, in one arm and reached out with his other arm for his Wife and Daughter. They all came together in one tight four-way embrace. Tears flowed freely as they became reacquainted with Miranda once more.

Selene looked over at the embracing family, then walked straight over to Forkbraid.

"You finally did something right", she said, before wrapping her arms around him, their lips coming together in a passionate kiss.

They kissed and hugged for quite a while before Forkbraid asked, "What happened to your hair, Selene?"

Selene shrugged, "I'm not really sure. A side effect of the battle I think."

Forkbraid nodded, looking carefully at the long white streak before giving Selene another kiss.

'I'll have to look into this', he thought to himself about the white streak in Selene's hair.

Charlene ran to Marcus and embraced him in a hug that took him completely by surprise. Then, when Charlene's lips met his, he simply went with the moment and returned the kiss.

"It was so horrible, Marcus", Charlene told him, "I was in the bunkers with everyone else. The whole Academy shook violently. We thought the walls were coming down on us."

Special Agent Murphy was standing with Cormac and Candy. The three felt like loose ends.

Cormac looked at the Swann family as they continued to hug each other, "I guess our job is done then, Candy", he said to his Wife.

"Yes, Cormac", Candy replied with teary eyes, "We certainly did well, didn't we."

After several minutes Special Agent Murphy said "Huh, hmm. Huh, hmm", as if clearing his throat, and everyone turned around to look at him.

"Now that I've got your attention, Ladies and Gentlemen", Special Agent Murphy began, "This is Cormac Farmer and his Wife, Candy."

Forkbraid then added, "Yes, and we owe them a great debt of gratitude."

Everyone looked at Forkbraid questioningly.

"Catherine, Peter", Forkbraid continued, "Cormac and Candy rescued Miranda from the terrorists. Had they not done so, Miranda would still be in mortal danger."

Catherine and Peter, with children in tow, walked over to Cormac and Candy.

"It seems we're indebted to you both", Peter said to them.

"No, not at all", Cormac replied, "We only did what any decent folk would do."

"You brought our little girl back to us", Catherine told them with tears in her eyes, "We will be forever grateful."

Candy knelt down in front of Miranda, running her fingers through Miranda's blonde locks.

Looking up at Catherine Swann, Candy replied, "It was our pleasure. We were glad to help."

Forkbraid turned to Selene and whispered into her ear, "Cormac and Candy are Martian psychics. Cormac's a low level eight and Candy's a high level seven."

Selene looked at Forkbraid with a query upon her face.

"Yes, and religious psychics as well", Forkbraid informed her with a smile, then he added, "Cousins as well, as it turns out."

"Really", Selene replied, "You're going to have to explain that one to me."

"I will a little later, my darling", Forkbraid told Selene.

"Now where's Roseanne?", Forkbraid enquired.

"Roseanne is in the infirmary", Selene replied.

"Is she okay?", Forkbraid asked.

"We believe she will be", Selene replied adding "The battle was a harrowing experience. Roseanne watched as a friend of ours died horribly. It was quite a shock. Roseanne lashed out with a fury that had to be seen to be believed."

"So she's in shock?", Forkbraid enquired.

"Yes", Selene replied, "But we expect she'll be fine in a few days. She just needs time."

"Tell me the details of what happened later", Forkbraid replied.

"I will, my love, I will", Selene promised.

The Prophet had been watching the news feeds. The attack on the Elysium colony had been played over and over again. As much destruction as the news feeds showed, the Prophet saw no real evidence that they'd succeeded in striking the Psychic Academy. Captain Scar had managed to return having lost half of his small squadron. Not one of their six Raiders had returned. Over and over the Prophet watched the news feeds.

Leroy and Matthew were in the church, formerly the pub known as The Black Pullet. They, too, watched the news feeds on the video screen.

"Did we or did we not succeed?", the Prophet asked.

"My lord, we caused enormous damage. There are a lot of dead", Leroy remarked as yet another corpse was shown on the screen.

"But they're all women!", the Prophet spat out, "We can't have just killed only women!"

"It's impossible to have only killed women, my Lord. The odds of that happening are ridiculously long", Matthew explained, "They're deliberately showing only the female victims."

"Only the female victims!", the Prophet spat out, "Do you know what that makes us look like!"

Both men remained silent.

"They're making us look like misogynists! Like women haters! Like murderers of women!", the Prophet screamed at them.

"My Lord, we can't control what images they release to the media", Leroy replied.

"No we can't", the Prophet replied, "And those demons are making us look like the evils ones."

Matthew froze the screen on one particular image. He stood up and walked over to the screen.

"What is it, Matthew?", the Prophet asked.

"My Lord, it's confirmation that we hit their precious Psychic Academy", Matthew replied.

"How do you figure that, Matthew?", Leroy asked.

The image on the screen showed a woman lying dead at the top of a structure. There was debris scattered all around her, and parts of the structure clearly showed visible damage. Matthew ran his finger along the top of a rooftop wall. He tapped his finger at the image of the rooftop wall several times. It was so obvious. They'd released these particular images by mistake.

"I still don't get it, Matthew?", Leroy queried.

"Crenellations!", Matthew exclaimed.

"Crenellations?", the Prophet queried.

"The Elysium Colony is a standard colony", Matthew began, explaining "Buildings in standard colonies do not have crenellations on their rooftops."

"Go on", the Prophet requested.

"All the Psychic Academies on Earth are built like fortresses. For all intents and purposes, they look like huge castles, complete with crenellated battlements and moats. Like on Earth, so with Mars", Matthew explained, again tapping his finger on the image.

"So this image of that dead woman was taken on a battlement at their Psychic Academy?", the Prophet stated, requesting confirmation.

"Yes, my Lord", Matthew replied, confirming, "That picture depicts part of their battlements. It was taken at their Psychic Academy."

The Prophet smiled, "So we did manage to strike them."

Leroy also smiled, "There looks to be quite a lot of debris lying about. Quite a bit of damage as well. My Lord, it appears that we were more successful than they wanted us to know."

The Prophet smiled again, this time a very broad smile, "And the clincher, Gentlemen! That dead woman is wearing a witches cloak! She was a Witch!"

Leroy looked again at the screen, he smiled, "My Lord, I do believe you're right."

Matthew again looked up at the screen, "Hmm, how did I miss that!", he exclaimed.

Just then a news flash appeared on the screen. It drew their attention as it was the only news flash all day that had not been about the attack at Elysium. Instead, it was about the Aurorae colony.

"The few witnesses that are talking are saying that it was a wild gun fight. This is the old quarter of Aurorae and in true old quarter fashion, no one is giving any real details away", the newsreader informed their audience.

Matthew and Leroy watched the news feed with fascination, the Prophet watched with alarm.

"So far the carnage has affected the waterfront and at least one building in the nearby streets, where the fighting may have begun", the newsreader continued, *"It appears a variety of weapons, explosives, machine guns, light rail guns, lasers, and even swords were used during the fighting. Some sources have said dark magic was afoot, but these have been discounted by the authorities."*

The Prophet turned to Leroy and Matthew, he said nothing as the newsreader continued.

"So far the death toll has reached ninety-five, although the Aurorae police and security forces are saying the death toll is expected to rise as more bodies are discovered", the newsreader gasped slightly as she continued, *"Many of the deceased at the waterfront*

were horribly mutilated. Severed limbs and other body parts were strewn about everywhere."
The Prophet shook his head in disgust.

The newsreader continued with the news flash, *"Sources in the Aurorae police department have been quoted as saying that the gun fight was between rival militant criminal gangs. We will have more information about this incident for you on the global news network at five pm tonight."*

"I requested a simple assassination of an eight-year-old Witch", the Prophet chided, "And this, this is what I get", the Prophet pointed to the screen.

"Make it look like a robbery gone wrong! Isn't that what I said?", the Prophet shouted at them.

Leroy's face went bright red, "We did give them your orders, my Lord. They just seem to have gotten a little bit out of control."

"A little bit out of control?", the Prophet queried, not expecting an answer, "I'd hardly call a gun fight with nearly a hundred dead, and mutilated corpses a little bit out of control!"

"Our people at the Aurorae colony are an unruly bunch, my Lord", Leroy explained, "More criminals than believers to be entirely honest."

"My Lord", Matthew interjected, "The news feed did say the authorities think it was a battle between rival criminal gangs."

"Well thank our Lord for that, Matthew", the Prophet replied, "Because the last thing we want right now, is to be the subjects of an organised planet-wide hunt. We simply can't afford any more screw-ups, Gentlemen!"

"My Lord, next time we'll send our own people to deal with it personally", Leroy recommended.

"Will there be a next time, Leroy?", the Prophet asked.

Leroy didn't answer, instead he just looked to the floor.

"What happened to that little Witch? What happened to the abomination?", the Prophet asked.

Leroy looked up, "We'll find out, my Lord."

Matthew looked at the Prophet, "We'll start our enquiries straight away, my Lord."

"Make sure you do that!", the Prophet replied.

Forkbraid and Selene walked along the battlement of the outer south tower. From here he could view the whole battle scene. A pulsed plasma cannon was still lying on the battlement where it had been dropped. Forkbraid could see that it had been stripped down and modified for hand held use.

As the thought, *"Who"*, crossed Forkbraid's mind, Selene's mind answered him, *"It's Varak's. It's his light pulsed plasma cannon."*

"Light!", Forkbraid muttered under his breath.

South of the Academy lay the wreckage of six Raiders, still smouldering upon the rolling meadows of the Elysium plateau. Forkbraid turned around and looked at the central keep. Its beautifully ornate onion dome had completely collapsed. Such beautiful workmanship, ruined. Lady Selene's apartment had been on the top floor, just beneath the dome.

"You won't be using your apartment any time soon, Selene", Forkbraid remarked.

"My apartment is fine, Forkbraid", Selene replied, "The access is a little awkward though, with the wreckage of the dome blocking the upper three floors. I can still use the outer balcony though."

Forkbraid looked at Selene seriously, "How many did we lose?"

"We lost eight in all", Selene replied, her voice heavy with sadness, "We managed to get nearly everyone into the bunkers. Then we tried to hold them off with only two dozen level nines."

"A third of your defenders", Forkbraid said softly, "I should have asked Captain Carmichael for more gun batteries. You could have done with three times as many batteries out there."

"That may have helped", Selene nodded, then added, "You know, you forgot to take that stupid Bat Wing of yours off its DNA lock."

"Oh, no, Selene", Forkbraid replied, "I didn't forget. My Bat Wing uses a [71]NIC system. There's no one else on Mars that can fly it but me."

"Neural interlock!", Selene replied, "You know that's dangerous don't you, Forkbraid."

"Yes, Selene, but not for me. I'm one of the few people who can use it."

Selene shook her head, "You always take risks, Forkbraid."

"Calculated risks, Selene, calculated risks", he replied.

Forkbraid walked over to where Selene had been standing during the battle, he held his hand above the spot, "You were standing right here? Weren't you, Selene?"

"Yes, about there", Selene confirmed.

Forkbraid dropped onto his knees and felt the air just above the spot where Selene had stood.

"What is it, Forkbraid?", Selene asked.

"This is why you have that white streak in your beautiful dark hair, my love", Forkbraid replied.

"The battle was quite a strain. I was exhausted afterwards. This streak of white is just a natural response I expect", Selene explained, holding the long streaks of white hair in her right hand.

Forkbraid stood up and shook his head, "No, Selene. You didn't ground yourself. I can feel it."

---

71 NIC – Neural Interlock Control. Direct control of the interceptor via neural interconnection and human thought.

"I always ground myself, Forkbraid. I couldn't have taken down those two Raiders if I hadn't", Selene replied pointing to the smouldering wreckage of two Raiders out in the meadows.

"No, Selene. You didn't ground yourself. You drew on your core strength and your staff amplified it. Just as it would have if you were inside an off-world colony", Forkbraid explained.

"No, no, Forkbraid", Selene replied, "I grounded myself, I'm certain of it."

"Okay, Selene. Try it now. Ground yourself", Forkbraid instructed.

Selene gave Forkbraid a wry look and then attempted to ground herself to the Martian surface.

After ten or so seconds, Selene shifted her weight and attempted to ground herself once more.

"Something's wrong", Selene stated with surprise in her voice, "I can't connect to the Earth."

Forkbraid clapped his hands together, "And there you have it, Selene, my love. This is Mars, not the Earth. The air you're breathing is Martian air, not Earth's air. That's Martian soil out there, not the Earth's soil", he gestured to the surrounding Martian meadows.

Selene looked up at Forkbraid, realisation upon her face.

"Selene, my darling", Forkbraid said softly, "You've been so concerned and worried about your people connecting to Mars and regaining their abilities, that you've neglected yourself."

"But I've always been able to use my gifts off-world", Selene reminded Forkbraid.

"Yes, yes. So have I, Selene", Forkbraid began, "But when we did so, we had no connection to the Earth. We couldn't ground ourselves. We relied purely on our core strength and our magical tools to amplify our abilities."

"But I'm not off-world now", Selene countered, "I have a whole planet beneath my feet."

"Yes, but it's not the Earth, Selene", Forkbraid explained, "This is Mars. You are instinctively trying to reconnect to the Earth. You need to readjust your instincts, readjust and connect to Mars."

Forkbraid was right, Selene could see it now, she had neglected herself.

Selene changed the subject and showed Forkbraid where Joanne Seato had died, her blood still stained the battlement. Blow-by-blow, Selene recounted the battle leading up to Joanne's death.

Then slowly with teary eyes, Selene recounted precisely how Joanne died, explaining that Roseanne saw it all, close up and personal.

Forkbraid was surprised by Selene's description of how Roseanne reacted.

"Roseanne sliced the Raider in two. Just like that?", Forkbraid asked.

"Yes. Just like that", Selene replied, "Before the battle I gave Roseanne Gnomulus to protect her, but even so, the amount of raw power she channelled was phenomenal."

Forkbraid nodded, then he asked, "I'm still not clear why Roseanne wasn't in the bunkers?"

"Roseanne is not just a powerful young Witch, Forkbraid", Selene replied, noting, "She is a very stubborn one as well."

"Stubborn you say", Forkbraid replied, remembering how stubborn Selene had been as a teenager, "Like mentor, like apprentice."

"Oh, yeah, thank you for that, Forkbraid. I told her to go to the bunkers, and she leapt off the top battlements up there", Selene replied pointing to the top of the keep, "following me down to here, right before the battle began."

"As you said, one very stubborn Witch.", Forkbraid agreed.

"Yes", Selene replied, "And when Roseanne is fully trained, one to be reckoned with."

Later during the day Forkbraid and Special Agent Murphy contacted the Cruiser Spartan in Martian orbit high above the Elysium plateau.

"Captain the anti-aircraft batteries were a success in that they did shoot down two of the Raiders. However, four Raiders still got through", Forkbraid informed him.

Special Agent Murphy added, "Had the enemy attacked from multiple directions the batteries would have been more effective. Unfortunately, they came in a tight frontal assault."

Captain Carmichael nodded, he understood, "And the batteries were overwhelmed."

"Precisely", Special Agent Murphy confirmed.

"We need at least three times the number of anti-aircraft batteries, Captain", Forkbraid recommended, as Special Agent Murphy nodded in agreement.

Captain Carmichael thought for a moment, "I have some more equipment you can have, but probably not enough for what you need."

"Whatever you can spare, Captain, we'll be grateful", Special Agent Murphy replied.

"I'll send another team back over to Deimos", the Captain told them, "I'll give them orders to scrounge up anything useful and bring it back with them. Whatever they find, it's yours."

"That'll be great, Captain", Forkbraid replied adding, "But don't forget those last four Wisps."

"Ah, yes, Forkbraid. They'll be arriving tomorrow morning", Captain Carmichael confirmed.

"Excellent!", Special Agent Murphy exclaimed.

"And Captain", Forkbraid began, "We now know where the militant's lair is."

"Now that is excellent news", the Captain replied.

"Not as excellent as I'd like", Forkbraid told the Captain.

"Why is that, Forkbraid?", Captain Carmichael questioned.

"Two reasons, Captain", Forkbraid replied, adding, "Their base is an old colony from before the terraforming called New Tortuga. They've effectively embedded themselves into the heart of a civilian population centre. A fair sized civilian population at that."

"Collateral damage will be high", the Captain suggested.

"Yeah, that's the problem", Forkbraid replied, adding "We're going to have to plan this one out carefully, real carefully."

"What's the second reason?", Captain Carmichael queried.

Special Agent Murphy replied, "The Aurorae colony, Captain."

"What about it?", enquired the Captain.

"It's crawling with militants as well. Hard core ones at that", Forkbraid informed him.

"A lot of them, down in the old quarter", Special Agent Murphy added.

"Well, that does complicate matters even more doesn't it", the Captain stated.

"That it does, Captain", Special Agent Murphy replied, adding "There may be a lot more pockets of militants down here than we thought."

"Captain, remember that figure of seventy-five thousand you once told me?", Forkbraid asked.

"Yes, I do", the Captain replied, remarking, "That's how many people are living on Mars… in my humble opinion."

"Yeah", Forkbraid replied, then dropping the clanger, "The true figure is at least double that. At least a hundred and fifty thousand and then some."

"No. No, Forkbraid. That figure's way too high, surely", Captain Carmichael scoffed.

"No, Captain, it's right on the money", Forkbraid responded, adding "Remember the original colonists. The ones from before the terraforming project began?"

"Yeah, they were all evacuated… Well before operation ice drop began", the Captain answered.

"That's the thing, Captain", Forkbraid replied, noting, "A lot of them didn't leave, Captain. Unofficial colonies that weren't recorded on anyone's books. They stayed behind."

The look on Captain Carmichael's face was priceless.

It took several seconds for Captain Carmichael to swallow Forkbraid's last statement, and then he let drop a bomb of his own.

"I've had word from L-Five, Forkbraid", the Captain informed them.

"Yeah. What's happening back there?", Forkbraid asked.

"Banyan's got the terrorist situation under control. Agent Murphy's Special Agent colleagues have performed their duties exceedingly well", the Captain replied.

"Well then, that's good news at least", Special Agent Murphy remarked.

"Yes, it is, Gentlemen", the Captain replied, "It's the latest report from the Hyper Dynamics Corporate colonies that's got me flummoxed, though."

"How so?", Special Agent Murphy questioned, "You said the terrorists were under control."

"They are, Agent Murphy", the Captain replied, "This is different."

"In what way, Captain?", Forkbraid asked.

"Clinton Usarian, the Hyper Dynamics Corporation's CEO", the Captain replied.

"What about Clinton Usarian?", Special Agent Murphy asked.

"He's dead, he fell on his sword", the Captain informed them, "At their annual general meeting of shareholders. He pulled out a sword, stuck it hilt down on the floor in front of him and just fell on it. Right there, in front of all their shareholders."

Forkbraid and Special Agent Murphy looked at each other with surprised looks.

"Just thought you'd want to know", the Captain finished, "Over and out."

"Fell on his sword", Special Agent Murphy repeated in disbelief.

Forkbraid looked at Special Agent Murphy, "Jim… Back at the Hyper Dynamics Corporate colony, I told Usarian that he ought to resign at the next annual general meeting. I told him that he should fall on his sword!"

"Let me get this straight, FB. You told Clinton Usarian to fall on his sword?", Special Agent Murphy requested clarification.

"Yes, Jim. I told Clinton Usarian to fall on his sword", Forkbraid replied, quickly adding "It was just a metaphor. He was just meant to resign, not bloody well kill himself."

"Well, FB, there is only one thing that I can say", Special Agent Murphy stated.

"What's that, Jim?", Forkbraid enquired.

"In future", Special Agent Murphy began, "Be bloody careful with your metaphors!"

Matthew had received word back from the Aurorae colony about the disaster at the water front. Not trusting anyone in Aurorae to give him a proper explanation, he sent one of his own men to find out what went wrong. He was now informing Leroy of the situation.

"Miranda Swann was not on the Shilo, Sir", Matthew told Leroy.

"What do you mean she wasn't on the Shilo?", Leroy queried.

"None of our people saw her, Sir", Matthew replied, "After the gun fight or whatever it was, the passengers on the Shilo were all escorted off the ship and out of the water front by the police. We still had some people around the water front, and they were watching very carefully. No one matching Miranda Swann's description, nor Cormac's or his Wife's, were on board the Shilo."

"Then what the hell happened?", Leroy questioned.

Matthew was silent for a long moment before answering, "Apparently there was a Wizard on board the Shilo, Sir", he replied.

"A Wizard", Leroy asked, "On board the Shilo?"

"That is what I have been told, Sir", Matthew replied.

"Are you sure?", Leroy asked.

"Magical staff, magical wands, magical shielding", Matthew replied, "And right at the end of it all, he vanished into thin air."

"A Wizard... Well that would explain all the carnage at the water front", Leroy replied.

"Then where's that abomination? Where's Miranda Swann?", questioned Leroy.

Matthew didn't want to answer, but he had to, "We don't know for sure, Sir, but if I were to hazard a guess, I'd say that that little Witch is in Elysium."

"Elysium!", Leroy exclaimed, "That's the absolute worst case scenario, Matthew. Are you sure?"

"No, Sir", Matthew replied, "I can't be certain of anything. It's just a wild guess, but if I'm right, then Miranda Swann is in Elysium, along with Cormac Farmer and his Wife."

"We need to confirm this, Matthew. Urgently!", Leroy told him.

"We can't", Matthew replied flatly, "Sir. If they're in Elysium, then they're at the Psychic Academy. We have no way to test that theory."

"I hope you're wrong, Matthew", Leroy replied adding, "Because if you are not, we are all dead men walking!"

"Are you going to tell the Prophet, Sir?", Matthew enquired.

"Are you insane, Matthew?", Leroy replied, questioning rhetorically, "Just what would we tell him? That you think... maybe... just maybe... that the little abomination is at their Psychic Academy. I will not tell him that, Matthew and neither will you."

Matthew nodded in agreement, "Yes, Sir. There's really nothing we can tell him then."

26. Discoveries

Forkbraid entered the room, with Special Agent Murphy close behind him. Seated before them at the table was Selene with Miranda's parents.

"Selene… Charlene was just telling me that you had Miranda's DNA tested", Forkbraid noted.

"Why, yes, Forkbraid", Selene replied, "Given the strength of Miranda's abilities I thought it might be useful if we knew a bit more about her ancestry."

"Selene, DNA won't tell you a whole lot about ancestry unless you have someone else's DNA to compare it with", Forkbraid explained.

Selene smiled broadly, "Ah, Forkbraid, but I do. Several people in fact."

"Who?", Forkbraid asked.

"You and I for starters. Then there's Cormac and Candy", Selene replied.

"What? You think we might all be related to Miranda?", Forkbraid asked.

"You yourself said there was some kind of nexus developing here on Mars", Selene reminded him, explaining, "You and I are distantly related, what? Ninth Cousins, aren't we? Then, there's Cormac and Candy. It turns out that they're our ninth Cousins as well."

Forkbraid nodded, "True enough, but the odds of little Miranda being a Cousin as well would have to be astronomically long."

"Yeah", Selene replied, rhetorically questioning, "But there is that nexus of yours, isn't there?"

Selene looked over to Peter and Catherine Swann. Peter was holding a file which Selene had given to him only minutes before Forkbraid and Special Agent Murphy entered the room.

"I gave Peter the results just a few minutes ago. None of us have seen them yet. I thought that the Swanns should be the first.", Selene informed Forkbraid.

Peter Swann opened the file and read the contents. After a couple of minutes Peter looked at his Wife, and then he looked up at Forkbraid.

"According to the results of the DNA comparisons, there is a high probability of a common ancestor approximately ten generations ago", Peter informed them all.

Forkbraid looked around the room at the faces before him, "Our eighth great-grandfather."

"Quite possibly, Forkbraid himself", Selene replied.

"Selene, you do know that's going to be extremely difficult to verify", Forkbraid informed her, "Sharing of memories does not occur among the ordinary folk."

"You're absolutely right, Forkbraid", Selene lamented, "We won't have any shared streams of memories to trace at all."

"And we are on Mars", Forkbraid continued, "It's not going to be easy to prove."

Special Agent Murphy had been listening intently to the conversation, "You could always do things the ordinary way."

"Ordinary way?", Selene queried.

"Government records", Special Agent Murphy replied, "You can trace a person's ancestral lineage through the birth, deaths, and marriage registers you know."

"We know all about genealogy, Jim. The birth, deaths, and marriage records on Earth have always been stored in a myriad of registers, scattered across literally hundreds of sites all across the globe. Very few of which have ever been linked together. Many of those records have been lost as well, or they are incomplete or just plain unreadable. It makes tracing ancestral lineages a wee bit iffy", Selene explained.

"That's the beauty of Cis-Lunar L-Five", Special Agent Murphy explained, "Every birth, death, and marriage is meticulously recorded in Colonial Central Command's archives. Genealogy is a really big thing at Cis-Lunar L-Five. It's really quite simple, you just request a pedigree listing from the archives, and then they send you the result. I've even traced my family tree. My great-grandfather left Earth for Cis-Lunar L-Five just over a hundred years ago."

Peter Swann then informed them, "Agent Murphy is right. A lot of folk at Cis-Lunar L-Five trace their family trees. It's a really big thing, especially if you find an ancestor is one of the original colonists on the very first colony."

"Have you ever traced your family tree, Peter?", Forkbraid asked.

"Yes, of course, we have", Peter replied, "I can trace my ancestry at Cis-Lunar L-Five back nearly two hundred years."

"Impressive", Forkbraid remarked, then he asked, "Were you able to trace your family tree back beyond that, on Earth?"

"No", Peter frowned, "Lady Selene is right. The vital statistics databases on Earth are a complete mess. Very few are interlinked and there's no central archive to requisition a pedigree listing from."

"That's a real shame", Forkbraid replied, knowing full well what Peter was talking about.

"Yeah, it is", Peter replied, "Catherine's tree is much more impressive though."

"How so, Peter?", Selene asked.

"Catherine had an ancestor on the very first colony to be constructed at Cis-Lunar L-Five", Peter replied.

"Really!", Forkbraid exclaimed.

"Yes. Back then colonists were all still called Astronauts", Peter replied.

All eyes turned to Catherine Swann, whose face turned bright red.

"It's true. I had an ancestor in the very first colony. [72]O'Neil it was called, named after some famous scientist from hundreds of years ago", Catherine informed them.

"That would be well over three hundred years ago", Special Agent Murphy told everyone.

"I can provide you with the data if you like", Peter offered, "We brought all of that with us."

"Catherine... You wouldn't happen to remember this ancestor's name?", Forkbraid asked.

"Why, yes, her name was Lovisa Carolinya Jacobson", Catherine replied.

Both Forkbraid and Selene smiled in unison.

"Lovisa Carolinya Jacobson was the granddaughter of Folcrom Tafazah", Selene informed them.

"Catherine, you and your Daughter are scions of Tafazah's second Daughter", Forkbraid added.

"More Cousins", Special Agent Murphy noted, adding, "Wait till Cormac and Candy here about this. They'll be stoked. They're really big on Cousins here on Mars."

"That's a fact", Forkbraid nodded in agreement.

"Your nexus is really starting to take shape, Forkbraid", Selene smiled again.

"Well, it certainly explains a lot, FB", Special Agent Murphy stated.

"What do you mean, Jim?", Forkbraid asked.

"You once told me that the colonists will adapt, even in the off-world colonies like at L-Five. Only that for the off-world colonists it will take many generations", Special Agent Murphy reminded Forkbraid.

"Yes, I remember, Jim", Forkbraid replied.

"Well, Miranda's ancestors joined the L-Five colonies right at the very beginning, more than three centuries ago", Special Agent Murphy pointed out, "That sounds like plenty of time to adapt."

Forkbraid nodded in agreement, "Yes, it is, Jim, yes, it is."

"Maybe we should test Roseanne's DNA as well, Selene", Forkbraid suggested.

"I did that during our flight out here on the Ptolemy", Selene replied.

"And the result?", Forkbraid enquired.

"No relationship to any of us I'm afraid", Selene replied with a slightly puzzled look on her face, "Roseanne's a complete wild card."

"Interesting", Forkbraid stated, "With all these other relationships coming to light, it's odd that Roseanne's not among them."

"It gets even stranger, Forkbraid", Selene replied, noting, "Analysis of

---

72 O'Neil – The first L-Five colony. Twin cylinders of the O'Neil type. Named after Gerard O'Neil, its original designer.

Roseanne's DNA showed her psychic abilities are more likely the result of a random genetic mutation, coupled to her experiences in her coma at the age of five."

"That is unusual", Forkbraid considered, "Usually psychic abilities travel in ancestral lineages."

"Have you ever traced your family tree, Forkbraid?", Catherine Swann asked.

"All psychics have their family lineages traced, Catherine. It's just done as a matter of course", Forkbraid replied without any elaboration.

"It's something that we do as a matter of course", Selene confirmed, "Usually we rely on our shared memories. We can follow those memory streams back several centuries in most cases."

"Yes, but surely you have traced your ancestral trees the way we ordinary folk do?", Catherine queried.

"Yes, we have", Selene confirmed, explaining, "But as I said before, the records on Earth can be a bit iffy. It's a lot harder than simply requesting a pedigree listing from a central archive. To do what you take for granted at L-Five requires a team of dedicated genealogists. They do all the research, travelling the globe as necessary to check the various registers and verify all the data."

"Sounds like a time-consuming process", Peter remarked.

"Very time-consuming. That's why we have dedicated genealogists to do it", Forkbraid replied.

"So… How far back can you trace your family tree, Forkbraid?", Peter asked.

Forkbraid was quiet for an uncomfortably long time. All eyes were turned to him.

Finally, Forkbraid answered the question, it was not what they expected, "Selene and I can trace our ancestral lineages back well over five thousand years."

Jaws dropped, and astonished looks were all around Selene and Forkbraid.

"Did we hear you correctly?", Special Agent Murphy asked, "You did say five thousand years!"

"Yes, Jim", Forkbraid confirmed, noting, "Well over five thousand years, closer to five thousand six hundred years, give or take a score of decades."

"Didn't Selene say that the records get a bit iffy?", Catherine queried.

"Yes. The records do get a bit iffy", Selene replied, "Before the vital statistics records, we have to reach back into recorded history and then other sources, then we augment those records with our shared streams of memory where possible."

"Five thousand six hundred years!", Peter repeated.

"Yes, Peter, thereabouts", Forkbraid confirmed once more, "And you know, that means we can trace Catherine's ancestry back that far as well. Catherine is our Cousin after all."

Peter looked to his Wife, "Catherine, your family tree just got a whole lot bigger."

Catherine smiled and replied, "It certainly did", then she asked Forkbraid, "Would you be kind enough to share your data?"

They all laughed.

Later that afternoon, Forkbraid and Selene were talking to Cormac and Candy. All four of them sat on comfortable couches on a balcony overlooking the green rolling pastures of the Elysium plateau to the north. The topic of discussion was the shared memory streams and family ties.

Forkbraid explained, "Tafazah laid down four distinct streams of memory sharing, two pigeon pairs, so to speak."

"Pigeon pairs?", Selene queried.

"You know, male and female streams. One pair for his Earth children and another pair for his Martian children", Forkbraid elaborated.

"So what did you discover about these four memory streams?", Candy enquired.

"Well, I found each pair, male and female, could be zipped together like helical strands of DNA. So the four memory streams combined into two planetary memory streams, just like a double helix. One Martian, the other Earthling", Forkbraid explained, adding "However, that is as far as I managed to get."

"Surely if you worked out how to stitch the pigeon pairs together, it couldn't be much harder to stitch the planetary memory streams together?", Cormac questioned.

"I wish that were so, Cormac", Forkbraid replied, "Combining the planetary memory streams requires a key. A key that I do not have."

"A key?", Cormac questioned, "Is there anyway around this key?"

Forkbraid laughed, "Sure, if I don't mind descending into a pit of total and complete insanity."

"Oh no, that doesn't sound good", Cormac replied.

"Don't you dare Forkbraid!", Selene cried out.

"Don't worry Selene. I'm not going to take the risk", Forkbraid assured her.

"Don't worry! Don't you, don't worry, me!", Selene shouted, "I know you too well, Forkbraid. You take risks. I have to worry, because the heavens surely know you won't."

"Do you know what the key is?", Candy asked.

"Ah, well that's the thing, Candy. If I'm right the key is something simple. Very simple. Something very similar to the memory streams themselves", Forkbraid replied.

"Another memory stream?", Candy queried.

"No, it's not another memory stream", Forkbraid replied, "I've traced down all the memory streams. Each, and every one of them."

"Are you certain?", Candy questioned.

Forkbraid checked off the list, "Six children on Mars, three Sons and three Daughters. Six children on Earth, again three Sons and three Daughters. Two shared memory streams for Mars, one for the Sons and another for the Daughters. Same deal for the Earth, two shared memory streams, one for the Sons and another for the Daughters. Have I missed something?"

Candy leant forward and exclaimed, "What about children of the mind's eye!"

"Children of the mind's eye?", Forkbraid questioned.

"Forkbraid!", Selene exclaimed, adding "A wight of one's will is a child of the mind's eye", Selene reminded him.

"Ah, yes, of course!", Forkbraid exclaimed, clapping his hands together.

"Perhaps that staff of yours is the key", Cormac suggested.

"Yes, yes. It's been handed down for generations", Candy reminded Forkbraid.

"Yes, Candy. Father to the eldest Son, all starting with Tafazah", Forkbraid replied.

"And each new owner reconsecrates the staff, imparting a wight of their own will", Selene stated, noting "If each consecration is concatenated together in series from the first till the last, the result could be considered a stream of memories."

Forkbraid sat still for a very long moment contemplating this new concept. It was a distinct possibility. Slowly Forkbraid reached into his robe and pulled out his staff out from his impossible pocket. Forkbraid held his staff before him, staring intently at the rune carved artefact. It was literally centuries old.

As the others watched, Forkbraid concentrated on his staff. Slowly and carefully he located the wights of his ancestor's wills. Gradually, cautiously, with intense visualisation and concentration, he bound them together into one long stream of will wights. Once completed, Forkbraid then bound his own will wight to the end of the memory stream, the final wight in the chain.

The others were right, his staff was a child of the mind's eye and each consecration had provided a link in the chain that was indeed, an analogue of a shared stream of memories. The staff stream.

Forkbraid internalised this new memory stream and then looked inwards into his own mind. There he found the planetary pairs of shared memories. Slowly and ever so cautiously, lest he fall into an endless pit of madness and insanity. Forkbraid compared the key that was provided by his staff with the lock that was an integral part of the two planetary streams of shared memories. This new staff memory stream was close, ever so close, but no, it was not the key!

"It is not the key!", Forkbraid opened his eyes, shook his head and exclaimed.

"Are you sure?", Candy questioned.

"Yes, yes, I'm certain of it", Forkbraid replied, "It's close, so very close, but it's not the key."

"We're still missing something", Selene suggested.

Cormac was not usually the big thinker in his household. Typically, Cormac let Candy do all the thinking and was satisfied to go along with her decisions. Yet as the others spoke, Cormac pointed out something that they had all missed.

"Pigeon pairs", Cormac said softly, so softly that the others nearly missed it.

Candy turned to her Husband, "Cormac, you have an idea?"

"Pigeon pairs, Candy!", Cormac replied more strongly and with more urgency.

"Of course, my Husband", Candy replied, squeezing Cormac's cheeks, then repeating, "Pigeon pairs. You are brilliant, Cormac!"

"Forkbraid, my Cousin, do you perchance have any other artefacts that were passed down from *He who asked The Great Question*?", Candy asked.

"Why, yes, Candy", Forkbraid replied, "A great many artefacts, in fact."

"These will be very prominent artefacts!", Candy cried out, then more softly, "One will be male, and the other will be female."

Forkbraid thought for a moment, then replaced his staff back into his impossible pocket. Slowly Forkbraid reached back into his robe with both hands and pulled out two of his wands from his impossible pockets.

The wand in his right hand was made of oak. Down the very centre of this wand was a length of thin, magnetised metal, connected to powerful magnets hidden inside its hilt. Wrapped around the hilt was copper wire, turned blue from oxidation over the centuries. This wand was male.

The wand in his left hand was made of rosewood and deeply coloured. Down the very centre of this wand were various lengths of crystal. Seven crystals to be precise, each made of a specific mineral and each placed in a precise order and alignment. Likewise with the other wand, these crystals connected to powerful magnets hidden inside its hilt. The hilt itself was also wrapped in copper wire, likewise turned blue with oxidation. This wand was female.

Forkbraid held the wands before him. Three pairs of eyes watched on.

"Same deal", Selene said to Forkbraid, "Consecrations! Wights of their wills, Forkbraid."

"Male and female streams of shared memories", added Candy, "Pigeon pairs!"

Forkbraid held the two wands before him. Slowly and carefully he located the wights of his ancestor's wills in his oak wand. Again with intense visualisation and concentration, he bound them all together into one long memory stream analogue. Once completed, Forkbraid then bound his own will wight to the end of the memory stream. It was a male memory stream! Quickly Forkbraid internalised this memory stream.

Then having done so, Forkbraid repeated the entire process for the rosewood wand, carefully binding his ancestor's will wights together into one long memory stream analogue and binding his own will wight to the end of it. It was a female memory stream! As with the first, Forkbraid quickly internalises this memory stream. Quickly Forkbraid replaced his two wands back into his impossible pockets once more.

Forkbraid turned his mind inwards. In his mind's eye he now had five shared memory streams. The two planetary memory streams, one Martian, the other Earthling. Both previously stitched together from pigeon pairs of male and female memory streams of shared memories. Just as with the previous pigeon pairs, Forkbraid stitched the shared memory streams from his wands together. Male and female, they zipped together like two helical strands of DNA. The wand memory stream was now combined. Now he was down to four sets of memory streams.

Forkbraid concentrated on the memory streams in his mind. The other three watched on, using their gifts they could see what Forkbraid was attempting. It was well beyond Cormac or Candy, even Selene would think twice about doing what Forkbraid was attempting. Skilled as Selene was, this was truly dangerous. A deep pit of madness and insanity lay in wait for any who failed.

The two planetary streams of shared memories came together, yet could not interlock. The key was missing. Slowly Forkbraid integrated the wand memory stream into the planetary streams. Again all three memory streams came together and again they could not fully interlock.

Now however, Forkbraid could see that the key required was ever so subtly different. Slowly Forkbraid brought the staff memory stream into close proximity to the other three memory streams. In his mind's eye, Forkbraid could see that this key would fit this lock perfectly! Ever so closely Selene, Cormac, and Candy watched the event unfold.

Forkbraid inserted the staff memory stream of shared memories into the midst of the other three. The other three streams of shared memories shifted ever so slightly and interlocked, the staff memory stream slipped into the other three with a perfect fit. The entire assemblage of memory streams began to swirl around and around in Forkbraid's mind. A strong feeling of vertigo came over Forkbraid as the assemblage of memory streams continued to swirl faster and faster.

Fear and panic arose in the minds of those watching. Cormac and Candy could stand no more and backed away, withdrawing their minds well away from the swirling assemblage of memory streams. Selene out of sheer love for Forkbraid held on firm and continued to watch on closely.

Forkbraid focused his mind on the swirling mass of memories, swirling faster and faster around in his mind. With a huge effort of will, Forkbraid reached deeply into the swirling mass and held firm with his mind. The mass of memories twisted and contorted in Forkbraid's mind, yet Forkbraid held firm. The mass of memories began to fold in upon itself, twisting and writhing in his mind like a tangled mess of snakes. Still Forkbraid held firm.

Then with a suddenness that caught Forkbraid completely by surprise, the writhing mass of memories began to take form. The writhing quickly stopped, and slowly a face began to solidify in Forkbraid's mind. A face Forkbraid recognised, but had only ever seen in pictures and shared memories. The long deceased face of Lord Folcrom Tafazah, the first Folcrom, stared back at Forkbraid with an impossible living consciousness. It smiled broadly at him.

He who had asked The Great Question had awakened.

The tiniest swirling vortex began to appear in the centre of the forehead of the face that was now within Forkbraid's mind. The vortex was tiny, as Forkbraid looked upon it, he realised it was infinitesimal. It was an infinitesimally small, yet infinitely powerful, pinpoint of radiant and luminous energy. So very tiny and yet so powerful, that Forkbraid could not resist it. Slowly, inexorably Forkbraid was drawn down deeper and deeper into the tiniest, yet most powerful of vortices. Selene looked on in horror as Forkbraid's mind entered the vortex.

Selene screamed out to Forkbraid with her mind, "*No, Forkbraid! No!*"

It was far too late, for suddenly, Forkbraid's consciousness disappeared completely into the vortex, and he was gone! That tiniest of vortices then suddenly snapped shut.

Tears streamed down Lady Selene's face as she screamed inconsolably. Selene held Forkbraid firmly in her tight embrace. Try as she may, Selene could not reach Forkbraid's consciousness. The place in Forkbraid's mind, where his consciousness should have been, was an empty void, except for the smiling face of *He who had asked The Great Question*. Indeed, Forkbraid's consciousness appeared to have completely disappeared. It no longer existed!

All that could be seen as Selene frantically searched for Forkbraid's consciousness was the long deceased face of Lord Folcrom Tafazah staring back at her. The vortex in the forehead of Tafazah's face had closed and Forkbraid lay prone and unconscious on the couch.

The sublime smile of Folcrom Tafazah's face looked out from the darkest depths of Forkbraid's mind and yielded Selene nothing as to what had happened to her man. Forkbraid's body breathed and functioned, yet he, himself, was no longer present.

It took a considerable time for Cormac and Candy to pull Selene away from Forkbraid. While Candy held Selene tightly, trying as she might to console her, Cormac sent his mind out urgently, screaming for help. Help came swiftly as friends and colleagues pushed their way through Selene's apartment to the balcony. Try as they might, there was nothing that they could do. Lord Folcrom Forkbraid had left the building!

For three days now Forkbraid had lain unconscious in the bedroom of Lady Selene's apartment. A nasal gastric feeding tube had been inserted, catheters had been inserted. His body lived, but his consciousness was completely absent. Lady Selene took care of his every need, bathing him when he needed bathing, adjusting his prone body when it needed moving, talking to him when she thought he needed talking to. Spending her time either sitting by Forkbraid's side or laying beside him on their bed. Lady Selene refused to leave Forkbraid's side.

Batteries of tests had been performed. Forkbraid's body was functioning normally, yet all brain activity had ceased, no signs of consciousness were present. The doctors that were on staff, had whispered to their colleagues that Forkbraid, was for all intents and purposes, brain-dead.

Lady Selene was hearing none of that, "He's not dead", she had screamed at them, explaining cryptically and tearfully, "Forkbraid is just sleeping... The pilot has merely left his vehicle... Forkbraid will be back!"

It was on the evening of the third day that several people approached Lady Selene's apartment. Charlene Fewkes knocked upon Selene's door. There was no answer. Charlene knocked again and again, yet each time there was no answer. Charlene waved her index finger in the shape of a certain bind-rune, in front of the lock in Lady Selene's apartment door. The lock clicked open and Charlene quickly opened the door.

Charlene led the way into Lady Selene's rooms. Marcus, Cormac, Candy, and Special Agent Murphy followed her into Selene's rooms. Charlene walked over to Selene's bedroom and then turned around to the others.

"You three stay right there", Charlene told the three men, pointing to the couches and chairs.

"I'd like to help too", Marcus told his Girlfriend.

"No, Marcus, you'll stay here with the others", Charlene insisted.

Charlene opened the bedroom door and stepped through. Candy followed her into the room and closed the door behind them. Before them on the king-sized bed lay an unconscious Forkbraid. Lady Selene was laying naked on the bed beside Forkbraid, with her back turned to the bedroom door. Slowly, Lady Selene stroked Forkbraid's long, almost sandy blonde hair.

"Lady Selene", Charlene quietly interrupted, "Lady Selene."

Selene stopped stroking Forkbraid's hair and slowly rolled over, sitting up on the side of the bed.

Never had Charlene seen Lady Selene look so unwell.

"Selene, you look so tired! You're not sleeping, are you? Have you even eaten today, Selene?", Charlene questioned.

Tears welled up in Lady Selene's eyes, "Forkbraid won't wake up", she cried softly.

Candy pulled some robes from out of a closet and walked over to Lady Selene.

"Cousin, this simply will not do", Candy told Lady Selene, "Come on, put some clothes on."

Lady Selene stood up shakily and allowed herself to be dressed by Candy.

Once dressed, Lady Selene looked back at Forkbraid once more, and then she turned back to Candy, "He won't wake up. It doesn't matter what I do, he just won't wake up", she cried.

Candy hugged Selene firmly and whispered into her ear, "Cousin, we will sort this out you know. We won't stop until we find a cure."

Candy then helped Lady Selene sit back down on the edge of the bed.

"Charlene, ask Cormac to prepare some food and drink. Something light", Candy said to Charlene, "I'll help Selene fix herself up."

Charlene disappeared back out the bedroom door and was gone for several minutes.

Candy then sat on the bed beside Lady Selene, "You've got to pull yourself together Cousin. Your people depend on you. Now come on, I'll help you get ready."

When Charlene reappeared through the bedroom door once more, Candy was busily brushing Selene's hair, "Our Lady is almost ready", Candy informed Charlene.

"Now, up you get, Cousin. Let me wipe those tears from your eyes", Candy told Selene.

Charlene looked at Lady Selene, gently saying to her, "You can't spend all of your time in bed."

Lady Selene smiled slightly and replied, "That didn't stop you and Marcus for two days."

Charlene blushed, turning bright red, "Selene! That was different."

"Not so different", Selene replied, "Forkbraid may be unconscious, perhaps even brain-dead, but he is still my man."

"He is not brain-dead, Selene", Charlene reminded her, "As you keep telling us, the pilot has merely left the vehicle. At some point, he will climb back in, and come back to us."

Lady Selene smiled once more and allowed herself to be led out the door.

Once in the lounge room, the three women sat down on a comfortable couch. Marcus and Special Agent Murphy each greeted Lady Selene in turn and then got down to business. Cormac had gone to gather some food. The defence of the Psychic Academy and the training programmes still had to continue, even with Forkbraid out of action and Lady Selene out of sorts.

"Captain Carmichael has sent down the other four Wisps as he'd promised", Special Agent Murphy informed Selene, "With the six that survived the attack, we now have ten all up."

"That's not enough to defend our Academy, Jim", Selene replied bluntly.

"No, it's not, Selene", Special Agent Murphy replied, noting "The Captain's men are out in the meadows building anti-aircraft gun emplacements. Within a few days we'll have two dozen anti-aircraft batteries set up and ready."

"Will they be enough?", Selene asked.

"You only had eight last time, with twenty-four, you'll be able to blast anything out of the skies", Special Agent Murphy assured her.

Lady Selene nodded, wishing Forkbraid was there to reassure her as well.

"The training schedules have been adjusted", Marcus told Selene.

"In what way?", Lady Selene asked.

"The games programme you requested earlier", Marcus explained, "Charlene tells me it has been working well. Everyone is loosening up and not worrying about their abilities so much."

"It allows their abilities to naturally resurface", Charlene elaborated.

"Yes, but with the latest changes we're making real progress", Marcus added.

"The latest changes?", Lady Selene queried.

Charlene gave Marcus a harsh look. They weren't going to mention the latest changes.

"Before Forkbraid was afflicted, he suggested certain grounding exercises", Charlene replied.

"Grounding exercises?", Lady Selene asked, remembering her conversation with Forkbraid.

"Yes", Marcus replied, adding "Forkbraid liked the games programme. He thought it was a great idea, but he felt it might be prudent to augment it with specific grounding exercises."

"To help our people connect with Mars on a fundamental level", Charlene explained.

Lady Selene nodded, "Has it worked?"

"Yes, Selene, it's been working very well indeed", Marcus happily informed her.

"Better than we'd hoped", Charlene confirmed.

"In a few months, maybe you'll be able to put together our first Martian Grey Council", Marcus assured her.

"The first Martian Grey Council", Lady Selene mouthed. It was like a dream, long forgotten and only partly remembered. That was their plan, to reacquire their abilities, set up Wyvern Remote Viewing teams, and form a new Grey

Council.

"We need to build up our Wyvern covens first, Marcus", Lady Selene advised.

"I expect we could have the first Wyvern covens ready in a few weeks", Marcus replied.

"A few weeks?", Lady Selene questioned, thinking, *"Am I dreaming, have I gone mad?"*

Candy and Charlene both caught the thought. Lady Selene was obviously under the weather, personal thoughts never floated to the surface like this normally.

Candy squeezed Selene's hand reassuringly, transmitting *"You are not dreaming, Selene, this is real, Cousin."*

Charlene explained, "The new programmes are working extremely well, Selene."

Marcus, who had also caught the loose personal thought, added, "Once we figured out the correct techniques, adapting to Mars became a lot easier."

Then Cormac walked back into the room. He had with him a selection of sandwiches, three different salads and a large bottle of fruit juice. He quickly placed the food and drink on the dining table in another room and returned.

"Someone might want to point out where the crockery is", Cormac remarked.

Candy rolled her eyes as she stood up, "Men! Don't worry, Cormac, I'll find them."

Charlene had another surprise in store for Lady Selene, "Cormac also had a good suggestion."

"Cormac?", Lady Selene queried, "What was his suggestion?"

Cormac seated himself beside Marcus, "Cousin, there are a lot of gifted here on Mars."

"Gifted?", Lady Selene queried.

"Yes. Like me and Candy", Cormac explained.

Lady Selene nodded in understanding, "Forkbraid was saying that just the other day. Mars apparently has more than a few of its own Witches."

"Exactly", Cormac replied, "Normally we hide our gifts. Persecution can be quite rife in the wild country and misunderstandings are more than common. So we tend to be very cautious."

Again Lady Selene nodded in understanding, every psychic knew about persecution.

"Anyway", Cormac continued, "I was thinking. What if we brought some of our gifted here? Wouldn't that help?"

"The gifted", Lady Selene thought as she considered this new idea, "Yes. If you think they'd fit in, Cormac?"

Candy had returned to the lounge room, "Fit in, Cousin? Of course, they'll fit in. They'll be like peas in a pod."

Cormac smiled at his Wife, then turned back to Lady Selene, "The gifted would be more than happy to help. They are nearly all Cousins you know."

"Good! I'm glad that's all settled", Candy stated, "Now let's eat. Supper is served!"

Forkbraid awoke, he looked around himself. For as far as the eye could see there was nothing, and beyond that, the nothingness continued endlessly. There was neither darkness nor light, all around him was a grey twilight of pure emptiness. There was neither sky, nor ground, everywhere around him was an all-pervading grey none sky.

Forkbraid strained to see anything at all, then realised he had no eyes with which to see.

Forkbraid tried to hear anything at all, but there was no sound, nor did he have any ears with which to hear.

Forkbraid gasped for air, straining to breathe, yet there was no air to breathe, and he had no lungs with which to breathe anyway.

Forkbraid tried to move, yet this non-place was not a place in which one could move, nor did Forkbraid have any limbs with which to move anyway. This place was strange, it was weird, yet strangely Forkbraid thought, somehow he recognised it.

Forkbraid shouted out as loudly as he could, yet he had no mouth with which to speak, nor lips, nor tongue to articulate words. This place was a non-place, it wasn't real and yet, it was the most real of places he'd ever been. It was a place of flagrant contradictions. It was, and yet, it was not.

The only thing that Forkbraid knew was real and existed, was his mind.

This was a place of pure mind.

With all of his force, Forkbraid shouted out with his mind, *"What is this place?"*

Then he heard a reply.

"Haven't you figured it out yet?", the voice asked him.

"Figured out what?", Forkbraid asked.

"Where you are, of course", the voice replied.

"Why don't you just tell me?", Forkbraid asked of the voice.

"It is not my task to tell you", the voice responded.

"Why don't you just let me go?", Forkbraid asked of the voice.

"You are free to leave, whenever you wish", the voice answered.

"Then why can't I leave?", Forkbraid demanded.

"First you have to know where you are", the voice explained.

"Your destination requires that you first know your point of origin", the voice continued.

Forkbraid was quiet for what seemed like an eternity before he asked the voice, *"Who are you?"*

"You know who I am", the voice responded.

Forkbraid thought for a moment then questioned, *"Folcrom Tafazah! Is that who you are?"*

"That is I, Lord Folcrom Tafazah", the voice responded.

"But you're dead. You died centuries ago", Forkbraid told the voice.

"One's death is merely the beginning, not the end", the voice replied.

"Then where is this place?", Forkbraid demanded.

"You already know", the voice replied.

Forkbraid considered that statement, *"This is not limbo!"*

"Correct, this is not limbo", came the response from the voice.

"And I know it's not anywhere on the astral planes!", Forkbraid told the voice.

"Correct again", the voice replied, *"You see, you already know where you are not."*

"That's not very useful to me. I'd rather know where I am", Forkbraid cried out.

"You only need to consider where you are, to know where you are", the voice replied.

"It is in the consideration that the elucidation comes to light", continued the voice.

"Stop speaking in riddles", Forkbraid demanded.

"I'm helping you as best I can", the voice responded.

"Then why won't you just tell me?", Forkbraid asked.

"That would be cheating", the voice replied adding, *"Even here there are rules."*

"Is this a test?", Forkbraid enquired.

"No. It is not", the voice replied, *"The shared memory streams were the test, and you passed those"*, then thinking to itself, *"Three centuries I have waited."*

"And you say that I already know where I am?", Forkbraid asked for clarification.

"Yes, you already know where you are", the voice confirmed.

Again there was a period of quiet that felt like an eternity, before the non-silence was broken.

"Perhaps you should ask yourself, what are you?", the voice advised.

"What I am?", Forkbraid considered, then remembering how he felt when he first awoke.

"What I am?", Forkbraid thought to himself.

"I am mind", Forkbraid shouted out.

"Correct", confirmed the voice.

"These must be the mental planes, the places of mind!", Forkbraid stated boldly.

"Incorrect, Forkbraid, incorrect", the voice replied in the negative.

"Well, it's certainly not heaven, nor any of the fairy or gandharva realms", Forkbraid remarked pointedly.

"No, it is not. You have already stated that this place is not among the astral planes", the voice reminded Forkbraid.

"Then where the hell am I?", Forkbraid demanded.

"You already know", the voice replied.

"So you keep saying. You are not helping at all", Forkbraid told the voice.

"You are, where I am, Forkbraid", the voice replied.

Forkbraid considered that one statement for a long time.

It was as if an eternity had passed once more.

Where was Folcrom Tafazah? He was dead, three centuries earlier.

"You're dead, but that's not what you mean, is it?", Forkbraid stated.

"Precisely", the voice confirmed; somehow it seemed happier, if that was at all possible.

Forkbraid recalled the lore pertaining to his ancestor and his subsequent death.

Folcrom Tafazah had considered that the hell or the limbo realms for that matter, to be unacceptable places for reincarnation.

Likewise, Tafazah had considered incarnating in a heaven, a fairy, or a gandharva realm, to be acceptable but nonetheless, unsatisfactory, as neither offered one the opportunity to break the cycle of birth and death, with its endless reincarnations.

Even reincarnating on the earthly plane, although acceptable, was not perfect, although it did provide the opportunity to break the cycle of life and death.

Tafazah's ancient saying had been *"Why settle for heaven, when heaven is merely second best! Return to that place from whence all things have come!"*

Lord Folcrom Tafazah had always stated he would not reincarnate, instead he would return to that very certain place. A place that he was said to have visited many times during his life.

"This is the Well-Spring! Nirvana! The mind of the Supreme Deity! God! Call it what you will!", Forkbraid shouted out.

"Yes Forkbraid", the voice replied, *"Finally you understand. This place is beyond all and every possible manifestation."*

"This is the pneuomena from which all phenomena are derived!", Forkbraid shouted out aloud.

"You are correct", the voice replied.

Forkbraid laughed aloud, *"I can do anything here!"*

"Anything you wish for, but be careful what you wish for, you might actually get it. Here that is a real possibility", the voice replied.

Forkbraid flexed his powerful mind. Slowly ripples formed in the vast grey non-sky that was this non-place. The ripples formed into a vast expanse of ocean, rippling with waves. Land formed from the waves and rose higher and higher out of the ocean. Grasses, plants, and trees grew out of the land. Animals appeared, and abundant life began to thrive in this new creation. It was beautiful beyond any comparison.

"I could create entire worlds if I wished", Forkbraid thought to himself.

Forkbraid's new creation collapsed and vanished back into the ripples of nothingness from whence it came. Then the ripples themselves vanished and the vast grey non-sky reappeared in all its grand and glorious nothingness.

Forkbraid flexed his powerful mind once more. Ripples appeared in the grey nothingness, then the ripples began to take form. An entire star field appeared in the grey non-sky. Slowly one star came into focus and approached him. It was an orange, yellow dwarf slightly smaller than the sun.

Around this star was a disk of collapsing dust and gas. In his mind, Forkbraid willed a planet to form in the developing thermally habitable zone of this small star. Low and behold, the gas and dust began to collapse and coalesce, at the exact point Forkbraid had chosen.

Slowly it coalesced, growing into a planetesimal. Forkbraid could see that given time, a habitable world would grow and develop. Life would appear and given enough time, perhaps even sentience.

An entire world would develop, and it would be needing Forkbraid's intimate care and guidance.

Forkbraid, for all intents and purposes, had become a God in his own right.

Realising this, Forkbraid faltered, *"I am not ready for this!"*

The voice that was Forkbraid's ancestor, Tafazah, took over the newly created planetesimal, and it vanished from Forkbraid's mind, along with its Sun and the entire star field around it.

"Just another planet for me to manage", Tafazah thought to himself, *"I'll look after it for him and keep it developing along nicely, until he returns."*

"No, Forkbraid, you are not ready for this", the voice informed him, *"Though you will be given more time."*

"I have to go back don't I?", Forkbraid enquired.

"Isn't that what you wanted?", the voice asked.

"Yes, yes, it is", Forkbraid replied, sadly realising the power he would be giving up.

"Whatever you need, Forkbraid, whatever you need", the voice stated, *"I will be right here watching over you."*

"Yes", Forkbraid replied, *"I understand that now."*

"And, Forkbraid, a piece of my mind will be with you always from now on. My knowledge will be your knowledge, all that I know, you shall know, thou shalt know", the voice trailed off, *"Thou shalt know",* repeating endlessly in Forkbraid's mind.

Forkbraid felt himself descending. Lights began to flash, various coloured balls of light appeared all around him. Sounds began to be heard, loud raucous sounds. The cacophony of light and sound continued growing in intensity, light and sound, light and sound. Noise upon noise and light upon light. All around him was intense, chaotic, discord.

Forkbraid now found himself in a place he recognised. Forkbraid was in the intermediate states, he was between realms. It was the place of choosing, the place where deceased, disembodied souls chose their next incarnations. Usually this required prodding by a cacophony of frightening sights and sounds. The prodding guided by experiential karmic predispositions.

Some who were fortunate, recognised the intermediate states, and they were able to guide themselves to beneficial rebirths. Others, still, far fewer in number, were able to break the cycle of birth and death altogether and exit into the far higher mental realms. Perhaps, even the Well-Spring, that noumena from which all phenomena were derived.

Forkbraid, now knew of the highest realm, beyond all manifest realms, beyond even the mental realms, for he had seen it for himself. For Forkbraid, heaven was a poor second best, he now knew when his time came, he could choose the highest realm of all, the Well-Spring.

Forkbraid's current decision was to return to the life he had not yet finished. The life he had yet to complete, however, with the cacophony of light and sound, it was difficult to see the right path.

"How do I find my body?", Forkbraid thought to himself.

Then his own mind answered and was heard above the cacophony, *"Take the shining path."*

The shining pathway lit up before him and Forkbraid willed himself towards it with all his might. The cacophony of lights and sounds began to fade away and gradually disappeared into the distance, as Forkbraid followed the shining path.

Before him now was the physical reality of which the Earth's solar system was merely a tiny infinitesimally small part. The Milky Way galaxy was spread out before him and he quickly fell towards it. Guided by his own will, Forkbraid quickly spied the Sun, with its encircling retinue of planets. He located the Earth, then a little further out, was a somewhat smaller planet, Mars. Downwards Forkbraid spiralled towards it.

Downward Forkbraid spiralled, spinning faster and faster, then everything went black. From the infinite depths of this blackness, an infinitesimally small pinprick of light was suddenly seen ahead of him. Forkbraid shot towards it at lightning speed. Swiftly, Forkbraid pierced this light and shot back out into familiar territory. Forkbraid's consciousness was now clearly back within his mind.

Looking back the way he'd come, Forkbraid could see the face of his ancestor, Lord Folcrom Tafazah, *He who had asked The Great Question*, that sublime smile still upon his face. The smallest of vortices Forkbraid had just been propelled through, was still momentarily open. Then all of a sudden, a vastness of brilliant golden light propelled itself through that tiny, open vortex. The vortex then quickly snapped shut once more.

It was blinding, the entire bedroom where Forkbraid's immobile body lay, was bathed in brilliant light. So much so that a sleeping Lady Selene was shocked into awakening.

"Was that a dream?", she thought to herself of the golden light.

Forkbraid awoke!

He choked and gagged on his nasal gastric feeding tube. Beside him, his naked woman, the Lady Selene awoke fully and startled by Forkbraid's awakening, she let out a loud scream. Quickly recovering and composing herself, Lady Selene did her best to calm Forkbraid down, as she removed the nasal gastric feeding tube.

Once the nasal gastric feeding tube was removed, Lady Selene grabbed Forkbraid and held him tightly to her breast. Tears of joy erupted from her eyes.

Uncontrolled sobbing began as Lady Selene repeated over and over, "Don't you ever leave me! Don't you ever leave me, Forkbraid!"

Forkbraid, who was still weak from his ordeal, asked with a weak voice, "Was it all a dream?"

Lady Selene, still sobbing, replied, "No. No, my love. You've been unconscious for a week!"

Charlene Fewkes opened the bedroom door and quickly stepped through it, Candy was quickly behind her. The two women had been staying in Selene's apartment, looking after her.

"Forkbraid's awake!", Charlene shouted out loudly.

Candy turned and ran back out of the bedroom shouting, "Forkbraid's awake! Forkbraid's awake! Forkbraid's awake!", her mind transmitting like a beacon.

Friends, family, and colleagues came running from all directions.

Charlene reached for a night gown and quickly covered Lady Selene, knowing that any second the room would be crowded with well-wishers.

It was several hours before Lady Selene and Forkbraid could get a moment's peace. Since his awakening, Lady Selene's quarters had been filled with well-wishers. A constant procession of people, all genuinely happy to see Forkbraid awake once more.

Now the procession was over, Charlene and Candy had chased everyone out declaring, "They need their rest."

Forkbraid had thought to himself, *"Rest! I've just slept for a week!"*

"Where were you, Forkbraid?", Selene asked, "Your mind was completely empty, your consciousness was… It was gone!"

"It's kind of hard to explain, Selene", Forkbraid replied, "I was out of it. Way out of it."

"You certainly were", Selene replied, stating "The doctors wanted to declare you brain-dead."

"That's not what I meant, Selene", Forkbraid answered, "I was beyond... Beyond everything."

Selene looked at Forkbraid with an uncomprehending look.

Forkbraid thought for a moment then simply said softly, "I was in the Well-Spring."

This Selene understood, "You were in the Well-Spring?"

"Yes, the Well-Spring", Forkbraid replied.

"Isn't that where Tafazah went?", Selene asked.

"Precisely", Forkbraid replied, "Tafazah drew me into the Well-Spring."

"I thought only the most powerful Witches could attain that", Selene replied, "And then, only when they pass away. You're still very much alive."

"Yes. I know, Selene", Forkbraid answered, stating "I'm still alive, yes."

"Why you?", Selene asked, "Why of all people did he choose you?"

"He didn't choose me, Selene", Forkbraid replied, "I was merely the one who passed his test."

"His test?", Selene queried.

"The shared memory streams. Combining them was a test. I passed it", Forkbraid answered.

"What was the test for?", Selene questioned.

"Ah. That's a good question", Forkbraid replied, "I've been to the Well-Spring. I know how to get back there too... And everything, everything that Tafazah knew, I now know."

"What do you mean?", Selene queried.

"Just that. Everything that Tafazah knew, everything, all of his knowledge. I have access to it now. All of it", Forkbraid replied.

"All of it?", Selene asked.

"All of it, Selene!", Forkbraid replied, noting, "He left a piece of his essence inside my mind."

"What will you do with it?", Selene enquired.

"Hmm. I don't really know yet", Forkbraid replied, "Whatever I will, I guess."

"It's a funny thing, Selene", Forkbraid stated.

"What is?", Selene asked.

"Tafazah died before the Psychic Academies on Earth were built", Forkbraid replied, continuing, "Yet all of their locations and their blueprints are all in his memories. All of them."

"I don't see how that's possible", Selene told Forkbraid sceptically.

"Possible or not, it's true", Forkbraid replied, "Even the location of the Elysium colony, the blueprints to this Psychic Academy. All of it, it's all in his memories."

"Forkbraid! I chose the locations of both the Elysium colony and this Psychic Academy. I designed this Academy. I had the blueprints drawn up to my specifications", Selene replied.

"Yes, I know you did", Forkbraid replied, adding "But where did you get your inspiration from?"

"I don't know, Forkbraid", Selene replied, her mind began racing, trying to think of her original inspiration, "It was just an idea that I came up with. I ran with it and developed it."

While Selene was still in thought, Forkbraid stated "Shared memory streams, Selene."

"What do you mean?", Selene asked.

"If I'm right, Tafazah's memories have been reasserting themselves over the past three centuries", Forkbraid stated, adding "I think his memory streams have been instrumental in inspiring a great many of our people over the centuries."

"But how, Forkbraid?", Selene queried.

"He had twelve children, Selene, and his children and grandchildren were also prolific. His memory streams were shared among his descendants and over the centuries with many, many other psychics as well. His memories have travelled far and wide."

"But I still don't get it, Forkbraid! How?", Selene asked again.

"Tafazah didn't reincarnate, Selene", Forkbraid replied, explaining "He ascended to the Well-Spring. From there, he can awaken any memory he so wishes, when he decides the time is ripe."

"And in the right person, the awakened memory brings inspiration", Selene continued the thought.

"Precisely, my darling, precisely", Forkbraid nodded in agreement to Selene's statement.

"Just how much influence has he had?", Selene asked, as she realised the potential for guidance.

Forkbraid frowned, he knew the answer, "A hell of a lot, Selene, a hell of a lot."

"And you know, because you know what he knows?", Selene asked as the penny finally dropped.

"Yes, Selene. I know, because I know what he knows", Forkbraid confirmed.

Selene sat back and considered the ramifications, "Give me another example."

"No, Selene, I shouldn't", Forkbraid replied, "He's weaved a lot into the tapestry. I must be careful how much I divulge, it could just as easily all unravel."

"Just one more example. You know I'll keep it to myself", Selene requested.

"The Venusian cloud resorts and the Venusian cloud cities", Forkbraid replied.

"Now I know that can't be right. That entire concept pre-dates Tafazah", Selene replied.

"Yes, the concept does, but nonetheless it was his memories that awoke and inspired their eventual development", Forkbraid explained.

"But why? What was so important about cities and cloud resorts on Venus?", Selene enquired.

"It's not the cities and the cloud resorts themselves, Selene. It's about the pollution they produce", Forkbraid replied.

"I don't get it. Pollution? Considering Venusian conditions are more like hell than anything else, why would anyone worry about pollution?", a confused Selene asked.

"The biological pollutants are adapting to the Venusian environment, Selene", Forkbraid responded, explaining "Given enough time, they'll potentially terraform the entire planet!"

"He's terraforming Venus?", Selene asked.

"Yes, he is, ever so slowly mind you", Forkbraid replied, adding "And nobody knows about it! Nobody! Nobody knows!"

"Tell me another, Forkbraid", Selene requested

"Selene. You said just one. Now you're taking liberties", Forkbraid replied.

"I know I did. Just one more! Only one! I promise", Selene requested again.

"Okay, okay", Forkbraid replied, "This is the last one. No more after this."

"Okay what is it?", Selene asked.

"Star ships", Forkbraid replied.

"What do you mean star ships?", Selene enquired.

"I have the complete specifications to a star ship in my mind", Forkbraid replied, "Tafazah designed it when he was a teenager. He wants me to build it."

"You're going to build a star ship, Forkbraid?", Selene asked sceptically.

"Yes, I am, as a matter of fact", Forkbraid replied, adding "But not just yet, that's for the future."

"Well, just so as you know, Forkbraid, wherever you fly it, I'll be going with you. And No! You don't have a choice in that. No choice whatsoever!", Selene informed him.

27. Aurorae Two — The Light of Troth

Lord Folcrom Forkbraid was seated at a large round table. On his right was Lady Selene, on his left was Special Agent Murphy. Captain Carmichael sat across the table from them. To the right of Lady Selene were Charlene and Marcus. To the left of Special Agent Murphy were Cormac and Candy Farmer. An agitated Varak did not sit, he preferred to stand.

"We have the anti-aircraft batteries in place", Captain Carmichael stated, "If they come back here, they'll be facing a ring of certain death."

"True enough", Special Agent Murphy agreed, "They have the latest targeting systems. They will be formidable."

Forkbraid nodded, "We should have done this in the first place. It would have saved lives."

"They got through last time!", Varak spat out.

"We only had eight batteries last time, Varak", Special Agent Murphy replied, adding "Now we have three times as many."

"Yes, but will it be enough?", Varak questioned, his large hands pressed against the table as he leant over his empty chair.

"That is also my concern, Varak", Lady Selene added.

Captain Carmichael replied, "Their Raider's wouldn't have made it as far as the airfield if we'd had this many batteries in place."

"And we can be sure of this, Captain?", Lady Selene questioned.

Varak nodded, also wanting to know the answer.

"Yes, Lady Selene", Captain Carmichael replied, "You can be sure of it."

Varak shook his head, "My Lady. It is not enough."

"Varak, I have a Heavy Cruiser orbiting right above us. We have two dozen antiaircraft batteries set up in the meadows out there. You have ten Wisps ready to launch at a moment's notice. I assure you, if they come back, you'll wipe them out", the Captain replied.

"Not to mention our psychics will be much better prepared in the event of another attack", Forkbraid added.

"It is still not enough!", Varak insisted.

Forkbraid sat back in his chair, he folded his arms behind his head, "You're right, Varak. It's not enough, it will never be enough."

"Forkbraid!", Captain Carmichael protested, "We can handle anything they throw at us!"

"For now, yes, Captain", Forkbraid replied, adding, "But they will come back. They'll bide their time, they'll rebuild their forces and then, then they'll be back."

"It makes no difference. We can handle them", the Captain insisted.

Forkbraid brought his arms forward once more and rested them on the table, "The Spartan can't stay in orbit indefinitely, Captain. And this, this is a Psychic

Academy, not a real fortress. At some point life has to return to normal."

"I'll keep my ship here for as long as it takes", the Captain replied.

"And if Colonial Central Command orders you back to L-Five?", Forkbraid enquired.

Forkbraid was right, the Captain knew it, "Then we'll cross that bridge if and when we get to it."

"You have to take the fight to the enemy", Cormac told them.

"Cormac's right! You can't sit around waiting for them, you have to take the fight to the enemy", Candy added, backing up her husband.

"Forkbraid has already told me where they are Cormac", the Captain replied, adding "If I send in the colonial troops, it will be a bloodbath. Collateral damage would be extremely high."

"There is a way, Captain", Cormac replied, "I've already discussed this with Forkbraid. You can get your colonial troops into New Tortuga without them being seen."

"Is this true, Forkbraid?", the Captain asked.

"Yes. There's a back way into New Tortuga, Captain", Forkbraid replied, "Cormac and Candy know the way in."

"That changes things", the Captain replied, "Once I have the details, I'll have my tactical officers run some simulations. We may yet send in our colonial troops."

"There is another issue to deal with as well", Forkbraid informed the Captain.

"Another issue?", the Captain enquired.

"The Aurorae Colony", Forkbraid replied.

"Ah, yes. You did say it was crawling with militants", the Captain replied nodding, "From what I've learned from Aurorae's security personnel, the old quarter is largely a lawless place. Apparently, it always has been."

"That's exactly it", Forkbraid replied, informing them, "It's not so much a fundamentalist issue, as it is a criminality issue."

"I'm not that sure I understand, FB", Special Agent Murphy stated, "When we were in the Aurorae colony, they pretty much seemed hell-bent on killing you."

"True enough, Jim", Forkbraid replied, "But most of the attackers were simply being paid. The credits were too good for them to say no. There were only a few true believers amongst them. They were the ones pulling the strings."

Captain Carmichael sat in thought for a few moments before answering, "Criminals or fundamentalists, we have to eliminate them."

"I'm not so sure, Captain", Forkbraid replied.

"Not so sure?", Special Agent Murphy questioned, "What are you thinking, FB?"

Lady Selene had been carefully following the conversation. Suddenly it dawned upon her what Forkbraid had in mind.

"You can't be serious, Forkbraid?", Lady Selene asked.

Special Agent Murphy looked over to Lady Selene confused, "What have I missed?"

"Forkbraid is going to go back to the Aurorae colony's old quarter. He's going to try to influence them", Lady Selene replied.

"Influence them?", Captain Carmichael enquired.

"Convince them to surrender", Lady Selene explained.

All eyes turned to Forkbraid.

"That was the general idea", Forkbraid told them.

"That's madness!", Lady Selene exclaimed, "It will be another bloodbath, just like the last one."

"I'm not so sure, Selene", Forkbraid replied, noting, "At Aurorae… When I ended the battle last time… There was a moment!"

"A moment!", Lady Selene exclaimed, "Forkbraid! I don't want you taking any more risks!"

"I'm serious, Selene", Forkbraid replied, "When I ended the battle last time, there was a moment… A moment when they all stopped firing… I could feel the relief in their minds… They were glad it had stopped!"

"So you're just going to drop yourself into another bloody meat grinder, just because you felt a moment?", Lady Selene questioned, transmitting telepathically, *"I don't want to lose you again, Forkbraid!"*

Forkbraid felt Selene's concern, *"You won't lose me"*, he transmitted back before replying, "I can sway them, Selene. I can make them surrender!", adding just a few moments later, "Most of them anyway. Some of them are hard core."

"And what will you do with the ones that don't surrender?", Selene asked.

"I was going to cross that bridge when I got to it", Forkbraid replied.

Lady Selene sighed and shook her head, transmitting *"You take too many risks, Forkbraid!"*

"Calculated risks, Selene. Carefully calculated risks", Forkbraid transmitted back.

"So how is this going to work?", Captain Carmichael asked.

"Well, it's really quite simple", Forkbraid replied, "Jim and I will fly into the Aurorae Colony's old quarter, and we'll land our Hummer on its new pier."

"Thanks for volunteering me, FB", Special Agent Murphy remarked.

"You're welcome, Jim", Forkbraid replied, continuing, "I'll get out of the Hummer and confront the militants, getting as many as I can to throw down their weapons and surrender."

"And after they've surrendered?", Captain Carmichael asked.

"We'll notify the Aurorae colony's security and police forces in advance",

Forkbraid replied explaining, "The police can arrest the militants after they've surrendered."

"Seems all very simple, assuming you can convince them to surrender", the Captain replied, "But as Lady Selene just asked. What about the ones that don't surrender?"

"Well, they will be a bit of a problem. Captain", Forkbraid replied, "But remember, it can't be any worse than the last time, can it?"

Special Agent Murphy leant towards Forkbraid and reminded him, "FB, there were well over a hundred deaths last time."

Forkbraid leant back into his chair, "There will be a lot less this time!", he assured him.

"How can you be sure?", Marcus, who up until now had been silent, asked.

"Last time I didn't give them the option to surrender", Forkbraid replied, "This time I will!"

"And you're sure this will work?", Lady Selene asked.

"Well no, quite frankly", Forkbraid replied, "There's nothing certain about it at all. It's just… There was that moment!"

"Forkbraid, you're just taking another risk!", Lady Selene exclaimed.

"Selene, it's an option. I have to try it", Forkbraid replied, before commenting, "If I don't, the alternative is far worse."

"What could possibly be far worse?", Lady Selene asked rather loudly.

Captain Carmichael answered for Forkbraid, "Sending in the colonial troops and hunting them down house by house."

Forkbraid put his hands up in front of him, "And there you have it!"

"Collateral damage would be very high", Captain Carmichael continued, "House to house, close quarters combat usually has that trait."

"You see, I have to try it!", Forkbraid insisted.

"Now… What about this back way into New Tortuga?", the Captain enquired.

"There's a hidden cave system that leads into the back of New Tortuga", Cormac replied, "Nobody knows about it, except for me and mine."

"So what? We just land our colonial troops at the cave entrance and march them in?", the Captain asked incredulously.

"No. That won't do at all", Cormac replied, "New Tortuga's got defences. They'll see you coming. We have to plan this out carefully"

"Then how, Cormac?", the Captain asked.

Cormac smiled, "On Hebes Island… The north side… There's a little town called Sweetness."

"Sweetness?", Special Agent Murphy enquired, "It's not on any map that I've ever seen."

"Most of the towns and villages on Mars aren't", Cormac replied.

"So, what about this town called Sweetness?", the Captain asked.

"You have your drop-ships fly low. Under the radar so to speak", Cormac replied, adding "Land them near Sweetness. It's a blind spot on New Tortuga's defences."

"A blind spot? How so?", Special Agent Murphy enquired.

"Sweetness is special", Cormac informed them.

"Oh, yes. Sweetness is a very special place", Candy added.

Forkbraid smiled a knowing smile.

Cormac continued, "From Sweetness, you can have your colonial troops march overland to the mouth of the cave system. Those evil sligs at New Tortuga won't even know you're coming."

"Okay", the Captain nodded, "So far so good. What happens next?"

Cormac smiled at the Captain, "Well, we are going to need a few Witches. Ones that know the lay of the land."

"Witches that know the lay of the land?", the Captain queried.

"Yeah, but that's okay. We'll pick them up along the way", Cormac replied without elaborating.

"I'll explain the rest of the plan to you when we get there, Captain", Forkbraid told him.

"So you have a plan then, Forkbraid?", the Captain asked.

"Oh, yeah", Forkbraid replied, "We'll flesh it out properly when we get to Sweetness."

"Very well then", the Captain replied, "But just so as you know, my colonial troops won't be going anywhere until I approve it."

Forkbraid nodded, "I wouldn't have it any other way, Captain."

"First things first, Jim and I will go to the Aurorae colony's old quarter and deal with the militant problems there. Selene, I want you to go to Sweetness with Cormac and Candy. Take the Captain with you. As soon as I've dealt with the militants at Aurorae's old quarter, Jim and I will fly across to Sweetness and meet you there."

"What do you want me to do?", asked Marcus.

"Nothing, Marcus", Forkbraid replied, "You and Charlene will be managing the Academy while we're all gone."

"I'd rather be at your side at the Aurorae colony", Marcus stated boldly.

"That's not your choice to make, Marcus", Forkbraid replied, "You'll be needed here."

"I'm not really qualified to run the Academy", Charlene informed them, "and neither is Marcus."

"That's true", Marcus added, "Neither of us are level nines."

"You only need to be level nine or higher to be part of a Grey Council", Lady

Selene replied, continuing "You guys are more than capable of running things while we're gone."

Forkbraid nodded in agreement.

"Varak, how are the repairs going?", Forkbraid asked.

"Coming along fine, although we could speed things up if we had more droids", Varak replied.

"Requisition as many androids as you need from the Elysium colony", Forkbraid recommended.

"Will they not need them down there?", Varak enquired.

"Of course, they will, Varak", Forkbraid replied, "However, they are needed up here first. The Elysium colony is manned by a skeleton staff at the moment. Nearly all the civilian population is actually up here in the Academy."

"Rebuilding our Psychic Academy is the priority, Varak", Lady Selene commanded.

"I will requisition the extra droids straight away, my Lady", Varak replied, and then he briskly walked out of the room.

"Good then", Forkbraid stated as he stood up, "We all know what we need to do. Jim, I'll meet you down by the Hummer in sixty minutes."

"Sixty minutes. Not a problem, FB", Special Agent Murphy replied as he stood up and walked to the door.

"We all know where we need to be, people", Forkbraid reminded everyone as he walked out the door behind Special Agent Murphy.

"I'll arrange for my Hummer to be refuelled", Captain Carmichael told the others.

"It'll need to be a long range Hummer", Cormac advised the Captain.

"It is Cormac", the Captain replied, adding, "I assume you have the co-ordinates for that town called Sweetness."

"That we do, Captain, that we do", Candy replied in place of her Husband.

"As Forkbraid said, sixty minutes", the Captain told them, "I'll meet you all downstairs."

With that, Captain Carmichael stood up and walked out of the room.

"We'll check on the little one before we go", Candy said, referring to Miranda, then she told her Husband, "Come along, Cormac."

Cormac and Candy both stood up and quickly vacated to the room.

"Well then, that leaves me", Lady Selene stated as she stood up.

"Don't worry, Selene, we'll take care of everything while you're away", Marcus reassured her.

"I know you will", Selene replied, adding, "Just two little extras though. Make sure Miranda and her family are safe. And keep an eye on Roseanne, make sure she doesn't do anything silly."

"Silly?", Charlene queried.

"Yeah, silly", Selene replied, "You know. If you tell her to do something, make sure she does it."

Charlene remembered Roseanne's actions on the battlements, "I think I know what you mean."

With that Lady Selene followed the others out the door.

"Well then, it's official, we are in charge", Charlene told Marcus.

Before heading down to the Hummer, Forkbraid caught up with Varak in the Psychic Academy's communications room. Varak had just finished requisitioning an extra fifty androids from the Elysium colony.

"Varak, I have a little task for you", Forkbraid called out as he entered the room.

Varak looked up, "And what would that be?"

Forkbraid pulled out a data crystal. It had taken Forkbraid hours the night before to collate the data and store it in the crystal. Forkbraid handed the data crystal to Varak.

Varak stared at the crystal before placing it in the crystal reader.

"What is this then?", Varak asked.

Forkbraid sat down beside Varak and brought the blueprints up onto the screen.

"It is a ship!", Varak exclaimed, and then he looked more closely at the designs, "It has a basic disk, and sled design."

"Yeah, but there's a bit more to it than that, Varak", Forkbraid replied as he pointed out some of the ship's key features.

"Is that what I think it is?", Varak enquired.

"Yep. That's exactly what it is", Forkbraid replied.

"You do know that nobody has ever managed to get one to work", Varak told Forkbraid.

"Well, that statement is actually incorrect", Forkbraid replied, "The inventor of the Searl levity disk actually made several working prototypes."

"I find that very hard to believe", Varak stated, and then asked, "How did he solve the problem with the alignment of the electromagnets, and they're interoperability?"

"He didn't", Forkbraid replied, then adjusted the view screen to show more details.

Varak looked more closely at the levity disk's detailed blueprint, "Where is the circuitry? It has no internal circuitry?", he asked.

Forkbraid didn't answer, he simply smiled.

"I can see the major control circuits. I can see the electro-magnetic components, but where is the circuitry for the electro-magnetics? It is missing",

Varak asked again.

"There isn't any, Varak. That's why you can't see it. Those aren't electromagnets, they are permanent magnets", Forkbraid informed him.

"Permanent magnets?", an astonished Varak queried.

"Yes, Varak, permanent magnets", Forkbraid confirmed, and then adjusted the view of the blueprints to show the interior of the twin under-wing mounted nacelles.

Varak looked closely at the nacelles. They contained a series of cones, seven in all, each aligned one after the other along the length of each nacelle. Apart from circuitry to control their activation and interlocking, no other circuitry was present.

"Permanent magnets again?", Varak queried incredulously.

"The Hamel thruster variant uses permanent magnets as well, Varak", Forkbraid confirmed.

"How the hell will this thing fly?", Varak asked, not believing the blueprints were serious.

"This ship has the ability to fly just like any other ship", Forkbraid replied as he called up other components onto the screen.

"You see, Varak, it has seven antigravity lifters. It has in-wing mounted electromagnetic drive units and in-wing mounted fusion thrusters", Forkbraid explained.

"Then why does it need those other esoteric components?", a confused Varak enquired.

"Those other esoteric components as you called them, Varak, react with rotating gravitational masses, and planetary, stellar and galactic magnetic fields", Forkbraid informed Varak.

"I don't get it", Varak stated.

"And neither did anyone else who saw those designs, Varak", Forkbraid replied, explaining, "The processes are not well understood at all. It's something that has to be taken on faith."

"On faith?", Varak questioned incredulously, "A ship that flies on faith!"

"I'll try to explain it for you, Varak", Forkbraid began, "Planets and stars have mass, right. Any mass exerts a gravitational influence on its surroundings, right."

"Planets and stars sit at the bottom of gravity wells", Varak stated in agreement.

"Exactly Varak", Forkbraid continued, "And every direction you approach from, the gravity well appears to be the same, or near enough, right"

Varak nodded.

"Stars have magnetic fields as well, don't they?", Forkbraid asked.

"Planets have magnetic fields as well, if they have a liquefied or molten interior, and they rotate", Varak replied in agreement.

"Exactly, Varak", Forkbraid replied, adding "So you have planets with gravitational fields and magnetic fields. And they rotate."

"That is an over simplified generalisation, but, yes", Varak agreed.

"That rotation creates frame dragging events", Forkbraid began.

Varak cut him off, "That is a theoretical, and I might add, a highly controversial temporal concept. There is no current proof of it at all."

"Bear with me, Varak", Forkbraid requested, and then continued, "Now, planets are embedded within a star's gravitational and magnetic field, and again, there are frame dragging events occurring."

"I am not sure that I follow you, Forkbraid", Varak confessed.

"That's okay, Varak", Forkbraid assured him, "It has to be taken on faith, remember. Anyway, there is an interaction, a turbulence between the greater gravitational and magnetic fields of the star and the lesser gravitational and magnetic fields of its embedded planets. These esoteric components, react with this turbulence and allow a ship to transfer from one point in space-time to another, very, very quickly."

"How quickly?" Varak enquired.

"It's kind of like faster than light, Varak, but not actually faster than light", Forkbraid replied.

"I honestly do not see how you can go faster than light, Forkbraid", Varak shook his head.

"The frame dragging events create temporal distortions that make it possible, Varak, although it's more like a wormhole or a slipstream than true faster than light traversal", Forkbraid replied.

Varak was quiet for a moment before asking, "What about planets that don't have magnetic fields, Forkbraid?"

"Magnetic fields are essential for generating a wormhole", Forkbraid replied, "For the giant planets, Jupiter, Saturn, Uranus and Neptune, it works very well. For the smaller rocky worlds, it's rather hit-and-miss. Earth is no problem, but Mars, Venus, and Mercury lack global magnetic fields. So in our solar system, Earth is the only terrestrial planet we can actually use."

Varak gave him another incredulous look.

Forkbraid adjusted the display and brought up a detailed image from the ship's scanners.

"That module", he said, pointing at the screen, "measures these turbulences. It maps the gravitational and magnetic interactions, identifies the temporal distortions created by frame-dragging events, and calculates the transfer windows."

"Transfer windows?", Varak queried.

"Yes. They're brief regions where space-time becomes unstable enough for the ship to transition from one region of space-time to another. Around the Earth, there are hundreds of these windows every single day. Around Jupiter, there are tens of thousands. Of course, only a small fraction are actually useful for generating a slipstream wormhole."

"What you said about Mars, Venus, and Mercury?", Varak asked.

"They're all heavily constrained," Forkbraid admitted. "Mars has no global magnetic field, so perhaps a dozen transfer windows appear each day, if that. Useful ones would be exceptionally rare. Mercury fares little better. It does possess a weak magnetic field, but its extremely slow rotation means the frequency of usable windows is about the same. Venus is worse still. No global magnetic field and a retrograde rotation make useful windows exceedingly uncommon. Not all terrestrial worlds were created equal, Varak."

"Is that why you included the more conventional propulsion systems?", Varak enquired.

"Exactly. Getting from Earth to Mars is relatively easy. Getting back isn't. Unless you happen to catch a suitable window of opportunity, which would be exceedingly rare, you'd have to rely on more conventional drive systems", Forkbraid confirmed.

"So these exotic components are simply another, much faster means of travel. If they use wormholes, or slipstreams, as you call them, then they are not truly faster-than-light."

Forkbraid smiled before telling Varak, "Oh, they're far more than that. The Sun itself is immersed in the Galaxy's gravitational and magnetic field, just as every other star is. These wormholes, or slipstreams, if you prefer, form tunnels linking distant regions of space. They don't violate relativity; they simply take a shorter path through space-time. They create an elegant solution to the problem of faster-than-light travel, as they aren't actually faster-than- light at all, they are just shortcuts."

Varak frowned, clearly unconvinced. Forkbraid enlarged another section of the display.

"The Sun's own gravitational and magnetic field interacts with the Galaxy's on a much larger scale, far beyond Neptune, near the inner edge of the Kuiper Belt."

Varak continued to stare blankly; he was still not seeing it.

Forkbraid suddenly looked up, "Varak... don't you see?"

Varak shook his head; he really did see it.

"These aren't the blueprints for just any Spacecraft, Varak...", Forkbraid paused for a moment, "They are the blueprints for a Starship."

Varak's eyes widened, "Holy fuck!"

It was several long minutes before Varak could compose himself. Forkbraid waited patiently, while the information sunk into Varak's mind.

"Why are you giving me these blueprints?", Varak finally demanded.

"I know your background, Varak", Forkbraid replied, "Your reputation speaks for itself."

"But a Starship?", Varak queried.

"Varak, I've been told you're the man who can build anything", Forkbraid told him.

"But a star ship, Forkbraid?", Varak repeated.

Forkbraid held his hands up in front of him. He joined his thumbs together and carefully framed Varak's face in the view between his hands.

Forkbraid focused on Varak's face, "Varak, can you build this?", he asked.

Varak turned to the blueprints, he carefully scanned as much of the details as he could. It was many long minutes before Varak answered; he was deep in thought.

"I am going to need a lot of very specialised materials and lots, lots of Polyceramalloy. I will have to smelt that myself. It is not as if I can just procure it… I am going to have to develop some new manufacturing equipment just to put this thing together as well… We are going to need a special construction hangar and an assembly floor… Not to mention industrial scale three-D printers… We will also need a lot more droids… Yes, Forkbraid… I can build this!", Varak replied, but then questioned, "But will it work? Can you even fly it?"

"Varak, you build it", Forkbraid commanded, "And leave everything else to me."

Varak nodded, "I can build this", he repeated with conviction.

Forkbraid smiled, "And, Varak, keep this one quiet. Need-to-know basis. For the moment, that's just you and me."

"Understood, Forkbraid", Varak replied.

"Excellent", Forkbraid stated as he stood up.

"Forkbraid… Where did you get these blueprints?", Varak asked.

"That's a very long story, Varak", Forkbraid replied, "Suffice to say, from a long dead ancestor."

"Long dead ancestor?", Varak questioned, not understanding Forkbraid's reply, "How long?"

"More than three hundred years", Forkbraid replied.

"Really?", Varak queried.

Forkbraid nodded, "Yeah", and then he left the communications room and headed for Captain Carmichael's Hummer.

Candy gave Miranda a huge hug, "Now you take care, little one", she said.

Cormac squatted down beside Miranda, "And be good for your Mother and Father", he stated as he gently squeezed Miranda's nose.

Miranda giggled, "Where are you going?", she asked.

"We're going back over to Hebes Island, to see some kin-folk of ours",

Cormac told Miranda.

"Your Cousin Joseph in Krell?", Miranda enquired.

"Oh no. We're going to another little town on the north side of the island", Cormac replied.

"It's called Sweetness, and we have a lot more Cousins there", Candy explained.

"Are you going to be alright?", Miranda asked.

"Little one, you need not worry about us", Cormac reassured Miranda, "Amongst our kin-folk, we'll be just fine."

Cormac kissed Miranda on the forehead and Candy gave her another huge hug, then they both headed for the door.

"Go on then, Miranda", Peter told his Daughter, "Go and wave goodbye to your Aunt Candy and Uncle Cormac."

Miranda ran out the door and followed Cormac and Candy to the hummer. Peter and Catherine Swann followed, walking slowly behind them.

"Aunt Candy and Uncle Cormac?", his Wife, Catherine, whispered in his ear questioningly.

"Well, yes, Cath. Miranda and Chiron are going to need some Uncles and Aunts, and we don't have a whole lot of relatives out here on Mars, do we now?", Peter explained.

"Fair enough", Catherine replied, adding "They are distant Cousins after all, I suppose."

"Exactly!", Peter exclaimed, adding, "And distant Cousins make excellent Aunts and Uncles."

"Later on, when things have settled down, you know these troubles", Catherine began, "We could always bring my Mum and Dad out here as well."

"I suppose we could, darling", Peter replied, hiding the frown on his face and thinking to himself, *'I was quite enjoying having my in-laws on the other side of the solar system.'*

"I'm sure they'd love it out here", Catherine replied.

"I'm sure they would too", Peter replied, suggesting "We could bring out my parents as well."

"Why not", Catherine replied, adding "I'm sure a lot of our relatives would love to live on Mars."

The Swanns arrived at the hangar just in time to see Forkbraid and Special Agent Murphy take off in one long-range Hummer. Miranda waved at the Hummer as it hovered above the Psychic Academy momentarily, before it sped away to the southwest and disappeared into the distance.

A second long-range Hummer had been prepared. In the hangar behind this Hummer, ten Wisps sat neatly lined up in two rows, waiting for any future attack. On the far right of the Wisps, was Forkbraid's own Bat Wing interceptor. This small squadron was a reassuring sight for the Swanns.

Lady Selene was already inside the second Hummer, as was Captain Carmichael who could be seen at the controls.

Cormac and Candy Farmer were about to climb aboard the Captain's Hummer when Miranda shouted out, "Aunt Candy! Uncle Cormac!"

They both turned around and looked back at the Swann family.

Miranda's salutary shout had caught Candy by surprise, and she had a questioning look upon her face, as she looked back to Miranda's Mother.

Catherine Swann nodded to Candy as she mouthed the words *"Aunt Candy."*

Candy ran back to the Swann family and gave Miranda's Mother a huge hug, "Bless your heart", she said to Catherine as tears began rolling down her cheeks.

Then Candy gave Miranda another huge hug as she told her "You take care now, little one. Your Aunt Candy loves you."

"Why are you crying, Aunt Candy?", Miranda asked.

"Tears of joy, little one, tears of joy. Now you take care", Candy replied as she let go of Miranda and ran back to the Hummer.

Cormac and Candy climbed aboard the Hummer and took their seats. Less than a minute later the Hummer began to slowly ascend. Miranda waved goodbye as the Hummer hovered momentarily above the Psychic Academy, before it too, sped away towards the southwest.

Miranda looked back to her Mother, who was now also crying.

"Why are you crying, Mum?", Miranda asked.

"I don't really know, little one", Catherine Swann replied, "Tears of joy I guess."

Miranda gave her Mother a hug, "You called me, little one."

"So I did, so I did", Catherine replied.

The Swann family then walked back to their apartment.

Special Agent Murphy and Forkbraid had just been communicating with the Aurorae colony's security forces, as their Hummer approached the colony. The chief of security had thought they were both mad. An L-Five Special Agent and a psychic from Earth, telling him they were going to make the criminal gangs in the old quarter hand in their weapons and give themselves up. It was completely ludicrous, but they had been quite insistent.

At first the chief of security had refused their request for, *"As many men and vehicles as would be necessary to pick up and transport the criminals for processing."*

He was certain it was some kind of joke. Then an image appeared on his communications screen. It was the [73]Psi Corps crest. No mistaking it, the ornate

---

73 Psi Corps, the name of the organisation responsible for organising and controlling the remote viewing teams.

crest with three symbols emblazoned in red, flanked by a dragon and a gargoyle. He had only ever seen it once before and that was many years ago in a manual, during his security training. That manual hadn't done it justice. The crest bore deeply into the security chief's mind. He became totally compliant.

A now far more compliant security chief had accepted their requests. As many men and vehicles as would be necessary, were made available and on stand by. They were prepared and stationed just outside the old quarter of the colony, ready and waiting. The security officers and police involved were all fully armed, but only told to expect the peaceful surrender of a great many troublemakers. Like that was ever going to happen.

Special Agent Murphy carefully controlled the descent of their Hummer. The new pier was wide enough and strong enough to land on, nonetheless the landing would still be tricky. No ships were berthed at the pier and very few people, mainly dockworkers, were about. The Hummer landed with a gentleness that showed the true skill of its pilot.

Forkbraid climbed out of his seat and walked over to the hatch.

"FB", Special Agent Murphy called out, "No meat grinders today."

Forkbraid smiled a wry smile, replying "Hopefully not, Jim", as he stepped out onto the pier.

Forkbraid routinely scanned the minds of the folk on or in the vicinity of the pier. Not much was happening, things were relatively calm.

One man had thought, *"Oh no not again"*, upon seeing Forkbraid and had quickly taken cover.

As a precaution, Forkbraid reached into his robe and pulled out his staff from his impossible pocket. He tossed the staff behind him as usual, and it followed him obediently as Forkbraid strolled casually down the pier.

As quiet as the day was, word spread quickly and before Forkbraid had reached the halfway mark along the pier, many more people had appeared in the waterfront streets. Forkbraid scanned the mind of these newcomers. Many of the onlookers were merely curious, they'd scatter if any trouble started. Some were more than curious, they had crawled out of the wood work looking for round two and their numbers were growing. They were also armed.

As Forkbraid scanned the growing numbers of onlookers, he found many in the crowd were armed with guns, rifles hidden under coats, pulsed plasma pistols and other assorted weaponry. The curious onlookers were now clearing the waterfront, leaving only those that were spoiling for a fight. They had lost many of their comrades in the last battle and revenge was clearly on their minds. By the time Forkbraid had reached the foot of the pier, there were well over fifty of them and their numbers were still growing. Forkbraid stopped walking and patiently waited.

"What is he waiting for?", was the thought on many of the minds that Forkbraid scanned.

Forkbraid waited just a little longer, until the number of militants began to stabilise at around a hundred and thirty. Forkbraid considered it both interesting and auspicious that none amongst the gathering army of men had opened fire. He scanned the armed men yet again. There were fewer than ten true believers amongst them. Most of them were frightened, remembering full well what happened the last time. This was that moment. It was happening all over again.

"I am not here to kill you", Forkbraid transmitted his thoughts to his enemies.

One of the militants shouted back, "Then what? Are you here to die?"

Nervous laughter erupted amongst the gathered men.

"I am neither here to die nor kill", Forkbraid transmitted.

Another of the militants shouted, "Then why the hell are you here?"

Forkbraid transmitted to the minds of all those around him, *"The last time I was here, there was too much death. This cycle of death must end."*

"The cycle of death will end when we decide to end it", another amongst the gathered army yelled.

"And that is why I am here. So you can decide to end the cycle of death", Forkbraid transmitted.

Confused chatter started up amongst the gathered men.

Forkbraid silenced the chatter with the thought, *"On the day that so many died, for what purpose had you been gathered?"*

One of the gathered men shouted back, "To kill a demon, hiding in the guise of a child!"

Forkbraid informed the militants, *"Demons do not walk amongst men. You were ordered to murder an eight-year-old girl."*

The same man who had responded shouted, "You lie! You are a demon! You walk among men!"

"I am as human as any of you", Forkbraid responded, *"As is the child you sought to murder."*

The man spoke out again, stepping forward and shouting, "He lies! Shoot him! Kill this demon!"

"And so a true believer steps forth", Forkbraid thought to himself, then transmitting to the crowd, *"The only evil ones here, are the ones who tell you to kill!"*

The armed men looked to their leader, then back to Forkbraid.

Forkbraid shouted deeply into their minds, *"Thou shalt not kill!"*

The armed men did not shoot.

Again their leader shouted, "Shoot him! Kill the demon! Kill him!"

Forkbraid shouted deeply into their minds once more, *"Thou shalt not kill!"*

Another man stepped forward and ran over to their leader. Forkbraid eaves dropped on their conversation.

"Sir, our men are hesitant", the man said to his leader.

"What? You think I can't see that", the leader replied, then shouted once more, "Shoot the demon! Kill him, before he infects you with his lies!"

Forkbraid shouted deeply into their minds once again, *"Thou shalt not bear false witness!"*

The armed men turned to their leader, clear derision upon their faces.

Forkbraid shouted deeply into their minds again, *"Thou shalt not kill!"*

Forkbraid could see the frustration in their leader's eyes.

"Who can we trust?", the leader asked the other man.

"There are a few good men, Sir", the man replied.

Their leader shouted, "Men! You are being tested! You must not let this demon confuse you! We must strike this demon down!"

He raised his pulsed plasma pistol and fired a single shot at Forkbraid.

Forkbraid's shield was instantly raised. The pulse of plasma flew towards Forkbraid, only to explode against his shield in a shower of brilliant blue sparks. The man with the leader then raised his gun and fired. The bullet stalled in mid-flight, fizzled and then dropped to the ground. Several other men amongst the militants stepped forward and fired. More bullets fizzled and dropped to the ground. Forkbraid remained untouched and unharmed.

"You cannot harm me", Forkbraid transmitted, continuing *"Should I wish it, I could kill you all. It is not, it is not my wish! This cycle of death must end! Thou shalt not kill!"*

Their leader screamed at the top of his voice, "Kill him! Kill him, you fools!"

Forkbraid's voice screamed back into their minds, *"Thou shalt not kill! Thou shalt not kill!"*

The armed men looked from one to another in confusion, they fired not, the stand-off held.

Forkbraid searched the surrounding minds. Fear and confusion was ripe. The men did not fire, but it was only a matter of time before all hell broke loose. At some point, the shooting would begin. That path would lead to many deaths. That path must be avoided at all costs.

Forkbraid reached deep into his own mind and there, tucked away in a neat little corner was a small swirl of nothingness. Forkbraid concentrated upon it and it immediately expanded. The face of his long deceased ancestor, Lord Folcrom Tafazah stared back at him.

"I know what you know", Forkbraid said to the face, and then Forkbraid faced the armed men once again, his eyes full of certainty and conviction.

Forkbraid's eyes rolled back. Golden light erupted from Forkbraid's forehead. Spreading out in an expanding sphere. It soon covered the entire waterfront, in front of the pier. All the armed men were encapsulated by the golden light. Not a soul moved. All the armed men stood frozen in fear.

Forkbraid sent out a simple message, *"Fear not!"*

A soothing warmth crept into the armed men, their fear began to wane, and it was soon gone.

A strange feeling of bliss enveloped them, and they found themselves, content.

Forkbraid sent out another simple message, *"This is the golden light of troth!"*

At once, all the armed men turned to look at Forkbraid.

They could see the truth of Forkbraid's words. They could see that he would only harm them, if they tried to harm him or others. Furthermore, they could see a small, young girl with bright blue eyes and long, flowing golden locks. Then they could see an even younger child, the girl's Brother, who was soon followed by the girl's Parents. They were just an ordinary family from L-Five.

The girl was special, they could see this, but she was human nonetheless. The young girl with the golden locks was not a demon. Then they saw Forkbraid once more, different, yes, powerful, yes, but human nonetheless. He was no demon either. The truth was clearly apparent to them all.

As one the group of armed men turned towards their leader. He was sweating profusely. He himself knew he was wrong, he himself knew he was deluded, yet he refused to admit it, even unto himself. This, they could all see. So clearly could they see the lies this man had told them. So clearly could they now discern the truth.

Their leader was a sick, deluded individual who was not to be believed. His lies were infectious, and like a disease they spread, quickly turning good men towards a path of evil. Likewise, the other true believers who stood with him even now. They were the believers of lies.

Then the golden light of troth vanished as quickly as it had emerged.

One by one the armed men threw down their weapons onto the ground in front of them. Guns, pulsed plasma pistols, rifles, knives, and even machetes clattered to the ground.

Their leader screamed out in rage, "What are you doing? Have you all gone mad?"

They didn't listen. Several of the men began to collect the weapons and gather them into a pile.

Their leader scream out again, "You idiots! Pick up your guns! Kill this demon!"

He and his sycophants began to harass the others, waving their guns at them.

Forkbraid used his telekinetic abilities and one by one, he quickly whisked the guns from out of the sycophants hands. These too were dropped onto the pile of discarded weapons. The other men grabbed the sycophants and held them firmly in place. The sick bastards weren't going anywhere.

Then their leader was all alone.

Their leader held his hands to his head as he shouted, "Are you all mad? Are you all insane?"

He marched forward towards Forkbraid and pointed his pulsed plasma pistol at him, point-blank.

He pulled the trigger. The pulse of plasma flew forth and scattered against Forkbraid's shield.

"Damn you! Damn you to hell!", he threw his pulsed plasma pistol at Forkbraid.

Forkbraid pulled it out of the air with his mind and sent it clattering onto the pile with the others.

Forkbraid reached out and touched their leader's forehead, "Sleep", he told him.

Their leader collapsed to the ground in a deep slumber.

One by one Forkbraid walked up to the other true believers. One by one he made them sleep.

Special Agent Murphy watched from their Hummer at the end of the pier through his binoculars.

The situation was under control. It was time for the police to move in.

Special Agent Murphy reached for his communicator and put through the call.

Within minutes dozens of patrol cars poured onto the water front. Prisoner transport vans soon followed. It wasn't long before the Aurorae security and police forces started handcuffing prisoners and taking them to the vans. Forkbraid was careful to point out the ring leaders, the true believers, that needed special treatment.

The chief of Aurorae security approached Forkbraid, "How the hell did you do this?"

"With the light of troth", Forkbraid answered him without elaborating.

"The light of troth?", the chief of security questioned.

Forkbraid did not answer him.

"Well, whatever it is, it's certainly cleaned this lot up", the chief of security stated.

Forkbraid looked over at the pile of discarded weapons and pointed to them, "Don't forget that lot. You ought to have them destroyed."

The security chief nodded to Forkbraid, then walked off to detail a trio of officers to take charge of the weapons. As he did so Forkbraid walked off down the pier towards their Hummer.

As Forkbraid climbed aboard their Hummer, Special Agent Murphy told him, "You're certainly giving me plenty of stories to tell my Grand-kids."

"You don't have any Grandchildren, Jim", Forkbraid reminded him.

"True enough, FB, but when I do, the stories I'll be able to tell them", Jim replied.

Forkbraid smiled at Special Agent Murphy, "Let's go, Jim. The next lot won't be this easy. We can be sure of that."

28. A Town Called Sweetness

Captain Carmichael's Hummer was flying low across the southern reaches of Lunae Planum.

Captain Carmichael was a fair pilot. He flew their Hummer as close to the ground as he could.

"Dusting the fields", is how he'd described it.

They were flying well and truly under the radar.

Much of Lunae Planum was a dust bowl, but that was further to the north. Here in the southern reaches, were vast grass lands and meadows. The winter snows had well and truly melted and the verdant green of early spring growth was now clearly evident everywhere.

Before long Captain Carmichael angled their flight path further to the south. As the tree line of the coniferous forests approached, Captain Carmichael increased their altitude. They were now skimming across the tree tops. Trees here on Mars, with its much lower gravity and higher concentrations of carbon dioxide in the atmosphere, grew considerably taller than they could ever have done on Earth.

Captain Carmichael had reassured them, that as long as they stayed close to the tree tops, New Tortuga's scanners could not pick them up.

Cormac had commented that, "If they flew any closer, they would be able to harvest the pine nuts by simply reaching out the window."

Captain Carmichael had responded by increasing their altitude ever so slightly, but then countered this action by flying down the deeper valleys that led towards the Hebes Sea.

After flying just above the tree tops, the passengers were all greatly relieved when the Hebes Sea became visible in the distance. Their relief was, however, short-lived. As soon as their Hummer crossed the shoreline, Captain Carmichael dropped their altitude once more. Now their Hummer was skimming just above the wave tops, so closely that the spray from the waves was forming rivulets of water running down their Hummer's front windows.

Candy's face has gone through several shades of white, then several shades of green, then back again. Candy had squeezed her husband's right arm so tightly, that deep fingernail marks remained every time she moved her grip. Cormac grimaced every time Candy did so.

Lady Selene preferred not to look out of the windows, having closed her eyes and trying to meditate for much of the last part of the flight. A flight that had resembled the tracks of a roller coaster, far more than any flight plan.

Captain Carmichael seemed completely unperturbed by their lack of altitude, he also seemed completely oblivious to his passengers discomfort.

At one point the Captain had stated, "Skin dancing and surface skimming were a standard part of every colonial fighter pilot's training."

Apparently the Captain was one of the best when it came to skin dancing or surface skimming, having excelled in his original training and having kept his pilots credentials in top order with many hours of flight time. This was hardly reassuring for his passengers.

Captain Carmichael made a beeline for the coordinates that Cormac had given him. As they approached Hebes Island, the Captain slowed the Hummer's flight, ever so slightly.

"Are you sure these are the correct coordinates, Cormac?", the Captain asked.

"They sure are, Captain", Cormac replied.

"I'm not picking up anything on my scanners", the Captain informed him.

"And you won't either, Captain", Cormac told the Captain, adding "Just head straight for those coordinates, and you can't go wrong."

As they approached the Hebes Island coast, a narrow cleft in the cliff face became visible. The coordinates of the town of Sweetness, were just beyond the other side. The Captain flew the Hummer through the middle of the cleft. The cleft was a little over five kilometres long. Towering cliffs soared skywards on either side of them.

"This gap is only about six hundred metres wide", the Captain informed them.

"That's what it's called alright", Cormac replied.

"What that?", the Captain enquired.

"It's called the Gap", Cormac informed The Captain.

"Oh", the Captain nodded.

On the other side of the Gap was a large, almost circular bay. Towering cliffs hid the bay completely from the sea. The bay was lined with broad sandy beaches. A fair sized valley sat at the rear of the bay. Green rolling hills covered with pastures and forests filled the valley. Towering cliffs could be seen further in the distance. They almost completely encompassed the valley.

"I can see why you'd call this place Sweetness", the Captain remarked.

To which Cormac replied, pointing to the east of the bay, "Speaking of Sweetness."

The Captain adjusted their course slightly to the east and shortly thereafter, the small township of Sweetness suddenly appeared before them. Behind the township, were rolling hills covered with crop fields, vineyards, and orchids. The entire scene was picturesque and beautiful.

"Funny", the Captain remarked, "There's still nothing showing on my scanners at all."

"Yet there it is, Captain", Cormac replied with a wry smile on his face.

Lady Selene looked carefully at the fast approaching township.

Carefully scanning with her mind, Lady Selene remarked, "Oh my. Oh my, oh my."

"What is it?", the Captain asked.

Lady Selene smiled, "You can't see them on your scanners, Captain, because they're hiding from us. The whole town, in fact."

"Hiding? From us?", the Captain questioned.

"Not so much us in particular", Lady Selene replied, explaining, "They're just hiding in general."

"Why? Why are they hiding?", the Captain enquired.

"Sweetness", Lady Selene paused, "is a town full of psychics."

"What!", the Captain exclaimed.

"Sweetness is a town full of psychics, Captain", Lady Selene told him again.

Cormac laughed out loudly, then stopped suddenly as Candy gripped his arm.

"Captain, we'd better pull over", Cormac recommended.

"Pull over?", the Captain asked, "Why? Where?"

"Over there on that spit of land", Cormac pointed towards the coast and a nearby spit of land, adding "You'd better be quick, unless you feel like cleaning up a whole mess of puke."

Captain Carmichael quickly manoeuvred their hummer over to the spit of land and then landed as quickly as he could. Cormac quickly helped his Wife out of the Hummer's hatch. Less than half a minute later they were all treated to the sounds of a technicolour yawn in full progress. Candy was extremely ill, courtesy of their roller coaster flight path. It was several more minutes before Candy could compose herself.

Cormac helped Candy to her feet. By now Lady Selene had also climbed out of their Hummer and was helping Candy as well. Captain Carmichael climbed out their Hummer and walked over to his three passengers.

"We have company", he told them.

They all looked up and followed the Captain's gaze. Where the spit of land connected to the beach, was a small delegation of townsfolk. Lady Selene, ever cautious, reached into her robes and pulled her staff out from its impossible pocket. Casually, Lady Selene tossed her staff behind her, where it hovered obediently. Reaching into her impossible pocket once more, Lady Selene pulled out her wand, Gnomulus. Astonished gasps arose from the small delegation on the beach.

Candy reached for Lady Selene's hand and held it gently, "It okay, Cousin. These are friends of ours", she said reassuringly.

The small delegation of two men and one woman approached. They were dressed in the same fashion as any country folk on Mars. Nothing about them stood out, they seemed quite ordinary. Yet there was not the slightest hint of fear in their eyes. They seemed very confident in their approach.

"We know you, Candy Farmer. We know your Husband, Cormac, as well. These other two, are unknown to us", the closest of the delegation accused them.

He was a tall man, quite old, with thin wispy grey hair with silver streaks.

The woman stepped forward. Like the tall man, she was quite old. Her long hair was completely grey.

The old woman scolded, "This other man is not one of the gifted. Nor was he born here on our world. This man does not belong here, Cormac Farmer!"

"It was necessary to bring him", Cormac replied defiantly, adding "Machinations are afoot."

The old woman ignored Cormac and turned to Lady Selene, "You girl! What manner of creature are you? I look into your mind and all I see is myself, looking back at me."

"It's a defensive measure", Lady Selene replied, explaining "My mind is a mirror to those who would peak without my invitation."

The old woman cooked an eyebrow and looked to her companions, *"Gifted and well-trained"*, was the thought she transmitted.

One of the other men, several inches shorter than the tall man and somewhat more rotund, remarked, "The girl does not even try to conceal what she is!"

"I can see that, Gareth", the old woman replied questioning, "Girl, you dress like a Witch. You use the gifts of a Witch. Yet you don't even try to conceal what you are?"

"I have never seen the need to conceal who and what I am", Lady Selene told them as she retrieved her staff and replaced both it and her wand, Gnomulus, back into her impossible pocket.

"You're not from around here, are you, Girl?", the old woman asked.

"No as a matter of fact I'm not", Lady Selene replied, adding, "I am from Earth."

"And Him? Where is He from?", the old woman asked.

Captain Carmichael answered, "I am Captain Carmichael, from Colonial Central Command at L-Five in Cis-Lunar space."

"Your words match your mind, Captain", the tall man replied, "No hint of deception in your voice whatsoever."

Cormac stepped forward, pointing out the tall man, introducing him, "This is Cadmus, he's the town's Chief Elder."

Cormac then pointed to the old woman and introduced her, "This is Mystal, another of the town's Elders."

Cormac finally pointed to the other man and introduced him, "This is Gareth, he's also one of the town's Elders."

Cormac turned to Lady Selene and Captain Carmichael, "As you can see, they're not really keen on strangers around these parts."

"And for good reason, Cormac, reasons you know very well", Mystal, the old woman scalded.

Cormac nodded, then introduced Lady Selene, "This Lady Folcrom Selene from the Flinders Psychic Academy on Earth."

Almost at once, the atmosphere seemed to change and the stern looks became far softer smiles.

"Greetings, Lady Selene", Cadmus stated warmly, continuing "Welcome to our humble refuge. We call it Sweetness."

"Thank you, Cadmus", Lady Selene replied, "I wish we were here for a pleasurable visit, unfortunately as Cormac mentioned, there are machinations afoot."

"Yes", Cadmus replied, continuing "But this is not the place to discuss… machinations."

"No, it's not", Gareth agreed, "Climb aboard your craft and fly it into town. Land at the back of the town hall. We'll meet you there."

"My Wife will need to freshen up", Cormac told them.

"Yes", Lady Selene added, "It has been a rather unpleasant flight."

"There was nothing wrong with my flying", Captain Carmichael disagreed.

"True enough, Captain", Lady Selene replied, "Your flying was perfect, although our stomachs unfortunately do disagree with you."

"I run an Inn near the town hall", Mystal informed them, "You can freshen up there. Cormac and Candy know where it is."

"We are expecting another Hummer to arrive", Captain Carmichael informed them.

"Another Hummer?", Cadmus queried.

"Yes", Lady Selene answered, "It will have two occupants. Special Agent James Murphy from Colonial Central Command at L-Five and Lord Folcrom Forkbraid from the Flinders Psychic Academy on Earth."

As the last name-dropped, three sets of eyes opened widely.

"The heir of he who asked The Great Question?", Cadmus queried telepathically.

Cormac answered him, "Yes, Cousin… And he's coming here today."

"These are indeed auspicious times", the old woman, Mystal remarked.

"Auspicious, yes", Gareth agreed, "But let us not forget who Lord Forkbraid is."

"Too true, Gareth. Auspicious times indeed, but I suspect dangerous times as well", Cadmus stated in agreement.

Lady Selene nodded in agreement as well, "Machinations are afoot and these are indeed dangerous times."

Special Agent Murphy had flown his Hummer low and fast over Ophir

Planum. This was all high plateau country. Snow and ice were still visible on the ground. Spring was yet to take hold at these altitudes. This was a dry country and once the ice and snow finally melted, the scant spring rains would be insufficient to quench these dry and rocky plains. As Ophir Planum dropped behind them in the distance, Forkbraid had commented on how the environmental niches of Mars would in time be as numerous and varied as those on the Earth itself.

They passed over a deep, flooded chasm, not unlike the Hebes Chasma, although somewhat larger. Special Agent Murphy had adjusted their course, more to the west, and they were soon flying low over high plateau country once more. It was still a relatively dry landscape, although here and there to the south, scattered stands of conifers could be seen. How far the tree line would eventually extend into these dry lands was yet to be seen.

The scattered stands of trees gradually grew more numerous and larger, until they were flying over forests, with numerous well grassed clearings. Special Agent Murphy flew swiftly, but safely across the tree tops. Eventually the grassy clearings became fewer and fewer, and then thick forests covered the lands beneath them as far as the eye could see.

They flew across the Hebes Sea from the east, skimming just above the wave tops as Captain Carmichael had previously done. Special Agent Murphy had been studying and memorising maps of Mars during his time aboard the Spartan on the flight out from Cis-Lunar L-Five to Mars.

"Over on the far western end, the Hebes Sea has an outflow", Special Agent Murphy remarked.

"An outflow?", Forkbraid enquired.

"Yeah. There's a river on the western end. It flows over hummocky country. Lots of water falls. Some of them are apparently quite high. Then it flows into Echus Chasma before turning north. The river becomes quite wide and splits into several tributaries. Flat, marshy country for hundreds of kilometres. It's one huge swampland, the Swamps of Kasei Valles, it's almost two-thousand kilometres of swampland."

Special Agent Murphy swung their hummer slightly to the north as Hebes Island appeared on their port side. It wasn't long before the cleft in the cliffs appeared' and Special Agent Murphy swung their Hummer through the Gap, flying low over the water with towering cliffs on either side.

"Don't expect to see anything on your scanners, Jim", Forkbraid informed him.

"Some sort of jamming device?", Special Agent Murphy enquired.

"You could call it that, Jim", Forkbraid replied, adding, "When the cleft opens up, Sweetness will be slightly to the left on the other side of the bay. I'll point it out."

Special Agent Murphy scanned the far side of the bay. Still nothing appeared on his scanners.

"Whatever they're using to jam my scanners, it sure works", Special Agent Murphy noted.

In the direction Forkbraid had pointed to, a small and picturesque township suddenly appeared from nowhere. One second there was nothing ahead of them, then all of a sudden it was there.

Special Agent Murphy looked at Forkbraid, then looked back at the town once again, "What in the blue blazes?"

"It's alright, Jim", Forkbraid assured him, "They're using psychic subterfuge to hide their town. We in the trade, call it a glamour."

"A glamour?", Special Agent Murphy queried, "How the hell does that work?"

"In your mind, you would have had an image of the township and its surroundings", Forkbraid explained, "They simply overlaid that image with an image of pristine wilderness. It obscures the truth, hides them from untrained eyes."

"So you could see them all along", Special Agent Murphy asked.

"Sure, Jim. Anyone who's had psychic training would have seen through their glamour."

A few minutes later Special Agent Murphy had their Hummer hovering above the small township of Sweetness. Forkbraid directed him towards a fair sized building in the middle of the town. Sitting on the ground at the back of the building was Captain Carmichael's Hummer. Special Agent Murphy settled his Hummer down gently beside it. As they climbed out of the hatch, they both noticed Lady Selene standing at the rear door.

"Gentlemen. So glad you could make it", Lady Selene greeted them, "What took you so long?"

"You know me, darling, I took the scenic route", Forkbraid replied as he walked up and put his arm around her.

"Scenic route. Right. You can tell me all about that later", Selene replied as they entered the hall.

Lady Selene led them into the hall's main meeting room. It appeared the whole town or close to it, had turned out for the meeting. Cormac and Candy Farmer were surrounded, catching up with friends and relatives. Captain Carmichael sat at a large bench with several other individuals. As Lady Selene led Forkbraid and Special Agent Murphy into the room. The Captain waved his hand and called them over.

Captain Carmichael stood up as Forkbraid and Special Agent Murphy approached.

"Forkbraid, this is Cadmus, Gareth and Mystal. They're a few of the town's Elders."

"Pleasure to meet you. I'm Folcrom Forkbraid and this is Special Agent James Murphy."

"Yes, Lady Selene told us that the *heir to he who asked The Great Question* would be coming", Cadmus replied, referring to Forkbraid's ancestor.

"From what the Captain has been telling us, you need our help", Mystal stated.

"To a degree, yes", Forkbraid replied, "New Tortuga, on the other side of the island, has a problem with militant fundamentalists. They've been causing all sorts of issues. A great many people have been killed as a result of their actions. We are aiming to neutralise them."

"Yes, we have heard of this. How can we help you, Forkbraid?", Gareth asked.

"We need a handful of local psychics", Forkbraid explained, "Psychics who have been inside New Tortuga previously."

"What would you have our people do?", Gareth enquired.

"Save lives", Forkbraid stated.

"Save lives?", Mystal questioned.

"Yes. We can get inside New Tortuga. We can deal with the militants", Forkbraid paused for a moment, "However, we need to get the innocent people out first, before we move in."

"You want our people to take the innocent folk to safety?", Mystal asked for clarification.

"Yes. That's exactly what we want to do", Forkbraid confirmed, adding "Once the innocent townsfolk are safely out of the way, we can move in with the colonial troops and neutralise the militant fundamentalists."

"Just how are you going to get into New Tortuga?", Cadmus asked.

"Cormac and Candy know of a rear entrance to New Tortuga", Forkbraid replied.

"You mentioned colonial troops", Gareth commented.

"Two drop-ships will be landing from my Heavy Cruiser, The Spartan. They'll be bringing sixteen squads of colonial troops with them", Captain Carmichael informed them.

"Captain… Your drop-ships will not be landing here", Cadmus told the Captain with the sound of finality in his voice.

"We need to bring them in under New Tortuga's scanners", the Captain replied, explaining "Coming through the Gap and landing here, where they can't be detected is the perfect place."

"Nonetheless, we can not allow you to land your colonial troops here", Cadmus was adamant.

"That won't be a problem, Cadmus", Forkbraid informed him.

"How so, Forkbraid?", enquired Cadmus

"We don't need to land the drop-ships in town", Forkbraid replied, explaining "We can land the drop-ships further to the west. Nearer the western mountains, but still within this valley."

"That will work. We'll still be hidden from New Tortuga's scanners, and we'll be closer to that cave system Cormac told us about", the Captain remarked, nodding in agreement.

"And the drop-ships won't even know the town of Sweetness is here", Forkbraid stated.

Cadmus sat in thought for a long moment before asking, "They won't know we're here?"

"You'll be jamming their scanners the same as usual. They won't be coming anywhere near the town itself", Forkbraid assured him.

"In that case, Captain, your drop-ships can land", Cadmus decided, "Just as long as they're nowhere near us."

"Agreed, Cadmus", Captain Carmichael stood up and shook Cadmus's hand.

Cormac and Candy came over to their bench, "We have our volunteers", Cormac informed them.

"Volunteers?", Gareth questioned.

"To go back into New Tortuga and lead the townsfolk to safety", Candy replied.

"We haven't even made a decision on that yet, Candy", Mystal informed her.

"Well then, you'd better get a wriggle on, because we have twelve Cousins all ready, willing and able to help", Candy replied as she placed her hands on her hips, signifying this was a done deal.

Mystal looked at Cadmus and Gareth, "Agreed?", she asked.

"Agreed", they both replied.

"And a good thing too I might say", Candy told them.

"It had to be, people", Cormac told them, explaining "Many of our Cousins were born in New Tortuga, and they still have family there even now."

While Special Agent Murphy was still standing, he looked around the room. He noticed many of the town's folk were staring at Lady Selene and Forkbraid. Those town's folk who weren't staring would glance over at them regularly.

"What gives with the crowd?", Special Agent Murphy asked.

"Look at how they're dressed", Lady Selene instructed him.

Special Agent Murphy looked around the room once again, "They're dressed just like any of the ordinary folk."

"And when you look at Forkbraid or Me?", Lady Selene asked.

"You're both dressed in your normal attire, well normal for Witches anyway", Special Agent Murphy replied.

"Exactly", Lady Selene replied, explaining "This is a town in hiding, Jim. They dress just like ordinary folk here, so that if anyone stumbles upon their town, they won't suspect that it's a town full of Witches. On Mars, Witches aren't as free as they are on Earth. It's unusual for them to see Witches, dressed so overtly as Witches in the open… They are just being curious."

"We prefer the term, Gifted", Mystal informed them.

A young couple approached their bench, the man bowing before Lady Selene and Forkbraid, the woman courtseyed.

"That isn't necessary", Forkbraid assured them.

The man spoke, "Cormac and Candy Farmer were saying that there's a Psychic Academy in Elysium, an Academy for the gifted", the man then nodded to Cormac and his Wife.

Candy introduced the couple, "This is Alaric and his Wife, Elysa."

Lady Selene smiled, "Cormac and Candy spoke correctly, Alaric", before confirming, "There is a Psychic Academy. It's being prepared as we speak. I suppose you could say I'm its head mistress."

"My Wife and I were just wondering", Alaric continued after a brief pause to find his words, "We have two young children. A boy and a girl. They'll be ready for school in a few years."

"And you were wondering, when we'd be ready for enrolments", Lady Selene answered.

"Yes, that's right", Alaric replied, with a hopeful smile on his face.

"We still have a lot of work to do before we'll be ready for enrolling students", Lady Selene informed them both.

The smile on Alaric's face dropped slightly, his Wife, Elysa squeezed his hand, "If they're not ready, Alaric, then they're not ready", she told him.

"How old is your oldest?", Lady Selene enquired.

"Our Son, Jarred, he's nearly two", Elysa replied.

"Then we have three, perhaps four years to be ready", Lady Selene told them, adding, "That should be plenty of time."

Alaric's smile picked up once more, Elysa smiled broadly as well.

"Assuming everything goes well, we'll have our Academy in order in two years and be ready for taking enrolments in the third. Our first classes will open in four years", Lady Selene decided.

Alaric and Elysa hugged each other, then turned back to Lady Selene, "Thank you, my Lady", they both said almost in unison.

"We'll keep in touch with your town's Elders and advise how and when to apply for enrolment", Lady Selene told them, adding "Let your family and friends know. Pass the word around."

"Yes, we will do that. Thank you ,my Lady", Alaric replied and then led his Wife back into the crowd of gathered townsfolk.

"More Cousins?", Special Agent Murphy smiled as he asked Cormac.

"Well, yes, actually", Cormac replied, adding, "Alaric is the Son of my third Cousin Jarred."

Candy then added, "And Elysa is the Daughter of my second Cousin, Alwyn."

Cadmus laughed, "We're all one big happy family on Hebes Island."

Lady Selene looked around the crowded meeting room, "We weren't expecting to have our Academy open for enrolments, for perhaps a decade or longer."

"So, you've sped up your schedule somewhat?", Mystal enquired.

"Yes, somewhat", Lady Selene replied, "When we built our Psychic Academy, we had no idea that there were psychics, gifted, already on Mars. Now that we know there is an existing need for our services, we'll make sure that we are ready for students in four years, perhaps less."

"That's a good thing", Gareth told Selene, "We teach our own as best we can, but it's more traditional homeschooling here. There is nowhere else to go for true formal training."

Mystal then enquired Selene, "What about our older students?"

"In the meantime, we can probably offer some kind of tutoring services", Forkbraid suggested.

"Yes", Lady Selene agreed, then thinking aloud, "We can send tutors here to Sweetness to provide some formal training. Any students who show exceptional ability, we can bring back to our Academy in small groups, perhaps for three-month intensive training programmes."

Mystal nodded, "Yes, that would do nicely."

"We do have a few things to take care of first", Captain Carmichael reminded them.

"We haven't forgotten that, Captain", Forkbraid replied, explaining to the Elders, "Before we can offer any services, we first have to make our Psychic Academy safe."

"And that means tackling the militant extremists at New Tortuga?", Cadmus queried.

"Precisely, Cadmus", Forkbraid replied, adding, "That and repairing the damage their attacks have already caused. Once we've dealt with those issues, we'll be opening up for business."

Cadmus smiled, "Then let's make it safe!"

Gareth and Mystal both added, "Agreed", in unison.

Matthew was busy working on the Delilah's navigation systems. He was carefully pre-programming several course scenarios. The Prophet stepped onto the bridge and startled him.

"My Lord!", Matthew exclaimed.

"Matthew", the Prophet replied, asking, "I'd like to know what you're doing?"

"Just taking some precautions, my Lord", Matthew replied.

"Precautions?", the Prophet enquired, "You've moved the ship closer to the entrance. You've had the ship fully refuelled and taken on a full complement of supplies. What's happening Matthew?"

"Precautions, my Lord", Matthew replied.

"But why Matthew?", the Prophet questioned.

Matthew carefully looked around, then got up out of his seat and looked back down the corridor.

"My Lord, has Leroy told you?", Matthew asked.

"Has Leroy told me what?", the Prophet asked.

"About the Aurorae colony. About the old quarter", Matthew replied.

"No. Leroy's still waiting for information to come in", the Prophet replied.

Matthew shook his head, "Leroy's lost the plot, Sir. You can't trust him."

The Prophet asked bluntly, almost angrily, "What are you talking about, Matthew?"

"We've had reports from Aurorae, my Lord", Matthew replied, "Leroy didn't want to tell you."

"Leroy didn't want to tell me what, Matthew?", the Prophet asked.

"There was a Wizard on board the Shilo when it docked at Aurorae", Matthew spat out.

"A Wizard?", the Prophet enquired.

"Complete with magical staff, magical wands, magical shielding, the works", Matthew informed the Prophet, "And right at the end of the battle, he just vanished, straight into thin air. Just like that", Matthew clicked his fingers.

"Now things are beginning to make sense", the Prophet commented, as he realised why the carnage at the Aurorae waterfront had been so high.

"Why didn't you tell me this, Matthew?", the Prophet asked.

"Leroy didn't want to say anything, my Lord", Matthew replied, explaining "I concluded that Cormac, his Wife and the child Witch, Miranda, were in all probability at that Psychic Academy in Elysium by now. Leroy's afraid, my Lord."

"Are you afraid, Matthew?", the Prophet asked.

"Yes, my Lord", Matthew replied "That's why I'm taking precautions."

"Now I see", the Prophet remarked.

"My Lord. If anything happens, anything at all. Come straight to the ship", Matthew stressed.

"Your precautions, Matthew?", the Prophet queried.

"Yes, my Lord. My precautions", Matthew nodded, "If things go pear shaped and the colonial troops roll in, I can have this ship in space, quick as lightning."

"That's good thinking Matthew", the Prophet congratulated him.

"Thank you, my Lord", Matthew replied.

"Are you certain that the abomination is in Elysium?", the Prophet asked.

"I can't be one hundred percent certain, my Lord", Matthew replied, adding "But Aurorae is only a Hummer's flight from Elysium. If they're anywhere, that's where they are."

"Then you were right to take precautions, Matthew", the Prophet replied, adding "Rest assured, if things go... pear shaped... I'll come here as quickly as I can."

"I have already prepared your stateroom, it's all ready for you, my Lord", Matthew replied.

"Matthew, make sure the crew are on board and ready at all times", the Prophet commanded.

"I've already seen to it, my Lord", Matthew replied.

"Good. Good, Matthew", the Prophet replied, adding "And Matthew... Don't tell Leroy about our conversation."

"As you wish, my Lord", Matthew replied.

The Prophet left the Delilah's bridge and walked back down the corridor.

Matthew watched him leave before continuing with his navigation programs.

Charlene Fewkes stepped through the doorway and out onto the western battlement.

"Marcus! I've been looking for you everywhere."

"Why? What happened?", Marcus asked.

"I can't find Roseanne anywhere", Charlene informed him, "I've checked her rooms. I've checked the infirmary. I've checked the training halls. I've checked everywhere."

"This is a big complex, you can't possibly have checked everywhere", Marcus replied.

"You know what I mean... Well have you seen her?", Charlene asked.

"No, I haven't. Not since yesterday", Marcus replied.

Charlene looked out over the western plains to where Marcus had been staring, "Well, I expect she'll turn up... What are you staring at anyway?"

"That building over there", Marcus pointed to a structure that was just beginning to take shape.

"It's new isn't it. It looks like a hangar of some kind", Charlene replied.

"Yeah. I've asked Varak about it. He says it's something Forkbraid requested", Marcus informed Charlene, adding "He said that he wasn't at liberty to discuss it."

"Aren't we in charge?", Charlene queried.

"Apparently not when it comes to that", Marcus pointed to the large hangar-like structure again.

Charlene turned around and looked at the Academy. Varak had requisitioned a good number of androids, all of which were busily working to repair all the damage. Charlene turned around and looked back at the strange new hangar. Varak apparently had plenty of androids. A good number were also working on his mysterious hangar.

"Wouldn't those androids be better utilised working on the repairs?", Charlene asked.

"I've already checked over the repair schedules with Varak", Marcus replied, adding "We're way ahead of schedule on all works. Varak requisitioned that batch specifically for Forkbraid's pet project, whatever it is."

"Great. Then all I have to worry about is where our stubborn little walk-in is", Charlene frowned.

"Our stubborn little walk-in has a name, Charlene", Marcus reminded her.

Charlene laughed, "I should be careful, Roseanne is far more powerful than anyone else here."

"Powerful, yes, but not fully trained and Roseanne is still a child", Marcus reminded Charlene.

Charlene nodded, "Well, I expect Roseanne will turn up when she's hungry. All teenagers do."

Roseanne Rhein made a quick sweep of the vehicle hangar. It was the hangar in which the ten atmo rated Wisp's and Forkbraid's Bat Wing had been stowed. An android followed her. Ignoring the Wisps, Roseanne made her way directly to the Bat Wing. Upon arriving at the Bat Wing, Roseanne gave it a quick inspection, then opened the cockpit hatch. Roseanne noted the ship was on DNA lock, as she had expected.

"Android", Roseanne addressed the android, "This ship is DNA locked. Can you disable the DNA lock for me?"

"This ship will have been DNA locked for a very good reason", the Android replied.

"Its owner is on the far side of the planet, and he will need it", Roseanne told the Android, "They can't come back here for it. It needs to be flown to them. Can you disable the DNA lock?"

"The DNA lock can be disabled", the Android informed her.

"Good. I want this DNA lock disabled", Roseanne told the Android.

"As you wish, Madam", the Android replied, and then began to dismantle the DNA lock.

It took the Android nearly fifteen minutes to disable the DNA lock on Forkbraid's Bat Wing. Having done so, the Android removed the DNA lock, packed it up neatly and stowed it safely in the Bat Wings tool locker.

"Task completed", the Android informed Roseanne.

Roseanne had performed a quick study of an interceptor flight manual. Knowing that she would be working with a Bat Wing, she had specifically called up the correct Bat Wing flight manual. Not an easy task considering that the Bat Wing Interceptor was an antique.

Using special memory and learning enhancement techniques she had learnt in her psychic studies, Roseanne had quickly absorbed the manual. Now Roseanne was actually standing beside vehicle. She climbed into the cockpit. Much to her annoyance, Roseanne found that the controls fitted to the Bat Wing, did not resemble anything she had absorbed from the manual. Roseanne climbed back out of the cockpit, perplexed.

"Android", Roseanne addressed the Android once again, "The flight controls in this vehicle do not comply with its manual. Analyse the controls. Explain them to me."

The Android climbed into the cockpit and began a careful analysis of the flight controls. A little more than five minutes later it climbed back out.

"Task completed", the Android informed Roseanne.

"Divulge the results of your analysis", Roseanne instructed the Android.

"Detailed or summary?", the Android asked.

"Give me a summary... And dumb it down, I'm only Human after all", Roseanne replied.

"All back end controls remain as stipulated by the original vehicle blueprints", the Android began, continuing "All front end controls have been replaced by a neural interlock system."

"Neural interlock system?", Roseanne queried, then issued the instruction, "Explain."

"Neural interlock systems allow direct control of technology via interlocking with neural networks", the Android informed her.

"Concerning this vehicle, neural interlock system? Explain", Roseanne ordered.

"Concerning this vehicle, its neural interlock system controls all flight systems, navigation systems, weapons systems and all other computational functions", the Android informed her.

"Concerning this vehicle, interlocking with a neural network? Explain", Roseanne ordered.

"The neural interlock system of this vehicle is designed to work with a biological neural networking source", the Android explained.

"Concerning this vehicle, define biological neural networking source", Roseanne ordered.

"This vehicle is controlled by direct input from a Human brain", the Android told Roseanne.

"Sweet!", Roseanne exclaimed, then turning to the Android once more,

"How?"

"Via the flight Helmet's neural interface and feed back system", the Android explained.

"How does one control this vehicle via the flight Helmet?", Roseanne asked.

"Direct thought control", the Android replied.

"Elaborate", Roseanne instructed the Android.

"Bat Wing interceptor flight instructions, issued by thought control", the Android replied.

"So? I put on the Helmet and follow the instruction manual?", Roseanne asked.

"Affirmative", the Android replied.

"Oh, this is too easy!", Roseanne exclaimed, and then turned back to the Android, "Android. Forget our conversation ever happened. Now go back to your usual duties."

"Yes, Madam", the Android replied and then walked off.

Roseanne Rhein climbed into the cockpit of Forkbraid's Bat Wing interceptor. Slowly, Roseanne sat herself into the flight seat and put on the flight Helmet, noticing the two strands of neural net cabling attached to either side of the Helmet.

Roseanne thought to Forkbraid's Bat Wing interceptor.

"Check all systems."

The ship replied, *"All systems are functional."*

"Check fuel levels."

The ship replied, *"All fuel tanks are full to capacity."*

"Activate antigravity lifters."

The ship replied, *"Affirmative."*

"Hover at three feet altitude."

The ship replied, *"Affirmative."*

"Manoeuvre one hundred feet forward", putting the Bat Wing in the open courtyard.

The ship replied, *"Affirmative."*

"Hover at an altitude of two hundred feet."

The ship replied, *"Affirmative."*

"Navigation computer, calculated a flight plan to the following coordinates", Roseanne gave the navigation computer the location of the town of Sweetness, which she had carefully lifted out of Varak's mind.

The ship replied, *"Affirmative."*

"Adjust the flight plan. Last five hundred kilometres for lowest possible altitude approach", remembering that New Tortuga had highly effective scanners.

The ship replied, *"Affirmative."*

"Activate main drive on warm up sequence."

The ship replied, *"Affirmative."*
"Activate flight plan on my command."
The ship replied, *"Affirmative."*
"Launch."
The ship replied, *"Affirmative."*

Forkbraid's Bat Wing interceptor sped westward at high speed on a course for the town of Sweetness. Within minutes the interceptor was soaring high in the Martian stratosphere.

Still standing on the western battlements, Charlene looked skyward as the interceptor flew past them at high speed. It was swiftly approaching the western horizon.

Charlene pointed to the fast moving craft, "Isn't that Forkbraid's Bat Wing?"

Marcus put his hands up to shade his eyes as he strained to see the now distant interceptor.

"That was definitely Forkbraid's Bat Wing", Marcus replied.

"I don't remember Forkbraid saying he had an automatic recall on his ship", Charlene remarked.

"He doesn't, Charlene. Some-one is definitely flying it", Marcus informed her.

"Some-one?", Charlene queried, then her mind tweaked, "Oh, Gods! It's Roseanne! Roseanne's flying Forkbraid's Bat Wing!"

"It could well be", Marcus replied, adding "We'd better have everyone check the Academy for Roseanne. Best to make it a priority."

"I have a feeling we won't find her, Marcus", Charlene advised, "The odds are that she's flying that bloody Bat Wing."

"I believe you're right, Charlene, but we still need to check, just in case", Marcus replied.

"We'll have to get a message to Forkbraid", Marcus remarked.

"And Selene. I doubt either of them are going to be very happy about this", Charlene added.

"It's going to be difficult getting word to them", Marcus considered, "They'll be in silent communications mode."

"But we can get word to them, can't we?", Charlene asked.

"Oh, yeah. We'll just have to send it via The Spartan", Marcus informed Charlene, "They'll pass the message on when they land with their drop-ships."

Charlene was doubtful, "By then Roseanne will already have arrived in Sweetness."

"That is possible", Marcus agreed, mentally noting how fast Forkbraid's Bat Wing had sped away. The damned thing was fast! Seriously fast!

29. On the Trail

Captain Carmichael had flown his Hummer from the town of Sweetness. He had headed towards the western mountains to locate a suitable landing site for the Spartan's two drop-ships. The Captain located a large flat clearing at the foot of the mountains. It was still well within the valley of Sweetness. It was an ideal landing site. Both of the Spartans drop-ships could land here with ease. The drop-ships could approach Hebes Island completely undetected.

Before landing in the clearing, Captain Carmichael took several scans of the surrounding mountains. There seemed to be quite a few trails leading up into the hill country and perhaps a few passes that might yield access to the other side. No doubt Cormac and his Cousins would know these trails and passes by heart. Nonetheless, the Captain studied the information carefully before saving the information on his computer. Captain Carmichael then took his Hummer down for a gentle landing.

Once landed, Captain Carmichael climbed out of his hummer and set up a small beacon. Carefully, he adjusted its output power levels, so it would be undetectable from outside the valley. As soon as the drop-ships entered the valley, they would detect the beacon and immediately make a beeline straight for it. This in turn would trigger a response on The Captain's sensors. It was only a matter of waiting for them to arrive.

Captain Carmichael pulled a comfortable camp chair out of his Hummer's luggage compartment and walked a short distance away from his Hummer to a broad, shady tree. The Captain unfolded the chair, set it up under the shade of the tree, and then he sat down to await the arrival of his drop-ships.

Less than an hour later the first of the drop-ships triggered Captain Carmichael's sensors. The Captain quickly rose to his feet and put his field glasses to his eyes. Searching towards the Gap, Captain Carmichael adjusted the focus until he had a clear view of his approaching drop-ships. Greatly magnified by the field glasses, the Captain could see his ships had already adjusted course and were making their way straight towards him. He smiled, knowing they would be landing shortly, then they could begin to make their move against New Tortuga.

As he watched the drop-ships approach, Captain Carmichael noticed a small ship zip through the Gap behind them. It was a Bat Wing! There was only one Bat Wing known to exist on Mars, namely Forkbraid's Bat Wing.

"What the bloody heck is going on?", the Captain muttered to himself, knowing with their current radio silence, that he'd have to wait for someone to explain this new development later.

Special Agent Murphy pointed across the bay towards the Gap. The Spartan's two large drop-ships were approaching low through the Gap. No sooner than they'd reached the bay, they veered west towards the mountains and Captain Carmichael.

"They'll be landing within minutes", Special Agent Murphy advised them as a reminder that they too needed to make a move in that direction.

As they watched the drop-ships progress across the bay, Lady Selene noticed something small out of the corner of her eye. It was approaching through the Gap and quickly zipped through behind the drop-ships. Lady Selene tilted her head slightly sideways as she strained her eyes to make out what it was she was seeing.

"Isn't that your Bat Wing, Forkbraid?", Lady Selene asked.

Forkbraid turned and looked back towards the Gap. After a few seconds he replied, "I believe it is. That is my Bat Wing."

"Did you recall it?", Special Agent Murphy enquired.

"Jim, it doesn't have a recall unit", Forkbraid replied.

Forkbraid's Bat Wing interceptor stayed on course, coming straight towards the town of Sweetness. Swiftly it flew above them, passing them by and heading towards the town hall. It hovered above the town hall for several minutes, before dropping in altitude and performing a perfect soft landing next to their Hummer.

"Who's flying it?", Special Agent Murphy asked.

"No-one, Jim", Forkbraid replied, adding "It just performed an auto-piloted landing."

Forkbraid had a worried look upon his face.

"Auto-piloted landing?", Special Agent Murphy queried, "This is a fairly primitive town, FB. There's no [74]DCI down here."

"Jim, it doesn't need DCI, my Bat Wing's on board computer system has simply picked a spot close to the nearest landed vehicle. Our Hummer in fact", Forkbraid explained.

Lady Selene started walking towards the town hall at a fast pace, Forkbraid quickly fell into step behind her. Both had exchanged worried looks, before heading towards Forkbraid's Bat Wing.

"What's the hurry?", Special Agent Murphy asked.

"Roseanne is on board", Forkbraid shouted back over his shoulder, adding, "And she's unconscious."

Special Agent Murphy exclaimed under his breath, "Oh, shit!", then he quickly followed them.

It only took a few minutes to reach the rear of the town hall. There, next to their Hummer was Forkbraid's Bat Wing interceptor. Several townsfolk had already gathered around the vessel. As they approached, two more townsfolk

---

74 Docking Computer Interlock. Interlocking of ships navigation computers for automated docking.

appeared around the corner of the town hall carrying a stretcher. The common thread among the townsfolk was the concerned look upon their faces.

Forkbraid and Lady Selene walked straight up to the Bat Wing. Special Agent Murphy stood back and watched as Forkbraid opened the cockpit hatch and stepped inside the craft. He quickly stepped back out of his Bat Wing with an unconscious Roseanne Rhein in his arms. There were small trickles of dried blood coming from Roseanne's nose. Lady Selene quickly felt for a pulse in Roseanne's neck. The concerned look on her face lightened slightly.

"Will she be okay?", Special Agent Murphy asked as Forkbraid placed Roseanne carefully onto the stretcher.

"We think so, Jim. Touch wood", Forkbraid replied hesitantly.

Lady Selene added, "We need to keep her under observation for a few hours."

"When Roseanne wakes up, she'll have one hell of a headache", Forkbraid remarked.

"Let's hope that's all she'll have", Lady Selene stated as they followed the stretcher bearers to Mystal's Inn.

"Shouldn't someone call a doctor?", Special Agent Murphy enquired as he followed them.

"The doctor is already on his way, Jim", Forkbraid assured him.

"Oh, yeah, the town's full of psychics", Special Agent Murphy replied, "I keep forgetting."

"What happened to Roseanne anyway?", Special Agent Murphy asked.

"She tried to fly my ship", Forkbraid replied without elaborating.

"I don't get it, flying a ship doesn't normally render the pilot unconscious", Special Agent Murphy replied.

"It does if the ship uses a [75]NIC system and the pilot hasn't been trained in its use", Forkbraid explained to him.

"Shit! Well that explains a lot", Special Agent Murphy exclaimed, adding "Let's hope Roseanne's still got her faculties when she wakes up."

"We think that she'll be fine", Forkbraid told him, "The ship's computer logs showed that Roseanne passed out right at the beginning of the flight, straight after issuing her flight instructions. The amount of neural traffic generated by the NIC must have overwhelmed her."

"Which means that when she wakes up, Roseanne will have me to deal with", Lady Selene stated as they walked up the stairs and entered the Inn.

"*Selene, go easy on her. The headache she'll have will be punishment enough*", Forkbraid silently transmitted to Selene.

"*I don't think so, Forkbraid*", Selene transmitted back, "*Roseanne could have killed herself today. She has to learn from her mistakes.*"

---

75 NIC – Neural Interconnect Control. Direct control of the interceptor via neural interconnect and human thought.

Forkbraid frowned slightly, *"I suppose you know best."*

Several hours later, Roseanne was still unconscious. One of the town's two Doctors had given Roseanne a quick examination and had pronounced, *"The young girl ought to recover soon enough, although she would have one nasty headache."*

Nothing that Lady Selene did not already know. Regular scans performed by Lady Selene and Mystal showed that Roseanne was recovering from her misadventure, albeit slowly.

Forkbraid had been busy making preparations with Cormac and Candy. Due to Roseanne's unplanned arrival, Cormac and Candy were going ahead to meet up with Captain Carmichael in the clearing by the mountains, where the drop-ships had landed. They would be taking a dozen or so of the townsfolk, their Cousins, with them to act as scouts and guides, as the Captain's men crossed over the mountains to New Tortuga.

Forkbraid and Lady Selene would leave later, after Roseanne regained consciousness and then catch up with others before they began their journey over the mountains. Cormac and Candy had left on foot, quickly leading their Cousins out of town and onto the trail that led to the clearing where the drop-ships had landed.

"Any change?", Forkbraid asked as he entered the room.

"No", Selene answered, adding in almost a whisper, "She's still sleeping."

Mystal remarked, "This little one will be fine."

"Are you still going to punish her?", Forkbraid enquired.

"Of course, I am", Selene answered quickly, "We can't let her get away with stealing your Bat Wing interceptor."

Forkbraid nodded in agreement with Selene.

"Selene, perhaps it's not my place, but if I may?", Mystal remarked silently.

"Yes, Mystal?", Selene enquired.

"I've been carefully following the threads of her past", Mystal offered, "Normally I wouldn't, but as this young lady has just stolen an interceptor, so I thought it might be prudent to find out why."

Forkbraid nodded, "Understanding why Roseanne did this would be useful."

"What have you found, Mystal?", Selene asked.

"This child lost her parents when she was quite young", Mystal informed them.

"When she was five or six, if I remember correctly", Selene replied.

"Yes. Since that tender young age, Roseanne has been a ward of the state, living in government orphanages and then later, one foster home after another", Mystal remarked.

Selene nodded as Mystal continued, "Roseanne never stayed with a foster family for more than a year at a time. Every six months or so she would be moved to a new home. Continually changing from one family to the next. It was hardly a stable up bringing."

"We already know this, Mystal, can you please make your point?", Selene asked abruptly.

"Lady Selene. Roseanne is no longer a ward of the state. This young one is in your charge. She's here on Mars and with her new family, namely you, you and Forkbraid. Roseanne looks up to you as a Mother figure", Mystal stated.

"Well if that's the case, why did she steal Forkbraid's Bat Wing?", Selene asked.

"A good question", Forkbraid added, "I've been wondering that myself ."

"Because it was the fastest way to get to you, Selene, the fastest way to get here", Mystal replied with a smile.

"The fastest way to get to me?", Selene asked.

"Yes, of course", Mystal replied, adding "You are her family now. You left her back at the Academy, and she was worried, very worried."

"Worried about what?", Selene enquired.

Mystal gave a quiet chuckle, "Worried about you. Worried that you wouldn't be coming back."

"That's ridiculous. I've always had every intention of going back", Selene replied.

"You're about to go into battle, Selene", Mystal pointed out, "You can't guarantee the future."

"So what, Roseanne stole Forkbraid's Bat, so she could fight by my side?", Selene asked.

"Simply put. Yes, Selene", Mystal replied, adding "That's exactly what she was doing. Her intention was to fight by your side with you and share your fate."

Selene stared at Mystal for several long moments, then turned to Forkbraid, who nodded in agreement with Mystal's assessment.

Finally, Selene turned to look at Roseanne once more, then reached out and took Roseanne's hand in her own, squeezing it gently.

"What am I going to do with you, young lady?", Selene asked of her unconscious charge, as Roseanne's eyes slowly began to open.

"Selene? What happened?", Roseanne's soft, almost feeble voice asked.

"Don't you say a word, young lady! I am so very angry with you!", Selene snapped back, then squeezing her hand and softening her stance somewhat, "Just rest now, Roseanne. We'll discuss this issue in a couple of hours when you're feeling a little better."

Roseanne closed her eyes and allowed herself to drop into a light slumber.

"You're not going to punish her, are you, Selene?", Forkbraid whispered in Selene's ear.

Tears welled up in Selene's eyes, and she quickly wiped them away with her sleeve.

"How can I punish her?", Selene whispered back, "She's had such a hard life."

Mystal smiled at them both, then led Selene and Forkbraid out of the room.

The Spartan's drop-ships took up considerable space in the clearing. The colonial troops had climbed out of the ships and quickly set up a base camp. Captain Carmichael kept an eager watch out for the others he had left behind in the township of Sweetness.

"Where are they?", the Captain asked himself, "They should have been here long ago."

Then as if to answer his quietly spoken question, Cormac and Candy appeared in the clearing, as if from out of nowhere. They were armed with local weaponry.

A startled Captain Carmichael asked, "Where the hell have you been?"

"We had a little problem show up", Cormac replied, in his usual fashion, he did not elaborate.

Captain Carmichael correctly surmised the problem and asked, "Yeah, what was Forkbraid's Bat Wing doing showing up here?"

Cormac answered him, "Roseanne stole it from its hangar and flew it here."

"Stole it? Flew it here? What, all the way from Elysium?", the Captain's questions poured out.

"Stole it, yes", Cormac replied, "Flew it all the way from Elysium, well that's debatable."

Candy added more pertinent information, "The young one passed out early in the flight. The ship pretty much flew itself here."

"What was she thinking?", Captain Carmichael asked, "If the enemy detected her, they'd know we're coming."

"Agent Murphy checked the flight logs. The ship flew here under the scanners, same as we did."

"Well that is reassuring, Cormac", the Captain replied, "What the hell was she doing?"

"We don't rightly know", Cormac answered.

Candy quickly added, "The ship's NIC system knocked her out cold. The others stayed behind to keep an eye on her, until she recovers. They'll be here shortly."

Captain Carmichael shook his head as he thought to himself, *"Bloody hell"*, then he asked, "So you're the only two here then?"

Cormac and Candy both smiled as Cormac replied, "No, Sir."

Cormac then whistled and without warning a dozen local folk appeared in the clearing. It was as if they had appeared from out of a fog. There was no sign of their presence one minute, then the next they were all standing in front them. They were all armed with local weaponry, the same as Cormac and Candy were.

Several of the colonial troops were startled by their sudden appearance and brought their own weapons to bear.

Captain Carmichael was quick to raise his hand and bark out an order, "Stand down!"

His men put down their weapons and went back to their duties, although several kept a weary eye on the newcomers.

"Jesus, Cormac! You can't just do stuff like that!", the Captain exclaimed.

Cormac smiled a broad smile at the Captain, "Obscuration. It's an artful talent."

Several of Cormac's Cousins chuckled at the colonial troops' discomfort.

After several minutes of further small talk, Captain Carmichael pulled out a map his men had produced from his scans of the mountains. He placed it on a table that had been set up by his Hummer and stretched it out across the table.

"My scans indicate that we should be able to use any one of these four narrow passes to get through to the other side", the Captain informed them.

Cormac looked at the map and nodded.

"Which would be the most efficient passage for my men and equipment?", the Captain asked.

"None of them will do you very much good, Captain", Cormac replied.

"What do you mean?", Captain Carmichael questioned.

"They're all dead ends, blind passages", Cormac replied, "They'll lead you deep into the mountains, and then they just stop."

The Captain stared at Cormac for a long moment, then looked at the map once again, before turning back to Cormac.

"Well, if these are no good, which pass do we take?", the Captain asked.

"This one right here", Cormac replied pointing to a passage on the map and tapping it with his fingertip, one that appeared to be a dead end.

Captain Carmichael rubbed his chin as he looked where Cormac had pointed. Looking back to Cormac he asked, "Are you certain, Cormac?"

"Absolutely", Cormac replied, "It's the only passage through the mountains. There ain't no others. That's the only one."

Candy then looked at the Captain and added, "This time of year, there'll still be snow on the ground, but nothing your colonial troops can't handle. They look like a hardy bunch."

Cormac followed his Wife's lead, explaining further, "There's a short stretch towards the top that goes through a tunnel in the mountain. The tunnel's an easy walk, only several hundred metres."

Candy continued the flow of information, "Then when we're on the other side, there's a narrow trail that leads down out of the mountains to the coast. We don't take it all the way down though."

Cormac picked up the discourse again, "The cave system that leads to New Tortuga is about halfway down that trail. It's well hidden, you won't find it without our help."

Captain Carmichael nodded in appreciation, this information would prove most useful, "Well then, now we're getting somewhere", he replied with a smile.

Lady Selene had returned to Roseanne's room with the town Elder, Mystal. A couple of hours had passed and Mystal had brought Roseanne some chicken broth.

"You gave us quite a scare, little lady", Selene scolded gently, "What were you thinking?"

"I don't know", Roseanne replied sheepishly, "I just wanted to get here."

"And here you are", Selene replied, "And here you're going to stay."

"No, No", Roseanne shook her head and almost shouted, "I'm going with you."

"Oh, no you're not", Selene told her firmly, "This is serious, Roseanne. You are going to stay here. End of story."

"But you'll need me", Roseanne implored, "I can help you."

Selene smiled at Roseanne, "Roseanne, you're only partly trained. You have a long way to go before you're ready for this."

"I am ready'", Roseanne insisted, "I am ready now."

Selene smiled at Roseanne once more and squeezed her hand, replying softly, "Roseanne, you're not ready. And you're not going. That's final."

Roseanne thought to Selene, "*Who'll look after you?*"

Selene smiled once more, "*I'll be fine, Roseanne. Forkbraid will be with me. And trust me, Forkbraid won't let anything happen to me.*"

"You'll be coming back?", Roseanne asked softly.

"Of course, I will ,Roseanne", Selene replied, "As soon as we've dealt with these extremists, I'll be back to take you home."

Roseanne was silent for a moment, before asking in a quiet voice, "Home?"

"Yes, home, silly", Selene replied, "You know, our Psychic Academy. That's our home."

Mystal coughed lightly to catch Selene's attention, "Perhaps, Roseanne could do with some food?"

"Yes, yes, of course", Selene replied, then turning to Roseanne once more, "Roseanne, this is Mystal, one of the town's Elders. Mystal is going to look after you while I'm away."

Roseanne nodded to Mystal, but did not say a word.

"Roseanne, I want you to be on your best behaviour while I'm gone", Selene continued, adding "I'll be back in a few days, so don't worry."

"How many days?", Roseanne asked worriedly.

"I expect no longer than a week", Selene replied, "Now behave yourself for Mystal, promise."

"Okay, I promise", Roseanne promised her.

"Good then, now eat your supper, and I'll see you in a few days", Selene told Roseanne as she left the room to find Forkbraid.

Lady Selene found Forkbraid by Agent Murphy's Hummer. They were discussing some plans that Forkbraid had just hatched. Selene noted that the Hummer's [76]AGLs were already humming.

"Going somewhere are we?", Selene enquired.

"Yes, we are", Forkbraid replied, adding "Agent Murphy's going to fly you to the Captain's base of operations."

"Fly me? What will you be doing?", Selene questioned.

"I'll be taking my Bat Wing", Forkbraid informed her.

"You and that bloody Bat Wing of yours", Selene scoffed, "I wish you'd left that damned thing back on Earth."

"Actually, it's a good thing that I brought it", Forkbraid replied.

"If you hadn't brought it, Roseanne wouldn't have been able to steal it", Selene stated with a tinge of anger in her voice.

"Ah, yes", Forkbraid began, "While it was unfortunate that Roseanne stole it, it was quite serendipitous that she did so."

"Serendipitous?", Selene questioned.

"FB, plans to use the Bat Wing as a diversion", Special Agent Murphy informed her from the Hummer's hatch.

"A diversion?", Selene asked.

"Yeah, a diversion", Forkbraid replied, "We're going to need one and my Bat Wing is going to provide it."

"You might want to explain that one to me, Forkbraid", Selene told him bluntly.

"No time to explain now, darling", Forkbraid replied, adding, "I'll explain it to you when we catch up with the others."

"Your explanation better be good", Selene told him as she climbed into the Hummer.

"It will be", Forkbraid called to her as he headed for his Bat Wing.

Within minutes both craft were flying swiftly towards the clearing where the Spartan's drop-ships had landed.

A short while later Special Agent Murphy's Hummer landed in the clearing by the Spartan's two drop-ships. Forkbraid's Bat Wing wasn't far behind. The clearing was starting to look a little crowded, with ships and troop tents now

---

76 Antigravity Lifters. Devices used to nullify gravity and allow vessels to fly.

taking up much of the available space.

The table that Captain Carmichael had spread out his map on, was now inside the command tent. The first map had been discarded and now a second map, with more information provided by Cormac and his Wife, Candy, took its place.

The trail they needed to take to cross the mountains was clearly marked, as was the location of their target, New Tortuga. Several small hamlets and villages along the southern coast of Hebes Island were also marked on the map, among them the little hamlet of Krell.

Forkbraid studied the map before him. Many of the landmarks stood out. Having [77]shared with Cormac and Candy some time ago on the Shilo, Forkbraid's mind contained many of their memories and among these were the hamlets, villages, and landmarks of Hebes Island.

"So Forkbraid, Agent Murphy here, tells me that you're going to use your Bat Wing as a diversion", the Captain stated, and then enquired "Precisely how is that going to work?"

"Fairly simple actually, Captain", Forkbraid replied, Lady Selene was also listening intently, "I'm going to program my Bat Wing to fly to New Tortuga. The computer will automatically scan the port facilities and attempt a landing."

"So you're not going to fly it yourself", Selene enquired.

"Oh, no, of course not", Forkbraid replied, "I'll be with you lot in the caverns."

"I'm not entirely certain how landing your Bat Wing in the port will create much of a diversion, Forkbraid", the Captain stated.

"Well, Captain, my Bat Wing will create quite a stir when it enters their port. It is probably the only Bat Wing on Mars at the moment", Forkbraid reminded him, adding, "And besides, it won't be landing in the port exactly. I fully intend to have it land in the middle of their town square."

Captain Carmichael's right eyebrow cocked up, "Middle of the town square. Well, I can see how that would create quite a stir."

"Especially when they'll suspect that a Witch is onboard", Forkbraid suggested.

"Why would they think that?", the Captain asked.

"Who else would be audacious enough to land a Bat Wing in New Tortuga's town square?"

Captain Carmichael smiled at Forkbraid, "You're right, they'll think it's you."

"The timings got to be perfect though", Special Agent Murphy suggested.

"It will be, Jim, it will be", Forkbraid agreed.

For the rest of the night they discussed the details of their plans step by step. It was several hours later before they finally turned in for the night. The next

---

77 Sharing of consciousness, telepathic two-way transmission of memories, consciousness, and experiences.

morning they would be up early and on the trail to New Tortuga. They estimated it was a two-day hike by foot with Cormac, Candy, and their Cousins leading the way.

Captain Carmichael had the entire clearing awake and ready well before first light the next day. At the crack of dawn they began their march along the trail leading up into the mountains. The forest on either side of the trail was thick with a mixture of various conifers. Bracken and scrub covered the ground and partially obscured the trail. Cormac and his Cousins walked ahead of the column, slashing back the undergrowth and scanning the trail ahead for pitfalls. The column moved at a good pace, inexorably towards its destination.

At strategic points along the trail, Captain Carmichael's communications technicians placed small communications relays. These would enable the Captain to communicate with his base camp and his drop-ships, without being detected by the enemy.

By mid-morning the trail had become much tighter, becoming more of a passage than a forest trail. They found themselves travelling up a narrow valley, the walls of which seemed to grow steeper with every step.

The trees of the forest clung thickly to the sides of the valley. The very air they breathed smelt as green as the surrounding forest. Mountain wild flowers sprung from the humus at the base of the trees. Early spring growth was all around them and carpets of flowers were seen here and there amongst the trees.

"What the!", Lady Selene exclaimed, "Is that a bee?"

The *"bee"* had landed on Lady Selene's sleeve.

Candy walked over to Lady Selene and inspected it.

"Yep, that's a bee alright", Candy informed her.

Lady Selene shook her sleeve and the bee flew away, "You've got to be joking, Candy, that thing must have been an inch or more long."

"Yeah, that's about right", Candy replied, "You don't have to worry though, they're stingless."

"Stingless?", Lady Selene queried.

Candy informed her, "Yeah. We don't have honey bees up here on Mars, like they do in the colonies, or on Earth for that matter."

"Why not?", Lady Selene asked.

"Apparently the honey bees don't like Martian gravity. You know, point three eight gs messes with their internal gyroscopes sort of", Candy explained, sort of.

"Oh, well if you don't have honey bees, what was that?", Lady Selene asked.

"That was a genetically modified stingless bee from Earth, from Australia I believe", Candy identified it for Selene.

"Candy, I grew up in Australia. I've lived there all my life. I can tell you,

Australian stingless bees are tiny little things, about the size of small fly", Selene told Candy.

"Well, yeah, they were when they were first brought here too", Candy replied, explaining "That was two hundred years back. Since then they've grown somewhat."

"Grown somewhat!", Lady Selene exclaimed, questioning, "What would make them grow so big?"

"Well, the lower gravity helps, but mainly it's the atmosphere", Candy replied.

"The atmosphere?", Selene queried.

"Yeah. The atmosphere here is much thicker than on Earth, it has much more carbon dioxide in it", Candy explained, "We need it for the green house effect. Otherwise, it would be much colder here than it currently is."

"Yes, I know that Candy, but why would that make the bees grow so big?", Selene asked.

"It doesn't. What most people don't realise, is that the Martian atmosphere has more than twenty-five percent oxygen", Candy informed Selene, explaining, "It's the oxygen that makes the insects grow bigger. Carbon dioxide, on the other hand, helps the fruit and vegetables grow."

"Candy, you did say insects, didn't you?", Selene asked.

"Oh, yeah. The richer oxygen levels affect all the insects on Mars", Candy replied.

"Are they any, we actually need to worry about?", Selene enquired.

"Hmm, let me think, there is one you need to watch out for", Candy replied, adding, "They weren't brought as part of the colonisation. They hitched a ride with a consignment of stingless bees."

"And what would they be?", asked Selene.

"Ants", Candy informed her without further elaboration.

"Ants?", Selene questioned, continuing, "They would have been Australian ants, like the bees wouldn't they?"

"Yes, of course", Candy replied, "From the same place as the bees."

"What species were they?", Selene enquired.

"Oh, I don't know what their species is called", Candy replied, "We just use their common name, same as they had back on Earth."

"And that was?", Selene enquired hoping to get the answer.

"Blue bottles", Candy replied, adding "Nasty little buggers, you don't want to be stung by one of them, trust me on that."

"Candy! Blue bottles!", Selene exclaimed, "They grow about an inch long on Earth, sometimes a little bit bigger."

"Yeah, well, here they grow to about", Candy paused for a moment in thought, "I don't know, four inches long. Although I have heard of some much bigger than that."

For the rest of the hike, Lady Selene kept a close eye out for giant blue bottle ants.

By late afternoon the trail had become a narrow, winding track, with rock clefts on either side. They were climbing quite a lot now and the going was much rougher. Patches of thick moss covered the ground and lichen covered the rocks. Trees grew out of every crack and crevice in the rocks, in which they could gain a foot hold. It was more of a mountain goat track than a trail.

The Winter's snow lay in patches here and there upon the ground. It made the climbing slippery and somewhat dangerous. The column was moving much slower now, yet they were still making good progress, courtesy of the lower Martian gravity. The higher they climbed, the more snow they encountered, until the snow finally covered the ground in a thick blanket of white. Rocks protruded here and there, marking their trail.

Now they found themselves pushing ahead through the snow. Climbing higher and higher, it was close to dusk when they finally reached a narrow crevasse. Cormac led them into the crevasse, his Cousins having already gone in ahead of him. Nearly two hundred feet into the Crevasse, they reached its end.

Before them stood a man-made tunnel. It had been bored through the mountain by a powerful tunnel boring laser. The tunnel was circular, dead straight and perfectly smooth. At intervals along the walls, brackets had been mounted. These contained torches, which had been lit by Cormac's Cousins. The column moved into the tunnel and slowly made their way to the other side.

"How old is this tunnel, Cormac?", Captain Carmichael asked.

"Don't rightly know, Captain", Cormac replied, adding, "It was built a long way back, sometime just after the Long Rains."

"The Long Rains?", Captain Carmichael queried.

"Yeah, after the sky fell, it rained almost continuously for many years", Cormac told him.

Captain Carmichael shook his head and asked, "Sky fell?"

"Captain, that's what the locals call it when thousands upon thousands of asteroidal ice chunks are dropped onto a planet", Special Agent Murphy informed him.

"Oh", the Captain replied, "And the long rains would have been all that water precipitating out of the atmosphere."

"Now you get the picture", Special Agent Murphy laughed.

"Forkbraid did tell me a lot of the original colonists stayed on the surface and refused to be evacuated when the terraformers arrived", Captain Carmichael replied.

"That's right, Captain", Cormac confirmed, "Many of them went underground. There were lots of smallish colonies scattered around the planet back then. New Tortuga was one of the largest ones, although there were some bigger ones."

"And this tunnel was bored back in those days?", the Captain questioned once more.

"Either before the terraforming or shortly after the long rains, I'm not sure which", Cormac replied, adding with a smile, "There was a lot of tunnelling done back then. You'll find tunnels like this scattered all over the place."

"Really?", the Captain asked.

"Yeah", Cormac replied, "There's a lot of them. I only know a couple of dozen or so. There are a hell of a lot more, most of them are long forgotten though."

"After this is all over, I should organise a proper survey", Captain Carmichael stated, adding, "There's a hell of a lot about this planet that needs to be known."

When Captain Carmichael reached the other side of the tunnel, he found it opened into yet another crevasse. Night was falling, and it was getting dark outside now, travelling down the mountain would be dangerous in the extreme. Even Cormac and Candy's Cousins had stopped just a few feet into the crevasse. They were already setting up their camp for the night. Captain Carmichael took the hint, then turned around and gave the order for his men to make camp. This night, they would spend in a laser bored tunnel, high in the mountains of Hebes Island.

The next morning when Captain Carmichael walked towards the crevasse he noticed that Cormac's Cousins were nowhere to be seen, neither was Cormac for that matter.

"It's all right, Captain", Candy called from behind, "Cormac and co have gone down the trail a little ways. They're checking the trail and scouting ahead."

"I don't remember giving that order", Captain Carmichael replied.

"You wouldn't", Candy laughed, "They headed off while it was still dark, while you and everyone else was still asleep. I stayed behind to let you know what's up."

Special Agent Murphy chuckled to himself when he saw the look on the Captain's face.

"What is it?", Forkbraid asked as he approached.

"Nothing important FB", Special Agent Murphy replied, "It was funny for a moment though."

Forkbraid walked up to Captain Carmichael and stared down the crevasse from the tunnel entrance, the Sun had risen, and it was quite light outside.

"We'd better get moving, Captain, we're losing daylight", Forkbraid advised.

The Captain shook his head, "You too, Forkbraid? Everyone's a bloody comedian this morning."

Captain Carmichael turned and walked back into the tunnel, he shouted out loud, "Get a move on men, we move out in five minutes. Pass the word down the line."

Five minutes later the column of colonial troops started marching out of the tunnel. The crevasse on this side of the tunnel was longer than on the other side and somewhat harder to traverse. Steep drops occurred in several sections and rope ladders were required to traverse them. Cormac and his Cousins had set these rope ladders in place as they'd passed through and scouted ahead.

When they finally arrived at the entrance to the crevasse, thick foliage blocked the way. Candy led them left, to the edge of the rock wall and the column skirted between rocks and tree foliage until they finally came out onto the trail. The view was extremely disappointing, tall trees grew everywhere and visibility was limited.

A small clearing opened up in front of them, small being an understatement. Thick foliage and tall trees confronted them again on the other side. The trail leading out of the clearing was narrow, winding, steep, and difficult to navigate. Very little snow was on the ground. The trees, however, held quite a lot of snow and every now, and then a large clump of snow would drop from the branches as they passed underneath.

The column travelled this narrow, winding trail for most of the morning, with Candy leading the way. The Captain's communications technicians positioned relays along the trail, but the distance between relays was much closer than on the other side of the mountains. Such was the thick nature of the foliage and the terrain. By midday the trail had opened up somewhat and the hiking became a little easier. No sign of Cormac or his Cousins had been seen since they'd left camp in the tunnel that morning.

Shortly after two pm they were almost halfway down the mountain. Cormac was sitting on a rock by the trail. The trail itself continued onwards down the mountain, still resembling more of a goat track than any path a person might take. Candy walked straight up to Cormac and immediately gave him a hug. The column stopped as Cormac motioned for Captain Carmichael to come forward.

"My Cousins have checked the trail further down from here. It's all clear", Cormac informed him.

"Good", the Captain replied, and then he asked, "How long till we get to the caves?"

Cormac smiled a broad smile and pointed to the Captain's left, "Just up that trail yonder."

"So we're not going down there?", the Captain pointed to the trail that Cormac said was clear.

"No", Cormac replied, "That would be silly, we don't want to go to Krell."

"Then why did you say it was clear?", Captain Carmichael asked.

"To let you know that no one would know we'd passed this way", Cormac replied.

"Oh", the Captain replied, "So this trail leads to the caves?"

Captain Carmichael stepped onto this new trail, if you could call it that. It was rough, severely overgrown and hardly looked like a trail at all.

"Pass the word down the line", Cormac told the Captain, "Push through the foliage, but try not to break any branches. We don't want this trail to look like a trail."

Cormac then jumped onto this new trail and led the way, Candy was close behind him.

As the column moved up the new trail, Cormac's Cousins appeared out of the scrub.

Candy turned around and advised, "Our Cousins will do their best to hide any signs of our passing."

A little over thirty minutes later the column pushed through more dense foliage and eventually came across a small, hidden cave entrance. One by one they climbed through the cave entrance and into the cavern beyond. The cavern was easily large enough to house the whole column of colonial troops. Cormac walked to the far side of the cavern and reached into a crack in the rocks. A large rock slid out of the way revealing another cave entrance.

"Here be the road to New Tortuga", Cormac stated as he smiled his broad gap-toothed smile.

"How long will it take?", Special Agent Murphy asked.

Captain Carmichael nodded in agreement, "Yes, how long?"

"We should be at the back of my house, in", Cormac rubbed the rough stubble on his chin, "Candy, how long do ya reckon?"

"Three hours and a half, Cormac", Candy replied with certainty.

"Yes, three and half hours", Cormac agreed, "The missus is always right."

The column of colonial troops followed Cormac and Candy into the cave system, each with glow lights lit and lighting the path before them. The walking was far easier now, although somewhat claustrophobic. True to their word, three hours and thirty minutes later they reached the end of the cave system. A short, thirty foot tunnel led from the natural cave to a dead end.

Cormac motioned for Captain Carmichael to approach as he shone his light down the tunnel.

"Beyond that stone door is our home", Cormac informed the Captain, "And beyond that is New Tortuga."

Captain Carmichael nodded and started walking down the tunnel. Cormac grabbed his arm.

"Not now, Captain", Cormac told him, "Best your men camp here for the night. We'll enter New Tortuga before the first light tomorrow. The rock is fairly soundproof, but just to be on the safe side, keep all noise to a minimum."

"Noted Cormac", Captain Carmichael replied, "We'll need to know what's on the other side."

"Me and Candy will fill you in on the details", Cormac informed him, adding, "Before your colonial troops go in, I'll lead my Cousins in first. We'll need about three hours to sort things out. We'll bring as many of the ordinary folk as possible into the safety of the hydroponics farms. Then whatever happens, is up to you."

Captain Carmichael nodded in agreement, "I'll make sure my men know there are civilians in the farms, Cormac. We'll do our best to keep them safe."

"Good", Cormac replied, "Make sure of that. Now, I recommend that your men get some rest."

30. New Tortuga Two

It was just two am in the morning and Cormac and his Cousins were crowded into the tunnel leading into the rear of his old house. His old house was carved out of the bedrock at the very rear of the cavern in which New Tortuga had been built. Forkbraid was with them.

Forkbraid pressed his ear to the rock door that separated them from the house. Slowly Forkbraid closed his eyes and let his mind wander through to the other side.

After a few minutes Forkbraid pulled his ear away from the rock, "Cormac, your house is completely empty."

"You're sure now, Cousin", Cormac replied, "We don't want to walk into any grief now, do we?"

"It's empty, Cormac", Forkbraid replied, adding, "The other houses on either side aren't though. I detected the presence of sleeping families."

"Ordinary working folk, Cousin. Farmers just like me and Candy. We'll try not to disturb their slumber as we pass", Cormac replied.

Forkbraid nodded, he had assessed the minds of the sleepers, they were indeed ordinary folk.

"Cormac Farmer!", an angry voice was heard behind them, "You didn't wake me!", it accused.

Cormac frowned, "I was hoping the missus would sleep in", he whispered to Forkbraid.

Then to Candy he replied, "To right. I didn't wake you, Candy, this business could get nasty."

"Nasty or not, I'm still coming", Candy insisted.

"There's no stopping you, is there, Candy?", Cormac smiled, knowing full well the answer.

Candy smiled back, "You know me well enough, Cormac", then to the others "Good morning, Cousins."

Candy flicked a switch and the stone door slid silently open, revealing a wooden panel. Candy then pushed a small button and the wooden panel in front of them opened.

"Now, Cormac", Forkbraid put his hand on Cormac's shoulder, "You know what to do, just remember, it has to be done quietly. Very, very quietly."

Cormac nodded, "Either that or we'll be in right trouble."

"Exactly", Forkbraid replied, "At six am, we'll be coming through with the colonial troops."

"Four hours isn't enough time, Cormac", one of Cormac's Cousins muttered.

"It's all we've got, so it will have to do", Cormac told him.

"Are we finished lolly gagging?", Candy asked, "Good, then let's get moving",

Candy then stepped into the closet, opened the door and stepped through it and into her old house.

Cormac and his Cousins quickly followed her. Forkbraid watched them pass through, and then closed the passage behind them.

Cormac led Candy and their Cousins through their old house. They quickly passed down the spiral staircase and along the corridor that opened onto the ledge high above the main cavern floor.

It was dark in New Tortuga and very little light could be seen from the main town on the far side of the hydroponics farms. The farms themselves had night lighting to help increase crop yields. The lighting, however, was nowhere near as bright as during daylight and instead gave the farms an eerie glow. Nothing stirred, and the silent night beckoned them forward.

Cormac and Candy then led their Cousins across the rock ledge to the main spiral staircase, leading down to the cavern floor seventy feet below. Fourteen silent figures descended the spiral stairs in the dead of night. Several minutes later they were standing on the cavern floor. Cormac stepped carefully out of the stairwell and into the hydroponics farms. He carefully scanned the area before them telepathically. It was all clear.

"No one about", Cormac whispered back to Candy.

Candy stepped out and walked into the hydroponics farms, their Cousins quickly followed.

"They're all down at the town", Candy whispered to Cormac, adding, "They don't pay much mind to the back of the cavern."

"More fool them", Cormac whispered back.

They made their way as quickly as they could through the extensive hydroponics farms. By the time they reached the other side of the farms, it was past two thirty am. The eerie glow of the hydroponics farms ended abruptly and the darkness of New Tortuga's night beckoned. The township of New Tortuga had very few street lights and those that there were, were to be avoided.

After a few quick telepathic exchanges, the group split into two. Candy led six Cousins towards the eastern terraces, Cormac led their other six Cousins towards the western terraces. Both groups climbed the terrace stairs as quickly as they could. It wasn't long before Cormac reached the first of the houses that had been carved deep into the terrace's bedrock.

Cormac walked into the entrance to the first house and scanned the minds of the family inside. They were ordinary folk and not at all interested in the politics, religious or otherwise of the fundamentalist militants that now controlled New Tortuga. Cormac quietly opened the door and stepped inside. Carefully he sent a telepathic wake-up call to the house owner who slept soundly in his bed in one of the back bedrooms.

The house owner awoke, climbed out of bed and quickly made his way to Cormac, he had a bewildered look on his face.

Cormac sent reassuring thoughts to the house owner as he approached, then just as the bewildered man was about to question him, Cormac raised his fingers to his lips, "Shhh."

"I can't explain fully", Cormac Farmer whispered to the man, "Things are happening, and you need to be absolutely quiet."

The Man recognised Cormac, "Why? What's happening, Cormac Farmer?", he questioned in hushed tones.

"The colonial troops will be here by morning", Cormac informed the Man, adding, "For your safety and that of your family, you need to take refuge at the back of the cavern beyond the hydroponics farms."

"Colonial troops? Safety?", the Man questioned.

"There's no time to explain", Cormac replied more strongly, "You need to take your family to the back of the hydroponics farms."

The Man nodded and asked "How soon?"

Cormac shook his head, then said, "Straight away. There's no time to waste. And you have to be absolutely quiet. No noise at all, and no lights. Grab your family and just take them to the very back of the caverns."

The Man nodded and whispered, "Beyond the back of the hydroponics farms?"

"Yes, that's right. Now get a wriggle on and get your family to safety. Don't worry about anything else, just your family", Cormac replied, then he added, "Make sure that you're all absolutely quiet and no lights." Cormac turned around and walked back out the door.

Cormac's Cousins were waiting for him when he came back out of the house, "Just like that, Cousins, we need to warn the townsfolk", he told them quietly.

"Every house, Cormac?", one of Cormac's Cousins whispered.

"No, not every house", Cormac replied, adding "If the householder has any affiliation or sympathy for those militant sligs, then move on to the next house. Save those that want the sligs gone. The colonial troops can have the militants and their sympathisers."

"What if they don't want to leave?", another of Cormac's Cousins asked.

"Then ask them to lock themselves in and take refuge at the rear of their house", Cormac replied.

Cormac then turned to his Cousins once more, "If you find a house with a militant slig living in it, use your spray, one red dot above the door on the lintel. The colonial troops will deal with them later. We just have to mark where the evil sligs are."

Cormac's Cousins quickly double-checked their packs for their spray cans, all were present.

Cormac's Cousins nodded then moved off on their appointed tasks. A couple of the Cousins moved down the terrace they were on, the rest climbed the stairs to the higher terraces. One by one they checked the houses. One by one they carefully warned the house owners. As Cormac looked back the way he'd come, a small, but growing stream of townsfolk were quietly making their way towards the hydroponic farms.

Cormac reached across to the eastern terraces with his mind. He felt the gentle touch of his Wife's mind greet him. Candy's group was also making headway and a growing stream of townsfolk were seeking refuge in the hydroponics farms, walking away from their eastern terrace homes.

"*No time to chat now, Cormac*", Candy transmitted to him, "*We have so much work to do and so little time in which to do it.*"

Cormac smiled his gap-toothed smile and transmitted back, "*Then we'd better get a wriggle on.*"

Three hours later, as six am was rapidly approaching, Cormac transmitted a single message to Candy, "*It's time, Candy.*"

Candy replied by transmitting back a single word, "*Agreed.*"

Cormac and Candy both changed tack.

A great many townsfolk from both the eastern and western terraces were now making their way towards the back of the hydroponics farms. So far things had gone well. Everyone had done their best to seek safety and refuge quietly. Very little noise had been raised. Soon, however, it would be six am. Shortly thereafter, the town lighting would come on once more and artificial daylight would greet New Tortuga.

In the light of day the movement of townsfolk seeking safety would be noticed. It was now too late for further townsfolk to make their way to the hydroponics farms unseen. Now Cormac, Candy, and their Cousins, instructed all the townsfolk they warned, to lock themselves inside and seek refuge at the rear of their houses, deep inside the bedrock.

Just before six am, Candy's Cousins regrouped with Candy. As Candy explained to the last family the urgent need for them to take refuge at the rear of their house, she also asked permission for herself and her Cousins to take refuge with them. Cormac and their other six Cousins did likewise on the western terraces. Both groups now took refuge with the very last family they had each warned. They had only managed to bring their warning to half of the townsfolk.

Cormac sent a simple message to his Wife, "*Be safe, Candy.*"

Candy sent Cormac a simple reply, "*You too, my sweet man.*"

Now they all waited. For dawn was approaching and with it a brand-new day.

Forkbraid sat patiently in the kitchen of Cormac's house. They had come through from the tunnel about five am. Lady Selene was with him and had prepared a light breakfast as they waited. Special Agent Murphy was with Captain Carmichael making their final preparations.

All seemed to be quiet, yet Forkbraid and Selene knew that everything was going to plan. The minds of many townsfolk that had made their way into the hydroponics farms were easily detected by them. A great many people had gathered in the hydroponics farms below them. They all waited patiently and quietly.

Forkbraid and Selene sent telepathic messages to the gathering crowd below. Messages of encouragement. Messages reminding them of the need to be quiet and above all, messages to let the townsfolk know, not to be frightened when the colonial troops arrived. At six am, Special Agent Murphy and Captain Carmichael walked into the kitchen.

"I've sent word to the drop-ships", Special Agent Murphy began, "Your Bat Wings is on its way."

"Then it's time to get moving", Forkbraid replied.

Captain Carmichael smiled, "Indeed it is", he then spoke instructions into his communicator.

Forkbraid stood up from his chair and offered his arm to Selene, "My Lady."

"Why thank you kind, Sir", Selene replied, and together they walked to the corridor and followed it to the front of Cormac's house.

Once outside, Forkbraid and Selene walked to the stairwell that led down to the cavern floor.

Forkbraid turned, faced Cormac's house and raised both arms above his head. He slowly lowered his arms and using his abilities, sent the families living in the houses on either side of Cormac's house into a deep and extended slumber.

"It's probably best if they sleep through what transpires next", Forkbraid explained to Selene.

"I agree completely with you, Forkbraid", Selene replied.

Captain Carmichael and Special Agent Murphy stepped out from Cormac's house, a squad of colonial troops quickly fell into formation behind them.

"Men, secure these houses", Captain Carmichael ordered.

Forkbraid responded quickly, "No need, Captain. These families aren't militants."

Selene quickly added, "And Forkbraid's just put them to sleep for the next ten hours or so."

The Captain gave Selene a funny look.

Forkbraid replied to the Captain's look, "That's right, Captain. They're all asleep, and they won't wake up until later this evening."

The Captain turned to his men, "Men. Cancel that order", then he turned to Forkbraid, "Can you make the Militants sleep?"

Forkbraid shook his head, "These families were already asleep, I merely extended their existing state. The militants will be another kettle of fish entirely."

Forkbraid held his arm out once more for Selene, and together they began walking down the main spiral stairwell to the cavern floor. Special Agent Murphy and Captain Carmichael quickly followed them and behind them followed a column of fully armed colonial troops. Twelve squads in all, armed and ready for action.

It wasn't long before Forkbraid and Selene reached the cavern floor and stepped out into the hydroponics farms. The hydroponics farms' lighting had begun gradually increasing in intensity and would shortly reach their maximum brightness. Frightened families were huddled here and there among the greenery. There were a great many of them. Concerned looks appeared on the faces of the parents as they watched a Witch and Wizard step forth from the stairwell's entrance.

Straight away Forkbraid and Selene sent out strong telepathic messages of reassurance, asking the people not to be afraid and to be patient and quiet. When Captain Carmichael and his colonial troops started marching out of the stairwell, Forkbraid and Selene sent out messages reassuring the people that the colonial troops were not a threat to them. They were only here to deal with the fundamentalist militants in control of New Tortuga.

The magical pair then continued to transmit these messages as they led the column of colonial troops across the hydroponics farms towards the township of New Tortuga.

It was after six thirty am when they approached the far edge of the hydroponics farms.

Captain Carmichael remarked, "It would have been nice to have darkness on our side."

Special Agent Murphy looked back the way they'd come, "You think your colonial troops could have navigated that in the dark and done so quietly?"

Captain Carmichael looked back over his shoulder, "I suppose you're right, Agent Murphy."

"You won't need darkness, Captain", Forkbraid reassured him, "They won't see your colonial troops coming."

"I still don't get how that's going to work", the Captain replied.

Forkbraid smiled as Selene informed the Captain, "It's called a glamour. Remember how you couldn't see the town of Sweetness as we approached it."

"Yes, I remember. It was quite extraordinary", the Captain replied as he remembered.

"Well, this is very much the same", Selene continued, "We'll be obfuscating their sight. They may look, but they won't see. Your colonial troops can approach unseen."

"More correctly speaking, their minds won't register what their eyes see", Forkbraid explained, adding, "Having my Bat Wing turn up as a distraction will make it so much easier for us."

Forkbraid reached into his impossible pocket and pulled out his staff. He tossed it behind him, where it hovered obediently. He then reached back into his impossible pockets once more and pulled out his wands. Lady Selene had done the same, her staff hovered obediently behind her and in her right hand she held her wand, Gnomulus. Together they stepped out from the foliage of the hydroponics farm and onto the trail that led to the township of New Tortuga.

Selene waved her arms towards the eastern terraces, as Forkbraid waved his arms towards the western terraces. There was a slight ripple in the air, as if one was looking into rising heat. Apart from that, everything else seemed normal, yet from the other side, this subtle ripple in the air, would hide an approaching army.

Captain Carmichael gave a simple order to his men, "Do not advance ahead of Lord Forkbraid and Lady Selene. Stay behind them until otherwise ordered."

Special Agent Murphy then instructed, "Remember, if you see a house door with a red spot on its lintel, secure it and everyone inside. They are militants."

Captain Carmichael nodded in agreement, then ordered three squads over to the eastern terraces and another three squads to the western terraces. The remaining six squads were to advance with the Captain and Special Agent Murphy on either side of the trail behind Forkbraid and Selene. Slowly and quietly, the small army moved forward towards the township of New Tortuga.

Matthew watched his screen as the small ship approached. The little ship had flown very low, under New Tortuga's main scanners. It has approached almost undetected.

"What the hell is that?", he whispered to himself.

It was small, it was alone, and it was approaching swiftly. As it came closer Matthew realised what it was. It was a Bat Wing Interceptor! He shook his head in disbelief.

"It's an antique", he said to himself in astonishment.

The small ship did not request [78]DCI, instead it scanned the cavern entrance as it approached. Then as it slowed and entered the cavern, the ship then scanned the port facilities and bypassed them completely. It was heading towards the town centre.

Matthew jumped to his feet and ran down the corridor to the Delilah's hatch. Quickly he leapt out of the Delilah and ran towards the town square. The Bat Wing interceptor had already landed in the centre of the town square by the time

---

78 Docking Computer Interlock. Interlocking of ships navigation computers for automated docking.

he reached it.

Leroy McGuvan approached the town square from the church, formerly known as the Black Pullet. It was an odd sight. Just gone six thirty am and a small craft had landed in the centre of the town square. Not the sort of thing that you'd expect at this time of the morning. Especially considering that ships were meant to land in the port, not the town square. The Prophet's men were coming from all directions, as was the Prophet himself. With their weapons drawn, the Prophet's men had the small ship completely surrounded.

"What is it, Matthew?", the Prophet asked.

"My Lord, that is a Bat Wing Interceptor", Matthew replied, adding, "It's an antique."

The Prophet cocked an eye-brow at the last remark.

"What's it doing here?", the Prophet questioned.

"I don't know, Sir", Matthew quickly replied, before adding, "It flew in low, under our scanners, it bypassed the port and came straight here to the centre of town."

"Any ideas, Leroy?", the Prophet asked.

"None, My Lord, but I'm fairly certain that this isn't good news", Leroy replied.

"Where's Captain Scar? Maybe he'll know what to make of this", the Prophet stated.

Matthew looked around the growing crowd of militants. Captain Scar was not among them.

Matthew then looked farther afield and caught sight of Captain Scar. The good Captain, Mort Kendal, was holding back, he was watching from a distance near the tavern called the Kraken.

Matthew watched as Mort Kendall climbed to a good vantage point, then having caught site of the Bat Wing, he appeared to stumble backwards. Matthew watched as Mort Kendal, alias Captain Scar, regained his footing and quickly headed in the direction of the port.

"That can not be a good sign. He knows something", Matthew thought to himself.

"My Lord", Matthew addressed the Prophet in a hushed tone, before asking, "Do you remember that conversation we had the other day in the Delilah?"

"Why, yes, Matthew, of course, I remember", the Prophet replied.

"Well, my Lord, it's right about now, that I recommend that we go straight to the Delilah and prepare for immediate evacuation", Matthew explained.

"Immediate evacuation?", the Prophet queried rather loudly.

Leroy caught the Prophet's query and turned to Matthew, "What's that?"

Matthew looked back at the Prophet, "My Lord. I just caught sight of Mort Kendal making a beeline for the port."

"Mort Kendal? Oh, yes, Captain Scar", the Prophet acknowledged.

"He knows something that we don't. I'd bet he's about to take flight", Matthew informed them.

Leroy looked to the port, then back at the Bat Wing Interceptor in the town square, "What do you mean Matthew? It's just one small ship."

"My Lord, Bat Wing Interceptors are very rare these days. Antiques. It was a Bat Wing that nearly killed Kendal during our first attack on Elysium. That has got to be the same Bat Wing", Matthew explained.

Leroy looked back at the Bat Wing Interceptor, asking, "Matthew, who's flying that thing?"

Matthew looked at Leroy, then turned to the Prophet and told him, "The odds are, my Lord, it's the Wizard himself. Who else would be so audacious?"

Leroy's thoughts hung on those last sentences, he stared at the Bat Wing for a long moment, then looked about the town square, "There aren't many townsfolk about this morning", he said feebly.

Matthew looked about the town square once more, then scanned his keen eyes farther afield.

In the distance towards the hydroponics farms, he could see a slight shimmering in the air. Rising heat as the early morning warmed up. He scanned his eyes along the terraces to his left and then to his right. Again, there were so few people up and about this morning.

"My Lord, Leroy's right. There aren't many townsfolks about. There should be far more people up and about, going about their daily business."

The Prophet looked around, "Now that is odd, isn't it, especially with all this commotion."

"My Lord, this is just another reason to get to the Delilah", Matthew stated, and then insisted more forcefully, "My Lord, for your own safety, we must leave now!"

The Prophet quietly thought about the situation, as Matthew's keen eyes scanned the cavern that housed New Tortuga. Along one of the lower, nearer, western terraces, Matthew caught sight of a small red dot on the lintel above a house door. A shocked look appeared on Matthew's otherwise Stoic features. He scanned the terrace further, here and there were several other red dots. They seemed to correspond to the houses where the Prophet's men and recruits had been billeted.

"They're already here", Matthew said quietly, almost under his breath.

"What was that?", Leroy asked.

"They're already here!", Matthew said far more loudly, "The colonial troops are already here!"

"What? How?", Leroy demanded.

Matthew pointed to the near western terrace and the first red dot he'd spotted.

He then pointed to the other red dots, "It's strange how red dots have appeared above the doors of the houses where our men have been billeted."

Leroy stared at the nearest door with the red dot, "That doesn't mean a thing, Matthew."

Matthew turned to the Prophet, "My Lord, we must leave now!", he was most insistent.

The Prophet was swayed by the concern on Matthew's face, "We're going to the Delilah now. Leroy, have that ship secured."

Leroy gave an order to his nearest Lieutenant, "Have that Bat Wing Interceptor secured!"

"Yes, Sir", the man replied.

Leroy then turned and followed after Matthew and the Prophet who were already quickly making their way to the Delilah.

By the time The Prophet had reached the space yacht, Delilah, Forkbraid and Lady Selene were very close to the town square. Special Agent Murphy and Captain Carmichael had given orders to the colonial troops to take up positions and prepare for battle.

Then at the appointed moment, Lady Selene had clapped her hands together, *"Clap!"*

This was no ordinary clap. The sound was loud, awesome, almost deafening, it echoed off the walls of the cavern. It was heard by everyone far and wide. Then as the echoing stopped…

Matthew climbed up the Delilah's boarding ramp steps and looked back towards the town square and beyond. A startled Prophet had quickly followed him and also scanned with his eyes towards the rear of the cavern.

Forkbraid and Selene's glamour vanished, the shimmering in the air was gone and there, for all to see, was a couple, a man, and a woman. They stood some distance beyond the town square. Their attire gave them away at once, they were a Wizard and a Witch.

Matthew pointed to the eastern terraces. There were armed colonial troops taking up positions on the terraces. Matthew then pointed beyond the Wizard and Witch, again armed colonial troops were taking up positions, numerous numbers of them. Matthew could not see the western terraces from his current position, but he knew the same was happening there.

"How? How did they get in here?", the Prophet questioned.

Matthew shook his head, "There's no time to worry about that now. We have to get out of here."

Leroy had also climbed the boarding steps and stared in shock at what he saw, "Holy Mother of God! We are in trouble!", he exclaimed.

Matthew had stepped into the Delilah's hatch and was making his way directly to the bridge.

The Prophet quickly stepped through the hatch behind him, then turned and stopped as Leroy was about to step through the hatch. The Prophet raised his hand in front of Leroy.

A startled Leroy stopped abruptly, "My Lord?", he enquired.

"Leroy. I need you to fight a rear guard defence", the Prophet told him, explaining, "I need you to buy us the time we need to escape."

"My Lord", Leroy replied as he glanced over his shoulder at the Wizard, the Witch and the colonial troops, "That... That would be an act of suicide, my Lord."

"Martyrdom, Leroy, Martyrdom, not suicide", the Prophet corrected, "Your Sacrifice will be greatly rewarded with a place in heaven, sitting at the right-hand of our almighty God."

The Prophet pushed the hatch switch and the hatch began to close.

Leroy gulped and replied meekly, "Thank you, my Lord", as the Delilah's hatch closed tightly, he thought to himself quite simply, *"Dead is dead!"*

Leroy then jumped to the ground as the boarding ramp and steps abruptly retracted.

"Holy fuck!", Leroy spat under his breath as he climbed to his feet.

Leroy stepped back and stared at the space yacht, Delilah, he shook his head and then turned around and made his way back to the town centre.

"This is the reward I get for all of my years of service!", he thought to himself as he ran back towards the town square.

As he approached the town square, he noticed his men were now ignoring the Bat Wing and taking up defensive positions to face this newer, far more deadly threat.

Leroy stepped forward and addressed his enemies, "If you think we're going to surrender, then you've got another thing coming", he yelled as loudly as he could.

Forkbraid yelled back with an amplified voice, "Surrender or fight. It makes no difference to us. You'll lose either way. At least if you surrender, you might still live."

"Maybe you haven't brought enough troops. Have you thought about that?", Leroy shouted.

Selene yelled back, her voice amplified, "Even if we'd left the troops behind, you'd still lose!"

Leroy looked to the terraces on his left and his right. Further back in the distance, quite a few doors had already been kicked in. They all had one thing in common, a red dot on their lintels.

Prisoners had already been taken. The colonial troops were somewhat closer now, they had the high ground and were heavily armed.

Leroy spoke quickly with one of his Lieutenants, "You there, get some men up onto those terraces. We must hold the high ground!"

"Yes, Sir", the man responded as he gathered several men together and sent them to the eastern terraces, and then he then gathered several more men together and sent them to the western terraces.

"Sir. We are going to need more men up there", the Lieutenant recommended.

"Don't you think I know that already?", Leroy replied, spitting under his breath, "Idiot!"

Leroy then pointed to the doors with the red dots on their lintels, the ones that were still well out of the reach of the colonial troops.

"How many of our men are still fucking asleep?", Leroy asked his Lieutenant.

"I don't know, Sir", the Lieutenant replied.

"Have every house checked", Leroy ordered, "I want every available man, armed and ready. Get as many men as you can up onto those terraces. We must hold the high ground!", he reiterated.

"Yes, Sir, right away, Sir", the Lieutenant said as he ran off to carry out his orders.

Leroy then turned his attention to the town's other defences.

Lady Selene shouted to the militants, "You're all going to lose! You all know it! If you throw down your arms and surrender, you will survive! If you don't, you will all die!"

"Why don't you let me worry about that?", Leroy shouted back as he went about checking New Tortuga's defences.

"You haven't got much time. Surrender or die!", Forkbraid levelled his ultimatum.

"I tell you what, I'll think about it", Leroy shouted back, "What say you call me back tomorrow."

Forkbraid shook his head, noting telepathically, *"He's just stalling for time."*

"Of course, he is", Selene replied telepathically, *"Give him ten minutes and no longer."*

"Ten minutes it is then", Forkbraid replied to his Wife, then he shouted out loudly, "You have ten minutes. That's all. Then you either surrender or die!"

Leroy stopped for a brief moment as he considered the last remark, *"Ten minutes"*, he thought to himself as he hastened checking the towns defences.

Matthew sat at the controls of the Delilah. He had switched on the Delilah's [79]AGLs and the space yacht was indeed hovering just above the cavern floor. However, as yet, Matthew had made no further moves towards escaping New

---

79 Antigravity Lifters. Devices used to nullify gravity and allow vessels to fly.

Tortuga.

"What are you waiting for, Matthew?", the Prophet asked, then demanded "Let's get out of here."

Matthew had no time for stupidity, "My Lord, would you please shut the fuck up and let me deal with this situation. If you want to live, you have to let me think this through."

The Prophet was taken aback by Matthew's response, "Matthew, I'm just wondering why you're hesitating", he replied curiously.

"I'm not hesitating, my Lord", Matthew replied, "I'm waiting for just the right moment."

"Just the right moment?", the Prophet asked curiously.

"Yes, my Lord", Matthew replied as he offered his master the co-pilots in front of his console.

The Prophet sat down and followed Matthew's gaze out of the Delilah's view portal.

Matthew pointed to the other side of the port, "There, my Lord, there."

On the other side of the port, where the Talons were stored, their pirates had all gathered. Mort Kendal, alias Captain Scar, was among them.

"Rats fleeing a sinking ship, my Lord", Matthew muttered softly to the Prophet.

The Prophet heard him loud and clear.

One by one the pirates boarded their ships. Then minutes later seven Talons and two Gull Wing Interceptors took flight. Less than a minute after that, one of the two remaining Raiders took flight as well and quickly followed the fighters into the blue skies of Mars.

Matthew switched on his tracking module and followed the trajectories of the fleeing pirates.

"That's what I've been waiting for", he told his master as he prepared the Delilah for flight.

Forkbraid shouted to the militants, "Your time is up."

Leroy shouted back, "What? So soon? I'm still thinking about it?"

"Don't think you can run away in the Delilah again", Forkbraid shouted.

Leroy turned back to the Wizard and Witch once more, "Why not?", he shouted, "It worked a treat the last time didn't it?"

"Everyone of the Spartan's Wisps is currently patrolling above Mars", Forkbraid replied, adding, "Most of them are patrolling above this very region."

"Shit! Shit!", Leroy said to himself, then shouted cheekily back to Forkbraid, "What? Does Usarian want his yacht back? Well he can't bloody well have it!"

Forkbraid looked to Selene telepathically noting, *"This is getting nowhere fast."*

Selene agreed, *"What do you suggest?"*

"Force their hand", Forkbraid replied, *"We're already shielded up, let's advance on*

them."

"So mote it be!", Selene replied verbally.

"So mote it be!", Forkbraid repeated.

Then they both advanced on New Tortuga with the colonial troops following them.

Leroy watched as the Wizard and Witch advanced, "Shit!", he swore under his breath, then he yelled out as loud as he could, "Open fire!"

The militants opened fire with rifles, machine guns and pulsed plasma pistols. Bullets and plasma pulses flew across the town square, aimed squarely at Forkbraid and Selene. They were perceived as the greater threat.

Matthew launched the Delilah and quickly flew the space yacht out of New Tortuga's port.

Forkbraid frowned as the Delilah slipped into the Martian skies. Matthew swung the Delilah west and kept her trajectory low, all the time watching his tracking module.

"What are we doing, Matthew?", the Prophet asked.

"Tracking the fleeing rats, my Lord", Matthew replied, explaining, "Escaping can't possibly be as easy as simply taking off and running away."

All the pirates were fleeing Mars and heading straight for high orbit, hoping to lose themselves on some of the more lawless Martian high orbital colonies. As Matthew and the Prophet watched the tracking module, the pirates entered space.

"How are you tracking them, Matthew?", the Prophet questioned.

Matthew laughed, "I've got low-jack on their ships, my Lord."

"Low jack?", the Prophet queried.

"I've placed tracking beacons on them", Matthew explained, before remarking, "I figured, that if things went pear shaped, it would be handy to know what happened to our, shall we say, friends."

As Matthew watched, one by one, the tracking beacons went out.

"What's happening?", the Prophet asked.

Matthew activated the Delilah's scanners. During his stay on Mars, he had modified them considerably, enhancing both their power and accuracy. A swarm of the Spartan's Wisps appeared on his ship's scanners. They were chasing down and destroying the fleeing pirates, one by one.

"There you have it, my Lord", Matthew pointed out, "They've unleashed a storm and our so-called friends are caught in the middle of it."

Mort Kendal, alias Captain Scar, watched his scanners as the Wisps approached from nearly every direction. He forced his Talon to duck and weave, to perform manoeuvres far beyond his Talon's normal capabilities. To his credit, he killed four Wisps before they finally took him down.

Such was the ferocity of the attack, Mort Kendal didn't have time to think beyond his desperate attempts to stay alive. His life did not flash before his eyes. In an explosion of brilliant blue, his Talon was torn into a billion pieces of debris. Mort Kendal, alias Captain Scar, died as he'd lived, on the edge. He was an arsehole, and he would not be missed, not even by his long-suffering Wife.

Soon all the tracking beacons were dead. They were all gone, all blown to smithereens!

"Seven Talons, two Gull Wings and one Raider", Matthew remarked, "All dead."

"Well, we can't leave the planet", the Prophet replied, stating the bleeding obvious, before asking "How did you know, Matthew?"

"Tactics of mistake one-o-one, my Lord", Matthew replied.

The Prophet gave Matthew a funny look, to which Matthew explained, "If you provide your enemy with a perceived way out, it has two major effects. One, any who would desert, will do so, probably before the battle even starts. Our so-called Pirate friends. Two, your enemy won't fight so hard if they think that they have an escape route. Instead of fighting like cornered foxes, they have the option to run like fleeing rats."

"You did say 'perceived' way out, didn't you, Matthew?", the Prophet enquired.

"Our enemies found a way in through the rear of the cavern. Probably Cormac Farmer gave them that information. They distracted us with that antique Bat Wing Interceptor, but they didn't blockade the port. They left it wide open. Only it wasn't wide open, was it, my Lord?", Matthew tapped on the Delilah's scanners pointing out the swarms of Wisps still patrolling just above the atmosphere.

Matthew kept the Delilah on a low, westerly trajectory. He was quiet for many minutes as he pondered their current situation.

"What do we do now, Matthew?", the Prophet asked with serious concern.

Matthew began to think aloud, "We can still leave the planet", he remarked, adding, "Just not today. There will be a time in the future when we'll be able to slink away, just not today."

"Yes, but what do we do now ,Matthew?", the Prophet asked again.

Matthew turned to the Prophet and smiled, "We survive, my Lord, we survive!"

Roseanne woke up screaming, her young body drenched in sweat. Mystal, Elder of the town of Sweetness, came running quickly into Roseanne's room. By now Roseanne was on her feet, she had dressed herself in her usual dark Academy robes and cloak.

"What are you doing, Roseanne?", Mystal desperately asked.

Roseanne's reply was almost gibberish, "They, she, he. Trouble. Death. I have to help. Bullets flying, plasma everywhere. Hell on Earth. Evil things!"

"Roseanne, get a hold of yourself. We are on Mars. You're dreaming", Mystal replied as she grabbed Roseanne by the shoulders and shook her gently.

Roseanne pushed Mystal away, "I have to help. Selene is in trouble."

"Selene is with Forkbraid, she'll be fine, Roseanne", Mystal assured her.

"Who will look after, Selene, if Forkbraid falls into darkness?", Roseanne questioned, her eyes had rolled back, only the whites were showing, her visage was viperous.

Mystal hadn't seen a visage such as this. There were no level nines or higher on Mars, outside of those who had recently arrived from Earth.

Raw power exuded from every pore of Roseanne's body. Raw power poured out of her eyes.

Mystal, herself a high functioning level eight, took several steps backwards in fear and found herself pressed hard against the wall of the room.

There was a sudden flash of light, a sudden beam of light extended from the floor to the ceiling. Roseanne stood amidst the very centre of this beam. Another flash of light erupted from Roseanne's torso, then all of a sudden, Roseanne Rhein was gone. The room was completely empty, except for a very frightened Mystal.

Forkbraid and Selene braced themselves for the onslaught, their defensive shields at their maximum. All of a sudden, between them and their attackers, there was a sudden explosion of bright light. A pillar of light extended from the cavern floor to the cavern roof, far above them.

The pillar of light contracted downwards and then there was a sudden flash at head level. Suddenly before them stood Roseanne Rhein. Her defences were up, she glowed with raw power. Bullets and pulses of plasma exploded into brilliant scintillations before her.

Forkbraid looked to Selene with an uncomprehending stare. Selene stared back at him, just as dumbfounded. They both picked up the exclamations from their evil adversaries in the town, the most common one being, "Holy fuck!"

"*What's going on?*", Selene questioned.

"*I don't know*", Forkbraid answered.

"*Where did she come from? How?*", Selene questioned again.

"*Roseanne [80]jaunted, she mind-walked. Give me a second*", Forkbraid replied as he quickly turned his own mind inwards.

With his defences still up, Forkbraid turned within.

The sublime, smiling face of Lord Folcrom Tafazah stared back at him, "*You know what I know*", it whispered to him.

---

80 Jaunt. The ability to step from one distant place to another, through a sheer act of will. Refer to Mind-Walker.

"You were a [81] mind-walker, weren't you?", Forkbraid asked.

"Yes, indeed, I was... Oh, the places my mind has walked", Tafazah's face replied.

"I need that knowledge and I need it now!", Forkbraid demanded.

The sublime, smiling face of Lord Folcrom Tafazah sighed, *"You know what I know! You already have the knowledge that you are demanding!"*

"I have the knowledge!", Forkbraid realised.

"You always have!", Tafazah replied, *"Even before you met me, you just never used it before."*

Forkbraid was caught off guard by Tafazah's last statement, his mind wondering how many times he could have used this knowledge in the past.

Selene had picked up on Forkbraid's previous thought and asked, *"You have the knowledge?"*

This brought Forkbraid back to the present, *"Yes, I have the knowledge"*, Forkbraid replied.

"Good, then go over there and get Roseanne out of here, now!", Selene demanded.

Forkbraid thought cautiously to himself, *"I can't do it. If I take Roseanne out of here, I'll be leaving Selene to stand and fight alone!"*

Forkbraid replied to Selene, *"You have to do it, Selene!"*

"I'm not a mind-walker! I don't have that power!", Selene's mind screamed back at him.

"You do now. Selene, with you, I share a piece of my mind!", Forkbraid replied, and then he transmitted the necessary knowledge directly to Selene's mind.

In a single instant, Forkbraid transferred all the knowledge Selene would need to be able to take Roseanne out of the current situation. Selene was startled by the flow of intricate knowledge. How simple it was, to mind-walk. Jaunting was actually simple, it was just a variant of blinking!

"Why me?", Selene questioned.

"If I do it, Roseanne will just jaunt back here to be with you", Forkbraid explained, stressing *"You have to do it, Selene."*

"When this is over, I'm going to give Roseanne such a talking to", Selene replied shaking her head in exasperation.

Selene began to run. Swiftly crossing the distance between her and Roseanne, Selene slipped through Roseanne's defences and wrapped her arms about her. There was another sudden, almighty flash of light. Another pillar of light reached from the cavern floor to the cavern roof. A second flash of light erupted from Selene's torso, then all of a sudden, Selene and Roseanne were gone.

The bullets and pulses of plasma that had been exploding harmlessly against Roseanne's defences, suddenly flew through the now vacant space and exploded in brilliant scintillations against Forkbraid's own shield.

---

81 Mind-Walker. One who has the ability to travel vast distances by way of mental teleportation. Refer to Jaunt.

Forkbraid thought to himself, *"As it should be. I was born for this task."*

Candy sat in the room with six of her Cousins. Their hosts were a young couple, with two children. It was here that they had taken refuge from the upcoming battle. The room was at the very rear of the couples' house. It was quite a large room, having been carved out as a billiards room. At present the only furnishings were a few couches. The couple had yet to acquire a billiards table; they were a very rare item on Mars. They all sat quietly, patiently waiting for the events outside in the town to run their course.

All of a sudden, there was a sudden flash of light. A pillar of light erupted from the floor to the ceiling. It quickly contracted and flashed again at chest height. Then before them stood two women, one older, and the other, both wearing the attire of Witches.

Candy stood up and stared in amazement, "Selene! Roseanne! What the hell? What's going on?"

Selene steadied herself and replied, "Hi, Candy. I'm not sure that I can explain. Suffice to say, Roseanne popped up in the middle of the battlefield and I thought that was kind of unsafe. So I grabbed Roseanne and we popped up here."

"Okay… You might want to run that past me again later", was the only reply that an awe struck Candy could come up with.

Candy had seen a lot of strange things in her life, but this one took the cake.

Selene then turned to the householders and asked, "Is it okay if we rest here for a while?"

The children all sat with their mouths wide open, their jaws agape.

The Wife looked to her Husband, equally stunned.

The Husband opened his mouth to speak, but just stuttered.

After several attempts, he finally mouthed the very soft reply, "Yeah, sure."

Forkbraid raised both of his wands and the colonial troops returned fire. Bullets and plasma flew in both directions. The colonial troops slowly advanced. Forkbraid advanced towards the town without the slightest hesitation. Both wands swinging, Forkbraid unleashed death without mercy. Streams of blue light erupted from the tips of his wands. Militant after militant, flashed into transparency and collapsed to the ground, dead, before him.

Forkbraid looked to his left and to his right. The colonial troops were fighting against a solid resistance on the terraces. The enemy was fighting hard and desperate to keep control of the high ground. That, Forkbraid thought, simply would not do.

Forkbraid held his arms up once more, the tips of his wands pointing towards the terraces on either side. Blue light leapt forth from the tips of his wands, as Forkbraid strafed the terraces ahead of the colonial troopers. Militant after militant flashed into transparency and collapsed to the ground. Other militants began to run in a total panic as the streams of blue light approached them.

Many were swept off the edge of the terraces and fell to their deaths. The colonial troops then sensed that they had the upper hand and surged forward.

"Excellent", Forkbraid said to himself as he returned his focus to the town square ahead of him.

Captain Carmichael had watched Forkbraid dispatch the militants on the terraces.

"He doesn't mess about, does he?", the Captain remarked rhetorically.

"No, Captain", Special Agent Murphy replied, "Forkbraid certainly does not mess about."

Streams of blue light flashed, militants died. Bullets flew in both directions. Pulses of plasma shot here and there. Steadily Forkbraid and the well armed colonial troops advanced. Leroy was fighting a losing battle and he knew it. Many of his men were already dead, many more were going to die, he himself was going to die.

"Fall back", Leroy screamed with an unparalleled urgency, "Fall back to the port."

The fighting had taken the whole day, night had already fallen hours ago and outside the caverns of New Tortuga, the Martian skies were dark.

Slowly the militants withdrew from their positions and retreated towards the port, continuing to return fire as they did so. Several pockets of militants were cut off from the rest and unable to retreat, for them, it was a fight to the death.

Several were trapped in the tavern, the Kraken. Forkbraid aimed both his wands at the tavern and with two viscous streams of raw blue might, levelled the pub, raising it to the ground and killing all of those within it. A squad of colonial troops overran the old Black Pullet, killing the militants within with grenades. Captain Carmichael's colonials were now hunting down militants house to house in the township of New Tortuga itself.

Forkbraid could see the port clearly now. Most of the militants were clearly routed, and were withdrawing from the town as fast as they could. Many were gunned down in a hail of bullets as the colonial troops advanced. The militants appeared to be heading to the western branch of the port, where several freighters were stowed. A last ditch effort to escape. Forkbraid quickly chased after them, streams of blue light still blazing from his two wands.

Finally, Forkbraid reached the port, he stopped and replaced both of his wands back into his impossible pockets.

The cavern in which New Tortuga was built consisted of three branches. The central branch being by far the largest, was where the township had been built and beyond that the hydroponics farms. It was a monstrously large, deep cavern.

The eastern and western branches were somewhat smaller and used for the port facilities. The western branch being by far the larger of the two.

Forkbraid stood in the very centre of the three branches of the New Tortuga cavern system, facing the western branch, into which the remaining militants had retreated. Perhaps they had hoped to fly out on one or more of the freighters stowed within it. With Forkbraid blocking their path, that was not about to happen.

The Antigravity Lifters on a couple of the freighters sparked into life.

Forkbraid shook his head and shouted into the cavern, "You are not going anywhere!"

Forkbraid raised his hands before him and focused all of his might and main into the western branch of the cavern. Forkbraid allowed himself to connect with the very bedrock beneath his feet, grounding himself to the planet Mars itself. His eyes rolled back, only their whites showed. The whole southern flank of Hebes Island began to shudder and shake, violently. Then the shuddering increased in intensity and then it began.

The outer section of the cavern walls before him, began to crack and crumble like poorly mixed concrete. Then the roof of the western branch of the cavern began to collapse. Sweat poured from off of Forkbraid's brow, strain clearly showed upon his face. Rocks fell and boulders tumbled.

The freighters and the militants were crushed under an avalanche of rock and rubble. Fuel tanks ruptured and exploded. Men screamed in crushed and burning agony. Still Forkbraid concentrated, until finally the outer wall of the cavern completely collapsed and slid violently into the Hebes Sea.

Then Forkbraid focused on what was now the completely collapsed roof of the western branch of the cavern. With one almighty thrust, Forkbraid swept this, along with the buried freighters, the dead men and the entire western port out into the Hebes Sea.

The whole western port of New Tortuga had been cleansed.

Captain Carmichael and Special Agent Murphy approached Forkbraid. Wide-eyed and amazed, they both stared at the result of Forkbraid's wroth. What had been the western branch of the cavern, was now a large, broad, flat ledge. Everything else had been swept completely away, and was now sitting at the bottom of the cold, deep Hebes Sea.

Captain Carmichael spoke softly, "There's nothing left!", and then he turned around, and he looked at Forkbraid.

Sweat still poured from Forkbraid's brow.

The battle was largely over.

Only the occasional gun shot was heard, as yet another militant in hiding was flushed out and terminated. There were not many of them left.

Special Agent Murphy slapped Forkbraid on the shoulder and said, "It's over now, FB."

"No it's not, Jim", Forkbraid replied, before noting "The Delilah flew out of here before the battle even started."

Captain Carmichael informed them both, "Every single ship that left New Tortuga, but one, has been destroyed."

"The Delilah?", Forkbraid queried.

"That would be the one that got away from us", the Captain confirmed, commenting, "No space yachts have been sighted thus far above the atmosphere. They've gone to ground, Gentlemen."

"Well, they won't get off the planet. Not with the Spartan's Wisps patrolling up there."

"Agent Murphy is right. My Wisps will blow them all to hell, if they try to leave the planet", the Captain agreed.

Forkbraid was silent for several long moments, and then he turned to face the eastern branch of the cavern. This was where most of the smaller ships had been stowed. Apart from a few dismantled shells, the only ship left was a medium-sized freighter, which had been converted into a Raider. It sat on a landing pad, midway along the eastern branch of the cavern.

"What is it, FB?", Special Agent Murphy asked.

"Not all the militants ran into the western branch", Forkbraid informed them.

"Really?", the Captain enquired.

Forkbraid didn't answer, instead he walked forward a dozen paces and raised his right arm. The dismantled shell of a small ship lifted off the ground and flew against the far wall. Cowering behind it had been one single man. Forkbraid raised the man telekinetically off the ground with a simple gesture of his right hand and brought him forward. Then Forkbraid put him down on the ground before them. The man cowered before them shivering with fear.

"This, Gentlemen, was their commander", Forkbraid informed the others.

"He was the man in charge?", Captain Carmichael questioned.

"Not quite. He was the one left in charge after their leader fled in the Delilah. This, Gentlemen, was the Prophet's right-hand man", Forkbraid corrected.

Captain Carmichael asked the man, "Where's your leader hiding then?"

Leroy spat at the Captain, "I don't know and even if I did, I wouldn't tell you."

Forkbraid concentrated on the man, "His name is Leroy McGuvan… And Leroy doesn't have a clue where his master has gone. In fact, he's quite pissed off that his master left him here to die."

"He's not pissed off enough, if you ask me", Special Agent Murphy remarked, "Otherwise, he might actually tell us something useful."

"Unfortunately, Jim, he doesn't actually know anything useful", Forkbraid replied.

"That might be why his master dumped him here", Captain Carmichael suggested.

"Either way, he's not much good to us then is he?", Special Agent Murphy informed them both.

Forkbraid stared at Leroy McGuvan for a long moment before stating, "He's no good to us at all, Jim. However, Leroy McGuvan here is guilty of a great many crimes. This is one truly evil man."

"Evil! You're the only evil creature around here!", Leroy yelled as he glared back at Forkbraid.

Captain Carmichael took out his pistol, "Well then, this man deserves to die", he stated as he pointed the pistol at Leroy's head.

Leroy took two steps backwards, shivering in fear.

"Put your gun away, Captain. You are not an executioner", Forkbraid told the Captain, using a slight lilt in his voice to ensure it was done.

Leroy McGuvan began laughing at them nervously, "That's right, you can't do it. You have to take me back to Earth for a trial. There has to be a trial. I have my right to a trial in court!"

Leroy McGuvan continued to laugh at them, aloud, now a deep belly aching laugh.

As Captain Carmichael re-holstered his pistol, Forkbraid took a step towards Leroy McGuvan and gestured quickly with his right hand. A sweeping of his arm, a flick of his right wrist.

Leroy McGuvan suddenly flew through the air and out of the port. As Special Agent Murphy and Captain Carmichael both watched, Leroy McGuvan flew several miles out to sea and then tumbled towards the cold, deep dark waters of the Hebes Sea.

"You're not an executioner, Captain, but I am. It is highly unlikely that Leroy McGuvan will be able to swim to shore", Forkbraid told them, then he added, "Have your men secure that Raider. I might have a use for it later."

Forkbraid then turned and walked back towards the township of New Tortuga.

"That, that was really harsh", Captain Carmichael remarked to Special Agent Murphy.

"That's his job, Captain. He's sanctioned to do his duty", Special Agent Murphy replied, adding, "It's a dirty job, but someone's got to do it! If Forkbraid hadn't, I would have shot him myself."

"Well, I guess that means poor old Leroy won't get his trial", the Captain remarked.

A small smile came over Special Agent Murphy's face, "Captain… That was his trial."

31. Best Laid Plans

Lady Selene looked out from the window of Candy's house. Roseanne was sitting on a lounge, on the rock ledge that looked out above the hydroponics farms of New Tortuga. Roseanne seemed to be resting, her eyes staring aimlessly into the distance at nothing in particular.

"Roseanne's a little embarrassed", Candy said to Lady Selene, "Popping up suddenly in the middle of it all. She has no idea how she did it either."

Lady Selene turned away from the window towards Candy.

Candy continued, "We've had word from Sweetness. Mystal isn't sure what happened either. Roseanne was having a nightmare. Mystal went in to comfort her and poof! Then she was here."

"Roseanne's a natural", Selene replied, elaborating "She jaunted simply on instinct. I wouldn't expect her to understand how she did it, not yet anyway. One thing for certain, we're going to have to watch her very carefully from now on."

Both women turned to the window and looked out upon Roseanne once more.

"I was kind of wondering how you managed to jaunt?", Candy enquired.

"Forkbraid sent me the necessary knowledge", Selene replied, noting, "It was actually far easier than I thought it would be. Quite surprising really. It's just a more advanced blinking technique."

"Really? Perhaps it's something that I can learn?", Candy enquired.

Selene slowly shook her head, "Sorry Candy. It's a simple thing, yes, but it does require a certain level of natural ability."

"Natural ability?", Candy enquired.

"Level nine and higher, even then I suspect some of us may not be capable", Selene explained.

Candy nodded, understanding that natural talent did indeed play a large part in what the gifted could or could not achieve.

Forkbraid stepped into the room, he had heard a small part of their exchange, "And even those with the highest abilities, still make a right hash of it", he chided.

"Right hash of it?", Selene queried, "I haven't seen you doing a whole lot of jaunting lately."

Forkbraid smiled at Selene, "Jaunting is meant to be a subtle art. Huge light shows aren't meant to be a part of the process."

"Really? And what makes you the expert all of a sudden?", Selene enquired.

"The process of jaunting only requires the smallest portion of the power you exuded, Selene. The light show you generated during your jaunt, was just wasted energy expressing itself as light."

"Wasted energy?", Selene questioned, with a slight note of annoyance in her voice.

"I don't want to sound offensive, Selene, but exuding energy during the process is just a side effect. It's akin to exuding sweat when one exercises."

"So, the energy I gave off when I jaunted was what? Body odour?", Selene queried, this time feeling more than a little offended.

"No, no, Selene. That's just an analogy, a metaphor. I'm just saying, it's possible to jaunt and not exude massive amounts of energy. The light show's side effects can be controlled somewhat."

"Well, okay then, Mr Expert, show us how it's done!", Lady Selene challenged sarcastically.

Forkbraid concentrated, there was an ever so slight flash of light, it ran from the tip of Forkbraid's head to the base of his feet. Another smaller flash of light occurred simultaneously at Forkbraid's torso. The entire flash of light was contained within Forkbraid's body. Forkbraid himself had not moved a millimetre.

"So, that was it then was it", Selene chided, "I didn't see you going anywhere."

"That's because I jaunted on the spot", Forkbraid explained.

Lady Selene began to laugh, "Jaunting on the spot!", she exclaimed, barely able to control her laughter.

Forkbraid sighed, he concentrated once more, there was the smallest flash of light again, and he was gone. Lady Selene and Candy looked around the room. Forkbraid was nowhere to be seen.

Another small flash of light occurred, just a few feet from where Forkbraid had been standing, then from out of nowhere, Forkbraid reappeared before them.

"Okay, so the exuding of energy, the flash of light, all of that can be controlled?", Selene asked, having seen Forkbraid demonstrate it before her own eyes.

"Yeah, it can", Forkbraid confirmed, explaining, "It makes popping in and out of somewhere, a whole lot less noticeable."

"How do I control it?", Selene asked.

This time Forkbraid laughed, "You already know how, Selene. Yesterday, you were rushed, you didn't have time to study the information that I gave you closely enough."

Lady Selene looked up at Forkbraid curiously, then carefully reconsidered the information Forkbraid had given to her the previous day.

There was a sudden small flash of light and Lady Selene was gone. Another small flash of light and Lady Selene reappeared behind Forkbraid.

"I can see how this would be useful", Selene stated as Forkbraid turned around to face her.

"You see, it's much more subtle when you do it that way", Forkbraid replied.

"Yeah, it is, although putting on a huge light show can have its uses too", Selene pointed out.

"True enough, if you need to create a distraction or frighten an enemy", Forkbraid agreed.

Candy just rolled her eyes and sighed, "Well, all this light flashing is making me giddy, I'm going out to see how Roseanne's doing."

Candy then stood up from her chair and strode out of the room.

Selene chuckled lightly, "Gods, you can be so annoying, Forkbraid."

Forkbraid smiled at Selene, "I think we both excel at that talent at times, my darling."

"I thought you'd be down at the docks with the others?", Selene queried.

"Yeah, I'll be heading down there shortly", Forkbraid informed Selene, noting "Jim thinks he might be able to use New Tortuga's own defence system to locate the Delilah."

"Well that would be great, the sooner we catch their leader the better", Selene replied.

"And Cormac wants to discuss, how did he put it? The remodelling", Forkbraid remarked.

"Considering the amount of damage you caused, that was very diplomatic of him", Selene laughed.

"Yeah, I did make quite a mess of it, didn't I?", Forkbraid agreed.

"That you did, my darling, that you did", Selene told Forkbraid as she leant forward to kiss him.

Cormac stood in New Tortuga's port, staring in awe at the damage caused by Forkbraid. The entire cavern roof was opened up above the old entrance and all that was left of it to the west, had been swept away into the Hebes Sea.

"It's as if he reached up with his hand, peeled back the roof and then swept it and the outer wall away", Cormac whispered in astonishment.

"Not quite as elegant as that", Special Agent Murphy replied, "He brought the roof down on the militants' heads first and then the walls, before sweeping everything into the Hebes Sea."

"Such power! It must have been an incredible sight", Cormac remarked as he turned to Special Agent Murphy.

"Incredible, yes, but also frightening", Special Agent Murphy admitted, noting, "You can't imagine the terror that our enemies must have felt when the cavern roof collapsed on them."

"I don't need to imagine anything Agent Murphy", Cormac sighed, "All the gifted who were present would have felt it. I know I certainly did."

Special Agent Murphy nodded, accepting, yet not fully understanding what Cormac was saying. Not being a psychic, he could never really know.

Captain Carmichael watched as his ship's engineers carried out scans of what remained of the roof above the entrance of the caverns. The broad ledge that had been the western branch of the cavern was stable, having been declared safe earlier by his engineers. Both of the Spartan's drop-ships had flown in from the township of Sweetness and were in the process of landing on the broad ledge. A slight westerly wind was blowing, bringing with it a cold chill from off the Tharsis Bulge.

As the first drop-ship touched down, the Captain remarked, "With the port in the open now, New Tortuga can't hide any more."

Cormac replied, "Not that it matters, Captain, you know where we are now anyway."

"True enough, Cormac, true enough", the Captain replied.

There was a small flash of light and an instant later Forkbraid was standing before them.

"I really wish you wouldn't do that, Forkbraid, it is really disconcerting", the Captain told him.

"It's the fastest way between one point and another, Captain", Forkbraid replied.

"Just because you can, doesn't mean that you should, FB", Special Agent Murphy stated as he lightly slapped Forkbraid on the shoulder.

Cormac made a broad gesture about New Tortuga's western port, then stated with a stern voice, "I have some concerns about your remodelling, Cousin."

Forkbraid looked about the broad ledge that had once been the western branch of the cavern.

The second of the Spartans drop-ships was in the process of touching down. There was still considerable room left on the ledge to land yet more ships if necessary.

"The port has much more space than before Cormac. When the new port facilities are built, I should have thought the extra space would be a huge bonus", Forkbraid replied.

"Well, yes, the extra space will come in handy. We can land far more ships and, of course, bigger ships", Cormac replied, adding "But that's not my actual concern."

"Then what is?", Special Agent Murphy questioned.

Cormac put his finger in his mouth and wet it, then held it up to the breeze, "You feel that?"

Forkbraid could feel the chill breeze upon his cheeks, "A light westerly", he replied.

"Yeah, a westerly", Cormac agreed, "The prevailing winds are always westerlies here."

Cormac pointed to the old entrance to New Tortuga, "Before you remodelled the place, the westerly winds blew straight past that entrance."

Cormac then turned to the eastern branch of the cavern, "Now they're blowing straight into the eastern port, and even into the town. When the westerly gales start blowing, it ain't going to be good. We need a solution before then."

They could all see the problem. Opening up New Tortuga, also opened it up to the elements.

"I get the picture, Cormac, perhaps the Captain's engineers can come up with a solution", Forkbraid suggested to him.

"Yes, yes. Sectioning off the western port into compartmentalised landing bays will help", the Captain suggested, adding, "Putting a wind break across the main entrance here will help as well."

"Yeah, but who's going to pay for all that work?", Cormac questioned.

Forkbraid tugged thoughtfully at his beard, "We could organise some kind of War rebuilding fund. This was essentially a War."

"Good idea. Governor Anderson over at the Chryce colony seems to fancy himself as being the big cheese on this rock. Maybe he'd find rebuilding a newly liberated New Tortuga prestigious or something?", Special Agent Murphy recommended.

"Whatever Governor Anderson thinks, my engineers will pitch in and help wherever they can, Cormac", the Captain informed Cormac.

Forkbraid smiled a wry smile, "What Governor Anderson thinks is irrelevant, Captain. Just flash the Psi Corps crest at him and he'll authorise anything we request."

"You can't keep pushing people around like that, Lord Forkbraid", Captain Carmichael replied, calling Forkbraid by his title, then explaining, "It makes you appear worse than the very people you're hunting!"

Forkbraid put his left hand to his face and rubbed his chin as he looked at the Captain. He was more than taken aback, but understood where the Captain was coming from.

"You're absolutely right, Captain", he replied almost apologetically, and then he continued, "However, on this occasion, I don't think it would hurt to pressure the Governor into getting New Tortuga some first class port facilities."

The Captain shook his head, "Be very careful, Forkbraid, careful that you don't replace one kind of fascism with another."

Forkbraid nodded in understanding, replying, "So noted, Captain, so noted."

Special Agent Murphy was more interested in catching the leader of the militants, he started walking towards New Tortuga's security centre.

"If you follow me, Gentlemen, perhaps we can catch their leader. Then we won't need to be hunting him any more", he called to the others as he walked.

As they started to follow Special Agent Murphy, Cormac said to Forkbraid quietly, "Cousin, you do what you have to. Which is the greater evil? To hunt evil down and kill it or to let that evil flourish?"

They all stepped into the simple rooms that were New Tortuga's security centre. The equipment here was connected to instruments high above them on the plateau. It was undisturbed, left in exactly the same condition in which it was abandoned. Special Agent Murphy pulled a disc from out of his pocket. It was the security centre's data logs.

"I was searching their security logs this morning when I came across this", he explained.

Special Agent Murphy fired up a screen and displayed the data on it. A single Bat Wing Interceptor was seen approaching New Tortuga on the scan data. The small craft approached swiftly and entered the colony. Special Agent Murphy quickly skipped to the next section.

On the screen ten ships flew out of New Tortuga's port.

"Seven Talons, two Gull Wings and a Raider", Special Agent Murphy noted for the others.

Less than a minute later another ship flew out of New Tortuga's port.

"The Delilah!", Special Agent Murphy noted, and then instructed, "Now watch."

The first batch of ships all ran fast and hard, heading as quickly as they could into the Martian upper atmosphere and space. They were just as quickly challenged by the Spartan's Wisps, which suddenly converged on New Tortuga from beyond the scanner's range. One by one they were hunted down and destroyed, but not so with the Delilah. This was all clearly shown on the data logs.

Special Agent Murphy smiled as he tapped the lone image on the screen, "The Delilah! There she is, running fast, running low and heading west."

The Delilah continued to run fast and low, heading west. Eventually the Delilah disappeared off the screen, somewhere in the vicinity of the Tharsis Bulge.

"That's it then. They're hiding in the Tharsis region!", the Captain exclaimed.

"Tharsis is a big place, Captain", Cormac advised, "It's the most rugged place on the planet."

"Just how well do you know the Tharsis region, Cormac?", Captain Carmichael enquired.

"Quite well, Captain, quite well", Cormac replied.

"Yes, but how well does the Prophet know the Tharsis region?", Special Agent Murphy asked, pointing out, "That's the thing we need to know."

They all stood there quietly for a moment, considering that one point, and then Cormac smiled and informed them, "You had their second in command. It's the other one you need now."

Special Agent Murphy nodded, "Leroy McGuvan", then he asked, "Who's the other one?"

Cormac replied, "The young one, Matthew. He was the smart one."

Special Agent Murphy laughed, "Funny that, I have a Cousin named Matthew. Talk about coincidences."

Forkbraid frowned, "I think we can safely assume that he's aboard the Delilah."

Cormac agreed, "Good odds on that", he told them.

"The question, Gentlemen, is whether Cormac knows the Tharsis region better than Matthew, the Prophet's new right-hand man?", the Captain stated as he pressed a few keys and replayed the Delilah's escape once more.

Several more times they watched the Delilah's escape. Each time Special Agent Murphy wrote down more notes on possible trajectories they could have taken.

At one point Special Agent Murphy mumbled, "If this Matthew knew the range of these scanners, which is likely, he could have continued on one course until the Delilah was beyond the range of these scanners and then changed course and gone anywhere."

"Perhaps not", the Captain countered, "He might have expected us to think of that and instead continued on the exact same course."

"Or", Forkbraid began, "He might have been running fast and scared and have completely forgotten about the scanners?"

Special Agent Murphy looked at the others, and then he turned to Cormac, "What would you have done?"

Cormac tapped his finger on the screen and followed the Delilah's course "Pavonis Mons."

"Pavonis Mons?", Special Agent Murphy questioned.

"It's directly west of here. Lots of caves and lava tubes", Cormac replied, adding "Not that it matters though. Northeast there's Ascraeus Mons, southwest there's Arsia Mons. It's the same deal with all of them. Lots of caves, lots of lava tubes."

Special Agent Murphy sighed, "You're not helping Cormac. You're just giving us an ever expanding search zone. We need to lock down on something definite!"

Forkbraid raised his hand and they all fell silent.

After a moment Forkbraid asked, "What is it about these caves and lava tubes, Cormac?"

"What do you mean?", Cormac asked.

Forkbraid looked out the window at the New Tortuga port.

The remaining cavern roof was still visible above them.

The penny dropped.

"Caverns", Cormac told them.

"Caverns?", Special Agent Murphy questioned.

"Back in the days before Mars had breathable air, caverns were being touted as the best places to set up colonies", Cormac informed them.

"We know that, Cormac", the Captain replied.

"Yeah, yeah. The Russians originally built the colony here before New Tortuga was New Tortuga. Back then it was called, Nova Tortuga", Cormac explained, before noting, "There were a lot of other caverns around the Tharsis Monts that were being considered as well. Some big enough to hide a space yacht in, even one as big as the Delilah."

"You said that Cormac, 'Lots of caves and lava tubes', you said", Special Agent Murphy replied.

"Yeah, that's the point Agent Murphy, 'Lots of caves and lava tubes', but only some of them were useful", Cormac smiled his broad gap-toothed smile.

"Which ones, Cormac? Which of the three Monts?", Captain Carmichael asked.

"None of them!", Cormac replied, explaining, "Many of the caves and lava tubes were considered, except there was a problem. It turned out that the volcanoes weren't truly extinct, they are just dormant, so none of them were any good for a permanent settlement. Not unless you wanted to have your colony inside a lava tube that could suddenly fill up with lava."

"Cormac, that puts us right back at square one!", Captain Carmichael exclaimed.

Cormac smiled his gap-toothed smile once more, "Not quite, Captain!"

"Not quite?", Special Agent Murphy questioned.

"There was one peak that was too tempting. It stood so high its peak was almost in space. It was the first place that humans landed on Mars", Cormac informed them.

Forkbraid spoke the words softly, "Olympus Mons."

"Yes, exactly. Olympus Mons", Cormac replied excitedly.

"Why Olympus Mons?", Captain Carmichael questioned.

"It has lava tubes and caverns. One tube pierces the south side of the volcano, just above the rupes. It continues right into the heart of Olympus and connects to the volcanoes' throat. From there, you can take a ship straight to the peak", Cormac explained excitedly.

"How can we be sure they've gone there?", Special Agent Murphy enquired.

"At the top of Olympus Mons, buried into its caldera near its throat, there is an ancient research station", Cormac told them, noting, "No other bases were built into any of those other caves or lava tubes. None. None except for

Olympus Mons."

"It's the only one?", Forkbraid asked.

"It's the only one", Cormac confirmed.

Special Agent Murphy looked at the others before stating, "It's all a bit iffy. I mean, the Delilah could be hidden in any cave large enough to house her."

Cormac slapped his hand on the desk, "My money's on Olympus Mons."

Captain Carmichael replied, "Agent Murphy's right. They could have slunk into any hole big enough to hide them."

"Yes, Captain. They could have", Forkbraid replied, before adding, "But we do have to start somewhere, don't we now?"

"And Olympus Mons is as good a place to start as any", Captain Carmichael agreed.

Just then an ensign entered the room, he was holding a communique, "Captain, Sir!", he saluted.

"Yes, Ensign, what is it?", the Captain asked, returning his salute.

The Ensign held out the communique, the Captain took it. The Ensign then left the room.

"What is it, Captain?", Forkbraid asked.

"I sent off my report last night on the capture of New Tortuga and other recent events", the Captain replied as he opened the communique and quickly read it, "The Spartan has been recalled."

"Recalled?", Special Agent Murphy enquired.

"Recalled to L-Five", the Captain replied as he read the communique once more.

"Why?", Special Agent Murphy asked angrily, "The job's not finished?"

"My superiors consider that the capturing of New Tortuga and the execution of Leroy McGuvan completes our duties with regards to this investigation."

"Captain, I should point out that the Prophet is still at large, and he still has the Delilah", a concerned Forkbraid replied.

"Yes, they know that. With the capture of New Tortuga, the Prophet has no base to operate from. My superiors are treating him as a *'spent force'*, they don't see any further threat", the Captain replied, shaking his head.

"That's ridiculous!", Cormac spat, "We have to hunt this evil slig down!"

Captain Carmichael frowned, "They, my superiors, are opening up another investigation."

"Another investigation?", Forkbraid enquired.

"It seems that some bureaucrat has taken exception to my creation of atmo rated Wisps", the Captain replied, "On my return I'm to be suspended from my command pending an investigation."

"Do they know that the Wisps in question were transferred to the Elysium

Colony for defensive purposes? That you don't actually have any atmo rated Wisps on the Spartan?", Special Agent Murphy asked.

"It was all in my report, Agent Murphy", the Captain replied, adding, "It appears that I will have to explain it all to them personally."

Finally, Forkbraid asked the obvious question, "How long before you take the Spartan home?"

"Hmm, I've been given four days to get the return trip organised", Captain Carmichael replied.

"Captain, it seems we'll be needing that Raider after all. Do you think your engineers can have it spaceworthy before you leave?", Forkbraid enquired.

"You'll need it sooner than that, Forkbraid. The minute my Wisps stop patrolling Mars, the Prophet will in all likelihood, jump planet. He'll just fly off at the first opportunity."

"That's what I'm afraid of, Captain", Forkbraid agreed, "The minute he jumps planet, he's gone, we've lost him."

The Prophet sat quietly as Matthew flew the Delilah across the rugged terrain of the Tharsis region. The space yacht was flying fast and low, just barely above the surface and the Prophet was having trouble hiding the fear and trepidation he felt as they ducked and weaved across the terrain. Thick ice and snow covered almost everything at this altitude and the landscape was as bleak as it was rugged. The Tharsis region was a vast region of desolation.

"Do we have to fly so low, Matthew?", the Prophet asked.

"Only if we don't want to be spotted", came Matthew's swift reply.

It was some hours later that they skirted south of a large volcanic cone.

"Pavonis Mons", Matthew had whispered.

"Pavonis Mons?", the Prophet queried.

Matthew didn't answer, instead he angled their flight path to the western side of Pavonis Mons and raised their altitude a little higher. The Delilah slowed and approached a large section of flat plateau country, slightly to the west of Pavonis Mons. Matthew banked the Delilah so they could get a better view. Below them was a huge sinkhole in the plateau, more than big enough to hide their space yacht. The Delilah slowly circled the huge opening.

"Are we going to hide down there, Matthew?", the Prophet asked.

"I was thinking about it", Matthew replied.

"It's awfully desolate country out there", the Prophet pointed out.

"All the better to hide in, my Lord", Matthew replied.

"What is it exactly?", the Prophet queried.

"It's a cave. A rather large one, the entrance to quite a large lava tube", Matthew replied.

Thinking of New Tortuga, the Prophet asked, "Is there another colony down there?"

"No, no colonies down there, Sir", Matthew replied as he checked his instruments, "I'm not picking up any power readings from down there at all."

"Well, what are we waiting for?", the Prophet asked.

Then, when Matthew didn't answer he asked again, "Are we going to hide down there or not?"

"I haven't decided yet", Matthew replied, "There are a few of these caves around here. I'm just not sure how stable they are."

"They're unstable?", the Prophet asked.

"They could be", Matthew replied, and then he added, "It's possible that they'll look for us down here as well. These caves are an obvious place to hide, and we'll be blind."

"What do you mean?", the Prophet queried.

"If we hide down there, Sir, we won't be able to see them coming", Matthew replied.

A few seconds later Matthew turned the Delilah northwest and the ship sped across the rugged, desolate terrain once more.

"So you decided against the caves", the Prophet remarked, and then he asked "Where to now?"

Matthew turned to look at his master, "We need to be able to see them coming. More importantly, we need to be able to see when the skies are clear."

"Another colony?", the Prophet enquired.

"No, not a colony. I know of a place. It's old, it's abandoned. It's probably derelict, but we should be able to watch the skies from there", Matthew informed his master.

The Prophet sat back in his seat, it seemed that their journey would continue for some hours yet.

Sometime later the Delilah approached a massive volcano, it was a huge and awe-inspiring sight as they approached. The monstrous volcano was ringed with a cliff escarpment that was easily five thousand feet high. The volcano itself was much, much higher, its peak being permanently lost above the ever present encircling clouds.

"Just how tall is that thing?", the Prophet asked.

"Olympus Mons, my Lord, it's somewhat over eighty-eight thousand feet tall", Matthew replied.

The Delilah approached the massive volcano from the south and Matthew increased the ship's altitude. Soon they were flying above the escarpment, following the gradual slope of the volcano higher and higher. The entire mountain was covered in snow and ice and the vibration of the Delilah's AGLs caused more than a few avalanches.

Matthew slowed the ship and carefully scanned the surface as if searching for something. Then, when he'd found what he was looking for, he adjusted course and made a beeline straight for it.

"Another cave!", the Prophet exclaimed.

"Not just any cave, my Lord", Matthew smiled, "This one is useful."

It wasn't anywhere nearly as large as the cave at Pavonis Mons, which was an enormous sinkhole, a skylight in the roof of a collapsed lava tube. Although this cave was the entrance to yet another lava tube, it was one that had punched through the side of Olympus Mons and although smaller, was more than large enough to accommodate the space yacht, Delilah.

"I didn't think you were keen on caves, Matthew", the Prophet reminded him.

"My Lord, this one is special", Matthew informed him, "Wait, you'll see."

With that Matthew directed the Delilah into the mouth of the lava tube.

Matthew carefully guided their ship through the entire length of the lava tube. The lava tube was long, and they travelled for well over an hour. The Prophet had expected the lava tube to narrow as they continued, yet it didn't, instead remaining surprisingly wide and varying little in its width.

When they reached the end of the lava tube, it was the most surprising thing of all. The lava tube opened up into a far wider, roughly circular chamber. Matthew adjusted the ship's controls and began to carefully guide the Delilah upwards. He watched his instruments with eagle eyes.

"I don't get it", the Prophet exclaimed.

"We're in the throat of Olympus Mons, my Lord", Matthew informed him, explaining, "Below us are untold and uncharted tens of thousands of feet of the volcano's throat. Far above us, in the opening in the volcano's caldera. There's an old, abandoned research station up there. We may be able to make use of it."

"And we'll be safe here?", the Prophet enquired.

"As safe as one can be in the throat of a volcano, my Lord", Matthew laughed.

"Just as long as this volcano isn't active", a nervous Prophet remarked.

"Olympus Mons is dormant, my Lord", Matthew assured his master, "The odds of it erupting while we're here are minuscule."

A short while later the Delilah reached the caldera atop Olympus Mons. The space yacht breached the top of the volcano's throat and found herself in broad spectacular daylight. Matthew quickly scanned the terrain, then, having located the research station, lowered the Delilah back into Olympus Mons' throat once more.

"What are you doing, Matthew?", the Prophet asked.'

"Making sure we can't be spotted, my Lord", Matthew replied as he guided the Delilah to a broad ledge, hidden in the dark of Olympus Mons' throat. Carefully, Matthew settled the Delilah onto the ledge. Having done so, Matthew then adjusted the ship's systems to use as little power as possible, reducing its energy signature to a bare minimum. The Prophet looked out through the bridge view ports, it was dark outside, but still, they were on the ground.

"It will be good to get outside and stretch my legs", the Prophet stated.

"My Lord, if you do, make sure you suit up", Matthew advised.

"Suit up?", the Prophet questioned.

"My Lord, we are near the summit of Olympus Mons", Matthew advised, explaining, "We are almost above the atmosphere. There's no air outside, Sir."

Matthew smiled a wry smile, "Well, that's not completely true. There's air out there, it's just too thin to be useful. You'll need a counter pressure suit and an oxygen supply."

"What about the research station?", the Prophet asked.

"I'll be suiting up and going out to it shortly, my Lord", Matthew replied, noting "I'm hoping it's still in reasonable shape. We'll be needing its systems to keep a watch on the skies."

"What's so important about watching the skies, Matthew?", the Prophet asked.

"We need to be able to keep tabs on them, my Lord", Matthew replied, explaining, "If we can see them coming, we'll have time to get clear. More importantly, if they stop their patrols, we can leave this rock altogether and go elsewhere."

"And where, Matthew, just where would we go?", the Prophet enquired.

"I have an idea, my Lord. It's not perfect, but it should keep us safe", Matthew replied.

Just then, there was a disturbance in the main corridor behind the bridge.

"Where are we now?", Mrs Harmon's voice could be heard asking.

"We've landed, Mrs Harmon", one of the crewmen replied.

"Where? Where have we landed?", Mrs Harmon asked once more.

"I don't know, Mrs Harmon. I'll find out and let you know", the same crewman replied.

Matthew stepped out of his seat and walked towards the corridor, "Mrs Harmon, we've landed somewhere safe. That's all you need to know."

"Safe? Are you sure? Is that little abomination on board?", Mrs Harmon almost screamed.

"We are safe for now, Mrs Harmon. And that little Witch is nowhere near us. She's on the other side of Mars", Matthew reassured her.

"We should have burned her! Burn her we should have! If not for her, we'd all be safe."

"Mrs Harmon!", Matthew shouted.

Mrs Harmon stopped rambling and looked up.

"Mrs Harmon. You are disturbing, my crew. Go to your cabin and remain there. That's an order!", Matthew ordered in a somewhat softer, controlled voice.

Matthew nodded to the crewmen, who then led Mrs Harmon back to her cabin.

"I didn't know that woman was on board", the Prophet remarked.

Matthew frowned, "She came back aboard the day that little Witch disappeared. She said that she didn't feel safe in New Tortuga with *'That little abomination running around free'*. I'm afraid she has become somewhat more unstable since then."

"Unstable! That's an understatement. One of the reasons I had her moved to the very rear of New Tortuga with that little abomination was because I couldn't stand the sound of her incessant whining", the Prophet snarled.

"I'll try to make sure that she stays in her cabin, my Lord", Matthew suggested.

"You do that, Matthew, you do that", the Prophet replied.

Matthew and three of his crewmen approached the old research station. It had been an awkward climb with the scanning equipment they carried. Fortunately the lower Martian gravity made the task somewhat easier.

The crewmen carefully placed the equipment boxes by the research station's main hatch, as Matthew walked over to the control panel on its right. The control panel was locked, and it took Matthew several minutes to get it open. Then after pressing the appropriate buttons, the hatch door opened, revealing the airlock behind it.

As Matthew entered the airlock, his crewmen retrieved their equipment and followed him in. The outer hatch closed and after a few minutes the inner hatch allowed itself to be opened.

Matthew frowned, "Keep your helmets on, Lads, there's no air in here."

Matthew's crewmen grumbled amongst themselves.

Matthew led his men straight to the research station's main control centre.

Upon arriving Matthew ordered, "Get your equipment out and start hooking it up."

"You must be joking, Sir", one of the crewmen replied as he looked around, "This stuffs fucking ancient."

"Jury rig it", Matthew ordered, "Do what you have to do. I want eyes and ears up and running in less than an hour."

The same crewman looked around at the control room once more, sighed, and then replied, "Yes, Sir", before telling his comrades, "Come on, Lads, let's get this show up and running."

Matthew sat down at a control panel and started checking the station's control systems. They were old but functional was his assessment. Matthew turned on the research station's environmental control systems and adjusted the controls to its lowest settings. Within seconds a mixture of oxygen and nitrogen started to fill the station. Minutes later, the pressure gauge on the control panel started to shift as the station's air pressure increased.

Twenty minutes later, Matthew checked the control panel once more, and then stated, "Okay, men, we now have air."

Matthew's crewmen took off their helmets and gloves, then continued to install their equipment. Every now, and then, Matthew would inspect their work and make his own careful adjustments. Connecting modern scanning computers to the research station's ancient scanning arrays was an art. By and large the two systems were incompatible, but with the right bridging techniques, the old and new equipment would work adequately together.

They'd been in the research station for a little over an hour. The equipment was finally installed and Matthew was now carefully testing each component before bringing the entire system online. Matthew carefully checked the read-outs from the equipment once more and made his final adjustments, carefully tweaking the communications interface between the old and the new systems.

Matthew smiled as he switched the systems on. A slight purring sound could be heard in the control centre, small, almost inaudible beeps began to sound. The research stations scanning arrays came online in passive mode. Matthew now had eyes and ears watching the Martian skies around Olympus Mons.

Matthew's communicator suddenly beeped and he quickly answered it. It was The Prophet.

"Yes, my Lord", Matthew spoke into the small screen.

"You said you'd be back in less than an hour", the Prophet snarled.

"Yes, my Lord. I did say that, but we underestimated the age of the equipment over here", Matthew replied apologetically.

"So, can we see them coming or can't we?", the Prophet asked bluntly.

Matthew quickly checked one of the screens, noted several small blips and replied with a smile, "Yes, my Lord, we can see every Wisp patrolling this side of Mars."

"Good, good, Matthew", the Prophet replied, before adding, "Then you can get back here and deal with that crazy woman."

"Crazy woman?", Matthew queried.

"Yes, that Harmon woman", the Prophet snarled, "The minute you stepped off the ship, she came out of her cabin and has been ranting and raving up and down the main passageway ever since."

Matthew nodded, "Yes, my Lord. I'll deal with her as soon as I'm back. I just have to set up a secure communications link between the station and our ship first."

"Be quick about it, Matthew, I believe she may be infected", the Prophet stated.

"Infected, my Lord?", Matthew queried.

"The crazy woman may be possessed", the Prophet replied and then signed off.

Matthew frowned as he ordered, "Lads, I need a communications cable laid from this station to our ship, and I need it done yesterday."

One of the crewmen frowned; that would be his job, "Yes, Sir, right away, Sir."

Matthew grabbed his helmet and gloves, and then he walked towards the passageway leading to the main hatch, ordering "And make sure this station has a minimal energy signature before you return to the ship. I don't want anyone to know that we've been here. You muck up, and you won't get back in."

The other two crewmen looked up at each other; that would be their task, they both frowned before replying worriedly, "Yes, Sir."

Matthew entered the Delilah through the aft airlock and had only been back on board the ship for a few minutes, when he heard Mrs Harmon approaching in the main passageway. Matthew quickly stowed his counter pressure suit and headed off in the direction of the commotion.

Mrs Harmon was moving from cabin to cabin, searching, "I know that she's on board!", she screamed.

"Mrs Harmon!", Matthew shouted abruptly to get her attention, then in a softer tone, "What seems to be the problem?"

"She's on board! She's on board!", Mrs Harmon screamed.

"Who's on board, Mrs Harmon?", Matthew asked.

"That abomination", Mrs Harmon whispered, "That abomination is on board!"

"I can assure you, Mrs Harmon, that little Witch is not on board this ship. She's on the other side of the planet", Matthew reassured her.

"But she is here, Sir. She must be! She's in my head! She's in my head! Everywhere I go, she's in my head!", Mrs Harmon replied in a voice that started off soft and then quickly grew in volume until she was almost shouting.

"Mrs Harmon, trust me. That little witch is not on board", Matthew reassured, explaining, "There is absolutely no way she could be on board. That abomination left New Tortuga long ago."

Mrs Harmon ignored Matthew and started stalking the main passageway once more, her head moving from side to side, eyes wide open and scanning.

"She's on board. She's on board. I know she is!", Mrs Harmon was almost screaming.

Matthew followed quickly after her and upon catching up stated bluntly, "Mrs Harmon, you are disturbing my crew. I'm ordering you back to your cabin."

Mrs Harmon turned around, a horrified look in her eyes, she shook her head, "No, no, not there!"

Matthew looked at Mrs Harmon questioningly.

Mrs Harmon replied to Matthew's look, "She's there. In my cabin! In my head! Everywhere I go! She's everywhere I go!"

Matthew frowned, they had no medic on board, they had no sedatives on board, and they had no way to restrain her.

Thinking quickly Matthew came up with an idea, "Mrs Harmon. I know a place where that little Witch can't possibly reach you", he coaxed.

Mrs Harmon looked at Matthew trustingly, "You can get her out of my head?", she whispered.

"I think I can find a place where that little Witch can't find you", Matthew reassured her.

"Show me! Show me!", Mrs Harmon shouted, "Get that abomination out of my head!"

"Calm down, Mrs Harmon", Matthew requested, "There's a special room under the bridge. It's been designed to be demon proof", he lied, "You can use it as your new cabin."

"Demon proof?", Mrs Harmon questioned quietly, "Demon proof", she smiled, "Yes, yes, take me there. I want that abomination out of my head."

Matthew led Mrs Harmon towards the bridge, then down another flight of stairs to the lower decks. He then led Mrs Harmon to an innocent looking hatch, one that Mrs Harmon hadn't noticed before. She had never been on the lower decks.

Matthew opened the hatch, then stated, "Mrs Harmon, please enter. The special demon proof room is on the other side of this hatch. You just need to pass through this portal."

Mrs Harmon stepped through the hatch and Matthew quickly closed it after her, he then began working the control panel beside it.

Mrs Harmon turned around when she heard the hatch close. The hatch was tightly shut. Quickly looking around the room in which she found herself, it suddenly dawned upon Mrs Harmon where she actually was. The outer hatch of the Delilah's forward ventral airlock suddenly opened and the near vacuum beyond the ship suddenly sucked her into the cold dark of Olympus Mons' throat.

Matthew walked away from the airlock. It was set to close automatically after thirty seconds.

He didn't watch as Mrs Harmon was sucked into the almost airless landscape upon the ledge, high up in the dark throat of Olympus Mons. He didn't watch as

Mrs Harmon died an agonising death in the darkness upon the ledge, as her body fluids oozed from every possible orifice.

Mrs Harmon screamed an almost silent, soundless scream of agony in the dark, cold, almost airless cavern, then her demons were silent. The abomination was no longer inside her head.

Matthew quickly returned to the bridge of the Delilah.

The Prophet had been waiting impatiently for his return.

"Have you dealt with that crazy Harmon woman?", the Prophet demanded.

"Yes, my Lord. It's all taken care of", Matthew replied without elaborating.

"What about the research station?", the Prophet questioned.

"When our crew return, we'll be able to monitor every ship in orbit on this side of Mars."

"Good Matthew", the Prophet replied, then after a long silence he added, "This wasn't what I had in mind you know."

"I'm not sure that I understand, my Lord", Matthew replied.

"Hiding in the dark, in a hole, on Mars Matthew", the Prophet explained.

"I know, my Lord, it's not what I had in mind either", Matthew agreed.

"By now, we should have had complete control of L-Five", the Prophet explained, noting, "And with Cis-Lunar L-Five as our base and in our control, the entire skies above the Earth. We should have had the entire Earth at our mercy, Matthew. Ours to deal with as we saw fit. Yet here we are, stuck in a hole on Mars. This was never amongst my plans."

"Best laid plans of mice and men, my Lord", Matthew replied in a softer voice.

"Indeed, Matthew. Best laid plans of mice and men", the Prophet agreed.

"It's not all bad, my Lord", Matthew stated.

"How can it be any worse?", the Prophet queried.

"We just have to regroup, my Lord", Matthew recommended.

"Regroup?", the Prophet enquired.

"Yes, my Lord, regroup in the outer satellites", Matthew explained.

The Prophet sat in deep contemplation for many long moments, and then he smiled, "And then we'll come back! With an armada! With a vengeance!"

Matthew smiled.

32. So Tonight We Hunt

Lord Folcrom Forkbraid stood before his crippled Bat Wing Interceptor, he sighed. He'd known when he decided to use his own ship as a decoy that it might get damaged, or even destroyed. He had hoped, however, that it would come through the battle unscathed. That was not to be the case. As the battle had begun, one of the Prophet's men had lobbed a hand grenade under his ship. The damage was significant, and extensive. It would take a lot of work to repair his little ship.

"We can stow your Bat Wing aboard that Raider", Cormac pointed out, before noting, "As soon as it's ready, we can fly back to Elysium, maybe Varak can rebuild her."

"Maybe, Cormac, but we're not going back to Elysium, at least not yet anyway."

Cormac cocked an eyebrow and looked back at Forkbraid.

"We still have to catch up with the Delilah", Forkbraid informed him.

Cormac nodded in agreement.

Special Agent Murphy approached, he was at New Tortuga's port overseeing the repairs to the terrorists last remaining Raider.

"Not long now, Gentlemen", Special Agent Murphy stated as he approached.

Cormac looked up with an enquiring look.

"The Spartan will be flying back to Cis-Lunar L-Five within twenty-four hours", Special Agent Murphy elaborated.

"What about that Raider?", Forkbraid enquired.

"It's almost ready to fly", Special Agent Murphy replied, with a slightly uneasy look on his face.

"What's the catch, Jim?", Forkbraid asked.

"She'll fly, but she won't be space worthy", Special Agent Murphy informed him.

"It will be kind of hard to catch a spaceship, if we can't fly in space", Cormac snorted.

"There's not much that we can do about that, Cormac", Special Agent Murphy replied, before explaining, "When they converted that old freighter into a Raider, they breached the hull in a number of points. All around those weapons blisters. Too many to track down and repair in time. That Raider leaks, Gentlemen."

"But she'll fly?", Forkbraid double-checked.

"Oh, yeah, she'll fly", Special Agent Murphy confirmed, "We just have to stay within the atmosphere. Take her up into orbit, and she'll bleed out our air into space."

Cormac rubbed his chin, "When you say 'bleed', just how badly are you talking?"

"We'd have about an hour of air before incapacitation", Special Agent Murphy told them.

"So, Jim, we have to catch them while they're still here and hit them hard before they can flee", Forkbraid stated.

"That's pretty much it, FB", Special Agent Murphy agreed, "Catch them on the ground, and then hit them hard."

"The Raider's weapons?", Forkbraid asked.

Special Agent Murphy smiled, "The Raider's weapons are fully operational."

"Well then, there's our silver lining", Forkbraid replied, adding "Jim, Have my Bat Wing stowed aboard that Raider. After all this is over, I'll see if Varak can salvage her."

"I'll have it done straight away", Special Agent Murphy replied as he started walking back to the docks.

Special Agent Murphy had only gone a few steps when he turned around, "I nearly forgot. Before Captain Carmichael takes The Spartan back to L-Five, he's going to change orbit and reposition directly above the Tharsis region."

"Did he say why, Jim?", Forkbraid enquired.

"For when he recalls his Wisps", Special Agent Murphy replied, "He'll be right above the Tharsis Region. Keeping watch until the very last second before they perform their long burn for L-Five."

Forkbraid smiled, "That may just buy us some time."

"That's exactly what he's hoping for", Special Agent Murphy replied, before adding, "Come to the Raider before nightfall. We'll be flying out tonight."

"Sure thing, Jim", Forkbraid replied.

"So tonight we hunt?", Cormac stated as a question.

"So tonight we hunt", Forkbraid confirmed.

Matthew watched his scanners intently as the Prophet entered the bridge.

"You called, Matthew?", the Prophet enquired, his eye immediately focusing on the scanners.

"Something is happening, my Lord", Matthew replied.

"What's happening, Matthew?", the Prophet asked.

"I'm not sure", Matthew replied, adding "It's The Spartan. She's changing orbit."

"Changing orbit?", the Prophet queried.

"Yeah. If my calculations are correct, The Spartan will end up directly above The Tharsis Bulge", Matthew replied, a worried look upon his face.

The Prophet was quiet for several moments staring into the scanner's screen before asking, "What's your assessment?"

"I'm not sure what they're playing at, my Lord", Matthew replied, noting

"Their patrols have thinned out as well."

"Thinned out?", the Prophet queried.

"There aren't as many Wisps up there as there were a couple of hours ago", Matthew replied.

"That's a good thing isn't it?", the Prophet asked, a slight smile appearing on his face.

"Maybe, maybe not", Matthew replied.

"Explain?", the Prophet demanded.

"They may be trying to lure us out of hiding", Matthew speculated, before adding, "But then again, they are moving The Spartan closer to us."

"I don't understand Matthew", the Prophet stated.

"Either do I, my Lord", Matthew responded, before explaining, "If they were trying to lure us out, they wouldn't be repositioning The Spartan this way. It doesn't make sense from any tactical view point."

Matthew elaborated further, "Thinning their patrols out in a ploy to lure us out of hiding and then having Wisps at the ready for when we show ourselves makes sense. Putting The Spartan above the Tharsis region negates that. It doesn't make any tactical sense at all. There's no way we're going to make a run for it with The Spartan sitting in the skies above us. It would be suicide."

"It makes sense if they know where we are", the Prophet suggested.

"No, no, my Lord", Matthew replied, "I thought of that too. If they knew where we were, they'd put The Spartan right above us, not way off to the side. The Spartan's projected new orbit, will put her stationery above the Tharsis Bulge, not us. Close enough to be dangerous, yes, but not close enough to strike."

"So we're not in any immediate danger then?", the Prophet enquired.

"Not for the moment, my Lord", Matthew replied, adding, "We are quite safe, so long as we stay down here and don't show ourselves."

"Good then, Matthew", the Prophet replied, adding, "Keep a close eye on things and call me if the situation changes."

The Prophet then left the Bridge and headed back to his cabin.

Special Agent Murphy sat at the controls of their Raider, slowly working his way through the preflight checklist. Everything seemed to be in order. He glanced up briefly as Cormac and Forkbraid approached the Raider, then went back to his checklist.

A few minutes later Forkbraid entered the Raider's bridge, "We all ready to go then, Jim?", he asked.

"We sure are, FB. Everything is in order here", Special Agent Murphy replied.

Special Agent Murphy glanced out of the view port at the other ships in the port, "Are you sure you want to go now and leave that lot in charge?"

Forkbraid looked out of the view port, security forces from Chryce colony had landed during the day and were taking charge.

Forkbraid frowned, "They're here to keep the peace, Jim. At least until New Tortuga has its own security personnel in place."

Special Agent Murphy looked up at Forkbraid, "You trust them then?", he enquired.

"No, not really", Forkbraid replied, adding, "But I do trust Selene and, Jim, you can be sure, Selene can handle that lot."

Cormac smiled and added, "And around twenty or so townsfolk from Sweetness turned up this afternoon, just to help out with security."

"Okay, I get it", Special Agent Murphy smiled, "These guys just think they're in charge."

"And that's just the way I want it", Forkbraid smiled back.

"Better strap yourselves in, Gentlemen", Special Agent Murphy recommended, "We're taking off in ten, nine, eight…"

Forkbraid and Cormac quickly sat down and strapped themselves in as Special Agent Murphy finished his countdown. On the count of three Special Agent Murphy started the Raider's AGLs and then on the count of zero the Raider lifted off. A sharp vibration swept through the ship as she strained against the Martian gravity, then the ship lurched forward and was suddenly airborne. A strong, but low vibration continued to be felt through the deck plating.

Special Agent Murphy looked around at Cormac and Forkbraid, a single bead of sweat ran down his temple as he smiled, "She's old, she's battered, and she really should be scrapped, but she flies."

"Who are you trying to convince, you or us?", Cormac snorted.

"She'll hold it together won't she, Jim?", Forkbraid asked.

"She should do", Special Agent Murphy replied, adding, "But just to be on the side of caution, I'll try not to put her under any real stress."

"Put her under stress?", Cormac queried, before stating flatly, "It feels like we're flying up shit creek in a barbed wire canoe hunting for turds."

Cormac turned to Forkbraid, "Honestly, Cousin, I'm starting to have concerns about this little adventure we're on."

"Noted, Cormac", Forkbraid replied, "But you'll need to keep your concerns in check. We need to catch these terrorists before they have a chance to jump planet."

Special Agent Murphy chuckled to himself as he adjusted course for Olympus Mons, keeping the Raider as low as possible to avoid detection. The deck plating creaked and vibrated with every flight adjustment.

It was several hours later when they approached the behemoth that was Olympus Mons. It sat low and squat upon the horizon. A shield volcano with a base so large that it was hard to discern against the curvature of the Martian horizon. If not for its towering cliffs and extreme height, one might have missed it in the darkness of night. Its upper flanks merged with the cloud cover, and its summit disappeared in the darkness high above the clouds.

Cormac smiled as he noted, "We're in luck, not too many clouds tonight. This one's usually well shrouded. Phobos and Deimos are up too, so they are giving us a little light as well."

The two small Martian moons traversed the night sky, adding their faint and eerie glow to the Martian night sky.

Cormac stared through the view port looking for landmarks, pointing these out to Special Agent Murphy as they approached. It was many minutes more before their Raider angled upwards to ascend the escarpment. Their Raider groaned and vibrated as she fought against the Martian gravity once more. Cormac shook his head. Their Raider was a disgusting piece of engineering.

"She'll hold together, Cormac", Special Agent Murphy reassured him.

"Make sure she does, Jim", Cormac replied, "If this thing falls out of the sky, you'll have Candy to deal with, and she will not be pleasant."

They were still some distance away from their targets when something far above them caught Forkbraid's eye.

"We'd better get moving, Jim", Forkbraid recommended, before noting, "I have a feeling we're running out of time."

Far above and hidden within the summit of Olympus Mons, Matthew, Captain of the space yacht Delilah saw it too. Quickly he summoned the Prophet to the ship's bridge. It was only a few short minutes before the Prophet entered the bridge.

"What is it now, Matthew?", the Prophet enquired.

Matthew pointed to the overhead view port, pointing deep into the distance above the Tharsis region. What had been a small point of light, was now quite brilliant. It was moving and quickly gaining pace.

"What is it?", the Prophet demanded.

"My Lord, it's The Spartan", Matthew informed him.

"The Spartan?", the Prophet queried in surprise.

"I've been watching the skies most intently, my Lord", Matthew explained, "All of the Wisps that were patrolling have been recalled to The Spartan. Then the Spartan fired up her fusion thrusters about a minute or so ago."

"Why? Where is she going?", the Prophet asked.

"I'm not sure, my Lord", Matthew replied, noting, "One thing for certain though, it's a long burn and that is important."

"A long burn?", it was not a term that the Prophet was familiar with.

"We'll know in a few minutes, my Lord", Matthew replied, "A long burn is something that you do when changing orbits. Planetary orbits."

"Planetary orbits?", the Prophet queried, a broad smile appearing on his face,

"We'd better get moving, take advantage of this situation."

"Yes, but not just yet, my Lord", Matthew advised, before explaining, "We need to know where The Spartan is going."

"Why should we care where it goes?", the Prophet scoffed, "So long as we can rid ourselves of this wretched planet."

"The longer we watch, my Lord, the faster The Spartan accelerates", Matthew replied, adding "In a few minutes, she'll have so much momentum, she won't be able to turn about. She'll be committed to her new destination. Not long after that, we'll be well out of the range of her weapons systems. Then we can safely leave."

The Prophet stared out of the overhead view port. Matthew was right, already The Spartan had moved some considerable distance and seemed to be accelerating so quickly they'd soon lose sight of her.

Matthew turned to his scanner's screen and checked the Spartan's course.

"Well, we can be certain she's heading for the inner system. Just which planet, we'll know for sure when she throttles down her burn", Matthew informed the Prophet.

The Prophet took his eyes away from the view port and turned to Matthew.

"The longer the burn, the further her destination", Matthew informed him.

Matthew turned to the overhead view port once more and watched carefully. As if on queue, the Spartan's bright burning thrusters lost some of their brilliance. Still thrusting, still burning, but now with a tenth of their previous intensity.

"And there we have it", Matthew clapped his hands together.

"So where are they going?", the Prophet asked.

"They're going to Earth", Matthew replied, then corrected himself , "Cis-Lunar L-Five to be more correct."

"So we can leave? We're free?", the Prophet enquired.

"Yes, my Lord, we are free!", Matthew exclaimed.

The Prophet strapped himself into a nearby seat.

"Let's not waste any time, Matthew, let's get out of here", he ordered.

"We'll be up and out of here in a few short minutes, my Lord", Matthew informed him.

By now the Raider had entered the lava tube that led into the Throat of Olympus Mons. Vibrating and groaning with every adjustment, the Raider navigated the narrow passage. Forkbraid, Cormac and Special Agent Murphy had watched The Spartan thrusting towards L-Five. It was now a race against time. Would they or would they not catch their enemy.

"Bring all of the weapons systems online, Jim", Forkbraid recommended, "As soon as we have a chance, lock on and hit the Delilah with everything this ship has."

Special Agent Murphy nodded and started flicking toggle switches on the weapons console.

"We're now running with weapons hot", Special Agent Murphy informed them.

"Good", Cormac replied, "It's about time we got some payback."

They had almost reached the Throat of Olympus Mons, when a sudden burst of light appeared ahead of them in the lava tube.

"Damn it", Forkbraid spat, "Jim. Push this piece of shit to its limits."

Cormac turned to look at Forkbraid, his concerned look spoke volumes.

"Throttling up", Special Agent Murphy replied, and their Raider lurched forward.

Quickly they navigated the last length of the lava tube, and then swung upwards into the Throat of Olympus Mons. The groaning and vibrations felt through the deck plating gave them all an uneasy feeling. A distant receding light shone high above them.

As the Delilah lifted off, out of the Throat of Olympus Mons, Matthew, and the Prophet got a good look at the research station and all the surrounding machinery. It was all illuminated by the Delilah's photon thrusters. There were heavy cranes and long swing arm gantries and other heavy equipment that you'd expect to see at a large spaceport rather than a small research station.

"I thought you said that this was a research station, Matthew", the Prophet commented.

"As far as I know, it was, my Lord", Matthew replied.

"Then what's with all of this equipment?", the Prophet asked

"I don't know, my Lord", Matthew replied, speculating, "Perhaps this place was used as a base during the Outer Satellite Insurrection?"

Special Agent Murphy pushed their old Raider hard, and she quickly reached the Caldera of Olympus Mons, creaking and groaning the entire way.

Forkbraid screamed out, "Lock onto the Delilah with everything you've got!"

Special Agent Murphy was quickly on the weapons console and locked onto the Delilah's photon thrusters.

"We have a weapons lock", Special Agent Murphy confirmed.

"Fire at will, Jim! Don't wait for my command", Forkbraid ordered.

Special Agent Murphy hit the ship's Pulsed Plasma Cannons' fire buttons.

Four sets of twinned pulsed plasma cannons began to fire continuously at the fleeing Delilah.

The lighting suddenly dimmed to a red glow on the Delilah's bridge.

Matthew exclaimed, "Shit! They have us on weapons lock!"

"Who Matthew?", the Prophet demanded.

"Behind us, Sir!", Matthew replied, then pointed to a blip on the ship's rear scanners, "They're behind us, coming out of the Throat of Olympus Mons."

The Prophet sank back into his seat, "What can we do, Matthew?"

"Not much, my Lord", Matthew replied, before suggesting, "Praying might be a good idea."

"Indeed, Matthew, indeed", and the Prophet began to pray.

Forkbraid watched the forward view port intently as dozens of plasma pulses shot towards the Delilah. Should anyone of these strike, the Delilah would be finished. One by one, the plasma pulses began to fall away and drift off target. Slowly the plasma pulses began to disburse in the Martian upper atmosphere.

"What the hell, Jim?", Forkbraid demanded.

"They're out of range, FB!", Special Agent Murphy informed Forkbraid.

"Lock on again. Hit them with something else. Bring those bastards down!", Forkbraid commanded.

Special Agent Murphy began flicking switches on the ship's weapons console once more.

Matthew watched their rearview scanners' screen and sighed with relief as the plasma pulses began to fall short and disperse.

"We're out of range!", Matthew exclaimed.

The Prophet stopped praying and looked towards the scanner, "We're safe?"

"Yes, my Lord, your prayers have been answered", Matthew replied.

Special Agent Murphy had activated the Raider's rail guns and began strafing the skies high above them.

Bright tracers shot towards the Delilah, as tungsten slugs shot forth at a significant fraction of the speed of light.

The Delilah was still within range of this weapons system. Should they strike the Delilah, they'd carve through her hull like a hot knife through butter.

"I can't see us hitting her, Jim", Forkbraid commented loudly.

"That's because we haven't got a lock on her, FB", Special Agent Murphy replied.

"No lock?", Cormac queried.

"The Delilah's out of range, we can't lock on", Special Agent Murphy explained, adding, "I'm strafing her as best I can, but it's like trying to hit a board at a hundred kilometres with a dart."

Forkbraid sat back heavily in his seat and sighed; their enemy was getting away.

Tracers flashed past the Delilah on its Starboard side. Seconds later tracers flashed by on its port side.

Matthew's face showed a concerned look once more.

"We may be out of range of their pulsed plasma cannons, Sir, but they have rail guns, and they are still a threat", Matthew informed the Prophet.

"They don't seem to be terribly accurate?", the Prophet commented.

"We're out of weapons lock range", Matthew explained, and then he smiled, "They will be lucky to hit us."

"Or we'll be right unlucky if they do", the Prophet reminded him.

"Yeah, yeah, they could get lucky. That is true", Matthew agreed.

"Then what do we do, Matthew?", the Prophet asked.

"Not much we can do I'm afraid", Matthew replied, "Lets just pray they don't get lucky."

Special Agent Murphy continued to strafe the skies in the direction of the fleeing Delilah.

Forkbraid stood out of his seat and grabbed his shoulder, "Enough, Jim. Enough. They're out of range. We're just wasting our time."

Special Agent Murphy took his hand off the weapon's joystick and stopped firing, "Shit!", he cursed and then slammed his fists down upon the weapons console.

Forkbraid concentrated on the fleeing Delilah, reaching out with his mind.

"One quick jaunt", he thought to himself, *"Just one quick jaunt"*.

The air in the cabin began to crackle slightly about Forkbraid as he concentrated for the longest of jaunts. A jaunt that would take him across space to the fleeing space yacht, the Delilah.

Cormac looked out towards the fleeing Delilah, "She's an awful long way off, Cousin", he commented, his fear and uncertainty showing.

Doubt spread across Cormac's mind and it was contagious.

Cormac's fear, his uncertainty, and his doubt touched Forkbraid and Forkbraid faltered.

Forkbraid froze for a long second, failing to jaunt, instead launching a single thought at his fleeing enemies, *"Run while you can, there's nowhere you can hide."*

"Run while you can, there's nowhere you can hide", Forkbraid then repeated.

The thought echoed in the minds of everyone aboard the Delilah.

Matthew smiled with glee, "They've given up!"

Quickly Matthew checked the scanners. It was true, the Raider was slowing down and falling behind.

"They've given up!", Matthew stated once more, smiling like a Cheshire cat.

"They've given up!", the Prophet exclaimed, "We're free!".

The Cheshire cat's smile was also contagious.

Forkbraid looked at Special Agent Murphy, "Take us back down to Olympus Mons. Keep tracking them though, I want to know exactly where they're going."

Special Agent Murphy nodded and turned their Raider about, descending back towards the Caldera atop Olympus Mons.

"We'll need to tap into the research station if we want to trace their course", Special Agent Murphy informed Forkbraid.

"Do what you need to do, Jim", Forkbraid replied.

Cormac watched the view screen intently as the caldera approached, "I thought this was meant to be a research station", he stated with a perplexed look on his face.

As they descended into the caldera, more and more heavy equipment became visible.

There were heavy lift cranes, swing arm gantries, mobile cranes and mobile gantries, storage sheds and warehouse facilities. It looked more like a major spaceport.

"It looks more like a major spaceport than a research station", Cormac remarked.

"It may have been a military base during the Outer Satellite Insurrection", Special Agent Murphy suggested.

"If it was, it was a well-kept secret", Cormac replied.

A small still voice echoed in Forkbraid's mind, *"You know what I know."*

Forkbraid nodded to himself as the memories flooded into his conscious mind, and then he said to the others, "I'm pretty sure that this facility pre-dates the Outer Satellite Insurrection. I'll explain it to you both later. For now put the ship down on that ledge, Jim."

Special Agent Murphy did as Forkbraid requested and landed their Raider on the ledge, the very same ledge upon which the Delilah previously had been hidden. Their Raider's bow lights lit up a section of the ledge.

Special Agent Murphy pointed to a small crumpled mass at the rear of the ledge, almost in shadow.

"Is that a body?", Special Agent Murphy asked.

Forkbraid reached out with his mind and viewed the crumpled mass as if he was standing directly above it, "It's the body of a woman. It's only been here a few hours."

"A woman?", Cormac queried.

Forkbraid showed the woman's bloodied visage to Cormac.

Cormac frowned, he was shocked, "It's Mrs Harmon", he informed them.

"Mrs Harmon?", Special Agent Murphy questioned.

"She was in charge of the little one, Miranda", Cormac replied, adding, "She was quite an annoying person. I mean, really annoying. It seems her friends grew tired of her."

"Friends!", Special Agent Murphy snorted, "Friends don't space one another."

"There's not much we can do for her now, Gentlemen", Forkbraid told them before enquiring, "How long can we stay up here, Jim?"

Special Agent Murphy checked the internal sensor readings, "Thirty minutes, maybe an hour."

"Long enough to determine their destination?", Forkbraid queried.

"More than long enough", Special Agent Murphy replied, then checking the exterior scans, pointed to a detached cable hanging down the side of the cliff to their ledge, "Nice of them to leave their cables behind for us to use. Then again, they were in a hurry weren't they."

It took Special Agent Murphy only a few minutes to suit up and connect the cable. Then a stream of data began flowing into the Raider's computer systems. Special Agent Murphy adjusted the sensor arrays on the research station to concentrate on the fleeing space yacht, the Delilah.

It was only a short while later that Special Agent Murphy declared with confidence "They're heading for Ceres!"

"Ceres?", Forkbraid asked, "Are you sure, Jim?"

"Absolutely", Special Agent Murphy replied.

"Well then, that will be my next destination", Forkbraid replied.

"You won't be getting there in this old junker, Cousin", Cormac scoffed.

Special Agent Murphy frowned, "Cormac's right, this old junker's going to be scrapped as soon as we get back to Elysium."

Forkbraid frowned as he considered the delay, "How soon do you think we can book passage?"

It was Special Agent Murphy's turn to scoff, "Book passage!"

Cormac understood, he chuckled slightly.

"What's so funny, Cormac?", Forkbraid asked.

Cormac turned to Special Agent Murphy, "You want to tell him?"

Special Agent Murphy nodded.

"There are no regular services beyond Mars orbit, FB", Special Agent Murphy informed Forkbraid.

"Surely there must be some transport?", Forkbraid questioned incredulously.

"Yeah, there's transport, there's just no regular services", Special Agent Murphy explained.

"Cousin", Cormac interrupted, "All flights beyond Mars are cargo and profit driven."

"Cargo and profit driven?", Forkbraid questioned.

"When an Interplanetary Freighter has enough cargo to deliver and there's enough profit involved to warrant the trip, then the freight gets shipped", Special Agent Murphy explained, adding, "These freighters also carry passengers, only a few dozen or so."

"The problem is, Cousin, unless there's cargo to be shipped, you could be waiting around Mars for quite a while, several weeks at the very least", Cormac added.

"That's not acceptable", Forkbraid replied, "We need to get after them straight away."

"FB, unless you've got an interplanetary class spaceship up your sleeve or can commandeer one, there's not a whole lot we can do about it", Special Agent Murphy replied.

Forkbraid sank back in his chair, shaking his head.

"Besides, there's no point, Cousin", Cormac added.

"Why do you say that, Cormac?", Forkbraid asked.

"By the time we get to Ceres, the bastards will have already left", Cormac replied.

Special Agent Murphy nodded, "Cormac's right, FB. They won't stay on Ceres. As soon as they've refuelled, they'll leave."

"You can be sure of that?", Forkbraid asked.

"Absolutely", Special Agent Murphy replied.

"The outer regions aren't like L-Five. The colonies beyond Mars don't necessarily follow the gravity laws", Special Agent Murphy explained.

"Gravity laws?", Forkbraid enquired.

"Yeah, the Gravity laws", Special Agent Murphy replied, explaining, "All the colonies around Venus, Earth, or Mars follow the gravity laws. Artificial gravity shall not deviate from one Earth G, by more than plus or minus ten percent as applied to the colony's main living surface."

"Why does that mean they won't stay on Ceres?", Forkbraid enquired further.

"Ceres has far less gravity than even the Earth's moon", Special Agent Murphy replied, explaining, "Because the moon has only one sixth gravity, workers can stay their for only six months, or twelve months stints. Six months on the moon, then two years back in the colonies, twelve months on the moon, then five years back in the colonies.

"Yeah, but what has that got to do with Ceres, Jim?", Forkbraid asked.

"I'm getting to it", Special Agent Murphy began, and then continued, "It's all about protecting the human physiology, skeletal structure and all that. The laws are adhered to quite strictly within Mars orbit, but beyond Mars, they're treated as optional. Ceres doesn't follow the gravity laws at all."

"And without gravity, human physiology changes?", Forkbraid queried.

"Exactly. People have lived on Ceres with near zero gravity for generations. They're not the same as you and I. In the rotating colonies around Ceres, gravity to some degree, is more or less maintained, although much lower than one G, but on Ceres itself, there is virtually no gravity. Honestly, the folk on Ceres have lost so much bone mass, it's ridiculous. I can't see the Prophet staying there."

Cormac nodded in agreement, "He'll head straight for the Jovian Realms."

"Jupiter's Galilean L-Five colonies?", Forkbraid questioned.

"The largest colonies beyond Mars are in Jupiter's Galilean L-Five zones. They're mega-colonies just as big as Colonial Central Command", Special Agent Murphy elaborated,

"From there, he could head out to Jupiter's leading or trailing Trojans or even further out to Saturn and its colonies. If he really wants to hide, he could go even further out to Uranus, Neptune or beyond."

"That's a lot of possibilities there, Jim", Forkbraid noted with concern.

"He'll stay in the Jovian Realms, Jim", Cormac stated with certainty.

"How can you be sure?", Forkbraid asked.

"He'll like their politics", Cormac replied.

Special Agent Murphy nodded in agreement, "Yeah, that's very likely. The Jovian Realms are ruled by an elite, aristocratic, feudal dynasty. They're basically all principalities. Each Galilean Moon's orbital region is ruled by a descendant of the colony's original founder, High Prince Albert von Horridian. Even Jupiter's leading and trailing Trojan asteroid regions come under the Horridian dynasties rule."

As Special Agent Murphy spoke the name, Forkbraid reached back into his memories. High Prince Albert von Horridian had been an autocratic and dictatorial ruler. He had controlled the Jovian Realms with an iron fist. High Prince Albert von Horridian had conquered the leading and trailing Trojan asteroids colonies, adding them to the Jovian Realms.

Upon his passing, control of the Six Jovian Realms of Jupiter, Io, Europa, Ganymede, and Callisto, along with the leading and trailing Trojan colonies, passed to his four Sons. His Eldest Son, High Prince Godric von Horridian, succeeded him, and he was the one who started the Outer Satellite Insurrection. His first strike killed the hollowed out asteroidal world, Eros, along with its six million plus colonists.

Amongst the Horridian Dynasty of the Six Jovian system, devout Christians all, the Prophet would find fertile ground for his beliefs.

"They will like his message", Forkbraid commented.

Special Agent Murphy nodded, "Highly likely. They're already devout Christians. Convert them to his brand of fundamentalism and the whole of the Jovian Realms will follow suit."

"We can't let that happen, Jim", Forkbraid stated, "It would be a worst case scenario."

Special Agent Murphy thought for a short moment, "Another Insurrection? Another War?", he whispered.

"Another War", Forkbraid agreed.

"Well that's not a good thing!", Cormac noted.

Special Agent Murphy flicked his eye past the internal sensors, mentally noting their readings.

"Yes, Jim, it's time to go", Forkbraid stated as he skimmed Special Agent Murphy's mind, "Take us back to New Tortuga, Jim."

With Special Agent Murphy again at the controls, their old Raider lifted off and started its journey back down the Throat of Olympus Mons.

"You were going to tell us about that old research station, Cousin", Cormac noted.

"Ah, yes, I'd nearly forgotten about that", Forkbraid replied.

"Well, FB, what's the story?", Special Agent Murphy asked.

"It's a long story, so I'll try to keep it short", Forkbraid stated as he questioned, "How deep do you think this volcanic vent is?"

Special Agent Murphy looked perplexed, he took a quick guess, "It's got to reach all the way down to the volcano's magma chamber."

"True enough, Jim, but how deep do you think?", Forkbraid asked once more.

"At least as deep as Olympus Mons is tall", Special Agent Murphy replied.

Forkbraid smiled, "The Martian crust is thinnest under the Tharsis Bulge region and thinner yet under Olympus Mons. This volcanic vent sinks down sixty kilometres into the Martian crust."

"That deep!", Special Agent Murphy exclaimed.

"That's a long way down", Cormac agreed.

"Jim, what are the major power sources these days?", Forkbraid asked.

"You know that as well as I do, FB. Nuclear Fusion and Solar power", Special Agent Murphy replied.

"Do you remember Nuclear Fission?", Forkbraid asked.

Special Agent Murphy laughed, "Fission power stations have been banned for centuries, you know that, FB"

"Yes they have, Jim", Forkbraid agreed.

"For nearly two and a half centuries, from the mid nineteen hundreds, till the end of the Outer Satellite Insurrection, fission power reactors were a major source of power. During the early days of L-Five and the colonisation of the solar system, fission was the major source of power in space."

"That's pretty much standard history, Cousin", Cormac stated.

Special Agent Murphy nodded in agreement.

"Fission power reactors were banned because of the deadly radioactive wastes they produced", Forkbraid continued.

"As I said, Cousin, standard history", Cormac stated once more.

"Exactly, Cormac", Forkbraid replied, then he asked, "What happened to all that deadly waste?"

"Everyone knows that", Cormac answered quickly, "It was disposed of by dropping it into the Sun."

Special Agent Murphy helpfully added, "Before that, for many decades it was stored on the far side of the moon."

"That's the official history, Gentlemen", Forkbraid agreed, explaining, "All the fission waste by-products were lifted off the Earth and retrieved from everywhere in the solar system and all carefully stored on the far side of the moon, for decades. Then it was all carefully parcelled up and disposed of by dropping it into the Sun. Right?"

"That's the history of it", Special Agent Murphy agreed.

This time Cormac nodded.

"Wrong, Gentlemen, very wrong!", Forkbraid informed them.

"What do you mean?", Special Agent Murphy asked.

"Not a single milligram of radioactive waste was dropped into the Sun", Forkbraid informed them.

"So history is a lie?", Special Agent Murphy questioned.

"Concerning this, yes it is, Jim", Forkbraid replied.

"What happened to all that radioactive waste, Cousin?", Cormac asked, adding, "Two and half centuries worth is one hell of a lot of waste."

"Every last gram of it was dropped down the Throat of Olympus Mons", Forkbraid replied.

"That's insane!", Special Agent Murphy exclaimed

"What if the volcano becomes active again?", Cormac quickly asked.

"Nothing, Gentlemen. Nothing at all will happen", Forkbraid told them.

"I don't get it. Two and half centuries worth of radioactive waste, and you don't see a problem with that?", Special Agent Murphy asked Forkbraid.

"Jim, all that radioactive waste dumped into the magma chamber generates a huge amount of heat", Forkbraid replied, noting, "It's mainly all spent uranium and plutonium. Some of the heaviest and densest elements around. It began melting and sinking deeper and deeper into the Martian crust and mantle not long after they began dropping it down."

"So if Olympus Mons erupted tomorrow, no radiation would escape?", Cormac asked.

"No more radiation than you'd get from any normal eruption", Forkbraid replied.

"Why did they dump it down here?", Special Agent Murphy enquired.

"It was part of the terraforming process", Forkbraid replied.

"I don't see how dumping two and half centuries worth of radioactive waste into Olympus Mons has anything to do with terraforming", Special Agent Murphy stated.

"It's all about the Martian core heat, Jim", Forkbraid replied.

"Martian core heat?", Cormac asked.

"Yes, Martian core heat. All of that radioactive waste has formed huge molten globules. All of it sinking down deeper and deeper into the Martian mantle. Eventually it will come to rest somewhere close to the Martian core."

Special Agent Murphy thought for a moment then asked cautiously, "Is it enough?"

"Enough for what?", Cormac enquired.

"Is it enough to increase the Martian core heat sufficiently to allow the Martian core to rotate?", Special Agent Murphy asked again, this time elaborating.

"I don't know, Jim", Forkbraid replied, before continuing, "But if it is, Mars will find itself with a new magnetic field, perhaps even plate tectonics."

"And that's why they dropped all of that radioactive waste down here?", Cormac asked.

"Exactly, Cormac", Forkbraid replied, before noting, "If it works, Mars will have a new magnetic field and that will help protect the new Martian atmosphere for millions of years."

Special Agent Murphy swung their Raider into the lava tube and carefully threaded their way along it towards the opening in the side of Olympus Mons.

"How long will it take?", Special Agent Murphy asked.

"Centuries at least, Jim. It will literally take centuries before all of that radioactive waste reaches the core", Forkbraid replied.

"So the terraformers were working from both the outside and the inside", Cormac asked.

"That's pretty much it, Cormac", Forkbraid replied.

Their Raider was flying down the length of the lava tube when Special Agent Murphy stated, "You know, the banning of the fission reactors was one of the major causes of the Outer Satellite Insurrection?"

"That it was, Jim", Forkbraid replied.

"When the uranium mines on Earth began closing down the Outer Satellites were still dependent on fission power. The Jovian Realm's Horridian regime used that as an excuse to start their War and dragged the other Outer Satellites along with them", Special Agent Murphy continued.

Forkbraid nodded, "They were still dependent on the old fission reactors, yes, but there was never any refusal to supply the Outer Satellites with uranium. That was Horridian propaganda."

"First the Horridians annexed Jupiter's leading and trailing Trojan colonies. Then they started their War by killing an entire world, Eros, along with its six million colonists. A War that eventually killed forty million people before it ended. The results of that War are still being felt today. In my view, those two events alone set back our civilisation by many centuries", Special Agent Murphy lamented.

"I tend to agree with you on that score, Jim", Forkbraid replied.

"Even today, it's still a mystery as to how and why the Outer satellite Insurrection ended. That was never publicly released. One thing is certain though, Colonial Central Command agreed to build the Jovian Realms new fusion reactors to replace their old fission ones, all for free. Technically speaking, the Outer Satellites won that war", Jim continued on with his rant.

"History records it as a mutually agreed upon peace treaty, Jim", Forkbraid reminded Special Agent Murphy.

"Mutually agreed upon peace, my arse! What a joke!", Special Agent Murphy spat out, "Colonial Central Command mutually agreed to leave the leading and trailing Trojan colonies under permanent Horridian occupation. Our relationship with the Belter colonies, the Saturnian Demarchy, the Uranian Federation and the Neptunian Commonwealth never really recovered either. As I said, FB, the Outer Satellites won that War. The last thing we need is a second Outer Satellite Insurrection, another Horridian War. That would be a huge disaster."

The flight back from Olympus Mons to New Tortuga had been uneventful. Special Agent Murphy had been unusually quiet as he flew their old Raider back. Cormac on the other hand had been more than a little jittery as the vibrations coming through the deck plating grew louder with every course correction, then ebbed back to their *"usual"* background levels.

Forkbraid himself, remained oblivious to Special Agent Murphy's silence and noticed not at all Cormac's discomfort with the ship. Forkbraid's mind was focused on how to get back into the hunt for the terrorists once more. Their fundamentalist terrorist leader, the Prophet, needed to be brought to justice. Foremost in his mind, was an Ace up his sleeve, if only it would be ready in time.

When their Raider finally landed once more at New Tortuga, it was clear to see that works on the new port facilities would turn this one time smugglers' outpost into a first-rate colony. Forkbraid allowed his mind to reach out into the township. He was pleasantly surprised to find that everything was running smoothly in the aftermath of the battle and the subsequent occupation by security forces from Chryce Colony.

The security forces were in charge, or so they believed, but in the background Forkbraid could sense the subtle presence of the psychics from the town of Sweetness. There were several dozen of them at least and Forkbraid could see that they were all working diligently to maintain the peace.

New Tortuga was in good hands.

Cormac had leapt out of their Raider as soon as it had touched down on its landing pad, pressing his forehead to the ground in gratefulness that it hadn't fallen out of the sky during their flight. Candy quickly approached from the township, with Lady Selene and Roseanne following closely behind. Candy mentally noted Cormac's behaviour as he leapt out of the Raider.

"Was the hunt that horrific, Cormac?", Candy asked as she approached.

"The hunt was fine, Woman", Cormac replied bluntly.

"Then why the theatrics?", Candy queried.

"Trust me, Candy, when we get to Elysium, you'll be doing the same", Cormac informed her.

"Did you get them?", Lady Selene enquired as she and Roseanne approached.

"No", Cormac replied, shaking his head, he held up his right hand and formed a small gap between his thumb and index finger, "Missed them by that much."

"So they got away?", Lady Selene asked once more.

"Yeah, by now they'll be well on their way to Ceres", Cormac replied.

"Ceres?", Roseanne questioned, "Why Ceres?"

"We suspect that it's just a refuelling stop on their way to the Jovian Realms", Cormac informed them all.

"The Jovian Realms?", Lady Selene enquired, not expecting an answer, instead exclaiming, "That's Horridian territory!"

"And Agent Murphy thinks that it will be the beginning of a second Outer Satellite Insurrection. Another Horridian War", Cormac replied.

"That can't be good", Lady Selene replied before running up the stairs to the hatch.

"A second Outer Satellite Insurrection?", Roseanne questioned.

"Agent Murphy seems to think so", Cormac replied.

"I'm sure it won't come to that, Roseanne", Candy tried to reassure her.

"I should hope not", Roseanne replied, "Surely that lesson was learnt the first time."

Lady Selene entered the bridge of their Raider while Forkbraid was still wandering through the township with his mind, "They're subtle aren't they?"

Forkbraid looked up at Selene and smiled, "Very. Very subtle. Years of persecution taught them that no doubt."

"No doubt", Lady Selene replied, turning to Special Agent Murphy who was checking over the ship's controls, "Do you really think there'll be another Outer Satellite Insurrection, Jim?"

Special Agent Murphy looked up from his controls, "Who knows, Lady Selene, who knows?", his words were non-committal, yet the tone of his voice and worry in his eyes, gave his fear away.

"The Jovian Realms are a feudal society, Selene", Forkbraid stated, adding, "Their feudal Lords use Christianity and Biblical laws as a method of political control."

Special Agent Murphy looked up from the ship's controls once more, "The Prophet is a militant Christian fundamentalist. He'll begin preaching his own brand of hate as soon as he gets there."

"You think the Horridian dynasty will use religion as a pretext for war?", Lady Selene asked.

"I wouldn't put it past them", Special Agent Murphy replied.

"Let's hope they don't", Lady Selene told them.

"Selene, Darling, get the others on board and strapped in", Forkbraid requested, "We'll be leaving for Elysium in a few minutes."

"Why so soon?", Lady Selene asked.

"I need to talk to Varak", Forkbraid replied, "There's a special project I have him working on, and I need to check on its progress."

"And it can't wait for a few hours?", Lady Selene questioned.

"No, it can't wait. This is far too important", Forkbraid replied.

With that, Lady Selene quickly gathered together Cormac, Candy and Roseanne. Within five-minutes they were strapped into their flight seats.

Cormac reached for his Wife's hand and took it in his, "Here we go again", he mumbled.

"Give me break Cormac, I've adjusted the plasma injectors", Special Agent Murphy replied, reassuring them, "The flight will be much smoother this time. I promise."

Cormac merely rolled his eyes.

A few minutes later, Special Agent Murphy went through a quick ten-second countdown. On the count of zero their old Raider began to lift off once more. A sharp vibration swept through the whole ship as she strained against the Martian gravity. The ship then lurched forward suddenly and was quickly airborne. A continuous low vibration could be felt through the ship's deck plating.

Their old Raider then groaned loudly once more as Special Agent Murphy adjusted their course for the Elysium subcontinent and the New Flinders Psychic Academy.

"Oh, yes, so much smoother now", Cormac stated sarcastically.

Candy was squeezing his hand quite tightly, "Now I know what you mean", she whispered.

"It's just a little vibration people", Special Agent Murphy reassured them, "We will all get back to the Psychic Academy quite safely, I assure you."

True to Special Agent Murphy's word, several hours later their old Raider was landing safely at the airfield just outside the New Flinders Psychic Academy at Elysium. After disembarking, Cormac and Candy both pressed their foreheads to the tarmac in thanks for their safe arrival.

Forkbraid arranged for his damaged Bat Wing Interceptor to be repaired, and Special Agent Murphy gave orders for their old Raider to be scrapped and recycled. Then after a short hummer ride, all six of them were safely within the walls of the New Flinders Psychic Academy.

33. Elysium

"It's good to see you all back safely", Varak greeted as they stepped out of their Hummer.

"It's good to be back, Varak", Lady Selene replied with a smile.

Lady Selene looked to Marcus and Charlene, "I noticed you've made good progress on the repairs, but still, I expected more would have been completed in our absence."

"We've had a few labour issues, my Lady", Marcus replied.

"Labour issues?", Lady Selene questioned.

Forkbraid quickly spoke up, "That would be my fault, Selene. I have Varak working for me on a special project."

"Special project?", Lady Selene enquired.

"Yes, Selene, a very special project", Forkbraid informed her, adding "I'll show it to you shortly."

Candy took her Husband, Cormac, by the hand, "Well, while you lot are looking at special projects, Cormac and I will be getting some well deserved rest."

Cormac looked at his Wife and smiled his broad gap-toothed smile, "Good idea, Candy, I'm just about knackered."

The others nodded as Cormac and Candy walked off towards the entrance.

"It wasn't just Varak's special project that caused us a few labour issues", Charlene informed Selene.

"We did have another issue crop up whilst you were away", Marcus agreed as he held up his left forearm.

Neatly wrapped around his forearm was an [82]A.I. Grip, "I never thought I'd be wearing one of these things. Still, it has come in handy for running this place."

Marcus flipped his A.I. Grip open and with a few precise keystrokes on its holographic keyboard, produced its holographic picture.

"That's an ant", Forkbraid exclaimed.

"Yes, and it's to scale", Marcus informed them.

"To scale?", Special Agent Murphy questioned.

"Yes, this one was about five inches long", Marcus replied, noting, "They can get bigger."

"It's a Bluebottle", Lady Selene informed everyone, "Candy mentioned them while we were on Hebes Island."

"Yes, my Lady, it's a Bluebottle", Marcus agreed, informing everyone, "A large colony of them was uncovered after the last attack on our Elysium colony."

"What has this got to do with your labour shortages?", Lady Selene asked.

---

82 A.I. Grip. A small personal computer, communicator, and analyser that "grips" itself around the operator's forearm.

Charlene replied, "The other colonies recommended that we eradicate them. They can apparently be quite bothersome."

"We've assigned thirty percent of our androids to the eradication program", Marcus explained, before noting, "They've been scanning the southern Elysium coast for any further bluebottle nests and eradicating them as they find them."

"Only the southern coast?", Lady Selene asked.

"Yes, it appears they crossed over the Elysium Channel from the Aeolis regions", Charlene added, before explaining, "So we're concentrating on the southern coast, that appears to be where all the infestations are."

"As if we don't have enough problems", Lady Selene sighed.

"We can worry about the Bluebottle ants later", Forkbraid suggested, "For now, let's all get aboard the Hummer. I have a little project I want to show you all."

Forkbraid winked at Varak.

They all climbed aboard the Hummer once more and Varak flew the craft the short distance westward to a large hangar. The hangar was quite large, well over one hundred and twenty metres long and almost as wide. It stood a good fifty metres tall and sat about three kilometres from the Academy. It was new, very new. Of all those aboard the Hummer, only Varak, Marcus and Charlene had seen it before and of those three, only Varak had been inside it.

The large doors on the east side of the hangar opened automatically as the Hummer approached and Varak guided the craft to a gentle landing just inside the hangar. Everyone aboard the Hummer caught glimpses of the hangar's occupant as they entered, but none of them could appreciate the size and scale of the glimpses through the Hummer's small windows. It was only after they finally stepped out of the Hummer and were able to stare in awe of the hangar's occupant, that they could fully appreciate what they were looking at.

Along both sides of the hangar and mounted to gantries along the hangar's roof were all manner of manufacturing and repair equipment. Some of these machines were enormous in their own right, but it was the hangar's main occupant that held them all spellbound. Lined up in the centre of the hangar was the hull of a very large ship, a spaceship.

"Isn't she a beauty?", Varak told them.

And a beauty she was. The ship was of a disk and sled construction and around seventy-five metres in length. The main saucer shaped disk section at the front was around thirty-five metres across. The rear sled section, containing the main fuselage and large, downward curved, delta shaped wings that were forty metres long and almost forty metres wide in wing span.

"Both the inner and outer hull sections are a single piece of polyceramalloy", Varak told them proudly, before noting, "Built from scratch, atom by atom, molecule by molecule, laid down by industrial scale three-D printers that I designed and built myself. I even smelted my own polyceramalloy. You have no idea how difficult that is to do here on Mars."

That Varak took pride in his work was easily noted by the broad grinning smile on his face.

Special Agent Murphy was looking at the upper rear edge of the delta shaped wings. He noted space for four thruster outlets and then looking underneath the wing and fuselage, noted seven sections of hull where antigravity lifters would be fitted in the future. He wasn't quite sure what to make of the two, large, long under wing nacelles on either side of its fuselage.

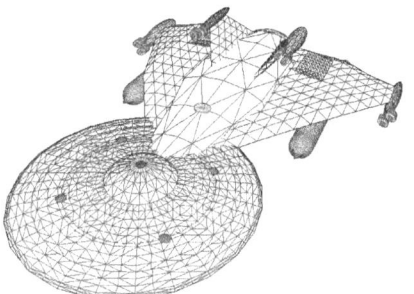

"Seven [83]AGLs", Special Agent Murphy noted loudly, then pointing to where the thruster outlets would in theory be positioned, "What's the main drive going to be?"

"Twin Micro-fusion drives", Varak replied, "One in each wing."

"Fusion thrusters?", Special Agent Murphy questioned, adding, "On a ship this small."

Starship Solstice - Topside

"Micro-fusion thrusters", Varak corrected, "One in each wing, each with two thruster nozzles."

"Micro-fusion?", Marcus asked.

Varak smiled, "Yes, I have not invented them yet, but I do not expect that it will take me that long. It is simply a matter of scaling down the size of existing standard fusion thrusters."

Special Agent Murphy pointed to the port Nacelle, "If she's going to have micro-fusion thrusters, why those nacelles? What are they for?"

"You better ask Forkbraid that one", Varak replied, "They are a bit too esoteric for me."

Special Agent Murphy turned to Forkbraid, as did everyone else.

"It's a new kind of drive system", Forkbraid informed them, "Those nacelles Hamel effect drives, and they'll work in tandem with a Searl levity disk in the main saucer section. The Searl levity disk reduces the ship's inertial mass and the Hamel effect drives give the ship a forward impetus. There's also another specially designed system in the bow that takes advantage of the gravitational and magnetic field effects that occur around planets and stars. Specifically frame dragging events and spatial-temporal anomalies."

"Frame dragging event and spatial-temporal anomalies?", Special Agent Murphy queried.

---

83 Antigravity Lifters. Devices used to nullify gravity and allow vessels to fly.

"Yes, Jim. If they work as envisaged, this ship will be faster than any other ship in the system", Forkbraid assured him.

It was other sections of the hull that had caught Lady Selene's eyes. At the far edge of the wings, both port and starboard were sections that looked as though they were being prepared for weapons systems. Again, atop the fuselage were smaller stabilisers, 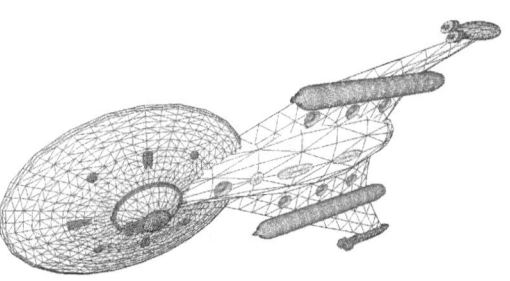 the tops of which were also being prepared for weapons systems as well.

Starship Solstice - Underside

"And what pray tell, are you mounting at the ends of those wings and on top of those two stabilisers?"

Varak looked to where Lady Selene had pointed, "Twin hyper resonant disrupter cannons."

"Twin disrupter cannons?", Lady Selene queried in disbelief, "You're mounting four of them?"

"Yes, my Lady, but they are twins, so technically there will be eight disrupter cannons in all", Varak replied as he turned to Forkbraid.

"Selene, my love, this ship is going to be capable of defending itself", Forkbraid informed her.

"What other weapons systems are you planning to put on this ship?", Lady Selene questioned.

Forkbraid rubbed his beard and then pointed to the disk section. Atop the disk were mounts for four other systems, equally spaced around the disk. The same pattern was repeated on the lower side of the disk as well.

"Phased laser array systems", Forkbraid explained, "Four on top and four below."

"Eight phased laser systems", Lady Selene replied while shaking her head in disbelief, "I know you, Forkbraid, what else are you planning? You never do anything by halves."

Forkbraid pointed to an assembly at the base of the saucer, "Quad pulsed plasma cannons."

Before Lady Selene could answer, Forkbraid pointed to another assembly higher up on the underside of the saucer section. It was a ring-like, circular feature with six small tubular openings. Two facing forwards, and two thirty degrees around the ring on either side.

"Six electromagnetic rail guns", Forkbraid continued, explaining "The ring rotates a full one hundred and fifty degrees to starboard and port, giving it the ability to fire backwards if necessary."

Lady Selene was about to say something, but Forkbraid was again too quick and continued. He pointed above the ring containing the rail guns. Two tubes penetrated the hull above the rail guns, there were another two at ninety degrees to port and another two at ninety degrees to starboard.

"Torpedo tubes", Forkbraid informed them, "Six in all."

"Is that the lot, Forkbraid?", Lady Selene finally questioned, "What on Earth do you need with", Selene paused to count in her head, "Thirty-two weapon systems?"

"If I'm going to track down extremists at the far reaches of the solar system, I'm going to need all the firepower that I can carry", Forkbraid replied unapologetically.

"What else is this ship going to have?", Lady Selene asked.

Forkbraid paused for a moment, and then answered, "Four atmo rated Wisps and my Bat Wing."

"For the love of God, Forkbraid", Lady Selene exclaimed, "Why do you need so much weaponry? That level of firepower is insane."

"Selene, I'm preparing for the absolute worst case scenario", Forkbraid replied, "I'm preparing for what Jim thinks is coming. And, by the way, the Prophet, and his followers are insane!"

Lady Selene turned towards Special Agent Murphy, "Jim?"

Special Agent Murphy replied, "Lady Selene, the Prophet has escaped. If he gets to the Jovian Realms, there will be another War. We will need this ship and all of those weapons systems."

Special Agent Murphy turned back to Forkbraid, "FB, you must have started planning for this weeks ago. How did you know?"

Forkbraid shrugged his shoulders and merely replied, "What can I say, Jim. Prepare for the worst, hope and pray for the best."

"So she's armed to the teeth", Marcus noted, "What defences does she have?"

Varak turned to Marcus, "When she is completed, she will have a standard high density deflector grid, but I am going to add some specialisations of my own."

"And exactly what will those be, Varak?", Marcus queried.

Varak smiled, a broad grin, "An extended defence shield. I have not worked out all the bugs yet, but it is going to consist of eight overlapping defence shields, each with variable frequency shifts. It should provide eight by eight layers of deflector shielding extended above the normal deflectors."

"Whoa, that should do the job", Marcus replied.

Charlene reached out for Selene's hand and gave it a gentle squeeze. Selene smiled gently in response, then turned her attention back to Forkbraid.

"Mark my words, Forkbraid", Lady Selene began a stern warning, "You fly that ship into Horridian territory, and you'll be starting the War!"

"I have no intention of flying this ship into Horridian territory", Forkbraid replied, before remarking, "At least if I can avoid it."

"Then what are you planning, Forkbraid?", Lady Selene demanded.

Forkbraid turned to Special Agent Murphy.

"Lady Selene", Special Agent Murphy began, "The Prophet's ship, the Delilah, has an easily identifiable exhaust stream. Her photon thrusters are identifiable, even from the scopes on Phobos. We can track the Delilah all the way to Ceres and the minute she leaves Ceres, we'll know."

Forkbraid took over, "The minute they leave Ceres, I intend to fly this ship after them. On an intercept trajectory. If all goes well, we'll overtake them well before they reach Horridian territory."

"Then it's game over", Special Agent Murphy tossed in with a smile.

"That's the plan?", a slightly less worried Lady Selene asked Forkbraid.

"That's the plan", Forkbraid confirmed.

"Varak", Forkbraid called out to draw his attention, "How soon will she be ready?"

Varak put his hand to his face and gently squeezed, "Difficult to say, I mean, some of this stuff is still being developed. I have to invent it first."

"Yes, but, Varak, how long?", Forkbraid asked.

Varak rubbed his cheeks, "Say about six months."

"Six months!", Forkbraid exclaimed, "No. No. That's way too long. We can't wait six months."

"When I said six months, I meant in Martian time", Varak replied.

"What? One standard year! We can't wait that long, Varak", Forkbraid shouted, "We need this ship up and running in six weeks!"

"Six weeks!", Varak replied with an astonished look on his face.

"At the very latest", Forkbraid confirmed.

"There is no way that I can have her ready in six weeks", Varak replied unapologetically.

"Varak. In six weeks, the Prophet will reach Ceres", Forkbraid explained, "We expect they'll stay long enough to refuel and then shortly thereafter, they'll launch for Jupiter's Jovian Realms."

"Then that is a problem, Forkbraid, because I cannot possibly have this ship ready in six weeks", Varak was adamant, "Even if I pull out all the stops, work around the clock, shave corners here and there, it will still take at least four months. And, yes, they will be Martian months."

"Varak, if you don't have this ship ready in six weeks. We'll have no possibility of intercepting the Prophet before he reaches the Jovian Realms", Special Agent

Murphy pointed out.

"That is neither here nor there, Agent Murphy", Varak replied, explaining, "Forkbraid has asked me to build the most advanced ship our species has ever seen. An Interstellar Class ship. That takes a lot of time!"

Special Agent Murphy cocked an eyebrow, "Interstellar Class?"

"Yes, Jim. A starship", Forkbraid confirmed, "It seems I've bitten off more than I can chew."

"Not at all, Forkbraid", Varak stated with conviction, "This ship will fly, she will do the job, but in six Martian months, not six weeks. This ship is a complex work of Art."

Marcus, who had followed the discussion closely, pointed out the obvious, "Gentlemen. If this ship isn't going to be ready in time."

"And she won't be", Varak pushed in.

Marcus continued, "We're going to need to come up with another plan."

Charlene then asked a question that would have been perfectly reasonable in most circumstances, "Can't we simply have an arrest warrant issued. And have the authorities on Ceres hold the Prophet and his crew until we get there?"

"An arrest warrant?", Special Agent Murphy queried.

"Yeah. Have Cis-Lunar L-Five Colonial Central Command issue an arrest warrant", Charlene repeated, "Then have it transmitted to Ceres."

A slight chuckle escaped from Special Agent Murphy's throat.

"What's so funny?", Charlene asked.

"Charlene, Colonial Central Command has very little authority beyond Cis-Lunar L-Five", Special Agent Murphy informed her, "The only reason we've had any co-operation here on Mars and in Mars orbit, is because L-Five's authority was backed up by a Colonial Heavy Cruiser and of course, Forkbraid here", he gestured in Forkbraid's direction.

"Agent Murphy's right, Charlene", Forkbraid agreed, "The Cruiser Spartan to back us up and the use of my abilities, have garnered all the cooperation thus far. Unless I'm actually standing on Ceres to back up the warrant, it will fall on deaf ears."

"Still, we can try", Charlene insisted.

"Charlene's right, It's better than nothing, Gentlemen", Lady Selene stated in support of Charlene.

"It couldn't hurt", stated Marcus.

"It won't work", Special Agent Murphy stressed, "At best they'll ignore it."

"It's better than nothing, Jim, let's at least give it a try", Forkbraid advised.

"I'll make it so", Special Agent Murphy agreed, "But personally, I think it will be pretty useless."

"Good, Jim. In the meanwhile, I'll try to come up with another method of getting to them. One that's not reliant on technology."

The next day Special Agent Murphy contacted Colonial Central Command at Cis-Lunar L-Five. Shortly thereafter, arrest warrants were issued for the Prophet and all of his crew aboard the space yacht, the Delilah. The authorities at Colonial Central Command then transmitted the arrest warrant to Ceres, more than that, they transmitted the arrest warrants to every known colony within the solar system.

Colonial news feeds carried word of the arrest warrants far and wide across the entire solar system.

On Mars, the evening news feed read, *"The authorities at L-Five Colonial Central Command Justice Department have issued Arrest Warrants for the alleged perpetrators and planners of both the Atrocities at L-Five, in which more than three thousand colonists were murdered and the fundamentalist militant attacks on the new Martian colony of Elysium, where hundreds more have been murdered. The main perpetrator and leader of the fundamentalist militant group calls himself the Prophet. No-one from Colonial Central Command's Justice Department was available for comment at the time of broadcasting, but it is believed that the perpetrators are currently fleeing to the Outer Satellites in a stolen space yacht, the Delilah. Meanwhile, colonial authorities on Mars are currently rebuilding the damaged colonies and have vowed to pursue the perpetrators until they are brought to justice."*

Six weeks later the space yacht Delilah was docked at the main docking bay in Ceres main surface colony, Utopia. A large domed structure several kilometres across and covered in thick sheets of clear aluminium. The main docking bay was outside the main dome of the colony. Two halves of a far smaller dome had lifted out of the tarmac to encapsulate the Delilah within it. The gravity at Ceres, being a dwarf planet, was minimal.

Matthew had noted at least eighteen colonies in orbit around Ceres as he'd flown in on their final approach. Fifteen of these orbital colonies were twin cylinders of the O'Neil-style variety, the other three being Toroidal structures. The increased size of the Solar collection mirrors was easily noticed on the colonies, situated as they were in the depths of the Asteroid Belt.

It was *"night"* on board the Delilah, or at least that portion of time denoted as *"night"*. As such, the Prophet himself was asleep. Matthew saw no need to wake the Prophet prior to landing and had decided to wake him after they were refuelled. That was the plan. A simple plan. Land, refuel, take off and set course directly for [84]Ganymede Prime in Jupiter's Moon, Ganymede's L-Five region. Matthew had always considered the simplest plans to be the best. No need for complications. Complications always force adjustments to simple plans and said adjustments are often undesirable.

---

84 Ganymede Prime. The Jovian Realms main colony, a twenty-four kilometre long single-cylinder O'Neil-style
mega-colony, situated in the Ganymede L-Five orbital region.

The space dock controllers had requested twenty-three thousand credits for the fuel. Quite a steep price considering the fuel was sourced and mined locally on Ceres. A largish Asteroid or small Dwarf Planet depending on how one viewed these things. Ceres was rich in volatiles with a thick layer of frozen water ice many dozens of kilometres thick beneath its outer crust of frozen regolith and rubble.

Matthew didn't argue the point. They were deep inside Belter territory and here the Belter's dictated the price and, of course, the method of payment. They wanted twenty-three thousand credits for fuel, but not L-Five credits. Matthew was instructed to make the payment in advance, in gold bullion. A material that was quite rare in the Belt. Fortunately, the Prophet had brought along a considerable amount of the metal for just these purposes and payment was not an issue. Payment already made, Matthew watched patiently through the view port as five rather tall, thin men in [85]power suits went about the business of refuelling his space yacht.

Matthew was still watching, when the five tall, thin men finally finished fuelling the Delilah. They walked off towards the hatch from whence they had come. It was then Matthew noticed a rather tall, fat man walking towards the Delilah. He too, wore a power suit. He was flanked by two other tall, thin, although slightly muscular men, again both wearing power suits. These two were quite heavily armed. Travelling alongside the tall, fat man was a small hover sled. It was controlled by a small remote attached to the tall, fat man's lapel. Upon it, appeared to be gold bullion.

Matthew blinked, he blinked again. "What!", he exclaimed to himself.

On that sled was the twenty-three thousand credits in gold bullion that he'd paid for their fuel!

"Crap", Matthew swore under his breath as he reached for his communicator.

"My Lord", Matthew spoke quietly, then more loudly, "My Lord, you are needed on the Bridge."

Some minutes later the Prophet stepped onto the Bridge, "What is it, Matthew?"

"We have a problem, my Lord", Matthew informed him.

"Please explain", the Prophet asked, in a tone that was more a demand than request.

Matthew gestured to the view port, "As you can see, my Lord, we have landed on Ceres, and I'm quite pleased to say, we have refuelled and hopefully can continue on our journey shortly."

"Hopefully?", the Prophet questioned, "You said hopefully, Matthew."

---

85 Power Suits. Exo-Skeletal suits. Counter pressure suites with built-in Exo-Skeletal supports to increase strength.

"Yes, my Lord", Matthew replied, explaining "There seems to be some problem with the payment for the fuel."

"What is the problem, Matthew?", the Prophet asked.

"I'm not sure, my Lord", Matthew replied, adding "I just watched an Official bring our payment back across to the ship. He should be here in a few moments."

A few moments later one of the ship's crew entered the Bridge, "Captain, Sir", he addressed Matthew, before gesturing to the tall, fat man and his two security guards as they stepped onto the Delilah's bridge.

The Prophet immediately noticed the sidearms that the two security guards were carrying.

He also noticed that the Official was really, really fat! Tall and fat!

Matthew spoke directly to the Official, "Was there a problem with our payment? You did request payment in gold bullion."

The tall, fat man answered, "I requested nothing of a sort", and he then paused for a moment, "And your credits are no good here anyway."

A large smile spread out across the Official's face.

"I don't understand", Matthew mumbled.

The fat official let out a boisterous laugh, "My dock master was not aware of your situation. I, on the other hand, am completely aware of your situation."

"Our situation?", the Prophet carefully probed.

Again the fat official laughed boisterously, "The Arrest Warrants, of course."

Both Matthew and the Prophet looked at each other.

The fat official laughed boisterously once more.

"Let me introduce myself", the fat official stated, continuing, "I am Horatio Moon. I'm the Administrator of the Ceresian Colonies."

The Prophet quickly replied, "It's a pleasure to meet you too, Sir."

"If only the circumstances were a little better", Horatio Moon replied.

"You mentioned arrest warrants?", the Prophet carefully probed.

"Hmm, yes, arrest warrants", Horatio Moon replied, explaining, "Apparently, Colonial Central Command at Cis-Lunar L-Five, has you on their most wanted list. On terrorism charges no less, with nearly four thousand murders under your belts. That is most impressive!"

"I assure you, Administrator Moon, we are not the terrorists", the Prophet quickly stated, adding, "We are refugees. Indeed, we are the victims."

"How so?", Horatio Moon asked, the smile dropping from his fat face.

"Those who were murdered, were murdered by the authorities at Colonial Central Command", the Prophet lied convincingly, "They are purging good Christians from Cis-Lunar L-Five. Those who they murdered are martyrs."

"And these attacks on Mars?", Horatio Moon asked.

The Prophet quickly responded, "We fled Cis-Lunar L-Five in this space yacht, the Delilah."

Matthew was quick to back up the lies, "And Colonial Central Command sent The Heavy Cruiser, the Spartan, after us. They even sent Witches and Wizards from Earth. A whole Interplanetary Liner full of them. Their persecution knows no bounds!"

"It's been horrendous I tell you, Administrator", the Prophet continued, "Continually defending ourselves from these damned Demons. In the end we had no choice, we had to flee Mars as well."

Horatio Moon gave the pair a stern look, and then suddenly a huge smile erupted across his fat face. He laughed boisterously once more.

Matthew and the Prophet both glanced at each other once more. *"What was the matter with this man?"*

"Terrorists. Refugees. It's neither here nor there to me!", Horatio Moon exclaimed.

The Fat Administrator continued, "Colonial Central Command at Cis-Lunar L-Five made a serious mistake when it issued those arrest warrants."

"A serious mistake?", the Prophet cautiously probed.

"Yes, oh, yes, very serious", Horatio Moon replied, before explaining, "They forgot to issue a reward and promises of payment alongside their arrest warrants.!"

"Reward?", Matthew queried.

"Yes, Boy, reward", Horatio Moon replied with a smile, "Without any monetary compensation, we at Ceres aren't going to lift a finger. No cash, no joy. That's the way we do things, Lad."

Matthew and the Prophet glanced at each other once more.

Horatio Moon laughed boisterously once more, before stating, "You two have a fan."

"A fan?", the Prophet enquired.

"Yes, oh, yes", Horatio Moon replied, "It seems the Horridians have taken an interest in you."

"The Horridians?", Matthew queried.

"Yes, yes", Horatio Moon replied, explaining, "The ruler of the Jovian Realms, High Prince Heinrich von Horridian himself has taken up your cause."

Matthew and the Prophet glanced at each other once more.

Horatio Moon laughed boisterously once more before slapping them both on the shoulders, a slap that felt quite limp for such a large man.

"Indeed", Horatio Moon informed them, "High Prince Heinrich von Horridian himself has paid us ten million credits just to keep you safe, and to have you sent safely on your way to Ganymede Prime, of course. As I said, your money's no good here, all of your expenses have already been paid. Your twenty-three thousand credits in fuel payment, should now be safely back in your hold.

Stock up with whatever supplies you need, rest as long as you wish, but when you leave, make sure you set your course for Ganymede Prime."

Matthew and the Prophet glanced at each other once more, broad smiles erupted upon their faces as they both began to laugh boisterously.

It was a few days later that the Delilah launched from Ceres and Matthew set course for Ganymede Prime. Back on Phobos, a dutiful Lieutenant Roberts' had ordered a close watch on the fleeing space yacht, the Delilah, as he had been instructed to do by Special Agent Murphy. His men had watched her approach Ceres, they had watched her final approach and landing. All this information had been dutifully reported to Mars, specifically to the New Flinders Psychic Academy.

Now his men watched as a ship had taken off from Ceres. They had calculated its course and found it to be a Jupiter intercept course. Spectral analysis of the ship's exhaust showed that it was definitely the Delilah. Later alignments of its course would yield a more precise destination within Jupiter's realm, but for now Lieutenant Robert's had enough data to report to Elysium.

Special Agent Murphy had received the report of the Delilah's departure from Ceres and had straight away informed Lady Selene, who in turn was now making her way to Forkbraid's rooms to inform him.

When Lady Selene arrived at Forkbraid's rooms, she found him in splendid isolation within his meditation room. Forkbraid sat cross-legged on a small, circular meditation cushion, he was quiet, barely breathing and quite unresponsive to Lady Selene's approach.

"His level of concentration must be extreme", Selene thought quietly to herself.

Not wishing to disturb her lover, Lady Selene picked up another circular cushion and placed it upon the meditation mat beside Forkbraid. Then Lady Selene sat herself down, cross-legged upon the cushion and began to meditate. Her aim was to inform Forkbraid of the latest developments in a meeting of their minds that would not detract from his meditation session.

Selene's breathing began to slow, as she concentrated, consciously watching her breathing.

Slowly Selene's body began to relax. Focused upon her breathing, her mind cleared of all and any thoughts.

Eyes open, breathing in, breathing out, Selene matched her breathing to that of Forkbraid.

Slowly, ever so slowly the world around her began to drift away, until there was only her breathing and that of her lover. Selene was sinking deeper and deeper into Samadhi.

Gradually the wall before her began to change. Selene did her best not to allow the vision to disturb her concentration, quickly bringing her mind back to her breathing. Breathing in, breathing out, breathing in, breathing out.

Slowly, an ornate doorway began to appear in the wall before her. Selene watched without watching, allowing her mind to do nothing more than concentrate on her breathing. Breathing in, breathing out, breathing in, breathing out.

Slowly the thought crossed Selene's mind, *"Forkbraid isn't meditating, he's astral projecting."*

Slowly Selene began to switch from meditation to astral projection. Carefully pulling herself up and out through her crown chakra, Selene stepped out of her body. Slowly Selene stepped forward away from her body. The doorway within the wall opened and with very little hesitation Selene stepped through the doorway.

After all, *"Forkbraid has come this way"*, Selene thought to herself.

Once through the doorway, Selene found herself high up on a mountain ledge, looking out over a world of great beauty. To her right, a narrow track led its way down to the foothills. A winding path, Selene followed it, not walking, her mind gliding down the path with the swiftness of a bird.

Towards the base of this path, Selene stopped to take in the vista. Before her stood a forest of sorts, although the trees were of a species totally alien to her. The path led its way through the trees of the forest. The Sun, this alien Sun, it seemed, would soon be setting strangely enough in the east. Above the horizon, Selene could see the crescents of two midsized moons.

"I haven't much time", Selene thought to herself, *"Forkbraid, where are you?"*

Swiftly Selene's mind glided through the forest, following the path up and down hills, over shallow brooks and streams, stopping only when she reached the far side. Selene looked back the way she had come. Many miles had been traversed so quickly. On the far side was a large meadow, covered in a ground cover, not unlike grass and yet, not grass at all. It all seemed familiar and yet at the same time it was strange and alien. Soft to touch, so much like grass and yet clearly, not grass.

The path led into this meadow and further beyond to a tall hill. Selene swiftly traversed the path into the meadow and within seconds was before the hill. Upon the hill top was a stone henge. Selene swiftly climbed the hill to the top, and stood before it.

Twelve stone posts stood in a circle, with twelve stone lintels above. A dome stood above the lintels, creating a solid stone canopy. Carefully crafted and elegantly built, it capped a beautifully formed temple. Inside the temple, the posts were marked with the twelve signs of the zodiac (one per post), as well as the twenty-four runes of the Elder Futhark (two to a post). Selene instantly noticed that they had been carved in reverse direction.

In the centre of the temple was an altar. The floor around the altar was inscribed with a pentagram. Above the altar, was the keystone to the dome. It was inscribed with a large six-pointed-star. On the four sides of the altar were signs for the four elements, Air, Water, Fire, and Earth. All seemed quite normal, except the signs of Water and Air were reversed.

Selene instinctively turned back the way she had entered. Selene had entered via the northeast entrance. Carefully Selene scanned the floor of the temple where she had entered. Nothing! Quickly Selene altered her gaze to the northwest entrance, again Selene scanned the floor. There it was, a Sigil embedded in the floor. It was the Sigil of Folcrom Tafazah, emblazoned in bright red on the floor of the entrance.

"The Sun sets in the East on this world", Selene thought to herself, *"East and West are reversed. Where in the names of the Supreme Deity is this world?"*

The question lingered upon Selene's mind.

Selene looked back to the altar and gazed upon its top surface. A Sigil had been carved into the altar. It was an ornate Sigil carved with deep meaning and carefully crafted. Similar to an Icelandic Helm of Awe and yet, quite unique and ornate, in some ways like a Hex sign. Selene found it to be both beautiful and somehow frightening all at the same time. Selene smiled as she followed the pattern of the Sigil carefully with her eyes. Carefully crafted in Runes, into the ornate pattern was the name Odhinn!

Selene faced the altar and raised her hands, outspread, high above her head, speaking loudly and with deep intonation, "All about thee stands the Pentagram of Fire and above thee stands the Six Rayed Star. Manifest!"

There was a sudden flash of light, then seated before her cross-legged upon the altar was Forkbraid, he looked up at Selene, "Clever Girl, Selene."

Forkbraid stepped off the altar and asked Selene, "What are you doing here?"

"Looking for you, of course", Selene replied, "And where is here anyway?"

"That's kind of hard to explain", Forkbraid replied, then asked, "So why have you come here?"

"To let you know, the Delilah is on the move again", Selene informed him.

"Then we need to get back", Forkbraid replied, before adding, "And right away."

Forkbraid took Selene by the waist, then flew swiftly out of the temple and back along the path, carrying Selene along with him. Very soon they were both on the mountain ledge overlooking the alien world before them.

"What are you doing?", a slightly angry Selene asked, "I can traverse this place myself you know."

"I'm just being cautious, Selene", Forkbraid replied, explaining, "This world is real. You don't want to get stuck here."

Forkbraid turned towards the doorway embedded in the cliff. Looking through it, he could see both himself and Selene in meditative pose, back on Mars. Selene looked back through the doorway, saw both Forkbraid and herself seated in meditation and began to falter. Fear, uncertainty, and doubt crept into her mind.

Without hesitation Forkbraid reached out and grabbed Selene by the wrist, then Forkbraid stepped through the doorway with Selene in tow. Once back inside his meditation room, Forkbraid turned to the ornate doorway in the wall. He clicked his astral fingers and the doorway closed, then vanished from existence.

Now safely back in his room, Forkbraid gestured to Selene's body, still seated in meditation. Selene stepped back into her body and Forkbraid followed suit, stepping into his. They both now awoke from meditation, stretched and stood up.

"Now what the hell was that about?", Selene asked angrily.

"I was being cautious", Forkbraid replied, explaining once more, "That world was real, Selene. It was the second planet of Alpha Centauri B."

"Bullshit!", Selene exclaimed, "It was nothing more than an outgrowth of your mind's imagination. A path working, a simple path working and nothing more."

"No. No, Selene", Forkbraid replied, informing her, "We were projecting across time and space. We were projecting to Alpha Centauri B, Planet Two. A world called Odhinn!"

Selene looked at Forkbraid carefully, "You're not joking are you?"

"No, I'm not", Forkbraid replied, "I'm being deadly serious."

Selene thought for a moment, and then asked, "We were really projecting to another planet?"

"Yes, Selene, we were and that's why I was being so cautious", Forkbraid replied.

"I still don't get the caution?", Selene asked, still a bit miffed.

"Perhaps, you'll understand if you consider what might have happened if you'd accidentally turned your projection into a teleportation. If you had jaunted!", Forkbraid stated.

"I might have gotten stuck on another planet in another solar system?", Selene queried.

"Yeah. Four point three light years from here, with no sure way of getting back, Selene", Forkbraid replied.

"Oh, my. No wonder you were being so cautious", Selene replied.

"Is that the only planet you've projected to?", Selene asked.

"No", Forkbraid replied.

"You've been to others?", Selene enquired.

"Four planets and one moons, so far", Forkbraid replied.

"You're joking?", Selene queried.

"I've been to Alpha Centauri A, planet's three and four, they're called Gaia and Aries. Alpha Centauri B, planet two, it's called Odhinn. Proxima Centauri Planet one, moon number six, which is called Kaliste, and Proxima Centauri Planet one's tidally locked leading Trojan planet, which is called Twilight."

"When were you going to tell me?", Selene asked.

"When I'd perfected the technique and I felt it was safe to share", Forkbraid replied.

"Why did you build the temple?", Selene asked.

"I didn't", Forkbraid replied, before explaining, "Tafazah built it. He built one on each of the worlds he jaunted to. So many worlds, Selene. Tafazah went to so many worlds, and he gave each of them a name."

"And you're following in his footsteps?", Selene asked.

"We all will, Selene", Forkbraid replied, adding, "One day, we'll all reach for the stars. Some by starship, some by jaunting, but we'll all get there in the end. I was just following the trail that Tafazah blazed a long time ago."

"Will this help us catch the Prophet?", Selene enquired.

"That was my original intention, Selene", Forkbraid replied, before remarking, "I tried to project to Ganymede Prime and I ended up on Gaia, four point three light years away."

"How the hell does that work out?", Selene asked.

"Biomass, Selene, Biomass", Forkbraid replied.

Selene nodded, she understood, "An earth-like planet makes a much bigger target, a colony is infinitesimally small in comparison", she muttered.

"Precisely, Selene, precisely", Forkbraid replied, adding, "I reached out for a colony and ended up projecting to an exoplanet."

"So, all of these worlds are habitable?", enquired Selene.

"Gaia and Odhinn are very much like Earth, Aries somewhat less so. Twilight is a habitable tidally locked eyeball world, and the moon of Proxima's Gas Giant, Kaliste, is only partially habitable", Forkbraid replied, explaining further, "Proxima doesn't move in Twilight's sky, so it's an ever-Sun. So Twilight is permanently hot on its Sunward side and completely frozen on the other. Kaliste is, of course, a moon, so it has strange seasons and odd tidal surges. Kaliste might even be a quasi moon, not a real moon at all; it's hard to say. Proxima's red glow doesn't help much either."

"At least we'll know where to go when your starship is built,", Selene suggested, "But how will this help us catch the Prophet?"

"If I can refine the technique, Selene. If I can use it to jaunt to the Ganymede Prime and the other colonies. Then we can go after him no matter where he runs to", Forkbraid replied.

Selene thought for a moment, "Perhaps you should target something a little bigger than your average colony, try projecting to Colonial Central Command next time."

"That's actually a good idea, Selene", Forkbraid replied, adding, "Then I can work my way down to smaller colonial targets. However, you do have to remember that Ganymede Prime is a mega-colony, it's just as big as Colonial Central Command, it's just further away."

"Now what's with these temples?", Selene asked.

"Folcrom Tafazah built one on each of the worlds he jaunted to", Forkbraid replied, explaining "Each world has its name inscribed within its Sigil on its altar."

Selene thought for a second, "To facilitate jaunting no doubt."

"Precisely Selene", Forkbraid replied, before noting, "Tafazah's first temple is on Earth."

"On Earth? Where?", Selene questioned incredulously.

"Yes, yes, Selene", Forkbraid replied, explaining, "In Tafazah's original pagan temple."

Selene thought for long moments, her mind reaching back into her memories of an historical pagan temple built by Tafazah in the hill country east of the city of Melbourne.

A Tower three levels tall, the lower level and structure being underground. Built using the sacred knowledge of the ancients and surrounded by Sigils and Symbols of deep and arcane meaning. The entire Temple itself was a complex Sigil.

"That Temple?", Selene whispered, "Tafazah's Tower?"

"Oh, yes, Selene. That Temple. Tafazah's Tower", Forkbraid replied, "From there Tafazah visited a hundred worlds or more."

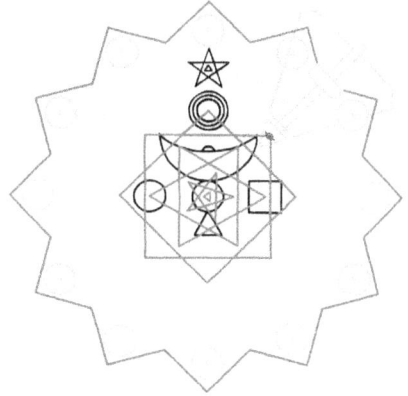

As it dawned upon her, the enormity of Tafazah's skills, Selene, knowing the structure of the original temple, asked, "Does each of these temples have a twist prism?"

"Oh, yes", Forkbraid nodded, "Each, and every one."

"Tell me, Forkbraid. Are any of these worlds already inhabited?", Selene asked.

"None with intelligent life", Forkbraid replied, elaborating, "At least none that Tafazah visited."

Selene nodded, considering how the future could now unfold, how colonies could be set up across the stars, with interstellar travel no longer reliant upon technology.

Forkbraid sighed as he caught Selene's thoughts, *"The mundanes will still need starships, Selene."*

"Of course, of course, Forkbraid", Selene replied, *"But will we need the mundanes."*

"Without them, we could not exist, we are an outgrowth of their evolution", Forkbraid explained, adding, *"When we eventually take our people to the stars, we will take the mundanes with us as well, at some point."*

Selene laughed lightly, "We can't even consider that, not until we've dealt with our civilisations issues of prejudice and disunity."

Forkbraid nodded in agreement, "Not until our house is in order."

Selene nodded as well and repeated Forkbraid's words, "Not until our house is in order."

Upon hearing that the stolen space yacht, the Delilah, had left Ceres, Special Agent Murphy had sent the Ceres administration a message, asking why they did not act on the Arrest Warrant issued by Colonial Central Command. It was several hours later that the reply from Ceres was received. Varak had received the reply in the Academy's communications centre. Prior to its arrival, another, more important message had been received from Earth.

"Which would you prefer first, the good news or the bad news ", Varak asked Special Agent Murphy.

"You may as well give me the bad news first, Varak", Special Agent Murphy responded, "After which, maybe, just maybe, the good news will take the bad taste out of my mouth."

"Well, if the good news doesn't, perhaps more of that Bourbon might", Varak stated with a touch of sarcasm as he passed Special Agent Murphy the message from Ceres.

Special Agent Murphy noted the sarcasm in Varak's voice, true he had been drinking a wee bit too much lately. He placed his glass of Bourbon on a nearby side table.

Special Agent Murphy was not happy with the reply, it simply read:

"We, the Administrators of the United Ceresian Colonies, are not in the habit of enforcing unlawful Arrest Warrants issued by Colonial Central Command or any other *'alien'* authorities. Furthermore, we are not in the habit of persecuting political and/or religious refugees. As such we sped the Delilah and all those aboard on their way to their desired sanctuary at Ganymede Prime."

"Well, that's that then, isn't it", Special Agent Murphy snarled, "Still we shouldn't have expected too much."

"You did say that they'd ignore any arrest warrants", Marcus who had just entered the room noted dryly.

"Yeah, but they didn't ignore the arrest warrant did they?", Special Agent

Murphy replied, "Instead they sped them on their way to their sanctuary."

Agent Murphy rubbed his face, it had become somewhat overgrown with a rough, stubbly beard of late, "So Varak, what's the good news?", and thinking to himself, *"I could do with a shave."*

"We have had a message from Earth", Varak informed him, "The next Interplanetary Liner to Mars will have more colonists on it. Psychic colonists."

"More colonists?", Marcus questioned.

"About three hundred families", Varak confirmed.

"Families?", Special Agent Murphy asked.

"Yes, families, Mothers, Fathers, Children", Varak confirmed, adding, "From all over the Earth."

Marcus considered Varak's last statement before questioning, "From all over the Earth?"

"Yes", Varak confirmed, "Apparently psychic families are volunteering to be Martian colonists from all over the Earth."

Varak passed the message transcript to Marcus, and then asked, "You do know the old saying, do you not, Lad?"

Marcus looked up slightly, whilst continuing to read the transcript.

Varak continued, "If you build it, they will come."

And coming they were, three hundred new psychic families. Volunteers from nearly every psychic academy and psychic community on Earth. Marcus read further, surprised by where the volunteers were coming from. A great many were coming from Iceland, quite a large number from Japan, a surprisingly large number from Polynesia. Most of the remainder were from the US, Europe and Australia, with small contingents from South America.

"If you build it, they will come", the thought repeated in Marcus' mind.

"No doubt, this batch will be only the first", Marcus stated as he looked back to Varak and Special Agent Murphy, "Others will follow."

Marcus passed the transcript back to Varak, "Varak, take this straight to Lady Selene. I'm sure she'll be most pleased."

"Right away", Varak replied as he sped out the door.

"Well then", Special Agent Murphy began, "We'll be needing a detailed passenger list."

Marcus nodded, "That can be arranged."

"Families will be needing accommodation", Special Agent Murphy noted, "We'll need to be assessing their qualifications as well, especially if we're going to be doling out jobs."

"There'll be plenty of both in the new Elysium colony", Marcus informed Special Agent Murphy.

Special Agent Murphy stood up and stretched.

"Is there anything else you'll be needing, Agent Murphy?", Marcus enquired.

"Yeah. A good shit, shower, and a shave", Special Agent Murphy replied as he rubbed his face once more, then as he walked out the door he turned around, "I suppose we should prepare for this population boom."

Several weeks passed and the Inter Planetary Liner arrived from Earth with its precious cargo of Colonists. More than three hundred families. Most of the Elysium colony was a buzzing hive of activity. Families were billeted accommodation, parents were offered jobs based upon their qualifications. All was proceeding smoothly, albeit at a faster pace than had been anticipated. The New Flinders Psychic Academy was preparing for its first intake of student boarders.

The Psychic Academy's schedule had been moved forward numerous times over the past several weeks.

Originally, it was expected that the Academy would not be taking on students for at least a decade. With the discovery of at least one psychic community, the township of Sweetness, on Mars, that schedule had been reworked to allow for students within four years. With the earlier than expected arrival of the new psychic colonists, complete with their families, the schedule was moved forward, once again.

Roving tutors were already running ad-hock classes in the Elysium colony and the township of Sweetness. Three month intensive tutorials would begin with the new Martian year. Then the first intake of boarding students would start the following year.

Life in the colony had become quite frenetic, with constant meetings and a constant flow of decisions taking up much of Lady Selene's time. Once everything was in place, once everything was organised, only then could the pace of life slow down and become more relaxed.

Special Agent Murphy had become quite the administrator, organising accommodation, working out who was the best fit for which jobs. Settling arguments and issues of security. Which was a good thing too, with Varak spending much of his time working on Forkbraid's pet project. This project too was nearing conclusion. Early systems tests had already begun on the new spaceship and flight tests would be beginning within weeks.

Forkbraid spent his time either overseeing the construction of the new spaceship and fine-tuning his astral projection and jaunting techniques. Already he had physically jaunted to the habitable worlds of the nearest star system, Alpha Centauri. Now he was honing his ability to lock down on the smaller colonies and teleporting to them. Choosing to practice first with the colonies of Cis-Lunar L-Five, starting with Colonial Central Command itself.

At the end of a long day, Forkbraid and Lady Selene sat comfortably on the balcony sofa of Selene's apartment. They enjoyed well-earned glasses of local Martian Sweet Cherry Red Wine, made by more Cousins of Cormac and Candy using Martian cherries from Cormac and Candy's own orchards.

The Sun was setting low in a glorious display of reddish, orange hues against the Martian horizon. Both beautiful and picturesque, the only sounds disturbing the scene, a slight breeze flicking at the drapes and the video news feeds speaking softly, almost unnoticed in the adjacent room.

One must remember that the tutelary deity, the Hindu Goddess Kali represents the duality of nature and that nature can be both cruel and kind. Likewise with life, life too can be both cruel and kind. Happy endings do not always come. Oft-times endings can be both cruel and harrowing, life happens, shit happens and sometimes people just die. Endings always lead to new beginnings, one must stand firm, and then when ready, march forward towards the light.

The news feed on the video screen in the adjacent room picked up significantly in tone. The young blonde newsreader read the news feed issued from Ganymede Prime throughout the colonies.

Sometimes happy endings don't come:

"High Prince Heinrich von Horridian of the Six Jovian Realms, with the unanimous support of the entire Jovian High Council has declared the persecution of Christians by the *'puppet'* Government of Cis-Lunar L-Five and the subsequent murder of several thousand Christian Martyrs to be a crime against humanity and an affront to God."

"Furthermore, High Prince Heinrich, again with the unanimous support of the entire Jovian High Council, has declared a State of War to exist between the Six Jovian Realms and the Governments of the Inner Solar System, specifically, the Governments of Earth, Cis-Lunar L-Five and Mars."

"We are now going to play the Royal proclamation from Ganymede Prime."

The proclamation began with High Prince Heinrich von Horridian's speech to the Jovian High Council:

"For too long have we watched in silence, for too long have we said nothing as our Brothers and Sisters of the Inner Planets have been persecuted for their beliefs. For too long we have watched as the twin evils of Witchcraft and Wizardry have taken control of the Earth. Now their control has spread, the *'puppet'* Government of L-Five has fallen to these same twin evils. The Government of L-Five now persecutes and murders the righteous. The planet Mars has also fallen to these twin evils. Witchcraft and Wizardry have taken control of Mars. That's right, the planet Mars has fallen and is now home to Witches and Wizards. Even now they plot against us. How soon before they attack us? How soon before they attempt to conquer us?"

High Prince Heinrich von Horridian paused, loud clapping and applause could be heard from the Jovian High Council.

"A Prophet of God is on his way to Ganymede Prime. He has fled this evil persecution, and he is now on his way to us. Too sanctuary, for we have offered it to him, our protection and the protection of the righteous."

Again the Jovian High Council could be heard offering loud applause:

"Having survived the murder of thousands of his followers, having survived the countless plots to murder him, both in the Cis-Lunar L-Five colonies and on Mars. This man, this Prophet of God, seeks sanctuary from us. And we shall give it. I hold the *'puppet'* Government of Cis-Lunar L-Five, fully responsible for the atrocities, in which thousands of the righteous were martyred. These were high crimes against Humanity and an affront to God himself. Now, my people, I must tell you, that a State of War now exists between us and the inner Planets."

Loud applause, clapping and shouts of agreement erupted once more from the Jovian High Council.

"No longer can we watch in silence. No longer can we allow our righteous Brothers and Sisters to stand alone. Henceforth, we are now at War with the Government of the Earth, with the Government of Mars and the *'puppet'* Government of Cis-Lunar L-Five."

The eruption of support drowned out the High Prince's words once again:

"We shall smite them, both in space and on their home worlds. We shall smite them and defeat them. We shall drive the twin evils of Witchcraft and Wizardry into Oblivion. Only then shall there be peace. Only then will this War end."

The applause erupted once more, this time taking several minutes to abate:

"I demand that the *'puppet'* Government of Cis-Lunar L-Five surrender, so that those responsible for the persecutions and murders may be tried for their atrocities. I demand that the *'puppet'* Government of Cis-Lunar L-Five, surrender its Armed Forces to the control of our Jovian Armed Services. That we might with minimal destruction, lay siege to the Earth and Mars, then drive the twin evils of Witchcraft and Wizardry into Oblivion. Only then, only then, may there be peace between us."

The sounds of support and applause erupted from the Jovian High Council once more.

War was coming.

What is now the Price of Peace?